Letters From Jack

By

J. J. Ramsay

Soli Deo Gloria

This work deserves a special mention to Lisa, without her love and fondness for the mystery and her support, this work would never have come about.

Preface:

This work is a historical fiction based on real events in history. The main character, Detective John Stone, is entirely fiction and any resemblance to a person alive or dead is merely a coincidence. The other characters are real persons in history and are all mentioned concerning their involvement in the Whitechapel murders, although any interaction with the main character is entirely fiction. John Stone's interaction with the coroner is made up by me, but one could imagine a detective playing this role as the Metropolitan Police had become so desperate to appease the constituents of the city, they would have done almost anything to apprehend the killer. Francis Tumblety is a real person whose flamboyance is supported by several newspaper articles that are cited and specific to their occurrence. Tumblety's interview at Scotland Yard is fiction, although the charges brought against him and his subsequent flight from England are a matter of record. Any interaction with the main character or police that Tumblety has in this story are fiction, as are the speculations of the man being an abortionist. His interactions with prostitutes and his lifestyle are taken from newspaper clippings. Tumblety's arrival to New York City was of interest to the New York City Police, but any other occurrences in this story are fiction. As are his date of arrival and his leaving New York City and the timing of the murder of Carrie Brown. It is, however, important to mention that there is no concrete evidence to prove that Tumblety was not in New York at that time.

Chapter One

I stood outside the New Scotland Yard building on the Thames and tried to fend off the memories of the years spent as a detective that came flooding into my mind with a tidal wave force. The moment was somewhat nostalgic, but at the same time it seemed fitting, in the sense of: in with the new, and out with the old. It left me almost relieved to be retired from the C.I.D. long before the new building was christened. I had started working as a detective after I was honorably discharged as a captain from her Majesty's Royal Army. That was more than thirty years ago almost to the day, making the day even more auspicious. In those days, the building was located in Whitehall. Then, it was simply called the Home Office of the Metropolitan Police Department. The building had backed onto a yard, where it was said that a Scottish Palace once stood, and where Scottish royals would stay on, while in London. The yard at the back was often called Great Scotland Yard. The name was taken up by the constabulary for the detectives attached to the branch of C.I.D. In those days, the constables were called bobbies by Londoners; after their founder Sir Robert Peel.

I walked away from the building with mixed emotions. I had looked forward to seeing some of the old faces that I had known in my youth; alas, they were few now. Those, I did see; were polite but dared not partake in too deep a conversation that might lead down dark paths in the past, that were best; left out of the light. Others in attendance seemed to ignore the past and seemed excited due to the arrival of the new century. I presumed that the coming of the twentieth century, was like, one of London's heavy rains that washed away the filth on the streets. I suppose that it was best that one leave the past in the past. I had talked to a few old friends, but the event seemed to have a dark cloud hanging over it; due to the prevailing mistrust of the public that had not changed since the force's beginning, and had re-emerged with the police failing to catch the Whitechapel killer. I found myself thinking that a new building and a new name might go a long way, but it could not erase the past.

Taking the train back to my home in Colchester. I was happy to be away from the hustle and bustle of city life. I did not venture far from my doorstep these days, and I was tired by the time I got back and sat on my porch to enjoy the afternoon sun. Alas, with the excitement of the day, I closed my eyes in exhaustion. As I sat there my mind wandered reluctantly back to the events that started on August thirty-first, 1888 that came flooding back again. They were events that were unprecedented for the time and would forever change my life and would enlighten the world of a district called Whitechapel in London's East End, and place it on the pages of the history books forever.

The day had begun like any other for me. August had set record temperatures for the coldest in decades, and the persistent rain had left everything saturated for days. Unfortunately, the weather was not the only thing that dampened even the best of Londoner's spirits. With the month on the close, most looked forward to a dry, crisp fall and a chance of a St. Martin's summer. However, the last day of August did not bring clearing weather. On the contrary, a dark cloud would hang over Whitechapel and remain, shrouding the city and those who lived in the metropolis for some time.

Nothing could have prepared me for what lay ahead. No amount of experience could have readied me for the appalling wickedness that had come to London in the wee hours of the morning. The unparalleled evil that had manifest in the East End would cause the world to shudder at the revelations that would be printed in the newspapers. Soon after, the women who walked the streets of Whitechapel would cringe at every sound in the night, and stories of unspeakable terrors would be told about the thing that went bump in the night.

Though my career as a detective in Scotland Yard was hardly on an upward swing in London's West End, when I had arrived in Whitechapel, I was of the opinion that my new assignment was tantamount to taking a step backward. I remember the conversation that I had with Inspector, Frederick Abberline head of C.I.D., in his office after I had handed in my resignation two days before.

The day had been a long time coming for me, The Yard was changing. For the last few years of my twenty year service as a detective, I had noticed an increase in the control of bureaucrats in the daily business of policing. It seemed that no matter which way a copper turned, both the internal and external politics of the day seemed to have a way of interfering, and more and more the politics won over hindering a copper from doing his job. I had waited outside Inspector Abberline's office for some minutes wondering why the inspector wanted to see me and I grew impatient. I hoped that my untimely resignation did not complicate the reference I wanted from Abberline. There was job working as an investigator for the Middlesex County Coroner and I wanted to apply and take a long vacation before I started.

"Detective Stone, come in, come in."

I was a little taken aback by the reception, which made me think that something was up. I had known Abberline for some years and I had received nothing more than a nod of the head in acknowledgment before now.

"Sit down Stone."

I sat, looking at the inspector more than a little curious and wondering what the man had in mind.

"I have your resignation letter."

"Good."

"It says here that you would like a reference for the coroner's office investigative position."

"Yes."

"I feel it necessary to ask Stone, why are you resigning?"

I really did not feel like answering, but as I watched Abberline thumb through the thick file on his desk, I assumed that the answers were already in front of him.

"Twenty years as a copper Sir, I think I have had my limit."

"I see," Abberline paused. "You love the work, but you hate the bureaucracy, is that it?"

"Yes, I suppose so."

There was a long moment of silence and I began to wonder if Abberline was going to tell me that he would not write me the reference.

"Is there a problem sir?"

"No. Though, I believe that I may have a proposition for you."

"Oh."

3

The word proposition threw me for a minute and I was beginning to feel like I would have to do something for the inspector in order to get my reference.

"I was wondering, how you would like a position with the coroner's office, but you would be answerable directly to me, whilst maintaining your position with the coroner Wynne Baxter?"

"How's that sir?"

"Stone, you are a good detective and though I hate to lose you here at The Yard, there is a good opportunity here where you can still be of use to us."

"Use, how sir?"

"We have two brutal murders in Whitechapel that remain unsolved Stone, but that isn't the half of it. The area is primed for a tumult. On one side we have this International Workers Club marching up and down London's streets creating riots due to unfair wages, on the other we have the city growing at an alarming rate, and moving ever eastward. Crime is running rampant in the East End, the Metropolitan Police are stressed, overworked and understaffed. To top it all off, I have just learned the Vigilance Committee is reforming to ease the lack of faith that the constituents have in the police. If that isn't enough, we have an increase in antisemitic trouble that leaves the Jews at the center of a powder keg that is ready to blow."

"And, I am to do what?"

"You would be in the thick of it, so to speak, keeping me informed of anything that looks like it could get out of hand."

"Like this Vigilance Committee."

"Yes."

"What would I be doing?"

"You would be officially on vacation and resigning at the end of the period."

"And unofficially?"

"Unofficially you would be doing your job, but behind the scenes, of whatever comes up?"

"Like these two cold murders?"

"Yes, they must be a priority Stone, two murders in as many months with no suspects."

"What about the coroner, does he know?"

"Absolutely not, you are under official direction, but unofficial in stance."

I thought about this some minutes aware that Abberline had his eyes on me the entire time.

"So, I am on leave before I resign, but I will be working for you," I said to make it clear?

"Yes."

"Doesn't sound like much of a vacation Sir."

"It will be a walkover Stone."

That was the way of it and that was where I found myself. Though investigating a murder was hardly new to me, working hand in hand with Wynne E. Baxter, the County Coroner for Sussex, was.

I had agreed to Abberline's proposal for two reasons. For one; I was a copper, and I liked being a copper. The second reason being; I was going to apply for the coroner's officer anyway, this would be a good way to get my feet wet, and see if the career move was right for me. One thing was certain, I had enough of the politics in The Yard, and this could give me the freedom I needed to work.

It was seven o'clock in the morning when the door to my office opened, and Wynne Baxter walked in with a steaming cup of tea. My office was located on the second floor of an office building in London's East End. The building also housed the offices of the coroner, Mr. Wynne Baxter, and the Police Surgeon, Dr. George Bagster Phillips. Working closely with the coroner, I had spent the last few weeks on the trail of a brutal murderer who was targeting prostitutes in Whitechapel. With a slight touch of a hand on my shoulder, I woke seeing the coroner standing over me. The man did not move until my eyes flickered in response.

I lay on the settee, unmoving listening to the spoon in Wynne Baxter's hand rattle around inside of the teacup, trying to motivate myself to put my feet on the floor. It had been late when I had finished writing my report on the investigation into the death of Martha Tabram. I had come to Whitechapel only a few weeks earlier to investigate the suspicious death of the woman who had been found near a stairwell at the George Yard buildings, in Whitechapel. In London's East End, crime was not uncommon. As a matter of fact, criminal behavior of all sorts was so commonplace most of the misdemeanors that would have been reported in other cities went overlooked due to the high demand on police. However, the crime perpetrated on Martha Tabram was unequaled to any crime I had investigated in my long career.

Though we had not met formally before my arrival to Whitechapel, Baxter was reputed to be a no-nonsense professional who already had more cases on his desk than one man could handle. I had read the newspaper's reports on the incidents before being assigned the case, but a murder in Whitechapel was hardly an eyebrow-raising event. The usual protocol for the reporting of murder in the East End in the past had been to place the column somewhere on the last page of the newspaper. This, however, was about to change for a murderer of a different sort had come to London, and his exploits would take up the front page of every newspaper around the world.

In London, in the year of our Lord, 1888, lawbreaking was rampant, especially in the East End. Here, human life, as terrible as it sounds, was cheap. This one case, however, was different from the norm; if murder, to anyone other than a detective; could be thought of in such a manner. These murders had a disturbing aspect about them that was out of the ordinary, and though ostensibly isolated, they would not be the last to make Londoners, and more specifically, the police to take notice. The two victims that I was looking into, were women that had been murdered in entirely different ways; seemingly, with no witnesses and were presumably unrelated. There were; however, some traits that stood out that made me take care before calling the crimes isolated incidences. Both women were of a similar walk of life and approximately the same age. The other aspect that caught my attention, that was somewhat troubling was that both murders seemingly lacked motive and were committed in the most peculiar and brutal manner. Before visiting the scenes and questioning witnesses, part of my preliminary investigation was to read the files and become acquainted with the cases. After reading both files there was something else troubling me about the cases, although, at the time, I could not put my finger on what exactly it was.

The woman, Martha Tabram was a thirty-nine-year-old prostitute, found lying near a dark stairwell with thirty-nine stab wounds to her body. Aside from the number of stab wounds, the sheer savagery of the crime was nothing like the Metropolitan Police was used to dealing with, even in the rookery. The ferociousness of the crime was enough for the order to be given for every constable to stay alert for a madman lurking in London's

East End. After spending several weeks on the case and having only the testimony of Mary Ann Connolly, to go on, the investigation had gone nowhere. Connolly, a known prostitute, and an acquaintance of the deceased, was the last person to see Tabram alive. There was no physical evidence to tie the murder to any particular suspect, and there was no reliable witness to state how the woman came to such a horrific end. At the inquest into Tabram's death, Dr. T. R. Killeen gave testimony on what I saw after being called to the scene of the crime by Police-constable Thomas Barrett.

[Sic] "Dr. T. R. Killeen, of 68, Brick-lane, said that he was called to the deceased, and found her dead. She had 39 stabs on the body. She had been dead some three hours. Her age was about 36, and the body was very well nourished. Witness had since made a post-mortem examination of the body. The left lung was penetrated in five places, and the right lung was penetrated in two places. The heart, which was rather fatty, was penetrated in one place, and that would be sufficient to cause death. The liver was healthy but was penetrated in five places, the spleen was penetrated in two places, and the stomach, which was perfectly healthy, was penetrated in six places. The witness did not think all the wounds were inflicted with the same instrument. The wounds generally might have been inflicted by a knife, but such an instrument could not have inflicted one of the wounds, which went through the chest-bone. His opinion was that one of the wounds was inflicted by some kind of dagger and that all of them were caused during life."

[Sic] The Coroner, Mr. G. Collier, Deputy Coroner for the South-Eastern Division of Middlesex, on Thursday, August twenty third in summing up, said that the crime was one of the most brutal that had occurred for some years. For a poor defenseless woman to be outraged and stabbed in the manner which this woman had been was almost beyond belief. They could only come to one conclusion, and that was that the deceased was brutally and cruelly murdered.'

The details of the doctor's testimony made me think that there was far more to the murder than just a crime of passion. The age of the deceased and the number of stab wounds inflicted was considered by me; to be something other than a coincidence. I had begun my investigation reading several police reports of complaints filed by some of the women in Whitechapel around that time. The single grievance made by most of the women who frequented the area was that of being robbed of the few pennies by those hungry enough to steal from an easy mark. I had also investigated a few reports in the past from women who reported that men called *'fancy men'* or pimps had started keeping several prostitutes in an area to work for them under the guise of protecting them from being robbed. However, the prostitute's complaints soon changed from being robbed by strangers to being robbed by the very protectors they paid to stop them from being targeted on the streets in the first place. In the three weeks since the murder, there had been no advancement in the case. During that time, I had been using a closet converted to an office down the hall from Baxter. The eight by ten room smelled of ammonia, and musty files. Though I tolerated the smell, I hoped there would not be sufficient opportunity for me to become accustomed.

Sitting up my feet, found the floor. Still half asleep, I opened one eye and inspected the coroner, who seemed rather chipper for the early hour. Taking the hot tea from Baxter, I cradled it in my two hands. Being a detective, made me a student of human behavior. I had spent many hours studying suspects in custody, taking note of their reactions during questioning. I had over the years grown accustomed to their body language. I had also become adept in identifying the small betraying signs that displayed anxiety, fear, and or dishonesty during an interview. Although helpful in my everyday investigations, I soon found I was unable to turn this quirk off. For better or worse, I found myself studying every person I met, and it had become a kind of second nature to me. Since their introduction, I had taken the time to consider the coroner. During my first impression, I found Baxter's gruff exterior and distaste for mortuaries incongruous with the man's role as coroner. However, after having the opportunity to study Baxter in action, I found that the man's brusqueness harmonized the man's dark penetrating glare, and both were quite effective, intimidating the most stubborn of witnesses who found themselves under the coroner's inquiry. The coroner had a quick step for a big man, and I guessed, that Baxter was in his early forties, greying at the temples with a large mustache that could not hide the perpetual smile on the man's round face. I had since learned that Baxter was a man of high personal integrity, something that I found lacking in the world I had become accustomed to as a detective. The ever-present smile and the man's tenacity for obtaining the truth made even the hardiest of witnesses uncomfortable on the stand. I had many times since our meeting considered; the incongruities of the man and saw Baxter as one who smiled at the world no matter the circumstances and wondered why the world didn't smile back.

"Get that into you, dear boy," Baxter said, gesturing with his teacup in hand. "I have a feeling you are going to need it.".

"Why is that?" I asked, as my lips tenderly touched the hot cup to drink in some of the soothing liquid.

"By Jove, there has been another murder," Baxter exclaimed. "And quite a ghastly one too, that is, if I have the story right."

"Where?" I yelped after spilling the hot tea on my knee.

"Buck's Row," Baxter replied. "I ran into a constable on my way into the office this morning; I'm surprised you haven't heard from your Home Office yet." Baxter related his story between sips of tea from his cup.

"Heard what?" I asked, bringing my cup to my lips, attempting to sip the scalding liquid again.

"Another prostitute has been found, this one with her throat slit straight across." Baxter commented, using his finger to draw a line across his own throat.

"Another prostitute!" I blurted.

"Yes, the poor creature was found across from Essex Wharf," Baxter explained.

Getting up from the settee, I changed my plans of not leaving the settee for at least a couple of more hours. Crossing the room, I went to a small table in the corner that held a pitcher and washbasin. Spilling the contents of the pitcher into the basin, I then pulled my shirt off and splashed the frigid water on my face and chest, toweling off with my shirt. Pulling a clean shirt from a hook on the wall, I reached for my jacket

"Where, are you off to Stone?" Baxter asked.

"Not me," I replied, reaching for my jacket. "We, Wynne, are going to Buck's Row."

"What, alright, I was going to the mortuary anyway," Baxter exclaimed, rising, taking another slurp from his cup.

"We can go there after we go to Buck's Row. I want to look at this crime scene, Wynne before it is too late."

"Too late," Baxter said, dropping his cup on the saucer after taking another gulp. "Too late for what Stone?"

"I will explain later!"

Buck's Row was approximately ten minutes' walk from Osborn Street. The deceased, who had as of yet to be identified, was found in a gateway used by the Brown's Stable Yard not far from the Brown and Eagle Wool Warehouse and the Schneider's Cap Factory. Arriving late, the victim had already been moved to the mortuary, leaving only a pool of coagulated blood to indicate where the body lay after the killer drew his knife across the victim's throat. To the left, only a few feet away from where the body had been found, a blood trail flowed towards the gutter in the street.

"The woman was killed only a few feet away from the gate, judging by the amount of pooled blood and where the blood flowed along the curb."

Wynne Baxter watched Stone as the detective sat on his haunches with a pencil in hand. The detective sifted through the small bits and pieces scattered in the gutter soaked with the unknown woman's blood, seeking anything that might be out of place. Not knowing the man well, I liked the tenacity of the man and was fascinated by the way his mind worked. Stone was in his fifties, a no-nonsense type, with a handlebar mustache and dark wavy hair that was rarely without the accompaniment of a bowler; propped soundly on top of his head. Stone was well over six feet in his socks, wide of shoulder, and thickly muscled. Two green eyes adequately proportioned apart below a stern brow, held a menacing gaze that seemed to just come naturally. There was not much to the story of the detective, but there were bits, and pieces, picked up from others that knew the man. Stone was a decorated veteran, and a detective for over twenty years, with a good record and well respected, if a little gruff in his dealings with his superiors. There was not much more; except that the man should have been a senior officer by now, but no explanation was given as to why not? His assignment working in the office of coroner was interesting, in fact, it was unheard of and highly irregular. As coroner, my first reaction was to flat out refuse, but these prostitutes kept turning up murdered in most peculiar ways, leaving London's citizenry in a hullabaloo. A letter from the lord mayor Sir Polydore de Keyser, explaining that Stone was on vacation and considering retirement seemed logical enough, and there was room for an investigator in my office due to the amount of work piling up on my desk. In short, the letter advised me to acquiesce; which was all that was needed to persuade me. Besides, with Whitechapel already being stretched east as far as it could go and with tensions running high, the community could use The Yard close at hand. So, by accepting the man into the fold, so to speak, the coroner's office made Stone welcome, with some reservations, of course.

"Well, Stone what do you make of it?" Baxter asked.

"Well, for one thing, the killer has left us very little evidence to collect. From all appearances, the murder took place here at the gateway to the stable yard where no footprints can be seen on the pavement, whether intentional or happenstance is anybody's guess. There are no street lamps, anywhere close by, although I did see one from the cab window at the end of the street. There are houses nearby, and on the opposite side of the street, the only buildings close by are a warehouse and a cap manufacturer, operating with only a day-shift."

"So, the area is dark and at that time of night; secluded," Baxter commented.

"Yes, but not only that, Wynne, this crime has the appearance of being premeditated."

"Planned," Baxter piped up. "Stone, are you telling me that you don't think that this is just some random act of violence?"

"I think it is safe to assume that this was not a crime of passion Wynne," I said, looking around. "I think this chap took his time searching for this very spot, a place of concealment with no lamps in the vicinity, and where no people would be walking about; that way, there would be no interruption."

"Why this spot Stone, of all places, there must be dozens of places that this bloke could have dumped his victim, and we may not have found her for weeks," Baxter commented.

"That is saying something, isn't it, Wynne."

"What?"

"This is a place of high traffic during the day. It is a place where his victim would be found quite easily, but secluded at night. You are right though about there being dozens of places where it might be weeks before the body is found, that is why, I think our killer wanted the body found soon after the deed was done. If I am wrong, why choose this place, you ask? I don't know; perhaps the woman lived nearby. Our killer may have visited this place before," I answered. "This man may even live close by, but I doubt it."

"Why?"

"Well, for one thing, I don't think the killer would kill close to his own home where a copper might remember him during routine questioning. I also doubt that this was simply a crime of opportunity."

"How do you know?" Baxter asked.

"I think that question could be best answered after I see the body at the mortuary, Wynne."

I walked passed the gate with Baxter following close behind muttering about my answers to his questions. Before leaving, they learned from a constable that the victim was taken to the Montague Street Mortuary. When they arrived, they found Inspector Helston. As the first responder, the inspector was the officer in charge of the investigation. Helston was still in attendance, as was Dr. Henry Llewellyn, the doctor was called to the scene soon after the woman was discovered at Buck's Row. After Inspector Helston finished questioning the doctor, I took a moment to talk to the inspector, and then, I followed Dr. Llewellyn into the autopsy room while Baxter hesitated at the door. The body lay naked on the wooden table prepped for the autopsy. As I studied the corpse, I made several mental notes on the condition of the corpse. Ignoring the cut to the woman's throat as the obvious cause of death, for the time being, I moved on to study the physical characteristics of the body first, and then, I worked back to the laceration at the woman's throat.

The body was that of a woman, who was approximately forty years old, five feet tall, dark-haired with a smattering of grey throughout. Taking a closer look at the face, I noticed that there was a bruise on the right side of her jaw, and some front teeth were missing. Though, upon closer examination, I saw no blood in the mouth, so I doubted that the missing teeth were from any recent altercation. At a glance, it was evident that the lady had not bathed in quite some time. On both hands dried dirt could be seen caked, under several cracked fingernails and rings of dirt could be seen around the wrists at the cuffs and around the neckline. Continuing around the table on which the woman was laid, I returned to the cause of death. The incision at the neckline ran from the left ear and continued eight inches around the victim's neck. The incision, according to Doctor Llewellyn, severed the carotid artery, slicing through all the soft tissue down to the vertebrae. Some other cuts were inflicted on the woman's abdomen. Upon closer study, these incisions were very deep and jagged. There was a cut that started two or three inches from the left side of the body and ran across the abdomen. Four more incisions could be seen on the right side. Though some incisions appeared hurried, others were jagged and gave the impression to be exploratory in nature. These incisions were applied with a degree of force behind them as if made by a dull knife.

"I assume that these incisions were all made after she was killed?" I asked Doctor Llewellyn, pointing at the jagged cuts on the victim's abdomen.

"Yes, they were all done post mortem, Detective. I am guessing by a left-handed man who sat straddled over the victim's legs." Llewellyn replied.

"Thank you, doctor, I do have one more question," I said, as I walked around the table. "The cuts that the killer made to the victim after she was dead, do you think that they made by a skilled hand."

"I highly doubt that Detective," Dr. Llewellyn replied. "It is my opinion that the cuts are random and hurried, more mutilating then purposeful."

Nodding, I glanced at the body one last time before leaving the mortuary. I heard Baxter following close behind with an eager step to be free of the smells of death and embalming fluid.

"I can't believe that a normal human being could be capable of doing such a thing to another Detective. Especially to one of the fairer sex," Baxter said, taking his seat.

For a long minute, I said nothing; waiting for the hansom to settle into its natural rhythm before commenting.

"Wynne, you asked me why, I did not think this crime was a crime of passion?"

"Yes, I did, now that you mention it," Baxter said, still holding his handkerchief up to his face.

"Wynne, this man did not kill a wife, a sibling, or for that matter a business partner. His victim was a prostitute and someone likely unknown to him before last night. I think we can further venture a guess and say that this man did not kill her for being a cheat or for any romantic interest. This killer sliced her throat so deep, according to a minor examination by Dr. Llewellyn, the blade of the knife sliced right into the vertebrae. There were

13

no defensive wounds on the woman's arms or hands, which means the two did not quarrel before her death, and she did not suspect that her life was in any danger right up until the knife was held up to her throat. Presumably, the woman felt comfortable enough around her attacker to turn her back on the man, having no suspicion that her life was in danger. The cuts, the killer made to the victim's abdomen, are cuts made after she was dead. Crimes perpetrated in the heat of passion are executed and then regretted, the moment the passion is finished. The perpetrator of a crime of passion usually panics and runs to escape punishment once the fury of the crime is satisfied, and when the rational man returns. In my experience with such cases, the culprit doesn't plan to dissect the body after the crime, and the victim is dead."

"What are you getting at, Stone?" Baxter enquired. "Is it your feeling that this killer was on some kind of rampage and did not stop until some kind of twisted appetite was satisfied?"

"Perhaps Wynne, if you accept the lunatic theory postulated by some at The Yard. It is quite apparent though that there is something more here than what meets the eye. The average man in his lust seeks out these women and pays them for their services and then goes on his way. This crime has all the appearances that this man is not satisfied in that way. I think it probable that this chap was not entirely satisfied with the quick end to the woman's life either. In most cases of murder, the realization of the act generally brings about fear and a need to get away to avoid being caught. I do not believe that the killer is satisfied to simply kill these women."

"Why?"

"His choice of the scene of the crime. The killer chose a place on a highly traveled lane, just off the walk in the dark shadows. Whether wittingly or merely indifferent to the idea that all the while a patrolling officer could be close by at any minute. This man kills his victim and then proceeds to mutilate the body. You made the point Wynne, that there were hundreds of places the killer could have left the body, and it might not be found for weeks. Plus, these cuts made to the abdomen are curious to me."

"How so?"

"Well, they appear to be probing and yet vicious at the same time Wynne."

"Meaning, what, for heaven's sake?" Wynne retorted. "Stone, you make it sound as if the killer was performing surgery."

"Meaning, the answer to whatever drove this man to kill this unfortunate woman, in this manner, is locked inside of the killer's head. This crime is made more fantastic not on its brutality alone but because I think the killer wanted the body found and the crime to be noticed soon after."

"By the by, now that I think of it," Baxter asked. "When the doctor said the killer was left-handed, you stopped in your tracks as if you were going to comment, and then you changed your mind, what were you going to say?"

"I think the doctor may change his mind on that point upon closer examination," I answered. "The incision made at the throat was from left to right, signifying..."

"Signifying that the killer was most likely right-handed," Baxter interrupted. "Yes, I know Stone, but if that is the case and you noticed it, why didn't Llewellyn?"

"I suspect that the doctor may be afraid that the public might get the wrong opinion if any perfunctory comments are made about the cuts in the abdomen. Llewellyn likely does not want the papers filled with the idea that a doctor could have committed the crime. Not to mention the illogical notion that some professionals still maintain that those who are left-handed are more apt to commit such atrocities, than a right-handed person. It's not unreasonable that Llewellyn in his efforts to protect his profession, would rather discount any science, and rely solely on superstition than leave it open to speculation."

"Be that as it may," Baxter said with a cocked eyebrow. "I suppose by tomorrow, when the inquest is held into the poor girl's death, we will get some answers."

The inquest proceeded at the Working Lads Institute on Saturday, September first. The hall was crowded when I arrived, more so than what a usual inquiry might see. How the woman had been killed had obviously aroused the morbid curiosity of the spectators. The coroner, Wynne Baxter, was standing at his desk, organizing his paperwork by the time I finally found a seat. The smack of the gavel on the desk quieted the room instantly. After a brief glance around at the spectators and the jury, Wynne Baxter called his first witness. The first called to the stand was Edward

Walker, the dead woman's father. Walker identified the woman as his daughter. The room hushed when the coroner told his first witness to proceed.

[Sic] Edward Walker deposed: I live at 15, Maidwell-street, Albany-road, Camberwell, and have no occupation. I was a smith when I was at work, but I am not now. I have seen the body in the mortuary, and to the best of my belief, it is my daughter; but I have not seen her for three years. I recognize her by her general appearance and by a little mark she has had on her forehead since she was a child. She also had either one or two teeth out, the same as the woman I have just seen. My daughter's name was Mary Ann Nichols, and she had been married twenty-two years. Her husband's name is William Nichols, and he is alive. He is a machinist. They have been living apart about seven or eight years. I last heard of her before Easter. She was forty-two years of age.

The Coroner: How did you see her?

Witness: She wrote to me.

The Coroner: Is this letter in her handwriting?

Witness: Yes, that is her writing. The letter, which was dated April 17, 1888, was read by the Coroner and referred to a place which the deceased had gone to at Wandsworth.

The Coroner: When did you last see her alive?

Witness: Two years ago, last June.

The Coroner: Was she then in a good situation?

Witness: I don't know. I was not on speaking terms with her. She had been living with me three or four years previously but thought she could better herself, so I let her go.

The Coroner: What did she do after she left you?

Witness: I don't know.

The Coroner: This letter seems to suggest that she was in a decent situation.

Witness: She had only just gone there.

The Coroner: Was she a sober woman?

Witness: Well, at times she drank, and that was why we did not agree.

The Coroner: Was she fast?

Witness: No, I never heard of anything of that sort. She used to go with some young women and men that she knew, but I never heard of anything improper.

The Coroner: Have you any idea what she has been doing lately?

Witness: I have not the slightest idea.

The Coroner: She must have drunk heavily for you to turn her out of doors?

Witness: I never turned her out. She had no need to be like this while I had a home for her.

The Coroner: How is it that she and her husband were not living together?

Witness: When she was confined her husband took on with the young woman who came to nurse her, and they parted, He is living with the nurse, by whom he has another family.

The Coroner: Have you any reasonable doubt that this is your daughter?

Witness: No, I have not. I know nothing about her acquaintances, or what she had been doing for a living. I had no idea she was over here in this part of the town. She has had five children, the eldest being twenty-one years old and the youngest eight or nine years. One of them lives with me, and the other four are with their father.

The Coroner: Has she ever lived with anybody since she left her husband?

Witness: I believe she was once stopping with a man in York-street, Walworth. His name was Drew, and he was a smith by trade. He is living there now, I believe. The parish of Lambeth summoned her husband for the keep of the children, but the summons was dismissed, as it was proved that she was then living with another man. I don't know who that man was.

The Coroner: Was she ever in the workhouse?

Witness: Yes, sir; Lambeth Workhouse, in April last, and went from there to a situation at Wandsworth.

By the Jury: The husband resides at Coburg-road, Old Kent-road. I don't know if he knows of her death.

Coroner: Is there anything you know of likely to throw any light upon this affair?

Witness: No, I don't think she had any enemies; she was too good for that.

[Sic]

After a brief recess, the crowd again was quieted by the coroner smacking the gavel on his desk. The entrance of Constable John Neil started the crowd to whisper again. Neil, was a constable patrolling Buck's

Row, except that the constable was nowhere to be found on the night in question when Andrew Cross and the other witness went looking to report the woman lying in the gate.

[Sic] John Neil, police-constable, 97J, said: Yesterday morning, I was proceeding down Buck's-row, Whitechapel, going towards Brady-street. There was not a soul about. I had been round there half an hour previously, and I saw no one then. I was on the right-hand side of the street when I noticed a figure lying in the street. It was dark at the time, though there was a street lamp shining at the end of the row. I went across and found deceased lying outside a gateway, her head towards the east. The gateway was closed. It was about nine or ten feet high and led to some stables. There were houses from the gateway eastward, and the School Board school occupies the westward. On the opposite side of the road is Essex Wharf. Deceased was lying lengthways along the street, her left hand touching the gate. I examined the body by the aid of my lamp and noticed blood oozing from a wound in the throat. She was lying on her back, with her clothes disarranged. I felt her arm, which was quite warm from the joints upwards. Her eyes were wide open. Her bonnet was off and lying at her side, closest to the left hand. I heard a constable passing Brady-street, so I called him. I did not whistle. I said to him, "Run at once for Dr. Llewellyn," and, seeing another constable in Baker's-row, I sent him for the ambulance. The doctor arrived in a very short time. I had, in the meantime, rung the bell at Essex Wharf, and asked if any disturbance had been heard. The reply was "No." Sergeant Kirby came after, and I knocked. The doctor looked at the woman and then said, "Move her to the mortuary. She is dead, and I will make a further examination of her." We placed her on the ambulance, and moved her there. Inspector Spratley came to the mortuary, and while taking a description of the deceased turned up her clothes and found that she was disemboweled. This had not been noticed by any of them before. On the body was found a piece of comb and a bit of looking-glass. No money was found, but an unmarked white handkerchief was found in her pocket.
The Coroner: Did you notice any blood where she was found?
Witness: There was a pool of blood just where her neck was lying. It was running from the wound in her neck.
The Coroner: Did you hear any noise that night?

18

Witness: No, I heard nothing. The farthest I had been that night was just through the Whitechapel-road and up Baker's-row. I was never far away from the spot.

The Coroner: Whitechapel-road is busy in the early morning, I believe. Could anybody have escaped that way?

Witness: Oh yes, sir. I saw a number of women on the main road going home. At that time anyone could have got away.

The Coroner: Someone searched the ground, I believe?

Witness: Yes, I examined it while the doctor was being sent for.

Inspector Spratley: I examined the road, sir, in daylight.

A Juryman (to witness): Did you see a trap in the road at all?

Witness: No.

A Juryman: Knowing that the body was warm, did it not strike you that it might just have been laid there, and that the woman was killed elsewhere?

Witness: I examined the road, but did not see the mark of wheels. The first to arrive on the scene after I had discovered the body were two men who work at a slaughterhouse opposite. They said they knew nothing of the affair, and that they had not heard any screams. I had previously seen the men at work. That would be about a quarter-past three, or half an hour before I found the body.'

The next witness was the physician, Henry Llewellyn. I glanced around the room, inspecting the crowd as the coroner waited for the room to quiet down. The medical profession at any inquest were generally the crowd's favorite witness; it never ceased to amaze me at the number of people who treated these inquiries like they were some sort of entertainment. The gossip about how the victim had been murdered was enough to draw a good-sized crowd. The fact that the woman had been mutilated after she was killed was enough to fill the room beyond capacity. Wynne Baxter stood up from his desk and walked towards the witness; the crowd silenced immediately, not wanting to miss one tidbit of the gruesome detail.

[Sic] Henry Llewellyn, surgeon, said: On Friday morning I was called to Buck's-row about four o'clock. The constable told me what I was wanted for. On reaching Buck's-row I found the deceased woman lying flat on her back in the pathway, her legs extended. I found she was dead, and that she had severe injuries to her throat. Her hands and wrists were cold, but the

19

body and lower extremities were warm. I examined her chest and felt the heart. It was dark at the time. I believe she had not been dead more than half-an-hour. I am quite certain that the injuries to her neck were not self-inflicted. There was very little blood round the neck. There were no marks of any struggle or of blood, as if the body had been dragged. I told the police to take her to the mortuary, and I would make another examination. About an hour later I was sent for by the Inspector to see the injuries I had discovered on the body. I went, and saw that the abdomen was cut very extensively. I have this morning made a post-mortem examination of the body. I found it to be that of a female about forty or forty-five years. Five of the teeth are missing, and there is a slight laceration of the tongue. On the right side of the face there is a bruise running along the lower part of the jaw. It might have been caused by a blow with the fist or pressure by the thumb. On the left side of the face there was a circular bruise, which also might have been done by the pressure of the fingers. On the left side of the neck, about an inch below the jaw, there was an incision about four inches long and running from a point immediately below the ear. An inch below on the same side, and commencing about an inch in front of it, was a circular incision terminating at a point about three inches below the right jaw. This incision completely severs all the tissues down to the vertebrae. The large vessels of the neck on both sides were severed. The incision is about eight inches long. These cuts must have been caused with a long-bladed knife, moderately sharp, and used with great violence. No blood at all was found on the breast either of the body or clothes. There were no injuries about the body till just about the lower part of the abdomen. Two or three inches from the left side was a wound running in a jagged manner. It was a very deep wound, and the tissues were cut through. There were several incisions running across the abdomen. On the right side there were also three or four similar cuts running downwards. All these had been caused by a knife, which had been used violently and been used downwards. The wounds were from left to right and might have been done by a left-handed person. All the injuries had been done by the same instrument."

Leaving by a side door as soon as Llewellyn gave his testimony, I was back at my office deep in thought about the absurdity of the doctor's statement. Llewellyn was emphatic in his assertion that the killer was left-handed, despite noting that the incision was made from left to right. I was sitting at my desk, thinking about Mary Ann Nichols when Baxter entered carrying a tray with tea and biscuits.

"Thank you, Wynne."

"That should hit the spot," Baxter commented. "By the by, when I came in the other morning, you looked a lot like the worse for wear. What did you get up to?" Baxter asked before sipping the strong tea from his cup.

"I was running down a lead in Spitalfields. It was quite late when I returned," I replied, not feeling in the mood for conversation.

"Spitalfields, you say," Baxter asked, turning from whatever was happening out on the street below. "May I ask what took you there so late?"

"I wanted to question Mary Ann Connolly again," I answered, seeing Baxter's head snap to attention out of the corner of my eye. "I was just following up on a statement that Constable Barrett had written down in his notes on the night that Martha Tabram was murdered."

"A statement that required immediate attention, so much so to have you track down Connolly at such a late date detective?" Baxter looked surprised.

"In Connolly's statement to Constable Barrett, Wynne, she remembered seeing a coal porter the night that Martha Tabram was murdered. I thought the coal porter might have seen something that could be of some help in the investigation."

"I questioned Connolly or 'Polly Poll as she is known, myself." Baxter offered. "She made no such statement at the inquest about seeing a coal porter in the area." Baxter turned towards the table that held the tea and biscuits, "So, what, if anything, did you find out?"

Baxter asked, pouring another cup of tea and then gestured with the pot in Stone's direction.

"Connolly told me that she saw a porter in the area of Wentworth Street. I went down to Spitalfields because I wanted to find out if she knew who the porter was. I also wanted to know why she had not mentioned anything about it to you at the inquest."

I saw Baxter's features soften after hearing my excuse. I understood why Baxter was curious. Being a stickler for detail, I knew that Baxter would blame himself for having missed such a thing.

"Wentworth is nowhere near the George Yard buildings where Tabram was found, dear boy," Baxter said, reaching for another biscuit.

"After making several inquiries, I found Connolly in a pub near where she and Martha Tabram met the Guardsman on August seventh the night that Tabram was found murdered. After threatening Connolly with obstruction, she recalled giving Constable Barrett the information on the coal porter, but Barrett, according to Connolly seemed less than interested. She told me that on her travels that night, she remembers seeing the porter but paid him no mind."

"Detective," Baxter interrupted. "I still fail to see any connection?"

"The coal porter is only a part of what my investigation has turned up," I said, watching Baxter dunk his biscuit in the scalding tea. "The point is that Martha Tabram and Mary Ann Nichols were found in areas of seclusion and of easy access and escape. The connection from Wentworth Street and Whitechapel High Street is..."

"Is the George Yard Alley," Baxter interrupted.

"That is right, Wynne, near where Tabram was murdered. The areas where both murders were committed are similar. Both are completely devoid of people and are dimly lit at night, while this recent victim was murdered in Buck's Row with just tenements on one side of a dark road and a stable yard close by. I think it is time to accept that a pattern might be developing here."

"A pattern?"

"Our killer could be someone doing a service that would place him in and around the scene. Or someone who has some excuse to be in the area without drawing undue attention to myself, like this coal porter, for instance. This man would be familiar with those living there and used to being seen at odd hours."

"Surely, there is enough police walking patrols that someone should have heard or seen something."

Stopped by a knock on the door, Baxter got up from his chair and opened the door.

"Please forgive me, sir, I have a telegram for Detective Stone; the boy said it was marked urgent."

"Thank you, Miss Davenport," Baxter responded, taking the telegram from his secretary and closed the door, and tossed it on the desk.

"It would seem that the citizenry does not share your opinion that there are a sufficient number of police in Whitechapel," I said, looking up at Baxter.

"Who, might that be?" Baxter asked, amid a swig of his tea.

"This telegram is from Inspector Abberline, Wynne."

"Well, well, do tell," Baxter commented, sitting back in his chair.

"Apparently, the Whitechapel Vigilance Committee has been reinstituted. The committee has informed The Yard that they will address the issue of poorly patrolled areas in Whitechapel by the police."

"Well, the Vigilance Committee has been of use in the past. Though, I shouldn't think that two dead prostitutes in Whitechapel are enough to make them think things have gotten out of hand," Baxter commented.

Thinking about what Baxter said, I wondered what had prompted the organization of the Vigilance Committee, I was still lost in the thought when Baxter continued.

"The Nichols' inquest resumes on Monday; I assume you will be in attendance, Stone?" Baxter asked, picking up the tray.

"Yes, of course, bright and early," I replied.

"Cheerio," Baxter said with a wave.

Chapter Two

On Monday, September third, the great room at the Working Lads Institute, was filling rapidly. By the time I arrived, the jury had been seated, and Baxter was standing at his table waiting to begin. Inspector John Spratling was the first witness to be deposed.

[Sic] Inspector John Spratling, J Division, deposed that he first heard of the murder about half-past four on Friday morning, while he was in Hackney-road. I proceeded to Buck's-row, where I saw Police-constable Thain, who showed me the place where the deceased had been found. I noticed a bloodstain on the footpath. The body of deceased had been removed to the mortuary in Old Montague- street, where witness had an opportunity of preparing a description. The skin presented the appearance of not having been washed for some time previous to the murder. On my arrival Dr. Llewellyn made an examination of the body, which lasted about ten minutes.
Witness said he next saw the body when it was stripped.
Detective-sergeant Enright: That was done by two of the workhouse officials.
The Coroner: Had they any authority to strip the body?
Witness: No, sir; I gave them no instructions to strip it. In fact, I told them to leave it as it was.
The Coroner: I don't object to their stripping the body, but we ought to

have evidence about the clothes.

Sergeant Enright, continuing, said the clothes, which were lying in a heap in the yard, consisted of a reddish-brown Ulster, with seven large brass buttons, and a brown dress, which looked new. There was also a woolen and a flannel petticoat, belonging to the workhouse. Inspector Helson had cut out pieces marked "P. R., Princes-road," with a view to tracing the body. There was also a pair of stays in fairly good condition, but witness did not notice how they were adjusted.

[Sic] The Coroner said I considered it important to know the exact state in which the stays were found.

On the suggestion of Inspector Abberline, the clothes were sent for.

The Foreman of the jury asked whether the stays were fastened on the body.

Inspector Spratling replied that he could not say for certain. There was blood on the upper part of the dress body, and also on the Ulster, but I only saw a little on the under-linen, and that might have happened after the removal of the body from Buck's-row. The clothes were fastened when I first saw the body. The stays did not fit very tightly, for I was able to see the wounds without unfastening them. About six o'clock that day, I made an examination at Buck's- row and Brady-street, which ran across Baker's-row, but I failed to trace any marks of blood. I subsequently examined, in company with Sergeant Godley, the East London and District Railway lines and embankment, and also the Great Eastern Railway yard, without, however, finding any traces. A watchman of the Great Eastern Railway, whose box was fifty or sixty yards from the spot where the body was discovered, heard nothing particular on the night of the murder. Witness also visited half a dozen persons living in the same neighborhood, none of whom had noticed anything at all suspicious. One of these, Mrs. Purkiss, had not gone to bed at the time the body of deceased was found, and her husband was of opinion that if there had been any screaming in Buck's-row they would have heard it. A Mrs. Green, whose window looked out upon the very spot where the body was discovered, said nothing had attracted her attention on the morning of Friday last.

Replying to a question from one of the juries, witness stated that Constable Neil was the only one whose duty it was to pass through Buck's-row, but another constable passing along Broad-street from time to time would be within hearing distance.

In reply to a juryman, witness said it was his firm belief that the woman had her clothes on at the time she was murdered.

I smiled at Spratling's report on the conduct of the two workers at the mortuary, describing them as mortuary *officials,* which is not quite, the word, I would have used. I was sure Spratling's description was added for the jury's benefit. In the past, there had been much to-do over mortuary conditions and attendants following the proper protocols when handling a body from a police surgeon. The next witness deposed was Henry Tomkins, a horse slaughterer, who worked for Messrs. Barber on Coventry Street. Very little was gained by presenting this witness. Tomkins worked until Friday, at twenty-minutes-past four in the morning. Leaving work soon after, Tomkins, took his usual way home and saw nothing unusual in his travels. The next witnesses deposed was Inspector Helson and then Constable Mizen.

[Sic] Inspector Joseph Helson deposed that he first received information about the murder at a quarter before seven on Friday morning. I afterwards went to the mortuary, where I saw the body with the clothes still on it. The dress was fastened in front, with the exception of a few buttons, the stays, which were attached with clasps, were also fastened. I noticed blood on the hair, and on the collars of the dress and Ulster, but not on the back of the skirts. There were no cuts in the clothes, and no indications of any struggle having taken place. The only suspicious mark discovered in the neighborhood of Buck's-row was in Broad-street, where there was a stain which might have been blood.
Witness was of the opinion that the body had not been carried to Buck's-row, but that the murder was committed on the spot.
[Sic] Police-constable Mizen: said that at a quarter to four o'clock on Friday morning I was at the crossing, Hanbury-street, Baker's-row, when a Carman who passed in company with another man informed me that I was wanted by a policeman in Buck's-row, where a woman was lying. When I arrived, Constable Neil sent me for the ambulance. At that time nobody but Neil was with the body."

Andrew Cross was a Carman; and the first to find the body of Mary Ann Nichols at Buck's Row. Cross' testimony would illuminate one crucial

26

detail, an aspect that I hoped; would be, brought to light at the inquest. Cross on his route had not seen a constable on foot patrol in Buck's Row, this fact, I had already made Baxter privy to, after, I had questioned Cross.

[Sic] Chas. Andrew Cross, Carman, said he had been in the employment of Messrs. Pickford and Co. for over twenty years. About half-past three on Friday, I left my home to go to work, and I passed through Buck's-row. I discerned on the opposite side something lying against the gateway, but I could not at once make out what it was. I thought it was a tarpaulin sheet. I walked into the middle of the road and saw that it was the figure of a woman. I then heard the footsteps of a man going up Buck's-row, about forty yards away, in the direction that I myself had come from. When I came up, witness said to me, 'Come and look over here; there is a woman lying on the pavement.' They both crossed over to the body, and witness took hold of the woman's hands, which were cold and limp. Witness said, 'I believe she is dead.' Witness touched her face, which felt warm. The other man, placing his hand on her heart, said 'I think she is breathing, but very little if she is.' Witness suggested that they should give her a prop, but my companion refused to touch her. Just then they heard a policeman coming. Witness did not notice that her throat was cut, the night being very dark. I and the other man left the deceased, and in Baker's-row they met the last witness, whom they informed that they had seen a woman lying in Buck's-row. Witness said, 'She looks to me to be either dead or drunk, but for my part I think she is dead.' The policeman said, 'All right,' and then walked on. The other man left witness soon after. Witness had never seen him before.
Replying to the coroner, witness denied having seen Police-constable Neil in Buck's-row. There was nobody there when I and the other man left. In my opinion deceased looked as if she had been outraged and gone off in a swoon; but I had no idea that there were any serious injuries.
The Coroner: Did the other man tell you who I was?
Witness: No, sir; I merely said that I would have fetched a policeman, only I was behind time. I was behind time myself.
A Juryman: Did you tell Constable Mizen that another constable wanted him in Buck's-row?
Witness: No, because I did not see a policeman in Buck's-row.'

27

William Nichols told the jury that the woman at the mortuary, was indeed, his late wife and had made a positive identification of Mary Ann Nichols. They had been separated, and it had been three years since Nichols had last seen his estranged wife. Nichols candidly told the coroner that she had left him, of her own free will, to be with another man. The man seemed grieved but seemingly, displayed no ill will for a woman he had been separated from for eight years.

[Sic] Emily Holland was the owner of a Thrawl Street lodging house in which Nichols had frequented. She had last seen the deceased on Osborn Street at half-past two, and she was very intoxicated. Nichols must have had a banner night for she told Holland that she had made and spent her lodging money three times that day aside from some other speculation there was nothing substantial to be heard from the three witnesses that closed day two of the inquest into the death of Mary Ann Nichols.

Back at my office, I put pen to paper and wrote down the events of the day, the results, as far as I was concerned, were disappointing, to say the least. Aside from Edward Walker and William Nichols making the positive identification of Mary Ann Nichols, no new evidence had been revealed. To date, the information accumulated included the victim's name, where she was killed, and the details of how Mary Ann Nichols met her demise. Who killed her, and why, seemed to be a mystery in which police could not solve or make sense of? Hearing footsteps coming up the hall, I knew that Baxter would be on his way to review the results of the day, as the coroner had done in the past. It had been a ritual with them to sit at the end of the day and chat since the Martha Tabram investigation.

I watched without comment, as Baxter plopped his bulky frame into the chair across from me. Though the day had not gone; as Baxter might have expected, the coroner was responsible for accumulating witnesses, and that was all. The office could not guarantee testimonies nor results, and though I knew, Wynne Baxter was fully aware of his duties, I suspected the day had been trying for the county coroner who took his job very seriously.

"Well, it seems after two days of testimony the only thing we can be sure of John, is the victim's name and her occupation," Baxter stated, accompanied by a gasp of frustration. "The cause of death perpetrated by person or persons unknown, is getting to be more a scapegoat than anything else."

"As hard as it is to say Wynne, I feel as though this inquest has done little more than heap up more questions than answering the many we have in store."

"Refresh my memory, Detective," Baxter snorted. "Aside from establishing the woman's identity, I fail to see that I was any help at all today."

"There is one thing, that I cannot get straight Wynne, after all of the testimony?"

"What?"

"I cannot stop wondering why Cross did not see Constable Neil on patrol."

Several questions had, as of yet, to be answered, but I asked the one question that had been troubling me since I arrived back at my office.

"Perhaps the constable was too far away from the scene?" Baxter replied.

"On the contrary, Wynne, here listen to this," I said, retrieving my notebook from my pocket. "I wrote this down when you questioned him. Constable Neil said, [Sic] *'the farthest I had been away that night was just through the Whitechapel Road and up Baker's Row, I was never far away from the spot.'* If Neil's statement is correct, that would mean Cross and the other man should have run straight into Constable Neil or, at the very least, by him. Instead, they did not see a constable. They did, however, find Constable Mizen, where the man was supposed to be."

"Perchance in his panic after finding the dead body, Cross missed Constable Neil, or the man went in the opposite direction from where Neil was patrolling," Baxter explained.

"It is possible, Wynne, however, Cross wasn't skipping up the street window shopping, and I am certain Mizen would have blown his police whistle more than once in his search for another constable after Cross found him. Why was Constable Neil, not alerted right away?"

"I see your point, where do you suppose Neil was?" Baxter asked.

"Your guess is as good as mine, but I suspect, that the constable was somewhere other than on foot patrol."

"Have you considered Doctor Llewellyn's statement on the handedness of the killer? The man is convinced the killer was left-handed?" Baxter countered.

"I am still developing my own theory on that aspect of his autopsy, Wynne," I said, as I watched Baxter stuff his pipe with tobacco. "I think that I will need to confer with Dr. Phillips and get his opinion on the subject."

"Subject, what subject is that?"

"Well, it might be easier to show you than explain it to you, Wynne. Stand up for a minute," I said, coming around my desk.

Gripping Baxter by the shoulders, I spun the coroner around to face away from me.

"Stone, what the devil are you up to?" Baxter huffed.

"Just stand still for a minute," I said, holding the coroner by the shoulders to steady him. "What if the killer came up behind Nichols like this," I explained, wrapping my right forearm around the coroner's neck, taking advantage of my height, I placed my left hand behind Baxter's left shoulder and tightened my grip around the coroner's throat.

"She didn't die of strangulation, Stone!" Baxter shouted.

"I am aware of that Wynne; what side is my right hand on?" I asked the coroner.

"It is on my left. Why?" Baxter asked.

Walking back to my desk, I picked up my notebook.

"I wrote Dr. Llewellyn's testimony down. Here it is, [Sic] *"On the right side of the face there is a bruise running along the lower part of the jaw. It might have been caused by a blow with the fist or pressure by the thumb. On the left side of the face, there was a circular bruise, which also might have been done by the pressure of the fingers. On the left side of the neck, about an inch below the jaw, there was an incision about four inches long and running from a point immediately below the ear. An inch below on the same side, and commencing about an inch in front of it, was a circular incision terminating at a point about three inches below the right jaw,"* I finished reading, and then walked back and turned the coroner around again.

"I think the killer turned Nichols around, and then under the guise of passion, this fiend brings his left hand around the front of the victim, and then grips the victim's face, like this, while he brings his right hand up

30

concealing the knife. He grips their throat hard with his forearm almost in a chokehold rendering the woman semi-conscious. Next, this man plunges the knife into their throat, while his left-hand grips her shoulder, pushing the victim's own weight into the knife." With a swipe of my right hand against Baxter's throat.

"I think you might be onto something there, Stone," Baxter said, as his hand tenderly massaged his throat after being released from the grip. "Not only would it explain the bruises on Nichols jaw, but it also would explain the deep slash of the throat, cutting deep into the vertebrae. However, why isn't there more bruising around the neck if this wretch is, in fact, choking them?"

"The bruises on the jaw could be a button on a coat or a cufflink Wynne. As far as bruising on the neck, there isn't any because the victim isn't being chocked by hands or strangled by a rope that would leave the wrinkled bruising or tearing marks on the tender flesh that such an action might leave. I think the killer compresses both sides of the neck where the carotid arteries are. This slows the flow of blood to the head, making his victim almost blackout. In that way, she is rendered almost helpless and unable to struggle or scream."

"I still think there would be a lot more bruising around the neck, Stone?" Baxter said, still skeptical.

"Not if the killer knew where and how to apply the pressure," I retorted defensively.

"How do you mean?"

"I think that is a question best left to a doctor, Wynne."

When the day ended, I went directly to my rooms. Sitting with a cup of tea by the stove, a knock brought me out of my daydreaming. Before I could answer Inspector Abberline forced himself passed my landlady, nodding in my direction while thwarting off the attempts of Mrs. Wilson to deliver tea and crumpets. Begging her pardon, Abberline closed the door and threw his overcoat and bowler on a chair.

I watched as the inspector in charge of detectives paced back and forth, waiting for the man to give some inclination for the visit, which was both unusual and highly out of the ordinary. Abberline was a medium height man of about forty-five, balding with a handlebar mustache and steel blue eyes. I had studied the man several times in the past. Each time, I could not

31

help but think Abberline looked more like a banker than an inspector attached to the world-famous detectives of Scotland Yard. This night, Abberline held a rolled-up newspaper, which was rhythmically slapped in his left palm while pacing back and forth. Waiting for Abberline to make the reason behind his visit known, I watched the inspector turn towards the window and focus all his attention outside on the street for several minutes before speaking.

"First of all, Detective, I hope that I don't need to remind you that you have been placed here to investigate the murder of Martha Tabram and though officially you are on vacation, that should not be your primary objective here. I assure you if it weren't for all the political strong-arming going on by the constituents in London, you wouldn't be here in the capacity you find yourself. This latest news hitting the newspapers of another prostitute being murdered in Whitechapel and the reforming of the Vigilance Committee has got my office crawling with politicians. Until, I find out otherwise, you are going to be here in Whitechapel, answering only to me. As if things are not bad enough down here already with the high crime rate, unemployment, and poverty, not to mention the growing anti-Semitic feeling in London, these murders could be the match that will blow this powder keg wide opened. We cannot allow police authority in this investigation to be challenged by this bunch of armed civilians patrolling the streets at night. This entire mess sounds like a recipe for innocent people to be killed."

Abberline walked to the chair and placed his hat firmly on his head, then shrugged into his overcoat. "These are the names of the committee organizers and members, if, in fact, they do rally you may need them." Abberline stuck out a thick envelope and then held up a hand in response to any questions. "No time, Stone."

The inspector jerked open the door, and then stopped halfway through the doorway.

"Be careful down here, Stone, if this group is assembled, they will have something to prove, there are political powers at work here that are not under our control."

With that said Abberline, closed the door behind him. Stunned by the abruptness of the call, and the knowledge that my position in Whitechapel had been extended, I did not know what to make of it. I had assumed that my assignment in Whitechapel would extend until the killer or killers were caught in the Tabram case. Now, it seemed that something else was afoot, that I had not anticipated. This '*political strong-arming*' that the inspector had referred to was something that I had noticed, that had begun to affect police business for some time now and was the reason why I had tendered my resignation in the first place. It seemed like my vacation was now on the backburner and the walkover the inspector had promised was not so much a sure thing as he had anticipated.

Ripping open the envelope, I dumped the contents out on my lap and began to read. The Vigilance Committee was made up of at least four businessmen who were instrumental in its formation. Their reason for organizing was under the guise of how the murders were affecting businesses in the area. Two of the members were in the business of cigarette manufacturing, and of course, the third was George Lusk, a well-known builder and the Chairman of the committee. The committee included Mr. Joseph Aarons, who was the landlord of The Crown Public House at Mile End Road, and B. Harris, the Secretary of the Committee. The rest of the members were a nondescript group, including even an actor. All in all, the Vigilance Committee numbered about twenty members. They met at The Crown at nine o'clock each night, staying until half-past twelve when the pub closed.

Placing the information that Abberline had left me back in the envelope, I threw the package on the table where I took tea and started to pace back and forth. The surprise meeting with the inspector had caused me to think about my future in Whitechapel and the newly formed, self-appointed vigilante group. Vigilantes had their place in history, that is, before a citizenry was committed to elect a government and a means to enforce the law. In London, this was done over seventy years previous. Once laws were instituted and a police force was established, these groups were no longer necessary. The instating of such groups was a cause for concern for anyone who wore a badge. Any group of self-appointed, armed men whose courage came from a bottle, was an unstoppable force when called into action. These men, although upstanding businessmen, had the power to influence a mob, and every police officer knows mob mentality took no heed when challenged by any type of authority. On the other side, if the group, were disarmed and patrolled alongside police, they could aid in the protection of the women of Whitechapel, but only if they kept a cool head, and they allowed the police to do their jobs. However, in my experience, such vigilantes were formed to uphold their own personal agendas; whose goal was to sway others and once they were provoked trying to control them was impossible. Walking to the window, I looked out into the night and cringed at the thought of where the committee would be patrolling this night.

Chapter Three

Unable to sleep, I dressed quietly and left my rooms. It was now well past midnight, and I sat at my desk, rubbing my weary eyes trying to concentrate on lessening the pile of files spread over the top of my desk. The files contained copies of every police report and witness statement in the murders of the three women in Whitechapel. Though officially, the Metropolitan Police Department's view was that none of these murders were connected. My assignment was to quietly look at all three murders and this Vigilance Committee. Of course, Abberline had not said this in so many words, but reading between the lines my position seems to have become more important to the inspector then what was originally anticipated. That was inferred by the inspector coming to my rooms so surreptitiously to hand me the names of the vigilantes. I had spent the last three days making copies of all the files on the murders as discreetly as possible. Abberline's visit in regards to the Vigilance Committee had been unexpected and most unusual. I did not know why, but I had known the inspector long enough to know that Abberline had never once asked where I lived, much less, had the inspector darkened my door in the past. The secrecy of my mission was never so poignant than to have Abberline show up and handle our business both out of sight and hearing of anyone at the Home Office. The idea worried me, less than what I might have thought.

The 'political strong-arming' expression used by the inspector told me that there were other influences involved here in Whitechapel. These I am sure involved the Vigilance Committee, the newspapers, and public opinion that made it harder for police to do their duties. Though the secrecy needed to update me, was unexpected, it made sense, I suppose, as it had something to do with my working with the coroner's office. After much consideration, I decided that, perhaps, a certain amount of worry was healthy, lest, I became a scapegoat.

I had been a detective for a long time and I knew all the ins and outs and the office politics that one sees in large organizations. The Metropolitan Police Department was no exception. I cared less about promotion than most of my colleagues, and therefore, I did not feel the need to become involved. I did, on the other hand, care about my record. In the past, I had seen good coppers dismissed from duty while protecting someone of higher rank than themselves. The dismissal was usually explained this way: *that the appearance of decorum must be maintained for the greater good*, or some such way, just before the poor sod was fired for dereliction of duty. Though this meant less to me now, that I had technically resigned my position in The Yard.

Opening the last file, my immediate thought was that all the records seemed to be missing vital pieces of information. The key feature of any investigation was a list of suspects. All three murders had no one that the lead investigator could point to as a probable culprit. Though, I did not think the investigators incompetent, nor did I think that Abberline had implied for me to check into the cases because the inspector thought that my investigative skills were superior to those heading the investigation. No, something else had spurred the inspector to act so, out of character, and I could only assume that Abberline had not told me all that there was to know when the proposition was made to me.

To keep my focus on the details of the case, I began to read, all the while fighting off watery eyes and the temptation to quit and use the settee. As I read, I concluded that it was becoming harder to agree with the home office about which direction the investigation should take. The chief inspector was adamant that three different killers needed to be found in Whitechapel, if he knew something I did not, I would have liked to know what it was? The standard procedure in any cold investigation was to follow up on the direction that the investigation had originally taken and hope something had changed since the crime was committed. Following protocol, I had done as any investigator would. However, my view had changed since my investigation began. From the beginning, I had seen similarities in each of the cases. As a result, it was becoming increasingly hard to convince me that three deranged individuals were killing prostitutes in London's East End. Unfortunately, my feelings were not enough to persuade anyone that the murders of Tabram and Emma Elizabeth Smith were connected to this latest victim Mary Ann Nichols. What I needed was to find evidence. As I read the files of each victim, I tried to determine a motive, but as of yet, I could establish no clear suspect, let alone a motive. Instead of fixating on the unknowns, I turned my attention to the facts of the case that were proven. Typical investigative techniques demanded that the investigator seek out known acquaintances and family members. This was standard procedure, due to the high percentage of cases that had proven that someone close to the victim was usually the guilty culprit. Although, with no suspects in any of the crimes, I turned my attention to determine; how the killer chose his victims.

I began by looking at the victims themselves. There were several similarities between all three women. The most obvious was that they were all prostitutes and all roughly around the same age. The one distinguishing feature in each case was not where or when the women were killed, it was the fantastic way in which they were murdered.

"Emma Elizabeth Smith, age forty-five, attacked April second, Osborn Street, died April third, in hospital due to complications of having a ruptured peritoneum.

Residence: 18 George St. Spitalfields. Investigator: Metro. Police H. Division, Whitechapel, Edmund Reid, said about the Smith's attire *'was in such dirty, ragged condition that it was impossible to tell if any part of it had been freshly torn.'* Reid later wrote in his notes. *'Her past was a mystery, even to her intimate friends.'* All she had ever told anyone about herself was that she was a widow who, more than ten years before had left her husband and broken away from all her early associations. The surgeon who resided at the London Hospital testified Saturday, April seventh.

[Sic] Mr. George Haslip, house surgeon, stated that when the deceased was admitted to the hospital, she had been drinking but was not intoxicated. She was bleeding from the head and ear and had other injuries of a revolting nature. Witness found that she was suffering from a

36

rupture of the peritoneum, which had been perforated by some blunt instrument used with great force.

Coroner: Mr. Wynne Edwin Baxter. Inquest notes were recorded from the London Times on April ninth, 1888.

Shuffling through the pages in the file, I continued to read out loud, in order to keep myself awake.

[Sic] Day of the inquest, Saturday, April 7, 1888.

Mr. Wynne E. Baxter, the East Middlesex Coroner, held an inquiry on Saturday [7 Apr] at the London Hospital respecting the death of Emma Elizabeth Smith, aged 45, a widow, lately living at 18, George-street, Spitalfields, who, it was alleged, had been murdered.

Chief Inspector West, of the H Division of Police, attended for the Commissioners of Police.

Mrs. Mary Russell, the deputy keeper of a common lodging-house, stated that she had known the deceased for about two years. On the evening of Bank Holiday [2 Apr], she left home at 7 o'clock and returned about 4 or 5 the next morning in a dreadful state. Her face and head were much injured, one of her ears being nearly torn off. She told the witness that she had been set upon and robbed of all her money. She also complained of pains in the lower part of the body. Witness took her to the hospital, and when passing along Osborne-street, the deceased pointed out the spot where she was assaulted. She said there were three men, but she could not describe them.

Mr. George Haslip, the house surgeon, stated that when Smith was admitted to the hospital, she had been drinking but was not intoxicated. Smith told me that at half-past one that morning, she was passing near Whitechapel Church when she noticed some men coming towards her. Smith crossed the road to avoid them, but they followed, assaulted her, took all her money, and then committed the outrage. She was unable to say what kind of instrument was used, nor could she describe her assailants, except that she said that one was a youth of 19. Death ensued on Wednesday morning [4 Apr] through peritonitis brought on by the injuries.

Margaret Hayes, living at the same address as the deceased, deposed to seeing Mrs. Smith in company with a man at the corner of Farrant-street and Burdett-road. The man was dressed in a dark suit and wore a white silk handkerchief round his neck. He was of medium height, but the witness did not think she could identify him.

Chief Inspector West, H Division, stated that I had no official information on the subject, and was only aware of the case through the daily papers. I had questioned the constables on the beat, but none of them appeared to know anything about the matter.

The coroner said that from the medical evidence, which must be true, it was clear that the woman had been barbarously murdered. It was impossible to imagine a more brutal and cowardly assault. It considered that the ends of justice would be better met by the jury recording their verdict at once than by adjourning to some future date in the hope of having more evidence brought before them. The jury returned a verdict of 'Wilful murder against some person or persons unknown.'

The police are making every possible inquiry into the case, but up to yesterday [8 Apr] had not any clue to the persons who committed the outrage.

There was something about Emma Smith's case, which caught my attention. In addition to the apparent lack of police empathy displayed in Chief Inspector West's statement, there was something else that bothered me. It could not be found written in the detail of Smith's life, but in the lack of detail found in the police file. There was something in the statement that suggested that the victim came from a life of means. It was little to go on but there was a suggestion that Smith had, in her, not so distant past, lived a far better lifestyle before ending up in London's East End. Her acquaintances and friends had testified that there was a touch of *culture* in Emma Smith's speech, unusual in her class. There was also a note in the margin of the report which read: '*Once when Emma was asked why she had broken away so completely from her old life she replied, a little wistfully: They would not understand now any more than they understood then. I must live somehow.*'

Martha Tabram, age thirty-six to thirty-nine, died August seventh, George Yard, stabbed thirty-nine times in the body and neck.

Residence: Commercial St.

Investigator: Brought to the attention of Police Constable Thomas Barett, H, Division, Investigator: Detective Inspector Reid.

Coroner: Mr. G. Collier, Deputy Coroner South Eastern District of Middlesex.

Mary Ann Nichols, also known as Polly Nichols, age forty-three, died, August thirty-first, Bucks Row. Throat cut.

Residence: Wilmott's Lodging House, 18 Thrawl Street, Spitalfields

Investigator: Constable John Neil. Body found by Carman, Charles Cross, and Robert Paul.

Constable Thain on street duty, at fifteen minutes past three in the morning, found nothing out of the ordinary; body then found by Constable John Neil, ten minutes to four in the morning. The physician called was Dr. Rees Ralph Llewellyn, who pronounces Nichols dead at the scene.

Hours later slumped over on the top of my desk, I woke, having succumbed to my exhaustion while rereading the case files on my desk. Pulling at my watch fob, I looked at the time; it was seven o'clock. The early rap on the door quickly shook the cobwebs from my mind. Getting up from my desk, I walked across the room in a trance; opening the door, I saw that it was Doctor Phillips.

"Please, forgive the intrusion; I saw the light on in your office."

Dr. Bagster Phillips, always impeccably polite was at his utmost this morning.

"No, intrusion Doctor, how can I help you," I asked, stretching, trying to focus through my sleep-deprived state.

"I thought you might want to accompany me to the Whitechapel Union Workhouse; there has been another murder."

"Another murder!"

I shouted, barely able to wrap my head around the three cases I had on my desk. I listened as Phillips informed me of the crime in a most mundane manner, as if the man were talking about taking a stroll in the country. I watched Phillips retreat up the hall, still trying to fathom another murder so soon after the last. Wiping the sleep from my eyes, I sloshed water on my face and tucked in my shirttail while reaching for my coat. Hurrying out of my office, I ran down the stairs to the waiting carriage. Climbing aboard the hansom, I was surprised to see that Doctor Phillips had already made it on-board before me.

"Driver, you may proceed," Phillips called out.

The mortuary, where the body of the unknown woman was taken, had been described as primitive, by Dr. Phillips could not have been more aptly depicted. For, in my mind, I could think of no cruder setting for a mortuary to have existed. It seemed almost disrespectful to see the poor, naked, creature lying on a makeshift table in a shed, for there was no other word to describe the building. Sidestepping Doctor Phillips as the man harangued the mortuary attendant for stripping the victim, I walked around the table where the body lay. Looking at the ghastly state that the poor woman had been left; I was quite taken aback. Ignoring the heated conversation between the doctor and the attendant, I studied the cut at the victim's throat, while sidestepping two nurses that stood whispering in a corner; gossiping about another murder being committed under the noses of Scotland Yard. I was not offended, nor did I blame the two nurses as it was the same topic of conversation that seemed to be on everyone's lips of late.

In answer to my question as to the name of the victim, Doctor Phillips was unable to answer. The dead woman could not be identified by those at the crime scene who had found the body, nor by any of those questioned in the vicinity. The corpse lay unidentified in a frozen moment in time, lifeless, and without mourning, denied the typical rites of passage from this world into the next.

Though, I was used to investigating all types of crimes where death was involved. The brevity of life and the frailty of the human vessel was never more poignant than when viewing a victim left stripped vulnerable, and unassuming on a mortuary table. I studied the woman's swollen face seeing bruises around the chin. The victim's tongue protruding slightly between the teeth, told me a story of how the woman had been stifled. My guess was, her killer likely rendered her near unconsciousness to keep her from calling out. That is if, my hypothesis of the killer's modus operandi was correct. The victim's belly was slashed open, and the cut around the neck was quite deep and jagged like the previous victim. I walked around the table several times, my eyes searching for any clue that might bring a killer from the dark alleys of London's streets out into the light. The ghastly cuts and the brutality inflicted on the body was astounding. The signature cut around the neck marked the deceased as a 'Jack the Ripper' victim as some had begun to call the fiend that walked the streets of

40

London. The cut to the throat, along with the other gruesome dissection done to the body seemed, in my opinion, to grow worse with each victim.

I looked at the woman who was an individual no more, or at least not until she was identified. After her identity was confirmed, from that time forevermore, she would be remembered as a murdered prostitute left dead in the streets of Whitechapel. To the mortuary attendant, that the doctor was chastising, she was just another dead body. To Philips, she was a puzzle, and the doctor's responsibility to retrieve the clues from the body that told the story of how she spent the last moments of her life. To me, she was another victim of a heinous crime, and it was my job to find out who had killed her. She no longer had a job or responsibilities, the hopes, and dreams she once had as a child, a wife, or even as a mother were no longer obtainable for her. All those things, she held dear to her were forever lost. Stolen by some maniacal figure lurking in the dark, who, by cunning or sheer luck, remained faceless, leaving no clue to his identity. The wretch would have remained nameless except for the moniker given him by some reporter with a zeal for fantastic reporting, oblivious of the feelings of the victim's family.

Looking in a corner, I saw the rumpled clothes of the woman, and the cause of Doctor Phillips' irritation levied on the mortuary attendant. Picking up the dress, I noted that there were no bloodstains on the front of the black dress; however, there were bloodstains around the neck of both brown bodices. Examining; the articles of clothing carefully, I noted that there were no other smudge marks nor any bloody handprints that might be used in evidence at the opportune time they had a suspect in custody. Sitting the clothes back down, I stopped suddenly as something unexpected caught my attention. Picking up the clothes again, I inspected them more carefully. Examining the dress, I noticed that there were no wrenches in the fabric. Nor was there evidence that the material was roughly handled when the killer undid the clothing. This could be seen in the way that the buttons were still held firmly in place. Each article of clothing seemed to be treated with some care, not merely cut away or torn from the victim's body. Indicating that the killer took his time undressing the deceased. This on its own, told me that the man was not compelled to rush and had the time to do so, before mutilating her body. Laying the clothes back down carefully, so they could be inspected more thoroughly by the coroner, I looked down at the body one last time. I watched as

Doctor Phillips prepared a table for his instruments. Behind me, I heard the Coroner, Wynne Baxter, arrive. Soon the room would become crowded, filled with investigators and onlookers gawking at yet another one of 'Jack's' victims. Looking across the crude table, I nodded at Wynne Baxter and went to talk to the coroner; when, I noticed two circular marks around the victim's left ring finger. The area of the finger was white, hidden until recently from the tanning effects of the sun's rays. Picking up the hand, I inspected the fingers observing a circle of dirt and traces of green signifying the victim wore either several brass rings or in the very least two or three cheap, gold-plated, rings that had left a green hue to the skin.

"Stone, how the deuce did you get here so early," Wynne Baxter asked, sliding his robust figure through the congested doorway.

"Doctor Phillips was kind enough to stop by my office early this morning on his way here," I answered, still studying the corpse.

"This is quite ghastly; this is detective, quite ghastly," Baxter repeated. "I thought we had just about enough of this wretch after the last murder, what," Baxter said, making his disgust evident to everyone in the room.

I listened to the coroner, knowing full well that Baxter hated autopsies and was thinking of a way to excuse them both before Dr. Phillips began.

"Doctor Phillips informed me that the call was to twenty-nine Hanbury Street, Spitalfields," I offered, allowing Baxter an escape from the autopsy. "Shall we, we can talk on the way."

"I will plan to hold the inquest on Monday, the tenth I should think that would be adequate time; I suppose it will be held at the Working Lads Institute. We will find out the identity of this poor lady then, if we haven't beforehand, Detective," Baxter stated as they headed towards his carriage. "What have you discovered, if anything, thus far Stone?"

"Dr. Phillips estimates the time of death at half four in the morning. The victim has bruises around her chin, and the tongue is protruding between her teeth."

"Choked," Baxter commented. "It looks as if your theory about how this wretch subdues his victim is correct Stone."

I looked at Baxter and nodded.

"This case is similar to the Nichols case, indicating that she was more than likely stifled in some manner keeping her from screaming and alerting anyone. The cut to the throat is deep and jagged and is likely the cause of death; the other wounds were done post mortem. Doctor Phillips thinks that the fiend has taken an organ from the body. What, though, do not ask me, for the man would not tell me until after his examination?"

"Well, if our suspicions before this murder were that we had three separate killers operating," Baxter paused and gasped. "Forgive the use of the word operating Stone," Baxter apologized. "Killing these streetwalkers in Whitechapel, what should we be thinking now?" Baxter vented, holding a handkerchief up to his mouth.

"My view has not changed from the onset of these crimes, Wynne," I spoke as Baxter whiffed fresh air through the window. "I maintain there is one killer, and I think the man has just become bolder in his endeavors to shock the public and mock police."

I spoke, maintaining my gaze on the street as the driver cracked his whip over the horse's ears.

"Bollocks; Stone," Baxter mocked. "I may be persuaded to hear any arguments you might have about two killers; however, might I remind you about the details in both the Tabram and Smith murders. Two crimes that you would have a hard time convincing a jury that only one hand committed them both," Baxter continued.

Ignoring the coroner, I remembered the cuts in the abdomen and wondered how a crime of such a degree could be perpetrated without the killer being noticed by someone. I considered every possibility, and yet I could not understand how some of the victim's blood did not end up on the perpetrator's clothes and hands.

"Stone, Stone!" Baxter shouted.

"Yes, Wynne."

"Where were you just now, Detective?'

"I was just thinking about the incisions to the victim's abdomen, Wynne."

"I was asking if there was anything you noticed in particular that set this crime above the others."

"I noticed that the deceased, up until recently at least, had been wearing rings on her finger."

"They are gone?"

I nodded in response.

"Do you think this could be a robbery made to look like a '*Ripper*' victim?"

"Not judging by the woman's clothes and the hour that she was on the street," I answered. "No respectable woman wearing anything of value would be anywhere in Spitalfields at four in the morning, Wynne."

"Yes, quite right, sir," Baxter answered, realizing the futility of grasping at straws without thinking.

"She was also dressed quite commonly, Wynne," I continued. "I suspect that the rings were an heirloom or of no great value except to the deceased. Perhaps she just recently sold them for the pennies they were worth, who knows, perhaps we will never know."

Number twenty-nine, Hanbury Street lay huddled between John Street and Brick Lane. The walk in front of the house, as well as the footpath into the backyard, was alive with neighbors from the surrounding area eager to see some gruesome detail or in the very least, expecting to hear some small tidbit of gossip they could spread later.

"Constable, get these people back across the road, will you please," I shouted at a nearby officer who had his arms up, keeping the crowd at bay.

I followed another constable along a passageway through a doorway into the yard at the rear of the building with Baxter trailing behind. The lot was large, with a shed near the back. One door led into the house, to the left was a covered stairwell leading most likely to a cellar. The area was enclosed by a six-foot paling on all sides, separating the perimeter of the yard from the premises on the left and the right of the house. The path was partially stoned for easier walking, and the rest of the area was hardpacked earth. The victim's body had been found on the left of the passageway between a set of stone steps and the fence, according to Sergeant Baugham, who had returned from the mortuary after conveying the body there. Inspector Chandler was left in charge of the scene. Chandler told me that the victim's body lay with her head towards the house and her legs towards the shed. The stone walkway was relatively clean with no blood spatters except where the head of the victim had been laid after the assault. I took note of the two or three spots of blood on the wall of the house, and the blood on the palings. Kneeling on the ground, I examined the ground where only a faint smudge could be seen in the soil where the body of the woman was found. There was no significant amount of blood to be seen on the ground; besides a patch of saturated ground where the head lay, in the area behind the neck. Though not the amount of blood that one would expect from a wound like the victim in the mortuary received.

"What do you make of it, Detective?" Baxter asked.

"I don't see much in the way of anything, Wynne," I grumbled. "The scene is characteristic with that of the Nichols case, and if these victims were killed by the same culprit, then the murderer seems to be maintaining a consistent pattern. The yard here is perfectly hidden by the six-foot-high palings. The killer chose a similar place where the walk would leave no footprints to follow or examine."

"The wound seems consistent, doesn't it?"

"The wound was jagged," I responded. "It started on the left and went around the woman's neck, but . . ."

"But what, John?"

"I don't see a tremendous amount of blood pooling that you might expect. A wound like the victim received would bleed a lot more than the blood you see here. The traces of blood that you can see on the wall or on the palings, I am guessing; are drops from the fiend wielding his knife during the dissection. See how the spatters have tails pointing away from the drops. There are no marks of a struggle, nor any marks on the ground left by someone dragging a body in here. That can only mean the victim came here of her own free-will, or she was carried here after she was killed. This crime scene has the same physical appearance as the last. Well-hidden and out of the way, so no chance of being seen by any casual passer-by. The killer had both the opportunity and the time to kill the woman without fear of being seen, or anyone seeing him leave afterward, for that matter," I answered, still examining the area where the body was found.

Taking in the whole area at a glance, I noted that the constables were still looking for clues along the perimeter of the two yards. I scowled, watching the clumsy way the men tramped about the area leaving no stone unturned in their passing.

"This yard may have been dark and out of sight from any who might pass by on the street, as you say, but if you ask me, Stone, this mad man took an awful chance that no one from the house heard anything amiss going on back here," Baxter concluded.

Looking at the proximity of where the body was found and the distance to the door and the one window above the stairwell leading to the cellar, I doubted that at that time in the morning if anyone in the house was stirring, but it did say something about the risks the killer was willing to take.

"Perhaps the killer was not afraid of being confronted by anyone, Wynne."

"Detective, you have a bloody fantastic knack for unsettling my nerves," Wynne protested. "Your depictions thus far; make me wonder if we have any chance at all of catching this fearless, risk-taking, fiend."

"Be that as it may, it is probable that the victim was dead before being brought to the yard. Therefore, the killer did not need to worry about alarming those who live here."

"That being the case, John," Baxter retorted. "How do you explain the drips of blood on the palings, and, why bring her here of all places?"

"Wynne, look here in this area. I do not see the amount of blood one might expect on the ground in the area where the head was positioned," I said pointing with the tip of his pencil. "I am just saying that it is possible that she was killed somewhere else, and the dissection was done here. That was how these spatters were made while the killer sliced the victim's abdomen. As far as this location, Wynne, it is possible that it was just convenient, but I doubt it."

Looking around the yard, I tried to see the appeal that had drawn the killer here of all places, but aside from the high palings, there was no other feature that made the scene stand out.

"I suppose that it will be too much to hope for that the detectives who were first on the scene collected some kind of evidence," I commented, getting to my feet. "It is unlikely though."

"Why?"

"Because Wynne, between the yard and the walkway, and between here and the street the area has been trampled underfoot, the entire scene has been contaminated, by gawkers and constables having no care," I spoke loud enough so anybody within hearing distance would hear me.

"Stone, I talked to Doctor Phillips before I left the mortuary," Baxter grimaced. "Phillips believes that the woman's uterus is likely missing," Baxter offered.

"What do you think now, Wynne," I said, looking at the coroner. "Do you still think there is more than one killer?" I asked the question that I already knew the answer to.

"I suppose not, John," Baxter said, with his mouth twisted in disgust.

So engrossed was I with thoughts of the type of killer they were investigating, I could not bear to consider where the body parts ended up. Certainly, this '*Jack*' was nothing like any other criminal I had ever come across before. I suspected that it was for that reason that the police were having such difficulty trying to find a worthy suspect in the murders of the four women. All the victims were killed in a very disturbing way, all were prostitutes, and I still maintained all were killed by the same individual. Though the crimes were so perverse in their nature that it went beyond rational thinking to try and paint a picture of the man they sought. I had investigated many murders, most of which had a clear set of suspects, and it was only a matter of time to eliminate the unlikely from the probable. This killer seemingly had no motive, or in the least, no motive easily distinguished by investigators. It was also likely that the perpetrator of the crimes only met the victim a short time before killing them.

I suppose, what was most trying, was that Scotland Yard was considered the world's foremost authority on crime-solving. The entire Metropolitan Police Force was being scrutinized, and despite what the papers printed, they were coming off looking quite badly. The Yard was experienced in dealing with all sorts of crimes. Unfortunately, London was a melding pot of those who came from all walks of life, from every part of the world, any of whom were capable of committing every crime known to man. However, the crimes perpetrated on these women were fantastic. Fantastic, in that, there were never any eyewitnesses to place the victim in an area before she was killed. If there were, they could draw from a list of suspects seen moments before, or at least, in the surrounding neighborhood. In most cases, the last person the victims had been seen with, was hours before their deaths. Before the homicides in Whitechapel, the police were used to investigating murders that were either premeditated or spontaneous, perpetrated in the heat of passion. The victim, most often than not, was found to have a close link in some way to the killer. Of course, there were those cases that involved a murder while a felon was orchestrating a robbery or some such crime. In such cases, however, there was no intent to kill. These murders, where no apparent motive could be found, had left investigators, for lack of a better word, stumped. Unfortunately, it did little for the detectives to be constantly told by Home Office that the crimes were the work of a lunatic or some such escapee and to look elsewhere was a waste of time.

Exhausted, I looked at my watch when I returned to my office. It had been twelve hours since Dr. Philips had knocked on my door. Sitting on the edge of a cushion on the settee, I tried to erase the images that repeatedly flashed in my mind's eye. With legs stretched out and eyes closed, I once again saw the image of the dead woman's body that lay on the wooden table in the mortuary on Whitechapel Road. Before falling asleep, I tried to turn my thoughts to something else, when an idea came to me quite suddenly and without warning. It was the overpowering feeling that the killer was after something or was satisfying some dark urge or desire. Although, what dark purpose the killer had in mind, I could not imagine. It was clear though that something was causing the man to seek out this class of women and slice up their bodies in such a way that it was disturbing to even the hardiest of investigators. Covering up with my jacket, I shuddered, though the feeling stuck with me for several more hours, and sleep would not come until the sky faded into twilight.

The day before the inquest in the death of the woman few knew to be Annie Chapman, at twenty-nine Hanbury Street, I had an unexpected visit from Wynne E. Baxter. The sheer look of distress on the coroner's face made me stop what I was doing as my friend walked into my office and sat across from me. I allowed a few minutes to pass in silence until the coroner finally chose to speak his mind.

"Stone, if I was to ask you to handle something discreetly, would you, as a favor to me, keep the name of the person who gave me the information out of any report you may have to submit?" Baxter asked looking sheepishly at Stone.

"I suppose that would depend, Wynne?" I replied.

"Depend on what John?" Baxter asked a little defensively.

"I guess, it would depend on, if this person held vital information that would lead to the apprehension of a criminal, or if this person had information that may help save the life of another or stop someone from being hurt in some way," I answered Baxter, more than a little curious now.

"Fair enough, John," Baxter replied.

I watched the coroner leave my office without another word and return, escorting a young woman by the arm. Rising from my chair, I bowed slightly in recognition of the woman, who kept her eyes averted, staring nervously at the floor the entire time that Baxter directed her to the chair in front of my desk.

"Detective Stone, this is Miss Mary Curtin," Baxter offered, as I sat on the corner of Stone's desk.

"It is a pleasure," I greeted the lady, who nodded but remained silent.

Studying the woman, I estimated her to be in her mid-twenties, she was dressed in a dark high collared dress that resembled a nurse's uniform. She was quite frail and rubbed her hands nervously as if she was in some kind of trouble. It was safe to assume that this was the woman who Wynne referred to as needing her name kept out of any formal investigation.

"Miss Curtin," Baxter spoke first. "I want you to tell your story to Detective Stone here, just as you told it to me, and don't be nervous, you are not in any trouble," Baxter said in reassurance.

After Wynne confirmed that the young woman was not in any kind of trouble, I slid my chair over for Baxter and sat on the corner of my desk. I had been mildly interested, but now I was curious as to what the young woman had to say, as Baxter patted her on her arm; to comfort her.

"It was a fortnight ago that it happened, sir. I was cleaning the offices at the Hospital Museum when I heard voices coming down the hall. I thought everyone had gone for the day; I was cleaning Dr. Openshaw's office. I know I wasn't to start the offices until later, but my grandmother has been sick, and I wanted to get home to her as early as possible. When I heard them coming into the office, I grew frightened, so I hid in the closet."

The tears started to well, so Wynne handed the woman a handkerchief, so they waited patiently while she pulled herself together.

"When the two men came into the office, I could hear their voices through the door, one of the men I could not guess who it was, it was certainly no one I recognized. The bloke had an accent and talked about America, so I assumed that was where he was from. The other voice, I heard was that of Doctor Openshaw," Miss Curtin wiped her nose, and took a drink from a glass of tea that Baxter handed her.

"Did you hear a name mentioned?"

"No, I heard only the end of a very heated conversation between the doctor and the other man."

"Heated, do you mean they were arguing?" I asked, studying the girl looking for the source of her anxiety.

"No, not really, the other man, the American was calm; it was Doctor Openshaw who seemed to be angry," Curtin replied.

"Do you remember what the doctor was angry about?"

"The American wanted specimens for some kind of medical study. The man was very specific, making a list, as if going to market, and the specimens were to be placed in glycerine, not spirits. The chap said that money was no object."

Looking over at Baxter, who caught my eye, both men turned their attention back to Curtin. The very idea that some American was willing to pay an unspecified amount of money for medical specimens caught both their attention. It would imply an eagerness, and perhaps the willingness to go outside the usual channels to obtain these specimens.

"What were the two arguing about?"

"Doctor Openshaw said he had never heard tell of the type of medical study where the specimens needed to be placed in glycerin, not to mention why the man needed them sent to America. I could hear the skepticism in Doctor Openshaw's voice when he asked the man why he didn't get his specimens in America. When no answer came, that was when the doctor said he could not help the man, and the American walked out of the office," Curtin finished her account while wiping her nose with the handkerchief.

"Did you see the other man at all?"

"No, I was too frightened; I stayed in the closet; until I knew everyone was gone for the day. That is why I came to see Mr. Baxter. I really need this job, sir. I have been working hard. I really want to be a nurse; I don't know what I would do if I lost this job. When I heard about these women being killed in Whitechapel, I knew I must talk to someone," Curtin began to cry again.

"I don't understand miss, what does one, have to do with the other," I said, looking up at Baxter. "Have I missed something here, Wynne?"

"The streets are filled with the gossip of these murdered women and how they are missing body parts," Curtin answered.

"Detective," Baxter interrupted Curtin. "The specimens that this man was trying to purchase from Doctor Openshaw were female organs, the uterus in particular."

I looked at the retreating sobbing creature as Baxter escorted her out of my office; everything seemed to be out of sync for a moment. I sat trying to come up with some quick solution or something I could say to put the young woman at ease, but I could think of nothing. On the one hand, I could confront Doctor Openshaw about this unknown American; however, this would not only put Miss Curtin's job in jeopardy, but it would also place me in the precarious position of explaining how I knew about the American's attempted procurement of the female anatomy. On the other hand, this American Doctor had done nothing wrong, as for my responsibility in the affair, I could only hope to question the man about his motive and the reasons for attempting to obtain the organs in London instead of his native land.

"So, what do you think about this woman's story, Stone?" Baxter said, walking back into the office.

"I don't know what to say, Wynne, I am in a quandary," I answered. "I was just thinking of a way that I could confront Openshaw and obtain the American's identity and protect the young woman's job all at the same time. I don't know how could I possibly mention the one without mentioning the other? Dr. Openshaw will surely want to know how, I came to know a topic of conversation that he had in private behind closed doors," I blurted out throwing up my hands in frustration.

"I am sorry for that, Stone, but do you think this individual, this American, would actually go so far as to commit murder to obtain anatomy needed for this study?"

"Even if the two are connected, Wynne, which I doubt," I interjected. "Are you suggesting that this American is 'Jack the Ripper,' and it is him going around Whitechapel to obtain these specimens?" I asked Baxter attempting to gain some insight into how the coroner made the connection between the two events.

"What I am saying, Stone, is that, I am not sure if these two cases are in fact linked or not, but what if they are, and we don't look into this man and find out what reason the man has for procuring these specimens. Perhaps then, and only then, can we ascertain if this gentleman is legitimate or not," Baxter shouted in response.

"It seems too bizarre Wynne, to even consider rationally. If what you are suggesting is true, and this man is involved in these murders, that would mean that we are dealing with a very sick man. A man who has no qualms about committing murder is one thing, but a man who cares so little for human life and the consequences involved, is quite another."

Looking at my friend, I was sympathetic to Baxter's need to chase any lead, no matter how small in getting the culprit for the murder of the four women. I also knew that the coroner's distress went far beyond the need for upholding the law. Baxter worked for the people, and it was to them where the coroner's duty lay, especially when that duty involved the people of the East End, who struggled daily in their efforts just to survive.

"Well, I will say this, Wynne," I commented. "This American, if the man is not involved, does seem to be seeking these specimens at a most inopportune time."

"Yes, I suppose so," Baxter responded. "It would be difficult getting anyone to believe a doctor capable of such behavior, even more so, of a foreign practitioner."

"Well, Mr. Baxter, how do you propose we handle this, and protect the identity of your eavesdropper at the same time?"

"Yes, I see Stone, well this does seem to be a quandary, doesn't it?"

Chapter Four

Monday, September 10th, was the first day of the inquest for the deceased Annie Chapman. Chapman's last known address, was Crossingham's Lodging House, at thirty-five Dorset Street, Spitalfields. Born Annie Eliza Smith in September 1841, she was forty-seven years old and probably dying of tuberculosis. She was a woman who had been separated from her husband and had taken to prostitution to endure the streets of London. Chapman moved from lodging house to lodging house in search of work or to stay close to the men she saw and those she temporarily lived with.

The coroner, Wynne Baxter, was a man on a mission when deposing John Davies, the man who first found the body of Annie Chapman, in the backyard at twenty-nine Hanbury Street. The coroner was his usual thorough and professional self, but there was something else that I noticed during Baxter's questioning of the witnesses. I attributed it to some new enthusiasm in the search for answers in the pursuit of the vicious killer. Whatever it was, something intense and riveting in Baxter's voice kept every spectator's attention in the room.

Baxter began his usual series of questions dealing primarily with the who, the what, and the where, in the case, but soon, the coroner switched the direction that the inquiry was taking. I doubted that anyone else detected it, but I guessed that it was likely out of sheer exasperation of getting no definitive answers thus far. Baxter continued by posing the question of why the police had failed to supply a plan of the yard at twenty-nine Hanbury Street so, that it could be examined at the inquest to the entire jury. With no good explanation forthcoming, Baxter made it known to the whole room, about the lack of professional conduct displayed by police in the matter. Later Baxter would add more inconsistencies in the investigation that started the spectators to whisper back and forth about the Yard's inability to catch the killer. After pursuing these queries that had no ready answer, Baxter regrouped and called on John Evans, the night watchmen at Dorset Street where Chapman lodged.

Mr. Evans identified the deceased as Annie Chapman, a woman, who had frequented the lodging house on Dorset Street. Evans began by painting a rather less than flattering picture of the deceased, prompted by his last meeting with Chapman before her death. According to Evans' testimony, Chapman had shown up at the lodging house at approximately midnight, in an inebriated condition. Which, according to Evans was not an uncommon occurrence? At that time, Chapman did not have enough money for lodgings, so the watchman sent her on her way. Evans stated that his knowledge of the deceased; was based on personal experience, which permitted him to comment that Chapman had been living a rough nightlife.

I sat through the inquest with mixed emotion, hearing nothing that would lead them in a new direction in their pursuit of their killer, so subsequently, I found myself paying little attention. What occupied my mind was the meeting in my office with Miss Curtin. There was no easy answer on how to deal with the situation, so I had started to work out, at least, twenty different scenarios in my head on how to approach Dr. Openshaw, and at the same time keep the young woman from losing her job. On the other hand, I was in a quandary whether to inform Inspector Abberline of the development. Try as I might, I found no easy solution, nor did I want to do anything rash that might hamper any investigation into this American. If, in fact, this American was involved in the murders. As it was, it was disconcerting to think that a doctor would go to such lengths to obtain specimens for research. By the end of the day, when all was said and done, I and the coroner were no closer to the apprehension of the killer known as '*Jack the Ripper.*'

Two days later, I was back sitting with the spectators at the Working Lads Institute to hear another day of the depositions. Day two found Fontain Smith, Annie Chapman's younger brother on the stand confirming that the deceased in the mortuary was indeed his sister, Annie Chapman. The day's depositions also included employees of a packing case plant near the scene of the murder, most of whom testified, they had neither heard nor seen anything out of the ordinary. Next, on the list of witnesses was the much talked about '*Leather Apron.*' The room was full and beyond overcrowded as people streamed in and lined up along the walls and stood in the doorways. The crowds had shown up to see the one that they had read about in all the papers, the ominous man known to most only as 'Leather Apron.' It seemed like everyone who lived within a ten-block radius of the institute on Whitechapel Road; wanted to hear the testimony of John Piser. A hush fell over the crowd when Wynne Baxter stood before the witness to question him.

[Sic] John Piser: I live at 22, Mulberry-street, Commercial- road east. I am a shoemaker.
Coroner: Are you known by the nickname of 'Leather Apron?'
Piser: Yes, sir.
Coroner: Where were you on Friday night last?
Piser: I was at 22, Mulberry-street. On Thursday, the 6th inst. I arrived there.
Coroner: From where?"
Piser: "From the west end of town."
Coroner: "I am afraid we shall have to have a better address than that presently. What time did you reach 22, Mulberry-street?"
Piser: "Shortly before eleven p.m."
Coroner: "Who lives at 22, Mulberry-street?"
Piser: "My brother and sister-in-law and my stepmother. I remained indoors there."
Coroner: Until when?
Piser: "Until I was arrested by Sergeant Thicke, on Monday last at nine a.m."
Coroner: "You say you never left the house during that time?"
Piser: "I never left the house."
Coroner: "Why were you remaining indoors?"
Piser: "Because my brother advised me."
Coroner: "You were the subject of suspicion?"
Piser: "I was the object of a false suspicion."
Coroner: "You remained on the advice of your friends?"

Piser: "Yes; I am telling you what I did."

Coroner: "It was not the best advice that you could have had. You have been released, and are not now in custody?"

Piser: "I am not. I wish to vindicate my character to the world at large."

Coroner: "I have called you in your own interests, partly with the object of giving you an opportunity of doing so."

Coroner: "Can you tell us where you were on Thursday, Aug. 30?"

Piser: (after considering): "In the Holloway-road."

Coroner: "You had better say exactly where you were. It is important to account for your time from that Thursday to the Friday morning."

Piser: "What time, may I ask?"

Coroner "It was the week before you came to Mulberry-street."

Piser: I was staying at a common lodging-house called the Round House, in the Holloway-road.

Coroner: "Did you sleep the night there?"

Piser: "Yes."

Coroner: At what time did you go in?

Piser: "On the night of the London Dock fire I went in about two or a quarter-past. It was on the Friday morning.

Coroner: When did you leave the lodging-house?

Piser: At eleven a.m. on the same day. I saw on the placards, 'Another Horrible Murder.'

Coroner: "Where were you before two o'clock on Friday morning?"

Piser: "At eleven p.m. on Thursday I had my supper at the Round House."

Coroner: "Did you go out?"

Piser: "Yes, as far as the Seven Sisters-road, and then returned towards Highgate way, down the Holloway-road. Turning, I saw the reflection of a fire. Coming as far as the church in the Holloway-road I saw two constables and the lodging-housekeeper talking together. There might have been one or two constables, I cannot say which. I asked a constable where the fire was, and he said it was a long way off. I asked him where he thought it was, and he replied: "Down by the Albert Docks." It was then about half-past one, to the best of my recollection. I went as far as Highbury Railway Station on the same side of the way, returned, and then went into the lodging house."

Coroner "Did any one speak to you about being so late?"

Piser: "No; I paid the night watchman. I asked him if my bed was let, and he said: "They are let by eleven o'clock. You don't think they are to let to this hour." I paid him 4d for another bed. I stayed up smoking on the form of the kitchen, on the right-hand side near the fireplace, and then went to bed."

Coroner: "You got up at eleven o'clock?"

Piser: "Yes. The day man came, and told us to get up, as I wanted to make the bed. I got up and dressed, and went down into the kitchen."

Coroner: "Is there anything else you want to say?"

Piser: "Nothing."

Coroner: "When you said the West-end of town did you mean Holloway?"

Piser: "No; another lodging house in Peter-street, Westminster."

Coroner: "It is only fair to say that the witness's statements can be corroborated."

It was quite something to see the crowd burst into a frenzy of conversation when they heard the witness had an alibi that could be corroborated by none other than a Metropolitan Police Constable. Most in the room had heard about Piser from the newspapers and the gossip on the street, and had already, made up their assumptions about the man. Now to hear that they might be wrong produced an unexpected adverse reaction. Some snorted, while others hissed in unbelief when the witness gave his last statement.

[Sic] When William Thicke was deposed: Knowing that 'Leather Apron' was suspected of being concerned in the murder, on Monday morning I arrested Piser at 22, Mulberry-Street. I have known him by the name of 'Leather Apron' for many years."

Coroner: When people in the neighborhood speak of the 'Leather Apron' do they mean Piser?

William Thicke: They do.

Coroner: He has been released from custody?

William Thicke: He was released last night at 9:30.

57

Day three of the Inquest into Annie Chapman's death was Thursday, September, the thirteenth. The first hours of the morning were filled with the testimony of Inspector Chandler, Sergeant Baugham, and Doctor Phillips, the Police Surgeon. Baxter again took a hard nose approach to the police handling of the crime scene and the conveyance of Annie Chapman's body to the mortuary. First, Inspector Chandler gave detailed testimony of the crime scene upon my arrival, and then Sergeant Baugham was deposed. I already knew that the treatment of the body by police and mortuary assistants after leaving a crime scene was a thorn in Doctor Phillips's side. I was very interested to see how Baxter handled the issue.

[Sic] Sergeant Baugham 31 H stated that I conveyed the body of the deceased to the mortuary on the ambulance.
Coroner: "Are you sure that you took every portion of the body away with you?"
Baughman: "Yes."
Coroner: "Where did you deposit the body?"
Baughman: "In the shed, still on the ambulance. I remained with it until Inspector Chandler arrived. Detective-Sergeant Thicke viewed the body, and I took down the description. There were present two women, who came to identify the body, and they described the clothing. They came from 35, Dorset-street."
Coroner: "Who touched the clothing?"
Baughman – "I did not see the women touch the clothing nor the body. I did not see Sergeant Thicke touch the body."
Inspector Chandler, recalled, "Told the jury I reached the mortuary a few minutes after seven. The body did not appear to have been disturbed. I did not stay until the doctor arrived. Police-constable 376 H was left in charge, with the mortuary keeper. Robert Marne, the mortuary keeper and an inmate of the Whitechapel Union Workhouse, said I received the body at seven o'clock on Saturday morning. I remained at the mortuary until Dr. Phillips came. The door of the mortuary was locked except when two nurses from an infirmary came and undressed the body. No one else touched the corpse. I gave the key into the hands of the police."
The Coroner "The fact is that Whitechapel does not possess a mortuary. The place is not a mortuary at all. We have no right to take a body there. It is simply a shed belonging to the workhouse officials. Juries have over and

over again reported the matter to the District Board of Works. The East-
end, which requires mortuaries more than anywhere else, is most deficient.
Bodies drawn out of the river have to be put in boxes, and very often, they
are brought to this workhouse arrangement all the way from Wapping. A
workhouse inmate is not the proper man to take care of a body in such an
important matter as this."

[Sic] The foreman of the jury called attention to the fact that a fund to
provide a reward had been opened by residents in the neighborhood, and
that Mr. Montagu, M.P., had offered a reward of £100. If the Government
also offered a reward some information might be forthcoming.

The Coroner: "I do not speak with any real knowledge, but I am told that
the Government was determined not to give any rewards in future, not with
the idea to economize but because the money does not get into right
channels."

Coroner: "Were you present when the doctor was doing his post-
mortem?"

Chandler: "Yes."

Coroner: "Did you see the doctor find the handkerchief produced?"

Chandler: "It was taken off the body. I picked it up from off the clothing,
which was in the corner of the room. I gave it to Dr. Phillips, and I asked
him to put it in some water, which I did."

Coroner: "Did you see the handkerchief taken off the body?"

Chandler: "I did not. The nurses must have taken it off the throat."

Coroner: "How do you know?"

Chandler: "I don't know."

Coroner: "Then you are guessing?"

Chandler: "I am guessing."

Coroner: "That is all wrong, you know." Baxter turned to the jury.
"He is really not the proper man to have been left in charge."

The assembly buzzed in response at the scathing retort Baxter heralded
to the crowd that sat behind the jury, in response to Chandler's offhand
comment about his dealings with crime scene evidence. Baxter let the
harangue continue for another minute or so, to allow Chandler to get the
message that he was not the only one in the room who was displeased. The
crowd sat at the edge of their seats when Doctor Phillips was deposed.
After Phillips gave his testimony of the condition of the body at the crime

scene, Wynne Baxter wanted the jury to get the entire picture of the horrifying shape that the victim's body was left, right down to the minute details, much to the chagrin of Doctor Phillips.

[Sic] The Coroner: The object of the inquiry is not only to ascertain the cause of death, but the means by which it occurred. Any mutilation which took place afterwards may suggest the character of the man who did it. Possibly you can give us the conclusions to which you have come respecting the instrument used.

Phillips: "You don't wish for details. I think if it is possible to escape the details it would be advisable. The cause of death is visible from injuries I have described.

The Coroner: "You have kept a record of them?"

Phillips: "I have."

The Coroner: "Supposing any one is charged with the offence, they would have to come out then, and it might be a matter of comment that the same evidence was not given at the inquest."

Phillips: "I am entirely in your hands"

The Coroner: We will postpone that for the present. You can give your opinion as to how the death was caused.

Phillips: From these appearances I am of opinion that the breathing was interfered with previous to death, and that death arose from syncope, or failure of the heart's action, in consequence of the loss of blood caused by the severance of the throat."

Coroner: "Was the instrument used at the throat the same as that used at the abdomen?"

Phillips: "Very probably. It must have been a very sharp knife, probably with a thin, narrow blade, and at least six to eight inches in length, and perhaps longer."

Coroner: "Is it possible that any instrument used by a military man, such as a bayonet, would have done it?"

Phillips: "No; it would not be a bayonet."

Coroner: "Would it have been such an instrument as a medical man uses for post-mortem examinations?"

Phillips: "The ordinary post-mortem case perhaps does not contain such a weapon."

Coroner: *"Would any instrument that slaughterers employ have caused the injuries?"*

Phillips: *"Yes; well ground down."*

Coroner: *"Would the knife of a cobbler or of any person in the leather trades have done?"*

Phillips: *"I think the knife used in those trades would not be long enough in the blade."*

Coroner: *"Was there any anatomical knowledge displayed?"*

Phillips: *"I think there was. There were indications of it. My own impression is that that anatomical knowledge was only less displayed or indicated in consequence of haste. The person evidently was hindered from making a more complete dissection in consequence of the haste."*

Coroner: *"Was the whole of the body there?"*

Phillips: *"No; the absent portions being from the abdomen."* ·

Coroner: *"Are those portions such as would require anatomical knowledge to extract?"*

Phillips: *"I think the mode in which they were extracted did show some anatomical knowledge."*

Coroner: *"You do not think they could have been lost accidentally in the transit of the body to the mortuary?"*

Phillips: *"I was not present at the transit. I carefully closed up the clothes of the woman. Some portions had been excised."*

Coroner: *"How long had the deceased been dead when you saw her?"*

Phillips: *"I should say at least two hours, and probably more; but it is right to say that it was a fairly cold morning, and that the body would be more apt to cool rapidly from its having lost the greater portion of its blood."*

Coroner: *"Was there any evidence of any struggle?"*

Phillips: *"No; not about the body of the woman. You do not forget the smearing of blood about the palings."*

Coroner: *"In your opinion did she enter the yard alive?"*

Phillips: *"I am positive of it. I made a thorough search of the passage, and I saw no trace of blood, which must have been visible had she been taken into the yard."*

Coroner: *"You were shown the apron?"*

Phillips: *"I saw it myself. There was no blood upon it. It had the appearance of not having been unfolded recently."*

Coroner: "You were shown some staining on the wall of No. 25, Hanbury Street?"

Phillips: "Yes; that was yesterday morning. To the eye of a novice I have no doubt it looks like blood. I have not been able to trace any signs of it. I have not been able to finish my investigation. I am almost convinced I shall not find any blood. We have not had any result of your examination of the internal organs."

Coroner: "Was there any disease?"

Phillips: "Yes. It was not important as regards the cause of death. Disease of the lungs was of long standing, and there was disease of the membranes of the brain. The stomach contained a little food."

Coroner: "Was there any appearance of the deceased having taken much alcohol?"

Phillips: "No. There were probably signs of great privation. I am convinced she had not taken any strong alcohol for some hours before her death."

Coroner: "Were any of these injuries self-inflicted?"

Phillips: "The injuries which were the immediate cause of death were not self-inflicted."

Coroner: "Was the bruising you mentioned recent?"

Phillips: "The marks on the face were recent, especially about the chin and sides of the jaw. The bruise upon the temple and the bruises in front of the chest were of longer standing, probably of days. I am of opinion that the person who cut the deceased's throat took hold of her by the chin, and then commenced the incision from left to right."

Coroner "Could that be done so instantaneously that a person could not cry out?"

Phillips: "By pressure on the throat no doubt it would be possible."

The Forman: "There would probably be suffocation."

The Coroner: "The thickening of the tongue would be one of the signs of suffocation?"

Phillips: "Yes. My impression is that she was partially strangled. Witness added that the handkerchief produced was, when found amongst the clothing, saturated with blood. A similar article was round the throat of the deceased when I saw her early in the morning at Hanbury-street."

Coroner: "It had not the appearance of having been tied on afterwards?"

Phillips: "No. Sarah Simonds, a resident nurse at the Whitechapel Infirmary, stated that in company of the senior nurse, she went to the mortuary on Saturday, and found the body of the deceased on the ambulance in the yard. It was afterwards taken into the shed, and placed on the table. She was directed by Inspector Chandler to undress it, and she placed the clothes in a corner. She left the handkerchief round the neck. She was sure of this. They washed stains of blood from the body. It seemed to have run down from the throat. She found the pocket tied round the waist. The strings were not torn. There were no tears or cuts in the clothes."

Inspector Chandler recalled: "I did not instruct the nurses to undress the body and to wash it."

After the deposition, the whispers of the crowd displayed a definite lack of confidence in the police. I even found myself slightly dismayed by the end of the testimony. It was hard to believe, but the stories in the newspapers about the Metropolitan Police bungling the investigation into the Whitechapel murders seemed to ring true in the jury's eyes. I had sat through the depositions for three days and heard more than once how police had mishandled evidence, resulting in their testimony to come under scrutiny. Getting up from my chair, I walked over to the table where the coroner was shuffling papers into his briefcase.

"Well, Detective, how do you think the proceedings are going so far?" Baxter asked, grim-faced.

"The Metropolitan Police Department seems to be coming off rather badly, doesn't it?" I said in answer to Wynne's question.

"I hope you don't think; I am deliberately trying to make the police look bad in their efforts, Stone?"

"Of course not, Wynne, you are just doing your job. A job, I might add, that is difficult enough without being bogged down by inept law enforcement. If anything, you are setting an example by maintaining a high level of integrity in the inquiry that is missing everywhere else, I wouldn't expect anything less."

"Thank you, Stone," Baxter replied, bowing his head respectfully. "My office works independently from official bodies and does not come with much support beyond the constituents, and when they become disgruntled, all eyes are looking to me to get the answers the police cannot seem to achieve."

"Wynne, if the police are looking poorly during this inquest, it is largely due to their prejudices, their unprofessional way of handling evidence, and their treatment of witnesses. As much as it distresses me to admit this about a colleague, Inspector Chandler gave the impression to the jury that procedure in dealing with a crime scene, its exhibits, and the handling of a body is less of a priority when dealing with a dead prostitute in Whitechapel."

I vented my harsh feelings for the first time to the coroner; however, it was not the first time that I had felt this way. Inspector Chandler's cavalier attitude about handling evidence in such a high-profile murder case was counterproductive, to say the least. I cringed at the idea, but then I suspected that every jury member and spectator at the inquest came away from the inquest feeling the same.

"That is why I must maintain a strict regimen in handling the police in these inquests. More and more, I find the citizenry displaying a definite lack of faith in their protectors. Every time an article is printed in the newspapers of how the police are not taking these crimes in this area very seriously, I feel that their faith dwindles."

"Wynne, we have a grave situation here, there is no room for sloppy police work, and there can`t be any mishandling of evidence if we are going to apprehend this maniac."

"Well, I must say, Stone," Baxter started to shoulder into his coat. "The confidence in the Metropolitan Police has diminished in such a way that there is talk that vigilantes would be doing a better job policing London's street on their own."

"That is all we need, Wynne, a bunch of civilians walking around the streets at night adding to the confusion!"

"This inquest sums up in about a week," Baxter said, placing his hat on his head. "That should allow the police the time they need to add whatever they can to this investigation. Although, I am sorry to say that I can't see anything of credence being added, if left in the hands of Inspector Chandler," Baxter said, with no amount of optimism.

"That will give me a few days to find out what I can about a foreigner trying to buy human organs in Whitechapel," I replied grimly.

Back at my office, I prepared my copy of the Chapman investigation.

Annie Chapman, age 47, died the 8th of September at 29 Hanbury Street, Spitalfields, her body mutilated, and her throat cut.

Residence: Crossingham's Lodging House, 35 Dorset Street, Spitalfields

Coroner: Mr. Wynne Baxter.

Investigator: Body brought to the attention of Inspector Joseph Chandler, the body having been moved to the Working Lads Institute on Whitechapel Road, by Sergeant Edward Baugham.

Reading each file over numerous times, and going over the minutes of each inquest made me feel like the foremost authority in each case; however, that wasn't saying much. With each passing day that went by, no new evidence was added by investigators, and the odds that the killer would be apprehended before another murder decreased considerably.

Reaching into my desk drawer, I retrieved a surgical text that I had borrowed from Dr. Phillips. Studying the anatomical diagrams of arteries and muscles, I then reread each file on where the victims were found and compared how each body was left after the victim was murdered. Except for Elizabeth Smith, all the victims were found on their backs with clothes disarranged around their waist. Bruising was evident on or around the jawline, along with a pool of blood around the back of the neck. No substantial blood spray was found on any of the victim's clothes.

Cross-referencing the police reports with the surgical text and inquest notes, I could see definite similarities with each victim the 'Ripper' chose. All of the victims, aside from Smith and Martha Tabram, had their throats cut. The crime scenes were secluded, surrounded by poorly lit alleys, warehouses, and vacant buildings. Each woman came from a broken marriage, largely as a result of their intemperance. Subsequently, likely to avoid the workhouses, the women had taken to prostitution to survive. All of the victims were alive when the killer's blade sliced their throat. The medical text read that only living tissue bled, meaning that there was no blood flow post-mortem. It was my belief that the women were likely close to unconsciousness but not out cold when their throats were cut; otherwise, there would have been no blood spray. The one disturbing point that I could not wrap my head around was how the killer left the scene with no noticeable blood on his clothes and how the front of the victim's clothing was not saturated with blood. The crime scenes also showed no significant amount of blood spray in the vicinity of the body.

Weary from a full day of watching inquest testimony and reading case files, I closed the text and pushed the police reports away from me. Too tired to venture out in the rain, I lay down on the settee, hoping that sleep would come quickly.

Chapter Five

The hospitals and what served as a mortuary in the city as vast as London were numerous. I soon found out, however, that in London's East End, there were no public mortuaries in the city up to Bow Street and beyond. Hence, the need for using the shed at the Working Lads Institute, as a morgue, in the Chapman case. So far, during my investigation, I found no particular person inquiring about, or wanting to obtain bodies for medical research. I knew from experience that bodies were not kept for any length of time at the mortuary. I also knew that depending on the season in which a body was shipped to a morgue; it was in the family's best interest to have the body buried as soon as possible. Much to my surprise, and subsequent disappointment, I heard more than once from those I questioned concerning obtaining medical specimens that anything could be had in Whitechapel for a price. During questioning of doctors or mortuary attendants, I made a point of not making any specific reference to any particular person seeking out bodies or body parts that might be purchased for medical research. The last thing I needed was to start another wave of fear to spread through Whitechapel like the one created by Burke and Hare in Edinburgh.

I had spent two days looking into all of the mortuaries in the East End, including Shoreditch, Montague (Whitechapel), St. Georges, Golden Lane, and Millbank Street Mortuaries, and each time I received the same answer. The only positive information I received was that I should be asking at the Pathological Museum of the London Hospital Medical College. I was not amused when I heard this bit of advice, knowing full well that it was

Doctor Thomas H. Openshaw, who was the curator at the college. The advice did spark my curiosity though, for it made me wonder if I was walking in the same footsteps as the foreigner looking for specimens sealed in glycerin.

My immediate response was to rush right up to the London Hospital Medical College and confront Doctor Openshaw with the knowledge that I had about this foreigner wanting to secure these specimens for some undisclosed reason. However, each time my anger was kindled against the doctor who found it unnecessary to mention something as noteworthy as this incident to police, my temper was cooled by a vision of the young, Miss Curtin, whose only ambition was to be a nurse, and that I alone would prevent any chance of that from ever happening. It also did not escape my attention that technically I was no longer in the position to do so. The other poignant detail and one that cautioned me before acting rashly, was the fact that, as far as I knew, the unknown American had not committed any crime in seeking these specimens. The only real evidence that I could respond to was hearsay on behalf of an employee of the college, whom I could not produce as a witness to the account. Even if a crime had been committed, soliciting said specimens, if it were established, would likely amount to no more than an immoral act listed in a chapter of London's ordinances. It was little to go on, but my gut told me that this foreigner was something other than some kind of doctor in need of specimens for research. During the span of my career, I had seen my fellow man perpetrate a variety of crimes for various reasons. However, never before had I imagined that a man would kill another human being simply for pieces of their body. It seemed too surreal to be believed by the rational mind. The crime had its basis in some story told by Mary Shelley, then anything in real life. There had to be some other reason behind this man killing these women other than taking pieces of their anatomy. It was indeed nothing, I had ever come across in all my years as a detective. Like it or not, I had to consider that this doctor could be instrumental in finding the perpetrator of the Whitechapel murders, or could, in fact, be, the fiend '*Jack the Ripper*,' himself.

My mind was busy with all sorts of scenarios, as was often the case when I was investigating a crime; and trying to ferret out the perpetrator. The one fact that I kept focusing on was that this foreigner was in London to purchase his ghastly tokens because the man dared not seek what his warped desires sought in his own country. I presumed that this was likely due to fear of apprehension from authorities there. Like it or not, the more I investigated, the more, I found myself delving into the purposes that such an individual would want or desire parts taken from the body of a murdered woman. A medical study to serve the advancement of medicine or the scientific community, in general, was acceptable to most if not understandable and could be viewed as honorable if it ultimately saved lives. This prospect of such a purpose, although reasonable, lost all legitimacy when I considered that the foreigner tried to bypass the proper channels in obtaining his specimens. Unfortunately, during my long career, I had learned not to contend with the disturbing fact, that to some, the value of human life was minimalized by the selfish desire of the individual who only saw a means to an end. In Whitechapel, I had known some to take a human life for as little as the shoes on a man's feet; I supposed that it was not a far stretch to believe that someone would commit murder, for pieces of the victim's anatomy.

By week's end, I had no new leads. Discouraged by my progress, I decided to broaden my investigation. Turning my focus in another direction, I decided to take a page from Mary Shelley's book, so I began looking into any reports of graveyard robbers that might be operating in the vicinity. However, this also turned out to be a fruitless undertaking. With no new leads and no other avenues to follow. I gave up exhausted from traveling all over London's East-end, not liking the premise of facing the coroner with nothing new to lend to the investigation after all of my efforts.

Day four of the inquest in the death of Annie Chapman, was on Wednesday, September the nineteenth. The six days that had been at the investigator's disposal had proven to be discouraging, to say the least. There was not one new shred of evidence, no description of the perpetrator, nor was there any eyewitness to be found that could be brought forward to give evidence. The crowd sat silently; as the coroner stood up from behind the table opposite to where Doctor Phillips sat. The doctor had been recalled to establish similarities in the Nichols murder and the other murders in Whitechapel.

[Sic] Dr. Phillips, divisional surgeon of the metropolitan police, was then recalled.

The Coroner, before asking him to give evidence, said: "Whatever may be your opinion and objections, it appears to be necessary that all the evidence that you ascertained from the post-mortem examination should be on the records of the Court for various reasons, which I need not enumerate. However painful it may be, it is necessary for the interests of justice."

Dr. Phillips: "I have not had any notice of that. I should have been glad if notice had been given me because I should have been better prepared to give the evidence; however, I will do my best."

The Coroner: "Would you like to postpone it?"

Dr. Phillips: "Oh, no. I will do my best. I still think that it is a very great pity to make this evidence public. Of course, I bow to your decision; but there are matters which have come to light now, which show the wisdom of the course pursued on the last occasion, and I cannot help reiterating my regret that you have come to a different conclusion. On the last occasion, just before I left the court, I mentioned to you that there were reasons why I thought the perpetrator of the act upon the woman's throat had caught hold of her chin. These reasons were that just below the lobe of the left ear were three scratches, and there was also a bruise on the right cheek. When I come to speak of the wounds on the lower part of the body, I must again repeat my opinion that it is highly injudicious to make the results of my examination public. These details are fit only for yourself, sir, and the jury, but to make them public would simply be disgusting."

The crowd immediately began to stir with anticipation, the very thought that the details that the doctor did not want to divulge were finally going to be made public caused the jury to hush, even I sat up straighter in my seat.

[Sic] The Coroner: "We are here in the interests of justice, and must have all the evidence before us. I see, however, that there are several ladies and boys in the room, and I think they might retire."

As the ladies and messenger boys left the courtroom, I could see several in the front row whisper between each other. One could almost hear the lengths of the tall tales and conspiracies that were being discussed in the room. With a perturbed expression, Doctor Phillips objected again to the coroner's suggestion to make every detail known to the jury. This new objection by Phillips made the jury voice their own objections. I could only imagine the doctor's reasoning was based on the grounds of what the surgeon thought was in good taste, but laying all proprieties aside the investigation had to take precedent.

[Sic]Dr. Phillips again raised an objection to the evidence, remarking: "In giving these details to the public, I believe you are thwarting the ends of justice."

The astonished look on Baxter's face revealed that the man was more than a little irritated with Phillips' repeated objections to the demands of the inquest. It was apparent that the very idea that Phillips was questioning the coroner's approach in the handling of the proceedings was offensive to Baxter. It was evidently a war of wills that was transpiring before the crowded room, each juror sat at the edge of their seats as the live drama unfolded before them.

The Coroner: "We are bound to take all the evidence in the case, and whether it be made public or not is a matter for the responsibility of the press."
The Foreman: "We are of the opinion that the evidence the doctor on the last occasion wished to keep back should be heard."
(Several Jurymen: "Hear, hear.")

I watched as the jury pounded on the arm of their chairs to affirm their agreement with the coroner forcing the doctor to disclose all the pertinent information found at autopsy. I could only assume that Phillips felt it was his sole responsibility, to assess and disclose at his own discretion the nature of the intimate details of how Chapman had been slain. It was also evident that the doctor considered that the jury could not be responsible for ascertaining the validity of said information. In my opinion, it was this very attitude that had slowed the investigation on several levels when dealing with officials who found it pertinent to withhold vital information from investigators that could have changed the course of the investigation.

The Coroner: "I have carefully considered the matter and have never before heard of any evidence requested being kept back."
Dr. Phillips: "I have not kept it back; I have only suggested whether it should be given or not."
The Coroner: "We have delayed taking this evidence as long as possible, because you said the interests of justice might be served by keeping it back; but it is now a fortnight since this occurred, and I do not see why it should be kept back from the jury any longer."

I looked on as Wynne Baxter thundered away at Doctor Phillips, due to his hesitation at giving the facts of the case; I could see the coroner's patience wearing thin. It was clear by the murmuring of the jury that they concurred. It went beyond reason that Doctor Phillips would continue to evade giving exact details of the case. The repeated claims of thwarting justice sounded suspicious, made worse by the man's continued objections. Judging by the atmosphere of the room, the consensus was felt by all the spectators, causing a general reverberation by the viewers that had grown due to the street gossip which had drawn people to come from miles around. The room was hushed again when Doctor Phillips finally began to speak once more.

[Sic] Dr. Phillips: "I am of opinion that what I am about to describe took place after death, so that it could not affect the cause of death, which you are inquiring into."
The Coroner: "That is only your opinion, and might be repudiated by other medical opinion."
Dr. Phillips: "Very well. I will give you the results of my post-mortem examination."
Witness then detailed the terrible wounds which had been inflicted upon the woman and described the parts of the body which the perpetrator of the murder had carried away with him.
Phillips: "I am of opinion that the length of the weapon with which the incisions were inflicted was at least five to six inches in length - probably more - and must have been very sharp. The manner in which they had been done indicated a certain amount of anatomical knowledge."
The Coroner: "Can you give any idea how long it would take to perform the incisions found on the body?"
Dr. Phillips: "I think I can guide you by saying that I myself could not

71

have performed all the injuries I saw on that woman, and affect them, even without a struggle, under a quarter of an hour. If I had done it in a deliberate way, such as would fall to the duties of a surgeon, it would probably have taken me the best part of an hour. The whole inference seems to me that the operation was performed to enable the perpetrator to obtain possession of these parts of the body."

The Coroner: "Have you anything further to add with reference to the stains on the wall?"

Dr. Phillips: "I have not been able to obtain any further traces of blood on the wall."

The Foreman: "Is there anything to indicate that the crime in the case of the woman Nichols was perpetrated with the same object as this?"

The Coroner: "There is a difference in this respect, at all events, that the medical expert is of opinion that, in the case of Nichols, the mutilations were made first."

The Foreman: "Was any photograph of the eyes of the deceased taken, in case they should retain any impression of the murderer."

I watched with curiosity wondering what Baxter's and the doctor's response to this question would be. I assumed that both wanted to dismiss the matter before the jury went off in a tangent of suggestions that borderline nothing more than the use of witchcraft. They were fast approaching a new century, and science was trying to carve a new course for itself and put down all of the antiquated methods that clung to modern man like vestiges of the past. Although, I had heard some cases since the introduction of the box camera that a few zealous photographers had taken pictures of the eyes of victims involved in a tragic death. It was believed by some that the eye acted much the same way as the modern camera, and it was hoped that the retina would retain the image of whatever the victim last saw before their death. As far as I knew; the idea was utter rubbish. It was apparent though, that there would be many that would try and keep ancient superstitions alive, while men of intellect were busy trying to introduce more scientific deductions that corresponded with and not in opposition to Biblical teachings.

Dr. Phillips: "I have no particular opinion upon that point myself. I was asked about it very early in the inquiry, and I gave my opinion that the

operation would be useless, especially in this case. The use of a blood-hound was also suggested. It may be my ignorance, but the blood around was that of the murdered woman, and it would be more likely to be traced than the murderer. These questions were submitted to me by the police very early. I think within twenty- four hours of the murder of the woman."
The Coroner: *"Were the injuries to the face and neck such as might have produced insensibility?"*
Doctor Phillips: *"Yes; they were consistent with partial suffocation."*

The next witness was Elizabeth Long, who positively identified the deceased in the mortuary. Long gave testimony that she had seen the deceased on the morning of Annie Chapman's death.

[Sic] Elizabeth Long: "I passed 29, Hanbury-street. On the right-hand side, the same side as the house, I saw a man and a woman standing on the pavement talking. The man's back was turned towards Brick-lane, and the woman was towards the market. They were standing only a few yards nearer Brick-lane from 29, Hanbury-street. I saw the woman's face. Have seen the deceased in the mortuary, and I am sure the woman that I saw in Hanbury-street was the deceased. I did not see the man's face, but I noticed that I was dark. I was wearing a brown low-crowned felt hat. I think I had on a dark coat, though I am not certain. By the look of him he seemed to me a man over forty years of age. He appeared to me to be a little taller than the deceased."
Coroner: *"Did he look like a working man, or what?"*
    Long: *"He looked like a foreigner."*
Coroner: *"Did he look like a dock laborer, or a workman, or what?"*
    Long: *"I should say he looked like what I should call shabby-genteel."*
Coroner: *"Were they talking loudly?"* –
    Long: *"They were talking pretty loudly. I overheard him say to her 'Will you?' and she replied, 'Yes.' That is all I heard, and I heard this as I passed. I left them standing there, and I did not look back, so I cannot say where they went to."*
Coroner: *"Did they appear to be sober?"*
    Long: *"I saw nothing to indicate that either of them was the worse for drink."*
Coroner: *"Was it not an unusual thing to see a man and a woman*

standing there talking?" Long: "Oh no. I see lots of them standing there in the morning."
Coroner: "At that hour of the day?"
  Long: "Yes; that is why I did not take much notice of them."
Coroner: "You are certain about the time?"
  Long: "Quite."
Coroner: "What time did you leave home?"
  Long: "I got out about five o'clock, and I reached the Spitalfields Market a few minutes after half-past five."
The Foreman of the jury: "What brewer's clock did you hear strike half-past five?"
  Long: "The brewer's in Brick-lane." [Sic]

The rest of the day dragged on for me. When it became apparent that the remainder of the inquest would be spent cross-examining witnesses, I took advantage of the lull and ducked out a side door. As I made my way, I could not believe the crowds that had gathered jammed-backed around the outside of the doors and windows of the building, each one seeking even the most minuscule of information from the inquest. I walked the streets in a daze; the limits to the barriers that stood in front of the investigation seemed to be overwhelming. Doctor Phillips's attempts to obstruct the proceedings; by refusing to give testimony at the inquest was proof of that. I was sure there was nothing malicious in the man's attempts, something you would be hard-pressed to convince the coroner of. However, the overactive sense of responsibility that the doctor possessed in addition to the man's stubbornness; did nothing more than cast more aspersions in the direction of the professionals handling the investigation. Besides, the attempt seemed almost senseless in itself, considering the newspaper reporting that had been going on since the murders began. Not to mention the fact that the jury had been allowed to view the body at the mortuary before the inquest began.

Back at my office, I shuffled through the files on my desk, just as I had done every day since the investigation began, searching for the one, overlooked clue that would lead me to a killer. After several hours, I saw very few answers in the making; unfortunately, there was no end to the queries as a result of the incomplete files in front of me. Every investigator was armed with the simple fundamentals of detecting. Scotland Yard had built a reputation of finding the who, what, where, when, and why, of a crime better than any other law enforcement body in the world. To date, the files were not shy in detail about where the crimes were committed. They could even boast and say they knew approximately the time of when the crime was committed as well, but that really mattered little, considering they had no eyewitness to place a suspect with the deceased before they were found dead. The difficulties with this particular aspect of the investigation were not entirely due to the ability of the detectives. The problem of obtaining a suspect lay primarily in the clandestine activities that the women partook in plying their trade that made it difficult to find a credible witness.

Elizabeth Long testified at the inquest that the man she saw Chapman with '*looked like a foreigner*' and she stated, '*the man looked like what, I should call shabby-genteel.*'

The information that Long gave at questioning was the same as that at the inquest. Long also stated that she had seen the pair at about half-past five in the morning. As I was reading, I did my best not to think of the man that Curtin had overheard talking to Dr. Openshaw. This man had called himself an American, who, by anyone's standards was considered a foreigner. The American also called himself a physician, who, given his profession may be thought of dressing in a '*shabby-genteel*' fashion. I searched the other files for any witnesses that may have a better description of the suspect but found nothing. Closing the files, I placed it on top of the pile; while wondering if there was something that I was missing.

A few minutes later, a very frustrated looking, Wynne Baxter burst into my office with a swift knock on my half-opened door.

"Phillips has tried to control these inquests from day one," Baxter vented. "Well, I will not have it. I never had such a disagreeable witness on the stand in my life like that blasted man was today!" Baxter exclaimed.

I looked up at the coroner and knew from experience responding would do not good until Baxter had a chance to vent his frustration.

"Phillips was asked simple and direct questions, and the man has turned the inquest into a circus, causing the jury to think there is some kind of a conspiracy going on in Whitechapel." Baxter finished by flopping into the chair opposite.

"What do you think is his motivation for not wanting to answer your questions," I asked. "I mean, aside from giving every ghastly detail in the woman's condition, a fact that has been made public, for at least a week given the gossip of police constables to journalists?"

I sympathized with my friend, having sensed the general feeling of the crowd when I left the inquest before it was finished for the day.

"It is the man's blasted conservative attitude! Philips is so uptight; the man thinks that the rest of the population is the same way. If it weren't for his delicate sensibilities and his assumption that anything that might be revealed will astonish or frighten the populace, this inquest would be further along."

"I do not think the doctor comprehends that his misgivings are doing more harm than good, Wynne."

"It is not just that, Stone," Baxter continued. "It is this timing of the woman Elizabeth Long, seeing Chapman at half-past five. The body was found by the carman at three-quarters of five. When the body was inspected by Doctor Phillips at twenty minutes past six, the doctor said it was still warm to the touch. That infernal man argued on the stand that Chapman was probably killed before half-past four. I don't know if the man is mistaken, which brings his professional conduct under scrutiny or if his goal is to hamper my authority in the proceedings."

Baxter's red face describing his dealings with the doctor on the stand was evidence enough to see how the coroner felt about Dr. Phillips.

"When do you sum up the proceedings, Wynne?"

I asked the question to change the subject.

"I guess it will be on the twenty-sixth of this month. Although the conclusions will not come as a surprise, it seems at this point that it will be just a formality. I just don't like this shadow of a doubt that Phillips has left overhanging the jury; it has all the appearances that we are trying to hide something." Baxter finished.

"What possibly could be gained by not revealing the whole truth?"

My question wasn't answered right away, causing some speculation to mount in my own mind.

"I have no idea, but there is no way that I am going to leave that jury thinking that they have been deceived when it comes time for me to make my summations."

Baxter stood up and started towards the door, and with a wave was down the hall.

September twenty-sixth came before I knew it. Day five of Wynne Baxter's inquest in the death of Annie Chapman had a cloud of unrest hanging over it. I stood off to the side and waited patiently to hear Baxter's summation. After seeing my friend in my office after the fourth day of inquest proceedings; I had been busy tracking down the foreigner, unfortunately, my efforts had come to nothing.

With the summation, the coroner reflected on the previous minutes of the inquest, congratulating the jury for their efforts. Next, the coroner delved into the victim's background, lifestyle, and residents. To all of this, the jury had very little response. Baxter then related the witness statements of the times that the deceased was last seen, right up to and including the events that led up to Chapman being found murdered. It wasn't until this portion of the coroner's summation that I heard a turn in the direction of Baxter's speech. At first, I wondered about where Baxter was headed, and then I realized that the coroner was making a full disclosure of facts.

[Sic] After a brief pause, he continued, "She was not in the yard when Richardson was there at 4.50 a.m. She was talking outside the house at half-past five when Mrs. Long passed them. Cadosh says it was about 5.20 when he was in the backyard of the adjoining house, and heard a voice say 'No,' and three or four minutes afterwards a fall against the fence; but if he is out of his reckoning but a quarter of an hour, the discrepancy in the evidence of fact vanishes, and he may be mistaken, for he admits that he did not get up till a quarter past five and that it was after the half-hour when he passed Spitalfields clock. It is true that Dr. Phillips thinks that when he saw the body at 6.30 the deceased had been dead at least two hours, but he admits that the coldness of the morning and the great loss of blood may affect his opinion."

Baxter paused again this time looking directly at Doctor Phillips. I could see the tension mount between both coroner and doctor when their eyes met across the room. Even at the distance from where I sat from Dr.

Phillips, I could see the doctor's cheeks flush. After only a short pause, Baxter continued making his opinion known to all in the room about his frustration in dealing with Phillips.

[Sic] *"and if the evidence of the other witnesses be correct, Dr. Phillips has miscalculated the effect of those forces. But many minutes after Mrs. Long passed the man and woman cannot have elapsed before the deceased became a mutilated corpse in the yard of 29, Hanbury-street, close by where she was last seen by any witness. This place is a fair sample of a large number of houses in the neighborhood. It was built, like hundreds of others, for the Spitalfields weavers, and when hand-looms were driven out by steam and power, these were converted into dwellings for the poor. Its size is about such as a superior artisan would occupy in the country, but its condition is such as would to a certainty leave it without a tenant. In this place seventeen persons were living, from a woman and her son sleeping in a cat's-meat shop on the ground floor to Davis and his wife and their three grown-up sons, all sleeping together in an attic. The street door and the yard door were never locked, and the passage and yard appear to have been constantly used by people who had no legitimate business there. There is little doubt that the deceased knew the place, for it was only three or four hundred yards from where she lodged. If so, it is quite unnecessary to assume that her companion had any knowledge - in fact, it is easier to believe that he was ignorant both of the nest of living beings by whom he was surrounded, and of their occupations and habits. Some were on the move late at night, some were up long before the sun. A Carman, named Thompson, left the house for his work as early as 3:50 a.m.; an hour later John Richardson was paying the house a visit of inspection; shortly after 5:15. Cadosh, who lived in the next house, was in the adjoining yard twice. Davis, the carman, who occupied the third-floor front, heard the church clock strike a quarter to six, got up, had a cup of tea, and went into the back yard, and was horrified to find the mangled body of deceased. It was then a little after six a.m. - a very little, for at ten minutes past the hour Inspector Chandler had been informed of the discovery while on duty in Commercial-street."*

I listened as Baxter finished making it quite clear how he felt about the times that key witnesses had testified about being in or around the back yard of twenty-nine Hanbury Street. Ultimately, though, it was the doctor's estimated time of death, which was now officially put into question. Up until now, the exact time of death in murder cases had been relative; to determine an approximate; time of death. That time then could be later used to ascertain the whereabouts of the deceased or a suspect in or around the crime scene. In the Whitechapel murders, however, with so many unknowns in the cases, the estimated time of death became vital to the investigation. It was that time used by investigators and coroners in hopes of eliminating unnecessary suspects, of which there were many. With a general time of death, investigators could then tie other factors into the case, such as the victim's movements, the time that the body was discovered, the arrival of the doctor, and the arrival of constables. The key was to substantiate all testimony, so that the time of death could be verified or contested. All of these bits of information were now used to link the deceased to known associates and track their movements on the night in question. Unfortunately, with so much discrepancy in witness accounts, the coroner had to rely on the expert testimony of doctors and investigators. However, when the validity of their testimony was under scrutiny, there was not a lot of evidence left to tie the last known movements of the victim to witness statements.

Baxter first touched base on the discrepancies in witness accounts and those of trying to pinpoint the actual time of death. The coroner also put any fears to rest on the supposition that a crazed psychopath was trying to recreate the deaths as part of covering other crimes of murder done to make it look like a '*Ripper*' killing. The final surprise came when Baxter did what up until that very minute, I would have considered to be unlikely.

[Sic] "The conclusion that the desire was to possess the missing part seems overwhelming. If the object were robbery, these injuries were meaningless, for death had previously resulted from the loss of blood at the neck. Moreover, when we find an easily accomplished theft of some paltry brass rings and such an operation, after, at least, a quarter of an hour's work, and by a skilled person, we are driven to the deduction that the mutilation was the object, and the theft of the rings was only a thin-veiled blind, an attempt to prevent the real intention being discovered. Had not the medical examination been of a thorough and searching character, it might easily have been left unnoticed. The difficulty in

believing that this was the real purport of the murderer is natural. It is abhorrent to our feelings to conclude that a life should be taken for so slight an object; but, when rightly considered, the reasons for most murders are altogether out of proportion to the guilt. It has been suggested that the criminal is a lunatic with morbid feelings. This may or may not be the case; but the object of the murderer appears palpably shown by the facts, and it is not necessary to assume lunacy, for it is clear that there is a market for the object of the murder. To show you this, I must mention a fact which at the same time proves the assistance which publicity and the newspaper press afford in the detection of crime. Within a few hours of the issue of the morning papers containing a report of the medical evidence given at the last sitting of the Court."

Baxter had the entire room sitting at the edge of their seats and every journalist in the room writing furiously on their notepads. The gasps and whispers of the jury were allowed to continue until Baxter's voice thundered, and the room fell silent again.

[Sic] "I received a communication from an officer of one of our great medical schools, that they had information which might or might not have a distinct bearing on our inquiry. I attended at the first opportunity, and was told by the sub-curator of the Pathological Museum that some months ago an American had called on him, and asked him to procure a number of specimens of the organ that was missing in the deceased. He stated his willingness to give £20 for each, and explained that his object was to issue an actual specimen with each copy of a publication on which he was then engaged. Although he was told that his wish was impossible to be complied with, he still urged his request. He desired them preserved, not in spirits of wine, the usual medium, but in glycerin, in order to preserve them in a flaccid condition, and he wished them sent to America direct. It is known that this request was repeated to another institution of a similar character. Now, is it not possible that the knowledge of this demand may have incited some abandoned wretch to possess himself of a specimen?"

I watched the crowd intently, curious as to their reaction, but the coroner had every spectator's undivided attention, with not a whisper to be heard. I turned my attention back to Baxter, whose voice resonated to the rafters of the room like some great orator on a stage. I listened intently after Baxter revealed the information, they had obtained second-hand, wondering if Baxter simply got caught up in the moment or if the man was prepared to divulge Curtain as the source of the information.

[Sic] "It seems beyond belief that such inhuman wickedness could enter into the mind of any man, but unfortunately our criminal annals prove that every crime is possible. I need hardly say that I at once communicated my information to the Detective Department at Scotland-yard. Of course, I do not know what use has been made of it, but I believe that publicity may possibly further elucidate this fact, and, therefore, I have not withheld from you my knowledge. By means of the press some further explanation may be forthcoming from America if not from here. I have endeavored to suggest to you the object with which this offence was committed, and the class of person who must have perpetrated it. The greatest deterrent from crime is the conviction that detection and punishment will follow with rapidity and certainty, and it may be that the impunity with which Mary Ann Smith and Anne Tabram were murdered suggested the possibility of such horrid crimes as those which you and another jury have been recently considering. It is, therefore, a great misfortune that nearly three weeks have elapsed without the chief actor in this awful tragedy having been discovered. Surely, it is not too much even yet to hope that the ingenuity of our detective force will succeed in unearthing this monster. It is not as if there were no clue to the character of the criminal or the cause of his crime. My object is clearly divulged."

The coroner of Middlesex continued with every eye peeled, and every ear listening to his every word. The entire room sat up at attention when Baxter revealed his own personal feelings about his findings during the investigation. I even recognized some of my own comments that I had made to the coroner, leaving me to wonder what Baxter's motivation was for yet another subtle turn in his inquest summation. There was no rule as to the direction that inquest proceedings were to follow. The goal of an inquest was primarily to introduce facts to the public in a wrongful death investigation, a death that had no suspect, or in this particular case, had no rhyme or reason. However, I had certain misgivings after hearing some of what the coroner said. I found myself wondering if Baxter was divulging too much to the jury, a thing that I had been critical of the newspaper reporters. As an investigator, I liked to keep specific facts and circumstances in a case from the public, some tidbit of information that perhaps only the perpetrator of a crime would know that could be used against a suspect to tie them to a crime. I could very well understand Baxter's frustration and the reasons why the revelation was made; however, I inwardly hoped that my friend did not expose too much that may help the '*Ripper*' elude capture from police.

[Sic] "His anatomical skill carries him out of the category of a common criminal, for his knowledge could only have been obtained by assisting at post-mortems, or by frequenting the post-mortem room. Thus, the class in which search must be made, although a large one, is limited. Moreover, it must have been a man who was from home, if not all night, at least during the early hours of Sept. 8th. His hands were undoubtedly blood-stained, for he did not stop to use the tap in the yard as the pan of clean water under it shows."

The coroner finished the inquest by addressing rumors that had been spreading from day one. Baxter revealed that most of the higher-ranking officers in the police department believed the killer was a man who recently escaped from a lunatic asylum. The seemingly senseless nature of the crime and the inability for the police to apprehend such a wretch had left the top brass reeling from their failure to apprehend the killer. Baxter then urged the jury and the general public in the East End to focus their attention on the only description of the multiple murderer. In this last statement, the coroner tried to get any who might identify the killer by the description given by Elizabeth Long to draw some positive attention from the news agencies, and to get the public involved in finding the '*Ripper.*'

[Sic] "If the theory of lunacy be correct - which I very much doubt - the class is still further limited; while, if Mrs. Long's memory does not fail, and the assumption be correct that the man who was talking to the deceased at half-past five was the culprit, he is even more clearly defined. In addition to his former description, we should know that he was a foreigner of dark complexion, over forty years of age, a little taller than the deceased, of shabby-genteel appearance, with a brown dear-stalker

hat on his head, and a dark coat on his back. If your views accord with mine, you will be of opinion that we are confronted with a murder of no ordinary character, committed not from jealousy, revenge, or robbery, but from motives less adequate than the many which still disgrace our civilization, mar our progress, and blot the pages of our Christianity. I cannot conclude his remarks without thanking you for the attention you have given to the case, and the assistance you have rendered me in our efforts to elucidate the truth of this horrible tragedy."

The Foreman: "We can only find one verdict - that of willful murder against some person or persons unknown. We were about to add a rider with respect to the condition of the mortuary, but that having been done by a previous jury it is unnecessary."

With the throng of people, I had no opportunity to talk to Wynne Baxter after the inquest. Eager to escape the mass, I walked away from the Working Lads Institute and hailed a cab around the corner from the mob that had gathered in front of the building.

"Stone, Detective Stone!"

Hearing the shouts coming from behind me, I turned and saw the red-faced coroner as the man pried himself from the crowd of people.

"My word, I am glad to be away from all the back-slapping and approval of that group."

I smirked at Baxter's obvious embarrassment from all the attention.

"Hurry, Detective let us get in the cab before any try to follow," Baxter said, carrying his briefcase in one hand and mopping the sweat from his brow with a handkerchief in the other. It was several blocks before Baxter finally broke the silence between them.

"Don't just sit there, man," Baxter piped up. "Confounded, I know that you are thinking that I may have gone too far and revealed too much. Be that as it may, the truth of the matter is, I felt it was necessary, and I will do anything to apprehend this monster!" Baxter sighed, still mopping the sweat from his brow.

"And Miss Curtin, what do we say to her, when she is identified as the one who has given you this information and is forced to testify as to how she came upon it?"

83

"I will not have these deaths come to nothing because of the questionable efforts of police and due to the few high-minded material witnesses, who in their own conceits, choose to be cavalier in their duties! No offense dear boy." Baxter stopped to apologize.

"None taken," I acknowledged the coroner's apology. "By the way, Wynne, who is this unknown sub-curator from the London Museum Hospital who brought this mysterious American to your attention?"

"I am sorry, John, I received communication by letter, and until necessary, this gentleman will remain anonymous."

"I see," I looked at the coroner, wondering if the curator was a figment of Baxter's imagination. "Do you think we may find out this gentleman's identity in the near future?"

"Detective, it has long been my feeling that the general consensus of police and a percentage of the public feel that these poor girls are just prostitutes and London is far better off without them, then with them. As far as the witness from the Medical College, I should think that the curator's response will be trifling, if any, in their efforts to minimize any more attention to the college then what would have to be explained." Baxter finished by pushing his handkerchief into the front pocket of his jacket.

With no response, Baxter sat quietly, staring out the window of the cab.

"What are you thinking now, John?" Baxter asked, seeking some kind of response.

"I would think we are going to have a time of it, Wynne."

"A time of what?"

"Of finding an American in a city with a population of approximately three million," I answered rather sarcastically.

Three days after the Chapman inquest had been put to rest, I had a cab drop me off at The Yard. My primary purpose was to report on the inquest, and the progress I had made in the Chapman murder. Secondarily, I was inwardly hoping that Inspector Abberline would honor my resignation. As much as I regretted my desire to leave Whitechapel, I saw no good end coming to the murder investigation. At every turn, I found that the investigation was being led down improbable paths by bureaucrats intimidating detectives to lead the investigation away from the probable into the unlikely, for unknown reasons. I would have thought that the unsolved murders of four women and the animosity between the Metropolitan Police and the citizenry were more than enough to deal with. However, the Metropolitan Police Department's mishandling crime scenes and evidence was enough to involve every man jack who had an opinion on policing. Not to mention the bureaucrats interest in saving face, and making excuses, rather than putting forth every effort to find out who the killer was.

As I walked into the building, I saw the stiff figure of Inspector Abberline talking to constables at the front desk. When my presence was known, Abberline motioned for me to come to his office. I had no more than sat down when the inspector slid a piece of paper across the desk towards me. Picking it up, I began to read aloud, unsure what to expect.

[Sic] *Dear Boss,*

I keep on hearing the police have caught me but they wont fix me just yet. I have laughed when they look so clever and talk about being on the right track. That joke about Leather Apron gave me real fits. I am down on whores and I shant quit ripping them till I do get buckled. Grand work the last job was. I gave the lady no time to squeal. How can they catch me now? I love my work and want to start again. You will soon hear of me with my funny little games. I saved some of the proper red stuff in a ginger beer bottle over the last job to write with but it went thick like glue and I can't use it. Red ink is fit enough I hope ha. ha. The next job I do I shall clip the ladys ears off and send to the police officers just for jolly wouldn't you. Keep this letter back till I do a bit more work then give it out straight. My knifes so nice and sharp I want to get to work right away if I get a chance, Good Luck

    Your Truly Jack the Ripper

    Dont mind me giving the trade name

PS Wasnt good enough to post this before I got all the red ink off my hands curse it. No luck yet. They say I'm a doctor now. Ha ha"

I took a minute to digest the correspondence, meticulously going over every detail. After several minutes, I read it again. Suddenly, my interest in resigning had become less important to me, at least, for the time being. I stopped reading and looked up at Inspector Abberline.

"When did Home Office receive this, Sir?"

"It was delivered to the Central News Agency by mail, they brought it here upon receipt this morning. The letter you have is a copy. The original is covered in red ink, made to look like the victim's blood described in the letter."

Dumbfounded, I read the letter to myself again, when I had finished, I laid the letter on my lap, astonished.

"This bloke is going to kill again! "

"I wish we could make these women in Whitechapel see what we're up against, Detective," Abberline sighed. "We have been keeping this letter confidential until the first of the week."

"Until the first of the week," I asked, somewhat surprised. "What happens, then, Sir?"

"My superiors seem to feel, if we release this to the press, there might be a chance to find out who may have written it," Abberline said, pacing back and forth.

"How?"

"The consensus here, is that someone might recognize the phraseology."

"What are the odds of that, Sir?"

"Be that as it may, Stone, it is better for us to use the newspapers; than to allow them any more latitude in their reporting. If this madman is exposed and loses his audience, then we can downplay the newspaper's fear-mongering." Abberline hesitated, then continued. "If we allow the papers to run wild, who knows what this man will do to keep his audience engrossed."

"What, if anything, can we do to stop them, Sir?"

"That is, just it, Stone. There is nothing we can do to stop them. But there is a plan in the works to hopefully put a different spin on these stories, so that police don't come off looking so badly."

Seeing the futility of the situation, I decided to change the topic of conversation back to the letter.

"Sir, is there any reason to believe this letter could be a hoax?"

"None so far, that is to say, there is nothing specific in this letter that links it to anything from the past homicides."

"Well, perhaps someone will recognize the handwriting, and we can move forward, but I wouldn't put all my hopes on the possibility."

"I too have my misgivings about putting the letter in the papers, seeing how; the news agencies are doing their level best to make us look like a bunch of buffoons wandering around like blind men," Abberline snapped and unrolled the paper in his hand and read the Times headline aloud. '*Another Whitechapel Murder.*' Now, the papers are calling him '*Jack the Ripper.*' These journalists are sensationalizing these killings to sell papers. Meanwhile, their headlines have all the appearances of goading this killer, so much so that this fiend is becoming more and more brazen. The fantastic method this '*Jack*' uses to kill these women combined with this ritualistic dissection becoming more ghoulish with each victim, the public doesn't need any more help to add to their anxiety."

"Londoners seemed to be gobbling up these stories, Sir."

"These newsagents, don't seem to understand that the more they write about our failure to catch him, the more they are blatantly slapping our faces in public. The East End of London houses more than 60 brothels, and there are 1200 prostitutes in the area in which to contend. Are we to hold their hands at night, we haven't the time or the manpower?"

After listening to Abberline's outburst, I now understood why the Assistant Commissioner, Robert Anderson, was allowed to take sick leave.

The stress that Abberline displayed told me how great the heavy burden the man under. It was out of character for the man to unload on a subordinate.

"So, what do we do now?"

I supposed that I knew the answer to the question before asking it; but it was only due to how uncomfortable I was feeling that the question was asked.

"We stay focused Stone. That is why your position in Whitechapel is so important right now, but we must keep it low key, you understand?"

I nodded in answer recalling my primary reason for seeing the inspector.

"I need you to check and recheck, and check again every statement given by every witness if needs be, and look again to every clue that we have." Abberline spoke defiantly.

After my meeting with Abberline, I finished filling out my reports and decided to go back to my office. As tired as I was, the letter from the killer had put every copper on high alert. Passing by the coroner's office, I poked my head around the opened doorway.

"Detective, what can I do for you?" Baxter asked cheerfully.

"Would you mind coming into my office, Wynne?"

"Not at all, I will be along directly."

True to the coroner's word, it was only a few minutes before Baxter walked into my office, carrying two cups of steaming tea.

"I know you have no way of heating water, Stone so, I went ahead and made us a spot of tea."

"Thank you, Wynne, I sure could use it," I said thankfully.

"What is this matter of great urgency?" Baxter asked, lifting the teacup halfway to his mouth, stopping mid-motion.

"I want you to look at something in the strictest of confidence, Wynne."

I spoke, watching Baxter sit his teacup down, giving me his full attention.

"Here, read this."

Reaching across the desk, Baxter took the letter and began to read.

"Signed, *Jack the Ripper*," Baxter whispered, finishing the letter by reading the salutation out loud. "When did The Yard receive this, John?"

"It was delivered by hand to the Home Office yesterday."

"Nobody else knows of this," Baxter asked?

"Only a handful, and now you, of course," I answered. "The rest of London will know at the first of the week."

"What do you mean, the rest of London will know at the first of the week?"

"I mean that the Home Office is going to release a copy of this letter to the papers."

"What is their motivation for making this public?" Baxter asked, sharply.

I looked at, Baxter understanding the reason for the question, for I had been thinking the same thing.

"They believe, by making this public, we might be able to find out if anyone can recognize the diction used in the letter."

"That is the most absurd thing I have ever heard!" Baxter flung up his hands in hopelessness. "Do you know what this means, Detective?" Baxter asked, shaking the letter in the air.

"Yes, that there is a possibility that there could be another prostitute dead in Whitechapel before morning." I said, folding the letter up and putting it back inside my vest pocket.

Baxter all but slammed the teacup on the edge of Stone's desk and then began to pace back and forth in front of my desk.

"Inspector Abberline hopes that if we don't let this leak until we have to, this '*Jack the Ripper*' may try to get in touch through the newspaper again," I said, trying to grasp anything positive from the situation.

"What, if anything, will that do?" Baxter asked, still pacing.

I could see the anxiety on the coroner's face, and understood, knowing that anyone that was involved with mortality as much as the coroner, anticipating another killing, so soon after closing an inquest only days earlier, was not something either of them wanted to think about.

"There is a plan in the works to perchance change the perception that the newsagents are printing about the police. The inspector feels, that the papers are exciting this killer's desire for attention. If he is right and this maniac does love the publicity about his ability to dodge the police, swaying public opinion may force the killer to do something rash that may give us a clue to his identity.

The idea sounded reasonable in the inspector's office, but after hearing it come out of my own mouth, the idea sounded as fruitless as bloodhounds mucking up and down crime scenes hoping to get the scent of the elusive killer.

"Regardless, if we respond or not, or if we try to keep the villain's alias out of the papers, this letter describes that it doesn't seem to matter, the '*Ripper*' will see to it himself. This letter clearly states that fact. Whether we like it or not, '*Jack*' is going to kill again, and there doesn't seem to be a way for the police to stop him." Baxter roared and then slumped into his chair.

"Wynne, some of the papers have painted a picture of a killer ridding the streets of London's undesirables, not the blood-thirsty villain we know him to be."

"Well, we cannot be responsible for what the newspapers write about this lunatic."

"That is just it, Wynne, perhaps we could change the direction of the reporting."

"How, would you go about doing that, Detective?"

"By giving the facts instead of gossip."

"How would your Home Office feel about that, Stone?"

I knew that Baxter was right, but there had to be some way of swaying public opinion.

"John, the papers have half the public believing that this killer is some deranged Robinhood. While the other half believe that an escapee is running loose in London slashing prostitutes."

"That is just it, Wynne," I explained. "If anything, my investigation thus far, has turned up quite the contrary," I explained. "This man is meticulous, premeditating, and calculating. I believe the perpetrator of these crimes studies these women. It is common knowledge that Whitechapel is the home of the indigent and criminal. What better place for '*Jack*' to choose to hunt."

"Stone, do you hear yourself? Baxter interjected. "You describe this monster, as if the man was out for sport, choosing these women as if they were game of some sort," Baxter shouted.

"Unlike the newspapers, Wynne, that is precisely the description of this man that we should be placing all of our energies in looking for. If we are to catch this monster as you call him, then we must think like him," I said, watching Baxter dunk a biscuit into his tea, allowing it to drip on the edge of his cup. "I believe that our killer lies in wait and becomes familiar with the habits of his next victim. I think it is possible that this man has taken days watching and waiting for the opportune time before striking. That is why there is no evidence left at the scene to speak of. '*Jack*' may even seek their invitations, but I doubt it. I think he may try to gain their trust."

"How the devil does a maniac do that?"

I heard the exasperation in Baxter's voice and empathized while trying to explain.

"I think '*Jack*' probably plies them with drink. We already know from both the Nichols and Tabram cases that these women enjoy the pub-life; they may even confide in him about their personal lives. The information our killer learns; is volunteered freely. Perhaps this is how '*Jack*' gains their confidence and how he chooses his next victim."

Baxter sat sipping his tea, remaining silent. I sat wondering if the coroner's thoughts were like my own thoughts, wandering down the dark alleys of Whitechapel speculating where and when the hunter would kill again. The idea that I could do nothing to prevent the killer from killing again disturbed me. Unfortunately, there was no other recourse to take until the man made a mistake and left some incriminating evidence that would lead police on the trail of a killer.

"So, all police can suggest to these women," Baxter retorted. "Is for them, not to walk down dark alleys alone until this man strikes again and takes another prostitutes life, and hope that the next time '*Jack*' kills that they will find some evidence that will finally lead them to him, is that it, Detective?"

"I am afraid so, Wynne," I said, apologetically. "They are doing everything humanly possible to catch this '*Ripper*,' perhaps sooner, rather than later, this chap will make some mistake that will give us some clue, or in the very least, something that suggests how '*Jack*'s' victims are chosen, so that we can at least warn these women."

"Stone, you sound as if this monster will keep killing until the police catch him," Baxter picked up his teacup and emptied it.

"Of that, Wynne, I am quite certain," I answered. "Make no mistake; judging by this latest letter and the boasts made that another victim is forthcoming, '*Jack*' won't stop until whatever started this glut for blood has been satisfied.

Chapter Six

September thirtieth was as warm a day; as any in July. The papers had finally started to print current events other than stories of the unsolved murders in the city of London. Even though, the death of Annie Chapman and her inquest were not a too distant memory. Nor was the knowledge that a killer of the most brutal kind was still at large in London's East End forgotten. Those women who walked the streets in the wee hours plied themselves with liquid courage to keep going out night after night, and nothing; not even '*Jack the Ripper*' would stop them.

In the days that followed the inquest, I kept up my regiment of going over witness statements and police reports. However, it was not long before I realized that each new piece of information turned out to be as futile as the previous lead. The letters offering information or suspects that poured into the Home Office numbered in the thousands, and yet Inspector Abberline insisted that each one was followed up with an interview and a report. Even though none seemed to lead police on the scent of a killer, the inspector's thorough and regimented discipline in the running of the case was ceaseless; nevertheless, there was still no suspect in the holding cells of Newgate Prison awaiting trial.

Arriving late to my rooms, I had looked forward to a steaming cup of tea, which I hoped would somehow revitalize me. Although the tea warmed my insides, it did little to help my spirits. Sitting in the dark, I watched the dancing shadows that were cast on my wall from the coal stove, its light and warmth penetrated the dark confines of the solitude I sought as I sipped the amber liquid, immersing myself in the comfort of my chair listening to light rain as it struck the thin windowpane.

The pounding on the outside door hours later made me shutter in my deep sleep, but it did not bring me out of my slumber. I did not rouse until I heard the pounding at my own door only a few feet away from where I sat. The deep sleep in which I was immersed tried to keep me bound into the painless oblivion I had found, nevertheless, the heavy pounding at the door continued stubbornly until it finally broke the clutches that remained, leaving a wave of nausea in its wake. Opening my eyes, I immediately sought the culprit that awakened me. Rising stiffly from the wing-backed chair, I groggily looked through the window at the black sky that had cleared, and the remaining clouds cradled a full moon. Walking towards the door and the faceless culprit on the other side, I yanked on the doorknob. On the other side, I found a large constable that all but burst into the room with a frightened-looking Mrs. Wilson standing behind, his arm extended with a fist still cocked to continue his barrage on the door.

"Detective, you are requested, sir!" The constable shouted, handing me a message.

"What for? What bloody time is it?"

I shouted at the constable, rubbing my face with my hands.

"It is half-past one sir, I have a carriage waiting for you downstairs."

"Half-past one!" I shouted as the constable fled down the hall. Turning, I looked at Mrs. Wilson who stood fingering a handkerchief in her hands.

"There has been another murder," Mrs. Wilson sniffled. "I will get you a cup of tea while you dress."

Running my hands through my hair, I ignored the gawks from the other boarders who had slipped their heads through half-opened doors and then slammed the door making their displeasure for being woken in the middle of the night known. Tucking in my wrinkled shirt, my surly mood softened as my landlady's words echoed in my mind as I ripped open the message.

Detective Stone, Inspector Pinhorn is on-site. I would like you to concentrate your efforts on the International Workers Club. This club has been under our suspicion for some time; perhaps we can learn something.

Inspector Abberline.

Suddenly very awake, I pulled my shirt over my head, taking no time to unbutton it. It took me only minutes to splash water on my face, don another shirt, and slip into my jacket. Seconds later, I opened the door meeting Mrs. Wilson halfway coming up the hall towards me with a cup and saucer forcing it into my trembling hands. Taking a quick gulp of the steaming liquid, I was grateful for the tea as it ran down my parched throat, setting cup and saucer on a table in the hall. Racing down the stairs I heard Mrs. Wilson urging me to be careful just before closing the door behind me. Climbing aboard the cab, the driver slapped the reins on the horse's backs, looking at the constable, the expressionless face offered no other information. I looked out the window as the racing hansom rumbled down the cobbled streets, the driver's whip snapping continually over the horse's ears urging the beast ever faster through London's East End. It took the cab only minutes to reach its destination on Berner Street. With a lurch, the driver hauled on the reins. Sliding across the seat, I opened the door before the cab came to a complete halt.

The body of 'Jack's' latest victim lay close to a wall of a two-story building in a lane called Dutfield's Yard. I took my eyes off the body long enough to have a look around. Numerous constables, carrying lanterns and torches were milling around to illuminate the dark drive. Dutfield's Yard was crowded between numbers forty and forty-two on Berner Street. The fact that the International Workers Club was number forty, did not escape my attention. The opening to the lane was a nondescript space separating the two buildings, that was shielded by a pair of nine-foot-high wooden gates that I learned were almost always closed. The gates; were now being propped open by two large stakes that were sunk into the ground. Inspector Pinhorn, the officer in charge, was questioning a constable, and judging by the man's tone, I could tell that the inspector was none too happy with the constable. During the inspector's interrogation, I heard Pinhorn ask if the patrolman was in the habit of opening the gates that shrouded Dutfield's Yard in darkness and checking behind them. The constable's answer was a decisive no. Averting my attention from the red-faced constable, I walked through the gates and examined the area where the body lay. I approached the scene as both doctors stood and reviewed their findings with each other taking note that the victim lay on her side and the discoloration of her cheeks. I also studied the deep laceration to the victim's throat, which upon my own preliminary examination seemed far more aggressive on the left than that on the right side. I did not miss the tightly knotted handkerchief around the victim's neck.

Removing myself as Doctor Phillips prepared to have the body transported to the mortuary, I looked at the buildings adjacent to the scene of the crime. The International Workers Club had been the topic of conversation by those who thought the club to be used by enemies of the government. The club had already been the focus of several police raids in their efforts to weed out immigrant anarchists from the streets of London. It did not bode well, that it was common police knowledge, that the club was also the hub for the gathering of a large portion of the Jewish population. This was likely due to the Yiddish newspaper printed there. I had heard from other detectives that the Social Democrats had met in conjunction with the members of the club to connect on any topics that both groups felt strongly enough to act upon. Up until recently, their combined efforts had produced more than a few marches and protests on London's streets.

Through the chaos, I watched yet another crime scene being molested by several constables, all searching for some clue, all the while oblivious of the irretrievable evidence that they could be trampling underfoot. I had made my feelings known that the areas should be cordoned off and inspected in the light of day, but my suggestions had been disregarded. Inspector Pinhorn nodded in my direction, and I responded in like manner. Though Pinhorn had been on the scene only minutes before me, the man was in complete control yelling orders to a group of constables to hold every member of the club until all of them had been identified and questioned. Up the street, I saw another racing cab coming around the corner with reckless abandon. From the corner of my eye, I could see two constables standing across the street of the entrance to Dutfield's Yard. My attention turned to the man who sat on the curb between the two constables. I studied the man, who held his hat in one hand, while the other rubbed a balding pate. I walked over to the two constables and questioned them as to who the man was that they were holding.

"He is the man who found the body, sir!"

The constable shouted too enthusiastically for two in the morning.

"Does he speak English?"

"Yes, sir."

"Give me a moment with him, will you," I asked, hearing a shout from beside me. I turned in time to see the carriage drive away.

As I stood looking at the witness, the man timidly looked up from the curb, obviously still in shock after finding the murdered woman.

"I am Detective Stone; I need to ask you some questions."

A simple nod was the man's only response.

"What is your name?"

"Louis Diemschutz," the man said, proudly. "I live here."

"When did you find the body?"

"At about one o'clock, I was returning from purchasing some jewelry, I always drive my cart into the yard when I return home," Diemschutz responded.

"Are the gates to the yard always kept open?"

"Only when I know there is a delivery, or if I know, I will be arriving home late," Diemschutz answered.

"The body," I asked, noticing the man grimace. "How was it that you found it in the dark lane, did you have a lantern on your cart?"

"No, I had no lantern. I may not have even noticed the body until the morning except my horse did not want to enter the yard, so I had to lead her in. I could sense that she was frightened, but I never could have imagined this."

"Is your horse generally skittish?"

"No, I have had the same horse for ten years, sometimes, I fall asleep, and before I know it, I am home safe and sound in the yard."

"Was the yard empty when you drove in, I mean besides the body being there?"

"Yes, if the horse had not shied, I likely would not have looked around. I grabbed the horse by the bit strap and led her in; that was when I saw something up against the wall. When I lit a match, I saw what I thought was a bundle lying on the ground. When I got closer, I noticed that it was not a bundle at all, but a woman. I nudged her with my whip handle, hoping to get her to leave the yard, but when she did not move, I grew frightened, and then I saw the blood still pumping from a cut in the woman's neck." Diemschutz said, rubbing his face in the efforts of trying not to think of the body.

"Constable," I shouted, still looking at Diemschutz. "Constable, who was first on the scene?"

"Constable Henry Lamb, Sir."

"Find him and make sure this man's statement gets recorded," I commanded.

Walking back to the entrance of Dutfield's Yard, I watched as Doctors Blackwell and Phillips readied the body for transport. Accompanying the doctors was acting Superintendent West, who was being reassured by Doctor Phillips that the body would be accompanied to the mortuary. As the yard cleared out, I waited, watching the chaos subside. As torches were doused, and constables took away lanterns, the lane was left as dark as it had been when '*Jack*' had visited the place hours earlier. The remainder of the constables, along with Pinhorn and Superintendent, West walked into the club to begin taking statements from the men being held there. Left to my own devices, I turned up my collar against the mist of rain that had started again, watching Diemschutz walk wearily passed me towards his rooms above the club.

"Diemschutz, do you have a lantern that I can borrow?"

"Yes, Sir."

I waited while Diemschutz groped around in the darkness before finding a lantern, and handing it to me without comment. Standing at the entranceway, I watched Diemschutz walk back into the yard. A few seconds later, a faint light spilled across the center of the yard with the opening door and disappeared when the man closed the door casting the yard in shadow again. I shook the dust from the lantern, hearing very little oil in the base, but enough for what I required. Diemschutz's story rang true, I found that out by asking the man for the lantern. The ruse told me two things: one, Diemschutz knew the yard well enough, to walk around in the dark without the aid of a lantern. Second, the man had to take the time to find the lantern, and judging by the dust accumulated on the fixture, it had not been used in some time, telling me that nothing within the yard had been staged before police arrived. Fishing a match from a vest pocket, I struck it and lifted the globe touching the flame to the wick. Closing the globe, I walked into the yard holding the lantern out at arm's length, and close to the ground. I covered the area by using a sweeping pattern until I came to the place where the body had laid. I did not know what I expected from my search. Perhaps it was simply to substantiate Diemschutz's story and eliminate the man as a suspect, and to satisfy my curiosity as to why the killer had chosen this place above any other.

The victim's blood had run, at least, a good pace away from where the body had been placed after her throat had been cut. True to the past crime scenes, there were no signs of a struggle, the area where the body was placed, was smooth, and the soft ground was flattened by the weight of the body. Kneeling, I felt the ground with the palm of my hand; it was damp but not wet. It was clear that the body had been placed on the ground after the rain had subsided, allowing time for the victim's clothes to absorb some of the moisture from the soil. Keeping the lantern close to the ground, I saw a heavy heel print only a few feet away from where the body had been, studying the print more closely; I also found the remains of crushed cachous pressed into the ground. The surrounding area was covered in footprints of all types, not excluding those of a shod horse. It was instantly apparent by studying the area that it would be next to impossible to distinguish those from the killer and the handful of constables and both the doctors who were at the scene. In the entranceway, I stopped, the marks of several deep shod hoof prints could be distinctly seen. It was clear that the horse had reared upon entering the lane, substantiating Diemschutz's statement that the horse had shied upon entering the yard. I assumed that it could have been the smell of the large quantity of blood that made the horse reluctant to enter.

Leaving the yard, I lifted the globe and blew out the flame, placing the lantern on a hook on the fence. Men slowly started to drift out of the International Workers Club, having been questioned and subsequently released. Remaining in the shadows, I studied each man, listening to the gossip about the murder and the usual complaints about being detained between those that gathered outside of the club entrance. Remaining in the shadows, I studied the faces of those that stayed outside of the club waiting for friends that had not been released yet. After several minutes, I had learned nothing, but I continued to wait, as a gathering crowd formed on Berner Street. Standing against the gates, I waited listening; knowing full well that any one of them could be a killer. When the crowd finally dispersed, and I had learned nothing from the overheard conversations, I left Dutfield's Yard; and walked up Berner Street, busy organizing my thoughts. As I walked, I was stopped twice by constables on Commercial Road, demanding that I identify myself. Every block from Berner Street to Whitechapel Road was being infiltrated by constables looking for someone with bloodstains on his clothing. Somewhere in the distance, I heard the bark of a hound used to track an invisible killer who left no trail. Opening the face of my watch, I looked at the time, it was twenty minutes to three. Still suffering from the effects of little sleep, I decided to walk to Leman station to clear my head and wait there for any news of suspects that might be apprehended by the searching constables.

The walk did me good, as it gave me a chance to examine what I had seen at Dutfield's Yard. The murder of the unknown young woman was different from that of Nichols and Chapman. I noticed right off that the cut at the woman's throat; wasn't as fierce as it had been in the other two cases. A right-handed man would naturally start on the victim's left, then move to the right with the cutting edge up all the while the weight of the body would be falling forward. If the man happened to be in the middle of cutting the throat and was forced to flee, the killer would likely apply less force on the blade, following through with his cut. The other more noticeable difference from the other two murders was that there was no other injury done to the body.

The thought came to me that the killer did not, or rather could not, finish whatever had been planned. Had Diemschutz disturbed the killer? There was a good chance that Diemschutz had come along just as the killer slid the knife across his victim's throat, which explains the blood still pulsing from the wound. As a result, 'Jack' could not finish whatever was intended for the third victim. A stranger in the yard, combined with the smell of blood, could very well explain the horse shying. Diemschutz had commented that his horse was accustomed to going into the yard on its own accord without any prompting, suggesting routine. Something, or someone moving in the horse's path, might startle an animal enough that his master would have to dismount from the cart and reassure the animal by leading him in the rest of the way. The more I thought of the body of the woman lying off to the side, the more my theory made sense. Diemschutz had returned before the 'Ripper' had a chance to mutilate the body. It was likely Diemschutz had startled the monster as the knife sliced into the neck of the woman, forcing the killer to carry the body off to the side and away from the horse. It seemed possible, that 'Jack' had narrowly escaped detection by Diemschutz. If that was the case, then the carter may have narrowly escaped harm himself.

The walk had refreshed me, though my thoughts remained occupied by images of the crime scene. I arrived at the Leman Street station house before I knew it. Outside the entrance to the station, a crowd had gathered, causing plenty of commotion with shouting and complaining after word of another murder in Whitechapel had hit the streets. The men and women were angry due to the police departments inability to catch the killer and for allowing another nameless victim to lie in another London mortuary. Avoiding the mob, I decided to go to my office instead and await any findings.

Rising well after noon, I stretched to get the kinks from my back. It had been close to dawn when I arrived at my office; I was tired from a restless sleep, the settee was not as comfortable as the bed in my rooms but had proven adequate in a pinch, like so many other times in the past. After sloshing water in a basin, I splashed water on my face, then brushed my clothes and prepared to return to Berner Street. Despite feeling that it was likely a fool's errand, I needed to get a good look at the crime scene in the daylight. A shout from the hall made me turn to open the door and look out in time to see Wynne Baxter come up the hall towards me.

"Have you seen the papers this morning, Stone?" Baxter asked.

I watched the coroner push by me while slapping a folded newspaper against my chest.

"No, I haven't, why?"

"Peruse the front-page, Detective; last night was a busy night for '*Jack*' indeed."

"If you are referring to the Berner street murder, Wynne, I was roused late last night by a constable."

"Read the headlines, Stone!"

Unfolding the paper, I scanned the front page.

"*MORE MURDERS AT THE EAST END*," I read the headline aloud and then stopped.

"What do you make of that Stone?"

"I can't believe it," I responded, sitting back in my chair. "There were two murders last night?"

"Read on, Detective, read on!" Baxter responded.

Straightening the crease in the paper, I read the details of the news report in the London Evening News which were surprisingly abundant, especially since the murder occurred only a few hours earlier. Looking at the coroner, I began to read the newspaper article aloud.

[Sic] "Having been disturbed in his first attempt, yesterday morning, the murderer seems to have made his way towards the City, and to have met another 'unfortunate,' whom he induced to go with him to Mitre-square, a secluded spot, lying off Aldgate, and principally occupied by warehouses. He took her to the south-western corner of the square, and there cut her throat, quite in his horribly regulative way, and then proceeded to disembowel her. He must have been extremely quick at his work, for every portion of the police beat in which Mitre-square is included, is patrolled every ten minutes or a quarter of an hour, the City beats being much shorter than those of the Metropolitan Police. Police-constable Watkins 881 passed through the square at about 1:30 or 1:35 and is quite certain that it was then in its normal condition. Within a quarter of an hour, he patrolled it again and then found a woman lying in the corner with her throat cut from ear to ear. On closer examination, he found that her clothes had been raised up to her chest and that the lower portion of the body had been ripped completely open from the pelvis to the sternum, and disemboweled, just as were Mrs. Nichols and Annie Chapman. Indeed, this last murder is in its main features an almost exact reproduction of the horrible tragedies of Buck's-row and Hanbury-street, and, humanly speaking, it is absolutely certain that it also was committed by the same man. There were certain deviations from the murderer's ordinary plan, but they are not inexplicable or very significant. He gashed her face in several places, but there is evidence to show that the woman at the last moment suspected his design and struggled with him, and it is not improbable that he stabbed her in the face before cutting her throat and committing the other atrocities."

I stopped reading the newspaper article and looked up at Baxter.

"Well, what do you make of that, Detective?" Baxter asked.

"There seem to be a few inconsistencies, Wynne. This last statement alone," I said, rereading the paragraph again. "*He gashed her face in several places, but there is evidence to show that the woman at the last moment suspected his design and struggled with him, and it is not*

101

improbable that he stabbed her in the face before cutting her throat and committing the other atrocities. That does not sound right at all, Wynne."

"What do you think, Stone, was it the 'Ripper,' or perhaps someone else who wanted to make it look like our killer?" Baxter asked.

"The mutilation sounds consistent with the other murders, despite this reporter's account, I'd be more inclined to believe it is 'Jack' when we get word from the doctor about the post mortem injuries, it may be too soon to tell."

"You are not changing your mind are you, John, and taking on your superior's stance that we now have four or five killers out roaming the city."

"No, Wynne. I am still certain there is only one killer here, though I am more likely to believe a police surgeon's report than anything found in the newspapers these days."

I answered after mulling over the report a minute longer, knowing full well that the mutilations described in the paper, were similar to those described in the Chapman and Nichols' cases.

The first day of October fell on a dreary Monday. The weather had changed quickly overnight, and the rain returned with the cold temperatures. As my cab rolled up to the curb, I could not help noticing the weary look of The Yard at 4 Whitehall Place. Construction had begun on a new building, but with the bad press, the Metropolitan Police had been getting of late, some were adamant that the new building wasn't all that the department needed for London's police to step into the twentieth century. I found Inspector Abberline's mood unchanged from their last meeting when I heard the sharp command that bid me enter the office.

"Detective, what is your report on the Berner Street, murder?" Abberline snapped without looking up from the file that lay open on the desk.

"The victim was discovered at one o'clock in Dutfield's Yard by a carter, named Louis Diemschutz, a steward from the International Workers Club, who also lives on the premises. Diemschutz was working late on the night in question, and upon returning home, the man found the body of a woman lying on her side, her throat had been cut, and according to his statement, the wound was still bleeding profusely. I arrived at one-thirty, Doctor Blackwell was already on scene, and Doctor Phillips arrived shortly thereafter, at twenty past one. My examination of the body revealed that the woman had a silk handkerchief wrapped around her neck that was knotted tightly with the bow on the left. There was a bluish color to the victim's cheeks; the cut made to the neck was made by a sharp knife, several inches deep on the left, the incision was not as deep on the right. There was no other mutilation done to the body. Constable Henry Lamb, of H Division, was first on the scene," I paused looking up from my notes at Abberline whose attention was still fixated on the file folder in front of him. "The other murder was committed at Mitre Square and is under the City Police jurisdiction."

"City Police, has since, asked for The Yard's assistance in their investigation," Abberline responded.

Several minutes passed before, I finally got up the nerve to say something about the newest murder when Abberline finally spoke up stopping me.

"Why not, mutilate the body at Dutfield's Yard, as the man did to the victim at Mitre Square?" Abberline asked flatly.

"My view is that the perpetrator of the crime likely had every intention of dissecting the body as was done to the victim at Mitre Square. I think; the killer was interrupted by Diemschutz and was forced to flee to escape detection. I would also add, sir, that it is possible that the first victim was used as some sort of a diversion, perhaps to keep police occupied, so the killer could accomplish what was really intended in the first place."

"But you don't think so, is that it?"

"No, sir, it is my feeling that Diemschutz startled the killer by his impromptu arrival, and I think the Police Surgeon's examination can give evidence to support this theory."

"How?"

"In my assessment, the slice to the throat is more superficial than the previous victims, substantiating my theory, Sir."

Abberline was well known for asking opinions from his subordinates. Right or wrong the inspector valued his minions' opinions and was receptive of their point of view, no matter how trivial.

"I think you should read this, Stone."

I looked at Abberline curiously before taking the sheet of paper from the inspector.

[Sic] *"I was codding dear old Boss."*

I stopped in mid-sentence and looked up at the inspector, who had turned his attention back to whatever was in the file in front of him.

[Sic] *"when I gave you the tip, you'll hear about Saucy Jacky's work tomorrow double event this time one squealed a bit couldn't finish straight off had not got time to get ears off for police thanks for keeping last letter back till I got work again.*

Jack the Ripper."

My voice trailed off into a whisper, and then I looked up at Abberline.

"Well, what do you think now?" Abberline asked, and then continued before receiving an answer. "This letter was delivered to the Central News Agency, and then it was sent to the Home Office." Abberline finished speaking and turned his full attention back to the file on his desk.

I sat in silence, not knowing what to say. I had conveyed my thoughts to the inspector, confident that I was right, but I had to admit that I was only speculating when I gave Abberline my theory. It appeared now after reading the description in the letter that was exactly what the killer had intended. In the minutes that followed, after careful consideration, I realized there was no need for the murderer to create such a diversion, for the police did not have any idea who the killer was or where the madman would strike next. The city of London was the largest in all England, and in the world for that matter. There were countless places that a body could be left where it might take years to discover. This man, known only as 'Jack the Ripper,' had murdered five women; each victim was found within minutes after their deaths. It was apparent that the 'Ripper' wanted his victims found right away. It was assumed that the fiend loved the publicity. However, now I was thinking that perhaps, the killer's motive for choosing the site to commit his crimes was in some bizarre way not to show disrespect to the victim.

The very idea that the mad man had proceeded a mile away to kill again proved the authenticity of the letter that was sent to the newspaper. It also placed the killer in a new light. For not only had the man wrote a letter describing his intentions to kill two women in one night, signified by the statement, '*double event this time*,' it might indicate that the Mitre Square victim may have been handpicked beforehand. It also intimated that the murder was carefully planned. That type of preparation and timing required a cool, meticulous, calculating mind, certainly not the type of madness possessed by the man that the superiors in Home Office had constables looking for. Looking at the inspector, I had long grown accustomed to the nerve-grating, long periods of silences that occurred during my reports. The inspector was particular in everything, wasting no effort on useless hyperbole or meandering thoughts.

"The letter, perhaps written days before the murder, would certainly dissolve any thoughts that the victims of these crimes were random," Abberline finally spoke. "Wouldn't it?"

"If that is, in fact, the case," I said after giving what Abberline said some serious thought. "This man seems to be relishing every minute of operating right under the patrolling copper's noses. Not to mention the fact that his activities seem to have become more daring. This letter seems to be flaunting '*Jack's*' ability to elude detection," I replied. "Not only that but, ..."

"But what, Detective?"

"I believe this killer appears to have some knowledge of our patrol routes, and our tactics."

The accusation, although unmade was put forth unintentionally, and once made, I could hardly retract it. I wondered if Abberline was thinking as I was, that there was a possibility that the murderer was either acquainted with the police or was, in fact, a dismissed constable. Though there were several other possibilities to contend with, before jumping to any kind of conclusions, unfortunately, the brush was made, and it would have to be looked at sooner than later. There were also other points made in the letter that needed to be addressed. First and foremost, the killer was providing information to the police that they were looking in the wrong direction for a certain suspect.

"Let's leave unfounded accusations where they belong, Detective. Having said that, I will tell you that the patrols, starting today, will be changed every shift. The constables will be changing patrol patterns, and their shift start, and completion times, with no exceptions," Abberline explained. "I have also been instructed by Chief Inspector Donald Swanson to offer City Police all of our assistance in their investigation. We are under the gun here, and every eye is on us to get this psychopath."

"So, what do you want me to do now?" I asked, hoping that I would be free from the post that I had been given and allowed to resign like I had intended weeks before.

"We are not going to sit around and wait until this killer strikes again," Abberline snapped. "We are here to do a job, and you have been given your assignment. We are falling short of the mark on this, and the longer we let it go on, the harder it is going to be to bring this wretch to justice. That will be everything, Detective." Abberline finished.

I left the office and walked up the hall. I had hoped to show the inspector that my placement in the coroner's office, although perhaps helpful politically, was doing little to further the investigation. As I walked, I turned my attention to the two murders that had been committed one hour apart. The Berner Street murder was foremost in my thoughts, as I exited the building and hailed a cab. The inquest, presided over by Wynne Baxter was already in progress at Vestry Hall, Cable Street, and St. George; in the East. Opening the door to the cab, I slid along the seat, still deep in thought. I did not hear the driver shouting at me seeking my destination until I realized the cab was not moving. I arrived late; the inquest had already begun at the Vestry Hall. Choosing a vacant spot along the wall next to the door, I listened to the coroner question his first witness.

[Sic] William West: "The large doors are generally closed at night, but sometimes they remain open. On the left side of the yard is a house, which is divided into three tenements, and occupied, I believe, by that number of families. At the end is a store or workshop belonging to Messrs. Hindley and Co., sack manufacturers. I do not know that a way out exists there. The club premises and the printing-office occupy the entire length of the yard on the right side. Returning to the club-house, the front room on the ground floor is used for meals. In the kitchen is a window which faces the

door opening into the yard. The intervening passage is illuminated by means of a fanlight over the door. The printing-office, which does not communicate with the club, consists of two rooms, one for compositors and the other for the editor. On Saturday, the compositors finished their labors at two o'clock in the afternoon. The editor concluded earlier, but remained at the place until the discovery of the murder."

Coroner: "How many members are there in the club?"

West: "From seventy-five to eighty. Working men of any nationality can join."

Coroner: "How do you know that you finally left at a quarter-past twelve o'clock?"

West: "Because of the time when I reached my lodgings. Before leaving, I went into the yard, and thence to the printing-office, in order to leave some literature, there, and on returning to the yard, I observed that the double door at the entrance was open. There is no lamp in the yard, and none of the street lamps light it, so that the yard is only lit by the lights through the windows at the side of the club and of the tenements opposite. As to the tenements, I only observed lights in two first-floor windows. There was also a light in the printing-office, the editor being in my room reading."

Coroner: "Was there much noise in the club?"

West: "Not exactly much noise; but I could hear the singing when I was in the yard."

Coroner: "Did you look towards the yard gates?"

West: "Not so much to the gates as to the ground, but nothing unusual attracted my attention."

Coroner: "Can you say that there was no object on the ground?"

West: "I could not say that."

Coroner: "Do you think it possible that anything can have been there without your observing it?"

West: "It was dark, and I am a little short-sighted, so that it is possible. The distance from the gates to the kitchen door is 18 ft."

Coroner: "What made you look towards the gates at all?"

West: "Simply because they were open. I went into the club, and called my brother, and we left together by the front door."

Coroner: "On leaving did you see anybody as you passed the yard?"

West: "No."
Coroner: "Or did you meet any one in the street?"
West: "Not that I recollect. I generally go home between twelve and one o'clock."
Coroner: "Do low women frequent Berner-street?"
West: "I have seen men and women standing about and talking to each other in Fairclough-street."
Coroner: "But have you observed them nearer the club?"
West: "No."
Coroner: "Or in the club yard?"
West: "I did once, at eleven o'clock at night, about a year ago. They were chatting near the gates. That is the only time I have noticed such a thing, nor have I heard of it."

I sat listening to the testimony with little interest, I had become distracted by several comments that I had heard whispered from spectators who sat near me. Apparently, the authorities were still having some difficulty identifying the victim. With the dismissal of William West from the stand, I turned my attention back to the coroner and his next witness, the carter, Louis Diemschutz.

[Sic] Lewis Diemschutz, "I reside at No. 40 Berner-street, and am steward of the International Workmen's Club. I am married, and my wife lives at the club too, and assists in the management. On Saturday, I left home about half-past eleven in the morning, and returned exactly at one o'clock on Sunday morning. I noticed the time at the baker's shop at the corner of Berner-street. I had been to the market near the Crystal Palace, and had a barrow like a costermonger's, drawn by a pony, which I keep in George-yard Cable-street. I drove home to leave my goods. I drove into the yard, both gates being wide open. It was rather dark there. All at once my pony shied at some object on the right. I looked to see what the object was, and observed that there was something unusual, but could not tell what. It was a dark object. I put my whip handle to it, and tried to lift it up, but as I did not succeed I jumped down from my barrow and struck a match. It was rather windy, and I could only get sufficient light to see that

there was some figure there. I could tell from the dress that it was the figure of a woman."

The Coroner: "The body has not yet been identified?"
The Foreman: "I do not quite understand that. I thought the inquest had been opened on the body of one Elizabeth Stride."
The Coroner: "That was a mistake. Something is known of the deceased, but she has not been fully identified. It would be better at present to describe her as a woman unknown. She has been partially identified. It is known where she lived. It was thought at the beginning of the inquest that she had been identified by a relative, but that turns out to have been a mistake."

I left the inquest with the name Elizabeth Stride on my lips. Diemschutz had testified as was expected, adding no new evidence. The day seemed to have been another wasted effort to catch the killer stalking women in the city. To make matters worse, having the victim's identity confused with another woman, also nicknamed 'Long Liz' only added to the confusion. With the victim's identity in question, the jurors were unable to close the inquest. Day two of the inquest into the woman's death was scheduled for the next day. I hoped for the coroner's sake that someone would come forward and give reliable testimony so, that the deceased could be properly identified.

Chapter Seven

Day two of the inquest started with the questioning of Constable
Lamb of H Division police station. I noted that Wynne Baxter had a
determined look, more so than usual, as the coroner faced the jury of
twenty-four men. Each juror looked as resolute as the coroner in their
efforts to place a name to the deceased who lay in St. Georges
Mortuary, unidentified.

*[Sic] Constable Henry Lamb: "Last Sunday morning, shortly before
one o'clock, I was on duty in Commercial-road, between Christian-
street and Batty-street, when two men came running towards me and
shouting. I went to meet them, and they called out, 'Come on, there has
been another murder.' I asked where, and as they got to the corner of
Berner Street, they pointed down and said, 'There.' I saw people
moving some distance down the street. I ran, followed by another
constable - 426 H. Arriving at the gateway of No. 40 I observed
something dark lying on the ground on the right-hand side. I turned my
light on, when I found that the object was a woman, with her throat cut
and apparently dead. I sent the other constable for the nearest doctor,
and a young man who was standing by I dispatched to the police
station to inform the inspector what had occurred. On my arrival,
there were about thirty people in the yard, and others followed me in.*

No one was nearer than a yard to the body. As I was examining the deceased the crowd gathered round, but I begged them to keep back, otherwise they might have their clothes soiled with blood, and thus get into trouble.

Coroner: "Up to this time had you touched the body?"

Lamb: "I had put my hand on the face."

Coroner: "Was it warm?"

Lamb: "Slightly. I felt the wrist, but could not discern any movement of the pulse. I then blew my whistle for assistance."

Coroner: "Did you observe how the deceased was lying?"

Lamb: "She was lying on her left side, with her left hand on the ground."

Coroner: "Was there anything in that hand?"

Lamb: "I did not notice anything. The right arm was across the breast. Her face was not more than five or six inches away from the club wall."

Coroner: "Were her clothes disturbed?"

Lamb: "No."

Coroner: "Only her boots visible?"

Lamb: "Yes, and only the soles of them. There were no signs of a struggle. Some of the blood was in a liquid state, and had run towards the kitchen door of the club. A little - that nearest to her on the ground - was slightly congealed. I can hardly say whether any was still flowing from the throat. Dr. Blackwell was the first doctor to arrive; He came ten or twelve minutes after myself, but I had no watch with me."

Coroner: "Did any one of the crowd say whether the body had been touched before your arrival?"

Lamb: "No. Dr. Blackwell examined the body and its surroundings. Dr. Phillips came ten minutes later. Inspector Pinhorn arrived directly after Dr. Blackwell. When I blew my whistle other constables came, and I had the entrance of the yard closed. This was while Dr. Blackwell was looking at the body. Before that the doors were wide open. The feet of the deceased extended just to the swing of the gate, so that the barrier could be closed without disturbing the body. I entered the club and left a constable at the gate to prevent any one passing in or out. I examined the hands and clothes of all the members of the club. There were from fifteen to twenty present, and they were on the ground floor."

Coroner: "Did you discover traces of blood anywhere in the club?"

  Lamb: "No."

Coroner: "Was the steward present?"

  Lamb: "Yes."

Coroner: "Did you ask him to lock the front door?"

  Lamb: "I did not. There was a great deal of commotion. That was done afterwards."

The Coroner: "But time is the essence of the thing."

Lamb: "I did not see any person leave. I did not try the front door of the club to see if it was locked. I afterwards went over the cottages, the occupants of which were in bed. I was admitted by men, who came down partly dressed; all the other people were undressed. As to the water closets in the yard, one was locked and the other unlocked, but no one was there. There is a recess near the dust-bin."

Coroner: "Did you go there?"

  Lamb: "Yes, afterwards, with Dr. Phillips."

The Coroner: "But I am speaking of at the time."

Lamb: "I did it subsequently. I do not recollect looking over the wooden partition. I, however, examined the store belonging to Messrs. Hindley, sack manufacturers, but I saw nothing there."

Coroner: "How long were the cottagers in opening their doors?"

  Lamb: "Only a few minutes, and they seemed frightened. When I returned Dr. Phillips and Chief Inspector West had arrived."

Coroner: "Was there anything to prevent a man escaping while you were examining the body?"

  Lamb: "Several people were inside and outside the gates, and I should think that they would be sure to observe a man who had marks of blood."

Coroner: "But supposing he had no marks of blood?"

  Lamb: "It was quite possible, of course, for a person to escape while I was examining the corpse. Everyone was more or less looking towards the body. There was much confusion."

Coroner: "Do you think that a person might have got away before you arrived?"

Lamb: "I think he is more likely to have escaped before than after."
Detective-Inspector Reid: "How long before had you passed this place?"
Lamb: "I am not on the Berner-street beat, but I passed the end of the street in Commercial-road six or seven minutes before."
Coroner: "When you were found what direction were you going in?"
Lamb: "I was coming towards Berner-street. A constable named Smith was on the Berner-street beat. I did not accompany him, but the constable who was on fixed-point duty between Grove-street and Christian-street in Commercial-road. Constables at fixed-points leave duty at one in the morning. I believe that is the practice nearly all over London."
The Coroner: "I think this is important. The Hanbury-street murder was discovered just as the night police were going off duty. (To witness): Did you see anything suspicious?"
Lamb: "I did not at any time. There were squabbles and rows in the streets, but nothing more."
The Foreman: "Was there light sufficient to enable you to see, as you were going down Berner Street, whether any person was running away from No. 40?"
Lamb: "It was rather dark, but I think there was light enough for that, though the person would be somewhat indistinct from Commercial-road."
The Foreman: "Some of the papers state that Berner Street is badly lighted; but there are six lamps within 700 feet, and I do not think that is very bad."
The Coroner: "The parish plan shows that there are four lamps within 350 feet, from Commercial-road to Fairclough Street."
Lamb: "There are three, if not four, lamps in Berner-street between Commercial- road and Fairclough Street. Berner Street is about as well lighted as other side streets. Most of them are rather dark, but more lamps have been erected lately."
The Coroner: "I do not think that London altogether is as well lighted as some capitals are."
Lamb: "There are no public-house lights in Berner Street. I was engaged in the yard and at the mortuary all the night afterwards."

Next to take the witness stand was Edward Spooner. Spooner was called to describe the scene, as the horse-keeper arrived only minutes behind Constable Lamb.

[Sic] Edward Spooner: "I live at No. 26, Fairclough-street, and am a horse-keeper with Messrs. Meredith, biscuit bakers. On Sunday morning, between half-past twelve and one o'clock, I was standing outside the Beehive Public- house, at the corner of Christian-street, with my young woman. We had left a public- house in Commercial-road at closing time, midnight, and walked quietly to the point named. We stood outside the Beehive about twenty-five minutes, when two Jews came running along, calling out 'Murder' and 'Police.' They ran as far as Grove- street, and then turned back. I stopped them and asked what was the matter, and they replied that a woman had been murdered. I thereupon proceeded down Berner-street and into Dutfield's-yard, adjoining the International Workmen's Club-house, and there saw a woman lying just inside the gate."
Coroner "Was any one with her?"
Spooner: "There were about fifteen people in the yard."
Coroner: "Was any one near her?"
Spooner: "They were all standing round."
Coroner: "Were they touching her?"
Spooner: "No. One man struck a match, but I could see the woman before the match was struck. I put my hand under her chin when the match was alight."
Coroner: "Was the chin warm?"
Spooner: "Slightly."
Coroner: "Was any blood coming from the throat?"
Spooner: "Yes; it was still flowing. I noticed that she had a piece of paper doubled up in her right hand, and some red and white flowers pinned on her breast. I did not feel the body, nor did I alter the position of the head. I am sure of that. Her face was turned towards the club wall."

I looked around the room watching the spectators whisper back and forth after Spooner testified that the victim's neck wound had been still bleeding when the body was found. The testimony revealed another obstacle that police had to contend. The fifteen people in the yard only added to the mass of tracks in the lane and made distinguishing them from the killers impossible. As I surveyed the crowd, both men and women gossiped back and forth. I was sickened by the thoughts that the press had succeeded in turning the inquests, and the murders as a whole; into some type of spectacle. In my mind's eye, I returned to the night that I had arrived in Dutfield's Yard. I had stood on the street watching the crowds of people as they gawked up the lane all with the weird curiosity that people have when they stop to look at some type of accident that has occurred, each one eager to see the grotesque scene, only to be repelled by the awful reality of death. There was nothing I could think of in the world to compare with the sight of a corpse, when the body lay void of all that had made life possible.

Shaken out of my thoughts by a rumbling in the crowd, I looked up in time to see the witness leave the room. The next person called was one Mary Malcolm, the sister of the deceased.

[Sic] Mary Malcolm: "I live at No. 50, Eagle-street, Red Lion- square, Holborn, and am married. My husband, Andrew Malcolm, is a tailor. I have seen the body at the mortuary. I saw it once on Sunday and twice yesterday."
Coroner: "Who is it?"
Malcolm: "It is the body of my sister, Elizabeth Watts."
Coroner: "You have no doubt about that?"
Malcolm: "Not the slightest."
Coroner: "You did have some doubts about it at one time?"
Malcolm: "I had at first."
Coroner: "When did you last see your sister alive?"
Malcolm: "Last Thursday, about a quarter to seven in the evening."
Coroner: "Where?"
Malcolm: "She came to see me at No. 59, Red Lion-street, where I work as a trouser maker."
Coroner: "What did she come to you for?"
Malcolm: "To ask me for a little assistance. I have been in the habit of assisting her for five years."
Coroner: "Did you give her anything?"

115

Malcolm: "I gave her a shilling and a short jacket - not the jacket which is now on the body."

Coroner: "How long was she with you?"

Malcolm: "Only a few moments."

Coroner: "Did she say where she was going?"

Malcolm: "No."

Coroner: "Where was she living?"

Malcolm: "I do not know. I know it was somewhere in the neighborhood of the tailoring Jews – Commercial Road or Commercial Street, or somewhere at the East-end."

Coroner: "Did you understand that she was living in lodging-houses?"

Malcolm: "Yes."

Coroner: "Did you know what she was doing for a livelihood?"

Malcolm: "I had my doubts."

Coroner: "Was she the worse for drink when she came to you on Thursday?"

Malcolm: "No, sober."

Coroner: "But she was sometimes the worse for drink, was she not?"

Malcolm: "That was, unfortunately, a failing with her. She was thirty-seven years of age last March."

Coroner: "Had she ever been married?"

Malcolm: "Yes."

Coroner: "Is her husband alive?"

Malcolm: "Yes, so far as I know. She married the son of Mr. Watts, wine and spirit merchant, of Walco Street, Bath. I think her husband's Christian name was Edward. I believe I is now in America."

Coroner: "Did he get into trouble?"

Malcolm: "No."

Coroner: "Why did he go away?"

Malcolm: "Because my sister brought trouble upon him."

Coroner: "When did she leave him?"

Malcolm: "About eight years ago, but I cannot be quite certain as to the time. She had two children. Her husband caught her with a porter, and there was a quarrel."

Coroner: "Did the husband turn her out of doors?"

Malcolm: "No, he sent her to my poor mother, with the two children."

Coroner: "Where does your mother live?"

Malcolm: "She is dead. She died in the year 1883."

Coroner: "Where are the children now?"

Malcolm: "The girl is dead, but the boy is at a boarding school kept by my aunt."

Coroner: "Was the deceased subject to epileptic fits?"

Malcolm: "No, she only had drunken fits." (Sobbing bitterly.)

Coroner: "Was she ever before the Thames police magistrate?"

Malcolm: "I believe so."

Coroner: "Charged with drunkenness?"

Malcolm: "Yes."

Coroner: "Are you aware that she has been let off on the supposition that she was subject to epileptic fits?"

Malcolm: "I believe that is so, but she was not subject to epileptic fits."

Coroner: "Has she ever told you of troubles she was in with any man?"

Malcolm: "Oh yes; she lived with a man."

Coroner: "Do you know his name?"

Malcolm: "I do not remember now, but I shall be able to tell you to-morrow. I believe she lived with a man who kept a coffee-house at Poplar."

Inspector Reid: "Was his name Stride?"

Malcolm: "No; I think it was Dent, but I can find out for certain by to-morrow."

The Coroner: "How long had she ceased to live with that man?"

Malcolm: "Oh, some time. he went away to sea, and was wrecked on the Isle of St. Paul, I believe."

Coroner: "How long ago should you think that was?"

Malcolm: "It must be three years and a half; but I could tell you all about it by to-morrow, even the name of the vessel that was wrecked."

Coroner: "Had the deceased lived with any man since then?"

Malcolm: "Not to my knowledge, but there is some man who says that he has lived with her."

Coroner: "Have you ever heard of her getting into trouble with this man?"

Malcolm: "No, but at times she got locked up for drunkenness. She always brought her trouble to me."

Coroner: "You never heard of any one threatening her?"

Malcolm: "No; she was too good for that."

Coroner: "Did you ever hear her say that she was afraid of any one?"

Malcolm: "No."

Coroner: "Did you know of no man with whom she had relations?"

Malcolm: "No."

Inspector Reid: "Did you ever visit her in Flower and Dean-street?"

Malcolm: "No."

Coroner: "Did you ever hear her called 'Long Liz'?"

Malcolm: "That was generally her nickname, I believe."

Coroner: "Have you ever heard of the name of Stride?"

Malcolm: "She never mentioned such a name to me. I think that if she had lived with any one of that name, she would have told me. I have heard what the man Stride has said, but I think he is mistaken."

The Coroner: "How often did your sister come to you?"

Malcolm: "Every Saturday, and I always gave her 2s. That was for her lodgings."

Coroner: "Did she come to you at all last Saturday?"

Malcolm: "No, I did not see her on that day."

Coroner: "The Thursday visit was an unusual one, I suppose?"

Malcolm: "Yes."

Coroner: "Did you think it strange that she did not come on the Saturday?"

Malcolm: "I did."

Coroner: "Had she ever missed a Saturday before?"

Malcolm: "Not for nearly three years."

Coroner: "What time in the day did she usually come to you?"

Malcolm: "At four o'clock in the afternoon."

Coroner: "Where?"

Malcolm: "At the corner of Chancery-lane. I was there last Saturday afternoon from half-past three till five, but she did not turn up."

Coroner: "Did you think there was something the matter with her?"

Malcolm: "On the Sunday morning when I read the accounts in the newspapers, I thought it might be my sister who had been murdered. I had a presentiment that that was so. I came down to Whitechapel and was directed to the mortuary; but when I saw the body, I did not recognize it as that of my sister."

Coroner: "How was that? Why did you not recognize it in the first instance?"

Malcolm: "I do not know, except that I saw it in the gaslight, between nine and ten at night. But I recognized her the next day."

The Foreman: "Had she any special marks upon her?"

Malcolm: "Yes, on her right leg there was a small black mark."

The Coroner: "Have you seen that mark on the deceased?"

Malcolm: "Yes."

Coroner: "When did you see it?"

Malcolm: "Yesterday morning."

Coroner: "Did you mention the mark before you saw the body?"

Malcolm: "I said that I could recognize my sister by this particular mark."

Coroner: "What was the mark?"

Malcolm: "It was from the bite of an adder. One day, when children, we were rolling down a hill together, and we came across an adder. The thing bit me first and my sister afterwards. I have still the mark of the bite on my left hand."

The Coroner (examining the mark): "Oh, that is only a scar. Are you sure that your sister, in her youth, never broke a limb?"

Malcolm: "Not to my knowledge."

Coroner: "Did you recognize the clothes of the deceased at all?"

Malcolm: "No. (Bursting into tears). Indeed, I have had trouble with her. On one occasion she left a naked baby outside my door."

Coroner: "One of her babies?"

Malcolm: "One of her own."

Coroner: "One of the two children by her husband?"

Malcolm: "No, another one; one she had by a policeman, I believe. She left it with him, and he had to keep it until she fetched it away."

Inspector Reid: "Is that child alive, do you know?"

Malcolm: "I believe it died in Bath."

It was astounding to hear and hard to believe the trouble the coroner was having identifying the deceased. I could understand the skepticism in Baxter's and Inspector Reid's responses to Malcolm's answers. I had to concur with both authorities that some suspicion was raised by Malcolm's replies while being questioned. Especially in the manner that the witness

119

used to identify a blood relative. Being a detective, and having interviewed thousands of witnesses myself, I could understand the limits of trust that an investigator must place in an eyewitness account. At times, I believed that most eyewitnesses used their feelings more than they used the senses that God gave them when asked to identify someone or recall some incident. As I considered Malcolm's testimony, I made a mental note to check the deceased for a black mark on her right leg. It seemed apparent that after the witness had some difficulty identifying the deceased, the constable must have asked Malcolm if there were any identifying marks on the corpse to be sure of her identification. I found it strange that the woman did not take the time that night to search for the mark to put her own mind at ease; as to whether the body of the dead woman was, in fact, her sister. I knew that Baxter, as coroner was obligated to have Malcolm testify even if there were doubts about her ability to either give the facts or clearly identify the deceased as her sister. In my own mind, Malcolm's credibility diminished rapidly when she could not identify the deceased just by looking at her.

My attention was drawn back to the front of the room by the entrance of the next witness. The entire room went silent, as Doctor Frederick William Blackwell walked across the room to the seat opposite the coroner's desk. Blackwell was a tall man, in his early forties, wearing a crisp dark suit, his full beard hung below his chin covering the top buttons of his collar, and in his left hand, he carried a top hat which was placed gently on the table in front of him before sitting. The doctor then crossed his legs and meticulously straightened the crease in his trousers. Blackwell then folded his hands properly on his lap and waited patiently for the questioning to begin. The coroner wasted no time asking Blackwell to identify himself, and then Blackwell proceeded directly without any prompting to provide all the pertinent information, after being called to Dutfield's Yard and his subsequent examination of the body.

[Sic] Mr. Frederick William Blackwell: "I reside at No. 100, Commercial-road, and am a physician and surgeon. On Sunday morning last, at ten minutes past one o'clock, I was called to Berner-street by a policeman. My assistant, Mr. Johnston, went back with the constable, and I followed immediately I was dressed. I consulted my watch on my arrival, and it was

120

1.16 a.m. The deceased was lying on her left side obliquely across the passage, her face looking towards the right wall. Her legs were drawn up, her feet close against the wall of the right side of the passage. Her head was resting beyond the carriage-wheel rut, the neck lying over the rut. Her feet were three yards from the gateway. Her dress was unfastened at the neck. The neck and chest were quite warm, as were also the legs, and the face was slightly warm. The hands were cold. The right hand was open and, on the chest, and was smeared with blood. The left hand, lying on the ground, was partially closed, and contained a small packet of cachous wrapped in tissue paper. There were no rings, nor marks of rings, on her hands. The appearance of the face was quite placid. The mouth was slightly open. The deceased had around her neck a check silk scarf, the bow of which was turned to the left and pulled very tight. In the neck there was a long incision which exactly corresponded with the lower border of the scarf. The border was slightly frayed, as if by a sharp knife. The incision in the neck commenced on the left side, 2 inches below the angle of the jaw, and almost in a direct line with it, nearly severing the vessels on that side, cutting the windpipe completely in two, and terminating on the opposite side 1 inch below the angle of the right jaw, but without severing the vessels on that side. I could not ascertain whether the bloody hand had been moved. The blood was running down the gutter into the drain in the opposite direction from the feet. There was about 1lb of clotted blood close by the body, and a stream all the way from there to the back door of the club."

Coroner: "Were there no spots of blood about?"

Blackwell: "No; only some marks of blood which had been trodden in."

Coroner: "Was there any blood on the soles of the deceased's boots?"

Blackwell: "No."

Coroner: "No splashing of blood on the wall?"

Blackwell: "No, it was very dark, and what I saw was by the aid of a policeman's lantern. I have not examined the place since. I examined the clothes, but found no blood on any part of them. The bonnet of the deceased was lying on the ground a few inches from the head. Her dress was unbuttoned at the top."

Coroner: "Can you say whether the injuries could have been self-inflicted?"

Blackwell: "It is impossible that they could have been."

Coroner: "Did you form any opinion as to how long the deceased had been dead?"

Blackwell: "From twenty minutes to half an hour when I arrived. The clothes were not wet with rain. She would have bled to death comparatively slowly on account of vessels on one side only of the neck being cut and the artery not completely severed."

Coroner: "After the infliction of the injuries was there any possibility of any cry being uttered by the deceased?"

Blackwell: "None whatever. Dr. Phillips came about twenty minutes to half an hour after my arrival. The double doors of the yard were closed when I arrived, so that the previous witness must have made a mistake on that point."

A Juror: "Can you say whether the throat was cut before or after the deceased fell to the ground?"

Blackwell: "I formed the opinion that the murderer probably caught hold of the silk scarf, which was tight and knotted, and pulled the deceased backwards, cutting her throat in that way. The throat might have been cut as she was falling, or when she was on the ground. The blood would have spurted about if the act had been committed while she was standing up."

The Coroner: "Was the silk scarf tight enough to prevent her calling out?"

Blackwell: "I could not say that."

Coroner: "A hand might have been put on her nose and mouth?"

Blackwell: "Yes, and the cut on the throat was probably instantaneous."

The inquest was then adjourned till one o'clock Wednesday, October, the third. Although everyone within the area anxiously awaited October the third to attend day two of the inquest, however, when it came, those in attendance were grossly disappointed. The inquest had come and gone and there was still, no new information acquired in the short time since the murder, and very little had changed in finding the identity of the woman found in Dutfield's Yard with her throat cut.

Day three of the inquest into the murder of the woman at Dutfield's Yard proved to be just as disappointing for coroner and spectators alike, as the previous day's inquiry. Most of the witnesses who knew the deceased testified that they knew her as 'Long Liz.'

Two witnesses, Elizabeth Tanner and Michael Kidney, both testified that they knew the deceased, and told the coroner that they had, in fact, identified the woman as *'Long Liz'* because she had a deformity of the hard or soft palate, a fact that proved to be misleading for the woman lying dead in the mortuary; had no such affliction. The testimony given by the witnesses proved to be even more troubling after Kidney later testified that the deceased was the same woman that had lived with him on and off for more than three years. Kidney, then had the audacity to comment that with the assistance of a young detective at his disposal, the murderer would be apprehended in no time. When questioned how the witness would go about apprehending the culprit, Kidney refused to elaborate.

Wynne Baxter responded to Kidney's answer. *[Sic] "You cannot expect that. I have had over one hundred letters making suggestions, and I dare say all the writers would like to have a detective at their service."*

This comment by Baxter caused the room to fill with laughter and a dismissed and embarrassed Michael Kidney stormed out of the inquiry. After several inconsequential witnesses: one Mr. Edward Johnson who was Doctor Blackwell's assistance was called to more or less corroborate evidence given by Blackwell.

Thomas Coram was next to testify about a knife found that was proven not to have been used in the murder, the room once again settled into their seats as Doctor Phillips was called before the inquiry. Every mouth was closed and every eye was riveted on the front of the room as the doctor who openly defied the coroner during the last inquest was about to give evidence. After several minutes of giving his account of the crime scene and the state of the body at the scene, the doctor paused and a juror piped up and asked the doctor a question that seemed to be on everyone's mind including the coroner.

[Sic] A Juror: "You have not mentioned anything about the roof of the mouth. One witness said part of the roof of the mouth was gone."
Phillips: "That was not noticed."
The Coroner: "What was the cause of death?"
Phillips: "Undoubtedly the loss of blood from the left carotid artery and the division of the windpipe."
Coroner: "Did you examine the blood at Berner-street carefully, as to its direction and so forth?"
Phillips: "Yes."

Coroner: "The blood near to the neck and a few inches to the left side was well clotted, and it had run down the waterway to within a few inches of the side entrance to the club-house."

Coroner: "Were there any spots of blood anywhere else?"

Phillips: "I could trace none except that which I considered had been transplanted if I may use the term - from the original flow from the neck. Roughly estimating it, I should say there was an unusual flow of blood, considering the stature and the nourishment of the body."

By a Juror: "I did notice a black mark on one of the legs of the deceased, but could not say that it was due to an adder bite."

Before the witness had concluded his evidence, the inquiry was adjourned until Friday, at two o'clock.

Wynne Baxter sat at his desk, rolling an empty glass around on its edge when I walked into the office and took a seat in a chair in front of the coroner's desk. Without looking up, the coroner spoke.

"Catharine Eddowes inquest starts Thursday, October the fourth, at Coroner's Court, Golden Lane. Mr. S. F. Langham, Coroner for the City of London presides," Baxter offered.

"How are you holding up, Wynne?"

I asked the question; sensing the desperation in my friend's voice after the turn of events of the day's proceedings.

"As good as can be expected, John," Baxter snorted. "It could be worse; we could have lost the body or some such thing and really looked incompetent in the public's eyes. Perhaps, I am being unreasonable, but much like the rest of London's citizenry, I expect after three days of inquiry; something as simple as a woman's name could be confirmed by witness examination, that is, unless the coroner of the district is inept," Baxter said, bitterly; with a touch of self-pity rearing its ugly head.

"That is putting too much responsibility on your plate, Wynne. What do you plan to do next?"

I was sympathetic to the coroner's plight, knowing full well how serious Baxter took his position and the extent that the man was prepared to go during the execution of those duties. There was, however, a fine line between doing one's duty and trying to hold yourself responsible for the efforts of others. Baxter had performed the duty of his office to get the answers constituents expected. Constituents may demand a quick effortless inquest, but the coroner could only deliver on the witness testimony that was presented.

"Inspector Reid has a lead on finding Elizabeth Stride's former husband. Reid, is as we speak, trying to locate him, and if able, the inspector will be bringing him to the inquest on the fifth. That should eliminate any question, once and for all, as to this woman's identity. Having said that, on Friday, I will recall doctors Phillips and Blackwell and refute all of the incorrect witness testimony about the deceased having a deformity of the hard and or soft plate, of which the deceased resting in the mortuary has neither condition," Baxter said, continuing to rotate the glass on the blotter on the top of his desk.

"I was as stunned as anyone when the juror piped up and asked Doctor Phillips about the roof of the mouth of the deceased," I offered.

"As was I, Stone, the man just beat me to it. What burns me is that with the papers going on and on about cachous being found near the body, now to add insult to the confusion, it is being rumored that grapes, of all things, were found at the scene. I should think that Phillips would have searched the inside of the mouth of the woman as well as the contents of the stomach during the autopsy, to put these questions to rest as well." Baxter vented.

Rising from my chair, I watched Baxter still rolling the glass on its edge. "Why don't you pick me up, and we will go to the Eddowes inquest together, Wynne?"

"I will have my carriage here in the morning," Baxter replied.

With a wave, I walked out of the office and headed to my rooms for the first time in several days.

Chapter Eight

Day one of the Catherine Eddowes inquest was on Thursday, October fourth, at the Coroner's Court, Golden-lane. Mr. S. F. Langham, put Eliza Gold in the witness chair after the jury was allowed to view the deceased in the mortuary next door. Eliza Gold proceeded to tell the jury that she had positively identified the deceased as her sister, and her name was Catharine Eddowes.

The next witness was John Kelly, who lived with the deceased, although Kelly had known Eddowes, as Catharine Conway. Kelly alluded to the jury that Conway would walk the streets at night if she did not have money for lodgings. The witness also stated that they had slept in common wards if they did not have money (the money having been spent on food and drink) for lodgings. Kelly testified that he had last seen her on the Saturday before her death. They had parted at Houndsditch, as Conway told Kelly that she was off to Bermondsey, to see her daughter Annie, she did not return. On Saturday afternoon, Kelly found out that Conway was in the goal for drunkenness and would be released on Sunday.

The next witness that Coroner Langham called to give testimony was Constable Edward Watkins.

Constable Watkin (Sic): No. 881 of the City Police. "I was on duty at Mitre-square on Saturday night. I have been in the force seventeen years. I went on duty at 9.45 upon my regular beat. That extends from Duke-street, Aldgate, through Heneage Lane, a portion of Bury-street, through Cree-

lane, into Leadenhall-street, along eastward into Mitre-street, then into Mitre-square, round the square again into Mitre-street, then into King-street to St. James's-place, round the place, then into Duke-street, where I started from. That beat takes twelve or fourteen minutes. I had been patrolling the beat continually from ten o'clock at night until one o'clock on Sunday morning."

Coroner: "Had anything excited your attention during those hours?"

Watkin: "No."

Coroner: "Or any person?"

Watkin: "No. I passed through Mitre-square at 1.30 on the Sunday morning. I had my lantern alight and on - fixed to my belt. According to my usual practice, I looked at the different passages and corners."

Coroner: "At half-past one did anything excite your attention?"

Watkin: "No."

Coroner: "Did you see anyone about?"

Watkin: "No."

Coroner: "Could any people have been about that portion of the square without your seeing them?"

Watkin: "No. I next came into Mitre-square at 1.44, when I discovered the body lying on the right as I entered the square. The woman was on her back, with her feet towards the square. Her clothes were thrown up. I saw her throat was cut and the stomach ripped open. She was lying in a pool of blood. I did not touch the body. I ran across to Kearley and Long's Warehouse. The door was ajar, and I pushed it open, and called on the watchman Morris, who was inside. He came out. I remained with the body until the arrival of Police-constable Holland. No one else was there before that but myself. Holland was followed by Dr. Sequeira. Inspector Collard arrived about two o'clock, and also Dr. Brown, surgeon to the police force."

Coroner: "When you first saw the body did you hear any footsteps as if anybody were running away?"

Watkin: "No. The door of the warehouse to which I went was ajar, because the watchman was working about. It was no unusual thing for the door to be ajar at that hour of the morning."

By Mr. Crawford: "I was continually patrolling his beat from ten o'clock up to half-past one. I noticed nothing unusual up till 1.44, when he saw the body."

By the Coroner: I did not sound an alarm. We do not carry whistles."
By a Juror: "My beat is not a double but a single beat. No other
policeman comes into Mitre-street."

After several witnesses were deposed, I found myself unable to
concentrate on the impossible amount of useless information. My attention
soon strayed and I turned the testimony over in my mind. Next, I
considered Frederick William Foster's testimony. Foster was the surveyor
who had been responsible for the original survey for the city planner and
had mapped the area from Berner Street to Mitre Square. Foster testified
that in his qualified opinion that it would take twelve minutes to walk what
the surveyor said to be; the three-quarters of a mile distance. The next
witness was Inspector Collard, whose testimony added nothing to the
Watkin testimony. After Collard testified, next on the witness list was
Doctor Frederick, Gordon Brown.

*[Sic] "I am surgeon to the City of London Police. I was called shortly
after two o'clock on Sunday morning, and reached the place of the murder
about twenty minutes past two. My attention was directed to the body of
the deceased. It was lying in the position described by Watkins, on its
back, the head turned to the left shoulder, the arms by the side of the body,
as if they had fallen there. Both palms were upwards, the fingers slightly
bent. A thimble was lying near. The clothes were thrown up. The bonnet
was at the back of the head. There was great disfigurement of the face. The
throat was cut across. Below the cut was a neckerchief. The upper part of
the dress had been torn open. The body had been mutilated, and was quite
warm - no rigor mortis. The crime must have been committed within half
an hour or certainly within forty minutes from the time when I saw the
body. There were no stains of blood on the bricks or pavement around."
By Mr. Crawford: "There was no blood on the front of the clothes. There
was not a speck of blood on the front of the jacket."
By the Coroner: "Before we removed the body Dr. Phillips was sent for,
as I wished him to see the wounds, I having been engaged in a case of a
similar kind previously. I saw the body at the mortuary. The clothes were
removed from the deceased carefully. I made a post-mortem examination
on Sunday afternoon. There was a bruise on the back of the left hand, and*

one on the right shin, but this had nothing to do with the crime. There were no bruises on the elbows or the back of the head. The face was very much mutilated, the eyelids, the nose, the jaw, the cheeks, the lips, and the mouth all bore cuts. There were abrasions under the left ear. The throat was cut across to the extent of six or seven inches."

Coroner: "Can you tell us what was the cause of death?"

Dr. Brown: "The cause of death was hemorrhage from the throat. Death must have been immediate."

Coroner: "There were other wounds on the lower part of the body?"

Brown: "Yes; deep wounds, which were inflicted after death."

(Witness here described in detail the terrible mutilation of the deceased's body.)

Mr. Crawford: I understand that you found certain portions of the body removed?"

Brown: "Yes. The uterus was cut away with the exception of a small portion, and the left kidney was also cut out. Both these organs were absent, and have not been found."

Coroner: "Have you any opinion as to what position the woman was in when the wounds were inflicted?"

Brown: "In my opinion the woman must have been lying down. The way in which the kidney was cut out showed that it was done by somebody who knew what he was about."

Coroner: "Does the nature of the wounds lead you to any conclusion as to the instrument that was used?"

Brown: "It must have been a sharp-pointed knife, and I should say at least 6 in. long."

Coroner: "Would you consider that the person who inflicted the wounds possessed anatomical skill?"

Brown: "He must have had a good deal of knowledge as to the position of the abdominal organs, and the way to remove them."

Coroner: "Would the parts removed be of any use for professional purposes?"

Brown: "None whatever."

Coroner: "Would the removal of the kidney, for example, require special knowledge?"

Brown: "It would require a good deal of knowledge as to its position, because it is apt to be overlooked, being covered by a membrane."

129

Coroner: "Would such a knowledge be likely to be possessed by someone accustomed to cutting up animals?"

Brown: "Yes."

Coroner: "Have you been able to form any opinion as to whether the perpetrator of this act was disturbed?"

Brown: "I think he had sufficient time, but it was in all probability done in a hurry."

Coroner: "How long would it take to make the wounds?"

Brown: "It might be done in five minutes. It might take me longer; but that is the least time it could be done in."

Coroner: "Can you, as a professional man, ascribe any reason for the taking away of the parts you have mentioned?"

Brown: "I cannot give any reason whatever."

Coroner: "Have you any doubt in your own mind whether there was a struggle?"

Brown: "I feel sure there was no struggle. I see no reason to doubt that it was the work of one man."

Coroner: "Would any noise be heard, do you think?"

Brown: "I presume the throat was instantly severed, in which case there would not be time to emit any sound."

Coroner: "Does it surprise you that no sound was heard?"

Brown: "No."

Coroner: "Would you expect to find much blood on the person inflicting these wounds?"

Brown: "No, I should not. I should say that the abdominal wounds were inflicted by a person kneeling at the right side of the body. The wounds could not possibly have been self-inflicted."

Coroner: "Was your attention called to the portion of the apron that was found in Goulston-street?"

Brown: "Yes. I fitted that portion which was spotted with blood to the remaining portion, which was still attached by the strings to the body."

Coroner: "Have you formed any opinion as to the motive for the mutilation of the face?"

Brown: "It was to disfigure the corpse, I should imagine."

A Juror: "Was there any evidence of a drug having been used?"

Brown: "I have not examined the stomach as to that. The contents of the stomach have been preserved for analysis."

Mr. Crawford ended the day's proceedings by announcing that the Corporation had unanimously approved the offer of a reward of £500 by the lord Mayor for the discovery of the murderer. Several jurymen expressed their satisfaction at the promptness with which the offer was made. The inquest was then adjourned until next Thursday, October eleventh.

Day four of the Elizabeth Stride inquest was scheduled for Friday, October the fifth. At two o'clock, in the afternoon. I sat across the room from the jury hoping that the coroner's inquest would result in some testimony that would positively identify the deceased as Elizabeth Stride.

Wynne Baxter's face was devoid of all expression when Doctor Phillips entered the room. The entire room was hushed as the witness started towards the front of the room. The jurors all sat stone-faced, and the spectators that stood four-deep against the walls stopped whispering. There was no shuffling feet, no clearing of throats, no whispers could be heard when the doctor finally took his seat. Every eye was on the two men that were at the top of the room, sitting only a few feet apart. Baxter remained seated taking his time, shuffling through some papers, as was his way. After another minute, Baxter stood and took two decisive steps towards Phillips, who sat almost motionless except for a slight quiver that erupted in the doctor's left leg. Doctor Phillips's face showed no surprise when the coroner barked out his first words that made several men in the jury sit up straighter in their chairs. I watched Baxter pace with arms crossed behind his back, head lowered looking at the floor. The expressionless face, the lack of greeting, spoke volumes to anyone who had attended the inquest days earlier. The crowd waited in anticipation for the doctor to continue. Each member of the jury anxiously awaited the results that were found after the coroner asked Phillips to re-examine the body. It was important for Baxter to have these answers to put an end to queries that were raised during the last day of the inquest involving the deceased's palette and stomach contents.

[Sic] Dr. Phillips, surgeon of the H Division of police, being recalled, said: "On the last occasion I was requested to make a re-examination of

the body of the deceased, especially with regard to the palate, and I have since done so at the mortuary, along with Dr. Blackwell and Dr. Gordon Brown. I did not find any injury to, or absence of, any part of either the hard or the soft palate. The Coroner also desired me to examine the two handkerchiefs which were found on the deceased. I did not discover any blood on them, and I believe that the stains on the larger handkerchief are those of fruit. Neither on the hands nor about the body of the deceased did I find grapes, or connection with them. I am convinced that the deceased had not swallowed either the skin or seed of a grape within many hours of her death. I have stated that the neckerchief which she had on was not torn, but cut. The abrasion which I spoke of on the right side of the neck was only apparently an abrasion, for on washing it was removed, and the skin found to be uninjured. The knife produced on the last occasion was delivered to me, properly secured, by a constable, and on examination I found it to be such a knife as is used in a chandler's shop, and is called a slicing knife. It has blood upon it, which has characteristics similar to the blood of a human being. It has been recently blunted, and its edge apparently turned by rubbing on a stone such as a kurbstone. It evidently was before a very sharp knife."

The Coroner: "Is it such a knife as could have caused the injuries which were inflicted upon the deceased?"

Phillips: "Such a knife could have produced the incision and injuries to the neck, but it is not such a weapon as I should have fixed upon as having caused the injuries in this case; and if my opinion as regards the position of the body is correct, the knife in question would become an improbable instrument as having caused the incision."

Coroner: "What is your idea as to the position the body was in when the crime was committed?"

Phillips: "I have come to a conclusion as to the position of both the murderer and the victim, and I opine that the latter was seized by the shoulders and placed on the ground, and that the murderer was on her right side when I inflicted the cut. I am of opinion that the cut was made from the left to the right side of the deceased, and taking into account the position of the incision it is unlikely that such a long knife inflicted the wound in the neck."

Coroner: "The knife produced on the last occasion was not sharp pointed, was it?"

Phillips: "No, it was rounded at the tip, which was about an inch across. The blade was wider at the base."

Coroner: "Was there anything to indicate that the cut on the neck of the deceased was made with a pointed knife?"

Phillips: "Nothing."

Coroner: "Have you formed any opinion as to the manner in which the deceased's right hand became stained with blood?"

Phillips: "It is a mystery. There were small oblong clots on the back of the hand. I may say that I am taking it as a fact that after death the hand always remained in the position in which I found it-across the body."

Coroner: "How long had the woman been dead when you arrived at the scene of the murder, do you think?"

Phillips: "Within an hour she had been alive."

Coroner: "Would the injury take long to inflict?"

Phillips: "Only a few seconds - it might be done in two seconds.

Coroner: "Does the presence of the cachous in the left hand indicate that the murder was committed very suddenly and without any struggle?"

Phillips: "Some of the cachous were scattered about the yard."

The Foreman: "Do you not think that the woman would have dropped the packet of cachous altogether if she had been thrown to the ground before the injuries were inflicted?"

Phillips: "That is an inference which the jury would be perfectly entitled to draw."

The Coroner: "I assume that the injuries were not self-inflicted?"

Phillips: "I have seen several self-inflicted wounds more extensive than this one, but then they have not usually involved the carotid artery. In this case, as in some others, there seems to have been some knowledge where to cut the throat to cause a fatal result."

Coroner: "Is there any similarity between this case and Annie Chapman's case?"

Phillips: "There is very great dissimilarity between the two. In Chapman's case the neck was severed all round down to the vertebral column, the vertebral bones being marked with two sharp cuts, and there had been an evident attempt to separate the bones."

Coroner: "From the position you assume the perpetrator to have been in, would I have been likely to get bloodstained? - Not necessarily, for the commencement of the wound and the injury to the vessels would be away

133

from me, and the stream of blood - for stream it was - would be directed away from me, and towards the gutter in the yard.
Coroner: Was there any appearance of an opiate or any smell of chloroform? - There was no perceptible trace of any anesthetic or narcotic. The absence of noise is a difficult question under the circumstances of this case to account for, but it must not be taken for granted that there was not any noise. If there was an absence of noise, I cannot account for it."
The Foreman: "That means that the woman might cry out after the cut?"
*   Phillips: "Not after the cut."*
Coroner: "But why did she not cry out while she was being put on the ground?"
*   Phillips: "She was in a yard, and in a locality where she might cry out very loudly and no notice be taken of her. It was possible for the woman to draw up her legs after the wound, but she could not have turned over. The wound was inflicted by drawing the knife across the throat. A short knife, such as a shoemaker's well-ground knife, would do the same thing. My reason for believing that deceased was injured when on the ground was partly on account of the absence of blood anywhere on the left side of the body and between it and the wall."*
A Juror: "Was there any trace of malt liquor in the stomach?"
*   Phillips: "There was no trace."*

I admired the way Wynne Baxter had professionally handled the testimony of Doctor Phillips and then made sure that this testimony was collaborated by the recalled Doctor Blackwell as well.

[Sic] Dr. Blackwell: [recalled] (who assisted in making the post-mortem examination) said: "I can confirm Dr. Phillips as to the appearances at the mortuary. I may add that I removed the cachous from the left hand of the deceased, which was nearly open. The packet was lodged between the thumb and the first finger, and was partially hidden from view. It was I who spilt them in removing them from the hand. My impression is that the hand gradually relaxed while the woman was dying, she dying in a fainting condition from the loss of blood. I do not think that I made myself quite clear as to whether it was possible for this to have been a case of suicide. What I meant to say was that, taking all the facts into

consideration, more especially the absence of any instrument in the hand, it was impossible to have been a suicide. I have myself seen many equally severe wounds self-inflicted. With respect to the knife which was found, I should like to say that I concur with Dr. Phillips in my opinion that, although it might possibly have inflicted the injury, it is an extremely unlikely instrument to have been used. It appears to me that a murderer, in using a round-pointed instrument, would seriously handicap himself, as he would be only able to use it in one particular way. I am told that slaughterers always use a sharp- pointed instrument."

The Coroner: "No one has suggested that this crime was committed by a slaughterer."

Witness: "I simply intended to point out the inconvenience that might arise from using a blunt-pointed weapon."

The Foreman: "Did you notice any marks or bruises about the shoulders?"

Blackwell: "They were what we call pressure marks. At first they were very obscure, but subsequently they became very evident. They were not what are ordinarily called bruises; neither is there any abrasion. Each shoulder was about equally marked."

A Juror: "How recently might the marks have been caused?"

Blackwell: "That is rather difficult to say."

Coroner: "Did you perceive any grapes near the body in the yard?"

Blackwell: "No."

Coroner: "Did you hear any person say that they had seen grapes there?"

Blackwell: "I did not."

After the two doctors gave testimony, Mr. Sven Ollsen of twenty-three Princes' Square St. George's in the east gave evidence. Ollsen a clerk of the Swedish Church there, had known the deceased in a past life and verified her name to be Elizabeth Stride. At the time when the clerk knew the deceased, she was the wife of John Thomas Stride. Ollsen's testimony could be verified by the church registry; of which the clerk was the registries keeper.

The next witness to be called was William Marshall of sixty-four Berner Street. Marshall recognized the deceased as a woman observed by him talking to a man at quarter to midnight Saturday night, three doors down

135

from his house. Marshall described the man as 'decently dressed, middle-aged, stout, and approximately five foot six inches. Marshall had no recollection of the man having whiskers or not.

Phillip Krantz, of forty Berner Street, was called next. Krantz was the editor of the Hebrew paper called 'The Workers Friend.' On the night of the murder, the editor was in his room that was attached to the printing office at the rear of the International Working Men's Club. Krantz entered his room at nine o'clock and had remained there until a club member came to inform him that a dead woman was found lying in the yard. After being questioned about hearing any noise coming from the yard, Krantz testified as did the other witnesses that no screams nor any commotion was heard coming from the yard during the time in question. The following witness was Detective-Inspector Reid.

[Sic] Detective-Inspector Reid said: I received a telegram at 1:25 on Sunday morning last at Commercial- Street Police-office. I at once proceeded to No. 40, Berner-street, where I saw several police officers, Drs. Phillips and Blackwell, and a number of residents in the yard and persons who had come there and been shut in by the police. At that time, Drs. Phillips and Blackwell were examining the throat of the deceased. A thorough search was made by the police of the yard and the houses in it, but no trace could be found of any person who might have committed the murder. As soon as the search was over the whole of the persons who had come into the yard and the members of the club were interrogated, their names and addresses taken, their pockets searched by the police, and their clothes and hands examined by the doctors. The people were twenty-eight in number. Each was dealt with separately, and they properly accounted for themselves. The houses were inspected a second time and the occupants examined and their rooms searched. A loft close by was searched, but no trace could be found of the murderer. A description was taken of the body, and circulated by wire around the stations. Inquiries were made at the different houses in the street, but no person could be found who had heard screams or disturbance during the night. I examined the wall near where the body was found, but could detect no spots of blood. About half-past four the body was removed to the mortuary. Having given information of the murder to the coroner I returned to the yard and made another examination and found that the blood had been

removed. It being daylight I searched the walls thoroughly, but could discover no marks of there having been scaled. I then went to the mortuary and took a description of the deceased and her clothing as follows: Aged forty-two; length 5ft. 2in; complexion pale; hair dark brown and curly; eyes light grey; front upper teeth gone. The deceased had on an old black skirt, dark-brown velvet body, a long black jacket trimmed with black fur, fastened on the right side, with a red rose backed by a maidenhair fern. She had two light serge petticoats, white stockings, white chemise with insertion, side-spring boots, and black crape bonnet. In her jacket pocket were two handkerchiefs, a thimble, and a piece of wool on a card. That description was circulated. Since then, the police have made a house-to-house inquiry in the immediate neighborhood, with the result that we have been able to produce the witnesses who have appeared before the court. The investigation is still going on. Every endeavor is being made to arrest the assassin, but up to the present without success."

With that end of the testimony, the day was almost spent, so the inquiry was adjourned for a fortnight.

The afternoon hours of the day were warm for October, and a pleasant change from the rain that had dominated the weather. I was preoccupied with the last testimony when I left the inquest in the death of Elizabeth Stride. Hailing a cab, I tapped my pipe on the curb before climbing into the hansom. It had been three days since the discovery of the headless and legless corpse, dubbed the 'torso murder'. I had been busy hunting down the allusive American when the torso was discovered and had not been active in the investigation. The papers had reported that the police were being mocked by the mad man that stalked London's streets, for the latest murdered woman was found at the Victoria Embankment, the site of the new '*Scotland Yard*' building. The discovery seemed to support the newspapers portrayal of the Home Office, and the image conveyed in their daily reports of the police as the laughing stock of all London. As detrimental as the reporting had done to the police image, that was not the worst of it. Gangs had started to rove the streets at night in pursuit of the '*Ripper*' looking for a chance to share in the five hundred pounds reward, unfortunately, that was not the worst of it. These gangs had begun to rob people in the streets and had even turned on police who were powerless to stop them.

The new Home Office of Scotland Yard, was located 35 Victoria Embankment; and when complete; would have a magnificent view of the Thames, London Bridge, and the Parliament buildings. The building was still under construction when I walked onto the site, but already the shape and size of the structure could be seen. Its foundations were of Portland stone, the outside walls of red and white brick. Walking around the busy site, I noted the construction trades coming and going. I guessed there were upwards to one hundred men, if not more, doing various jobs, with any one of them feasibly being the perpetrator who had killed and beheaded the unfortunate woman whose torso was found in the dark cellars of the building.

Walking along a narrow track used by laborers pushing wheelbarrows, I saw an entranceway that could be reached by planks to the main floor. Aware of being watched by a group of men who returned to their work when I looked in their direction; didn't bother me at all. I had been a Police Officer far too long not to have grown accustomed to being snubbed by the general public. Walking on the planked subfloor, I looked around for anyone who had the appearance of being in charge. Almost immediately, I saw a tall gentleman yelling orders and pointing to several areas on the site to a group of men in the center of the main floor.

"Excuse me," I interrupted the man, "Could you tell me if Frederick Wildborn or Charles Brown is here on-site?"

I saw the irritated look on the foreman's face and instinctively opened my jacket showing the badge pinned to my vest, to prevent any backlash from the man for being interrupted.

The man stopped and looked me up and down from head to toe then pointed, over his shoulder.

"Outside on the scaffolding near the doorway where you came in."

I watched the foremen return to what he was doing without giving me a second thought and continued shouting more instructions to the men who stood in front of him.

Outside, I saw three men on a lower platform of a scaffold.

"Excuse me; I am looking for Frederick Wildborn."

All three men stopped working on a window they were framing in and turned towards me.

"That's me. What do you want?" Wildborn snapped.

"Scotland Yard, Detective Stone, I'd like to ask you some questions, if you don't mind," I replied, not being put off by Wildborn's gruff manner. Upon hearing the words Scotland Yard, the other two men on the scaffold turned their backs quickly on me and continued their work.

"Ballocks, not you lads again, I told everything that I know to that other bill," Wildborn exclaimed, climbing down from the scaffolding.

"I am not interested in what you have said to the other officers; I am only interested in what you are going to tell me now. I need you to take me to the spot where you first noticed the body."

With more grumbling, Frederick Wildborn led me around to the Cannon's Row entrance, the only other access to the building was on the Embankment, on the Thames side. I took note as they walked around the building that there were hoardings of seven or eight feet high in place to keep people from entering the site from the streets.

"How many entrances are there to the vaults below?" I stopped Wildborn before entering.

"There are only two. Both entrances are well gated and locked as well." Wildborn offered.

Continuing on the path, I watched Wildborn walk around a large opened gate with a lock dangling from the catch, leading me further down a well-used footpath to a smaller gate with a single latch. I watched Wildborn shove his arm through an opening in the fencing and lift the latch leading the way in.

"Mr. Wildborn, how many people frequent the vaults during the course of a day would you say?" I asked curiously.

Wildborn turned on me perturbed to be stopped again and questioned. "Only those who are known workmen on this site or those who have business with the clerk of the works are admitted," Wildborn spoke frankly and then started to turn away.

"How many of those, do you suppose, know to skip the latch on the gate as you just did? "

"Anyone who works down here at this site, I'm guessing," Wildborn answered.

Walking along several large planks laid in a row, Wildborn led me into the dimly lit vaulted cellar. I followed the workman closely turning first left and then right a half dozen times along a well-worn path. Now that the upper floor was constructed, I could not help but think that the space was the perfect place that '*Jack*' would use to both conceal the body and embarrass Scotland Yard. The deeper into the bowels of the building they went, the darker it grew. I followed close on Wildborn's heels as the lantern cast long shadows between the vaults. The vaults according to Wildborn were arched ceilings so designed for strength, to support the floors above. The cellar was a maze of these vaults, and if it hadn't been for Wildborn's knowledge of the area there would have been no way I could have found my destination without proper direction. I could only imagine that anyone unfamiliar with the site would wander around for hours in search of his objective. At their destination, Wildborn led me around a large central column that split the passage, leaving a space of about six feet square at the end of the walkway.

"It was here where I found the body."

The carpenter held up the globe of a lantern that hung from a hook on the wall and struck a match.

Taking the other lantern from Wildborn, I inspected the vaulted space. Where the workman had halted was the rear corner of what would be described as a crawl space under the main floor of the building. Glancing around, I inspected the place with the additional lantern's light. The more I looked at the complete darkness that surrounded me, the more I thought it impossible that anyone without some previous knowledge of the vaults where the torso was found could have possibly navigated the place without a lantern. That is, after the floor was fixed overhead enclosing the space. It seemed probable to me that given the cool temperatures of the space and the dampness it was likely decomposition could have been slowed and thus, the smell that would have emanated from the corpse was not as severe as it would have been out in the open. I sniffed the air detecting the dank smells that would accompany such a place that was close to the Thames and that had been flooded at least once since construction began.

Turning back towards Wildborn, I studied the carpenter, thinking that at least some of the story told to police rang true, but that as far as I was prepared to go with the man who had been in and out of the space several times since the body was laid there. The time of death could have been retarded by the cool temperatures. However, on the grounds that the workman and several others were in the area performing their duties, I could see no way of the two or three frequenting the space to have not noticed some smell caused by the putrefaction of the torso that would have begun at the terminus of the victim's life.

Stepping around the carpenter, I looked into the dim light that shone from the lantern in my hand. I could vaguely see the dark stain against the wall where the killer had placed the torso. According to Doctor Thomas Bond's testimony, the torso had been in the vaults for some time before being found. The police investigation revealed that the vaults had been closed and locked after completion of construction on September the twenty-ninth. Wildborn had found the torso on October second.

Looking around, I thought of the twist and turns they took to get to the place where the torso was placed, and then I remembered that at least some of the floor would have been unfinished at the time the body was put in the vaults. The killer might have placed the torso inside the vaults when there was still natural light to guide his steps. It was the only plausible explanation. The vaults were dark, only a person with some knowledge of the place could navigate such a remote area. As much as I wanted to believe that the cool temperatures were instrumental in masking the smell, given the enclosed space and the close proximity of Wildborn's tools, I found it hard to believe that the man had not detected something amiss. Careful not to draw any conclusions, nobody knew better than I that there was a killer on the loose who was capable of murder most terrible and was cunning enough to elude police. However, after reading the police report by Detective Thomas Hawkins and the coroner's inquest report, I established that out of a construction site filled with tradesmen, there were only three or four men who stood out in my mind that were possible suspects. They just happened to be the same persons who had access and reason to be in the vaults.

I remembered reading in the file that George Budgen, a bricklayer's laborer, was in the vault a few days before the torso was discovered by Wildborn. Wildborn was in the vault on Monday. The carpenter at that time saw what appeared to be an old coat but didn't recognize it as anything suspicious. Budgen reported seeing nothing out of the ordinary a day later on Tuesday. Mr. Cheney, who was the bricklayer's foreman reported not being in the vaults since they were completed and locked four days before the torso was found. Next on my list of suspects, was Ernest Edge. Edge was a general laborer who held keys to the gates that led to the vaults. Turning my attention to an impatient Frederick Wildborn, I studied the man, I had chosen for my guide but I saw nothing that would lead me to believe Wildborn was guilty of anything other than a bad attitude.

"What made you come down here the day you found the torso?"

I asked the question, already knowing the answer from Wildborn's inquest testimony. Albeit, I was curious as to what the carpenter's response would be when asked again.

"I store tools here," Wildborn answered abruptly.

"Why here of all places?" I asked, eyeing Wildborn, looking for any sign of hesitation in his speech or nervous body language.

"We built the forms down here for the masons. When the vaulting was finished, we moved out of here, and they were kept locked. I have lost several tools on this site already; I didn't want the thieving blokes I work with stealing any more of my tools. Besides, I know who has the key."

"Who is that? Who has the key, I mean?" I asked Wildborn, knowing full well but again looking for any tell-tale signs the man might be hiding something.

"A boy by the name of Edge has a key. Edge is in charge of locking the gates up at night."

"How many others have a key?"

"I know the foreman has one, but I wouldn`t know who else has a key."

"Who has knowledge of this area as well as," I hesitated for a moment. "Say you, for argument's sake?" I asked walking around the carpenter.

"I'd say, anyone who has worked down here, I expect. Why do you ask?" Wildborn asked, defensively.

"I am just trying to get some idea how a headless, legless torso, that would weigh," I mused. "I am guessing in the neighborhood of one hundred pounds, would be found down in an area that is secured by locked gates, on a site that is surrounded by high fences and hidden beneath a newly constructed building that has a labyrinth that anyone who had never been down here before would find difficult to navigate?"

I could tell that what I said touched a nerve, if not, I had awakened the man's curiosity who perhaps had not, at least, up until then, given the idea any thought. I poked around the area while Wildborn stood eyeing me suspiciously. I hoped that like myself, Wildborn was trying to get some idea of how a body could be missed in a place used by just a select few.

"You testified that you recalled seeing what you thought was a coat in the corner, is that correct?"

"That's right. At the first of the week, I needed a nail punch, so I came down on my break to get it." Wildborn snarled.

"Follow my thinking, will you, for a minute. You brought your tools down here to be stored and to be secure. Is that right?"

I continued after I saw Wildborn nod in recognition.

"How secure was this location if it was being used by others. Didn't it concern you that someone other than you had access to the place where you had left your belongings?"

"I didn't give it much thought," Wildborn answered.

"Did you ask Edge if others were coming down here?"

"No, I was busy. Besides, seeing the coat slipped my mind. Why are you badgering me? I am not the one with the key." Wildborn shouted.

"I am just trying to solve a murder," I smiled. "You said that you were tired of losing tools so, you left them here where they would be safe, is that correct?"

"Yes!" Wildborn snarled.

"I am wondering after seeing the coat that did not belong to you, why you were not concerned as to who was using a space that you had believed to be out of the way and unused by anyone else?" I eyed Wildborn to see if I could break the crusty exterior, and force the man to reveal something.

"I already told you, I did not know others were using this area!"

"So, you did not suspect anyone had been in the area when you saw a coat in the corner that had not been there before?"

"I told you, I was in a hurry that day and had no time to look closer at the bundle or ask Edge if anyone else had been allowed down here!"

Try as I might Wildborn was not forthcoming with the answers I wanted. Which could mean the man was telling the truth or the carpenter was a very good liar and had recognized the coat, and was possibly protecting someone.

"Well, if you're done. I got to get back to work." Wildborn stated.

"I am just going to be a minute, and we will leave together with the lantern."

"No need, you can take the other lantern. Just stay left and follow the wall until you see the light at the end, that's the Cannon Row entrance if you go left you will find yourself going towards the Embankment. You understand?" Wildborn sneered at Stone.

"Yes. Stay to the left, is that it?" I asked.

"That's right," Wildborn replied sarcastically, and then turned abruptly to leave.

"Oh, one more thing Mister Wildborn. Could you tell Ernest Edge to be available when I am done here?"

Wildborn turned with a scowl, nodded, and then left.

Holding the lantern in front of me, I continued to study the ground, looking for a drop of blood or any sign on the hard-packed dirt floor to give evidence of how the murderer transported the body to such a remote spot. The ground was smudged by dozens of footprints from workers who had been down in the vaults during construction, not to mention the countless number of constables searching the area after the torso was discovered. After twenty minutes of scanning the floors, I could find nothing that might give a clue as to how the murderer brought the body into the vaults. Straightening my back from being hunched over for such a long period, I stared at the wick in the lantern as it fluttered when a draft blew up the tunnel. It was cool in the cellar-like passageway, the temperature was much like that of a cave. It was likely the reason why the few who had entered after the vaults had been completed, detected no smell from the putrefaction of the corpse. The fresh damp air that found its way from the Thames River, coupled with the chilly temperatures, had kept the body from decomposing too quickly. Moving deeper into the vaults, I carried the lantern close to the floor to examine the area carefully. I could find no blood spray on the walls or floor to give evidence the body had been dissected in the area where the torso was discovered. Nor did I find any evidence that the body had been dragged along the floor in a sack of some kind. The absence of such evidence told me that either, more than one person was involved in carrying the torso, or some other method was used to transport it. The construction site would have more than one wheelbarrow close at hand that may have been used. The latter seemed the more likely possibility.

According to the mason's foreman, the vaults were finished in three months, from start to completion. Three days later, the torso was found. Wildborn, Edge, and Cheney, all had easy access to the area.

"Along with at least one hundred other men," I whispered to myself.

Outside the sunny afternoon had faded, overhead, dark clouds had replaced the blue sky, and the wind blew unsuspecting leaves from their branches, sweeping them across the roadways where they came to a halt against the hoardings at the Cannon Rows entranceway. A spattering of rain had begun when I emerged, ceasing all work on the scaffolding that surrounded the New Scotland Yard Building. Seeing the tradesmen and laborers scatter for cover, I waited at the entrance studying the area and thinking about Wildborn's answers. The man had a valid reason for his presence in the vaults. The idea remained that anyone who was afraid to lose tools would immediately become concerned that his hiding place had been infiltrated and would do an immediate inventory. The extra time in the area would have made the man aware of the coat and or the smell causing him to inspect it, to discover who the culprit was, who had been in the area that he thought was secure. Though Wildborn seemed stubborn and perhaps a little dimwitted, a construction worker did not fit into my thinking. Up until that moment, a practitioner of some kind had been the culprit. It was possible that we now had two murderers in London, and one had nothing to do with the other. It was also conceivable that Wildborn had saw the coat and inspected it but chose to ignore it, so that he would not be implicated in the murder. For whatever reason, Wildborn's behavior during questioning had been guarded and the man had been little help.

The afternoon was near to a close, and I felt like climbing in between the sheets and staying there. The investigation in the torso, like that of the 'Ripper' case, had come to a screeching halt before it had really begun. On Monday, October eighth, the inquest into the 'torso mystery' would begin. I hated to admit that my trip to the New Scotland Yard building had added nothing to the investigation, just as most of my efforts to date. As the murder had been committed out of Baxter's jurisdiction, the inquest would be held at the mortuary at Millbank Street by John Troutbeck, Coroner, for Westminster residing.

Shouting for a cab, I was home an hour later, sipping tea at my flat and watching the rain pound against the thin pane of glass in the window. The idea that the murders had been committed under the noses of police was troublesome, but the continued practice of the killer to thumb his nose in the face of the police was exasperating. I tried to avoid my next thought but failed in my attempts. If the police did not find 'Jack the Ripper' soon, there would be another murder and more retaliation on police. Though I did not like walking away without a culprit in custody, I had to admit that Inspector Abberline was right. The newspaper's constant reporting on how badly the police were handling the investigation had diminished civic trust in the police. For a moment, I considered all that I had learned from my trip into the vaults and doubted that anyone on the construction site was the killer, despite the peculiar circumstances surrounding the coat and the proximity of Wildborn's stash of tools. I also had doubts that any further inquiry would provide a clue into the murder of a headless torso that was impossible to identify. I did not like having a defeatist attitude, but it stood to reason that until there was some way to track the killer known as '*Jack the Ripper*' there was not anything they could do to stop these senseless crimes.

At my office the next morning, I began the report on my investigation of the vaults under the New Scotland Yard building. In my report, I stated that although it was suspicious that all three men, Cheney, Wildborn, and Edge had been in the vaults at times when no other had access, it was unlikely that any could have carried out the vicious crime that had been perpetrated on the female torso found there. In the police reports Dr. Thomas Bond gave evidence that the body had been dead for a maximum of eight weeks and a minimum of six. I hated to admit it, but unless Bond's timing was wrong, the body could not have been in the vaults long, or someone would have noticed the bundle while working on placing the main floor above or finishing the work on the vaults. Unfortunately, it appeared as though all three men had been in the wrong place at the wrong time after the body was placed below. There was one thing to consider, however, if Bond's time of death was right, where was the body held to prevent decomposition before being placed in the vaults. Somehow, I suspected that Bond's timing was off, but had no way to prove my theory either way. Due to the conditions of the vaults, the torso had been somewhat preserved. But I found it hard to believe that in the time that Wildborn had been in such close proximity of the body, the man did not smell some odor. Nor had any of the others who had been in the vaults after the corpse was dumped there. Allowing for the maximum time of the woman's death to date, it would seem likely, the torso was placed in the vaults at a time when construction was ongoing. As a result, this put the remaining construction crews in or around the site at the same time, not to mention the insecure gating at both entranceways allowing the intrusion of outsiders at times when the work had ceased for the day.

Blowing on the wet ink to dry it, I placed the paper in the file folder. Pushing back from my desk, I dug into my vest pocket and found the key to the top drawer of my desk, unlocking the drawer, I pulled out the file that was secreted there. The file was a compilation of personal notes that I had written on each and every case. Shuffling through the documents, I found the case now dubbed the Whitehall Mystery. With pen in hand, I began to write:

Inspector Marshall, while investigating the vaults found pieces of the Echo and Chronicle newspaper near where the torso was found. The Echo Newspaper was dated August twenty-fourth, five days before the vaults were completed and locked; however, they were unable to ascertain the date of the Chronicle. Too many people had access to the secured vaulted area to seek a specific suspect. The general consensus is that the pieces of the newspaper may have been placed with the body, so that investigators may try to tie the crime with the reports of 'Jack the Ripper' murders found in those papers. However, it must be noted that the killer knew enough anatomical language to tourniquet the legs and arms to prevent blood spray during dissection. Tapping the ink from the tip of the pen into the well, I placed the file back in the top drawer and locked the drawer, replacing the key in my vest pocket. It would still be a couple of days before the inquest into the torso murder; I would have to wait until then, to continue.

Rising from my desk, I reached for my overcoat on the hook beside the door and went down the hall to the coroner's office. Finding the door locked, I left the building and shouted across the street for a cab.

"Where to Sir?"

"Scotland Yard!" I answered as I climbed in the back of the cab, just as a downpour threatened to drench all the unprepared pedestrians on the street.

It was dark when I finally left the Home Office; the dinner hour had already come and gone. The rain had long since turned to a fine drizzle, and a thick fog had rolled in reducing visibility to within a few feet. Climbing aboard the cab, I was deep in thought. I had spent the afternoon copying files on the Catharine Eddowes murder. The murder had been handled primarily by City Police, as it was in their jurisdiction. While at

The Yard, I had taken time to report in with Inspector Abberline on my investigation into the torso and handed in my report on my findings. With the jostling of the cab over the cobbled streets, I was lulled into a dream-filled sleep where 'Jack' screamed his intentions to murder all the prostitutes in London. Waking with a shudder, I sat upon the seat and wiped my face with both hands; the images that flashed before me of the dark figure lurking in the shadows of Whitechapel consumed my every thought. Looking at my watch, I held the face of the old timepiece to the lantern that hung from the roof of the cab and had a change of thought. Tapping the roof of the cab, I got the driver's attention.

"Driver, take me to H Division, on Leman Street."

"Right, oh!" The driver snapped the whip over the horse's ears, and the cab leaped forward again.

With the dense fog came a damp chill so, I rolled up the collar of my overcoat when the cab dropped me at the corner of Leman and Braham Street. Inside H Division, the station was in a bustle of officers doing their duty. The halls were crowded with those either reporting a crime or asking questions about someone in goal. People shoved and pleaded to be the one next to be heard by the sergeant on the desk; some were holding bandages on faces and hands having been a victim of some crime or arrested for allegedly committing one. The sergeant's desk was situated in the front hall of the Police Station making the sergeant the frontline to handle whatever came through the door.

"Sergeant!" I shouted above the cacophony and noise created by those trying to get the Sergeant's attention.

Turning, the sergeant looked with a leer to see who was shouting at him.

"Yes, and who might you be, Sir?"

"I am Detective John Stone, Scotland Yard," I answered, holding open my jacket to display my badge.

Seeing the badge, the sergeant pulled in his reins.

"Yes, Sir, what can I do for you?"

"I'm looking for Constable Long," I shouted over an argument that had taken place between two women standing behind me.

"If you two don't stop, I will come down there and throw you both in the poke." The sergeant shouted above the din, his face turning red with the telling. "You just missed him, Sir; Constable Long is on patrol."

Looking at the large clock on the wall, I tried to guess where the constable may be on his patrol at that time.

Turning to the sergeant, I interrupted again. "What area is the constable patrolling this night?"

"My guess would be, Braham Street." The sergeant returned to yelling over the crowd that stood before him.

Leaving by the main entrance, I headed down Leman Street and then turned left down Braham Street. The streets were unusually crowded, given the mist and the chill in the air. Crossing Aldgate High Street, I started my search for Constable Long, looking down streets, dead ends, and dark alleys, most of which were heaped with all manner of crates and trash. Propositioned by prostitutes and eyed by small groups of men who used numbers and the dark to prey on the unsuspecting, I ignored the all too familiar plight that infested the walks of London's East End. Walking down the narrow corridors in the dark, the familiar feeling like I was an intruder was almost always present. The streets here were continually moving with those who were pushed by patrolling constables from one doorway or bench to another, each man woman or child, having the sunken eyes that only sleeplessness and hunger can bring, moving in a daze, haunted by the cold and starvation. The sole remedy for some was a hot meal and a warm bed, but that was as unachievable as the job it took to afford such amenities.

Unfortunately, seeing the human race at its worst was an occupational hazard for a policeman. I supposed that I had grown calloused to the plight of the East End over the years. Now, for some reason, that long slumber had been stirred by the murders of the five women in Whitechapel. I had unexpectedly delved into the lives of these women more thoroughly than I had in any investigation before, as a result, I had seen living in the East End up-close, and I had been troubled by the misery. In the past, I had investigated the heart-wrenching effects of crime in all walks of society and every class. In the East End, 'Jack' had inadvertently drawn a spotlight on the women who had been destitute enough to fall back on a lifestyle that had magnified life in the ghetto as I had never seen it before. It was a raunchy world of the malcontent, the forgotten, and the outcast of society, seemingly left to aimlessly fend off the elements, hunger, and debauchery of every kind. They lived in gutters, and storefronts, holding out hands, in a plea for help. Those possessing a kind heart, must sooner or later, come to grips that they could never have enough resources to help them all.

This was not the first time; I walked the streets of Whitechapel at night. Over the years, I had become accustomed to every nook and cranny of London's diverse landscape. My job took me behind the scenes of people's lives, sometimes in places where others could not even imagine. However, after arriving in Whitechapel, I had the opportunity to peer closely into the lives of those who society had segregated. Unfortunately, after seeing the condition that the young woman Alenka had been left, I had become more personally involved in a case then I had ever allowed myself to do before. I saw the lodging houses where the women slept, I had encroached into their pasts and investigated their relationships, and during that time something in me had changed. I had become a part of the society that others shied away from. I understood, how; the East End had become a melding pot of all that society had come to loathe. These people were the homeless, the criminal, and the helpless. Each one scrounging for a bed, their next meal, or the cheap gin that would change nothing except dull the senses to perhaps get through one more day. Their life had begun to spiral out of control long before they had met their end. How they got into the predicament that they found themselves, was due to a set of circumstances some of which was beyond their control but later through self-pity and addiction they had accepted their plight and dove deeper into the abyss of the East End. Now, there was a killer to add to the plague of misery that those who lived in the east had to contend. 'Jack' was a predator seeking out the undesirable, and those that would never be missed, nor cried over. To add insult to injury, the people of the East End were now being blamed for shielding the criminal from the police.

Coming to a halt, I couldn't be sure where Constable Long was at that very moment without walking every step of the man's beat; I did know, however, where the man would ultimately end up. Cutting across Middlesex Street, I saw a sign reading Goulston Street; I then headed for the Wentworth Buildings.

Counting the numbers on the buildings, I stopped in front of a staircase with the numbers 106 to 119 painted on a post. It was a dwelling house with a long staircase attached to several others that led to the rooms on the upper levels. Turning sharply, I heard a door slam somewhere nearby. Across the street, there were angry shouts that ended with another slam of a door. These were the sounds I attributed to a city that did not sleep. In the dim light, I could see a crate turned on its side lying next to a tall fence. Turning the crate over, I sat down and waited. For several minutes, I sat in the dark tuning my senses to the night, I watched as a cart passed by, the driver's song, sung out of key. The darkness to me was as comforting as much as it could be fearful. In the dark, one could sit and listen, the ears picked out the funny curse of a passer-by, as a foot splashed in a puddle, or the rooting sound of an animal looking for morsels of food in the garbage. However, the dark concealed criminals like the 'Ripper' who stalked the streets for the unsuspecting. The night also held the secrets of London's many disfigured bodies that hid from the daylight. They covered their deformities with hoods and in baggy clothes that draped over their bodies, shielding themselves from the peering eyes of the curious. They were called aberrations and harassed by children, and shunned by the rest of Whitechapel that had in turn been outcast by the rest of London. The night was also the friend of the petty criminal, sheltering those dastardly creatures that used the cover of darkness to conceal their activities from the penetrating and accusing light of day.

I sat listening in the deep shadows for some minutes wondering if Constable Long would ever show up and then finally, I heard a tune being whistled and the creak of a rusty lantern handle swinging in stride as the constable came around the corner of the Wentworth Buildings.

"Constable Long," I spoke in a loud, clear voice, and then struck a match, so I could be identified.

"Who is it? Who's there?" Long shouted.

Holding up the match, in front of my face, I waited for the constable to approach. I noted that Constable Long's voice had been commanding, not nervous, or shaken; it said something about the man, I was about to meet.

"Detective John Stone, Scotland Yard," I replied.

"What the devil are you doing in the shadows, come out here, Sir!" Long said, holding up the lantern to see the approaching figure more clearly.

"I just want to ask you some questions about what you remember of the night that Catherine Eddowes was murdered. I thought that I would walk with you on your patrol. I hope you don't mind?"

"Mind, why should I, mind? You picked a devil of a time to do it?" Long stated.

Allowing the statement to go unchallenged, I walked towards the wall where the much gossiped about graffiti was written.

"I won't take much of your time constable; I just have a couple of questions," I said as I turned to look at Long.

"I suppose it's about that graffito, I found?"

"That's right; you found it at," I said, stopping turning to look at the constable. "When was it, five to three in the morning of the thirtieth, is that right?"

"Yes, Sir," Long stood back and held the lantern towards the wall where the graffiti had been written.

"You testified that on your patrol you past here at twenty minutes past two, and you saw no writing at that time, is that correct?"

"Yes, that's right."

"You saw no one about, heard nothing suspicious, and saw nothing out of the usual?" Taking a moment to look around the area, I stepped closer to examine the wall where the graffiti had been written.

"No, there was no one about. It was quite early, as you have stated Detective," Long turned hearing a scuffle behind him.

They watched as a young couple darted across the street, hand in hand.

"If you were here at this precise spot at twenty past two, and then didn't return until thirty-five minutes later, is that to say it takes you approximately that amount of time to complete your entire patrol every night?"

"That is an average I would say," Long answered, standing erect and at attention.

"Where exactly was the piece of Eddowes' apron found?" I asked, backing up to allow the constable room.

"Right here, under where I found the writing on the wall," Long pointed.

"Right here underneath the graffito where you would be sure to find it," I spoke, thinking out loud.

"What do you mean, Sir?" Long asked.

"Nothing," I said, catching a glimpse of defensiveness in the constable's tone. "Do you think the piece of material was dropped. Or, is it more likely, that it was deliberately placed where you or another constable might find it, directly below where you would see the writing on the wall?"

Walking towards the wall and gesturing to Long.

"I don't rightly know," Long hesitated. "I suppose that it could have been placed there by the killer so, I could see the message on the wall," Long responded.

I watched Long step towards the brick wall, raising his voice.

"How about the writing, how big was it, and where did it start and where did it finish?"

"The writing was about forty-eight inches high, and it was spread down the wall to about thirty-six inches in length," Constable Long spoke matter-of-factly, and without hesitation.

"Well, I have to say, that, that is a good description and precise too. So, let me get this straight. On that night, you walk around the building the same way you came tonight, you see this graffito written in white chalk, and then you look down and see the piece of apron, all in the dark."

"I have given all this information to Inspector Swanson, and testified at the inquest as well, Detective" Long turned to walk away.

"Just one more question if you don't mind Constable?" I spoke gruffly, stopping Long in his tracks. "Did you wash off the graffiti, or did someone else?"

"I pointed the graffito out to my superiors and then went about my patrol, finishing at seven in the morning. Is that everything, Detective Stone?" Long asked.

"Yes, thank you for your cooperation." Tipping my hat at Constable Long, I left the man standing in the center of the street with his mouth agape.

Deep in thought, I found myself three hundred yards away in Mitre Square before I knew it. Most of the questions I had asked Constable Long, I already knew the answers from the inquest report. Although what happened after the graffito was discovered and brought to the attention of Constable Long's superiors was not a matter of common knowledge. Who ordered the graffito washed from the wall, and why, was not common knowledge? That information was kept from everyone except the top brass. The very idea rankled me, not because the information may or may not have been helpful in the case, but because the bureaucrats decided that those beneath them were incapable to ascertain if the information was helpful or not.

Walking into Mitre Square, I could see that the location chosen by the killer had been the result of careful planning. The premeditation involved suggested a man who was in full command of his actions and the circumstances before and after murdering his victims. The intent and opportunity were apparent in the murder of Catharine Eddowes after 'Jack' killed Elizabeth Stride. I believed that the perpetrator of the crime then immediately and deliberately made his way to Mitre Square. To me, it was proof that the location, was chosen well in advance by the killer and not just some random site and a chance encounter with an indiscriminate victim. It was quite possible that the victim could have sat in the square after making a prearranged meeting with the killer days in advance. The three escape routes that Mitre Square offered, with only one lamp in the furthest corner from where the body was found, was in keeping with the other crime scenes. Mitre Square had all the same characteristics that the executor of the crime had used in the past. Each location the killer had chosen was, in my estimation at least, chosen beforehand. The locale offered favorable conditions to continue the dissection of his victim, keeping his movements concealed in darkness. All of these aspects were another building block in the case against the fiend, known to the public as 'Jack the Ripper.' These facts fundamentally ruled out the common consensus that the murderer was a mindless madman, recently escaped from some asylum that was wielding his knife at the prostitutes in Whitechapel. There was thought and planning that was evident in all of the murders, not to mention the contemplation of writing letters to newspapers and authorities giving details of the crimes about to be committed. The more thought I gave to the explanations and excuses made to the public, not to mention the sheer absurdity behind the suggestions made from Home Office to the detectives on the ground investigating these crimes, was mind-boggling. The murderer used every tactic imaginable to mask his presence and keep from leaving any evidence in his passing, whether by using paved walks to conceal footprints or the use of shrouded areas less traveled by the common folk as his chosen settings to commit these crimes. All the while allowing for more than one escape route that would leave constables guessing which path the killer had taken after the crime scene was detected. The killer employed strategies and characteristics that could only be carried out by someone with intelligence and wit. Hardly someone unstable could elude police for so long.

Walking around the square, I tried to envision the man they looked for. Certainly, a man who was used to the mechanics of a blade in hand, no matter the profession. Though the man I envisioned remained faceless, the killer, I imagined was not reckless nor haphazard in his movements. '*Jack*' employed both cunning and forethought, combined with daring in the execution of his crimes. These qualities spoke of someone with purpose, though; I refused to entertain any idea or reason for the warped sense of calling the man might have felt in the performance of his crimes.

I walked back up Wentworth Street and hailed a cab. Tired, I looked at my watch, the hour was late there would be no use going back to the office now. My plan had been to check the scene first hand at approximately the time that the crime was perpetrated. There was, of course, another reason for remaining in Mitre Square for so long. I had checked my watch when I had entered the square. I stood in the furthest corner of the Square out of sight for exactly thirty-five minutes, and failed to see a constable on patrol. Climbing in the cab, I slumped into the seat almost asleep by the time I reached my rooms on Whitechapel Road.

Chapter Nine

The inquests that I had attended to date, numbered three. There seemed to be no end to the questions asked by doctors, police, and coroners alike. What was the time of death, when the last time the deceased was seen alive, what was her destination? All were logical questions asked about an individual that had a name, a family, and friends. However, on Monday, October the eighth, the inquest that would be later known as the '*Whitehall Mystery*' held at the Sessions House, Broad Sanctuary, was anything, but ordinary. Here these questions were not asked of the police or the doctors, because the torso had no identity, there was no witness to identify her or give the details of a life that was lived by the deceased. There were no friends or acquaintances to provide intimate details into the last moments they saw the deceased alive, there was nothing usual or standard about the inquest at all. The details that were known of the torso were these; the body belonged to a woman, who was around the age of twenty-four, of fair complexion and dark hair. The torso found had no head so, there was no face in which friends or family could identify a missing loved one. There were no distinguishing marks that could be described in the newspapers to find who or where the woman might have come from. Nor, was there any other way of identifying the woman, who had been murdered, and her head, her arms and legs scattered around the city of London, her torso left in the unfinished vaults of the new Scotland Yard building.

Where did she come from, who was she, what was her date of birth? These were all questions left unanswered, sealed inside the head of the victim, and perhaps the murderer that killed without remorse, seemingly without motive, and without mercy. The murders of six women that were assumed to be killed by at least two individuals went unsolved. These heinous crimes, perpetrated by a faceless fiend who went unpunished, left the female population of the city afraid to walk the streets. Leaving the rest of the population unsatisfied by the results of the police thus far. The discovery of the torso had caused a flurry of newspaper headlines, with the Metropolitan Police as the brunt of their criticism.

Arriving at the Sessions House at the Broad Sanctuary, both I and Wynne Baxter were shown to a row of chairs reserved for police and professionals who attended the inquest. I knew very little of John Troutbeck, Coroner for Westminster, but Baxter assured me that Troutbeck's style, although slightly unorthodox, was still professional in his duties as coroner. Troutbeck's father was respected and well known as the Chaplains in Ordinary to Her Majesty Queen Victoria.

After several minutes of waiting for the inquest to come to order, I leaned over and whispered in my friend's ear.

"What do you mean, Wynne, when you say that Troutbeck has an unorthodox style?"

"It seems Mr. John Troutbeck and the Coroner's Act of 1887 have come under fire," Baxter whispered. "The man has also been criticized by the newspapers for barring them from his inquests. Troutbeck has even gone, so far as, to keep his inquests entirely private, by not disclosing any information at all to the newspapers."

"Can the man do that?"

"Can, and has done, on more than one occasion in the past," Baxter said, with a shrug of his shoulders.

Interested in this unique style of the coroner, I could not help but want to know more.

"What about the Coroner's Act of 87, put Troutbeck in hot water?"

"The portion of the act that was troubling by most coroners, and doctors alike, is the subsection that dealt with a coroner using a doctor to testify at an inquest that was different from the deceased's own physician, to collaborate testimony given by another doctor who was unavailable to attend," Baxter paused. "How do you think our Doctor Phillips would feel if I pulled that at one of my inquests?"

Averting my attention, I watched the figure of Frederick Wildborn walk up to the witness chair and take his seat. The testimony Wildborn gave was verbatim as to what the man had given to me after I had questioned the carpenter of Groves and Sons.

Budgen was in the vault at three o'clock on October the third; because the foreman, Mr. Cheney asked him to examine a parcel found there. After dragging the bundle into the light, Budgen then proceeded to cut the three or four strings that held the cloth around the package and discovered it contained a portion of a body.

[Sic] Thomas Hawkins a detective at A Division was next deposed. At twenty past three a Mr. Brown, an assistant foreman of Grover and Sons Company came to the station and reported a body that had been found in the vaults at the new police buildings. After viewing the remains of a woman's body wrapped in what appeared to be some kind of dress material, I went to report what I found at the station and to Doctor Bond. I returned to the vault with Detective Inspector Marshall at five o'clock who took charge, then directed all witnesses back to the station where their statements were taken.

Charles William Brown: "I reside at 5, Hampton-terrace, Hornsey, and am assistant foreman to Messrs. Grover, at the new police offices, Whitehall (sic). The works are shut off from the surrounding streets by a hoarding about 7ft high."

[Coroner] "How many entrances are there?"

Brown: "Three; two in Cannon-row and one on the Embankment. There are gates at the entrances as high as the hoardings."

[Coroner] "How long have these vaults been completed?"

Brown: "Three months."

[Coroner] "Who was admitted to the works besides workmen?"

Brown: "No one, unless they had business."

[Coroner] "Was any one kept at the gates?"

Brown: "No."

[Coroner] "So that any person who chose could walk in?"

Brown: "There was no one to prevent them. On Saturdays, all the gates are locked up, except a small-one in Cannon-row."

[Coroner] "Is there a watchman there?"

Brown: "No."

[Coroner] "Who are left on the premises at night?"

Brown: "No one. The small gate in Cannon-row is secured by a latch, and it is not everybody who can undo it."
[Coroner] "Is there any watchman outside?"
Brown: "No."
[Coroner] "What were the approaches to the vaults?"
Brown: "A road made of planks laid two abreast. Once down in the vaults it is very dark. The floors have to be laid there and the drains put down. Carpenters were at work there the week before the discovery."
[Coroner] "Did you observe anything about the state of the locks on the following Monday morning?"
Brown: "No."
[Coroner] "Did they look as if they had been forced?"
Brown: "I did not notice."
[Coroner] "Do you think previous knowledge was required to get to the vaults?"
Brown: "Yes, I do. I first saw the parcel about half-past two o'clock on Tuesday afternoon. I had been in the vaults on the Monday, but had not noticed any smell. I was there in the dark. On Tuesday the first witness called my attention to the parcel. I struck a light, and I saw in the corner what looked like an old coat with a piece of ham inside. I procured a lamp, and the parcel was afterwards got out and opened."
By the Jury: "Tools have been stolen on the works. I do not think it possible that anyone could have lowered the parcel from Richmond-mews."

"This is the testimony I have been waiting to hear," I said, glancing over at the coroner briefly as Ernest Edge took his seat.

John Troutbeck looked over a few papers in front of him, before continuing his questioning, while Edge squirmed in his seat nervously.

[Sic] Ernest Edge, a general laborer, living in Peabody's-buildings, Farringdon-road, deposed: "I was in this vault on Saturday week at twenty minutes to five in the evening, going there to get a hammer to nail the door of a locker. I struck a match, but nothing was in the vault then. I went across the trench, where we were measuring on the Friday. On the Saturday I was in the very corner where the parcel was discovered on the

Tuesday."

[Coroner] "There was no parcel there on the Saturday?"

   *Edge: "No. I might have been near the vault on the Monday; I certainly
was on the Tuesday."*

[Coroner] "The vault leads to nowhere?"

   Edge: "No."

[Coroner] "Are workmen constantly in the vault during the day?"

   *Edge: "Almost every day they go there to look for things. On the
Saturday I locked up after everybody had gone, and left everything secure.
As to the gate, which opens with a latch, I left that in the usual way. I am
sure it was shut. To open the gate, it was only necessary to pull the
string."*

*By the jury: "The string would not attract the attention except of persons
who knew about such buildings."*

I sneered at the last comment, recalling when I went to the vaults how
easily Wildborn had popped the latch at the gate when the gate was
supposed to be secured. It would have been immediately apparent that
anyone who hung about the construction site and paid any attention at all
to the comings and goings of the workers for a couple of hours would have
been able to pick up the fact that the gate was unlocked and could be easily
opened. I mentioned as much to Wynne, as the witness left the room,
Baxter drew my attention to the next witness to enter the witness chair.

Doctor Thomas Bond, had the appearance of a man well in his sixties, as
the doctor's hair was more salt than pepper with an almost grey mustache,
though I knew that the man was barely fifty years old. Bond wore a dark
wool suit and appeared to be anxious. I took note of the doctor's nervous
habit of twisting his hat repeatedly back and forth. Before I could think
any further on the subject, Bond began his deposition.

*[Sic] Mr. Thomas Bond: "I am a surgeon, and reside at the Sanctuary,
Westminster Abbey. On Oct. 2, shortly before four o'clock, I was called to
the new police buildings, where I was shown the decomposed trunk of a
body. It was there lying in the basement partially unwrapped. I visited the
place where it had been discovered, and found that the wall against which
it had lain was stained black. The parcel seemed to have been there for*

160

*several days, and it was taken to the mortuary that evening, and the
remains placed in spirits. On the following morning, assisted by my
colleague, I made an examination. The trunk was that of a woman of
considerable stature and well nourished. The head had been separated
from the trunk by means of a saw. The lower limbs and the pelvis had been
removed in the same way. The length of the trunk was 17 inches, and the
circumference of the chest 35½ inches and the waist 28½ inches. The parts
were decomposed, and we could not discover any wounds. The breasts
were large and prominent. The arms had been removed at the shoulder
joints by several incisions, the cuts having apparently been made obliquely
from above downwards, and then around the arm. Over the body were
clearly defined marks, where string had been tied. It appeared to have
been wrapped up in a very skillful manner. We did not find marks
indicating that the woman had borne any children. On opening the chest,
we found that the rib cartilages were not ossified, that one lung was
healthy, but that the left lung showed signs of severe pleurisy. The
substance of the heart was healthy, and there were indications that the
woman had not died either of suffocation or of drowning. The liver and
stomach, kidneys and spleen were normal. The uterus was absent. There
were indications that the woman was of mature age twenty-four or twenty-
five years. She would have been large and well nourished, with fair skin
and dark hair. The date of death would have been from six weeks to two
months, and the decomposition occurred in the air, not the water. I
subsequently examined the arm brought to the mortuary. It was the arm of
a woman, and accurately fitted to the trunk; and the general contour of the
arm corresponded to that of the body. The fingers were long and taper,
and the nails well shaped; and the hand was quite that of a person not
used to manual labor."*

[Coroner] "Was there anything to indicate the cause of death?"

Bond: "Nothing whatever."

[Coroner] "Could you tell whether death was sudden or lingering?"

*Bond: "All I can say is that death was not by suffocation or drowning.
Most likely it was from hemorrhage or fainting."*

*[Coroner] "Can you give any indication of the probable height of the
woman?"*

*Bond: "From our measurements, we believed the height to have been 5ft
8in. That opinion depends more upon the measurements of the arm than*

161

those of the trunk itself."
[Coroner] "Was the woman stout?"
   Bond: "Not very stout, but thoroughly plump; fully developed, but not abnormally fat. The inference is that she was a tall, big woman. The hand was long, and was the hand of a woman not accustomed to manual labor."
[Coroner] "Did the hand show any sign of refinement?"
   Bond: "I do not know that a hand of that kind is always associated with any refinement of mind or body, but certainly it was a refined hand."

   "What do you make of that Detective?" Baxter asked enthusiastically.
   "A woman bred of a good family; I would say, wouldn't you," I answered?
   "This woman certainly was not used to the toil in factories, public houses, or kitchens of those who live in the heart of London's East End, I will venture that. If I was a betting man, this was a woman that some man wanted to be done away with and made to look like one of 'Jacks' prostitutes.
   "I am inclined to agree with you, but how do you explain the uterus being absent from the body?" I whispered over my shoulder to Baxter.
   "Yes, quite right, John, there is that to consider. Do you suppose that the killer was mimicking Jack'?" Baxter offered.
   "That is entirely possible, especially the part about the cutting up of the body, Wynne. However, the average layman would do a botched job of extracting a uterus from the trunk, don't you think?"
   "I guess that brings us around to this mysterious organ purchaser again," Baxter said, grimacing knowing the effect that his statement would have.
   "Yes, a man that could be one, and the same, as the murderer." I agreed.
   "This Hibbert fellow," Baxter said, pointing across the room as the man's name was announced. "Is Doctor Bond's assistant."
   I nodded in recognition taking notice that the crowded room went silent as Hibbert took his seat in front of the coroner.

162

[Sic] Mr. Charles Alfred Hibbert, assistant to Mr. Bond, deposed: "I examined the arm on Sept. 16. It was a right arm, and had been separated from the shoulder joint. It measured 31 inches in length and was 13 inches in circumference at the point of separation, the wrist being 6½ inches round, and the hand 7½ inches long. The arm was surrounded at the upper part with a piece of string, which made an impression on the skin, and when it was loosened there was a great deal of blood in the arm. The hand was long, and the nails small and well-shaped. It was the hand of a female. There were no scars or bruises. The arm had apparently been separated after death."

[Coroner] "Did the arm seem to have been separated easily?"

Hibbert: "The operation was performed by a person who knew what he was doing - not by an anatomist, but by a person who knew the joints."

[Coroner] "Had the cuts been done by a very sharp knife?"

Hibbert: "They were perfectly clean. I found that the skin cuts of the arm corresponded with those of the trunk, and that the bones corresponded likewise. The same skill was manifested in both instances. The work was not the work of the dissecting-room that was obvious. A piece of paper was shown to me as having been picked up near the remains, and it was stained with the blood of an animal."

[Coroner] "Was there the mark of any ring on the finger?"

Hibbert: "No."

"I wonder what Bond will have to say to his assistant tomorrow, after hearing that his assistant testified that the dissection was done by someone who knew what end of a knife to use?" I spoke over my shoulder to Baxter.

"What do you mean, Stone?" Baxter asked.

"In the police report, Bond made his feelings known that the dissection of the torso was not done by a slaughterer of animals or any type of physician," I answered Baxter.

"One would think that a doctor and his assistant would be of the same mind, wouldn't you?" Baxter responded.

"You would think," I responded. "At least, we know the two did not try to collaborate on their answers, Wynne."

[Sic] Inspector Marshall, of the Criminal Investigation Department, said:

163

"About five o'clock on Oct. 2nd I went to the new police buildings on the Thames Embankment, and in the basement saw the trunk referred to by previous witnesses. The corner from which it had been taken was pointed out to me, and I saw that the wall was a great deal stained. Examining the ground, I found the piece of paper alluded to by the last witness, as well as a piece of string, apparently sash-cord. Dr. Hibbert handed me two pieces of material which had come from the remains. I at once made a thorough search of the vaults, but nothing more was discovered. On the following morning, with other officers, I made a further search of all the vaults, but nothing more was found nor anything suspicious observed. The piece of paper spoken to forms part of an Echo of Aug. 24th. Dr. Hibbert handed me a number of small pieces of paper found on the body. They are pieces of the Chronicle, but I cannot yet establish the date. It is not of this year's issue. With respect to the dress it is of broche satin cloth, of Bradford manufacture, but a pattern probably three years old."

[Coroner] *"Is it a common dress?"*

Marshall: *"It is made of common material. There is one flounce six inches wide at the bottom. The material could probably be bought at 6½d per yard. I have examined the hoarding round the works."*

[Coroner] *"Is it possible to get over it?"*

Marshall: *"There is a place in Cannon-row where a person could easily get over, but there is no indication of anybody having done so. The latch which has been referred to is not likely to have been noticed except by a person acquainted with buildings. The string with which the parcel was tied was a miscellaneous lot. One piece is of sash-cord, and the rest is of different sizes, and there is also a piece of black tape."*

[Coroner] *"Did you form any opinion as to how long the parcel had been where it was found?"*

Marshall: *"From the stain on the wall I certainly thought several days, but the witness Edge told me he was sure it was not there on the previous Saturday."*

Coroner: *Edge being recalled repeated his assertion that the remains were not in the vault on the Saturday, as they were discovered in the very place where I looked for the hammer.*

The Coroner: *"Do you think it possible that the parcel was there without your seeing it?"*

Edge: *"I am sure it was not there."*

After the crowd had thinned at the close of the first day of proceedings, I waited for Wynne Baxter to finish talking to Coroner Troutbeck, and then we both climbed into a cab and headed to our flats. Looking over at my friend, I watched Baxter stare out the window of the cab saying nothing. The rumble of the cab doing a steady clip was reason enough for no conversation, but I could not help but feel that something was troubling the coroner.

"These inquests seemed to be piling one on top of another," Baxter growled. "I am not sure if we are any further ahead today; than when we first started."

After a long pause, Baxter went silent again, I decided to refrain from comment and leave the coroner to dwell on his own thoughts.

"It seemed suspicious to me that Edge would finish his testimony the way that he did," I said after several minutes of mulling.

"I don't think I follow, Detective," Baxter answered.

"When Edge was asked if the parcel was in the vaults the man said definitely not, reiterating that there was nothing there on the Saturday. When recalled, the question was asked of him again. Edge testified having knowledge that people were going there regularly and that the workers on the site knew that the passage gate was not locked. Why did Edge not just say that there was no way to be sure when the torso was left there? Instead, the man adamantly says for certain that there was no wrapped bundle there on the Saturday in question."

"I am still not sure what you are getting at," Baxter queried. "So, Edge made it clear that there was nothing there on the Saturday, what of it."

"Why didn't the man testify having no knowledge of the wrapped bundle until his attention was brought to it? Instead, Edge went into great detail about looking for a hammer in the exact spot that the torso was found. Edge even makes it known that the bundle was not there on the Saturday when locking the doors to the vaults. Why would Edge not just say, anyone could enter the construction site without too much trouble, but the man makes it obvious to the members that no one but an employee could have entered the vaults."

"Perhaps the man was just making his position clear to the jury," Baxter replied.

165

"Possibly, Wynne," I responded. "Unfortunately, Edge has now inadvertently drawn suspicion to himself given the fact that a set of keys to the vaults were in his possession. I also think that Edge intended to draw suspicion to anyone other than to himself, which makes me wonder what the man has to hide."

"Are you sure that you are not reading too much into Edge's testimony?" Baxter commented.

"What do you mean, Wynne?"

"I understand how you feel, Detective, because I have done it on more than one occasion myself. I spend so much time seeking a suspect that when I finally have a prime candidate, I want to shoulder the entire mess on one person, sitting in front of me that I can hand over to the police and be done with it. Instead, we spend our time chasing this allusive faceless figure about the streets of London. This wretch may as well be a ghost for all the good we have done."

The conversation was left at that; I sat listening to the rumbling of the hansom cab's wheels on the cobbled street, lost in my own thoughts. I understood why Baxter had responded the way that he did, because I was feeling the same. All the murders were committed by someone whom the victims did not know. There was no long list of associates to talk to and question, and at times there wasn't even any immediate family to question. While other victims had no real contact with any family in years. As a result, the list of suspects was too few to add any real significant momentum to the investigation. To make matters worse, the inquests added no lurid detail nor any surprise witness that shed any light on any particular part of the case. The ugly truth was that the investigation into the murders was going nowhere. Unfortunately, the torso inquest did little more than add more questions, to an already floundering investigation. Regrettably, for the coroners in charge of the cases, the questions were piling up, while the constituents expected answers, and there were just none to be had.

The next morning, I decided to tackle organizing the mountain of paper work on the top of my desk. Picking up a piece of paper that I had scribbled on.

"Blood was still gushing from a wound in the neck," I whispered to myself.

"What's that you said, Detective?" Baxter asked, entering the office carrying a pot of tea.

Startled, I looked up from my reading to see Baxter walking into my office.

"I was just reading some notes I had written on the Stride case," I explained, sitting back in my chair reflecting on what I had just read.

"The first three days were rather confusing; I must say, John," Baxter replied, taking a seat.

"Have you any information forthcoming that will establish her identity beyond a doubt?"

"This was far more difficult than needs be, John," Baxter said, stirring his tea. "With the public scrutinizing my every move and the papers making it look like we have lost all control. It is no wonder I am still trying to ascertain the identity of the poor soul. To make matters worse there is the woman's relatives mourning or wanting to know if they should mourn, and all I have is the testimony and witness accounts to either put them at ease or tear their world down about their knees. The similarities in both Elizabeth Stride and Elizabeth Watts are overwhelming, to say the least. After the first day of the inquest, even I could not be sure of the identity of the woman at the mortuary. When a coroner is forced to close the first day of inquest proceedings without establishing an identity, it allows for all kinds of speculation to arise as you saw yourself, John. It was very unnerving, to say the least. Fortunately, Stride had married a carpenter, one John Thomas Stride," Baxter paused, looking over the rim of his cup. "Things were not summed up as easily as that, however. Detective- Inspector Edmund Reid, who was placed in charge of looking for Stride's husband found records that Elizabeth Gustafsdotter had married John Thomas Stride, a ship's carpenter of Poplar. It turns out, that Stride died in 84."

"Come again?"

I could well believe the twists and turns an investigation could take. Record-keeping was at times haphazard at best. Dates of birth were often kept in the family Bible and sometimes finding the family member who kept these records was difficult to track down or that person had died and the records lost.

"It gets better, John. It was to our good fortune; Stride had a nephew who was a police constable. Baxter stopped long enough to take a handkerchief from his jacket to clean his glasses.

"Constable Walter Stride."

"Yes, yes, that is right. Do you know the man?"

"No, I saw his name on a roster, recently."

"Constable Stride will be at the inquest, and under oath, to verify for once and for all that the unnamed woman lying in the mortuary is Elizabeth Stride. The constable will testify that the deceased married his uncle John Thomas Stride, and we have a photograph to verify it."

"What will your summation entail?"

"Why Detective, can't you wait like the rest of Whitechapel?" Baxter asked, sarcastically.

"Just curious, Wynne."

"Off the top of my head, it's believed that Diemschutz, startled the Ripper by his ill-timed return. The killer likely believed that time and opportunity were in his favor; and proceeded to commit the crime, in the dark lane beside the club. Hence the reason why there was no other mutilation to the body. That is if we believe that one man killed both Stride and then Eddowes an hour later."

"If we ignore the letter describing a double event and the premeditation of the crime, there are certainly a lot of similarities, Wynne."

"Yes, but the cut to the throat was different, wasn't it, Detective," Baxter responded.

"Understandably so, Wynne, if you consider the interruption by the steward. If you ask me, I think that Lewis Diemschutz narrowly escaped with his life."

Day two of the Inquest into the death of Catharine Eddowes was on Thursday, October the eleventh. I and Wynne Baxter took their seats across from the seated jury. Wynne Baxter had never met Mr. S. F. Langham, the City's Coroner, and was interested to see the inquest proceed. The first witness was Dr. G. W. Sequeira. The doctor arrived at Mitre Square at five minutes to two in the morning and was the first doctor to arrive at the crime scene. His testimony was consistent with Doctor Gordon Brown's. Corroborating that the victim was found in the darkest area of the square. Although Sequeira added something more. The doctor stated that the body could be seen despite the limited light offered by the lamps in the Square. Sequeira made a special point of mentioning the deviant of the crime had no particular skill in perpetrating the dissection of the body and continued establishing the time the killer needed was sufficient to carry out such a crime and not be detected by the constables who patrolled the area.

"Stone, it sounds to me that the City Police had a hand in the arrangement of these witnesses in the proceedings this day," Baxter whispered.

"I agree with you, Wynne, nice and tidy; taking the focus of the investigation from local physicians and the patrolling constables right off the hop," I whispered.

Annie Phillips was the daughter of Catharine Conway when her mother was married to Thomas Conway. Ms. Phillips testified that her parents separated due to her mother's drinking, Conway, her father, being a teetotaler. Conway testified that she had not seen her mother in over two years, and had no contact with her siblings for over eighteen months. She also stated that she had no knowledge of her father at all since her parents separated.

Next, to take the witness stand, was Detective Sergeant John Mitchell, who testified finding Thomas Conway. Thomas Conway, unfortunately, could not be identified by the deceased two sisters because neither of them had ever seen him before. After a few minutes of discussion, City Constable Lewis Robinson was called. Robinson was the constable who had arrested the deceased on the night of her murder for public drunkenness.

[Sic] City-constable Lewis Robinson, 931, deposed: "At half-past, eight, on the night of Saturday, Sept. 29, while on duty in High-street, Aldgate, I saw a crowd of persons outside No. 29, surrounding a woman whom I have since recognized as the deceased."
The Coroner: "What state was she in?"
Constable Robinson: "Drunk."
Coroner: "Lying on the footway?"
Robinson: "Yes. I asked the crowd if any of them knew her or where she lived, but got no answer. I then picked her up and sat her against the

169

shutters, but she fell down sideways. With the aid of a fellow-constable I took her to Bishopsgate Police-station. There she was asked her name, and she replied "Nothing." She was then put into a cell.

[Coroner] "Did any one appear to be in her company when you found her?"

Robinson: "No one in particular."

Mr. Crawford: "Did any one appear to know her?"

Robinson: "No. The apron being produced, torn and discolored with blood, the witness said that to the best of my knowledge it was the apron the deceased was wearing.

The Foreman: "What guided you in determining whether the woman was drunk or not?"

Robinson: "Her appearance."

The Foreman: "I ask you because I know of a case in which a person was arrested for being drunk who had not tasted anything intoxicating for eight or nine hours."

[Coroner] "You are quite sure this woman was drunk?"

Robinson: "She smelt very strongly of drink."

Next, to testify, was the goaler of Bishopgate station.

"This fellow has come under fire for allowing the inebriated woman out of goal in the first place," Baxter whispered, as the goaler took his seat.

I nodded in agreement.

"If the man had of kept her detained, I wonder if she would still be alive today?" I commented, glancing at Baxter as I spoke.

"Whatever does that mean, Stone?" Baxter asked.

"Meaning Wynne, with all 'Jack's' preparation and premeditation, I wonder if Stride's killer had not already picked Catharine Eddowes as his second victim before the crime was committed."

"I still think you are giving this wretch too much credit, Stone. In his letter 'Jack,' described a '*double event*,' I believe the man would have killed any cocotte that might have crossed his path, just to prove his point that his letters are to be taken seriously."

Without comment, I wondered for the second time, in as many days, if I was doing what Baxter had accused me of, giving 'Jack the Ripper' too

170

much credit. The activity at the top of the room averted my attention, leaving my response to Baxter's claim left unsaid.

[Sic] Constable George Henry Hutt, 968, City Police: "I am goaler at Bishopsgate station. On the night of Saturday, Sept. 29, at a quarter to ten o'clock, I took over our prisoners, among them the deceased. I visited her several times until five minutes to one on Sunday morning. The inspector, being out visiting, I was directed by Sergeant Byfield to see if any of the prisoners were fit to be discharged. I found the deceased sober, and after she had given her name and address, she was allowed to leave. I pushed open the swing-door leading to the passage, and said, "This way, missus." She passed along the passage to the outer door. I said to her, "Please, pull it to." She replied, "All right. Good night, old cock." (Laughter.) She pulled the door to within a foot of being close, and I saw her turn to the left."
The Coroner: "That was leading towards Houndsditch?"
Yes."
The Foreman: "Is it left to you to decide when a prisoner is sober enough to be released or not?"
Constable Hutt: "Not to me, but to the inspector or acting inspector on duty."
[Coroner] "Is it usual to discharge prisoners who have been locked up for being drunk at all hours of the night?"
Hutt: "Certainly."
[Coroner] "How often did you visit the prisoners?"

"What does that have to do with anything?" Baxter asked Stone critical of the coroner's style.

"No idea, Wynne," I said, with a shrug of my shoulders.

Hutt: "About every half-hour. At first the deceased remained asleep; but at a quarter to twelve she was awake, and singing a song to herself, as it were. I went to her again at half-past twelve, and she then asked when she would be able to get out. I replied: "Shortly." She said, "I am capable of taking care of myself now."
Mr. Crawford: "Did she tell you where she was going?"

171

Hutt: "No. About two minutes to one o'clock, when I was taking her out of the cell, she asked me what time it was. I answered, "Too late for you to get any more drink." She said, "Well, what time is it?" I replied, "Just on one." Thereupon she said, "I shall get a fine hiding when I get home, then."

[Coroner] "Was that her parting remark?"
Hutt: "That was in the station yard. I said, "Serve you right; you have no right to get drunk."

[Coroner] "You supposed she was going home?"
Hutt: "I did."

[Coroner] "In your opinion is that the apron the deceased was wearing?"
Hutt: "To the best of my belief it is."

[Coroner] "What is the distance from Mitre-square to your station?"
Hutt: "About 400 yards."

[Coroner] Do you know the direct route to Flower and Dean-street?
Hutt: "No."

A Juror: "Do you search persons who are brought in for drunkenness?"
Hutt: "No, but we take from them anything that might be dangerous. I loosened the things round the deceased's neck, and I then saw a white wrapper and a red silk handkerchief."

The day was filled with several witnesses, George Morris, night watchman of Messrs. Kearly, and Tonge's Tea Warehouse. Constable Harvey, on duty at Houndsditch and Aldgate, and off duty Constable Pearce, who lives at No. 3 Mitre Square, whose bedroom window overlooks the square. All witnesses testified that they neither seen nor heard anything out of the ordinary until alerted of the murder. Next came two witnesses, Joseph Lawende and Joseph Levy, that testified that they saw the deceased only hours before her death, when they left the Imperial Club, at Duke Street.

[Sic] Joseph Lawende: "I reside at No. 45, Norfolk-road, Dalston, and am a commercial traveler. On the night of Sept. 29, I was at the Imperial Club, Duke-street, together with Mr. Joseph Levy and Mr. Harry Harris. It was raining, and we sat in the club till half-past one o'clock, when we left. I observed a man and woman together at the corner of Church-passage,

Duke-street, leading to Mitre-square."
The Coroner: "Were they talking?"

*Lawende: "The woman was standing with her face towards the man,
and I only saw her back. She had one hand on his breast. I was the taller.
She had on a black jacket and bonnet. I have seen the articles at the
police-station, and believe them to be those the deceased was wearing."*
[Coroner] "What sort of man was this?"

Lawende: "He had on a cloth cap with a peak of the same."
*Mr. Crawford: "Unless the jury wish it, I do not think further particulars
should be given as to the appearance of this man."*

The witness Joseph Levy had less to offer than Joseph Lawende, as far
as identifying the man that they saw talking with Catharine Eddowes on
the corner of Church Passage after leaving the Imperial Club on Saturday
night. The man who both witnesses failed to identify was possibly the last
man to see Eddowes alive.

"Why, do you suppose, Crawford did not want the description of the
man they saw Eddowes with repeated to the jury?" Baxter asked, looking
curiously over at Stone.

"My guess, Wynne, is that Crawford does not want the man alerted, in
case the witness statements go public," I replied, just as the foreman of the
jury answered.

The Foreman: "The jury do not desire it."
*Mr. Crawford (to witness): "You have given a description of the man to
the police?"*

Lawende: "Yes."
[Coroner] "Would you know him again?"

*Lawende: "I doubt it. The man and woman were about nine or ten feet
away from me. I have no doubt it was half-past one o'clock when we rose
to leave the club, so that it would be twenty-five minutes to two o'clock
when we passed the man and woman."*

173

"Well, I guess that little ploy is worthless, there is not much good in having a description of a man if no one alive can identify him from a line-up," I snarled, looking over at Baxter, after hearing Lawende's answer.

[Coroner] "Did you overhear anything that either said?"
  Lawende: "No."
[Coroner] "Did either appear in an angry mood?"
  Lawende: "No."
[Coroner] "Did anything about their movements attract your attention?"
  Lawende: "No. The man looked rather rough and shabby."
[Coroner] "When the woman placed her hand on the man's breast, did she do it as if to push him away?"
  Lawende: "No; it was done very quietly."
[Coroner] "You were not curious enough to look back and see where they went."
  Lawende: "No."

The next witness's name had been on the lips of nearly every citizen who lived in London's East End. The topic that caused all of the gossip was that of the mysterious writing that Constable Alfred Long had found written on the wall at the stairwell entrance of a Goulston Street dwelling. The conspiracy theorists had a heyday with the writing that had been washed from the wall on the night of Catharine Eddowes' murder.

[Sic] Constable Alfred Long, 254 A, Metropolitan police: "I was on duty in Goulston-street, Whitechapel, on Sunday morning, Sept. 30, and about five minutes to three o'clock, I found a portion of a white apron (produced). There were recent stains of blood on it. The apron was lying in the passage leading to the staircase of Nos. 106 to 119, a model dwelling-house. Above on the wall was written in chalk, "The Jews are the men that will not be blamed for nothing." I at once searched the staircase and areas of the building, but did not find anything else. I took the apron to Commercial-road Police-station and reported to the inspector on duty."
[Coroner] "Had you been past that spot previously to your discovering the apron?"

174

Long: "I passed about twenty minutes past two o'clock."

[Coroner] Are you able to say whether the apron was there then?"

Long: "It was not."

Mr. Crawford: "As to the writing on the wall, have you not put a 'not' in the wrong place? Were not the words, "The Jews are not the men that will be blamed for nothing?"

Long: "I believe the words were as I have stated."

[Coroner] "Was not the word "Jews" spelt "Juwes?"

Long: "It may have been."

[Coroner] "Yet you did not tell us that in the first place. Did you make an entry of the words at the time?"

Long: "Yes, in my pocket-book."

Coroner: "Is it possible that you have put the 'not' in the wrong place?"

Long: "It is possible, but I do not think that I have."

[Coroner] "Which did you notice first - the piece of apron or the writing on the wall?"

Long: "The piece of apron, one corner of which was wet with blood."

[Coroner] "How came you to observe the writing on the wall?"

Long: "I saw it while trying to discover whether there were any marks of blood about.

[Coroner] Did the writing appear to have been recently done?"

Long: "I could not form an opinion."

[Coroner] "Do I understand that you made a search in the model dwelling-house?"

Long: "I went into the staircases."

[Coroner] "Did you not make inquiries in the house itself?"

Long: "No."

The Foreman: "Where is the pocket-book in which you made the entry of the writing?"

Long: "At Westminster."

[Coroner] Is it possible to get it at once?"

Long: "I dare say."

Mr. Crawford: "I will ask the coroner to direct that the book be fetched."

The Coroner: "Let that be done."

"Well, you really have to hand it to the constable," Baxter spoke as the witness left the room. "Long really held his ground."

"You are not giving this Crawford much credit are you, Wynne?" I spoke as the room exploded into whispers after hearing the last testimony.

"That is most unfair, John," Baxter replied, looking a little sheepish.

"Well, what if Crawford wanted the constable to repeat the incident for the newspaper's benefit, to clear up once and for all any gossip and innuendo," I responded, looking over at the coroner.

"You might be right, Detective, but it still doesn't bode well for the poor Jew of the East End does it," Baxter replied.

The bailiff called Detective Daniel Halse to the front.

"No, it doesn't," I responded cutting the conversation short. "This Halse is a good copper, I met him once. The man is thorough and knows his business. It will be interesting to hear what Halse has to say."

[Sic] Daniel Halse, detective officer, City police: "On Saturday, Sept. 29, pursuant to instructions received at the central office in Old Jewry, I directed a number of police in plain clothes to patrol the streets of the City all night. At two minutes to two o'clock on the Sunday morning, when near Aldgate Church, in company with Detectives Outram and Marriott, I heard that a woman had been found murdered in Mitre-square. We ran to the spot, and I at once gave instructions for the neighborhood to be searched and every man stopped and examined. I myself went by way of Middlesex-street into Wentworth-street, where I stopped two men, who, however, gave a satisfactory account of themselves. I came through Goulston-street about twenty minutes past two, and then returned to Mitre-square, subsequently going to the mortuary. I saw the deceased, and noticed that a portion of her apron was missing. I accompanied Major Smith back to Mitre-square, when we heard that a piece of apron had been found in Goulston-street. After visiting Leman-street police-station, I proceeded to Goulston-street, where I saw some chalk-writing on the black facia of the wall. Instructions were given to have the writing photographed, but before it could be done the Metropolitan police stated that they thought the writing might cause a riot or outbreak against the Jews, and it was decided to have it rubbed out, as the people were already bringing out their stalls into the street. When Detective Hunt returned inquiry was made at every door of every tenement of the model dwelling-house, but we

176

gained no tidings of anyone who was likely to have been the murderer."
By Mr. Crawford: "At twenty minutes past two o'clock I passed over the spot where the piece of apron was found, but did not notice anything then. I should not necessarily have seen the piece of apron."

[Coroner] "As to the writing on the wall, did you hear anybody suggest that the word 'Jews' should be rubbed out and the other words left?"

Halse: "I did. The fear on the part of the Metropolitan police that the writing might cause riot was the sole reason why it was rubbed out. I took a copy of it, and what I wrote down was as follows: 'The Juwes are not the men who will be blamed for nothing.'

[Coroner] "Did the writing have the appearance of having been recently done?"

Halse: "Yes. It was written with white chalk on a black facia."

The Foreman: "Why was the writing really rubbed out?"

Witness: "The Metropolitan police said it might create a riot, and it was their ground."

Mr. Crawford: "I am obliged to ask this question. Did you protest against the writing being rubbed out?"

Witness: "I did. I asked that it might, at all events, be allowed to remain until Major Smith had seen it."

Mr. Crawford: "Why do you say that it seemed to have been recently written?"

Halse: "It looked fresh, and if it had been done long before it would have been rubbed out by the people passing. I did not notice whether there was any powdered chalk on the ground, though I did look about to see if a knife could be found. There were three lines of writing in a good schoolboy's round hand. The size of the capital letters would be about 3/4 of an inch, and the other letters were in proportion. The writing was on the black bricks, which formed a kind of dado, the bricks above being white."

Mr. Crawford: "With the exception of a few questions to Long, the Metropolitan constable, that is the whole of the evidence I have to offer at the present moment on the part of the City police. But if any point occurs to the coroner or the jury, I shall be happy to endeavor to have it cleared up."

A Juror: "It seems surprising that a policeman should have found the piece of apron in the passage of the buildings, and yet made no inquiries in the buildings themselves. There was a clue up to that point, and then it *was altogether lost."*

*Mr. Crawford: "As to the premises being searched, I have in court
members of the City police who did make diligent search in every part of
the tenements the moment the matter came to their knowledge. But
unfortunately, it did not come to their knowledge until two hours after.
There was thus delay, and the man who discovered the piece of apron is a
member of the Metropolitan police."*

*A Juror: "It is the man belonging to the Metropolitan police that I am
complaining of."*

There was a slight pause as Detective Halse left the room, and constable
Long was readmitted.

"The Juwes are not the men that will be blamed for nothing," I
whispered to myself then looked over at Baxter, to get the coroner's
response. "What do you make of that, Wynne?"

"There may have been good cause to wipe the writing away, the way
things are in the East End."

"There is something that no one has brought up throughout the
questioning that makes me wonder about the authenticity of the writing."

"What is that, John?"

"Remember all the fuss about the printing of 'Jack's' letter to identify
the diction. It doesn't seem to be a concern now, does it?"

"No, it doesn't."

"Well, one thing is certain, the scrawl professed to be in 'Jack's' hand,
is no comparison with Halse's description."

"I'm wondering if the misspelling of Jew was deliberate."

"I am certain, that will be discussed for many a day to come, Wynne."

The crowd silenced, as Constable Long returned to his seat to give more
detail to his last statement referring to what was written on the Goulston
Street wall.

[Sic]Mr. Crawford: "What is the entry?"

*Witness: "The words are, 'The Jews are the men that will not be blamed
for nothing."*

*[Coroner] "Both here and in your inspector's report the word 'Jews' is
spelt correctly?" Long: "Yes; but the inspector remarked that the word*

was spelt 'Juwes.'

[Coroner] *"Why did you write 'Jews' then?"*

  Long: *"I made my entry before the inspector made the remark."*

[Coroner] *"But why did the inspector write Jews?"*

  Long: *"I cannot say."*

[Coroner] *"At all events, there is a discrepancy?"*

  Long: *"It would seem so."*

[Coroner] *"What did you do when you found the piece of apron?"*

  Long: *"I at once searched the staircases leading to the buildings."*

[Coroner] *"Did you make inquiry in any of the tenements of the buildings?"*

  Long: *"No."*

[Coroner] *"How many staircases are there?"*

  Long: *"Six or seven."*

[Coroner] *"And you searched every staircase?"*

  Long: *"Every staircase to the top."*

[Coroner] *"You found no trace of blood or of recent footmarks?"*

  Long: *"No."*

[Coroner] *"About what time was that?"*

  Long: *"Three o'clock."*

[Coroner] *"Having examined the staircases, what did you next do?"*

  Long: *"I proceeded to the station."*

[Coroner] *"Before going did you hear that a murder had been committed?"*

  Long: *"Yes. It is common knowledge that two murders have been perpetrated."*

[Coroner] *"Which did you hear of?"*

  Long: *"I heard of the murder in the City. There were rumors of another, but not certain."*

[Coroner] *"When you went away did you leave anybody in charge?"*

  Long: *"Yes; the constable on the next beat - 190, H Division - but I do not know his name."*

[Coroner] *"Did you give him instructions as to what I was to do?"*

  Long: *"I told him to keep observation on the dwelling house, and see if any one entered or left."*

[Coroner] *"When did you return?"*

Long: "About five o'clock."

[Coroner] "Had the writing been rubbed out then?"

Long: "No; it was rubbed out in my presence at half-past five."

[Coroner] "Did you hear any one object to its being rubbed out?"

Long: "No. It was nearly daylight when it was rubbed out."

A Juror: "Having examined the apron and the writing, did it not occur to you that it would be wise to search the dwelling?"

Long: "I did what I thought was right under the circumstances."

The Juror: "I do not wish to say anything to reflect upon you, because I consider that altogether the evidence of the police redounds to their credit; but it does seem strange that this clue was not followed up."

Witness: "I thought the best thing to do was to proceed to the station and report to the inspector on duty."

The Juror: "I am sure you did what you deemed best."

Mr. Crawford: "I suppose you thought it more likely to find the body there than the murderer?"

Witness: "Yes, and I felt that the inspector would be better able to deal with the matter than I was."

The Foreman: "Was there any possibility of a stranger escaping from the house?"

Long: "Not from the front."

[Coroner] "Did you not know about the back?"

Long: "No, that was the first time I had been on duty there."

The crowd was showing their impatience, with Constable Long, their grumbling was evidence of that. First, they huffed at the difference in testimony between what Detective Halse had remembered was written on the brick wall at Goulston Street and the difference between what Constable Long had remembered the graffito to say. The entire room growled in response to the apparent neglect of duty that Constable Long displayed in failing to follow up a clue. The testimony made the jury take notice and speak up. I considered the possibility that Constable Long may have been prompted to give his statement, or if it was, an issue of rivalry between the two police departments that Constable Long was given the nod to hang himself in front of the jury so that the London City Police would be seen in a better light. The politics of the police departments is something that most outside of the organizations would not see, nor care about. It was several minutes after hearing the testimony before Mr. S. F. Langham City Coroner spoke. It seems that after hearing the testimony, Langham was considering an adjournment and stopping the proceedings. By some means known only to himself, the coroner decided that it was unlikely that any further evidence could be found that would bring about a change in the jury's verdict, Mr. Langham then made the decision to make his summation.

[Sic] "That the crime was a most fiendish one could not for a moment be doubted, for the miscreant, not satisfied with taking a defenseless woman's life, endeavored so to mutilate the body as to render it unrecognizable." Langham said.

Then Langham instructed the jury that the evidence given should be that the murder implicated only one person and that it be willful murder against some man who, is of yet, unknown.

As the spectators began to depart, we remained in our seats until the crowd thinned. There was silence between us, for I think we were both in primarily the same mood. The inquest had summed up the circumstances of one woman found dead in the city of London. Before them, they now had six women in which there seemed to be no answer to friends and family alike as far as who had taken the life of their loved one. The investigation for me and the rest of the Metropolitan Police, for that matter, was far from over.

For a moment, I deliberated over the inquest conclusions which quite frankly left me at a loss for words. Unfortunately, the jury was vindicated in their findings, because there was no other answer other than that which they read as an official verdict minutes before. The murders were committed by someone willfully without explanation or purpose. The act was vicious, brutal, heinous, and savage. Having said that, they were still, no closer to finding the perpetrator of these crimes than they had been the day before the Catharine Eddowes inquest began.

It was several minutes after we arrived back at my office before, I felt like talking.

"What is your personal opinion, Wynne," I asked. "Do you think one man killed both Stride and Eddowes?"

I wanted to know if the coroner's opinion had changed.

"If one can rely on the witness testimony, which is something, I find precarious at times, if not absolutely difficult when dealing with those from Berner Street. However, I am inclined to agree with you, Stone that Diemschutz, did most likely startle this monster, we have skulking around our streets at night laying prey on defenseless women. Although it is my opinion, that all eyes would have been in the direction of this man Michael Kidney if there had of been more hard evidence, and if, I had been able to question Israel Schwartz, another key witness."

Baxter watched closely; while I dug into a police report. I found nothing and I looked at him curiously.

"You can't find it, can you?" Baxter asked.

"I don't see any mention of Israel Schwartz in the police file. The only information I have on Michael Kidney is that the man was Stride's lover and that the pair had a tumultuous relationship, likely due to their drinking cheap gin," I said, holding the file across the desk for Baxter, who waved a hand at me.

"You won't find what I have to tell you in your files Detective, because it was taken out."

"On whose authority, Wynne?"

"Why your office, who else would have that kind of authority?" Baxter stood up, unbuttoned his coat, and then walked over to the window lifting the shade. "There was another witness on Berner Street near Dutfield's Gate, on the night of September thirtieth," Baxter paused, and walked back to his chair and sat down.

"This man Israel Schwartz, you spoke of," I asked, directing my full attention on Baxter's every word.

After packing the briar-wood pipe and clamping it between his teeth, Baxter continued.

"Yes, Israel Schwartz, a Hungarian, Jew, who was near Dutfield's Yard at about 12:45 a.m. on the night Elizabeth Stride was murdered." Baxter paused again long enough to light the bowl.

"I don't understand, Wynne, I was called to the scene that night, I arrived late mind you, but I was there nevertheless, and I saw no such witness, nor was I made aware of anyone else other than Louis Diemschutz," I said, slamming my hands on top of my desk in frustration.

"Schwartz was taken away from the crime scene immediately, before, I am sure, you got there, Detective." Baxter paused again, setting another lit match to the bowl of his pipe.

"Sorry, Wynne, but I find this information most disconcerting," I apologized for my flare-up of temper. "Please continue."

"Be that as it may Stone, I found this information out quite by accident, myself, I assure you. My source told me that Israel Schwartz saw a man fitting what may have been the description of Kidney, but nothing could be proven. Then . . ." Baxter offered and then hesitated.

"Then the Goulston Street graffiti was found," I finished Baxter's sentence and slumped back in my chair.

"That is right, Detective," Baxter retorted. "Everyone was already up in arms about the police allowing these murders to go unchecked in the East End; by allowing news of this graffiti mentioning the Jews to get into the papers, the streets would have erupted in violence unparalleled to that of 'Bloody Sunday.' Our police force couldn't have handled another bout like that."

I listened as Baxter prattle on about events surrounding Annie Chapman's murder. Though, I knew all of the details already having attended the inquest which Baxter presided over. What I was interested in was this witness, this Israel Schwartz. I allowed the coroner to finish simply out of courtesy, wondering why I had not been informed about Schwartz being a potential witness, by Inspector Abberline, and why the man's name was kept out of the police reports.

"So, when the name Israel Schwartz came up, the man being a Jew, a Jew in the proximity of yet another murder. . .," I left my sentence unfinished when Baxter began again.

"Look at me, here I am rambling on when you know all or most of it already. Sorry, old boy," Baxter said, finishing his tea. "Right, so where was I."

"Israel Schwartz," I repeated, jarring Baxter's memory.

"Right oh," Baxter began. "With the people already up at arms and grumbling about the Jews, the City Police had to act fast. They knew that the citizenry wouldn't consider that this graffiti could be a coincidence. Your superiors feared that the city would allow their superstition, and fear to control their common sense, as the past has already demonstrated." Baxter said, refilling his teacup.

"What did Chief Inspector Swanson's report have to say about what Schwartz was doing in the area that night?"

"Schwartz, saw Elizabeth Stride standing with a man, with whom, she had words. The official statement made was Schwartz saw the unknown man throw Stride to the ground; apparently, she cried out as if she had been startled rather than hurt, although she did not cry for help. Schwartz started towards the woman to lend assistance, when another man across the street, who was lighting a pipe or some such thing, moved towards Schwartz, shouting the word '*Lipski*' of all things. Frightened, Schwartz started to walk away, leaving Stride to her own devices and was either followed, or the other man just wanted to put a scare into him. It seems that it worked."

"Lipski, what exactly does that mean?"

"Israel Lipski was a Polish Jew, Stone. I remember the case vividly. The police were called to a Batty Street residence, where a pregnant woman had been forced to ingest nitric acid. Her name was Miriam Angel. At the address, police found Lipski under a bed with acid burns inside his mouth. We later determined it was apparently attempted suicide, but there mustn't have been enough acid left over to complete the job, Lipski lived, and was taken into custody. Lipski was later tried and convicted of the crime of murder and was subsequently hung at Newgate Prison for that nasty bit of business." Baxter wiped his mouth and then shrugged his shoulders. "When Stride was killed it was determined that the man was shouting *Lipski*, as an anti-Semitic remark; therefore, it was ascertained that the man making the slur was obviously not a Jew. If you wait just a moment, I kept an article from the Illustrated Times, I will get it for you."

Confused, I was not sure what to think. On the one hand, there are three men in the immediate vicinity only a short time before Stride was murdered, one of whom was a Jew and the other two who seemingly were not, given the use of the anti-Semitic remark. If, the one man, was Michael Kidney who had knocked Stride to the ground, who was the third man?

"Here, you can read this, for yourself, Stone," Baxter said, handing over the newspaper. "Although it hardly gives more information than I have just related to the incident."

184

[Sic] Illustrated Times Saturday July twenty-third, 1887, In Whitechapel.

"At the Thames Police-Court, last Saturday, Israel Lipski, twenty-two, described as a walking stick maker, of 16, Batty-street, Commercial-road, St. George's-in-the-East, was again brought up, charged, on remand, with the willful murder of Miriam Angel, a married woman, on Tuesday, June 28, by pouring nitric acid down her throat. It will be remembered that the prisoner was discovered under the deceased's bed in an insensible condition, having evidently swallowed some of the same poison. Charles Moore said I was manager of an oil shop at 96, Blackchurch-lane. Witness was in the habit of supplying stick makers with nitric acid. On Tuesday, at nine o'clock in the morning a grown-up person purchased a penny worth of nitric acid, and the prisoner was the man. The house in Batty-street was about two hundred yards from witness's shop."

There was a little more but nothing of importance so, I stopped reading.

"You, more than, I can understand, Detective that since that awful business referred to as '*Bloody Sunday*,' which occurred in 87 at Trafalgar Square; your police department has been at their infernal best to keep from complicating social uprisings and conflicts to stop them from turning into bloodbaths in the streets of London. The arrest of *Lipski* is obviously still weighing heavily on the minds of East Londoners, not to mention the possible complicity of a member from this Workmen's Club. Although admittedly, most need no coercing when it comes to retaliating against the Jew for any reason, whatsoever. It seems the Jew could be blamed for any disaster, natural, or otherwise, and in most minds, it is entirely justified."

I listened and considered what Baxter said while scraping the bowl of his pipe with a knife.

"The Workmen's club is a front for a Yiddish Newspaper, isn't it?"

"Yes, but it's a lot more than that, John," Baxter answered, tapping his pipe into a waste paper basket. "The division of social classes in London has never been more sensitive an issue since the Trafalgar Square incident. Workers are forever marching from the east, to rally in the west in their fight for equality. To add to these difficulties, the Jews of London are becoming more vocal in their fight for their rights. They feel that they have already been pushed as far to the east of the city as they can go. The slums

185

and rookery of London's East End are their last frontier, so to speak. The *International Working Men's Educational Club*, as they like to call themselves, is an organization that houses both Democrats and anarchists. The club is attended by Jews, although frowned upon by most of the orthodox sect. Since the club's conception, it has been responsible for the planning of strikes, rallies, and marches that have filled our streets numerous times." Baxter paused long enough to light his pipe.

"What does all this have to do with Israel Schwartz?"

"It has nothing to do with the individual, but unfortunately, it has everything to do with the entire Semitic race that resides in the East End of this great city of London. After all the growing pains that London has suffered, we do not need another uprising Stone. Londoners are established in commerce and trade; and ready to move into a new century, we cannot allow another '*Bloody Sunday*' to occur. Something like that would only weaken our standing in the world economy, and worse might cause a civil war. Unfortunately, whether substantiated or not, some think the Jews in Whitechapel have something to do with this '*Jack the Ripper*.' Oh, you and I both know that is absolute rubbish, but it doesn't help that this last murder was committed next to a club frequented by an ethnic group which a large portion of London's population believes to be the cause of every social uprising that occurs in London."

"Who in their right mind would believe that, Wynne?"

I mocked, and then, at the same time knowing the limitless ways that prejudice can be made manifest, I could see why the Home Office had concealed the witness and the graffiti. I could also relate why politically the Yard's presence in Whitechapel was necessary.

"I think we can both agree, Stone, that it is likely the reason for your assignment here."

"I suppose so, Wynne," I answered.

I marveled at Baxter's ability to almost read my thoughts. Wynne's comment about my being stationed in Whitechapel, made me wonder how much the man knew or simply surmised about my being attached to his office.

"Prejudice is alive, and well even when we are so close to the twentieth century, Stone. But let us not leave out the maladjusted or even the envious. Believe it, or not John, there are more Jewish lenders in London than you can shake a stick at. There are also more than a few Londoners who hate the fact that the Jews are influential in commerce and would do anything to take what they have away from them," Baxter responded. "It has been the same story for centuries."

"Throw into the mix, this Goulston Street graffito near another brutal murder," I said, searching through the piles of papers on my desk.

"Yes, and the fearmongering of some right-wing political groups that have their own agendas in mind, and you have a recipe for a social uprising."

"*The Jews are the men that will be blamed for nothing.*"

I repeated the phrase that seemed to contain a double meaning that deliberately pointed at the Jews. It would seem that the Semitic peoples were used simply as a catalyst by some group to keep the civil unrest simmering in London's East End.

"I believe you have missed the argued about '*not*' in that sentence, Detective," Baxter interrupted. "*The Jews are the men that will not be blamed for nothing.* That is, according to Constable Long's notebook, even if the constable omitted the word '*not*' himself or he had been coached to do so before his testimony."

"Whether one leaves in the word '*not*' or takes it out, it is a curious phrase to write. Either way, the connotation seems to leave an accusation pointed at the Jew."

"Yes, and I believe, that was why it was wiped off Stone."

"Jews. As in, *J. U. W. E. S.*" I spelled the word out as it was written in Detective Halse's notes. "Why do you suppose Jews was spelled that way, Wynne?"

"It could be an ancient rendering, or perhaps it was deliberately misspelled, who knows," Baxter replied, shoving his pipe in the corner of his mouth and striking another match.

"Here it is on page three of Friday, October fifth's paper. Mr. S. F. Langham Coroner and Mr. Crawford a Solicitor, appearing on behalf of the police, "Crawford asks Constable Long:

[Sic] Was the writing on the wall, The Jews are not the men that will be blamed for nothing?
Constable Long: No. I believe the words are as I have stated. The Jews are the men that will not be blamed for nothing."

Coroner: Was the word Jew spelt Juwes?

Long: It may have been.

Coroner: Yet you did not state this. Did you make an entry of the words at the time?

Long: Yes, in my pocket book.

Coroner: Is it possible you have put the 'NOT' in the wrong place.

Long: It is possible but I don't think so.

Long recalled with his pocket book: The Jews are the men that will not be blamed for nothing

Coroner: Jews is spelt correctly.

Long: Yes, but the inspector remarked that the word Jew was spelt Juwes."

"Do you think Constable Long was prompted to omit that in his statement, Wynne?"

"Perhaps the constable is dealing with his own prejudice, but I am not judging the man, mind you, merely speculating?" Baxter answered.

"Or perhaps, Constable Long just wrote it down wrong."

Baxter shrugged and folded the paper.

"Why wasn't Superintendent Thomas Arnold questioned at the inquest, that is what I would like to know?" I asked the question realizing I already knew the answer.

"I am guessing for the same reason, Constable Long omitted the 'not,' in his first statement. Or, as you suggested, why wasn't the writing on the wall compared to the letter written to the newspaper? There are certain things that are best left to those in charge. If they make a mistake, it is better that they have to answer for their misdeeds, John."

"Be that as it may, Wynne, but if the citizens have the government watching over them, who is watching over the government to make sure they have the greater good in mind?"

"It is best to allow those in the upper echelon of government to figure out these things, John. Anyway, I believe that those in power thought the entire issue was best avoided. Perhaps, they were afraid that an in-depth investigation might point the finger too closely in the Jew's direction, and they wanted to nip it in the bud before it anything had a chance to start, in order to stop those that might take the law into their own hands."

"Like those who belong to the Whitechapel Vigilance Committee."

"Yes, Detective, like those that belong to the Vigilance Committee."
Baxter sighed, tired from working into the late hour. "Well, Detective, I
am all in, I would be glad to take this up again tomorrow," Baxter said,
glancing at his watch and then placing it back in his vest pocket.

I nodded at the coroner in agreement and watched as Baxter trod
slowly out of my office.

Chapter Ten

It was early the next morning when I and Baxter left our offices on
Whitechapel Road and hailed a cab. The cab stopped letting me out at
Duke Street, the beginning of the patrol route of Constable Edward
Watkins. The cab would continue on taking Wynne Baxter on to Mitre
Square, where the coroner would be waiting for me. The plan the two
concocted was to retrace Watkins' exact route on the night of Catharine
Eddowes' death. We would both record our times. I was to walk the
patrolmen's route, and compare the time it took Baxter to arrive at the
Square by cab. Referring to a diagram, I drew in my notebook of Watkins
route, I planned to mimic the movements of the patrolling constable.

As I walked, I thought about what I knew of the patrolmen. Watkins, a
constable for seventeen years. During which time, the man had displayed
the qualities of a reliable officer, never missing a day, arriving early before
his shift started, and maintaining a professional attitude on the job.

Constable Watkins started his patrol at Duke Street, and then proceeded
left on Heneage Lane, a right onto Bury Street, and then circled back onto
on Cree Church Lane. I took the same pace that I thought Watkins would
take as a patrolling constable and then took a left onto Leaden hall Street,
and then another onto Mitre Street. I then turned right into Mitre Square,
examining the square. Exiting the square, I then continued back up King
Street, and circled St. James Place, and then strode back out onto Duke
Street completing Watkins' route. Glancing at my watch, I estimated my
time to cover the route to be eleven minutes. Constable Watkins route

covered roughly three-quarters of a mile, I calculated that I had walked approximately two miles an hour.

Walking back into the square from the Mitre Street entrance, I looked from right to left. At this point, I stood underneath a gas lamp that was secured to the wall of the building occupied by Williams & Co. I took a moment to size up the location where Catharine Eddowes spent her last few minutes of her life, while Baxter climbed out of the cab behind me. I had taken the time to study a street map of the square, I assessed the area to be approximately eighty feet by eighty feet. Making up the square was the rear of the William & Co. building, two houses, one occupied by Constable Pearce, the other empty, the gated warehouse of Kearley & Tonge. On the opposite wall facing me was another Kearley and Tonge Co. building, and then next to it the Church Passage. On the right of the square from bottom to top, was the rear of the Horner & Co. building and a vacant yard that leads behind the Heydemann Co. Next, to it, there was an empty office building and two buildings belonging to the Taylor Frame Co., all of which faced Mitre Street.

Constable Pearce was off duty the night of the murder and was at home in his bed. According to the constable's testimony, it was possible to see the exact spot of the murder from the bedroom window of his flat. The constable told investigators that nothing unusual or out of the ordinary was heard coming from the square the night that Eddowes was killed. The house next door to Pearce's was unoccupied.

The Square was connected from Mitre Street to Cree church and Dukes Place. The patrols of Constables Harvey and Watkins were designed so that while Harvey was patrolling Mitre Street, Watkins was elsewhere and vice versa, allowing a twelve-minute overlap in patrols and yet during that time when both patrolmen were steadfast to their duties, a man entered Mitre Square with Catharine Eddowes unseen. '*Jack*' murdered Eddowes by slicing open her throat and doing unspeakable dissections to her body, taking with him pieces of her internal organs.

I stood for a moment, replaying the testimony of all those involved in the case over and over in my mind. The thoughts that the 'Ripper' left Eddowes dead in the darkened corner, with presumably, blood on his hands and clothing and not a soul witnessed the man come or go seemed too fantastic to be believed.

Taking out my notebook and a pencil from my pocket, I wrote down the times that were on record of the two constables patrolling in or around the area the night of the murder. I took special notice of the positions of the gas lamp to my left that hung from the wall on the Williams & Co. building. There was another in the Church Street Passage, and a free-standing lamp that stood in front of the Kearley and Tonge building that was a warehouse of sorts.

"Stride was killed at one o'clock," I spoke to Baxter; while reading from my notes.

"Give or take ten minutes," Baxter said, waiting patiently.

"Let's assume for argument's sake that Diemschutz did, in fact, interrupt the killer, at one o'clock Saturday night," I went on.

"Right!" Baxter answered.

"Foster, the architect, and planner of the Berner Street area testified that it was a twelve-minute walk from Berner Street to Mitre Square, an area of approximately three-quarters of a mile. I suppose, the killer could cut that time in half by running all the way," I concluded.

"Except, of course, 'Jack,' would not want to draw attention to himself so, if the chap hurried that time might be shaved to eight to ten minutes, let's say." Baxter interrupted.

"Alright, so, the killer could have shown up in the square at ten minutes past one on Saturday night, give or take a minute. Constable Watkins was last in the Square at half-past one. Constable Harvey was on his patrol which intersected with Watkins' route at Mitre Street, neither of whom reports seeing anyone or anything out of the usual. Constable Harvey was last in the vicinity of Mitre Street at thirty-seven minutes past one, Constable Watkins then discovers the body of Catharine Eddowes seven minutes later. That would give the killer anywhere from seven to thirty-four minutes, to slip into Mitre Square undetected and allow time to kill Catharine Eddowes and to dissect her body."

"Where do the two times come from, Detective?"

"That is seven minutes if Constable Harvey did, in fact, enter the square between the time Watkins entered, which doctors say was ample enough time for 'Jack' to kill Eddowes and dissect her body. Thirty-four minutes if Harvey did not enter the square at all. That gives 'Jack' another twenty-seven minutes to complete his dissection on Eddowes. Which, in my opinion, at least, sounds more probable."

191

"Dr. Frederick Brown had calculated in his testimony that the mutilation done on Eddowes' would have taken at least ten minutes to complete," Baxter retorted.

"From a doctor's point of view, that time may seem realistic Wynne. However, it seems highly unlikely, to suggest that a layman could dissect a body in seven minutes, and make his escape undetected."

I recalled the mutilated body of Eddowes lying in the mortuary the first day of the inquest on October the fourth. In my mind, there was nothing about the dissection of the body that would make me believe that the killer could complete all that was done to his victim in just seven minutes and then escape without being noticed.

"So, what are you getting at Detective," Baxter said impatiently. "Are you quibbling over two or three minutes?"

"Wynne, if the killer had left Dutfield's Yard at one sharp, that would put him in Mitre Square by let's assume twelve minutes past. That time is verified by Catharine Eddowes' release from the Bishop Street station and the approximate time it would take her to walk here after being released from goal. That would mean the killer had to be lying in wait somewhere here for four or five minutes, and yet both Watkins and Harvey reported seeing no one."

"You forget, Detective, that Constable Harvey arrived back at the square twenty-three minutes to two in the morning. Factor that in, and then, we are back to the seven to nine-minute margin for the killer to commit the crime." Baxter spoke emphatically and then clamped his unlit pipe between his teeth.

"I haven't been remiss, Wynne, because I don't think Constable Harvey was in the Square at twenty-three minutes to two."

"What are you basing this assumption on, Detective?" Baxter spoke up defiantly.

Ignoring Baxter for a moment, I returned to my notes, glancing at the notations one more time, I then put the notebook and pencil back into my pocket. Walking over to the south-west corner of the square where Eddowes body was found, I could see the remnants of the dark stain that remained where the body had been laid. Not the amount of blood that I would have expected to find at a crime scene where the body had suffered the kinds of wounds that Catharine Eddowes had suffered.

"I would have thought there would have been more blood on the ground," I said, continuing without waiting for a response from the coroner.

"With all due respect, Detective?" Baxter shouted. "What tangent are you off on now?"

My plan when I had left the office that morning was to try and find some hole in the testimony given by Constable Watkins or the that given by Constable Harvey, for that matter. In my calculations, the time of the event and the constable's patrols all seemed too neat and tidy. I went over the times again in hopes to make some sense of the time '*Jack*' arrived at Mitre Square, killed Eddowes, and then escaped unseen by Constables Watkins, Harvey, and Long. All three constables were in the vicinity of the murder that night, and no one saw anyone who looked suspicious, including Constable Long, on whose patrol the bloodied piece of Eddowes' apron was found. The piece of apron marked the Duke Street exit as the route the killer used for his escape. Taking out my watch, I handed it to Baxter.

"Bear with me for a moment, Wynne," I said, unbuttoning my jacket. "My theory is that the killer most likely held Eddowes from behind."

I took my time and I began to talk my way through the crime whilst estimating the time each action might take to complete.

"Stone, what the devil are you doing? Baxter shouted.

"I am trying to recreate the killer's steps, keep your eye on the watch," I answered while continuing my movements. "Eddowes was found on her back, her clothes rifled up about her waist and her palms facing outwards. The victim's garments were not cut, torn, or even removed roughly by the killer. In taking that kind of care '*Jack*' displayed a coolness paralleled only by someone who has killed before. Not only that, but this man was comfortable in his abilities and relaxed despite the knowledge that constables were patrolling all around him. Eddowes' face was terribly disfigured; including slices that had been made to her eyelids."

I narrated my macabre play for Baxter, as I recreated the killer's movements. As I related, my re-enactment of the crime, my thoughts returned to the day of the inquest of Catharine Eddowes. When it came time for the jury to view the body, I had stood in the corner of the room and waited for the jury to pass by exiting the room, before I was allowed to view the body. With the mortuary attendant and the coroner present, I examined Catharine Eddowes' wounds more closely. Even with the autopsy already completed, the jagged cut to the neck and the slices to the face established that the woman was a '*Jack the Ripper*' victim. I remembered thinking at the time that I was grateful that the poor creature had not been alive during those horrific moments when the killer had sliced at her face and performed the other cuts to her body.

Dr. Frederick, Gordon Brown arrived just after two in the morning and estimated the time of death to be thirty to forty minutes previous to his arrival. Aside from the neck wound which had taken Eddowes' life; Dr. Brown told the jury that all the other wounds had been done post mortem.

Continuing on in my narration, "Jack rolled his victim onto her back and then proceeded to cut eyelids, nose cheeks, and jaw. Moving on his knees perhaps straddling the body, he next started to unbutton both bodices as the killer had done to remove the victim's clothing, and then performed his surgery and rolled the victim over on her right side, and cut out the right kidney."

"How much time has passed, Wynne," I asked, looking up at the coroner?

"Your little drama has taken you all of six minutes," Baxter answered smugly.

"Six minutes," I shouted, astonished at how little time that my narration had taken.

"Detective, this proves nothing, in fact, this silly re-enactment of yours if anything proves, that seven to nine minutes was probably more than enough time for the killer to dissect his victim, especially if the man had some kind of experience in surgery," Baxter said, none too sympathetically.

"That is my point exactly, Wynne. Five minutes for our killer, who doctors adamantly testified, did not have the same knowledge that a surgeon would possess, to slash a woman's throat, mutilate her face and body, and then proceed to cut out two of her organs. I was simply narrating his movements having no idea where to look inside a body, let alone how to proceed in extracting human organs, and my re-enactment of the crime as you so aptly called it, took me six minutes," I countered; satisfied that I had finally gotten my point across. "The killer even took the time to undo the buttons of the woman's dress and did it, in the dark, knowing that two patrolling officers were in the vicinity Wynne."

"So, what do you propose Stone, that the killer with a skilled hand would need a full ten minutes to kill Eddowes and leave undetected?" Baxter asked.

Looking around the Square, I ignored Baxter while turning my attention to the three exits.

"I believe the Duke Street exit of Mitre Square is the only plausible, and quickest way for the '*Ripper*' to make good his escape."

"Why, Detective, there are three the wretch could choose from?"

"Yes, Wynne, but I think '*Jack*' took Duke Street, crossing Houndsditch, going up Gravel Lane, and then crossing Middlesex Street, to Goulston where Constable Long found the bloodied piece of apron torn from our victim's clothing. It is the only route that fits with the timing of our patrolling constables."

"That would fit with Sir Henry Smith's thoughts, that this man was returning back to Whitechapel, however, Detective that does not sit well in the pit of my stomach."

Walking over to the only free-standing lamp in the Square, I remembered the testimony of Constable Richard Pearce. Pearce said there was a clear line of sight into the Square from his bedroom window.

"Wynne do you remember Constable Pearce's testimony," I asked looking over at Baxter, who was pacing back and forth.

"Yes, the off-duty constable who lives beside Williams & Co. What of it?" Baxter answered, pointing to the rear of the house.

"Pearce testified being able to see into the Square from his bedroom window, though, it was poorly lit."

"Yes, I believe that was what the man said," Baxter answered, looking around for another lamp post in the vicinity.

"There is a lamp attached to the wall on the Williams & Co building, and yet Pearce said the Square was poorly lit."

Not waiting for Baxter to respond, I walked across the Square to the Church Street Passage that was at the opposite end of the Mitre Street opening. Here, well inside the passage was another wall lamp, although this lamp would have primarily lit the passage leading into the Square. Turning, I walked from Church Passage to stand under the only free-standing lamp in Mitre Square that stood in the corner between the two Kearley and Tonge buildings and the St. James Passage. Turning on my heel, I started to count paces from the lamp post across to where Catharine Eddowes' body was found.

"What the devil are you doing now, Stone?" Baxter grumbled.

"This is the only lamp post," I said, pointing to the post that stood near the St. James Passage. "In the Square and it wasn't working up to snuff. I wonder why Watkins did not inform his sergeant of the watch that a defective lamp needed to be fixed."

"By Jove, you are onto something there, Detective; it has been mandated since this madness began, that all constables are to note poorly working or broken lamps in the area of their patrol immediately on their return to the station," Baxter said, walking over to the lamp post that Stone stood near.

"So, why didn't Watkins report it, Wynne."

"Why didn't Constable Harvey report that the lamp was not working, for that matter, Detective?" Baxter said.

I knew from several conversations in the past, that Baxter hated any type of incompetence in city officials.

"Perhaps neither constable noticed it."

I stood unmoving for a moment remembering the mutilation done to the victim's body again, imagining the amount of blood that must have issued from the body. I could not rest easy with the thoughts that the murderer would have to have some blood somewhere on his clothes and hands, and if so, the killer would have been noticed after leaving the Square.

"What are you thinking now, Detective?" Baxter asked.

"I was just remembering some gossip I heard about Sir Henry Smith on the night of this crime," I mused.

"What is it, Stone, you have my attention," Baxter said, excitedly rubbing his hands together in mock pleasure.

"After taking charge of the scene, Sir Henry retraced; the supposed, steps of the murderer from Mitre Square. After finding Constable Long with the piece of an apron and the graffito on the wall, his detectives found a sink on Dorset Street with the traces of blood in the basin. It was assumed the killer used the basin to wash Eddowes blood from his hands."

"How could they be sure that it was Eddowes' blood?" Baxter queried.

"It was believed by City Police, that the killer had cut away a piece of Eddowes apron in the attempt to clean some of the blood from his hands, judging by the piece of the apron that was found a third of a mile from

Mitre Square. Sir Henry Smith reasoned that if '*Jack*' was headed in that direction, the man must be from the East End, hence the reason for the Metropolitan Police Department's involvement."

"I say bollocks to that Stone. This killer was on the run," Baxter huffed. "Smith could not possibly know where the killer was headed. It is entirely possible that the man went that way to throw constables off his trail"

Walking away from where Baxter stood, I returned to where Eddowes' body was found, near a rounded curb behind Taylor & Co. I estimated the distance to be roughly one hundred steps. Given that the lamp that hung on the Williams & Co wall would illuminate Mitre Street and the lamp that hung at Church Passage was more than eighty feet away, I could see why the '*Ripper*' chose that corner of the Square. I looked down to where the body was laid, the stain was dark and unmoving; the blood had flowed away from the body to the back corner of the converging buildings where a wooden paling had been erected to separate the back of the buildings.

"It is about one hundred paces from that lamp where you are standing Wynne, to where Eddowes' body was found and the only free-standing lamp post in the Square was apparently not working properly. This is where Eddowes was murdered, and given the distance from the wall lamps and the street lamp where you are Wynne, it certainly would have made this the darkest corner in the Square."

Turning, I looked at the wooden paling that stood on a two-foot-high brick wall. The paling held up a section of covered roof attached to the rear of the Horner and Son building. Next to it, I could see a vacant yard that skirted behind two other buildings that led up to the Heydemann Co. building.

"Take a look at this, Wynne," I said, watching my friend waddle towards me.

"What am I looking at, John," Baxter asked, seeing nothing unusual.

"This vacant yard Wynne. I suppose the killer could have stood here waiting for Eddowes. Perhaps during that time, our killer saw Watkins look into the square and continue on patrol. Our man is then assured that another fourteen minutes were at his disposal to finish the mutilation of the body then escape up the Duke Street passageway. Doctor Frederick Gordon Brown testified that this killer could be a man who had knowledge of anatomy," I said, reaching into my coat pocket for my notebook. "*Brown said, 'He must have had a good deal of knowledge as to the position of the abdominal organs, and the way to remove them.*' The doctor also testified; fourteen minutes was what the killer would need to make good his escape." I closed my notebook and looked at the coroner.

"You are basing your assumptions on unproven hypothesis, Detective. There is no proof that Watkins merely glanced into the square, Detective, and did not enter doing a complete sweep of the area. Plus, what about the chance passer-by Stone," Baxter commented. "How could a man walking down the street presumably with blood on his clothes and hands, not be seen. It confounds me to no good end how the killer left the Square without being noticed. London is a city that does not sleep, there are plenty of shift workers and twelve hundred other women like Eddowes walking around. I can't for the life of me figure out how this killer keeps disappearing into thin air?"

"He could disappear if there was a cab close by," I commented. "it would be even easier if our man had a driver and a carriage of his own. That could be the third man that Schwartz saw."

"That is a lot of speculation, Stone."

"There has to be something that were missing or discounting, Wynne. Maybe, the '*Ripper*' is familiar with the constables' nightly patrols, otherwise, how does the killer make his escape without being seen by either one or the other patrolling constables? Barring interruption and proceeding as one who has knowledge of the human anatomy, all the while working in the dark, you cannot dissuade me from thinking that the killer needed at least fourteen minutes to accomplish what was done to the corpse."

"Alright, Stone, but Doctor Brown said that this knowledge of anatomy could come from someone such as a butcher who was used to cutting up animals. The doctor also testified, correct me if I am wrong, that in his opinion five minutes would be all someone with that type of knowledge would need to do what was done to Catharine Eddowes," Baxter retorted.

"Yes, Wynne, the doctor did say that, but is it a doctor or a butcher who is looking for the same pieces of female anatomy that are missing from our murdered women?"

The silence allowed me to resume my thoughts while leaving the coroner to ruminate over what I had said. The square was quiet with no passerby. I stood in the corner where presumably, the killer stood in the dark perhaps waiting for Eddowes to meet him.

"Alright Wynne, let us, assume for now, that five minutes is enough for an experienced hand to kill Eddowes then cut up the body to disguise the true reasons for his crime. That left five minutes for the 'Ripper' to make his getaway. How does he exit the square and not be seen by one or the other patrolling constables?"

"What are you thinking, John?" Baxter asked.

"There are only two logical scenarios, Wynne."

"Which are, what?"

"One or both of the constables stopped somewhere on their patrol and didn't bother to enter the square until Watkin's found the body. That would give the killer thirty minutes or more to kill Eddowes and dissect the body."

"We had better tread lightly, Detective, if we are going to accuse one of your brethren of something like this, we would have the entire department on our heads!"

Baxter made a valid point, and I gave the suggestion careful consideration.

"Listen to this for a moment, Wynne," I said, digging through my pocket retrieving my notebook. "This is what I have deduced. Constable Long testified at the inquest on October the eleventh that he was at Goulston Street at twenty minutes past two on his usual patrol. Detective, Constable Halse at that time, was searching for the killer of Catharine Eddowes. Halse was also in the same area, and yet there is no report of the two meeting. It was Halse who found Constable Long standing where the graffito was written on the wall. What if Constable Long had stopped somewhere and did not continue his patrol until hearing the blast of Watkins' whistle. It would explain the disappearance of the culprit."

"What do you mean, John?"

"Well, when Halse found Long, the detective would assume that 'Jack' did not run past the constable, so Halse would quit his search in that area. Halse would have no reason to think that Long had been somewhere other than on patrol, would he?"

"No, I suppose not, but that is a stretch, Stone," Baxter rationalized. "We have no proof nor any way of knowing whether Long was performing his duty diligently or not."

"Be that as it may, Wynne," I commented. "It is common knowledge that most constables round their patrol times to the nearest five minutes, something that occurs only if an incident prompts them to make a report; otherwise, we really have no idea where each constable was at any given time unless their movements can be confirmed by another constable."

"If the police are indeed accustomed to making this time adjustment you speak of, Stone and Watkins and Harvey did add another five minutes to their time of arrival at Mitre Square that would still only give the killer another five minutes to perpetrate his crime against Eddowes," Baxter stated his point.

"Yes, Wynne, but another five minutes for our killer to do what the doctors are testifying took only five to ten minutes to perform. Having said that, Wynne, what if Constable Long was not at Goulston Street at twenty minutes past two?"

"Alright, what if the man wasn't?" Baxter answered.

"What if Constable Harvey had gotten into the habit of not entering Mitre Square at all, but instead walked right down Duke Street knowing full well Watkins was on the job. Watkins' fourteen or fifteen-minute absence from the Square would allow the killer an escape route from the scene of the crime. In addition to the absence of Constable Long that would allow the killer to escape right up Goulston Street unmolested."

"That is a lot of if's Detective," Baxter said, pulling pipe and tobacco pouch from his coat pockets. "How do you know that Constable Long was not where the man was supposed to be at twenty minutes past two, and what was the purpose of the killer writing the graffito at all?" Baxter asked inquisitively.

"Aside from Detective Halse, reporting that he did not see Constable Long anywhere while searching the Goulston Street area for Catharine Eddowes killer you mean," I retorted, looking at Baxter, waiting for a response.

"Yes, I suppose that does look rather suspicious, doesn't it," Baxter commented. "It is still, a lot of supposition though, and if what you surmise is true, then it would be an example of gross incompetence."

"If that is not the case, Wynne, the patrol times of the constables and the doctor's time of death would place the killer in the Square doing his worst to Eddowes right under one or both constable's noses. Either way, it does not bode well for our patrolmen."

"I don't know what I find more disturbing, Detective," Baxter said, packing his pipe. "Knowing our constables are doing such a slack job of it or knowing this blackheart is the most daring criminal in all London's history. It would take nerves of steel for someone to do what was done to this woman knowing full well a constable could catch him at any minute."

"I am sorry, Wynne, but I can't see it any other way," I apologized. "Either Constable Watkins or Harvey or both did not enter this Square at their scheduled time, or Dr. Brown's time of death of half-past one or, at the most, twenty past one in the morning is incorrect."

"What about this graffito," Baxter asked, taking his pipe from his mouth. "A man running from a crime generally doesn't stop to write a jest of some kind to get the police to look the other way?"

"As for the graffito, I am not sure that the killer wrote it. Having said that though, perhaps 'Jack' merely dropped the piece of apron to keep the police guessing and suspicion drawn away from where it should be. We have already discussed; how every time some transgression is committed in the East End, the Jew is looked upon as being the architect."

"That would make this killer quite diabolical, wouldn't it?"

"As well as cunning, Wynne."

"I wouldn't give this maniac, too much credit Detective," Baxter retorted.

"Perhaps not Wynne, but what would you call a man who has murdered at least five women that we know about, killing two in one night, a task, I might add, that must have taken planning, and still remain at large from police custody?"

When Baxter did not reply, I decided to allow the coroner to be alone with his own thoughts. Modus Operandi of all four women who were killed much in the same way, were all killed by one killer. The only other possibility that made sense was that there could be another killer mimicking the previous crimes to place police on the trail of one killer, the much-publicized 'Jack the Ripper.' Sitting on a nearby bench, I started to go over each of the crimes perpetrated on the four prostitutes.

"Tabram was stabbed thirty-nine times, her throat wasn't slashed," I said, thinking out loud. "The Guardsman, she was last seen with had opportunity and was able to produce a weapon, that would produce marks similar to those that the murder weapon made, howbeit, not one covered in blood. There is no possibility that the killer could escape without blood on his clothes or arms given the number of stab wounds in the victim's body. And yet nobody saw or heard anything out of the ordinary. Elizabeth

Stride, had her throat slashed, whether the killer was interrupted or not, the killer still had to have previous knowledge of both victims to go from Dutfield's Yard to Mitre Square in the short time allotted and murder the two women and escape. Nichols was found in a backyard where there was no evidence of a struggle, with blood pooling around the back of her neck, signifying a possibility that she was killed somewhere close by then placed on the ground where she was found. Officers patrolling the street saw nothing and reported nothing suspicious. There were also discrepancies in the constables patrolling times that have been put into question time after time. Andrew Cross denied seeing Constable John Neil in the area; however, Neil proclaimed to be never further than Bakers Row away the night that Nicholls was killed. There was not a drop of blood found on Eddowes dress; her throat slashed her body mutilated. There is another plausible explanation here Wynne…"

Looking over at Baxter, I hesitated to finish the thought knowing how Baxter felt about my theory that the killer was a doctor.

"What other explanation could there be, Detective?" Baxter said sheepishly.

"There is the possibility that this killer is using a carriage, allowing him the freedom and the ability to move after the murders are committed."

"The only trouble with this scenario that you have concocted Stone is how a carriage could move about in an impoverished area like Whitechapel in the middle of the night, and have its movements go unnoticed," Baxter asked.

"A doctor could Wynne; there are countless emergencies in the night that would warrant a doctor to move about unquestioned."

"I am not sure which one of your theories, I like better, Stone," Baxter answered. "The thoughts that our constables are allowing this fiend to carve up these poor creatures right under their noses or the fact that there is some deranged physician out there doing his worst to the prostitutes of Whitechapel and going about it without a care," Baxter added.

Chapter Eleven

Back at Mitre Square later that night, I confronted Police Constable Watkins on his patrol. After I introduced myself, I immediately detected a hint of uneasiness with the constable.

"You can stand at ease, Constable," I said.

"No, thank you, Sir. If you don't mind, could you tell me what this is all about?" Watkins said, remaining at attention.

"Just some routine questions dealing with your involvement in the Eddowes investigation," I answered, hoping to reassure Watkins' that there was nothing formal about my interest. However, at the same time, I noticed the constable's jaw tighten in response to what I had said.

"Begging your pardon, Sir, but all that information is in my report," Watkins answered.

"Do you have a problem answering my questions, Constable?" I asked, feeling my temper and my blood pressure start to rise.

"No, Sir, no problem. I would like to request that if you have any questions for me that you would ask them while my immediate supervisor is present. Is that everything, Sir?" Watkins said, replacing his helmet back on top of his head.

"Yes, that will be everything, for now, Constable."

Frustrated by the incident, I watched Watkins continue on his beat, and not for the first time during my investigation into the murders, I felt like, I was getting absolutely nowhere. My dealings with the coroners and doctors were far more productive than with the Metropolitan Police. Leaving the square, I returned to my office. Behind my desk, I sat wondering if Watkins had something to hide. It was most unlikely, the constable's demeanor, and the lack of respect, that irked me, they were; however, not the traits, I would have detected from someone guilty of dereliction of duty. It was likely that P.C. Long had complained about being questioned while on duty. Subsequently, the station had been told not to answer any questions without their immediate supervisor present. If the truth was known, I had no right to question anyone, suspect or constable, and the thought made me wonder if word of my resignation had been found out.

From day one, I had expected that there might be some opposition. I had heard subtle comments behind my back, I was sure, even some had suspicions that I was an informer. Being a police officer, I could well understand their feelings. Out on patrol night after night was no picnic, dealing with people who had little or no respect for the law, let alone those who had the good fortune of enforcing it. The job was demanding and could make even the most dedicated officers resentful for having their performance scrutinized.

Taking out the copies, I had of the police reports on all four women, I began to study them.

Catherine Eddowes, a.k.a., Kate Conway, and Kate Kelly. Age 46, found murdered in the south corner of Mitre Square. Cause of death, throat cut, her body mutilated, victim's left kidney, and part of the womb missing.

Residence: Cooney's Common Lodging House, 55 Flower and Dean Street, Spitalfields.

Investigator: Body found by Police Constable Edward Watkins at 1:44 a.m., Inspector Collard arrived from Bishopgate St. Police Station at 2:03 am. Murder Investigation led by Chief Inspector Donald Swanson. City of London jurisdiction investigation led by Detective Inspector James McWilliam, London Police.

Coroner: Mr. S. F. Langham City of London.

"Excuse me, if you please, Detective Stone?"

"Yes," I said, looking up, finding Dr. Phillips standing in the doorway of my office. "Come in, Doctor."

I had met Doctor Phillips for the first time at the Chapman inquest and found the man thorough if not, a little curt. I studied George Bagster Phillips as the doctor entered my office. Philips was a portly man; I would guess in his fifties by the greying at his temples. The doctor wore a full set of whiskers that traveled down the jawline leaving the chin and upper lip clean-shaven. I had been introduced to the doctor by Wynne Baxter, who found the doctor's immensely polite manner somewhat grating.

"Detective Stone, I do hope that I am not intruding, I knocked but there was no answer?"

"Not at all, I was just reviewing police files, please come in doctor."

"At our last meeting, you told me that at my earliest convenience, you had some questions that you wanted to ask me?"

Although, I knew of Baxter's personal feelings towards the doctor, I found the doctor's candor somewhat refreshing.

"Yes but . . ." I said, but didn't get a chance to finish.

"If you are not available; I do understand, Detective?" Phillips apologized.

"No, no, please come in Doctor Phillips," I replied, gesturing toward the chair in front of my desk.

"I have been going over the Stride and Eddowes murder cases, Doctor. I would like to ask you some questions and perhaps get your medical opinion about a theory of mine, if you don't mind?"

Waiting for the doctor to be seated in the chair across from me, I continued.

"I am sure you are quite familiar with each of the cases after conducting the Stride autopsy and testifying at the inquest. I believe that you were also asked by Dr. Brown to look in on the Eddowes autopsy?"

"Yes, Detective, I am quite familiar with both cases."

I acknowledged the Doctor, watching the man straightened his lapels on his jacket making himself comfortable.

"Being a police surgeon, I have many files placed on my desk; however, these Whitechapel murders are somewhat of a priority when my services are required," Phillips answered, stuffily.

"Doctor at the inquest you, stated to the coroner that," I paused as I reached for the sheet of paper I required on my desk. "Here it is, allow me to refresh your memory. You said, '*I think the mode in which they were extracted did show some anatomical knowledge.*' Is that correct, Doctor?"

"Yes," Phillips replied.

"You, also testified Doctor, if you would please allow me to continue reading your testimony," I said, reaching for another sheet from a file. [Sic] *"I think I can guide you by saying that I myself could not have performed all the injuries I saw on that woman, and affect them, even without a struggle, under a quarter of an hour. If I had done it in a deliberate way, such as would fall to the duties of a surgeon, it would probably have taken me the best part of an hour. The whole inference seems to me that the operation was performed to enable the perpetrator to obtain possession of these parts of the body.*"

"Yes, that sounds like my testimony, Detective, what is it, you would like to know pray tell that my testimony does not clarify?" Doctor Phillips responded.

"If you would be patient with me, Doctor, I will explain," I responded, reaching for another file. "John Davies discovered Annie Chapman's body at six in the morning. John Richardson was at the address at quarter to five and saw nothing out of the ordinary," I paused to rummage through the papers on my desk.

"I am sorry, Detective, but what is the question?" Phillips interrupted.

"Please, if you will allow me, Doctor, I just want to make sure my facts are correct. I estimate that the killer had indeed one hour and fifteen minutes to complete the dissection performed on Chapman. In your testimony, you said it would take you, a practiced skilled surgeon, at least an hour to perform these exact procedures."

"Yes, Detective, however, I said it would take me that long to perform those exact procedures," Dr. Phillips answered.

"Meaning that a skilled hand with a scalpel would have made neater cuts. Is that what you meant, Doctor?" I asked the question waiting for an answer with a raised eyebrow.

"Yes, I suppose so, Detective, I still don't see your point?" Phillips persisted.

"My point, Doctor is just this. If in fact 'Jack' needed an hour and fifteen minutes to perform his dissection. I think it only stands to reason that this man is of your profession and not someone with a little anatomical knowledge to use your diction," I stated.

I waited for a moment, watching Phillips who said nothing in response, but merely waited for me to finish.

"You also testified that Chapman was dead at least two hours if not longer, is that correct?" I said, looking at Phillips eager for his response.

"That is what I stated, Detective," Phillips responded.

"If that is the case, how do you account for the time between John Richardson inspecting the cellar door and finding that it was locked at quarter to five in the morning and finding nothing out of the usual? Then an hour and fifteen minutes later, John Davies found the body of Annie

Chapman. You established that Chapman had been dead for about two hours perhaps longer."

My questions for the doctor were all geared toward the time of death. My hope was to ascertain how precise medical techniques were in the process of measuring the time of death at the scene of a homicide.

"I estimated the Algor mortis ....," Phillips answered.

"Algor mortis Doctor Phillips," I interrupted, could you explain how this determines time of death for me please.

"Certainly, body temperature is 98.4 degrees, Detective. Algor mortis is the cooling of body temperature after a person is deceased," Phillips answered. "The body cools in summer .75 degrees every hour, in winter, 1.5 degrees every hour, we have been using this calculation since the time of the ancient Greeks."

"What technique do you use at the crime scene, Doctor to confirm this calculation?"

"Newton's Law of cooling states that the rate of cooling of a body is determined by the difference between the temperature of the body and that of its environment. Nysten's Law, established in 1811, states that rigidity travels downward beginning with the face, and then the neck, trunk and arms, and finally to the lower limbs. Using these two guidelines, this scale was established. *Warm and not stiff: not dead more than a couple of hours. Warm and stiff; the body is dead between a couple of hours and a half-day. Cold and stiff; the body is dead between a half-day and two days. Cold and not stiff; dead for more than two days.*"

"So, by using this method of calculating the time of death, it is far from pinpoint accurate?"

"Perhaps not as precise as we would like, but I assure you, Detective, it is accurate within fifteen minutes to an hour."

"What were your findings at the Chapman crime scene?"

"In Annie Chapman's case, she hadn't been dead more than a couple of hours. In respect to Elizabeth Stride, the body and the face were warm, while the hands were cold. After determining the ambient temperature, I calculated that death had occurred between the time that I arrived on the scene and a couple of hours before," Phillips summed up.

"Doctor Frederick Brown testified at the Eddowes' inquest," I replied, continuing to look through the inquest minutes. "That on Thursday, October fourth, there was only blood under the neck of the deceased and on the pavement where she was found. There was no blood found anywhere on the front of Eddowes` clothes."

"Detective, I am not sure that I can make a qualified statement in that case, I was the attending surgeon at the post mortem, not at the crime scene," Phillips explained.

"Yes, I know Doctor, however, I am interested in your professional medical opinion," I said, hoping to get some answers to questions that had been bothering me. "When a throat is cut, there is a tremendous amount of blood loss," I continued.

"Why yes, especially if the carotid artery is cut as it is in these cases," Phillips responded.

"The artery cut in at least four of the women murdered here in Whitechapel?"

"Why yes, of course."

"If the carotid is cut, Doctor Phillips, I am assuming that there should be a tremendous amount of spray like it was under pressure?"

"Yes, that is exactly right," Phillips answered.

"No blood spray on the pavement and none on the front of the clothes; I think it possible that she may have been killed somewhere other than where the body was found."

"Yes, I suppose that is possible, Detective, but if you will excuse me for saying, I am not a detective, I am a surgeon. I am not sure, how I can be of any further assistance to you in this matter, Sir?"

"Please bear with me another moment, Doctor," I replied, hoping to get the answers I looked for. "When a person dies, does that same blood stay under pressure, and would it spray like it would if a person is alive?"

"After death, the body will show some signs of blood leaking from a wound depending on the area being cut open, but generally a post mortem wound does not bleed, there is no pressure of blood running through the body because the heart has stopped beating," Phillips answered. "Therefore, blood pools in the body."

"What if a person was unconscious, would that affect the blood pressure, Doctor Phillips?" I asked, getting up from my chair and walking around to the front of the desk and sitting on the edge.

"The blood pressure would be somewhat lower, but it would still be present. Blood spray is significantly increased when a major artery is cut," Phillips answered.

"Like the carotid," I queried, pointing to the side of my neck where the artery was located.

"Yes, Detective, the carotid artery is the artery that pumps blood into the brain. There is a tremendous amount of blood flow due to the arteries size," Phillips replied.

"Is it possible, Doctor, if someone could place an arm or a silk scarf like the one Elizabeth Stride wore, tight enough to prevent her from screaming and to render her unconscious?" I asked, waiting for an answer.

"Why yes, Detective, if someone knew where to apply enough pressure for an extended period, then the victim would eventually blackout," Phillips answered.

"Doctor, I have seen many fatalities, and I can identify a strangled victim. The telltale sign of which is a tremendous amount of bruising on the neck. Is it possible to do what I previously described without leaving the bruising that," I paused, thinking about my next statement? "A victim might have if they were strangled by hands or a rope?"

I waited with anticipation, for the first time in months, I began to see a clearer picture of the killer that had started to form from the beginning of my investigation. All that needed to be added was the killer's face.

"I suppose that a person would be able to render someone unconscious if they had some knowledge of the arteries and their position on the neck, but there would still be some noticeable bruising," Phillips answered.

"You mean that a person would have to have knowledge of the artery, its function, and location. If all of these criteria were met, there still would be bruising; though minimal."

"Yes, of course, but even if the killer were knowledgeable in the function of these arteries, during the intercourse of the crime, bruising would be prominent, given the nature of the act itself."

"Doctor, would that bruising be here under the line of the jaw, of the victim?" I pointed along the side of my jaw where at least three victims had signs of bruising.

Doctor Phillips nodded in response.

I understood why the Doctor might be reluctant to speak about; what I suspected they were both were thinking. It would be difficult for a doctor to imagine that one of his fellows who had taken the Hippocratic Oath and had become a practitioner of medicine could turn out to be a deviant. That 'Jack the Ripper' could possibly be a man of the medical profession was hard for even me to stomach. The papers had hinted about it, my friend, the coroner, had implied it in his questions at the inquests of the dead women, but none had as of yet stated that the man who was killing women in Whitechapel was a practitioner. As happy as I was to finally get answers to questions that had caused many sleepless nights for me, the fact was, that I too found the knowledge disturbing. No one wanted to think that a man sworn to preserve life, could be a murderer. I could only sympathize with Dr. Phillips and treat the man and his profession with respect.

"If I was to hazard a guess doctor," I said, getting up from the desk. "I should think that the killer places enough pressure on the sides of the neck to accomplish this, but very different from the rough hands of a man under the throes of uncontrollable anger, so as not to leave a large amount of bruising on the tender flesh. Our man would also have to be someone powerful, and confident enough to be able to approach from behind and place his hands on his victim in the heat of passion without alerting her and so that she would, at least at the beginning, be a willing participant," I continued, describing what my thoughts were on how the killer approached his victims.

"I suppose that is understandable, Detective," Phillips replied.

"Doctor Frederick Gordon Brown arrived at the scene where Catharine Eddowes was killed at 2:20 am. The doctor testified that Eddowes' throat was cut straight across, the body was mutilated, still quite warm, and no rigor mortis was detected. Dr. Brown estimated that Eddowes was killed at approximately 1:40 am. There was no blood found on the front of the victim's clothes," I referred directly from the inquest report.

"I must stress again, Detective, that I was only involved in a small part of the autopsy," Phillips repeated.

"Yes, I know, Doctor, if you would be patient and allow me to explain," I said, looking up at the doctor making my thoughts known for the first time. "I have a theory on how the women were murdered, would you humor me for a minute?"

"As you wish, Sir."

"I think the 'Ripper' gets familiar with each of the women that I kills."

"Familiar, Detective," Phillips, interrupted. "In what way?"

"Being prostitutes," I continued. "I believe 'Jack' studies each of the women before approaching them. It is my opinion that this man then establishes a relationship, if not a friendship with the women for a brief time. Plying them with alcohol, meals, what have you, and then, when they are comfortable in his presence that is when the killer strikes?"

"Do you mean that this man perhaps knows these women, or are you inferring that this killer is well known in the community?" Phillips asked.

"No, not known, as in this man resides in the area where these women live. I think our killer travels among them, learning their habits and friendships. It is quite possible that 'Jack' hand-picks one special woman in his travels. I don't believe that our man engages them at first, if at all."

"Why do you assume that?"

"I believe the killer seeks one thing, I doubt that there is any attraction at all except to gain the means to an end, if there was, why mutilate their bodies," I explained. "The cuts on the face would indicate that our man despises these women, for who or what they are."

"Am I, to believe that this killer seeks out specific victims?"

"Of that, I am certain, what characteristics these women have that draws him to his victims, I am still working on."

"And why do you think this man just chooses prostitutes for his victims, Detective?"

"Perhaps our killer is a social outcast," I answered. "This man could be the shy type; who has trouble talking to women or perhaps a physical defect makes him seek women in the dark corners of the slums of Whitechapel. It is quite conceivable that our man comes to London's East to seek out what cannot be found elsewhere. 'Jack' may watch the individual of his choice for days, and then attempts to befriend her, all the while making her feel comfortable around him."

"Detective, when you talk about this 'Jack' you conjure up images of a Quasimodo-type in a storybook!" Phillips stated.

I continued knowing that I had the police surgeon's attention.

"Maybe you are right, Doctor, perhaps our killer is a type of outcast. A recluse of sorts, or perhaps his ailment is not physical; it could be that the killer is maladjusted in some other way. There is no telling what creates a monster like 'Jack,' or what motivates him."

"If you are right, Detective, and this madman does get friendly with each woman, what happens next to lead to such a horrific end for the victim?" Phillips asked.

"I believe after a few meetings 'Jack' plans their last encounter." Walking around my desk again, I continues to ply the doctor with my theory. "This is how I think the killer approaches his victims. All the women had signs of being choked in some way, made evident by way of a swollen tongue or bruising on and around the chin. I think, our killer uses a scarf, it could be a gift given to them the night they are murdered. Stride was wearing a silk one, and Chapman was wearing a handkerchief. The perpetrator perhaps comes up from behind and makes as if to affectionately caress them. 'Jack' then wraps the scarf about the neck, protecting the delicate skin of the neck. The killer then wraps his arm around the woman's neck and squeezes on the right and left of the victim's neck with his bicep on the right and his forearm on the left, stifling the woman so she can't scream. At the same time, cutting off the blood flow to the neck, squeezing only enough until they are close to blacking out. Carefully our killer cradles them against himself. Reaching for his knife 'Jack' stabs the blade in and then slices across the throat. The weight of the body plunges the knife to the hilt making the cut jagged and pushes the blade deep into the neck slicing into the windpipe and vertebrae. The blood sprays away from the killer onto the ground. In this way, no blood spray gets on his clothes. Laying the victim on the ground the killer is free to continue to mutilate the body."

After describing my theory on how the killer carried out his murderous task, I waited patiently to see what the doctor's reaction might be.

"Well, Detective, you certainly have given this 'Jack the Ripper' a considerable amount of thought and consideration. Explain to me, if you please, what makes this man, this 'Jack' kill in the first placed?"

"That, Doctor, is entirely up to supposition. I can only surmise that 'Jack's' attraction to these prostitutes is for different reasons than what these women think, 'Jack' perhaps finds their attraction to him misleading, while they seek only his money, our man, in turn, is perhaps seeking some form of misdirected affection. There has never been a forced sexual attraction, leading me to believe 'Jack' is not interested in these women in that way. 'Jack' kills in such a way that it is difficult to comprehend rhyme or reason. The cutting of the throat could be presumed to be merciful in a twisted way, and yet when you try to ascertain the reasons for the mutilation you lose sight of that purpose. I can only deduce that the mutilation is the result of some all-consuming hatred for the one these women represent. His actions are maniacal, to say the least; right down to the taking of the victim's internal organs. Which in itself could, perhaps be some type of memento if you could call it that."

"If you are correct in your hypothesis of this killer's methods, what good if any, does this information do to get us closer to finding out his identity?"

"Well, Sir, I believe that the man, we seek has some skill in dissection," I answered, seeing Phillips about to protest.

Holding up my hand, I stopped the doctor.

"With all due respect, Doctor, I have been to the mortuary and seen cadavers cut open. I have been to crime scenes that would make most cringe in horror, not to mention, I am also a veteran of war. I can honestly, beyond a doubt, tell you, sir, until you offered me an anatomy textbook from your laboratory, I could not have told you where a human kidney was located, let alone cut it out as precisely as this monster has done to Elizabeth Eddowes. Would you concur?"

I asked the question all the while, waiting with anticipation as the doctor rubbed his forehead and then looked up at me.

"I find this most heart-wrenching and disturbing, Detective. I refuse to believe that one of my colleagues is out there in the dead of night murdering women. I just refuse to believe it, Detective!" Phillips said, gathering his coat and hat in hand. "I bid you, good night, Detective."

I remained seated as Doctor Phillips walked out of my office. A few minutes later, Wynne Baxter walked in with a bewildered expression on his face.

"Detective, what on earth is wrong with Bagster Phillips," Baxter huffed.

"We were going over the cases that the doctor has been involved with. I may have insulted the doctor with the theory that 'Jack' may be a..."

"Stone, don't tell me you are still parading around your theory that this sadistic murderer is a medical doctor?"

"I am not as disbelieving as you, Wynne, or Doctor Phillips, for that matter," I tried to empathize.

"How do you explain why 'Jack' mocks police in his letter at the notion that they may be entertaining the idea of him being a doctor?"

"Nothing would give me greater pleasure to let this go and agree with you and Doctor Phillips, Wynne. I don't relish, nor want to believe the idea any more than either of you. You must accede, however, that we are dealing with an individual of very high intellect, who could very likely have gone to medical school. I will concede that it is possible that our killer could be a veterinarian. However, I will not give up thinking that whatever his profession, this sadistic killer we call 'the Ripper,' who comes out at night and slices up these women has some knowledge and skill with a knife."

"I say, Stone, it seems like sometimes you are taking your theories right from fiction," Baxter retorted. "That story, Dr. Jekyll and Mr. Hyde, almost comes to mind!"

"I cannot assume to know what makes this 'Jack the Ripper' tick, Wynne," I explained. "But I suspect that the man has some hatred for the women and the profession. Perhaps this hatred is due to a mother, a girlfriend, or even a wife that manifests itself in the horrific treatment of his victims."

"Do you mean this man has some type of psychosis, Detective," Baxter asked.

"What else would cause this man to go into the shadows of the East End to kill and mutilate his victims, Wynne."

"Well, you and I both know the East End has all sorts that have been ostracized and confined to the darkest corners of London's ghetto?"

"I am guessing at this stage of course when I say this, but I believe our killer has something wrong that is entirely invisible to the naked eye. Something lurid and twisted that keeps 'Jack' lurking in the slums of London."

"Who else feels as you do, John?" Baxter asked, sitting down with a grim expression.

"I believe that Inspector Abberline and I both are thinking along the same lines, Wynne. We are of the assumption that if the papers keep sensationalizing these murders in their efforts to sell more papers, the crimes will not only continue, the killer will get more brazen, and more women will die."

"Well, that is not very encouraging, Detective."

"Wynne, the Metropolitan Police Department has one thousand constables walking beats on every street corner in London. The Police Commissioner, Charles Warren, keeps hiring more constables to walk the beat, but more manpower and this idea of bloodhounds scouring the crime scenes are not going to make one bit of difference. We need more detectives, men that know how the criminal mind works. We haven't even scratched the surface of this killer. Our police were thought to be able to handle every crime known to the civilized world, except one," I said, pacing the floor trying to explain what I saw was the apparent problems with hunting a killer like 'Jack the Ripper.'

"Are we still talking about murder, Detective?" Baxter asked.

"Yes, but it isn't the crime of murder that has changed, Wynne".

"What element of murder are the rest of us missing that you seem to hold the key to, Detective?"

Understanding Baxter's frustration, I allowed my friend's tone to go unchecked.

"It is not the crime that has changed in this case, Wynne, it is the nature of the crime."

"I am not sure I follow, Detective?"

"Wynne, how do you apprehend a criminal, that perpetrates a crime, with no apparent gain, or motive?"

"You have gone barmy old boy!" Baxter huffed. "Every crime has some purpose, besides those accidents that cannot be foreseen by the perpetrator."

"Let me explain, Wynne," I said, organizing my thoughts. "I believe that we are hunting a man that has no ties to any of the victims. There are no friends, no relatives, nor any employer to question. There are no eyewitnesses to the crime because no one sees him coming or going. The police are hunting someone, who kills like an animal kills its prey, and then after mutilating their bodies most horrifically, this madman moves on to the next victim, leaving no clue behind. To make matters worse, this 'Jack' then dares to write letters to the newspapers and Scotland Yard to boast about his ability to confound police and rub their very noses in the fact, we have no clue to his identity or where to look for him next. The Yard has the best detectives and every tool at their disposal, and we still have no way of knowing when or where this killer will strike, nor do we have any idea of how to stop him."

"Surely, this killer has to have some motivation, something driving him that will tip his hand and reveal some way of catching him," Wynne suggested.

"That is the bare bones of it, Wynne, there are thousands of criminals in Newgate Prison right now that have murdered for money, hatred, envy, and jealousy. These elements are the factors that motivate the perpetrator to do the crime, but there is also the tie that binds each criminal to the victim. There is some type of relationship with the victim, or the very least, the victim has something the killer desired which they take by force, sometimes ending in murder."

"Our killer can't just run around picking his victims at random, there has to be some thread, something 'Jack' sees in them, aside from the fact that they are all women and prostitutes?"

"That is just my point, Wynne, I believe there is."

"What do you mean Stone," Baxter huffed. "First you say there is nothing to tie the murderer to the crimes, and now you say that there is."

"That one element Wynne, unfortunately still escapes us, I am afraid. My hope is that there is someone in the East End who has seen something or heard something, maybe they are scared to come forward or are simply unaware of its relevance. So, I am going back to the crime scenes, and I am going to talk to every prostitute in London's East End," I said, slamming my palm down on top of my desk.

"You are what!" Baxter shouted. "Do you know how many women you are talking about, Stone?"

"Yes, I have already been informed that there are roughly twelve hundred known prostitutes in the East End. I don't have to interview them all, Wynne, just the women in the vicinity of each murder."

Opening my desk drawer, I withdrew a map of London, while Wynne Baxter stood and walked around to join me at my desk. As the coroner hovered over my shoulder, I took up my pen from the ink well and let the access ink drip from the tip.

"What are you thinking, Stone?" Baxter asked, absorbed in the details of the map.

"I am going to mark out all of the locations where each of the four women was found first," I said, pointing my index finger on the map, seeking out all of the streets of interest in Whitechapel.

"Well let's see," Baxter said, rubbing his chin. "Eddowes was found in Mitre Square."

With my finger, I traced out a line on the map. "Tabram was found in the George Yard Buildings at Whitechapel High Streets. Chapman was found at Hanbury Street, Spitalfields. Nichols was found at Bucks Row, near Osborn Street, and Stride was found at Dutfield's Yard next to the International Workers Club on Berner Street, St George."

When we had finished marking out all the locations, I drew a rough circle around the area.

"That would be about one square mile wouldn't you say, Wynne?" I asked, looking up at the coroner, who nodded in agreement.

"It will probably take us a month of Sundays, but I am game if you are." Baxter offered, walking around to the front of the desk, collecting his hat.

"Us...! What on earth do you mean us, Wynne?" I bellowed at the coroner.

"Listen, you are supposed to be Scotland Yard's aid to the Coroner's Office. There are 80,000 people in London's East End; it will be easier if we both start bright and early in the morning. Wouldn't you agree?" Baxter asked.

I looked long at the coroner, whose enthusiasm seemed to have run amuck. I smiled wondering if Baxter's comment was somehow meant to tell me that he knew the real reason behind my assignment here in Whitechapel.

"Sounds good, Mr. Baxter, there is only one thing though."

"And what might that be, Mr. Stone?" Baxter did a mock bow.

"The women we are seeking to talk to will be out all night given their profession; most won't be up and, on the street, again until after supper, Wynne," I answered smirking at my partner.

"Oh right, I see your point, John. I guess I will see you, say, this afternoon." Baxter replied, looking sheepishly.

I waved my goodbye as I watched my friend walk out of my office not knowing if Baxter knew what he was in store for. There were a countless number of reasons to dissuade the coroner and only one needed to persuade myself to allow Baxter to tag along. It was simple, I could use my friend's help. I had always worked alone, but in this case, Baxter had a way with the people of the East End. Sometimes people were less cooperative when they were showed a badge. Most were not inclined to cooperate at all, and would be more likely to run the other way when approached by police. It was difficult to guess the reactions of some but not so of those living in London's East End.

Chapter Twelve

During the next two days, we walked the cobbled streets of London's East End. With every step of the square mile where the murders were committed; we delved into the habits and relationships of the five murdered women. Everywhere we looked, the streets were choked with carts, wagons, bales of merchandise, and the faces of almost every nationality in the world. London, one of the biggest cities on the globe, had become the target of the industrialized world to sell their wares to the four corners of the globe. With industry; came the rampant growth; and boom expected of the industrial revolution bringing with it the engineers and professionals that were needed to keep the new machines running. Thousands left the countryside and whatever meager existence they had become accustomed to, seeking employment in the developing cities that promised a wage for every worker. They left homes and families and a simpler way of life that was governed by climate and pestilence that could strike the unsuspecting and the unprepared, leaving the afflicted with nothing to look forward to but suffering in the wake of the devastation.

However, even a city as large as London could not house all that came looking for a better life. With every new industry, London grew, pushing its boundaries ever eastward, and with its growth, London's vast immigrant population grew with it, eventually pushing not only the warehouses ever east but the immigrant that came with it. No city in the world that grew so devastatingly fast could have accommodated the exodus of people that arrived. Those who came looking for employment had turned their backs on the hardships of one life, only to be confronted with an entirely new set of privations that they had not foreseen, nor were they equipped to handle. In the city, they discovered overcrowding, no housing, and the employment that they had sought, nonexistent. Soon the cobbled streets that they walked night and day seeking any opportunity became a grim reminder of all that they had left behind. Starvation became their constant nemesis, forcing some to do things that they would have never imagined in their past lives, to gain the pennies needed for food and a place to lay their heads at night.

With starvation comes fear, and with it, desperation. Soon, the crime rate grew beyond the cities expectations and out of the control of the Metropolitan Police Force. Every nationality imaginable came flooding into the city, arriving on trains and ships, others arrived with their carts piled high with their possessions, families, and dreams. Before long congestion, and overcrowding became obstacles that the city fought desperately to overcome. The new arrivals crowded into any available flat, paying exorbitant rents, and when the costs of housing started to escalate, those with extra rooms began to sublet a single dwelling into two living spaces. In most cases, the division didn't end there, the rooms that once accommodated two people soon housed a family of four. Some families due to the high unemployment were forced to take in a boarder, now one room held as many as five and six people. With the onslaught of people arriving daily, greedy landlords continued to raise their rents. With the rising cost of housing, the prices of food began to escalate, forcing the unemployed to move further east into the ghetto.

With the urgent need for accommodations, tenements and lodging houses sprang up on every corner to meet the high demand. However, the demand was great, and soon every building that could be converted to housing the flood of people was used. New laws were put into place to control these tenements which allowed that each building had to be licensed and subject to constant Police supervision. To be supervised by police, lodging houses had to display a sign easily seen and read by constables, stating the number of beds for which it was licensed. In London, on the day when they walked the streets of the East End, there were, at least, one hundred and forty-six licensed lodging houses, accommodating more than 6000 beds.

In the east, the streets and tenements became more deplorable with every step they took into the Ghetto. Here, rubbish lay in every corner, gutter. With each step, one quickly realized that every available space unaccounted for was infested with every sort of vermin. Both the refuse of beasts of burden and that from privies ran along the gutters of the street and walks gathering on wagon wheels and the shoes of the unsuspecting who trod along the cobbled streets. Through open windows and doors, women dumped pails of waste and washing water indiscriminately, until it lay in pools under windows and on top of sheds and overhangs, adding to the stench that rose up from the street and assaulted their noses. Every odor imaginable could be added to the collection of fragrances. In the Whitechapel Market, stalls with braziers cooked every kind of dish imaginable, catering to all a man wanted or needed, from bread to tanned leathers. Men and women who were too old to earn a few pennies could be seen digging through the garbage and counted themselves lucky if a hawker's barrow tipped on its way to the stalls. A mob could be counted on to scrounge over a few tidbits that had been missed up against the curb. Unfortunately, it was not only the old and unemployed that suffered. Around every corner, the darkened hollowed eyes of hungry children could be seen, sitting huddled in doorways and on window sills. The older urchins wandered the streets eager to participate in petty thievery to ease the rumble in their shrunken stomachs.

As in every society infested with crime, there are still those who want to live respectable lives; they dream of schools for their children and of churches to worship in. They are the young and old alike, standing in long lines waiting endless hours for a chance at day labor to put a meager meal on the table for that day. For those unlucky souls who remain in lines after the day's laborers are chosen, these become the homeless who crowd park benches sleeping by day because city ordinances are enforced to prevent the homeless from sleeping during the night on public benches or in parks. The lucky few who find employment that has no family to provide for can often afford rooms in workers' houses. These rooms are filled with the young and old squandering away pennies with their dreams in the hopes of moving out of the ghetto one day to a home and a family of their own.

They walked along Commercial Street from Spitalfields to Whitechapel, moving southward as far as Leman Street to the docks. They searched night after night in the darkened doorways and still darker alleyways, for any clue that might have been missed knowing the deeper into the shadows they searched, danger lurked around every corner. The men who had tried to find employment and failed had given up and had resorted to all types of rookery in hopes to survive. Crimes in the East End were reported on every street corner and soon multiplied tenfold overnight, causing the good citizens to scream that there were too many newcomers in the city and not enough police. The unemployed grew restless from too much time on their hands and the hunger that gnawed at their insides forcing them to become hunters in a world where the innocent or unsuspecting became their prey. These petty criminals lurked in the deep recesses of the city where everyone that walked was fair game, and there was no rule, golden, or otherwise to keep them restrained. Pickpockets and thieves prowled, wherever people congregated. These miscreants waited in corners in markets, stations, and on launches, anywhere those who were too occupied to notice their purses being pinched or were too naive to fear the streets that were plagued by the parasites who preyed on the law-abiding and innocent citizen.

Buildings replaced green spaces; trees and bushes were cut down along verges and lanes, replaced by muddied paths and rutted roadways. With the industry came warehouses and smokestacks that spewed exhaust that covered rooftops and sills in fine ash. The stacks stood pinnacle-like against the skyline, while the coal smoke that filtered out blackened the sky.

Soon more roads were cobbled, and the clip-clop of horses' hooves pulling freight and hansom cabs could be heard on every street at all hours of the night and day. With the requirement for transportation to move the manufactured goods, came the need for carts and wagons and for more horses. Stables were at the end of every street, and dung-filled carts hauled the tons of manure away that piled up every day. With the exploding population raised the necessity for more provisions and more markets and with it higher prices to meet the supply and demand. As they walked along Bucks-row, the slaughterhouses were too many to count, to supply the demand for fresh meat to those who could afford it. They saw butchers standing in doorways with bloodied aprons and hands. All along the way, the stench of death from carcasses and hides was in the air. With the growth of the city came the need for hawkers, sweeps, and carters. However, with a population as vast as the city of London, there were nine men lined up for every job available, and not enough jobs to go around.

With rents to be paid, and food to buy, and no jobs to be found came despondency and the anxiety that comes with failure. As a result, some women left their families in crowded rooms to walk the streets at night selling their bodies to put food on the table and a roof over their family's heads. I could well imagine the pathway that Tabram, Chapman, Nichols,

Stride, and Eddowes' lives had taken, caught up in a world of gin-soaked numbness to do whatever they could; to survive. Sadly, in the end, they lost homes, families, husbands, and all they had of value, to be consumed by the life of a prostitute. Immersed in a life that they hated; these women hid their pasts from those they knew, taking on a new identity. They roved the streets earning pennies in a futile attempt to survive only to lose their lives at the end of a butcher's knife and to be made a spectacle on a mortuary slab.

The women had family and friends, those who knew them before they had left their lives to walk the streets at night. I wanted to talk to these, or at least, talk to those who could shed light on their plight, and on how they lived. However, by the week's end, they saw the futility of their mission to find these intimates. The friends of the deceased they sought had moved on from the addresses given to constables or the coroner at inquest. In some cases, rents had doubled forcing them to other lodgings. They soon realized that the people of London's East End had become unwilling nomads. They wandered the streets in hopes that they might find even the most menial labor; while searching for the cheapest rents where work might be had. In other instances, the women they talked to had been acquaintances at best with the victims. Those people pressed together in a population where the need for companionship a few hours every day while they stood in soup lines, or stood in pubs exchanging comments over a dram of gin that was so cheap and so readily available in the slums, that it was preferred to water.

These were the precarious circumstances that the two men faced as they dug deeper into the women's past. They looked for ex-husbands, fathers, mothers, children, and siblings in the off chance that they had spoken to their families of some small thing that could lead them to a killer. As before the detective, and the coroner struck out again. In all the cases that they investigated, the families had not seen or heard from their daughters, sisters, or mothers in months or years. The few who had seen their loved one before their death often occurred in a brief exchange of conversation and the plea to borrow money so, they could find lodgings to avoid sleeping on the streets. These persons, that they interviewed professed either out of guilt or shame that they knew nothing of the life their family member had been living to survive the mean streets of London town. Even the rudimentary relationships the women had cultivated at lodging houses, few knew of the life the deceased women lived before they chose to sell their bodies. Others chose to ignore the knowledge that out of desperation these women had been forced into their lifestyles to pay for a night's lodgings. They could only assume that it was out of humiliation or the fear of being disgraced by family or those they knew that the five victims had kept their personal lives to themselves. Going as far as not even giving their real or full names to friends they met.

In Spitalfields at a lodging house in Dorset Street, they found Mary Ann Connolly, more commonly known as Pearly Poll. Connolly had known Martha Tabram only by the name, Emma. I had talked to Poll in a previous interview, however, this time, I and Baxter tried desperately to jar some memory of the fateful night when she last saw her friend alive. After several minutes Poll seemed convinced the Guardsman that Tabram had last been seen with was the guilty party, not some allusive killer, walking the streets of London. They warned Poll to be careful of going down alleys with strangers, although their warnings had little effect on the woman. Poll merely shrugged and gave a hearty laugh before walking away into the night.

They went to East Greenwich, to number six River-Terrace and interviewed Tabram's husband at his residence. The man had not seen his wife for eighteen months. The two had been separated for thirteen years there was no reason to believe that Tabram had any relevant knowledge or was involved in any foul play with his estranged wife.

They interviewed Edward Walker, the father of Mary Ann Nichols, who had not seen or heard from his daughter in two years. Walker did not know that his daughter's last known address was in the Lambeth Workhouse. Unfortunately, the man had no intimate knowledge about where his daughter had been living since, nor what she did for money. Mary Ann Nichols' husband, William Nichols of Coburg Road, told them that he had no contact with his wife in the past eight years. Nichols was forthright during the interview and told them his marriage had ended due to his wife's drinking habits. Next, they interviewed Emily Holland, of eighteen Thrawl Street, in Spitalfields. They had established that Holland was the last person to see Nicholls before her death. Holland told them that she had spoken to Nichols a few hours before her death. Holland seemed sincere when she told them that she knew nothing of her friend's personal life. Nor did she see her with any men of any kind. Holland added nothing new to the testimony she gave at the inquest.

They questioned Amelia Palmer of thirty-five Dorset Street, Spitalfields again, who knew Chapman for five years in common lodgings. Palmer informed them that Chapman's husband had died eighteen months previous to her death and that the pair had been apart for four years before that. Chapman was known by some as Mrs. Sivvy because she had lived with a sieve-maker but admitted that she did not know the man's name. Palmer told them that Chapman used to crochet antimacassars' and sold flowers in Stratford. Palmer also told them that the last day she saw Chapman alive, that she had asked Chapman if she was going to Stratford to sell her wares. Chapman said that she didn't feel well, and she wouldn't be going, adding that she would have to go somewhere to pay for her lodgings, but where Chapman went or how she got the money Palmer didn't know. They found Fontain Smith at his work, employed as a printer's warehouseman. Fontain was Chapman's younger brother. Smith told them that he had last seen his sister two weeks before her death. At that time, Smith gave his sister two shillings for lodgings but did not know which lodging-house she frequented, or what she did for a living. Smith added that his sister did not freely offer confidential information about her lifestyle to him, nor was it his business to press her to find out.

Late on Wednesday night, they found Elizabeth Tanner. Tanner said she knew Stride only as Long Liz. Stride had once told Tanner that her family had died when the Princess Alice sank in 1885. Tanner admitted that she knew Stride to stay out all night, but aside from cleaning rooms at the Lodging House at thirty-two Flower and Dean Street, she did not know how her friend lived. Tanner had said she recognized Stride because she had a problem with the inside of her mouth. Tanner had last seen Stride at the Queen's Head public house on Commercial Street. At that time, Stride had been quite sober. Michael Kidney would not answer any questions when they contacted the man. Kidney was adamant that Stride had a problem with the roof of her mouth. Kidney informed them again of his possession of specific information that would lead them to catch the killer, but no one would listen to him. With that said, Kidney walked away.

Wynne Baxter was all for hauling Kidney into a station to force the man to reveal this information. It took several minutes to calm the coroner down, until he was able to convince his friend that I could see no new information to be had by the effort. Frustrated and tired, the two men got into a hansom cab and headed back to the office.

An hour later, over tea, exhausted by their foray into the night, they discussed all that they had learned. There had been only three people in attendance at the inquest of Catharine Eddowes, apart from professional men. There was Eliza Gold, who was Eddowes' sister, Annie Phillips, who was Eddowes' daughter, and John Kelly. Their statements did little or nothing to shed any light on the murders.

Annie Phillips had not seen her mother in over two years, while Mrs. Gold saw her sister four weeks previous. Unfortunately, neither of them had anything new to add to their previous testimony. Neither of the women knew where the deceased lived, nor what she did for money.

John Kelly was the other witness they hoped to gain something of interest from. Kelly had lived with Eddowes for seven years. Kelly repeatedly claimed that I knew nothing of what Eddowes did for a living. They assumed that the man denied having knowledge of Eddowes' lifestyle, out of loyalty, and not to tarnish the dead woman's character. Though, it was more likely that the man's refusal to accept the fact was likely not to bring focus on the lack in his own character. Kelly also claimed that Catharine left him to see her daughter in which she was going to obtain money and never returned.

Sitting in my office, Wynne Baxter flung up his hands in defeat.

"I have questioned hundreds of people in my career, Detective, however, I must say, that I have never received so little information from, so many interviews," Baxter said, slumping in his chair, holding his head in his hands.

"Perhaps now you understand, how, I arrived at my theory that our killer seeks out these specific types of women," I replied.

"Specific," Baxter said. "What do you mean, Detective?"

"It's clear, isn't it, Wynne," I said, looking over at Baxter. "Remember when, I mentioned to you before that '*Jack*' looks for women that have no apparent ties. If we have learned anything else after all of these interviews, it should attest to that. In almost every case, family members have not seen nor had any communication with the deceased in months or years. Even the victim's friends or acquaintances had little or no knowledge at all of what they did or with whom. These women lived in secrecy, keeping their relationships private from family and anyone they were acquainted with.

They concealed even the most trivial insignificant details about themselves from any they came in contact."

"Why would they go to such extremes? In most cases, aside from some excessive boozing, they had no need to hide out," Baxter queried?

"Wynne, they were not hiding from the law. They were hiding from themselves," I explained, pouring myself more tea and returning to my desk.

"What the devil is that supposed to mean, Stone?"

"Think about this for a moment, Wynne," I said. "These women had lives, homes, families. For the most part drinking in excess was a cause for their troubled marriages, however," I explained as I searched through the heaps of files on my desk always referring to the police reports to support my theories. "Annie Chapman had three children, the youngest was born with some form of physical ailment. The firstborn daughter died of meningitis, and then she and her husband separated. After all the tumult in her life, Chapman's health later begins to fail.

Catharine Eddowes took to drink after several failed relationships. Elizabeth Stride, she, on the other hand, took to prostitution quite freely, and early on in her life. It is known that Stride had a baby girl that died after birth. Later, consumed by the life she decided to live, she began to tell all her friends and acquaintances that her family was killed and that she was all alone. I think by lying about her family, she willingly abandoned all the remaining ties that reminded her that once in her past, she had a family and a seemingly normal life. Polly Nichols also was known to suffer from the drink, deserted her husband and five children."

"Alright, Detective, I see a pattern, but what if anything does this prove?"

"I believe Wynne that the pattern establishes that all of these women were running from failed marriages, the death of children, unemployed husbands, or simply from poverty. It is quite conceivable that these women tried everything in their power to keep their home from falling apart, but sadly, in the end, it was themselves that fell apart."

"I still don't see how this is of any use?"

"It establishes the type of women '*Jack*' targets, Wynne," I said, noting the grimace on my friend's face. "If nothing else, it helps us to understand a little about '*Jack's*' motivation."

"But really Stone, isn't it generally the understanding that all these women have abandoned homes and lives and burned their proverbial bridges, so to speak?"

"Yes, I suppose so, but let's take Elizabeth Stride for instance. Why would she tell her friends that her family had died in that awful sinking of the Princess Alice when there is no truth to it?"

"That was her way of abandoning her past."

"Exactly Wynne, it is why most of these women did not use their real names. Or why they kept moving from lodging house to lodging house. It is all due to the shame they felt for leaving their families and living the life they were living. It is easier for someone to forget what they were or what they left behind than it was for these women to live up to the reality of what they had become. Abandoning children, families, and homes, must have left some scars."

"But why leave their family," Wynne retorted. "I should think that they could have done better with their family intact than walking the streets at night alone."

"I am not so sure you are right, Wynne. You saw the way some of these people are forced to live in the slums of the East End, they are floundering in a city that boasts all the amenities, yet they can't find jobs. I don't know how, I would react if I were forced to watch my children grow thinner day after day, living in a slum with no hope of ever getting out. The feeling of despair must have been incredible; perhaps they thought it was the only thing left for them to do."

"Perhaps you are right, John. I must admit that I have had enough for today," Baxter said, reaching for his hat and walking stick. "I am going home to hug my wife. Good night, Detective."

"Good night, Wynne."

I remained at my desk listening to my friend's fading footsteps. A few minutes later, I blew out the lamp on my desk and walked out of my office. Standing on the street, I felt the cool breeze of autumns return on my face. I stood watching the crowds shuffle by my doorway, struggling with packages and burdens, while carts and wagons ambled down the center of the street oblivious to pedestrians who hustled out of the way. I looked at the faces of the women and men, having their own cares and concerns trying to make a living, provide for families, and find happiness mingled somewhere in the middle of it all. I pulled up my collar and was about to call a cab when I saw a constable walk across the street towards me.

"Excuse me, Detective Stone, is it?" The officer's tone and manner were short and gruff.

"Yes," I answered.

"I have this message from The Yard; it was delivered to the station this afternoon."

I took the message from the constable tearing open the cable, I read it and immediately hailed a cab.

"Where to Sir?"

"Scotland Yard and hurry," I shouted at the cab driver as I slammed the door behind me!

With a crack of the whip over the horse's ears, the hansom lurched forward. The cab sped down the street darting passed, the crowd all rushing to get out of the way of the racing cab. I looked out the window paying attention to nothing, in particular, my mind occupied with thoughts of what would demand my presence at The Yard so urgently, and at night away from prying eyes. There was only one thing that came to mind, that was another murder in Whitechapel.

Chapter Thirteen

Using one of my knuckles, I rapped on the office door of Inspector Abberline and was instantly beckoned to enter. As I opened the door, I sidestepped out of the way of the MP Samuel Montague and Superintendent Arnold as they passed by me leaving; the office. I knew the two only by sight, nodding my head slightly in recognition as both men left without saying a word.

"Stone, I take it you know who both of those men are," Abberline spoke, breaking the nervous silence.

"Yes, Sir," I answered respectfully, thinking that the furtive meeting at such an hour seemed a little out of character for two such prominent citizens.

"I have just been informed by those gentlemen. That the Vigilante Committee, chaired by one George Lusk, has written to Lord Salisbury to get the British Government to offer a reward to the public. They hope to get the citizenry to hand over the murderer terrorizing London's streets. The Home Secretary, Henry Mathews, has flat out refused. It has been brought to my attention that the Vigilance Committee has decided to offer a reward of its own, for any information leading to the apprehension of 'Jack the Ripper.' There seems to be some sort of consensus that because the murders are happening in the East End, there are those that have knowledge as to who this madman is and are concealing his identity." Abberline huffed and then sat down, rubbing his chin.

"Sir, has something happened that the Vigilance Committee feels it is necessary to take these measures?" I asked the inspector, curiously.

I watched as Abberline pulled a box from a drawer.

"Have a seat, Stone and take a look at this," Abberline answered, shoving the package across his desk.

Looking at the box, my mind was abuzz. I studied the box not knowing what to expect, given the inspector's vagueness as to the nature of the container. The box was nondescript, about four inches square and two inches deep. I imagined several different possibilities before picking up the box, then several more by the time I lifted the lid. Looking inside, I found what appeared to be a blood-stained letter. Setting the box on the edge of Abberline's desk, I looked up at the inspector, seeking some clue or suggestion from Abberline, but that proved fruitless. I had long ago become accustomed to the fact that Frederick Abberline's reactions to any situation were impossible to read. At the best of times, the man's face was completely devoid of expression. Taking the folded letter out of the box, the paper cracked when I unfolded it , due to the dried blood. The absence of anything else in the box suggested that whatever had been in the box with the letter had been removed long before it arrived at the Yard. Pulling apart the hardened creases of the paper, I began to read.

[Sic] *"From Hell*

Sor

I send you half the Kidne I took from one women prasarved it for you tother piece I fried and ate it was very nise. I may send you the bloody Knif that took it out if you only wate a whil longer.

Signed

Catch me when you can Mishter Lusk.

"Sir, am I supposed to believe that a woman's kidney was actually in this box?"

I asked the question, looking at the inspector, the mere suggestion of such an idea sickened me beyond anything I could put into words.

"Yes, Stone, the fiend is now turned cannibal, or so it would seem. As near as we can tell, we think the kidney that the '*Ripper*' has sent to Lusk, was the left kidney of Catharine Eddowes, but that has yet to be determined."

"We, sir?"

I was still trying to wrap my head around what I had read in the letter, rubbing my hands repeatedly on my pant legs to rid myself of the remains of the residue on my fingers from the letter.

"George Lusk, Chairman of the Vigilance Committee, received this in the evening mail. However, it was only after some influence by other members of the Committee, thar Lusk took the kidney to Doctor Thomas Openshaw. The doctor verified that the article in the box was, in fact, a human kidney. Doctor Openshaw then proceeded to tell the Committee that our murdered woman Catharine Eddowes had the left kidney removed, and the investigators were unable to find it. So, you see, Stone not only do we have this group of civilians wandering around the streets at night with torches and lanterns looking to string up any unsuspecting fool ignorant enough to be out at night and finds himself at the wrong place at the wrong time. Now, this self-appointed Committee is doing their own investigating and seems to be doing their level best to keep police out of it," Abberline vented.

"How long did they have this evidence before they thought to bring it to us, Sir?"

I asked, not sure if I should participate in the discussion at this point or remain quiet and find out what Abberline wanted me to do next.

"As near as I can figure, two or three days. According to Lusk, the box was received in the evening mail on October the sixteenth. At first, Lusk thought it might be some kind of hoax tossing the package in his desk drawer. The next day Mr. Lusk brought the package to the attention of a Committee member, who then persuaded him to contact the other members. It was during the course of that session that it was suggested that it would be easy to find out if the substance in the box was real by consulting a physician. In answer to your question as to who knows about this package, let me see, there is Doctor Openshaw, all of the Vigilance Committee and then the papers, we are the last to learn of this atrocity."

"So, what was done with the kidney?"

"Why?" Abberline barked again.

"I would think Doctor Phillips, or another police surgeon, would like to take a look at it."

"I suppose that couldn't hurt, Stone," Abberline agreed.

"Inspector, about assigning me to the coroner's office, I am not sure that my efforts are making one bit of difference?"

231

"Stone, believe it or not; you are doing exactly what I need. You are the eyes and ears on the ground that is unimpeded by any bureaucracy. You can move where I can't and deal with those that I cannot, so please continue until we get a handle on these murders?"

"Yes, Sir."

"I want you to go to George Lusk and interview him. This, of course, must be kept unofficial. I need you to find out what you can about those members of the committee and their involvement. Lusk's address is number one; Alderney Road, Mile End. We must do what we can; before the papers get wind of this story." Abberline finished.

"Is there anything else, Sir?"

"Yes, after you submit your report, I want you to put all your efforts and concentration on these letters that we have been receiving."

"Is there any particular letter you want me to concentrate on, or all the letters we have on file?"

"Just the letters from '*Jack*,' Stone. We have received in the neighborhood of two thousand letters from the general public to date who claim to be the '*Ripper*' and those who think they know who this wretch is. I have constables questioning every person in connection to the letters we receive. These people believe they are helping, but in most cases, they are merely wasting valuable time and manpower, that could be used in other areas. Unfortunately, we cannot stop looking into every possibility; for fear, there might be a legitimate lead there. Stone, we are dealing with a criminal so deviant that there is no telling where or when this '*Jack*' might strike again. We must be thorough and professional in our endeavors. That is why your presence in Whitechapel is critical. To date, we are looking at several suspects, but unfortunately, if we don't catch this fiend in the thick of it, we don't have a spot of evidence to convict anyone. I believe that I have a definitive direction on where this investigation is going. That is why; I need you to be close to the coroner and find out all you can about this man in the hospital that sent Baxter the information on this American. You may feel like you are wasting your time and energy, but I assure you, Stone, all your work has not been in vain." Abberline finished and walked around his desk, standing behind his chair.

"Yes, Sir."

"Stone, something tells me that there is more to these letters than meets the eye."

"Yes, Sir. Is there anything else?"

"No, that is all. It is late so, start fresh in the morning." Abberline answered.

Turning, I walked out of the inspector's office. It was some blocks and a cold evening rain that shook me from my thoughts after I left The Yard. I had been feeling a little useless and discouraged in the past weeks. At every turn of the investigation, I seemed to be revisiting old ground only to come to the same conclusions about facts and leads that the investigators before me had already discovered. Coming to the same deductions and results, left little room for any advancement in the murder cases. Although much to my surprise, I had been making sure nothing was missed in the investigation, precisely what Inspector Abberline had wanted me to do all along.

One thing that troubled me; was this curator at the hospitable that the inspector wanted to know about, that had confided in Baxter about the American. I had no way of knowing if Baxter had made the man up or if he had simply disguised Miss Curtin to protect her identity. When taking this assignment, I had no idea that part of my duties would be to spy on Wynne Baxter. It did not sit well with me now, that I had grown to like the man, nor would it do me any good to seek a job in the man's office if I was found out to be a spy. Hailing a cab, I climbed in feeling that my vacation had been cut short and my work load had doubled on my return.

Although morning brought with it a leaden sky, matching my enthusiasm for the investigation. The cab took me up Whitechapel Road, turning directly onto Mile End and then onto Alderney Road. It was here that I asked the cabman to stop before reaching my destination. I found walking along the street more expedient when studying my surroundings as opposed to looking from a cab window. A cab often drew unsolicited attention when one wished his approach to go unnoticed.

Alderney Road was less congested than the main thorough ways in the heart of London. The houses here were built in long rows, each one as similar to the one beside it; the only defining feature was the number that hung over the door. Starting up the street, I walked along until I found the house with the number one over the door. Taking the stairs two at a time, I crossed the large veranda and gave a stout knock with the heel of my hand on the door. After a moment of waiting, the door opened, and I was greeted by an elderly maid. She nodded at everything I had to say and then opened the door to usher me in. The maid prompted me to enter a comfortable parlor, and then quickly disappeared down a hall. On one end of the room was a fireplace that hissed and crackled at the other were shelves with row upon row of books with hardly a spine that had been cracked.

Only a few minutes passed, and I was greeted by Mr. George Lusk. Lusk was shorter than my six feet; I detected a slight swagger when the Chairman of the Vigilance Committee walked into the room. I had grown accustomed to such behavior, and more often than not it was accompanied by an aggressive attitude. It was noticeable in smaller statured men when they took note of my above-average height. Though I was willing to give George Lusk the benefit of the doubt before making any rash first impressions. I estimated Lusk to be the other side of fifty, with a sizeable greying mustache that matched his greying temples, a contrast to the man's dark hair. Lusk wore a tight-fitting vest with a gold watch fob hanging from a pocket over a white collarless shirt. I knew George Lusk was a builder by occupation, specializing in music hall restorations. These were my thoughts when Lusk walked into the room and gripped my hand a little too firmly. Although dressed as a gentleman, I could feel the calloused hand of a man who probably felt more comfortable in overhauls than a tailored suit.

"Sit down, Detective," Lusk said gruffly.

As I sat back in a comfortable winged back chair, I watched as Lusk walked over to a small table in the corner; and pick up a cigar box. Pulling out a large cigar, the builder bit off the end and spat it on the floor and shoved it in the corner of his mouth. Lusk then gestured to me with the box. Smiling, I held up a hand, refusing the offer.

"Make yourself comfortable, Detective," Lusk spoke through clouds of blue billowing smoke that followed him across the room to a matching chair that was placed in the corner directly across from where I sat.

"Now, what can I do for you, Detective?"

Lusk asked me the question as if the man had no idea of what would bring the police to his door.

"I am here about the box that was delivered to you, Sir," I answered, watching Lusk continue to puff on his cigar.

"Oh, I have already talked to the other Detective. I thought this was about something else?" Lusk, stood up walking to a decanter on the same table that the cigars were kept, pouring himself a generous glass full.

"I only found out about the box yesterday, Sir," I explained, not put off by Lusk's reaction. "It would seem, there was some delay in Scotland Yard obtaining the evidence, and then it was, shall we say, missing some important evidence," I retaliated, watching as Lusk's harsh expression softened a little.

"Though my actions may seem a trifle unorthodox, there is an explanation, Detective," Lusk answered, walking back across the room and pulled the top off of the whiskey decanter and poured himself another generous portion. "At first, I thought it was some kind of prank. It is certainly not something you find in your mail every day. I must admit, Detective; I was dumbfounded at first, and then sickened by it. My initial reaction was to throw the box away then after thinking about it, I called some associates from the Vigilance Committee. My associates and I thought it best if we take the box to a doctor and find out if what the letter described was to be taken seriously. You cannot possibly understand what it's like to have this 'Ripper' use you as some kind of conduit to get his message to the police?"

"Who did you call?"

"Only Mr. Aarons, and Mr. Harris."

I watched Lusk pour another glass of whiskey and drink it down in the same manner as the first two glasses.

"Conduit, Mr. Lusk, what exactly do you mean by that," I asked.

I studied the man who stood before me and detected something I had not noticed before. Lusk seemed more agitated by the incident than a man might expect after receiving a box with human remains in it, which in its self, would upset any normal human being. However, I sensed something else that I could not put my finger on.

"I mean these letters this killer keeps sending me, of all people. Why did this maniac choose me? I am just a family man, why pick me?" Lusk shouted.

"Letters," I asked. "The killer has contacted you more than once?" I responded, wondering why the inspector had not informed me of the other cases.

"Yes, of course," Lusk said, quickly leaving the room, returning with another letter. "Here, take a look at this, Detective," Lusk demanded, turning back to the decanter on the table.

[Sic] "Say Boss

You seem rare frightened, guess I'd like to give you fits, but can't stop time enough to let you box of toys play copper games with me, but hope to see you when I don't hurry too much

Bye-bye Boss."

"Well, Detective, what do you make of that?" Lusk asked, pacing the floor.

"It seems to me that whoever wrote this letter, sees you as some kind of an adversary. By sending you these letters, I believe '*Jack*' wants you to be aware that you are included in his plans."

"What do you mean my adversary, Detective?" Lusk shouted, yanking the cigar from his mouth. "Why pick on me, of all people?"

"What I mean is that '*Jack the Ripper*' seems to want to include you in his plots."

"What plans, this is not some game we are playing at?" Lusk shouted again. "What in the world are you talking about, Detective?"

"To you and I, this can only be viewed as some sick and twisted correspondence, Sir. It seems evident that whoever sent these letters to you, wants you to see him as an important person, someone to take notice of. This madman may continue to contact you."

"That hardly explains why this maniac has chosen me?"

"I have been developing a theory on this, and perhaps this proves my theory correct," I said, rereading the letter.

"Would you care to impart your wisdom, Detective?"

Ignoring Lusk's sarcasm as I considered the diction in the letter.

236

"If I were to guess, I would say that '*Jack*' believes himself to be the embodiment of a man who is doing London some good. You, on the other hand, are the one the person who is trying to stop him," I replied. "Do you have any idea who may have written it?"

"Stone, I can't believe Scotland Yard would have such a dimwit on staff," Lusk said, throwing up his hands roaring. "Isn't it obvious, Stone, that it was the killer of these prostitutes?"

I had to conceal a smirk, because, at first glance, the comment did seem dimwitted. However, with the sudden appearance of these letters that Lusk had been receiving, I had to ask myself if the letters were a ploy to keep the Vigilance Committee active. I decided to keep up the façade to see if Lusk was involved in some way.

"I'm sorry, how do you know that it was the '*Ripper*' who wrote the letters to you?"

"Who else could it be?" Lusk asked sarcastically. "I am the Vigilance Committee Chairman; hence the phrase catch me if you can...."

Lusk stopped in mid-sentence; the look on the man's face was one of despair. I watched Lusk walk across the room, and pick up a picture off the mantle of the fireplace and hand it to me. I took the picture from Lusk and immediately recognized the source of Lusk's rage. The picture was of Lusk standing with three beautiful daughters ranging from age twelve to eighteen or nineteen years of age.

"Do you think it could be somebody else, Detective?"

Lusk's voice softened for a moment showing the characteristics of a frightened father, only to return to the tough, bellowing chairman of a powerful Vigilance group.

"Tell me what you think, Detective, not what I want to hear?"

"I think there is a strong possibility it could be someone else."

"Someone else!"

"Look here," I said, standing up and crossing the room to Lusk, trying to put the man somewhat at ease by softening my tone. "In the letter, you received with the remains in the box; the author addresses you as 'Sir' in salutation and the postscript as 'Mr. Lusk.' In this new letter, the man addresses you as 'Boss.' I will have to study this letter further, but I would wager that we are dealing with two different people."

"Two different people," Lusk gasped. "Are you saying there are a couple of psychopaths wandering our streets all wanting to use me to boast of their crimes?" Lusk asked and then turned his back and poured himself another drink.

"I believe there is one killer who wrote you a letter and perhaps sent you a piece of a victim's anatomy. I believe that the other letters you have received are written by someone else, not two killers but two different people writing the letters. One of these letters is likely written from someone who wants you to sit up and take notice, or perhaps someone who just wants to play some joke on you to scare you because of your position in the Vigilance Committee."

"And this other person, why send me a letter portraying himself to be this killer, if nothing could be further from the truth?"

Lusk asked sounding defeated, and I could not blame the man. I did not know how I would react; if someone was sending me letters proclaiming to be a sadistic murderer of women.

"I would guess that this person is someone who has something to gain by copying this '*Jack the Ripper's*' correspondence."

"Are you implying, Detective, that someone may be using me to gain some advantage?"

"We have to look at this logically Mr. Lusk. What could someone gain; by making these letters public, and keeping the fear that '*Jack the Ripper*' is still lurking in the shadows of Whitechapel?"

"Are you referring to the Vigilance Committee, Detective?" Lusk asked before putting the glass to his lips.

"Would the committee have anything to gain by writing letters to you and the newspapers professing to be this '*Jack the Ripper*'?"

I asked the question, studying Lusk closely for any sign of guilt.

"That is the most ludicrous thing that I have ever heard of Detective," Lusk retaliated. "What could the Vigilance Committee possibly gain; by writing fake letters to me of all people? The Vigilance Committee is set up by the people, for the people, and run by the people; there isn't anything to gain." Lusk stated and then jammed his cigar back into his mouth.

"It could be someone within your organization that may want to influence the local politics in Whitechapel."

"How could they do that pray tell?"

"By keeping the '*Jack the Ripper*' stories in the papers. By using fear-mongering as a tactic, it could give the appearance that the officials in the East End are incompetents to fuel the discord in the city."

238

"Is that supposed to make me feel better, Detective? A killer is slicing up women only blocks from where I live and you are standing here telling me that there is someone else copying the letters of this killer in hopes to scare the public, for some political gain. Both of whom want the attention of the Vigilance Committee. I don't happen to agree with you, Sir. I will be taking my family out of London to protect them. In the interim, the Vigilance Committee will triple their patrols if needs be, to do the job, that our law enforcement agency cannot." Lusk said, slamming down his glass on the mantle and then turned on his heel. "Now if you will excuse me, I am going to bid you, good night."

I watched the man; some might consider one of the most influential in all Whitechapel, walk out of the room, looking defeated and lost. Putting on my overcoat, I saw myself out. Walking along the rain-soaked street, my mind was busy with the conversation I had with the Chairman of the Vigilance Committee. For the first time since starting my investigation, I now realized how many lives the *'Ripper'* had changed and affected since his appearance six months before. *'Jack the Ripper'* wasn't just killing prostitutes in the slums of the city that no one cared about, as some would believe. This killer of women was affecting the lives of people and families all over the city. People who got up for work and did not want to have to live in fear and chaos every day, wondering when this killer would strike again.

George Lusk appeared to be a man who viewed circumstances affecting his world, as cut and dried or black and white. I imagined that Lusk chose to believe that there was no middle ground and no gray area to concede. Unfortunately, during my career as a police officer, I found some in the world worked entirely inside the gray areas to achieve their own selfish desires. These people, in their dealings with others, thought nothing of manipulating any circumstance or person to satisfy their own greed. These were seemingly indifferent to the collateral damage they left in their wake.

Amidst all the intrigue that I suspected was going on, there were the streets of Whitechapel to consider. The East End fell into an area that could only be construed by most of London to be a large gray area. All the planning and decision making for the city of London was left up to the few, not the many. These select few oversaw all that was London. Their view was that development was good for the economy and for all who lived in the city. Expansion meant more taxes, and new jobs, pushing the city into the modern age and a new century. As a result, the East End became the brunt of the politician's need to move the city limits ever eastward under the guise to control crime and eliminate the ghetto. Unfortunately, with growth, as more often than not happens, the rich grew richer, and the poor grew miserable, and that was the black and the white of it. The gray area was the people wedged in the middle, who became the collateral damage caught in unemployment, and high rents, that were being pushed systematically into the ghetto. The politicians saw the ghetto as the result of the growing pains of a city that grew too quickly, and it was the acceptable cost of doing business and the by-product of all that was done for the good of its people. However, not one of those politicians had the foresight to see the cause and effect that expansion would bring. Nor had they put into place programs that would help those caught in the struggle between growth and poverty. The engineers and the planning departments saw the ghetto only as a series of dilapidated buildings that could be demolished for the implanting of more industry. They did not see the faces of the individuals and their families who did not care about bottom lines or expenditures.

The ghetto was where the hungry and the poor lived, who scraped and scratched for the few pennies they could make for food to survive through the day. Theirs was the plight of the desperate who did not think about tomorrow or next month or next year. The needs of the poor in London's East End were simple; it was survival. They spent little time thinking about the repercussions brought about by the greed of the few, disguised as industrial growth. The indigent was consumed with thoughts of where their next meal would come from, and where they would sleep that night. They did not think about the future for they lived for the moment, for the moment was all they had. Tomorrow, for most of Londoners, was viewed with promise and hope. Unfortunately, for those who lived in the ghetto, tomorrow was another day to scratch and fight, and to feel the rumble of hunger in their bellies. Their dreams were simple; they wanted to live in a city where they went to work every day. They wanted to watch their families grow up in a home and to enjoy a normal life. Unfortunately, they were caught between the blurry lines of race, progress and the ghetto. The East End had become a cesspool which, to some was where only the criminal and the dregs of society had come to live among its own. Caught between expansion and modernization, the only mechanism that the government was prepared to install to help those whose plight was to live in the ghetto was the police service. The Metropolitan Police was the last bastion in place; to keep those who lived in the East End from infiltrating the rest of London. Unfortunately, when the police showed signs of stress in keeping the lines of society separated, the new plan was to mow the ghetto down and build anew. The ghetto had now become enthralled in the middle of industrialization, politics, and a maniacal killer, who in his own twisted way by seeking recognition for his murderous machinations, 'Jack the Ripper' had brought attention to the slums in Whitechapel.

Chapter Fourteen

The next morning, it became a priority to find out what had become of the portion of the dissected kidney sent to George Lusk. I kept an open mind, but I was inclined to believe public opinion that the organ was just some medical student's joke, thus alleviating Lusk's fears that his family was in any foreseeable danger. However, the more I investigated, the mystery deepened, and I became less convinced that the letter was, in fact, a prank. Although, I was positive that Lusk's daughters were in no immediate danger, as they did not fit the pattern of '*Jack's*' usual victim, I doubted, I could have convinced Lusk of that.

Two days later, I received a telegram from Inspector Abberline informing me that Chief Inspector Swanson, had ordered Major Sir Henry Smith to send the portion of the alleged kidney to be inspected by, the Metropolitan Police Surgeon Doctor Gordon Brown. The telegram also informed me that Doctor Phillips' services would not be required and my presence was requested at The Yard again later that evening. Glad for the interruption, I had grown tired of chasing the whereabouts of the kidney that seemed to have disappeared. I had also become exceedingly more disturbed that I could not obtain any concrete answers as to whether the anatomy that George Lusk had received was a hoax or was indeed a portion of an organ removed from the body of Catherine Eddowes. Although I was relieved to be able to move onto other matters, I was troubled by the interference of the chief inspector. The fact that Inspector Swanson had taken the time to deal with this matter on his own, made me suspicious. The more I considered Abberline's inability to get any answers, I became convinced that the interference from Home Office had the appearance that his superiors were attempting to sweep certain facts of the case under the rug without informing him first.

The only positive outcome that came from the introduction of the latest piece of evidence was a growing feeling that a medical student may have been involved in obtaining the dissected kidney. It seemed to date that my only advocate as to the murderer having any medical experience was Dr. Frederick, Gordon Brown. Doctor Brown; in his expert medical opinion, claimed that there was no way of telling if the renal artery on the dissected kidney sent to George Lusk was from the murdered woman, as the portion of the renal artery remaining in the body of Catherine Eddowes was too small to make any comparison. Dr. Brown also established that the fragment of the organ was taken from a female, of approximately the age of forty-five. However, the mystery deepened, and the credibility of Brown's statement was put under question after I interviewed Doctor Sedgwick Saunders. Saunders openly criticized Brown's comments about the portion of the kidney being that of a female. Doctor Saunders was quoted in the Liverpool Daily Post saying, [Sic] *"there is no difference between the human male and female kidney."* Saunders also told me, off the record, that it was utterly ludicrous to believe that anyone could tell the exact age of the woman that the portion of the kidney had come from. The comments made by Doctor Saunders had ultimately put Doctor Brown's assertion that the killer had some medical training under fire from the rest of the medical profession.

An hour later, with the report in hand, I waited outside Abberline's office. Although the inspector's message revealed nothing as to the nature of the summons, I suspected another letter had surfaced. Unfortunately, I had no time to think any further on the subject; as Abberline's door was opened and the inspector, ushered out Doctor Thomas Horrocks Openshaw.

Abberline gestured towards the Doctor. "Detective Stone, you are acquainted with Doctor Openshaw, I assume?"

"Yes, Sir. Good day Doctor."

"Good day, Detective, Inspector." With that said, with a curt nod, Doctor Openshaw retreated down the hall.

It became suddenly apparent that something had transpired between Doctor Openshaw and the inspector. I detected a grave atmosphere when I entered that permeated throughout the office. Watching Abberline walk around his desk, I couldn't help but feel impending doom.

"Detective, if you please," Inspector Abberline said, holding out an ushering hand to a chair. "I am truly at wit's end here, Stone. I cannot understand how the world's greatest detectives in the world cannot find one man running around London sending letters to newspapers and everyone but the Queen herself, and we can't seem to get one shred of evidence to catch me. This Vigilance Committee is now calling for the resignation of the Home Secretary for his refusal to offer a reward, which in turn has prompted them to write Queen Victoria, who is reported to be taking a personal interest in the murders here in Whitechapel. The Vigilance Committee is offering a reward, and the Member of Parliament, Samuel Montague, is offering a reward of his own. At this very minute, there is in the neighborhood of twelve hundred Pounds in accumulated monies offered to anyone with even a shred of information. However, it seems we have no one in a population of five million people who knows anything of this wretch, '*Jack the Ripper*.' We have over eight thousand constables patrolling the streets, and what do we have to show for it?" Abberline shouted, throwing up his arms in desperation. "I will tell you, Detective, we have nothing."

Without a word, Abberline picked up a piece of paper from off his desk and handed it to me, and then turned his back on me to gaze out of the office window. Looking at the paper, I instantly recognized it for what it was. As I began to read, I was immediately overwhelmed by a feeling of nausea; apparently, I had not read enough of the twisted correspondence to be immune to the killer's use of levity in describing his victims. If the truth was told, it was the knowledge that the fiend was still sending letters to not only the newspapers and the Police Department but to citizens like George Lusk and now Dr. Openshaw. The very idea made every copper in London bristle at being mocked by the maniac dubbed '*Jack the Ripper*.' It was rather sobering receiving another letter from the maniacal killer. It put down any optimism that '*Jack*' had gone underground in the month since the Catharine Eddowes murder. The mere idea that the killer was still out there put everyone in a police uniform back on high alert, wondering when another corpse would turn up. Looking at the wrinkled paper that the letter was written on, I began to read aloud, wondering all the while why the killer had decided to correspond with Dr. Openshaw.

[Sic] "Old boss

You was rite it was the left kidney i was goin to hoperate agin close to your opitle just as i was goin to dror mi nife along er bloomin throte them cusses of coppers spoilt the game but i guess i wil be on the job soon and will send you another bit of innerds.

Jack the ripper

O have you seen the devle with my microscope and scapul a –lookin at a kidney with a slide cooked up."

Unable to comment, I gaped up at the inspector with a half-opened mouth, waiting for instruction as to what the new plan of attack was to find this killer.

"Well, what do you make of it, Stone?" Abberline questioned.

"Did the doctor receive this letter today," I asked, trying to figure out the circumstances that may have prompted another letter from '*Jack.*'

"Yes, this afternoon," Abberline responded.

"Correct me if I am wrong, Sir, but it appears to me as though the killer has some firsthand knowledge that Dr. Openshaw was the doctor that the Vigilance Committee took the piece of the kidney to for verification," I answered, studying the letter, for more clues.

"I assume that you had a chance to interview George Lusk about it, Detective," Abberline snapped.

"Yes, I did Sir, and receiving this letter could substantiate a theory of mine about some of the letters we have been receiving, supposedly from '*Jack,*' could be forgeries," I said, sticking my neck out like the proverbial chicken ready for the slaughter.

"Enlighten me, Detective."

I waited while Abberline pulled out his chair and sat down, giving me his full attention.

"When I talked to Mr. Lusk, I was made aware that there has been more than one letter sent to his house, each time he informed Mr. Joseph Aarons, who was the landlord of The Crown Public House at Mile End Road, and Mr. B. Harris, the Secretary of the Committee."

"How many letters has the man received?" Abberline snapped.

"Mr. Lusk showed me another besides, the one you read. However, I think it worth mentioning, Sir, that it is possible that the letters were written by different people."

"You can verify your theory, of course, with some evidence you have discovered, Stone?"

"Sir, if you study both letters, the authors of each uses two different salutations and postscripts. This so-called 'Letter from Hell' mentions Mr. Lusk by name, the other is similar to this letter Dr. Openshaw received, referring to the recipient as 'Boss,' both in salutation and postscript. The letter makes no mention of a victim or any reference to a future victim," I said, nervously looking at Abberline wondering what the inspector's response would be.

"This mention of the hospital and looking at the kidney, the author of these letters may have gleaned from the newspapers, Detective," Abberline responded, his tone not softening since his first tirade.

"Yes, but the reference to the microscope and scalpel sounds more like the writer of the letter was present during the procedure then it does someone speculating about how Dr. Openshaw may have examined the portion of the kidney. At the very least, I believe the person who wrote this letter has some knowledge of such methods," I offered.

"I concur, Stone, it does seem to reek of a fabrication. However, the content of the letter is not all that could be scrutinized. Examine the grammar and spelling, Detective," Abberline suggested. "You would be hard-pressed to tell me the letter was written by an educated man."

"As per your instruction, Sir, I have taken the opportunity to look at the letters more closely. After careful consideration, I believe it not improbable for an educated man to fabricate a letter and deliberately misspell words to misdirect the investigation."

"Yes, I see your point, Stone, that would be rather crafty of the wretch, wouldn't it? That would mean that we are dealing with someone who is not only intelligent but someone who has something to gain from copying '*Jack's*' letters." Abberline said, rising from his chair, seemingly deep in thought. "I suppose the question we should be asking is who would want to do such a thing in the first place?"

"It may seem rather unlikely, Sir, but it is my thinking that it might be someone inside Lusk's own organization," I suggested, and then immediately wished that I hadn't, not knowing how receptive Abberline would be of the idea.

"Why would a member of the Vigilance Committee want to write letters pretending to be the 'Ripper'?"

I looked at Abberline, knowing that the inspector's mind worked much like an abacus, always calculating every aspect before making a rash conclusion.

"You said it yourself, Inspector, *there are political powers at work that are not under our control*," I answered, looking at Abberline wondering if the inspector agreed with my theory.

"Stone, you may have something," Abberline paused. "If you are right, we had better handle this with kid gloves, for now. The next question we should ask ourselves is why a member of the Vigilance Committee may want to interfere in this investigation?"

"If I might suggest, Sir, that it may be this reward business," I offered.

"Yes, I can see that being a possibility, but ensuring that a reward is posted may be small potatoes," Abberline offered. "The resignation of the Home Secretary might be the bigger game that they are after.

I sat thinking about what Abberline said, while the inspector gazed out the window, the silence becoming more irritating with every tick of the clock that hung on the wall. The prospect that a person or an organization could manipulate the newspapers by using the exploits of a multiple murderer was almost too surreal to be considered. Add the letters from 'Jack,' and one could see a conspiracy unfolding before their very eyes. I had only been toying with such an idea since my meeting with George Lusk. Now placing all the pieces of information together in front of me, I could see what could be construed as a diabolical plan to bring about some specific political agenda that might otherwise not have come to fruition. The idea that such a thing was possible was mind-boggling.

"This conversation Stone stays in this room, is that clear?"

The suddenness of the order made me wonder if, Abberline was guarded in case the insinuation was made in front of the wrong people. The inspector might have been wary due to the unknown foundations of such an organization. Offhand, I could think of at least a half-a-dozen powerful people who might hope to gain in some way by the Home Secretary, resigning from office. Which in my mind, would mean that the Secretary, leaving office, had more to do about placing another in that office, and less to do with the government offering a reward for the apprehension of a killer? Other ramifications had to be considered given the blowback from the newspapers about The Yard's inability to catch the killer. Perhaps Abberline was worried, given the fact that the Home Secretary was in charge of policing, and a new secretary could go in search of a new chief inspector.

"Yes, Sir," I said nervously. "What do we do now, Inspector?"

"Do, Stone? We catch this '*Jack*,' that is what we do. I want you to keep digging into these letters if you are right, and I think you might be onto something, then maybe there is more here than what meets the eye."

"Yes, Sir," I spoke quickly, wishing the inspector was clearer in his explanation.

"That is all Stone!" Inspector Abberline barked.

Walking along Parliament Street, I felt the cold blast of autumn's wind cut through my light suit jacket; however, it wasn't half as cold as the stare the inspector had leveled at me when I told him my theory. With each step, I thought of each letter that had been sent either to private citizens, Scotland Yard directly, or to the newspapers. I tried to think of the killer's motives and wondered if there was one underlying tone in each of the letters. Some point the killer wanted to make or gloat over, or a small shred of information that the man either consciously or subconsciously added to give some hint to his identity. After the first three murders, it was always in the back of my mind that '*Jack the Ripper*' was headed down some path or reaching towards some climax of sorts, allowing for each murder to become more daring and more horrific than the last. Aside from the referral to Boss, in some of the correspondence, the other letters were addressed to specific individuals or to the general public. Unfortunately, there was no exact location in which the letter referred, nor was there any time allocated. There was nothing that would place the killer in a specific part of town or on any street for that matter. Nor was there was anything peculiar or identifiable in the killer's dissection that bore the signature of a particular surgeon or even a butcher. There was no pattern in anything '*Jack*' did, that is, aside from killing prostitutes down dark alleys.

As I walked along, oblivious to the congestion on the street, I read and reread each letter over and over in my mind. Unfortunately, I could not think of anything in the letters that revealed any precise message or any detail that the writer of the correspondence could not possibly have obtained by perusing the newspapers.

I began with the first '*Dear Boss*' letter received by the Central News Agency, next came the '*Saucy Jacky Letter*,' which was the first letter sent to George Lusk. Next came the letter '*From Hell*,' and the letter to Doctor Openshaw. In each case, the recipient was referred to as *Boss, dear old Boss, Dear Boss, say Boss*, and *old Boss*. Nothing in any of the appellations could be used as a reference to any specific recipient. In fact, the letters could have been mailed to anyone. Although something kept nagging me about the content of the letters, but as of yet, I could not put my finger on it? Rolling up my collar, I saw a cab at the corner, slapping the door with the palm of my hand to get the driver's attention; I shouted my destination and then climbed in, thankful to be out of the winds piercing fingers.

The morning was dull with a fine mist in the air, sitting at my desk with copies of '*Jack's*' letters in front of me, I started to list all the similarities and differences that I could see in the letters. Slowly, I began to recognize a pattern in the writing of some of the letters. So, focused on the correspondence, I failed to hear the knock on my door.

"Detective!" Baxter, barked.

"Wynne, I'm sorry, I was preoccupied with what I was doing," I said, rubbing my tired eyes.

"I see that John, what are you working on anyway, something to do with the '*Jack the Ripper*' case I expect?"

"I am looking into the '*Ripper*' letters to see if there is any detail overlooked that may tie any particular suspect we have on file to these murders, Wynne," I replied apprehensively.

"Are you looking at anyone in particular, Detective?"

"Right now, I would be happy, Wynne, if I could find just one detail or some common denominator in the writer's diction. Or anything that the killer utilizes in his writing style that might give us some clue as to his background or education."

I looked away from my work in time to see Baxter take off his suit jacket and start to roll up his sleeves.

"What are you doing, Wynne?"

"I have no inquests to hold for the next few days and this looks like something two heads would be better suited for. Wouldn't you agree, Detective?"

"Thanks, Wynne."

"Alright, where do we begin?" Baxter asked, enthusiastically.

"Well, I think what you should do, is read each letter Wynne, while I compile what I have found as far as inconsistencies or similarities between the letters. I have these originals only for a brief time before I have to return them. As I read them, you could mark each point down and give me your opinion on what I have found in each case. Agreed," I suggested.

"Agreed."

Baxter picked up the letters and retreated to the chair opposite and sat down to read.

An hour later, they had compiled two parallel lists and variations found in the letters, and then they began to exchange comments and suggestions across the desk to each other.

"Ok Wynne, this is what we have so far. Five letters use a derivative of '*Boss*.' The first letter is signed '*Jack the Ripper*,' as is the second, third, and fourth. However, in the first and second letters, the writer refers to himself as '*Saucy Jacky*.' The fourth letter is the letter that was sent to George Lusk, the one fondly known to those at the Yard, as the '*Letter from Hell*,' I said, sarcastically. "There is no 'boss' reference, addressing Lusk as '*Sor*,' the postscript reading, '*catch me if you can Mishter Lusk*.' The fifth letter, we examined, we will call the '*Openshaw letter*.' The writer refers to the good doctor as '*Old Boss*' and signs it '*Jack the Ripper*' with a lower case '*r*.'" Accepting Baxter's nod in recognition satisfied me.

"Alright then," I continued. "These are my thoughts; in the first letter, the writer refers to himself as, '*Saucy Jacky*.' That sounds more like a name, a mother calls a child who is a naughty little boy. There is also a reference to 'codding,' which is Irish country slang for fooling someone; in this instance, we are left to assume it is in reference to the police. The killer then promises '*to take the ears off of my next victim*,' and that there will be more victims to come. The letter is signed, *'Jack the Ripper.'* The author makes use of the name *'Ripper'* given him by the newsagents in addition to the first name *'Jack'* differentiating himself from the name *'Leather Apron.'* Not only does this label our author as the sole perpetrator of the murders, but it establishes that this man is proud of his sins and his desire is for the public to see him as someone playful, not just a sadistic killer."

"Letter two," I continued, my critique of the letters, while walking back in forth behind my desk. "This letter is somewhat larger in content. The killer has a lot to say, about this *'Leather Apron'* moniker and making a point of informing the police that they don't have a clue as to his identity. His *'down on whores'* statement authenticates that this man is a misogynist, and hates all women but especially those associated with prostitution. The correspondent continues with more referrals to being a naughty child, calling his murders, *'funny little games.'* I suppose our killer, believes that all policemen are fools and he gets extreme pleasure by taunting them. I also think our killer perceives himself as someone far superior to everone else, especially the police. I believe, *'Jack's'* victims are not random, but each one is chosen, although what specific characteristic or trait centers out each victim remains a mystery. It could be just because they are prostitutes, but somehow, I doubt that *'Jack's'* reasoning is so simplistic. What else?" I asked, referring back to my notes.

"This man loves the papers calling him *'Jack the Ripper,'* and chooses his victims specifically, the killer, thinks himself superior to others." Wynne said, reading my notes.

"Yes, thank you, Wynne," I said, finding the place where I had left off. "The games that *'Jack'* refers to; could be as simple, as making these women think his advances are genuine. Our killer then either grows weary of the games or perhaps these women tire of him, bringing about the end of the relationship. After *'Jack'* murders his victim and mutilates their features so, that they are no longer attractive, our man steals away with a piece of their anatomy. I believe this action in the killer's mind, is suggestive of taking a memento, or establishes the sense of control this man desires over his victim. His postscript says, *'Dont mind me giving the trade name.'* This, not only bespeaks of his eagerness to take up the nickname the newspapers have given him, but it also establishes his intentions to keep living up to it."

251

"Letter four..."

"Wait a minute, Detective, back up for a second," Baxter barked, still furiously scratching away with my pen making notes. "What is this memento, taking business?"

"Sorry, Wynne, I assume that this killer takes his victim's ears or womb, or even a kidney, and keeps it in memory of the occasion! You know that Catharine Eddowes kidney and uterus were both missing; even the torso found at Whitehall was missing the uterus. I believe that the more often '*Jack*' kills, the more fixated this man becomes. From the first victim, until this last, this man has been spending more time on each victim after death has occurred, it appears that our man is no longer afraid of being caught, nor content with just slicing his victim's throat."

"Detective, how can you be so sure of what you are saying," Baxter balked. 'You almost sound as if you have some intimate knowledge of this man. I fear you are taking too much license here Stone?"

"In a way, I suppose, I am. But try to understand my thinking here, Wynne. By studying these letters and these victims, I am trying to get to know this man. I think I can understand how this killer thinks, by understanding how these women come to be '*Jack's*' next victim."

"Such as?" Baxter queried, looking up from scribbling in the pad propped on his knee.

"Such as, why or how this villain chooses each of his victims. What sets each victim apart from the others, and how and when '*Jack*' strikes. I think we can learn a lot about this man by studying these letters. It is the only link we have, and I am convinced the answer to how this man thinks is here. As far as my speculation that this wretch likes to kill, I do not think that my thoughts are so, farfetched considering that this killer is sending the police letters, gloating, and telling them of his plans. You don't have to be a doctor, Wynne; to know that with each consecutive victim; the amount of dissection has increased. The amount of time that the killer spends carving the victim's face and their bodies displays a cruel nature that goes beyond a man seeking organs for a medical study. His actions speak of a repressed psychosis, which is made more evident with each crime becoming more and more ghastly than the last."

Baxter looked at Stone without saying a word.

"Moving on to the fourth letter, referred to as the '*Letter from Hell.*' Our letter starts with a formal salutation, using '*Mr. Lusk* and *Sor.*' '*Jack*' does not refer to himself in the third person, nor is the pseudonym '*Jack the Ripper*' used. The reference '*from Hell*' insinuates some connotation of pure evil. I believe the writer wants the reader to imagine that the killer has an association perhaps with some dark forces. It seems our author is using any measure to astound and frighten the reader. To be quite honest Wynne when I first read the letter it near sickened me," I offered, glancing up from the correspondence at the Baxter.

"I must say, Detective, if the killer is resigned to astound all who reads this grisly, correspondence than I'd say, the man is doing a smashing job of it," Baxter commented without looking up from the piles of notes in front of him.

"You are quite right, Wynne, I think this killer wants us to be horrified and disgusted, which leads us to ask the question, did '*Jack*' actually eat the piece of what we are to assume was Eddowes' kidney in the box? Or was this some ploy to just make us believe him capable, to keep the streets full of fear and gossip?"

"I'd say '*Jack*' is doing a bloody good job of convincing us that there is a good chance of him doing it, Detective," Wynne replied, getting up from his chair to pour himself a cup of tea.

"Be that as it may, Wynne, there is no new information in the letter, at least nothing that couldn't be gleaned from the papers to assume that this letter is written by the same author as the first two letters."

"What are you getting at Stone," Baxter interrupted. "Are you suggesting that there is more than one person responsible for writing these letters?"

"I believe Mr. Baxter that there are at least two authors for sure, but most likely three."

"Three! Where the devil are you getting this information from, Stone?"

"In the '*Dear Boss*' letter, dated September 25th and the '*Saucy Jacky*' postcard, there are distinct similarities in the formation of the letters."

"How so, Detective?"

"To begin with Wynne, look at the way the letter slants away from the right margin, then tightens towards the bottom of the page. There are similarities in both letters in the size of the upper case '*I*' and the spacing between the words. Then look at the crossing of the '*t*,' it is on the right and in some cases, doesn't touch. In both correspondences, the dot of the

253

'*i*' is to the right of the letter and the pen is pressed very firmly. In both letters, there are also apparent similarities in the formation of the letters '*b, p,* and *s.*' The '*b*' and '*p*' are not closed, and the formation of the '*s*' is tall and spiked. These are the most apparent details, there are other less predominant characteristics but similar to a lesser degree."

I watched the coroner look from one letter analyzing all the characteristics that I had pointed out and then refer to the other letters. As the minutes ticked by and the Baxter's response still had not surfaced, I sat down and poured myself more tea.

The minutes, slowly ebbed by and then, the coroner finally looked up from the letters in his hands.

"Stone, how in the world did you discover these differences?" Baxter continued without waiting for an answer. "You must have studied these letters under a bloody microscope."

"The idea first came to me after I read an article by Alphonse Bertillon," I explained.

"A bloody Frenchman!" Baxter interrupted.

"Yes, but never mind that Wynne," I responded to the coroner's comment. "In the past few weeks, I began to study the letters as a clue rather than merely reading the content. I began to look for the characteristics displayed by the person behind the pen, not just in the wording," I reasoned.

"I must say, Detective, I find you're reasoning astounding and even entertaining, if I may be allowed go so far, but is anyone else going to take you seriously?"

"Well, I suppose that I will have to cross that bridge when I get to it, Wynne, let us continue," I said, changing the subject.

I was resigned to focus on the task at hand; rather than give any more thought to the very point that nagged at me since I had begun the task. I could only field my ideas to my superiors, what they did with the information was up to them.

"Look at each of the letters again Wynne," I asked. "If '*Jack*' is the ego maniac, that I believe these letters let on, then why did the killer not sign all of the letters '*Jack the Ripper*,' I asked. "I would think, that should be this man's stamp of genuineness, which is why I believe our killer wanted to set the record straight about any misunderstanding that arose with Piser, being considered a suspect."

254

"I don't understand, John?"

"I think our killer was offended when the girl's thought Piser was the killer," I answered.

"But Detective…"

"Just a minute," I said, holding up my hand to stop Baxter from interrupting me. "This man further states, '*send you the knife.*' Why would '*Jack*' relinquish his weapon? This knife is his signature, it would be like signing his own death warrant," I finished.

"Hear, hear Detective," Baxter objected. "I think that you are leaving too much to supposition, are you not?" Baxter sighed.

"I don't think so, Wynne. As we have discussed in the past, this man does not think like you or I. Perhaps this fellow lives in a world of fantasy and sees himself as some necessary evil ridding the world of the immoral of the East End."

"Judge, jury, and executioner, by ridding London's streets of its prostitutes."

"Perhaps that is how '*Jack*' envisions himself, who is to say, Wynne."

"Enough of that, Stone, what more have you on these letters?"

"The other major difference in this letter, compared to the others, Wynne, is the spelling," I said, changing the subject. "I am convinced the words are deliberately misspelled and have a feel as if someone was dictating the letter to the writer."

"What do you mean?"

"The words: '*Sor, Prasarved, tother, Mishter,*' all sound like verbal slang. Also, the words '*knif* and *whil,*' are words that have a silent letter, like '*k*' in the word knife, '*h*' in the word while, yet these letters are not the letters that are omitted. Doesn't that strike you as odd, Wynne?"

"I suppose that is odd once you explain it like that, but let us for a moment assume you are correct, Detective," Baxter said, holding up a letter. "What about this third letter, the one written to the Echo, for I imagine, Israel Schwartz?"

[Sic] "You though your-self very clever I reckon you informed the police. But you made a mistake if you though I dident see you. Now I known you know me and I see your

255

little game, and I mean to finish you and send your ears to your wife if you show this to the police or help them if you do I will finish you. I t no use you trying to get out of my way. Because I have you when you don't expect it and I keep my word as you soon see and rip you up.

Yours Truly, Jack the Ripper."

"This is the third letter, posted on October sixth," I answered. "I think this letter was written deliberately to astound its readers and intended only to sell newspapers, nothing more. It does use the pseudonym '*Jack the Ripper,*' but that is where all similarities end from the first two letters. Again, Wynne, this is just supposition but, the author deliberately misspells '*thought*' by excluding the '*t.*' I also believe the word '*dident,*' to be a poor way of plagiarizing the other letters as if someone knew there was glaring spelling errors in the first two letters and was deliberately trying to copy from them. The writer also makes a miserable attempt at suggesting that Schwartz is a threat, by mentioning his wife, then adds a postscript in the margin of the letter, writing, '*You see I know your address,*' but doesn't bother to mail it or deliver the message directly to the address by messenger. Instead, the letter is given to a newspaper publication."

"By jove, Detective, I think you might be onto something there," Baxter said.

"There are only so many possibilities, Wynne. These five letters that we have been focusing on, have too many variations in style and too many inconsistencies not to address them with some scrutiny," I reflected, retreating behind my desk.

"If you are correct Stone, then who do you suppose these other authors are," Wynne said, before slurping the last of his tea. "And, who could possibly gain by terrorizing the city? I mean, I suppose the newspapers would be the more apparent culprit, in their attempts to profit by newspaper sales, but that seems too easy a target?" Baxter questioned.

"That is precisely what I have been asking myself all day Wynne. If I am correct, and I think I am, I believe that there are at least three different

256

authors," I answered. "First, I think, we have a man out there who enjoys the publicity and being called '*Jack the Ripper*' almost as much as committing the crimes. I am certain that this individual did, write the first two letters. The other letter to George Lusk, I believe the Vigilance Committee had a hand in writing that one."

"Your daft man," Baxter growled. "What on earth would they have to gain?"

Baxter stood up and tossed the letters on the edge of Stone's desk.

"The Vigilance Committee has had an interest in this from the beginning Wynne."

"From the beginning, John?"

"Yes, Wynne," I argued. "This organization has written the Home Secretary, requesting that the government offer a substantial reward, albeit, their request was refused because the English Government does not offer rewards for the apprehension of criminals. After the government refused to offer any help, the committee deliberately wrote an editorial in the London Times, knowing that it would be brought to the attention of the Queen. I have a feeling they were instrumental in swaying public opinion to get the Home Secretary to resign."

"How could they accomplish that Stone," Baxter argued. "After all, they are not that influential."

"By using the threats against George Lusk to get their point across."

"I have been introduced to Mr. Lusk; I find it hard to believe that the man would be involved in such devious behavior, John," Baxter suggested.

"Wynne, I interviewed Lusk myself," I explained. "I came away with the same impression. Though if I am right, I find it hard to believe that Lusk suspects any impropriety at all. However, my theory is based largely on this kidney business. I think the idea came to me after both Doctor's Sutton and Brown, offered ..."

Pausing, I began to look for the scrap of paper; I had written on.

"Just a minute, Wynne, I have it right here someplace," I said continuing to sift through the piles of papers on my desk. "Here it is, [Sic] '*the kidney removed had been put in spirits within a few hours of its removal.*' I ask you Wynne, who but someone with medical experience would know to do that?"

"Certainly, a doctor, but that was what you wanted to hear, isn't it, Detective? I must say though immersing in spirits has been a way of preserving for different applications for centuries."

"It does stand to reason," I answered. "If '*Jack's*' plan was to eat the kidney, why did the man wait until the sixteenth of the month to write about it? The only conclusion I am left with, Wynne, is that the organ was dissected by someone who knew what they were doing, perhaps a physician, most certainly someone with medical knowledge. The specimen could have been taken from some physician's training lab and put in a box the same day that it was sent to George Lusk, with the letter '*From Hell*' attached."

"There are far too many possibilities for my liking Stone," Baxter replied. "This could have been '*Jack*' as you say, but it also could have been any number of men or women for that matter that work at a hospital. We both know that there are those who are fascinated by the publicity in a case and do silly things like this without realizing the hindrance to the case that they cause, simply to get some kicks from playing a lark."

"That is precisely my point, Wynne," I answered. "The letter to Dr. Openshaw mentions details about scalpels, microscopes, and slides, giving a little too much information for the laymen to have, wouldn't you agree?"

"It would be easy to just agree with you, John, but several other occupations use similar equipment," Baxter suggested. "However, I will ask you, would a physician tip his hand by placing those specifics in the letter, even if the man tried to shroud his knowledge by using misspelled words."

"I see your point, Wynne, but that is where my theory about different authors makes sense, given the inconsistencies these letters contain."

"Yes, I see your point, and it is valid, John."

"That being said, I feel we must return to the dispute about the time it took for our killer to remove organs from his victims," I commented. "Not to mention, this foreign gentleman that is somewhere in London, looking for specimens for medical research to consider."

"Yes, there is, isn't there," Baxter mused. "I have not given that chap much thought of late."

"You are right about one thing though, Wynne," I responded.

"Oh," Baxter said, perking up a little. "What was that?"

"When you say that there is far too much speculation going on, to be sure of any one point for certain. Nor, is there enough evidence to point a finger in any one direction at this time."

"What can we really be sure of then, Stone?"

"I think there is a definite political motive here, but like I just stated, how could you prove such a thing, if it's true," I stated. "I also believe that it would be a big mistake to rule out the involvement of the newspaper syndicates."

"How can you be so entirely sure that you are right in that regard, Detective?" Baxter retorted. "I am sorry, my friend, but I must say that you are pulling at straws with no real proof to back up anything that you speculate."

"Wynne, the citizens of this city, are tired of being frightened at every turn," I began. "They are living in uncertainty, and wondering where this madman will strike next. I don't think it any stretch to say that the consensus in Whitechapel is that government doesn't care about their plight. Whoever wrote this letter is exploiting that fear and the agents that print these outlandish letters are contributing to it, not helping matters. I am not sure what is worse, the government for allowing this fear to run rampant in the streets or the agents for printing that those in charge of the streets of Whitechapel are bunglers, too incompetent to be in control. This is how they, whoever they, may be, shake and manipulate the foundations of the government," I responded.

"That seems rather farfetched, Detective," Baxter criticized. "Who would be powerful enough to manipulate so many to get the government to offer a reward, something, I must say it seems no extraordinary thing to ask. What of Lusk, why keep him entirely in the dark?"

"We have already seen how the public's fear can be used to bring about change in police habits and their thinking. Why, is it so impossible to believe that the constant shouts of distress by a city's citizens can be effectively used to get a response from the government Wynne? As far as the Vigilance Committee's intentions, they seem to have the best interests of the community in hand, but I believe that they may have had a hidden agenda. As far as Lusk, the man is a public figure, I think whoever is behind this scheme needed a man like him to authenticate their plan so, to be sure their ploy was believable without making anyone suspicious," I retorted.

"What other agenda would the Vigilance Committee have, besides meeting the needs of the people in a time when they are frightened, and the police are failing miserably?" Baxter asked.

"Exactly, Wynne," I replied. "When a committee is set up to meet the demands of the citizen, which in my opinion, could be considered a tall order. When a self-appointed committee like this one has all the support of the people, they have nothing to fear; until the people's demands are no longer being met. Then, the citizenry can turn on the Vigilance Committee just as fast as they did the police. Wynne, I ask you, what have the Vigilance Committee done to date?"

I watched Baxter shrug his shoulders in response.

"The Vigilance Committee are patrolling the streets, just as are the police, but the murders have not ceased, they really have done nothing to validate their development or existence. This letter and the specimen of a kidney, delivered to George Lusk could prove that this criminal in Whitechapel is beyond the arm of the law. It has been suggested more than once in the columns of every newspaper in London that police have lost control, and now, this criminal is not just happy to kill prostitutes but has taken to threatening a prominent citizen and his family. To add insult to injury, this '*Jack*' has also escalated to the most terrible of crimes known to mankind."

"Since you explain it that way, Stone, I may come around to your way of thinking. What do you mean escalated to the most terrible of crimes?"

I watched Baxter yawn as the hour was late, and the coroner obviously was having a hard time focusing.

"Cannibalism, Wynne!"

Chapter Fifteen

The next morning, I woke in my office as I had done a countless number of times, staying long at my desk after sending Baxter home the night before. I had continued to work until false dawn lit the sky. From a basin and pitcher, I splashed water on my face and toweled off. Glancing at the clutter on my desk, I wasn't sure what to do with the information that I had accumulated. While Wynne Baxter was well respected in his field and had become an invaluable asset and colleague, not to mention the coroner's collaboration on the work they had done investigating. In the grand scheme of things, it matter little to the investigation and there were still those at The Yard that needed to be considered. The only question that remained was what to do with all the information that I had compiled about the letters from '*Jack*.' My immediate thoughts was to waltz into Abberline's office and drop the files on his desk to show that I had not been sitting on my hands in Whitechapel. Although as fast as I had conceived the thought, I dismissed the idea. Aside from having no actual proof and no suspect to substantiate my theory, what it all boiled down to was supposition. Not to mention the fact, that I was accusing ten different newspaper publications and a powerful organization like the Vigilance Committee of tampering with a criminal investigation. I could only imagine the response at The Yard after I tried to explain my theory of how these organizations had written at least three of the letters signed '*Jack the Ripper*' and then at the same time proceed to accuse these organizations of giving false statements to police. I could only guess the kind of reception; I would receive when I could give only innuendo and supposition to support my theory and present no real proof for my allegations. I might as well tell them that I was acting entirely on a gut feeling, the reaction would have been the same. After careful consideration, I decided the information was best left on the top of my desk until some further evidence presented itself.

The last thing on my mind during the wee hours before exhaustion finally forced me away from my desk was to compile a list of suspects for my files. I had examined each profile much the same way as I had done with the '*Jack the Ripper*' letters. Glancing at the list of suspects that I had compiled, I had to be honest with myself that it was far from promising. None of the suspects had been seen in the vicinity of any of the crimes by an eyewitness, nor did any one suspect have a previous relationship with the other victims. This was significant, if the consensus was to be believed, that all five women had been murdered by one killer. It went without saying that the criminal investigator's first task was to establish a list of suspects that were in proximity to the crime. These were generally; accumulated from a pool of persons within the victim's close personal relationships. What lay on my desk was the list that I had compiled following the standard conventions of criminal investigative techniques. Unfortunately, none of the suspects fell under the guise of those conventions.

Henry Turner X
Michael Ostrog X
John Pizer X
Grenadier Guardsman PVT George
Michael Kidney X
Henry Samuel Tabram X
James Kelly X

Thomas Conway X
William Nichols X
John Chapman X
John Kelly X

The list of suspects collected to date for the murder of the five women was not long, nor was it distinguished. I had tried to be selective in my collection of the most obvious, but with so few to consider, it was challenging to have more than one suspect for each of the murdered victims. Examining the names, I knew several could be eliminated at first glance. Most of the obvious were added simply to reduce any further suspicion, or in the very least, to add credibility to the investigation. Having established a clear, if not, a disappointing set of suspects, I also considered a couple of names that Scotland Yard had taken into consideration from the beginning, but to me, these were; as unlikely as the rest to even be regarded as likely candidates.

"Good morning, Detective, will you join me for some tea," Baxter asked, carrying a tray rattling with cups and saucers.

"Wynne, you are looking chipper this morning."

"I shouldn't be," Baxter said, pouring tea into two cups. "I could not sleep a wink thinking about these infernal letters that I read last night John."

"Thank you," I said, taking the teacup and saucer. "I hope delving into this killer's thoughts did not distress you too much, Wynne."

"Give it no thought, John. Dealing in death should be second nature to me, but it is not, such is the life of a coroner. What are we covering today?"

"Key suspects, I should think, Wynne," I said, looking up at the coroner who cautiously sipped the scalding liquid from my cup.

"For now, if you don't mind, John," Baxter said, settling in his chair. "I will sit and listen and drink my tea if that is alright. Cheers." Baxter said, cradling the teacup between his hands.

"Martha Tabram," I began without hesitation, focusing on the papers in front of me. "She was married to Henry Samuel Tabram, who left her in 1875, due to her '*alcoholic fits*' as Mr. Tabram put it. The couple tried to reunite, but Martha Tabram was living with Henry Turner at the time. Jealousy could possibly be a motive; however, the couple had been separated for thirteen years, and Tabram has no other connection to the other women.

Henry Turner lived with Tabram on and off for twelve years. Turner, like Tabram before him, left due to his wife's excessive drinking. Martha Tabram had spent the last year in and out of Lodging Houses having no

263

fixed address. She took to prostitution to pay for her lodgings. Henry Turner last saw her the Saturday before her death, again its possible jealousy could be a motive, or Turner could have resented the fact that his wife took to prostitution; however, there is no connection between Henry Turner and the other four women to speak of.

Private Law and Private Leary were in the neighborhood on the night in question between two and six in the morning. During questioning, Private Leary told police that Private Law had gone on his own, for 2 hours in which time Leary did not know his friend's whereabouts. We assume that Law was in the vicinity of the murder.

On August fifteenth, Mary Anne Connelly picked out Private George in a line-up of Guardsmen, who she claims was with Tabram on the evening of August seventh. Connelly also claims she was entertaining a Private Skipper on the same evening. Connelly; however, was mistaken in her identification of the Guardsmen on both counts, when questioned at the inquest. It is unfortunate, but Guardsmen uniforms can be mistaken quite easily by those who are not familiar with the different regiments.

I think we can safely exclude Henry Samuel Tabram and Henry Turner from the list of eligible suspects. Without any further evidence or witnesses who might have seen Martha Tabram with a Guardsmen, there is no tangible evidence to link Privates Skipper or George to the crime either. Unless some new evidence is discovered implicating either man, it is safe to assume that we can safely eliminate these two as well.

In the case of Mary Ann '*Polly*' Nichols, she and her husband, William Nichols, were separated for eight years before her death. Mr. Nicholls had repeated quarrels with his wife due to her drinking habits, and she had subsequently left him. Mr. Nicholls admitted having known that his former wife was living with a Blacksmith and had later left him and had taken up with another man unknown to him. Mary Ann Nicholls had since been living in common lodging houses, having no fixed address. Both Polly Nichols and William Nichols have had no connection whatsoever for years. Thus, eliminating jealousy due to his wife living with other men as a possible motive. William Nichols has no known connection to the other victims. Mary Ann Nichols' occupation after leaving her husband was unknown; she admitted to no one that she had taken to prostitution to pay her rent.

I believe it is safe to eliminate William Nichols from the list of suspects due to the length of separation between him and his wife. It might be worth making a note of the fact that there is no previous connection between Nicholls and any of the other suspects, thus eliminating collusion.

In the murder investigation of Annie Chapman, her husband had been deceased for eighteen months previous to her death. She was known to have lived with a sieve-maker; his name and whereabouts are unknown. Chapman, since the death of her husband, has lived in common lodging houses having no fixed address. To make ends meet, she sold hand-made articles and resorted to prostitution if needed to pay for lodgings. Chapman was last known to be seen with a pensioner by the name of Edward Stanley, a bricklayer's laborer. At the inquest held in Chapman's death, Stanley denied living with Chapman.

Before Elizabeth Stride's death, she was married to John Thomas Stride in 1869, a man thirteen years her senior. She was admitted to Poplar Workhouse in 1877; upon her release, she temporarily reunited with her husband; however, the circumstances that caused the couple to separate must have remained unchanged; for they separated soon after, permanently this time. John Thomas Stride died in 1881. Since that time, Stride has been in court on numerous occasions on drunk and disorderly charges. Michael Kidney, a waterside laborer, had been living with Elizabeth Stride for several years when she accused him of assault on April sixth, 1887 but, Stride failed to appear in court to answer to the charges. Michael Kidney claims to have last seen Stride on the day of September twenty-fifth, 1888, five days before her death. Mr. Kidney also claimed to know nothing of her prostitution, and it was due to Stride's drinking that made her leave for days at a time. Kidney is a peculiar personality and somewhat odd in his manner, but hardly the type to kill."

"That man should be put in the asylum to be evaluated," Baxter commented. "That is my opinion, anyway."

I heard Baxter's comment, understanding the coroner's dislike for Kidney due to the man's behavior on the witness stand.

"Continue, Detective," Baxter said, rising from his chair long enough to pour another cup of tea.

"In the case of Catharine Eddowes, she was married to Thomas Conway; Eddowes left her husband in 1880. In 1881, she was living with a man known as John Kelly at Cooney's Common Lodging House, at fifty-five, Flower and Dean St. Money was seemingly not an issue, Eddowes regularly used prostitution as a means to pay for her vices. Eddowes, on the night before her death, was found drunk on the road at Aldgate High Street on September twenty-ninth by Police Constable Louis Robinson. She was in custody until one a.m. at Bishopgate police station on September thirtieth. She was last seen in Church Passage at the entrance to Mitre Square by three witnesses. Joseph Lawende, Joseph Hyam Levy, and Harry Harris saw Eddowes at 1:35 talking to an unknown gentleman; she was found ten minutes later by Police Constable Watkins.

We can eliminate John Kelly as a suspect, that is, if can we rely on the eyewitness description given by the three witnesses who last seen Eddowes alive. All three witnesses told the coroner that they most likely could not identify the man they saw with Eddowes, if said man, was found at a later date. Whether out of conscience sake of not seeing the man in the proper light, or fear of reprisal for mistaken identity, it is not known.

All four victims had nothing in common except their occupation. There are no relatives or acquaintances to tie any one of the victims to another. Aside from Tabram, all women were known for their fondness for drink; as a result of this affliction, these women had suffered the loss of their spouses. Living conditions being as hard as they are in the East End, gainful employment is hard to come by, and all had fallen on desperate times. All the women, lived private lives. The victim's relatives, and closest acquaintances testify of having no knowledge whatsoever as to how they paid for their meager lodgings. Even the men, the women cohabitated, claimed to know nothing about their prostitution. Although the deputies of the lodging houses must have had their suspicions, the victims moved quite frequently from one common house to another and kept their movements entirely secret. Their need to seek out family members to borrow money instead of brokering in their trade is evidence that they were not totally comfortable with their lifestyles. It is possible that at sundry times, these women had bouts of sobriety in which they were ashamed and tried to change their lives in which they had to resort to prostitution to survive."

"I find it hard to believe Stone that friends, acquaintances, and family members knew nothing of how these women supported themselves," Baxter intervened. "The East End isn't so big that these people would not see each other from time to time."

"I agree, Wynne," I said, taking time to sip my tea. "I believe that a lot of these people who knew the victims chose to look the other way, choosing not to think about what they may have suspected."

"Hmm." Baxter groaned.

"Be that as it may, I think that we can also eliminate John Pizer as stated by evidence given at the Nichols' inquest as a suspect. As you know Wynne, Pizer's alibi would suit any man who would require one, having spent the hours in question when the Nichols woman was murdered with a police constable during the Docks fire on Friday, August thirtieth. The remaining suspects are few, and most seem as unlikely as they could come, including the Bogey Man."

"Grenadier Guardsman, Private George, who Mary Anne Connelly picked out of a lineup of Guardsman on August the fifteenth, is still a suspect in my view. Nevertheless, Connelly's eyewitness account was blemished by her inability to make a positive identification of the men that she and Martha Tabram had been entertaining the night of Tabram's murder. To make matters worse, Connelly even confused the Guardsman's units and their ranks. At first, she had identified the two Grenadier Guardsmen as corporals, but there wasn't a Guardsman to fit the description in the Grenadiers. Connelly then testified that she remembered that the two Guardsmen wore white bands around their hats. This only made matters worse because it proved that the two men were Coldstream, not Grenadier Guardsmen. It was also determined that the two men that Connelly picked out of a lineup had alibis for the night in question. To further complicate matters, the corporal she did choose out of a line up turned out to be a Private George. Pvt. George had been with his wife at 120 Hammersmith Road. The other soldier Connelly identified was a Private Skipper who was in barracks at 10:50 p.m., his alibi was confirmed by his commanders."

Exasperated, I finished the report and tossed it on my desk.

"Well, where exactly does that leave us as far as suspects go, Detective?" Wynne asked, slurping the last of his tea.

"I think at this stage of the game, Wynne, we would have a better chance of catching the aforementioned *Bogey Man* than '*Jack the Ripper*.' Both of whom have proved to be as elusive as any character you would read about in a storybook."

Sipping my tea, I paused to open a file that I had received from Inspector Abberline containing a list of suspects. In the corner of the file folder, I saw a name written in pencil, with a small note attached. Severin Antoniovich Klosowski was a man of Polish descent, arriving in England sometime in the late 1880s. Klosowski had been apprenticed by his father as a surgeon in Warsaw, Poland. Leaving Poland, Klosowski had soon after been hired as a barber's assistant in London and had recently opened his own barbershop on Cable Street. That was the extent of the note that Inspector Abberline had written in the margin of the page. I examined the entire folder for any further mention of Klosowski, but found nothing more; puzzled, I made a mental note to question the inspector on the why and how Klosowski had made it as a suspect in the most notorious criminal investigation in England.

There was one more name in the file. The name of Michael Ostrog had been tucked away as a likely candidate for the murders. However, after studying the man's police file, I saw only a description of a habitual criminal, not a deranged murderer. Judging by Ostrog's file, it was not difficult to see that the man had little regard for the laws of society; his police record was evidence of that. Ostrog was imprisoned from 1863 until the spring of 1888 for several offenses, although mostly for theft. It was, however, interesting to see that Ostrog's release dates coincided with the times of the murders of the five women in Whitechapel. Although there was no record of the man being anything other than a petty thief and nothing concrete to tie him to the Whitechapel murders.

"Tell me something, Stone; are you still chewing on this doctor idea as the likeliest candidate for the killer?

"I am blatantly aware, Wynne that all of the testifying doctors, aside from Doctor Frederick Brown that is, have a hard time swallowing this theory," I said trying to empathize. "What other explanation is there for the time required to murder and slice these women's bodies as the killer does and allow for the dissection and removal of organs in the few minutes that '*Jack*' has? I can come up with no other intelligent answer on how someone without anatomical knowledge could do what has been done to these women, escape, and then vanish without a clue. That is unless this man kills his victims somewhere else than dumps their bodies where they are found."

"What new theory are you considering now, Stone?"

"Nothing new, Wynne, the same theory that I have been trying to convince you of, from the beginning, my friend."

"You might be able to convince me that this man has some anatomical knowledge," Baxter relented. "But you are way off the mark in this, John. This wretch couldn't go traipsing all over the street carrying a dead prostitute in his arms."

"Wynne, listen to my explanation and then make up your mind."

I watched Baxter, nod in approval before proceeding.

"My theory is based on three details," I explained. "First, the blood at the crime scene is found predominantly behind the victim's neck and nowhere else. Second, there are no signs of a struggle where the bodies are found. Third, the constables patrolling the areas where the crimes are committed, never see anything or anyone out of the ordinary. In addition to the corroborated times of the constable's patrols and the doctor's time of death, coupled with the amount of time it is estimated for '*Jack*' to kill and disfigure his victim, and escape, a carriage lying in wait is the only way to support the timing that doctors have estimated for him to perform the dissections on the bodies and avoid detection by the patrolling constables."

"But in his letter, this fiend who calls himself the '*Ripper*,' laughs at the notion that police think him a physician," Baxter, interrupted.

"I think we are missing the simplest of answers, Wynne," I answered.

"Such as, Detective?"

"We do not want to believe that this man is a gentleman and even more offensive, would be to consider him a physician. There is no mistaking the maximum amount of time that would be required to complete the mutilation done on Eddowes and escape undetected. The times are too close, leaving no room for the faint of heart, all the while working in the dark. If we do not take into account the near expert training in dissection, all the while operating under these types of extreme conditions, we are only fooling ourselves, Wynne."

I watched Baxter digest what I said, before continuing.

"I also believe that this man has our constable patrol routes mapped out long in advance. Just as I suggested that the killer handpicks certain women from an endless pool of prostitutes, I believe our killer takes his time and studies the police patrols, taking note of the times when constables come into contact with each other or if they stop along the way."

"You don't believe that at such a critical time our constables are lollygagging about with some doxy do you, Stone?" Baxter sounded incredulous.

"Maybe not with some doxy as you say, Wynne, but it is human nature to bend a rule or sneak in somewhere on a cold night, we have all done it. What I am saying is perhaps '*Jack*' has perhaps seen our patrolling constables dip in and out of a pub more than once while, plotting his stratagems and then used the situation to his advantage. The killer has time, patience, an agenda, and a target. The Stride and Eddowes murders involved preparation in getting from one crime to another and make an escape without being seen coming or going from both scenes. These qualities describe the nature of the man who has taken to murder."

"What makes him kill these poor defenseless creatures in such a horrific way, Stone?"

"Who knows, perhaps we will never know, Wynne," I answered. "Something is driving this fiend to some sort of climax. It may be the thrill of the hunt or the chase, or it could be that this killer only has a fiendish lust for blood. His victims haven't changed so, we can assume that the victims are the key to catching this monster, but his manner and temperament have escalated to the degree that warrants some rationale. This killer's, motive though oblivious to us, is locked somewhere in his head. His desire and the brutality of the crime have increased to heights that would seem to be more organized than frenzied. It would also appear that the killer is, satisfying some insatiable desire, and the more often '*Jack*' kills, the harder it is for him to resist these urges that spur him to seek his next victim."

As I was explaining my thoughts to Baxter, I tried to put a face on the killer from the list of suspects, but to no avail.

"All of this is true, John, this monster has killed more often, and the violence of the crimes is unquestionable, but to what end?"

"Only our killer would know that, Wynne. After completing his last murder, this man has been walking around looking for his next victim. I still believe these letters have some hidden clue, but I have racked my brain thinking about them and have come up with nothing. It is possible that just as the letters have stopped, '*Jack*' will stop killing just as abruptly."

270

"I have been thinking about your ideas on these letters, Stone," Baxter commented. "I am not one hundred percent convinced in your theory that '*Jack*' wants police to play some sort of match with him. It just doesn't make any kind of sense that a murderer would keep police informed as to what will happen next. That would be like the man placing the noose around his own neck," Baxter offered.

"Wynne, don't misunderstand what kind of criminal that we are dealing with," I explained. "Jack has a very high intellect and more than likely narcissistic. He relishes in the knowledge that the police haven't a clue as to his identity. As such, our killer thinks himself smarter than the police, whether or not '*Jack*' is, remains to be seen, but the man has been doing a fairly good job making the public believe it," I answered Baxter.

"Alright, Detective, what is our next move; do we sit idly by until this killer strikes again?" Baxter growled.

"Unfortunately, Wynne, we are at an impasse, and our only hope is that with the doubling of police patrols and the public's awareness that we can eventually close '*Jack's*' hunting ground down. However, the women walking London's streets at night refuse to stay at home. Perhaps because it is their only way of survival, whatever the case, right now the killer has an endless supply of prey. If nothing else, we may get lucky, and a witness might get a description of this murderer and be able to put him in goal before he kills again."

"There must be someone out there who has seen this blackheart. The streets are filled with people in this city no matter what time of day or night," Baxter retorted.

"That is why the top minds in Scotland Yard are willing to allow the printing of '*Jack's*' letters in the newspapers Wynne. It is their thinking that someone in the East End knows who this man is and might be willing to offer him up, for a reward, but . . ."

"But, what, Detective?"

"It is my opinion, Wynne, that the more we advertise to the public, that we are at our wits end in our investigation of these murders, the more ammunition, we give to '*Jack*' who is using the public to attract attention to these crimes."

They sat in silence for several minutes before I heard Baxter yawn.

"Well, Detective, like the day, I am spent."

"Good night, Wynne."

"Good night, John."

Like the coroner, I was spent, but instead of going to my rooms, I blew out the lamp and lay on the settee and closed my eyes wrapped in my jacket.

Chapter Sixteen

The hour was late, the rain that drenched the streets and walks had persisted throughout the day into the night. Rolling up my collar, I waited in the shadows of an alley in Spitalfields. My day had started as it had every other day since coming to Whitechapel. I had spent the morning in my office pouring over countless files and witness statements looking for the one detail that might lead me on the trail of a killer. However, the trail I now followed was already weeks old, swept clean by time and the elements. Yet, I was not alone in my pursuit; the greatest detectives in the world had swept every nook and cranny in the East End, along with a pack of bloodhounds that had sniffed and scratched and turned over every rock and grain of sand. As a result, even the greatest noses in London could find no trace of the killer who left no sign or evidence of his passing, or a clue as to who his next victim might be. The absence of any substantial evidence left every copper that walked a patrol on edge, wondering when

'*Jack*' would kill again. Every possible suspect had been looked at again, and each crime scene had been inspected a second and third time; in hopes to find something that might have been missed the first time. Yet, the killer of the double homicide of Stride and Eddowes and three others had once again eluded Scotland Yard's every effort of apprehension. I had hoped that my time in the area of the crime scenes might turn up something. Perhaps 'Jack' would return to his killing ground. Unfortunately, as of yet, the only thing that my countless hours of surveillance had gotten me was wet. Returning to my office, I picked up where I had left off that afternoon.

Exhausted and preoccupied, I had not heard the steps in the hallway, as it was very late. The many days of little sleep had caught up to me, so I slipped on my overcoat and blew on the wick of my oil lamp, extinguishing the flame, and I headed for the door. I had no sooner placed my hand on the knob and swung the door open when I came face to face with the coroner.

"Wynne," I said, taken aback by the abruptness of the coroner's arrival, and then, I took note of the odd expression on his face. "What is the matter?"

"Detective, I wonder if I might impose upon you this night," Baxter asked.

"How can I be of assistance," I asked, unsure what to expect when I saw the small, frail creature come from the shadows of the hall from behind Baxter.

"This dear lady requires some help; she has come to me because she knew me by reputation. I have heard bits and pieces of her story, and it seems her granddaughter has found herself in a spot of trouble. The poor woman is so frightened, she didn't know where else to turn. I have a carriage waiting if you don't mind, I will explain more along the way."

The coroner did not wait for me to answer but proceeded immediately down the hall with the lady in tow. Sensing the urgency of the moment, I turned and locked my office door and then hurried after the pair. Outside, I noted that the rain that I had heard slapping against my office window; showed no signs of letting up. Opening the door of the carriage, I hesitated when I saw Doctor Bagster Phillips sitting on the bench across from the coroner and the old woman. The shrug of the doctor's shoulders; indicated to me that Phillips knew no more than I in regards to the strange circumstances surrounding the woman's appearance in the middle of the night. Grabbing the handle on the side of the door, I closed it behind me taking my seat; seconds before the carriage lurched forward. The trip lasted only about ten minutes, but I paid little attention to the time, being preoccupied with thoughts as to where they were headed and why it was necessary for me to tag along.

An hour had passed since Baxter's unexpected arrival at my office door. I had been standing in the shadows of two dilapidated cottages in Batty Gardens, just off Berner Street, feeling useless and in the way. The rain dripped from off the eaves overhead and landed on the brim of my hat, and somehow found its way down the back of my neck, soaking into the collar of my shirt. The hour was late, and I resisted the urge to strike a match to look at my watch. I stood oblivious to the rain, trying to find words to a prayer my mother had taught me as a child. Somewhere in the distance, I heard a carter, snap a whip over a reluctant horse's ears. Close by, I heard several doors slam from the comings and goings of those that chose the night hours to do their business. These were accompanied by the usual singing of an overindulged patron of a public house, that faded as the man staggered by. The seconds ticked by, as the rain made a distinct plop in a nearby barrel propped under an eve to catch the rain off of the roof of the cottage. I heard every slosh and every footstep of the passers-by, but nothing else from the shadows where I had chosen to take refuge out of the weather. I had opted to wait outside, escaping the smell of blood in the close quarters of the dilapidated shack that the old lady called her home. Upon entering, I immediately understood the reasons for the woman's urgency. As curious as I was, I had stepped out of the way to allow Doctor Phillips to go directly to work. In the carriage before their arrival, the coroner tried to explain the details as given to him by the old lady whose name was Mrs. Gorski, her granddaughter's name was Alenka. It seems, her granddaughter had gotten into trouble with a fiancé who had not the patience to wait for their wedding night. Upon hearing of her pregnancy, Alenka's fiancé had abruptly ended the engagement. Broken-hearted, she had sought advice from a friend, who told her that there was a doctor who could end her pregnancy, taking away her problem so, the man she loved would return to her. That was the extent of the story; moments later, the carriage had arrived at its destination, and the trio followed the old woman into a one-room cottage that both the grandmother and granddaughter shared. Seeing the blood-soaked bedclothes and sheets, I did not need to hear the rest of the story. All three understood why the old woman was desperate for help; I also recognized the results of the young woman's attempt to abort her pregnancy. Leaving the overcrowded hovel, I went outside to allow the doctor to work. I stood under the shelter of a crooked eave hearing; sobs erupt from the old grandmother come from inside the house. Then not too long afterward, the coroner stood in the open door and motioned for me to enter. Taking off my hat, I tiptoed into the room, mindful of the old woman's grief. From where I stood, I could see the old woman kneeling at the girl's bedside whispering in Polish, clenching the hand of her granddaughter in her wrinkled hands. Judging by the serious faces of both Baxter and Doctor Phillips, I had little hope of the poor girl surviving her ordeal.

Twenty minutes later, through the help of a neighbor, they were told the entire story of how the old lady and her husband had arrived in London with their granddaughter Alenka two years before. They had left Poland looking for a better way of life; however, after arriving in London, her husband had died of phthisis. Out of necessity, both grandmother and granddaughter had begun to clean businesses to make ends meet. The work was hard on the old lady so, her granddaughter had taken another job. They had thought that they had found a light at the end of their tunnel; when her granddaughter had been betrothed to a young man, she had met at a church social. It seems, his family was of good name and owned a butcher shop in the East End. Giving in to the pressures of the young man who did not want to wait for their wedding night, her granddaughter had become pregnant. Ashamed of what her grandmother might think, she kept her pregnancy a secret. After telling her betrothed of her pregnancy, the young man grew distant and finally refused to see her. A friend pointed her in the direction of a doctor on Berner Street who could help her. According to the old woman, the physician was known only as Doctor D. After asking only the pertinent questions through the translator, I was able to put the rest of the pieces of the story together that had brought them out on a stormy night to find the young woman, clinging to the barest threads of life.

It seems that the doctor had given the young lady medicine of some kind, and after she had taken it, she began to hemorrhage. Unable to stop the hemorrhaging on her own, she went back to this Doctor D. seeking help. She told her grandmother that the doctor had flown into a rage. First, the man had tried to forcibly remove her from his office. When she would not leave, the doctor began to assault her. After fighting him off, she ran out of the office and returned home where her grandmother found her weak from the loss of blood. Unfortunately, by then, it was late afternoon, and the local doctor was nowhere to be found. Unable to stop the bleeding, the old woman dared not move her granddaughter. Not knowing where to turn, her neighbor told her to go to the coroner and ask for help. When the translator was finished, the old woman clung to her granddaughter's side, stroking her hair and the side of her face, muttering some song in Polish.

Doctor Phillips stood at the edge of the bed and gestured for the two men to follow him to one of the corners of the shabby room.

"She is fading fast; it won't be long now."

"Isn't there something we can do?" Baxter asked.

"I am afraid, there isn't anything more I can do," Phillips said, turning to look at his patient. "Perhaps if we had arrived sooner, there might have been some hope."

"What could make her bleed like that?"

I asked the doctor the question after a long moment of awkward silence.

"There are a number of things that some of these so-called physicians give to these poor unfortunates. They know that these women come to them out of desperation, and their patients are willing to follow whatever directions they tell them to rid themselves of their pregnancy," Phillips responded.

"Will an autopsy reveal what the doctor," Baxter huffed in frustration. "Forgive me, Doctor Phillips, what this wretch gave to the poor child?" Baxter interrupted.

"Possibly, though there are dozens of flowering herbs, such as tansy and pennyroyal that are made into teas and ingested that would be virtually undetectable. But I doubt we need worry about that Mr. Baxter."

"Why?"

"Because I suspect, she flushed herself with lye, in combination with taking something orally which made the fatal combination Mr. Baxter."

"What can we do for the child?" Baxter asked, looking despondent.

"There is nothing much I can do except to make her comfortable. These poor creatures use anything from knitting needles to toxic herbs prescribed

276

under the direction of these so-called physicians who are supposed to uphold the Hippocratic Oath but unfortunately, all these men care about is lining their bloody pockets. They care nothing at all about these women once they leave their office. Now if you will excuse me, gentleman, I think I can be of more use with the patient."

Phillips' somber mood could be heard in the description the man gave in the limits of the help that anyone could offer the woman in her critical time of need.

"I am only in the way here, Wynne," I whispered.

"What are you going to do, Detective," Baxter asked.

"I am going home, but rest assured first thing in the morning, I am going to go down to Berner Street and hunt this Doctor D. down!"

"I am going to stay with this dear lady. If nothing else, I can offer her comfort. Take my carriage and have the driver return after dropping you off at your flat," Baxter said.

"Thanks, Wynne, but I think I am going to walk, but try to get an exact address of this Doctor D.'s office on Berner Street from the old woman."

I did not wait for a response, closing the door behind me, I walked into the night and the pouring rain.

Early the next morning, unable to sleep, I left my rooms before sunrise to visit the Leman Street Police station. It was in my mind to see if there were any recent complaints made about illegal abortionists operating in the area. When I started, I was somewhat optimistic about the results of my search based on the statement that Alenka's friend referred her to the doctor. The referral proved common knowledge of the doctor's practice. However, after looking in the registry for doctors practicing in the area, I could not find one. Nor, could I find any record of a charge made against an alleged abortionist, let alone any complaint made about one. After several hours of questioning constables in the area, I was unable to get any leads, nor could I find any recent grievances made at the station by women who may have suffered at the hands of this Doctor D. Widening my search proved useless. As far as the constables that patrolled Berner Street were concerned, there wasn't, nor had there ever been, a doctor, operating in the area by that name. Frustrated by yet another failure, I decided to go back to my office and wait for the coroner to return.

Doing my best to keep my mind occupied while I waited, I sat examining the list of suspects, when Wynne Baxter and Doctor Phillips showed up at my office door at ten in the morning. Both looked the worse for wear with grim expressions pasted on their faces. It seems the two had just left the side of the poor Polish woman who had held onto life as long as she was able and had passed only an hour earlier. Rising from my desk, I put my overcoat on. Doctor Phillips gathered the necessary paperwork from his office and left needing to fill out an unnatural death report and a death certificate at the police station. Leaving my office, we climbed back into the coroner's carriage.

Berner Street lay in the heart of London's rookery. Here every type of petty thievery, mugging, extortion, assault, and murder could be had for a price. Although crime was not limited nor isolated to Berner Street, it was here in the East End where more criminals congregated than any other street in London. It was also where the so-called 'back-alley butchers' found a venue to ply their trade in small shops disguised from the prying eye of the Metropolitan Police. These professed doctors made a living by practicing their rudimentary skills here. Berner offered, anonymity and their trade took on many forms. For some, it was in the illegal act of abortion and the use and sale of abortifacients, drawing on the woes of frantic young women who sought these medicines to end their pregnancy. Although abortion was illegal and punishable by law, there were still more than a few physicians willing to step outside of the bounds of the law. Besides, these were the many women who practiced midwifery and a multitude of others who charged exorbitant amounts of money to young women who wanted to terminate their pregnancy. It was here, down dead-end alleys amongst nondescript boarded up shacks and dives, that Baxter took me to locate a Doctor D. who might be working in the area.

They studied the street from the hansom, armed with a vague description, a partial name, and with only a rough idea of an address, all of which was given to them by the grieving old Polish woman. Although the hour was still early, the streets and walks were already alive with activity. I held no great hope of apprehending the salesman of the toxic elixir that Alenka had purchased. Though I kept my feelings from the coroner, who only wanted to correct a terrible wrong and give satisfaction to an old woman. The outcome of their search became clear to me when they came to the alleyway where the doctor's office was said to be located. The office, if that was what it could be called, was behind a barbershop. The plain door with no sign was left ajar, and with the force of my knock, the door swung open, revealing a vacant space. As I had suspected from the beginning, they could find nothing of any importance after a preliminary search.

"The office was most likely vacated moments after Alenka returned here for help," I commented, staring at the bare walls.

"What miserable luck Stone."

"My guess is, Wynne, that this man could see charges being brought against him so, our culprit, fled this location to mix with the diverse population of Berner Street. It is likely that this rogue will lay low for a few days and then set up another office under another name to begin his business all over again."

"Our efforts are wasted," Baxter retorted.

"Sorry, Wynne," I tried to sound sympathetic; unfortunately, the years on the police force had prepared me for just such an outcome.

"What do we do now, Detective?" Wynne asked, discouraged by the outcome of the past days' events.

"I am afraid we have to keep looking, but I don't want you to get your hopes up, Wynne. These people come and go," I reasoned. "The odds of us finding this quack, with the little information we have, are slim."

"You mean the odds of us ever catching this 'back-alley butcher' are slim, to say the least!" The Coroner retorted.

"I am afraid so, Wynne, unless we have a witness or catch him in the act," I paused, looking at Baxter wishing I could give my friend some reassurance. "Unfortunately, the way that this man's business transactions end the chances of us finding a living witness is going to be rather difficult."

After spending the morning canvassing the shops in the area, the only information that could be had was the name of the owner of the building where the doctor had set up practice. After questioning the owner of the barbershop, they learned that the leasing of the space; was left in charge of a landlord who lived on the premises. They woke the landlord who identified himself as Thomas Crumb, and soon the two investigators found that they were no further ahead than before questioning the man. Crumb was a scrawny, toothless man who smelled much like the bottom of a gin bottle. The landlord had met the man who rented the office only once, remembering very little of what the man looked like recalling only that the gentleman was a foreigner. Crumb also recollected that the gentleman said that he was a doctor of some kind and had paid six months' rent in advance. Crumb did not need to see the man again until the end of the six months when rent was due, having occupied the office for only three months.

Leaving the alley, I felt as discouraged as the coroner looked. I had displaced a lot of my anger about the death of the innocent woman on the futile notion that I could arrest the man that had murdered Alenka as sure as if it was done in cold blood. Without any leads and only a vague description of the man, any thoughts of capturing, the doctor seemed impossible. Glancing up the street, about half a block away, I could see several constables pounding on shop doors, in what appeared to be a broad sweep of the area. Calling a constable over to me, I revealed my badge.

"What is going on Constable," I asked, the reluctant young man who grimaced after seeing my badge.

"We are doing a door to door search, of the slaughterhouses and butcher shops in the area, looking for the 'Ripper,' Sir."

The constable stood at attention; the man's face expressionless.

"Well, I wonder whose brilliant idea that was," I asked out loud, without meaning to be heard, let alone answered.

"I believe it was the Assistant Commissioner's idea, Sir!"

"Carry on Constable," I said, dismissing the man after ignoring the comment.

"Wynne, you have had a long night, why don't you go home and get some rest while I look around a little more?"

"Right, oh, Detective, I think I will."

I watched Baxter climb into his carriage. Crossing the road, I thought about this Doctor D., who might as well be another murderer walking the streets of London. Though my gut told me it wasn't the last I would hear of the man.

At the top of the alley, I scanned the street, thinking of Alenka and the thousands of innocent girls that had visited the doctor before, and all the desperate girls that would see him or someone else like him in the future. It went without saying that there would be more desperate girls needing help, all to fall victim to these butchers. In the right or the wrong, the young women that sought these practitioners out had few resources to get the help required.

At the St. James Division station, I started searching through all the police files looking for any complaints filed at the station that involved abortion and a Doctor D. After several hours of rooting through the records, I narrowed my search looking for any claims made about foreign doctors known to be working in London under an alias. Finally, I ended my hunt by looking into any physicians that may have had complaints made or were suspected of wrongful or suspicious deaths involving any young pregnant women. Finding no complaints dealing with any physician in Berner St. or all of London for that matter, I gave up and decided to go back to my office. During the cab ride, I thought of the murdered women in Whitechapel and realized that something was disturbing to me that I had not given much thought to before. I had been looking for something that tied all the victims in Whitechapel together. It was the young polish woman Alenka that had given me a clue, not only were the victims all prostitutes, there was another common denominator in all the crimes that perhaps tied Alenka to the other murders in Whitechapel. All the victims to date were unmarried women. This latest event involving a woman with child who was compelled by her own set of circumstances and out of desperation to seek a solution for her unwanted pregnancy, by means that the law deemed unacceptable. Unfortunately, these young women were not only hiding a secret shame from friends and families, but they were also going outside the regular channels for help, and at the same time, they had willingly placed themselves in a precarious predicament. With few options remaining to them, these women had engaged an unqualified practitioner, thus having to suffer the consequences for their decisions by having placed their very lives in danger. It was frightening, but there could be hundreds of women every year who have been left to die in deserted offices or sent home to bleed to death leaving, the family no recourse but to hide the actual circumstances of their daughter's death either out of shame or ignorance. Regrettably, with little or no information to go on, the police involved in the investigation were left with no alternative but to file the death under natural causes during childbearing, which inadvertently could explain why there were no complaints filed against these illegal shops. It was these disturbing facts that left me concerned for the unfortunate girls, who would continue to seek out these physicians that were willing to practice outside of the law. The very idea left me to wonder how many women ended up in the same predicament as Alenka found herself. Unfortunately, until laws were reformed and police files were kept more up to date to keep better track of these criminals, more young women would end up like Alenka.

Finding Baxter in his office, I reluctantly told him that no information had been discovered about the doctor operating on Berner. Unfortunately, the information; left Wynne in no better mood. Yet, I did not take Baxter's lack of enthusiasm personally. The coroner was a man who worked for the interest of the people and held himself personally responsible that there was no one held accountable for the murder of the unfortunate girl.

I sympathized with my friend, for all too often, such cases turned out in much the same way. Of late, I, like the coroner, had found myself in the precarious position of being limited on what I was able to do to help the unfortunates of Whitechapel. If I was just another citizen of London that would be excusable; however, along with being a servant of the public came a sense of responsibility that I did not take lightly. Feeling useless to do anything to change the circumstances behind the girl's death was quite troubling, and not something I wanted to grow accustomed to.

Allowing Baxter, the time and the space needed to cope with the disappointing news, I left the coroner sitting at his desk. It had been in my mind to have Baxter check with other coroners in the hopes of any information they may have on a rise in illegal abortions being done in their areas. Though I saw the effort only as a way of being thorough, I could only assume that Baxter would have heard of an escalation of cases, had there been any. Unfortunately, they were likely to find the same problems as I had with families being unwilling to file a complaint due to shame or ignorance. Wynne Baxter was a coroner who carried the burdens of the people in his district on his shoulders. Any further badgering of the coroner this day; would likely make him feel as though his office had been failing miserably.

Though they had no leads, that did not excuse the reality that there was still, a young woman lying at the Working Lads Institute in London's East End, and her killer remained at large. If that wasn't enough to contend, there was also a brutal murderer, killing prostitutes in the slums of London that had to take priority over any other case. Though the burden did not fall entirely on my shoulders. Nevertheless, this realization did little to placate my feelings of helplessness. There was still a wolf in sheep's clothing, preying on innocent women, and this practitioner was taking advantage of their vulnerable state. I was cognizant of the fact that unless this man was stopped, countless more victims would fall prey and end up just as dead as the victims of '*Jack the Ripper*.'

The reality that life was short had never been so poignant to me than on the battlefield, where the people I knew were dying all around me. In the ghetto, death was nearer for some than others. That expectancy could be lengthened depending on living conditions and the availability of proper food. Death seemed to skulk around every corner in the slums; I could see it in the eyes of those who lived there. Hardships of all kinds overshadowed its residents every day. Survival could depend on being at the right place and the right time and obtaining work for the day, in order to be able to afford a hot meal. I had realized early in life that in the world, there would always be those who had and those who had not, though the separation of the classes had never before seemed more apparent than in London during those desperate years that I was stationed in Whitechapel. The imaginary line that separated the east from the west and London's classes was not enough for the elite. For those in the west, the east had become a stigma. Just as the west had become a blatant reminder to the poor that though all men were created equal, the division of the classes was put in place to remind the poor, that all men were not equal.

With the appearance of '*Jack the Ripper*,' the stench of the lower class threatened to flood past the line that had separated these classes for centuries. The citizens of the west had not raised too much of a fuss after the first few murders. However, when the death toll began to rise, the good citizens of London began to wonder if the maniac butchering women in the east could be stopped. Not only that, but they had real concerns if the blood would begin to flow in the gutters of their own peaceful neighborhoods. Cries of panic began to sound in the streets, and as a result, the citizenry began to wage war on the crime that seemed to run rampant in the east with no safeguards in place to stop it. The wealthy pointed their fingers at the ghetto, where in their opinions, no good thing could exist. When they had exhausted their efforts on the mysterious figure of '*Jack the Ripper*,' they turned their sights in the direction of the Metropolitan Police. With no other recourse, the top officials in the Metropolitan Police force began to resign. After hearing the disdain from their constituents in their ridings, politicians began to worry about their seats. Soon after, parliament implemented stiffer laws for workhouses and rooming houses, to keep what was deemed the 'riffraff,' responsible for unrest in the city, under control. The Metropolitan Police Department began to feel the pressures from citizens and bureaucrat alike that the city had seen far too much bloodshed on the streets that they were, sworn to protect. Soon the moniker '*Jack the Ripper*' became a symbol of all that was wrong in the East End, causing those in London to employ a crackdown on the ghetto. This, in turn, would not only rid the city of the criminal element and the maladjusted citizens that resided in the east, but it would also end the killing rampage of '*Jack*' that had caused the rest of the world to question London's failure to find one murderer. In retaliation, the people in the East End; began to rally together after hearing these rumors and began to organize political parties of their own after experiencing the brutality of the police in the past in their effort to clean up the east. Sadly, the reforms implemented did little more than to cause the rift between the classes to widen, and the survival of those in the ghetto had never looked so bleak.

The dismal rain that fell on the streets of London helped to clean the air and washed some of the filth from the streets. Feeling the rain on my face, I tried to clear my head. After several blocks, I realized that I had only gotten drenched, and my attempts to clear my mind had been in vain. I could not get the blood-soaked linen and the pale face of Alenka out of my mind. Shouting for a cab, I climbed aboard cognizant of the fact that I had not slept in forty-eight hours, and the limit of my strength had peaked long before the realization. Sliding across the seat, I yelled my destination to the driver eager, to be away from the trail of blood and the stench of death, at least for a little while.

Chapter Seventeen

Opening my eyes, I gasped; sitting up in bed, I reached my hands up to my throat. Swinging my feet to the floor, my sweat-soaked nightshirt clung to my back and chest. Wide awake, I could hear the wind and the rain as it rattled the panes of glass in the window. In the distance, a flash of lightning lit up the night sky and the walls in my room. Rising out of bed, I sloshed water on my face from a basin on my nightstand. Leaning against the stand, I tried not to think about the nightmare that had seemed all too real. Pulling off my nightshirt, my skin glistened with sweat, reaching for a tumbler next to my dresser; I poured a generous portion of water into the glass. Gulping the water down, I toweled off and lay back on the bed and shuddered. I tried not to think about the vividness of the dream. Time and time again, I told myself that it was only a nightmare, but it was little comfort. Outside, the lightning flashed again, and I heard the rumble of thunder as it rolled in the distance. The wind and rain pounded at the window, shaking the panes in their frames. I closed my eyes, but my dream stayed with me. The dark figure and the glimmer of light on the knife kept flashing before my eyes until the grey of false dawn stretched across the eastern horizon. Sunrise was hours away, and yet, sleep alluded me.

Rousing late, the sun shone across the foot of my bed when I next opened my eyes. I had tossed and turned for many hours before sleep had overtaken me, the nightmare still haunting me. There seemed to be no, comfort in the fact that the dream was not real but a figment of my imagination. I was sure that it was the police reports that I had made a practice of studying for months now, made the dream seem more real than possible. Washing and putting on a clean suit, I walked downstairs to the kitchen. Waking late, I had missed breakfast settling, for a cup of steaming tea to settle my nerves, I left my rooms for my office.

Enjoying the warmth of the sunny day, I decided to walk for a little while in hopes that the fresh air would be therapeutic. Unfortunately, after several blocks, the out of doors proved to offer an open theater for my mind to review the details of my nightmare. Passing by the Leman Street police station, I checked to see if there were any new reports on the doctor who had given the girl Alenka, her fatal prescription. Finding nothing, I started to go back to my office when I noticed a man reading a paper across the street from where I stood. Walking up the road another two blocks, I stopped again, turning to glance into a shop window, I saw the man was behind me at the corner with a newspaper in front of his face, pretending to read it. Walking quickly, I rounded the first corner and then ran a few steps into a blind alley and waited with my body pressed firmly against the wall. I didn't have long to wait; only a few minutes passed, and then, I heard footsteps running along the street in the direction I had just come. Taking a deep breath, I darted from the alley to stand in front of the man who pursued me. The shock on the man's face displayed that he had thought himself undetected. I stood unmoving, noting that the man did not attempt to run from the confrontation.

"Who are you, and why are you following me?"

My abrasive tone made the man's features tighten, but he seemed unaffected, as if there was no harm done.

Without saying a word, the man dug into his outside jacket pocket, displaying a press card. I looked at the card and took three steps towards the man, who stood his ground. Picking up the card that was attached to a string wound around a jacket button.

"Thomas, John Bulling, Central News Agency," I read the card and then reverted my glare back toward the man who stood unfazed by my closeness. "A pressman," I growled. "Alright, you have my attention, Mr. Bulling, what is it that you want from me," I said, not in the mood for being spied on but, I decided to give the newspaperman the benefit of the doubt for the moment. "You can start by telling me why you are following me?"

Deliberately, I turned my back on the man and started to walk back the way that I had come. It took only a few seconds before Thomas Bulling's step quickened, and the man kept in stride beside me.

"Alright, Detective, I do want something, I want an exclusive."

"An exclusive, on what exactly," I snarled, deciding to be allusive, and allow Bulling to explain himself.

"Oh, come on now," Bulling; laughed. "You, coppers got some lead on this '*Jack the Ripper*,' that's why you are all being so, bleeding closed-mouthed,"

"I am afraid, I don't have the slightest idea what you are referring to, Mr. Bulling," I responded, darting an upturned eyebrow at the pressman to caution the man's friendly tone.

"Detective, maybe we can work together. I have it on good authority that you are down here on special assignment from Scotland Yard."

I figured, judging by the man's age, that Bulling had been a newspaperman for more than a few years and had likely learned long ago that people only spoke freely when they had something to gain from what they were reporting. In my experience most pressman, cared little for the exactitudes of a story.

"If you have your information on good authority, why don't you ask the one who gave you the information in the first place," I asked mockingly.

"Detective, we're all on the same side here, I want this '*Ripper*' caught just as much as you."

Bulling shouted, grabbing at my overcoat sleeve. Turning, I glared at the hand on my sleeve until it was removed.

"We are nothing alike," I shouted. "You're interested in a by-line that sells papers, not in the truth or catching this killer."

"That's not true; I just print the news, that's what the people want, and if I may say so, that is what the people deserve," Bulling retorted, defensively.

"Listen, I am busy, and I neither have the time nor the inclination to listen to you while you defend your vocation," I said, turning to walk away from Bulling. "Just, get to your business," I said, glancing over my shoulder at the reporter, as I was starting to run out of patients.

"I have connections in Scotland Yard, you know," Bulling said, with a sneer.

"I am well aware of your connections, Bulling."

I turned to walk away and then stopped midstride. The word, from the Home Office, was to keep well away from all pressman. I had heard that the head of C.I.D., Sir Charles Warren, was going to urge the newspapers to print a more positive spin on the publicity that the department had received for not having someone in custody for the Whitechapel murders. Although I had not heard any news on what they were going to do, or who they were going to use to mend the police image in London, I had heard Bulling's name mentioned as a possible candidate to write a more favorable story about the police efforts to catch the killer. Looking at Thomas John Bulling, I couldn't help but think that there was something more to their meeting than just obtaining a story for a by-line. Bulling looked the part of a pressman, but there was something else about the man that troubled me. The newspaperman's clothes had the appearance of being slept in, and I detected the smell of alcohol on the man's breath when Bulling had grabbed at my jacket. My initial response had been to ignore the man, but something had stopped me. Perhaps it was the fact that Bulling worked for the Central News Agency, the very newspaper that had been sent the *'Dear Boss Letter'* dated September twenty-seventh. It dawned on me that I might benefit from having Bulling think that I was an ally rather than an enemy. So deep in thought was I that I didn't hear Bulling trying to get my attention.

"Detective!"

"Oh, right, you have contacts; you were saying," I answered. "I just may; have something for you Bulling. I have an appointment to get to right now, but I will be in touch, you can count on it," I said, turning to go about my business.

Eager for the reporter to leave me alone, I hurried up the street, allowing; Bulling to think that I had a scrap of news to give to him, when in reality; I had no intention of giving the pressman the time of day, let alone any story. Half a block away, I looked back, searching the street to see if Bulling still insisted on following me. I watched from a corner as the newspaperman crossed the street and headed in the opposite direction.

As I walked, I considered Thomas Bulling. The pressman's aggressive nature went with the job, although with Bulling, I had seen greater enthusiasm from a gravedigger. It seemed unlikely, at least to me, that Bulling would give up so easily if there was something to be gained by following me. Though Bulling seemed argumentative to a fault, the man did not appear to be the type to overly exert himself to seek a lead where one did not present itself. The mere suggestion that I may have something for the man seemed to satisfy the newspaperman.

Forgetting about that issue for the moment, I decided to concentrate on other pressing matters. My theory about 'Jack's' letters, having been written by more than one author, may have been supported by Bulling's sudden introduction. My first impression of Thomas Bulling, gave me cause to revisit an idea I had been mulling over, that a pressman could have written one or more of the letters. It was unlikely that there was more than one person involved in the writing of the 'hoax letters'; given the nature of the ruse. It would undoubtedly need the utmost secrecy to make the letters appear realistic. Throughout my career, I had been introduced to several pressman, and in my opinion most, gave the impression of being a conscientious lot, deeming the very idea of writing falsehoods in the newspaper; as unprincipled. I could only assume that someone willing to carry out such a plan would be a man who did not possess any such ethics. Bulling gave the impression that he would do almost anything for a story and not spend too much time worrying if his source was reliable or not. The idea made me question the intelligence behind the use of someone like Thomas Bulling, being employed to write favorable stories about the Metropolitan Police in the first place. I also had to ask, if it was coincidence or convenience for the department to choose the Central News Agency to fix their tarnished image. The same newsagent 'Jack the Ripper' sent his letters to. Walking along the street, I was preoccupied with the idea that had come to me unexpectedly. The more I thought about it, the more probable the idea seemed, that Thomas Bulling could be one of the authors of the letters.

Bulling, if chosen by C.I.D. could have been getting information from some source within the Metropolitan Police Department. Though, the pressman's ability to carry out this assignment successfully may have been next to impossible, given the increase in '*Jack's*' crimes, and the increased public outcry in response. The police image at this stage might have been unfixable. It was curious though that '*Jack's*' letters to the Central News Agency had stopped as suddenly as they had begun. That, of course, did not mean that the newspaper's angle behind writing forged letters to sell more papers was not probable. If Bulling wrote the letters, there would be no gain in it for the reporter unless '*Jack*' had sent the letters to Bulling. In doing this, '*Jack*' would make the reporter his only source, which would make Bulling indispensable in the process. But this may not have been the case. It was conceivable that someone else might, have been involved. Someone paying Bulling to report, only what they wanted the general public to see in the paper. It was plausible that Bulling went along with the scheme so, no one could question the authenticity of the letters.

Cutting across town, I considered the Central News Agency's involvement. After several minutes of mulling the idea around, I remembered that the newspaper had already been criticized by the Times about the lengths that the paper was prepared to go to embellish facts and be the first to report a story. The complaint had caused a myriad of stories to be written about the integrity of the reputed agent of the news. With that thought, I no longer questioned the possibility of my idea.

I decided my time was better spent, putting all my efforts into studying the crime scenes where the murders were committed. It was possible, if not probable, that the killer; may return to the same areas where the victims were chosen. Or, at the very least, the culprit might return to the scene of the crime to satisfy some morbid curiosity.

Unable to find a cab anywhere, I walked up Whitechapel Road. I spent the time thinking about Thomas Bulling. The man had been emphatic in his denial of following me. Over the years, I had grown accustomed to the reaction of most people during an inquiry. Having spent my entire career dealing with criminals whose common first reaction was the denial of all culpability. I had long ago concluded that the human condition was in a state of depravity, and not much surprised me. I had spent many hours studying the pattern of behavior of those who found themselves at odds with the law. Responses varied, depending on the guilt or innocence of the individual. However, the reaction of the guilty was almost always to lie and then to think about a defense later. Although I had believed Bulling, due in large part, to the man's reaction, the incident made me wonder why the man had chosen to follow me in the first place. Though I had no evidence, I was convinced that my theory of a newspaper reporter, writing one or more of '*Jack's*' letters, was sound.

As I walked, I considered '*Jack's*' letters. All the correspondences were written using an ordinary pen on ordinary paper. Both items could be purchased anywhere and it was not extraordinary for a pressman to have either in his possession. The letters could have been penned anywhere at any time, looking for these items was tantamount to looking for a needle in a haystack. However, I still refused to believe that my theories were wrong. After spending a countless number of hours examining the letters, there were too many anomalies in the letters not to come to that conclusion.

Taking my mind off of Thomas John Bulling for the moment, I noticed the throng of people on the street. I had been amazed by the endless myriad of human life in the East End; it was a part of the city that never seemed to lay dormant. The homeless walked about the streets, in a sleep-deprived fog, they shuffled about the cobbled walks, prodded by police or store owners to move out of alleys, and doorways or off benches and walks. They ambled from one place to another, oblivious to life about them.

In London, when the sun went down, all manner of skullduggery was formulated by the malcontent or desperate. It was usually the premeditated crimes that were committed after the sun went down. It was these criminal activities that were long thought about and schemed over, during many a night to bring them from the criminal mind to reality. Robbery and burglary are crimes of opportunity; most criminals use the cover of darkness to commit. The crime of murder however is complex and has various degrees that separates it from all other crimes. To determine these degrees the perpetrator's intent must be examined.

The motive of the vicious crimes in Whitechapel was one of the key aspects of the case that hampered investigators. The act of robbery was not a probable motive, as the victims were virtually destitute and seeking pennies from their patrons just to survive. Nor, was jealousy a factor. During the course of the investigation, detectives found no connection to a lover or ex-husband as a possible suspect. Detectives interviewed every possible witness and acquaintance, and there seemed to be no rhyme or reason for the crimes, except to say the killer was some kind of demented soul. One, who by repeating these atrocities had placed, himself in a category usually reserved for the insane. Though, these demented souls usually killed out of fear or out of being tormented, who lacked the capacity to understand right from wrong. These perpetrators in most cases, remain on the scene or return to a place of safety where they would be easily found and quickly arrested. It was in my experience that an individual who was not of sound mind could not formulate a plan to murder five women and continue to elude police. That wasn't to say the perpetrator of the Whitechapel crimes was of sound mind. This individual was placed in the category of the criminally insane, suffering a diminished empathy for his fellow man. However, there had to be some reason or gain for the culprit to continue his killing spree. What that reason was, unfortunately, had eluded me, along with the other eight thousand policemen working on the case in London.

These were the thoughts that engrossed me while standing in the dark outside of Dutfield's Yard. I had grown accustomed to hiding in thickets, alleys, or stairwells waiting for those who used darkness to perpetrate their crimes. At night, alone and waiting in the shadows was usually an opportunity for me to reflect on the circumstances of my life; however, of late, my position in the coroner's office had lost its appeal. The gruesome crimes in Whitechapel that had left me more and more disturbed of late. I had become a police officer because the work had suited me but, of late, I found myself unable to justify my position and had thought resignation was the best recourse. It had been three and a half weeks since the murder of Catharine Eddowes and Elizabeth Stride, and, so far, I had brought nothing to light in the investigation. Although critical of my own shortcomings, I stood in good company, for Scotland Yard in its entirety had done nothing to bring about the apprehension of the murderer known only as 'Jack the Ripper.'

My purpose for spending countless hours in the areas where the murders had been committed was to cover every possibility and leave nothing to chance. Investigative techniques ascertained that motive and opportunity were linked to a close relationship with the victim. Although after several weeks of investigating, I had turned up nothing. I was still convinced that my theory that the killer had contact with his intended victims long before the night of the murder, was correct. However, the motive for the killings had proven my theory weak. '*Jack*' had confirmed that the police investigative rules would have to be revised if they were going to catch the maniac still at large. To date, any key to whatever system the killer was using for picking out his victims was locked in the mind of the creature who continued to elude police and the greatest detectives in the world, had been unable to figure out the identity of the 'Ripper'.

Shielding a match, I checked my watch. Leaving my place of concealment, I knew that dawn would be breaking in minutes, and my nightly vigils had no favorable outcome. The days I had spent near Mitre Square, Dutfield's Yard, and Hanbury Street had proven to be another dead end. For all my hours of waiting in the shadows keeping the crime scenes under surveillance had brought me nothing but lost sleep and a lack of respect for the constable on the patrols. On more than one occasion, I found constable patrol times in some cases off by no less than five and as much as fifteen minutes. Though these times were construed as important in the investigation, what I discovered was that they were no more reliable than the weather and were not to be trusted as key factors in the investigation. If nothing else, it was further proof that '*Jack*' had indeed more than ample time to perpetrate his crimes then what the bulk of the doctors testified as a reasonable amount of time to murder his victim and dissect their bodies.

Moving out of the shadows, I startled a rawboned dog that was rummaging through a tipped over a trash can. Ignoring the mutt, I walked up the alley and broke up a group of hollow-eyed, desperate-looking young men hovering about a barrel converted into a fire pit. I watched the men depart after suddenly seeing me walk towards them either out of the eagerness to be left alone or for fear of being recognized by an officer of the law. They headed in the opposite direction all, rolling up collars and digging numbed fingers into pockets to shield them from the cold. Ignoring the men, I walked on, digging deep into my own pockets and nestling my chin down inside my overcoat to guard against the bite of the cold autumn wind. As the night faded into day, the shapes of other men could be seen as they started to move about trying to stay warm from the harsh wind. Walking up Mitre Street to Aldgate on my way to Whitechapel Rd., I saw a bundle in a darkened doorway. Thinking the worst, I moved closer. Hunched over, I reached a trembling hand for a corner of the soiled garment. In a flash, a gnarled hand darted out, clutching a butcher's blade only inches from my face. Underneath the edge of the worn coat, a weathered and wrinkled face snarled defiantly, clutching a small child in her arms. Holding up both hands in surrender, I tossed a few coins on the ground in front of the woman and then backed away leaving, the woman alone who was only trying to protect herself and the life of a child. Strolling back up the alley, I tried to force the image of the weathered old face of the woman from my memory. There were small miracles that each person had the ability in this life to participate in; I would have loved to have done more for the old woman and child, but there was only so much that one man could do. The East End was filled with the hungry and the desperate, I would love to help all the people I met but, there was only so much I could afford from my own meager resources.

Continuing on my way, a mist of rain began, and the grey light of morning proved to be as dark as my disposition. Skirting along the edge of the gutter on the street, I decided to go to my office instead of my flat to escape the drenching that was most surely on its way.

The halls in the office building were still dark when I arrived; the occupants were still several hours away from starting their day. Locking my office door behind me, I stretched out on the settee and covered up with my overcoat; sleep was only a minute away.

Chapter Eighteen

It took me a minute to understand that the pounding I heard at my office door was not dream induced, and another to open my eyes and focus. Swinging my feet to the floor, I rubbed the sleep from my eyes and wearily opened the door to see a pale-faced constable standing on the other side.

"Yes, Constable, how can I help you this morning," I spoke gruffly, looking through half-opened eyelids.

"My apologies, Sir!"

I saw the constable look at me sheepishly. Looking down at my rumpled shirt, my wrinkled pants and understood the young man's reaction, seeing me in this state at this hour of the day. I assumed that the man probably thought that I was sleeping one-off.

"Don't fret my, boy, I was up all night, now what is it," I said, defensively.

"A message, Sir, it is from The Yard," the constable answered, keeping his eyes straight ahead.

Taking the folded message from the constable's hand, I recognized Inspector Abberline's scribble immediately.

"Is there an answer, Sir?"

"No," I answered, folding the paper and putting it in my pocket.

"Very well, Sir."

I watched the fresh-faced policeman walk stiff-backed down the hall from the doorway. The new constables could be seen from a mile away, their dark blue wool uniforms not yet faded by the sun; their boots still held the shine from the factory. I couldn't help but think that the Metropolitan Police Department needed more constables like they need another '*Jack the Ripper*.' More bodies were not the answer to finding the Whitechapel killer. Someone needed to tell Sir Charles Warren they already had enough bodies wandering from crime scene to crime scene carrying messages and running errands. What they needed were more trained detectives.

It took me a fast twenty minutes to wash the sleep from my eyes, shave, and put on a clean suit that I kept at my office for those occasions that I did not make it back to my flat. Downstairs a hansom cab was waiting. Without waiting for directions, the driver sped away as soon as I closed the door and started heading towards Scotland Yard. Long before reaching its destination, the cab began to slow and had barely rolled to a stop when the door flew open, and Inspector Abberline climbed aboard.

"Keep seated, Detective. Driver!" Abberline shouted.

"Yes, Sir!"

"Twenty-two Batty Street and quickly. We haven't a moment to spare," Abberline shouted at the driver while entering, the cab.

"Yes, Sir!"

The driver responded with a crack of his whip in the air. Sitting rigid against the sway and bob of the cab as it sped swiftly down the cobbled streets, I wanted desperately to ask the inspector where they were going but, the question went unasked. With my head still full of cobwebs from sleep deprivation, I was somewhat unnerved by the abruptness of the events of the afternoon. I tried to think of something to say to ease the tension, but I couldn't think of anything. Grateful for the echo of the strike of wheels and horseshoes on the cobbles in the narrow street, I settled into my seat, gripping the door handle as they thundered down Whitechapel Rd. The abruptness of the meeting and the speed of the cab allowed no time to consider their destination, and most importantly, the urgency for their arrival. I had no sooner finished thinking of how awkward I felt when Abberline shouted over the cacophony.

"Well, Detective, I suppose you are wondering where we are off to?" Abberline asked.

"Yes, Sir," I sputtered. "It did cross my mind."

"It seems we have a lead," Abberline answered.

I watched the inspector turn to look out the opened cab window, saying no more. My curiosity was already peaked; yet, the comment made by the inspector made me sit straighter on the seat. My thoughts were only that the inspector referred to a lead on the identity of who '*Jack the Ripper*' was. Two more blocks and the cab came to an abrupt halt. The address the cab stopped in front of was a lodging house at Twenty-two Batty Street. Climbing out of the cab, Abberline was immediately addressed by three constables on the street in front of the house. The inspector quickly sent two constables around the back of the building, while the third; remained standing guard at the front door. Pushing open a gate, Abberline opened the front door and climbed a large staircase that led to the rooms on the second floor. Not waiting for an invitation, I followed, saying nothing.

At the top of the stairs, they were received by a very excited elderly woman who started into a long spiel in broken English and what might have been German. Standing behind the inspector, I did my best to follow the story, as difficult as it was. After a moment, I had the gist of what the old woman tried to convey. It seemed that Abberline understood more than I because the inspector quickly turned from the woman and started down the hall to the last room on the left. Rattling the doorknob, they found the door locked.

"Scotland Yard, open up!"

When no answer came, Abberline turned to the landlady who followed close behind. Holding out his hand, the landlady handed the inspector a key to the door. Taking the key, Abberline, unlocked the door. Standing behind the inspector, he held up his hand to the woman, whose curiosity was getting the best of her.

"Stand back, dear lady," Abberline spoke, hoping not to alarm the woman.

Abberline looked over at me; to see if I was ready to follow into the room. Nodding in recognition, I readied myself for whatever lay behind the door. When the inspector opened the door, I was prepared to rush in, not knowing what to expect, but was stopped suddenly halfway into the entrance; behind the inspector. Like the inspector, I couldn't help but be disappointed to find the room empty. Walking past Abberline, I entered the room and began searching through the armoire and a large sea chest that lay on the floor, both of which I found to be empty. Turning, I looked at Abberline, who walked out in the hall and down the stairs. Getting onto my knees, I looked under the bed then lifted the mattress to find no trace or answers as to who the occupant of the room was, how long the man had been gone, or if the individual was going to return to the lodging house. Following the inspector down the stairs, and out onto the street, they waited as a constable moved a small inquisitive crowd off of the walk.

"We have had this man under surveillance for two weeks now."

I saw Abberline look at me quizzically, and I had to admit that I was more than a little perturbed to be kept in the dark on what was going on for so long.

"Two weeks ago, our suspect up and disappeared. We thought at first that our man; may have left the country," Abberline stated. "When we were informed by the landlady that our man would be returning this evening, we believed that our chance had come to apprehended him, it appears that our quarry may have been tipped off or something spooked him."

"Who are we looking for, Sir?"

"A foreigner," Abberline began. "More specifically, an American, who, among other things, is suspected of having Fenian ties and some involvement in the explosion at Scotland Yard three years ago. This man also claims to be a physician, and maybe the abortionist you seek as well."

"I see," I answered, a little surprised.

"Our suspect is known to be quite eccentric, with means, who goes from city to city selling herbs or some such trifling, preferring the East End of London to practice his profession. This man is someone that I would like to question about the murders here in Whitechapel."

"Inspector!" A constable interrupted.

"Yes, Constable," Abberline snapped.

"We've searched all the clubs and public houses in the area, Sir. We found no one fitting the suspect's description."

"Canvas the area and question everyone in a three-block radius, if they have seen anyone fitting his description," Abberline ordered.

The inspector had suddenly become quiet. I had seen these moments of contemplation come over the man before, knowing full well that they could last for several minutes, and I still had several questions to ask of the man.

"Are we talking about the same doctor who had a hand in the death of the polish girl, Inspector?"

"Your Doctor T., Detective," Abberline sighed. "This man also goes by several other aliases, but we believe that his true name is Doctor Francis Tumblety," Abberline, answered and went back into the lodging house.

I watched Abberline walk into the boarding house. I stood thinking with my mouth agape, unable to believe my ears. I rehearsed the minutes since the cab had picked up the inspector unsuspecting of the turn of events that would lead me to this place. I considered this doctor; that for all purposes, I could now put a face and a name to. I whispered the name and began to gather the other tidbits of information tucked away that I knew about the man, painting a mental image of the suspect called Francis Tumblety.

"Stone!"

Entering the house, the inspector continued to question the landlady, who seemed somewhat calmer and more easily understood than at their first meeting. When I approached, the inspector suddenly turned and abruptly left by the front door again. Looking at the woman, I tried to read something on the woman's face that would give some clue as to what happened but, she had returned to talking in excited German again and, I could not make head or tails of what she was saying.

Outside, I walked up to the inspector and waited, not wanting to interrupt.

"Well, Detective, it appears that we have been wasting our time here," Abberline spoke after several minutes of intense quiet.

"What does this lady have to do with this Doctor Tumblety," I asked.

"Nothing Stone, absolutely nothing. It appears that we have been misinformed," Abberline huffed. "It seems that this lady at this lodging house was given a shirt with bloody cuffs," Abberline began. "She grew afraid, as most women are in the East End, and showed her neighbor, who informed the police. That was why we have had our constables staked out in this neighborhood in the last few days. It seems that the lady of twenty-two Batty Street takes in laundry, our man has never lived at this lodging house, and, I have just learned that the shirt she received to be laundered was bloodied by some accident," Abberline answered.

"Inspector Abberline!"

A constable interrupted, leading an elderly lady by the arm.

"What is it?" Abberline snapped without looking at the constable.

"This lady says she has seen the man we have been looking for."

I watched Abberline's head snapped around, and then the inspector took two swift steps towards the constable.

"Let's have it then, Constable," Abberline barked at the young man.

"It's Barry, Sir."

The constable's face went three shades redder and immediately continued.

"It seems that this lady lets a couple of rooms in her house, she seems to think she has had our man in one of them."

"Dear Lady," Abberline spoke softly. "What is your name?"

"Mrs. Pool."

I watched the old woman lift her chin with pride.

"Where do you reside, Mrs. Pool?"

"I live at number Three, Berner Street, Sir."

"And you say you think you have seen this man, this doctor that has been described to you?" Abberline asked.

"Yes, I think so. I have had a physician, a foreign man, living in my rooms off and on for the last two years. The man keeps to himself, obeys the rules, and keeps coming back. He tells me all the time that it's my cooking."

"A foreigner you say, what nationality is this man," Abberline asked quickly, interested in the old woman's response.

"An American, I believe," Mrs. Pool answered.

"And, when did you last see this man, Mrs. Pool?" Abberline continued to question the lady.

"It has been at least three, maybe, four days, I should think."

Abberline turned away from the lady and rubbed his chin deep in thought.

I looked at the inspector and mused that my superior was calculating in his mind, just as I was, the number of days that had passed since the death of Alenka, at the hands of the abortifacient's salesman, who called himself a physician.

"Constable, if you would, please escort this dear woman to my cab," Abberline snapped at Constable Barry.

"Should we remain here, Sir?"

"No, assemble the rest of the men and follow us to number three, Berner Street, double time!" Abberline ordered.

In the carriage, on the way to her address on Berner Street, the lady gave a full description of the man she had rented a room to in her house.

"My lodger," Mrs. Pool began. "Is a man of about five feet, nine inches tall, very broad-shouldered, with a fair complexion, and a bushy mustache curled at both ends. his appearance is more like that of a salesman than a doctor," Mrs. Pool said, beginning to recall all she knew about Francis Tumblety along the way, giving a full account of the doctor's habits.

After her lodger had moved in for the first time, she noticed that the man kept rather strange hours but soon grew accustomed to his daily comings and goings. After several weeks, she felt comfortable enough to inquire about the doctor's odd hours. She was told that his comings and goings at all hours were a result of his work at the hospital. Satisfied, she made no other inquiries. It wasn't until the last three days of his stay that Mrs. Pool noticed that Tumblety began acting rather peculiarly. When she attempted to make a subtle conversation with him, she noted that the man became very subdued. The next day Tumblety left early in the morning, and she had not seen him since. At first, this seemed less than unusual, because the man was a busy physician often, staying away for extended periods but always paying well in advance for the room, so the flat would be still available for him. However, this time, there was no offer of payment, and she suspected that the doctor would not be returning. It wasn't until yesterday that she was talking to her neighbor, who told her that she had been questioned by police about a man who fit the description of one of her lodgers. Then she grew suspicious of the man she knew as Dr. James Blackburn.

"Dr. James Blackburn," I whispered, catching the inspector's eye.

"That was the last time you heard from this Blackburn or spoke to him, madam," Abberline continued to question the landlady without hesitation.

"Why yes," Mrs. Pool sniffled. "After I heard that the man might be up to no good, I told my neighbor to tell the police. When I went home, I was in such a fright that this man might return, I didn't leave my room until your constable came to my door," Mrs. Pool answered.

"Dear lady, do you know where this Blackburn carries out his duties as a practitioner?" Abberline continued.

"Why no, Mr. Blackburn mentioned nothing other than his work at the hospital, which the doctor seemed to be regularly engaged for emergencies."

"How long are his absences from the lodging-house?" Abberline asked.

"Mr. Blackburn comes and goes. Although altogether, the doctor has lodged with me three or four times over the last two years and has been a good tenant, that is, at least, I think, until now." She offered, biting her lip, showing the strain she was feeling.

"Other than this instance, has this man given you any reason to be suspicious of him," Abberline asked, looking at the woman intently.

"No, if my neighbor had not told me about the police searching the area for this man, I would not have suspected him of anything. I give my tenants their privacy."

I watched the landlady sniffle in her handkerchief and suspected that the woman probably knew the second, her tenants broke wind and turned my attention back to the inspector.

"That is just fine, Mrs. Pool."

I considered Abberline's response, after taking down the details and closing my notebook, and placing it into my coat, as the cab came to a halt. If I was correct in my assumptions, the inspector was likely thinking along the same lines as myself, and the doctor was likely long gone by now. I waited as Abberline, helped the lady down, then escorted her into the house on Berner Street where Blackburn or the man described as Tumblety had been only days earlier. As I followed, a rage from unknown origins began to fester in the pit of my stomach. I tried not to think of Alenka, but a picture of her frail figure lying in a pool of blood kept flashing before my eyes. The very idea that this Blackburn or Tumblety, if they were both the same character, was the Whitechapel killer known as '*Jack the Ripper*' could be all one in the same man was staggering. Although it did prove my theory that '*Jack*' was a doctor, made conclusive by the knowledge that this *Doctor T*. on Berner Street was the same man. Although all that they knew was circumstantial, the pieces to the puzzle seemed to be fitting together quite nicely. Though admittedly, after some thought, they seemed to be fitting together almost too easy for my liking. For years, I had been honing my skills as an investigator; there were specific rules of investigating that I had developed and that I had never wavered from. One such rule was, if something seemed too good to be true, then it probably was. The other rule was always to find out if there was any money to be made. Money was a motivator for all types of criminal activity. If Inspector Abberline was correct and Doctor Tumblety was well to do and could afford to live anywhere, then why did the man live as a near-do-well lodger? I reasoned that it could be that Blackburn or Tumblety, was selling his herbs and abortifacients and performing abortions on the unfortunate women of Whitechapel as his source of wealth. The idea made sense; since there seemed to be a surplus of clients for him to access. The only piece of the puzzle that didn't fit was if *Doctor Francis Tumblety* was '*Jack the Ripper*,' why did the man not just murder Alenka, instead of giving her medicines to help her abort her pregnancy?

Following the inspector into the room, I immediately noticed that the small twelve by twelve room was impeccable. The bedsheets were crisp and folded with care; there were no personal items anywhere to be seen, nor was there anything to show that someone had lived in the room. Walking to the window while Abberline spoke to Mrs. Pool in the hall, I looked out at the hustle and bustle on the street. It seemed surreal that they had, with all intents and purposes, put a face to the doctor responsible for Alenka's death. Although, if all the evidence could be substantiated, they could not have found a more likely candidate then Tumblety as the murderer. Though several discrepancies needed to be dealt with in my mind before, I would jump on board and relent that Tumblety, was in fact, '*Jack the Ripper*' as well.

Alenka, called the back-alley butcher who had sold her the abortifacients, *Doctor D*. Although her English had been considerably better than her grandmothers, she may have been mistaken when her friend led her to the mysterious doctor and called the man *Doctor T.* or Doctor B. for that matter. The odds that the two were different people seemed too fantastic to consider. Both Blackburn and Tumblety were professed doctors by profession, whether real or made-up, and yet, they had no evidence to prove or disprove that both were the same man. One attribute that seemed conclusive was that the man was probably a sadist, judging by the account Alenka had given to her grandmother describing the brutal way that the man had treated her. Not only had the man no qualms about allowing her to bleed to death without treating her, but the wretch would have finished the job in his office to avoid any investigation if Alenka had not escaped. According to Inspector Abberline's information, Tumblety had taken lodgings in the ghetto out of convenience. It now seemed apparent that the man had discovered a way to make money off the unfortunate women who lived there. The East End proved to be a suitable haven for Tumblety to practice. Blackburn or Tumblety, seemed to be supplementing his income by performing illegal abortions, charging large amounts to troubled and frightened girls who felt as though they had no other recourse. According to the inspector's information, Tumblety's living in the East End would allow this man the freedom to live a lifestyle where prostitution could be had and was accepted more readily in the ghetto than anywhere else. If their suspect was, in fact, 'Jack the Ripper' than this lifestyle would also account for the absence of forced sexual contact with any of the women killed in Whitechapel before they were murdered. The man's behavior towards Alenka could confirm my suspicions that the killer was likely a misogynist, which could explain why 'Jack' made the statement of being 'down on whores.' Moving from lodging house to lodging house and from country to country would permit the man the anonymity that would be required to ply his trade and avoid prosecution. Traveling in the shady undercurrents of the back alleys of the ghetto, coupled with the use of several aliases, could be the reason why it was so hard to obtain an adequate description of their man.

Although the picture that I had formed of the man seemed to be coming together rather nicely, there was still one determining factor that kept nagging at me. If this doctor, was in fact 'Jack,' then why not kill all the women that came to him for an abortion instead of selling them medicines that may or may not do the job. The vast population in London could offer a broad range of women from all social statuses and backgrounds, giving Tumblety a seemingly endless client list. Tumblety deliberately chose those in the East End, knowing full well, these women had nowhere else to turn. The women that sought his services would all probably be young and unmarried like Alenka. Though being pregnant before marriage was not uncommon, the social construct deemed having a child out of wedlock, taboo. The young women would most likely not want to tell their parents, being ashamed of their circumstances. This practice of secrecy would allow Tumblety to continue and at the same time, keep his illegal practices arcane. In all probability, Tumblety saw the women who sought his services twice, perhaps in some cases only once, most likely guaranteeing that the combination of herbs and teas would cause an abortion, guaranteeing that patients would never have to see him again. In Alenka's case, however, she came back likely knowing she was in trouble, and that was why Tumblety flew into such a rage. The doctor could not allow a complaint to be made to the police, or even worse, have a patient die in his office. That would lead to too many questions, and most likely an investigation. That was why Tumblety's only recourse was to pick up stakes and move his office. There was only one characteristic that distinguished Alenka from the Whitechapel victims that stared me blatantly in the face, and I had not seen it until now. There was only one reason why Tumblety if the man, was in fact, '*Jack the Ripper*' did not kill Alenka or all the young women who came to him pregnant and afraid looking for help. It was because the man did not prey on women who were pregnant. Nor did the man seek out the homeless women of the East End, of which there was a vast amount. There was only one type of woman, '*Jack*' sought, and it was so obvious that I could not believe that I had not thought of it until now. The man hated prostitutes, the phrase in his letter was proof of that, '*Jack*' was '*down on whores.*'

The shout of my name from down the stairs brought me back to the problem at hand. Turning away from the window, I looked at the room one more time, feeling a little better that they were at least one step closer to finding Alenka's killer if not the killer '*Jack the Ripper.*'

Chapter Nineteen

The next few days seemed to meld one into another. The Commercial Street area and the surrounding areas of Batty Street and Berner Streets were the sections of London that the police concentrated on in a full, door to door search. They left no area untouched, every back-alley office was searched, every public house patron was questioned, and every lodging house was inspected in the search for Doctor Francis Tumblety or Doctor Blackburn. Despite all their endeavors at the end of two days, the search came to nothing and they were no closer to finding their suspect.

By day three, I had given up hope. However, the feeling would not leave me that Doctor Francis Tumblety had not only eluded them, but the man had most likely fled the city, as well. I spent the morning pouring over the police files at my desk in hopes that I had overlooked some fragment of information that could tie Tumblety to the killer '*Jack the Ripper*.'

By noon, I could hear Wynne Baxter, walking up the hall with a tray of tea to take up their usual formation on either side of my desk.

"Tea, Detective?" Baxter greeted me.

Over the short time that I had known the coroner, I quickly realized that Wynne Baxter, not unlike millions of other Englishmen, believed in the therapeutic properties of a steaming cup of tea, whatever the occasion.

"I would love some Wynne," I answered, watching Baxter place the tray on the edge of my desk and start to pour the steaming liquid into two teacups.

Sitting in the chair opposite me, Baxter put the edge of the cup tenderly to his lips, sipping on the hot tea and seemed to be relishing every moment.

"What are we working on today, Detective?"

"Case files Wynne," I answered, trying to sound optimistic. "I was just getting into the circumstances behind the torso found at Whitehall, Wynne."

"Oh, yes, that reminds me of that nasty bit of business down in Battersea," Wynne said, sipping at his tea.

"That must have been before my time, Wynne."

"Yes, of course, old boy, let's see perhaps that would have been September 1873, that would make it well on fifteen years ago now. I dare say time flies, doesn't it," Wynne replied, while continuing to sip on his tea.

"Yes, I suppose it does, Wynne," I answered, realizing that Baxter was not going to enlighten me any further without some prompting. "Bye the bye, what happened at Battersea that reminds you of this mysterious torso, which Scotland Yard seems to want to pin on '*Jack*,' as opposed to any other prospect," I asked.

"The Lancet published something on the subject, I believe, Detective, it was dated, I think September twentieth," Baxter mused. "Anyway, a body, or dare I say, a portion of a body was picked out of the Thames by a patrolman. I think it was the trunk, much the same as the Whitehall torso that was discovered," Wynne explained.

"So, the corpse was minus the head, neck, and all the limbs, is that it, Wynne," I asked curiously.

"Yes, that's exactly it, Detective. Only in this case over the next few days more parts were found, near Nine Elms. I believe it was the head, that was found at Limehouse, and another portion of the body turned up at Woolwich. It was in all the papers almost daily, causing a near panic up and down the Thames."

"Was the corpse ever identified?"

"What, oh no, the thing was too cut up, to be recognized," Baxter groaned. "The poor creature's entire face had been removed, the doctor, I believe it was Doctor Bond, had tried reconstructing the body but had no good results. The child's skull had been bashed in, and there was something about the carotid arteries. Detective!" In a snap, Baxter slammed his cup on the desk and was out of his chair and racing down the hall, returning after several minutes with a copy of the Lancet.

"Wynne, what is it?"

"Here it is Stone," Baxter said rifling through the paper. "Listen to this, [Sic] *"it would appear that after the victim had thus been stunned the body was immediately deprived of all its blood by a section of the carotid arteries in the neck, since there were no clots in any of the veins of the body. The tissues were, moreover, divided while they still preserved their vital contractibility, for, according to the evidence of Mr. Kempster, the muscles in the portions of the body that were first examined were fresh and retracted, so that death must have occurred within a very few hours. The scalp and skin of the face were probably next removed by making, a longitudinal incision through the scalp at the top of the head and a horizontal incision behind. The skin and peri-cranial tissues were then forcibly drawn forward and the skull thus laid bare, occasional touches of the knife being necessary to remove the skin of the face. Where the integument was thin or firmly adherent to the subjacent tissues, it was 'buttonholed,' and large portions thus remained attached to the bones. The face has in this manner—accidentally, perhaps rather than purposely— been rendered incapable of identification. The upper part of the nose is absent, as well as the inner part of the right cheek and the lower lip and chin, all of which would have required some time for their complete removal."*

Baxter hummed through the next portion skipping to the next section of importance.

"Here it is, old boy, [Sic] *"contrary to the popular opinion, the body has not been hacked, but dexterously cut up; the joints have been opened, and the bones neatly disarticulated, even the complicated joints at the ankle and the elbow, and it is only at the articulations of the hip-joint and shoulder that the bones have been sawn through."*

Baxter paused to run his finger across the text avoiding the less interesting facts, continuing, [Sic] *"notwithstanding the fact that Mr. Haden has skillfully adjusted the various parts of the body that have up to the present time been found, we fear that identification is next to impossible, except to those who are accurately acquainted with the very few marks which the body presents—namely, a scar as of a burn on the thorax."*

There was more humming then Baxter finished with the end of the article,[Sic] *"it is clear, then, that this is not a practical joke, and such an hypothesis must appear preposterous if, in addition to the evidence that the death was a violent one, it is borne in mind that the body bears no trace of dissection, or of having been used for operative surgery; for although we have said that the bones have been skillfully disarticulated, it is in a manner different from what obtains in the performance of any operation, for there are no flaps."*

"What do you think, Detective?" Baxter finished, tossing the Lancet on my desk.

"I think, Wynne, that there may have been a practitioner of some kind, murdering women in our midst for over fifteen years and this man has been cutting up his victims to render them unidentifiable. It also seems that the man is still getting away with it."

"It is obvious that you don't think that this body, found near Nine Elms was an isolated incident Stone," Wynne said, tapping his pipe in the wastebasket and blowing the sediment out of the bowl.

"I really can't see how, Wynne," I reasoned. "The man who killed this woman made cuts to the body like a surgeon. It is apparent that no novice did it, and while you are at it, you can forget about a husband hacking up his unfaithful wife in a rage."

"As long as you maintain this idea that this killer is a doctor, I am afraid, Detective that you will have few that will agree with you," Baxter said, stuffing his pipe between his teeth and scratching a match on the sole of his shoe.

"I understand your misgivings Wynne, I also understand the communities' reluctance to think that a medical man could ever void the public trust," I reasoned. "But I, contend that if not a physician, perhaps a student, I will even go so far as to say our killer is someone with medical training that never took the oath. What I don't understand, Wynne, is how you, of, all people can describe the cuts made to this body in Battersea to remove the skin of the face and still oppose the idea that this fiend is a surgeon or an expert of some kind with training?"

"I will concede that point, John," Baxter admitted. "However, I cannot fathom the reasons for anyone having the determination to accomplish such a feat, let alone the stomach for it," Baxter winced. "Perhaps this man was a physician's protégé or a student that washed out of medical school but certainly not a qualified physician."

"I don't know what the connection between these victims is Wynne, but my gut tells me that there is a connection."

"I find it quite odd that you have not mentioned Doctor Bond's connection to this crime and his statement that the cuts; on the woman's body had been done by a trained hand," Baxter queried.

"Doctor Bond must have had good reason to be forthright, though having not seen the body, I cannot compare the Whitehall torso to that of the Nine Elms body. On that note, as for Bond's statements it, may have been the doctor based his comments on the fact that the cuts to the two bodies were different, causing the doctor to form two opinions."

"How about this citing in the article about the woman's carotid artery being crushed, likely rendering the woman senseless? That fits in with your hypothesis of how this 'Ripper' leaves his victims senseless. Or, in the very least, it is quite similar to the method based on your theory," Baxter asked, relighting his pipe peering over the bowl.

"I, think it is worth mentioning, Wynne, that the author of that article also made mention that the body was not cut as one might see in a surgery. A physician is trained in the use of a scalpel and would perfect his skill over time with practice. However, Wynne, our killer is doing neither."

"Bollocks Stone! The woman was cut up like a Christmas goose," Baxter snapped.

"You misunderstand me, Wynne, obviously she was cut up, but not in any manner that could be identified with dissection or surgery."

"What are you talking about, Stone?"

"The killer in this case, in my opinion, Wynne, just wanted to cut her up. There was no finesse in the cuts that one might see in the saving strokes of a surgeon's scalpel, designed to save a life. There was no keeping of the anatomy to study in medical training for the next generation of surgeons. In that contention, I will agree with you, Wynne."

"What the devil are you talking about then, Detective?" Wynne asked, sitting up in his chair.

"Wynne, I believe that this unidentified woman was, cut up because the killer wanted to dispose of the body and to destroy any identifying features of his victim. For that reason and likely that was the only reason," I answered. "But, as you say, if not a surgeon or a mortician, who else could stomach such a task other than someone trained to do so. However, I believe there is one difference that sets our killer apart from the Nine Elms killer, then just his skill with a knife."

"What's that, Detective?"

"Our '*Jack*' enjoys cutting up his victims."

"Bloody hell!" Baxter exclaimed.

The look on Baxter's face, revealed that the coroner had tried all along to rationalize that the murders were committed by some madman running around killing with no thought or fear of reprisal. However, no matter how either of them tried to explain away the reasons for the killings, the fact remained that the Battersea killer was some type of deviant. A man with a compulsion, to kill, and no power or will to stop himself from doing it. '*Jack the Ripper*' was a man who walked the streets at night looking for his perfect victim.

The next morning when I returned to my office there was a newspaper folded at my door, with a note attached.

John,
I found this newspaper in a stack at home; I thought you might find it enlightening, Wynne.

Sitting at my desk, I unfolded the newspaper and ran my hand over it straightening the creases, then began to read.

The headline read, [Sic] HORRIBLE-MURDER IN LONDON, December 13, 1873.
An atrocious murder of a woman, it is supposed, has been perpetrated on or near the Thames, and the body, hacked to pieces, has been distributed over the river. A Thames policeman on the fifth of September, found in the mud off the Battersea Waterworks, the left quarter of a

woman's trunk which was taken to the Wandsworth Workhouse, where the divisional surgeon saw it, and pronounced it to be the portion of a body which had not been in the water more than twelve hours."

Flipping the page, I noticed that Baxter had added another note in the margin.

I have taken the liberty to underline the portions that I took special note of that were not mentioned in the Lancet.

Continuing down the article I traced with the tip of my finger along the paper until I came to the underlined portion then began to read aloud to myself skipping the details that Baxter had already read to me from the Lancet.

[Sic] *...found the right side of the trunk near the Nine Elms station. This part corresponded with the first part found and the headless trunk, it was apparent, had been severed with a very sharp knife and a saw had also been used. Soon after a portion of the lungs was found under an arch of old Battersea Bridge...*

Skipping along with my finger, I came to the next underlined portion then began to read again.

[Sic] *The search was now continued for the other parts of the body, the face with the scalp of a woman attached, was found off Limehouse. It was evident that the murderer or murderers had taken revolting precautions to prevent identification, for the nose was cut from the face but still hung attached to the upper lip.*

Stopping for a moment, I reread the section again about the nose being cut from the face of the victim, and then continued to read on.

[Sic] *The woman's age appears to have been about forty; she had dark hair, very thick, and cut short (as would be the case with a woman recently ill, or recently discharged from prison), and there was a scar, as of an old burn, on the left breast.*

Further reading revealed that the parts of the body had floated as far as the canals away. The article also stated that there was a misidentification of the remains by someone who was proven wrong when the missing person thought to be murdered, turned up alive and well. Suspicion was later cast at the owners of a barge that was docked in the area. It was reported that a woman saw aboard the barge fitted the description of the deceased. However, nothing came from the search of the barge, nor was anything further gained from a two hundred Pound Sterling reward offered by the government for the apprehension of the culprit. Baxter had underlined nothing more before the article came to its end.

[Sic] *"From the number of people who have been making inquiry, it would seem that there are many missing women of about forty years of age at this time in London and its neighborhood." I, read aloud*

"Ah, I see you have found the newspaper I left at your door, Stone," Baxter said, entering the office.

"Yes, Wynne, thank you, and as you put it in your attached note, it has been enlightening, very enlightening indeed."

"I too found some particulars that I had not gleaned from the Lancet, Detective," Baxter commented.

"The murdered victim's age height and hair color have caused me to rethink the similarities in the Whitechapel murders."

"I don't recall too many consistent similarities in any of the murders, Stone," Baxter retorted.

"If you look at the murders in Whitechapel, Wynne, in comparison to this Battersea case there are few similarities; however, if you look at the victims themselves, there are some curious similarities to the five women murdered in Whitechapel."

"Similarities, Detective, what similarities," Baxter said, shifting his chair around. "I mean aside from all the women being prostitutes."

"The hair color, Wynne," I answered, returning to my notepad. "Mary Ann Nichols had brown hair; Chapman has dark brown wavy hair. The two latest victims, Elizabeth Stride, has curly dark brown hair, and Catharine Eddowes has dark auburn hair."

"Aside from Eddowes, with auburn hair, the color of the hair is similar, anything else?" Baxter wondered.

"Wynne visualize the hair color, dark auburn at night. It could be interpreted as dark brown. There is also the age of the women, Wynne. All the women were not the same age, but they were all in their forties.

Tabram was age thirty-nine, Nichols was age forty-four, Chapman age; forty-seven, Stride; age forty-five, and Eddowes; age forty-six. This corpse found at Battersea; Doctor Bond estimated her to be in her forties as well."

"Detective, I get the idea behind the killer looking for similarities in hair color, but the age, how could '*Jack*' possibly guess their ages or much less care," Baxter gasped.

"It supports my theory, Wynne, that this man has studied these women from afar. I am surprised that I have not seen this before. There is also this statement made about the hair on the Battersea corpse being, sheared short, comparing her to someone who may have been, released from an asylum or prison."

"I wonder if that was put in the article to make the numerous workhouses aware," Wynne considered.

"I would have thought the investigating officers would have taken a description of the corpse to all the hospitals, asylums, and prisons, during the investigation, trying to ascertain an identification. It also confirms my theory that '*Jack*' chooses only those victims that will not be missed, or in the very least their disappearance, will not cause a lot of questions, to be asked."

"I am not sure, I agree with you there, John, look at the attention that this murder drew from the public."

"Yes, Wynne and look at the last line of the article that you underlined, [sic] *"From the number of people who were inquiring, it would seem that there are many missing women of about forty years of age at this time in London and its neighborhood."*

"If that is the case, John, why was there not some kind of massive search or hunt for these women at the time? There has to be somebody out there who wants answers to where their loved ones had disappeared to."

"Judging by that last statement, Wynne, I am willing to bet it never really dawned on anyone until the plea went out for the public's help to identify the woman. Until then, I am betting that no one even suspected that a problem even existed."

"What do you mean, John?"

"One problem, I have run into time, after time while investigating crimes into a victim's background is the lack of records. Paperwork is often left unfinished by detectives, files are poorly kept at Police Stations, and follow up is seldom done when a complaint has been issued. In most cases, a constable; is sent to an interview, but if no evidence is found of wrongdoing, the complaint; is merely dismissed."

"So, if someone is reported as missing, what then?"

"There might be an initial inquiry, but if no foul play is suspected, the odds of that happening are slim. This leads me to believe that more than one of these women is more than likely newly released from workhouses. There is a Union Workhouse at Wandsworth and Clapham, where the women upon entrance, are stripped of their clothing, their hair is cut short, as this Battersea victim, and they are given a prison type uniform to wear. Some of these women could be newly released from asylums or prisons after a long incarceration. Although, I would hazard a guess, and more likely to believe, that the bulk of the women chosen would be young to middle-aged women who have no families or who have run away from their families for whatever reasons, to come to London and are forced to become prostitutes to survive."

"Leaving their family back home to speculate what has ever become of them or wonder if they are alive or dead."

"It is becoming more apparent that this killing spree has gone on for a lot longer and on a larger scale than what authorities would like to believe or admit."

"Surely, some of these women have some kind of family waiting for them somewhere in London."

"I am sure some of them do, Wynne, and judging by the response police got when this article was written fifteen years ago, there must be some women that have disappeared that are missed, but I think this is a consideration made by the killer while choosing his victims. It would make sense that '*Jack*' seeks out the woebegone that would appear to have no one in the world to care for them. If one of these, goes missing then the police search won't be too wholehearted for the killer of some prostitute or a former inmate or two from Newgate or Dundee prison."

"As you have already suggested in your theory of the way 'Jack' seeks out his victims here in Whitechapel, is that it Stone," Baxter admitted.

"Yes, Wynne, consider this for a moment if you please. If a family has a child who is challenged in some way, what is the family most likely to do?"

"I have known families to keep the child hidden, or they send the child away to live with relatives," Baxter answered.

315

"That is generally the case, if a family is well off, they do look after the child; otherwise, they end up in an asylum somewhere. For some, it is a matter of not wanting the cost for the care of the child and, unfortunately, sometimes the embarrassment."

"Where they stay the rest of their lives, or if they are lucky enough to be eventually released, they look forward to the balance of their life begging on the streets where if they disappear, no one will miss them anyway," Baxter finished the sentence. "You know how to paint a bleak picture, John."

"Sorry, Wynne."

"Alright, Detective, supposing you are right, and these murders that took place over fifteen years ago are somehow connected to the Whitechapel murders," Baxter paused. "Why have they started again? Certainly, you're not suggesting someone has picked up the torch where this other madman left off?"

"To be honest, Wynne, I could not hazard a guess. Perhaps the killer was arrested and put in jail on a lesser charge, which would create a gap in his killing; wouldn't it."

"So, correct me, if I am wrong, John, but your theory is that this killer from fifteen years ago killed a lot of women up and down the Thames, then for whatever reason stopped, and has started to kill again.

"It is possible," I sighed. "But aside from the torso found at Whitehall, I doubt that this man and '*Jack the Ripper*' is the same."

"I must concur, John, aside from a few similarities in the women," Baxter agreed. "This fiend in Whitechapel isn't cutting up his victim in pieces and throwing them into the drink."

"Agreed, Wynne, although, if I am wrong, and there is no link at all, there is still no denying that the man who killed along the Thames River fifteen years ago, is still out there killing, the appearance of the Whitehall's torso is evidence of that."

"Fair enough," Baxter agreed. "So, we have a killer who looks for women who have no family to speak of and no one to look for them if they go missing. What about the victims aside from the hair color and age," Baxter asked? "There seems to be no other connection aside from the victim's all being prostitutes."

"I would think that alone should be enough to catch this killer, but somehow it isn't. We could have a thousand policemen on duty every night, and it does not seem to matter. These women will still be out there night after night on the street willing to follow any man who has a few pennies down the dark alleys of Whitechapel."

With evening well on its way and the coroner sitting opposite me sipping tea, I sat at my desk, unable to leave the stack of police files that had been sitting daunting me for several weeks now. Opening the first in a pile I had long ago pushed off to the side of my desk, I found a file with the date written on the top, July twenty-second, 1887, and nothing more. Inside was a single sheet from a newspaper dated *Saturday, July twenty-third, 1887*. The article was from *The Penny Illustrated Paper*.

"Wynne, listen to this."

[Sic] *"On Saturday evening last, the police of the S. division had their attention called by a man named William Gate, a laborer, to a parcel which I had discovered in the waters of the Regent's canal by Chalk Farm-road Bridge. This, on being opened, was found to contain the left thigh of a woman, and it was at first thought that it was another portion of the body of a woman parts of whom have been found at different times in the waters of the Regent's canal and the river Thames off Rainham and elsewhere. The remains were removed to the Albany-street police station, and there it was found that the thigh did not correspond in any way with the other portions found. It was the left thigh of a woman well advanced in years, and who had in her lifetime suffered from chronic rheumatism. The thigh bone, in being measured, was found to measure a little over sixteen inches, and had, in the opinion of the surgeon, been in the water about six weeks. The police authorities are having a strict watch kept by lock-keepers and bargeman on the Regent's canal, with the view, if possible, of discovering other portions of the missing body."*

I finished reading then looked up at Baxter, searching for a reaction.

"I assume that the police surgeon spoke of in the article would be either Doctor Kempster or Doctor Jenkins, and the coroner, in this case, would be Mr. A. Braxton Hicks," Wynne spoke up, offering this information, and then after a few minutes added. "You know, of course, Detective that the age of the victim does not fit in with your theory that the killer only kills those women around the age of forty."

"Yes, Wynne," I responded. "I am just doing a calculation of the number of women this fiend has murdered, and I am dumbfounded at the total I am coming up with."

"How many women do you figure have been murdered and tossed in the Thames, Stone."

"At first glance, Wynne, I am guessing five maybe six which we know of. That number is based solely on newspaper documentation and the police files that I have read, I was not attached to Whitechapel in those days, and there wasn't the sensational reporting then, as there is now with the '*Jack the Ripper*' case."

With Baxter's long silence came the return of the foreboding, feeling that they were dealing with a man or men quite inhuman. With a long gasp, the coroner sat his teacup on the desk.

"I don't know about you Detective, but I am feeling, more and more like these women are being killed for reasons other than some twisted lust for blood," Baxter said, holding up his hand to stop any interruptions. "Notwithstanding your theories Detective, I am seriously coming around to the thoughts of the rest of the community that this is some medical student's practical joke. There can be no other explanation!"

Watching his friend walk about the room, I considered the statement made by the coroner and contemplated why Baxter felt the need to have some type of explanation or reason for the murders. I supposed that it was an integral part of the man whether by profession or some innate quality bred within, not to consider that there was real unspeakable evil at work in the world. I supposed that it went against the grain to think that there were those that without reservation, conscience, or a second thought were quite capable of committing an injustice against their fellow man. To further complicate the picture. These seemingly normal, ordinary people would then go home, sit down to their supper, kiss their wife and child goodnight, and carry on like everything was right in their world.

"You are abnormally quiet Detective, there has to be something swirling around in that brain of yours."

I watched Baxter pour cold tea into his cup, sloshing some of it onto the desk top.

"I was just considering your explanation for the body parts found on the banks of the Thames," I answered. "I was trying to think of all the reasons why a student would throw bodies into the Thames Wynne."

I eyed my friend looking for the typical reaction, hoping that some rationale would present itself to the coroner. After several minutes of silence and no response came from the coroner, I continued.

"How are bodies received at the medical museum," I mused aloud, allowing my question to stir some reaction from Baxter; however, when none came, I continued. "Are they donated by the family of the deceased who can't afford a burial service. How are the bodies documented, for medical study, and who oversees these bodies, if say one is to go missing or let's say, five go missing," I said, tapping my chin with my finger?

"Oh, alright Detective," Baxter said, throwing his hands up in the air. "You made your point. It sounded better in my head than it did after coming out of my mouth."

"Wynne," I said, standing up behind my desk, pacing back and forth. "Perhaps it is too presumptuous of me to discount your theory or any other. We are, as in the dark here as we were fifteen years ago. Perhaps, what we should be thinking about is why," I paused, thinking for a moment, not caring for the answer to the question I was asking. "Why, we have not found this man, or '*Jack the Ripper*' for that matter. There are in the neighborhood of eleven women that we know of that have been murdered on the streets and in the alleys of Whitechapel or have been, butchered up and down the Thames River. The truth of the matter is, that we are no closer to finding either culprit today than at the beginning of this murderous rampage this killer or killers has been taking us on."

I paced back and forth, glancing at Baxter, not liking the look on the coroner's face.

"John, I am as astounded as you," Baxter responded. "I am an appointed official answerable to the same hierarchy as you. I am devastated at the lack of progress we have been making in these murder investigations. Every time, I am questioned by someone, or read these articles in the paper about how inept we are, I want to scream."

"I am just as frustrated, Wynne; it makes me wonder if I have been chasing the wrong culprit all of this time. Or if there is something more complex going on here, something so unspeakable that we cannot fathom its very existence."

"Whatever do you mean, John," Baxter asked.

I looked up and saw the coroner staring at me with his mouth unhinged, obviously curious as to what the answer might be.

"Perhaps there is not one killer here after all Wynne," I answered. "Maybe there are two, one man who has been operating in and around the Thames for years, the other, a physician who is taking anatomy from his victims for some study."

"John, that is preposterous?" Baxter said, slumping into his chair, taking his pipe from his pocket.

"Is there some other explanation, Wynne?"

"There must be?"

"Wynne, explain to me how fifteen years ago women were disappearing at such an alarming rate that when there were enough parts found and was pieced together by the enterprising Dr. Bond that there was a flood of people to react to the police call for the public's identification?"

"Alright, Detective, but I thought there were only a half dozen women that have been found?"

"That is all the bodies that have been found. I might be reaching here, but it has been over fifteen years, how many more bodies have been cut up and never found. I realize Wynne that this sounds like conjecture run amuck, but at this moment, what evidence is there to disprove my theory?"

With Baxter's shrug of his shoulders, I continued to think out loud.

"Is there a simpler explanation as to why women ranging from twenty-five to their mid-forties are disappearing, then to suggest that there is more than one maniac killing women and cutting up their bodies?"

"I cannot assume to know the answer John, I am as in the dark as the next man, and with that, I bid you goodnight."

Silently Baxter donned hat and cape, and with a nod, the coroner walked out of the office. Sitting in the silence of the darkening office, with the last rays of the sun dipping into the horizon, I listened to the snap of the wick in the lamp that sat on the corner of my desk. With Baxter's abrupt exit, I realized that the coroner had been taking each inquest home with him. Spending hours mulling over every detail of the deaths of these women, trying to justify the reasons why the killer or killers had not been apprehended long before now. Unfortunately, like me, the coroner had no answer, nor did any seem to be forthcoming. Wynne Baxter, had since accepting his appointment to the coroner's office, been faced with the arduous task of sifting through each case seeking answers that were not there to be had. Since coming to Whitechapel, I had been doing the same thing. Although as astounding as it seemed, it did not discourage me as much as I would have thought, it was quite the opposite. The lack of answers had encouraged me to keep seeking the truth with all the tenacity of a bulldog. That is why, instead of going home to a hot meal, I poured another cup of tea that had gone cold hours earlier. Reaching for one of the many files, recounting the details in which several pieces of corpses had been found along the Thames, I began to read.

On the eleventh day of September, a piece of human remains was discovered on the bank of the Thames off Pimlico.

The find had caused a great disturbance because the incident reeked suspiciously of the Battersea incident where several pieces of women's anatomy had been found all along the Thames River. Londoners were outraged, for not only did they have to put up with the maniac '*Jack the Ripper*,' but they now thought that the Thames torso murderer had returned as well. This latest piece of anatomy found on the Thames was an arm. It was in healthy condition, of the palm and fingers, both were free of calluses and scars and showed no sign of ever performing manual labor. No jewelry was present on the fingers. Having; no other pieces of the body to compare the arm to, the remains were put in spirits at the Hospital Museum, where it stayed until on September the twenty-eighth when another arm was found along the Lambeth Road. Again, the police were searching along the bank of the Thames for more remains and hoped that a body would surface soon, one that would match the two arms already at the museum. On October the second, a torso was found in the vaults below the newly constructed Scotland Yard buildings. The torso was that of a woman approximately twenty-five years of age, with one lung infected with severe pleurisy. Doctor Thomas Bond could only ascertain, given the limitations of the autopsy, that the woman did not die of suffocation or drowning. The killer had tourniquet both arms and legs to stop the flow of blood when the amputation was done. According to Doctor Bond's, opinion after a thorough examination, the person or persons who dissected the woman's body took no particular care or had no apparent medical background. After having determined that the body was indeed dead by the jury, the coroner, Mr. Troutbeck concluded, that the dissection done to the body was done to destroy the identity of the woman, not to mutilate the body for any purpose.

I slammed the cover of the file closed as I considered what I read. The one aspect that seemed to be continually shrugged off by both investigators and doctors alike was that yet another dead woman was found that showed signs of dissection with organs missing. I focused on the fact that the arm located on the bank of the Thames showed no sign of heavy labor that was a common characteristic among the folk of London's East End. This faceless woman had never been subjected to an arduous lifestyle, forced to toil in the mills, slaughterhouses, or workhouses, to survive. The hand gave evidence of this having no calluses, broken nails, or scars that would be noticeable on an individual who would be used to such hard labor. The dress was a common broche satin with a pattern that was at least three years old judging by the days' fashions. Inspector Marshall also found bits of paper from the Echo Newspaper dated August the twenty-fourth and the Chronicle Newspaper that was from an earlier year.

As I considered the newspaper clippings again, I found myself thinking that these bits of clues were all apart of some diversion. Designed to keep detectives searching in areas that had no connection to the woman whatsoever. A woman who was relatively healthy and showed no signs of having a hard life, from a family of means. If so, why hadn't the woman been reported missing? The woman might have been kidnapped from another city, or newly arrived on a ship, perhaps from another country? Which would explain why there were no inquiries made by the public. I began to suspect that the bits of clues left were of no importance at all to the investigation. As I sifted through the evidence, my mind began to work overtime, and I began to visualize a woman seduced by the killer, drawn away on some pretense of romance and then murdered. Her killer then dressed his victim in a cheap dress and discarded the parts of the body in the one place where the pieces could float for days before being found. All the torso cases had one common trait; the killer put all the body parts in a place where they would eventually be found. This last torso, the killer went so far as to place the body somewhere that would embarrass the police. I could not help but think that this odd behavior was all to satisfy the man's morbid amusement. I imagined the killer close by watching the police search for clues, thus fulfilling his lust for blood and his desire for attention. Unfortunately, when I had finished reading the file, I had done nothing but add to the many questions that I had no answers to. There seemed to be no answers in the choice of victims or in the few clues, and this troubled me, causing me to wonder if the killer was smarter than the police or if the man was just lucky. As I sat looking over the description, they had on the suspect known as Blackburn or Tumblety, I began to piece together a picture of the man who, at every turn, kept me guessing.

The final day of the inquest for the deceased known as Elizabeth Stride was October the twenty-third. Arriving at the Vestry Hall in Cable Street, I had been elbowed, stepped on, and shoved entering the overcrowded building. Just as I found a seat, the Coroner, Wynne Baxter, called his first witness.

[Sic] *Detective –Inspector Edmund Reid was recalled and announced that I had found John Thomas Stride former husband of the deceased, having been dead these some four years. Detective Reid examined the records at the Poplar and Stepney Sick Asylum, brought the records from the Asylum to the coroner verifying his findings, John Thomas Stride had in fact been a patient at the asylum and died of heart disease, in October of 1884. Reid had also located Mrs. Watts, now going by the name of Elizabeth Stokes, who was very much alive. Mrs. Stokes took the stand and showed the coroner her crippled foot, a characteristic that the deceased did not have. She apologized to the coroner having said her sister Mary Malcolm had given false testimony.*

The next witness was Constable Walter Stride, having recognized the deceased by a photograph as one Elizabeth Stride, who had married his uncle John Thomas Stride, in 1872 or 73. Stride's testimony had finally put an end to any doubt that may have still existed about the identity of the deceased, confirming once and for all that, she was in fact, Elizabeth Stride. The coroner, Wynne Baxter's summation, was thorough and informative; I listened carefully to the closing remarks.

[Sic] *"There were no signs of any struggle; the clothes were neither torn nor disturbed. It was true that there were marks over both shoulders, produced by pressure of two hands, but the position of the body suggested either that she was willingly placed or placed herself where she was found. Only the soles of her boots were visible. She was still holding in her left hand a packet of cachous, and there was a bunch of flowers still pinned to her dress front. If she had been forcibly placed on the ground, as Dr. Phillips opines, it was difficult to understand how she failed to attract attention, as it was clear from the appearance of the blood on the ground that the throat was not cut until after she was actually on her back. There were no marks of gagging, no bruises on the face, and no trace of any anesthetic or narcotic in the stomach; while the presence of the cachous in her hand showed that she did not make use of it in self-defense. Possibly the pressure marks may have had a less tragic origin, as Dr. Blackwell says it was difficult to say how recently they were produced. There was one particular which was not easy to explain. When seen by Dr. Blackwell her right hand was lying on the chest, smeared inside and out with blood. Dr. Phillips was unable to make any suggestion how the hand became soiled." The coroner finished his remarks*

The image, described by Baxter, stayed with me as the coroner finished his summation. As I sat in the crowd my mind, wandered to that fateful night nearly a month ago, when '*Jack the Ripper*,' lured Elizabeth Stride, under the pretense of passion into Dutfield's Yard. '*Jack*,' stands with Stride in a careful position in the yard that was chosen due to the location's high gates and the absence of intrusive light. Stride giggles wickedly as '*Jack*' turns her around so that she cannot see the fate awaits her. Stride feels; '*Jack's*' embrace as her suitor's; arms tighten around her. '*Jack's*' knife fills his palm and is poised when, unexpectedly, the carter Diemschutz arrives at the gate. '*Jack's*' plans for the woman are frustrated by the intrusion. With no time to waste '*Jack*,' turns the knife's sharp edge towards Stride's throat. In the dark, the movement; goes unnoticed, and with a flash, Elizabeth Stride is aware of only the bite of steel that sinks into the tender flesh of her neck. She holds her hand up as her warm lifeblood spills from the wound. Stride's body goes, limp and '*Jack*,' lowers her gently to the ground. '*Jack*,' quickly steps over Stride and slinks, away from the entrance of Dutfield's Yard, and waits for Diemschutz, to open the gate. '*Jack*' sees the horse rear sensing an intruder and during the commotion that ensues, the killer steals out of the yard, unnoticed, and melts into the night.

With the crack of a gavel on the desk, I dismissed my daydream, looking over at Wynne Baxter's resolute expression and intently listens to the coroner's final statements.

[Sic] *"There had been no skillful mutilation as in the cases of Nichols and Chapman, and no unskillful injuries as in the case in Mitre-square - possibly the work of an imitator; but there had been the same skill exhibited in the way in which the victim had been entrapped, and the injuries inflicted, so as to cause instant death and prevent blood from soiling the operator, and the same daring defiance of immediate detection, which, unfortunately for the peace of the inhabitants and trade of the neighborhood, had hitherto been only too successful. I myself was sorry that the time and attention which the jury had given to the case had not produced a result that would be a perceptible relief to the metropolis - the detection of the criminal; but I was sure that all had used their utmost effort to accomplish this object, and while I desired to thank the gentlemen of the jury for their kind assistance, I was bound to acknowledge the great attention which Inspector Reid and the police had given to the case. I left it to the jury to say, how, when, and by what means the deceased came by her death."*

I had been back in my office for an hour before Baxter, entered carrying a tray. I made no comment as Baxter, set the tray down, but did not pour the tea. Noting the coroner's expression, I reached across and poured two cups of the scalding tea and returned to my seat. Like those in attendance at the inquest, I had heard Baxter's last comments during the summation and was not affected in the least. I knew that the coroner had his own feelings about who the suspected killer was. I had not once tried to persuade or coerce my friend into thinking as I did, nor had the coroner criticized me for my theory that there was one man responsible, who was killing the prostitutes of Whitechapel.

Without saying a word, Baxter set the teacup with a rattle on the desk and poured more of the amber liquid into his cup and then sat down in the chair opposite with a gasp of exhaustion.

I watched the coroner pack his pipe with strong tobacco and place it between his teeth without lighting it. The two had come a long way since

325

their first meeting some months ago. A bond of respect and friendship had formed between them, one that I had come to rely on. I looked at the coroner for a moment and decided to remain quiet while my friend sorted out whatever was bothering him, and continued to look at the inquest report I had compiled of Elizabeth Stride.

"I can't, make heads or tails of this mess, Stone," Baxter said, finally. "I have presided over many inquests in wrongful deaths and murders, and always the jury was able to point the finger of guilt as the testimony directed and the culprit, paid fines and restitution or was taken for trial and hanged. What is it, about this '*Jack the Ripper*' that hinders our efforts and prevents us from bringing the man to justice? Is this wretch doing the devil's bidding, or are we stalking some ghost that goes about the streets of London and disappears in a wisp of wind not to be seen until the fateful night of his choice to exact his revenge upon the prostitutes of London," Baxter, shouted?

I understood that Baxter was not shouting at me, but at the killer who seemed as far from justice today as at the beginning of the inquests. I said nothing, as Baxter got up and walked out of my office, leaving his tea untouched.

As Baxter's friend, I had listened, allowing him to rant, knowing that it was the sound of a man who only wanted answers to a problem that seemed too far out of reach to obtain. It was the answers one needed when all avenues known to them were exhausted, and all help seemed far away, even though the threat of the enemy was near. That enemy still lurked in the darkened corners and alleys of every woman's mind that lived in Whitechapel. Whether '*Jack*' truly waited in the shadows or not, the fear they felt was not imagined. To the constables that walked the streets, the man known only as '*Jack the Ripper*' lurked in every alley or vacant yard. Each man who stood alone on a darkened corner asked the same question night after night, "*is tonight the night that Jack the Ripper*' will strike again? Every prostitute in the East End walked on pins and needles, and yet the fear of some deranged murderer that walked the same streets, as they, could not keep them from going out every evening to earn the pennies they needed to survive. Perhaps this lifestyle was all they had ever known, or maybe it was alcohol-induced bravado that kept the women going out on the streets night after night. Whatever the reason, the threat of a killer as vicious as '*Jack*' did not deter them from the men who came seeking them after dark. They went willingly down the back alleys and vacant yards to spend a few minutes of passion with the unknown men that came to call on them.

In a hushed meeting of police officials, it was rumored that Sir Robert Anderson suggested, '*That all women plying their trade after midnight were to be arrested. It was the responsibility of the police to warn them that it was impossible to protect them.*' Of course, the statement was the most absurd thing that I had ever heard. It made me shudder to think that another officer of the law would make such a statement. As it was, London did not have the manpower nor the time to arrest all the women out after midnight every night. Since they had no legal right to keep them longer than twenty-four hours, those same women would be arrested night after night.

To make matters worse, there was a consensus among those in the West End, along with a growing number of police, that felt the Jew was to blame for the police departments inability to apprehend '*Jack.*' Of course, this belief seemed to be held by the citizens whose prejudice allowed them the convenience to point fingers and cast aspersions at this small portion of the populace who made up only about one percent of London's entire population.

All the rumors and innuendo that floated around caused the citizenry in London's east to mistrust those who were the powers ordained to protect them. Most in Whitechapel gossiped that it was because the ladies were mere '*Judy's*' that the police did not care if '*Jack cut up a few prostitutes.*' Accusation ran rampant, and there was no easy fix. What made matters worse were the nuisances and meddlers, like Michael Kidney. Kidney spoke out publicly that he had information to apprehend the killer, but the police refused to listen to me. Not long afterward, the view that the police were running around in a stupor not knowing what to do next caused the police stations to be inundated with letters from citizens to tell them exactly how bad a job they were doing. This influx of mail to police stations in every district did nothing but add to the confusion, forcing every available officer to follow every useless lead to the end, leaving only a bone-weary police department in its wake. The collective assessment of police performance by those who lived in Whitechapel was that of complete incompetence, and that thinking was fueled by newspapers like the Illustrated Police News that were willing to tell on masse how pathetic

327

the police were doing in the course of their duties and how obsolete their investigative techniques were. Not to mention the endless pages of exaggerations that plagued the papers depicting the police as blind men and buffoons. With every murder that went unsolved, the newspapers printed more sensationalism, which in turn created more opportunity for publications to use the masse unrest that existed in the East End. The papers soon took every occasion to put into words a vision of poverty, unemployment, and overcrowding in the East for the world to see firsthand.

However, there was one voice that rose above the clamor of unrest that hovered over London. That was the voice of the newly appointed Vigilance Committee. No opportunity was allowed to go by that the committee did not take advantage of the occasion to speak out in rebuke of the police efforts to capture the perpetrator that stalked the women of Whitechapel. At first, the Vigilance Committee had the sole support of the common man; unfortunately, for all the organizations talk about instituting measures for the good of the people and its welfare, the committee had shown little results since its formation and had done nothing more than perpetuate the disdain and mistrust felt by constituents. With the Vigilance Committee on guard, the Metropolitan Police Department's actions were more than ever in the public eye, allowing for every reporter to place both organizations in the balance to critique the efforts of bringing '*Jack the Ripper*' to justice. '*Jack*' soon was described as a hooded figure, much like that of the grim reaper, that walked the back alleys; ridding London of the sinful, portrayed in the comics with captions overhead filled with phrases that were designed to frighten and make the reader laugh. After a murder had been discovered, the newspapers took it upon themselves to describe every morbid detail, right down to how the women were lowly prostitutes left to die in London's streets, and the police were depicted as helpless characters in the scenes. The articles captured every bit of the murders, right down to the horrific details of blood and gore; however, what the newspapers; did not depict was the lives that huddled on masse in fear that the next victim would be a friend or a family member that would be found lying dead in an alley. The newspapers gave the world a picture of five murdered women and the poverty in which they lived in the East End. The reports did a better than average job describing the fear that reverberated up and down the streets. Their reports depicted every detail of the grisly murders, designed to sell papers. Although their stories did not depict the circumstances that the women had to endure and how they had come to that point in their lives where fear of a killer that walked the streets did little to deter the overwhelming feeling of hunger in their bellies. Their reporting did not reveal the faces attached to the stories; there were no names of the families who suffered, no brothers, no sisters, and no parents that grieved due to their lost one. They neglected to paint a clear picture of what life was truly like on the mean streets of London, where a killer took center stage over the need for reform in one of the largest cities in the world.

The newspapers reported the murders, and the news went over the wire in every major city around the world from New York to Toronto and, the world heard about the horrid murders in Whitechapel. The killer's victims and the ghastly details may have been a source for news around the world, yet, the fantastic reporting did little for the image of London town. When the murders stopped, exaggerated versions of the stories began to circulate, and '*Jack*' was depicted as some type of hero for eluding police. The tales were repeated in every flat and public house, and the women of London that walked the streets where the killer lurked, waited for the next victim. However, '*Jack the Ripper*' was not a hero or an imaginary character. The man was flesh and blood, a faceless, cold-blooded killer, who went unpunished and continued to reap fear in the women of Whitechapel.

Chapter Twenty

The thick fog that rolled in covered everything in a thick blanket of moisture. The intense low that had hovered over London for most of the week forced the smoke from the city's chimneys down to street level, reducing visibility to only a few feet. The strike of a horseshoe on the cobbled street, the slam of a door, the hacking cough of some passer-by, was all that could be heard in the wee hours of the morning. I waited in a covered doorway across the street from a two-story building on the corner of Fairclough Street, between Berner and Batty Streets. With me were six constables covering the front and the back of the building. It had been two hours since I had received the tip from Sergeant Davis that an informer had seen a man fitting Dr. Francis Tumblety's description in the Berner Street area and, only a few minutes since, I had talked to the informer, a man named John Spooner. Spooner was a colorful, character who among other things, was a petty thief and a pickpocket, but more importantly, a valuable source of information about the happenings on the streets of London. After receiving the tip, I headed for Berner St. and met up with Davis and several constables from the Leman Street station and had the nondescript building where Tumblety was reported to be. Leaving my place of concealment for a moment, I walked around the corner where a waiting constable stood with a muttering Spooner, complaining about the damp chill in the night air.

"Are you sure that you saw our man in this area," I asked Spooner, gruffly, hoping I wasn't wasting my time.

"As I told this Blue Bottle," Spooner retorted.

"Mind your manners, you," the constable swung a slap at the back of Spooner's head.

"Like, I was saying, sir," Spooner said, sarcastically. "I'm not a blower; I just keeps my eyes open. When I saw this toff, near this flash house, I says to myself this bloke looks a bit out of place if you asked me, the toolers in the place were eyeing him up and down pretty good, but before any could make a move, this gent was out the door. Now me, I says to myself follow the pigeon Spoon, so I does, and this here bloke comes to this place all dark and looking abandoned and goes right up to the side door nice as you please, knocks three times, and to my surprise, the door opens, and your gent walks in. It wasn't until today when I got nibbed for poken me hand in a pocket, that I heard you coppers were up in arms about some bloke that fits this mark. So, I says to myself old Spoon now is the time to be using this pigeon to get myself out of the beak's way," Spooner finished speaking by adding a slight bow in mockery of my company.

I listened to Mr. Spooner, who could talk himself in or out of almost anything. Weary of false claims by those who operated on the streets, I had grown accustomed to those who would give incorrect information at the drop of a hat to escape a night in the goal.

"Should I hang onto this one, sir?"

"Yes, let him go only if our man is in fact in the building," I replied, glancing over at the scowl on Spooner's face.

"Detective there's somebody in the building alright," a constable interrupted. "I saw a light when a curtain moved in an upstairs window."

"Alright, Constable Smith, tell the Sergeant, I want him on the back door with you and two on the side door where Mr. Spooner says our man entered. Nobody moves until everyone is in place, and I give the signal, understand," I barked my orders.

With a nod, the constable was gone disappearing into the fog.

"Constable, I want you to hold Mr. Spooner across the road until I have my man, we may have use of him if our suspect is not among those in the house," I spoke to the young man holding the informant.

Sliding across the face of several buildings, I stopped at the front of the seemingly vacant building that we had under surveillance. Looking about, I waited for Sergeant Davis to come up behind me and whisper over my shoulder.

"The men are in position sir," Davis whispered.

"Good," I said as I readied myself to enter, and then I stopped. Holding up my hand in the direction of the sergeant. "Just a minute, I think I hear something."

"I think, I hear it too," Davis said, leaning towards the door. "Is that music, Sir?" Davis asked.

"I believe it is, Sergeant, so much for thinking the building might be empty, eh, Davis," I responded.

"What the bloody hell is going on in there do you suppose, Sir?" Davis asked.

"I don't know, but we're going to find out. Head around back and join your man there, we go in two minutes," I ordered.

"Ready men," I asked the two constables standing at my side.

Both men nodded apprehensively in recognition. I kept the two youngest constables with me so that I could keep an eye on them. It was apparent that the men were nervous, being young recruits, and not knowing what to expect. If the truth was made known, I was a little nervous as well. Whether from the hindering effects of the unusually thick fog or the excitement of catching the man I had spent weeks searching for, which, I didn't know. With a nod to the elder of the constables, I watched the man shove, his whistle between his lips and then blow; just as I lifted my foot to the door, the high pitched shrill shattered the silence. With a crash, the door jamb splintered under my foot, and the door slammed against the interior wall. The blare of the constable's whistle cut through the quiet of the night, within seconds, I heard the back-door shatter under Sergeant Davis' foot, the shrill of the whistle did the job they were intending; startling all the occupants of the building. Scrambling passed the broken door; I grabbed the front of one of the younger constable's uniform and shouted at him to get upstairs. Without hesitation, the recruit took the stairs two at a time, grabbing the other constable, I shoved him and yelled at him to follow his mate. The main floor was dimly lit, the windows had been covered in sackcloth to keep light from escaping out of the windows, and thus keeping up the appearance the building was unoccupied. The commotion; caused some of the occupants to scramble towards the back door where Davis met them and forced them back into the main room. Upstairs, I could hear my two young constables shouting and ordering the occupants down the stairs. Looking around the room, I scanned each of the faces of the men as they were brought into the main hall. The room had been occupied by several men all dressed as gentlemen, however, that was all that was genteel about them. The few men that came down the stairs were pulling on pants and shirts looking rather sheepish. After the men were all collected on the main floor and the confusion started to dissipate, I noticed the lavish decor, the absence of women, coupled with the covered windows and the apparent desire for privacy, I realized that I had uncovered a so-called, gentleman's club. Several men accustomed to the shakedown procedure still sat in chairs smoking with drinks in their hands, three or four men smoked out of hookah's, and by the smell in the room, I would guess that the hookahs were filled with opium.

"Alright Davis, get these men lined up, so we can take a good look at them," I shouted.

Turning to the pair of recruits, I looked for the timider of the two and chose him.

"You, go to the station and collect the wagon for our gentleman," I shouted.

"Yes, Sir."

"Sergeant Davis, do we see our man," I asked the question knowing the answer.

I had already studied all the faces in the room and had not seen Francis Tumblety among them. Unfortunately, the information Mr. Spooner had given them was false, or Tumblety had left before the constables had arrived.

"Detective Stone, there is an open window in the basement."

The shout from one of the young constables averted my attention.

"Well, don't just stand there," I retorted. "Get outside and see if you see anyone fleeing the area."

I watched the constable as the man left in pursuit of whoever had used the basement window to escape being apprehended with the others inside the club. I could very well understand the lengths at which the users of the building were willing to go to keep their meetings private and their personal lives even more so. Walking along the lineup, I saw the glazed eyes of the pair that had been smoking from the hookah; their manner was that of faint amusement. Looking at each man in the line more closely, I sought the one individual who might be a first-timer to the club. There was always one who had spent countless hours fighting the demons inside of him only to finally take the chance and find out what was waiting for him on the other side of the law. I knew from experience that there was always one in the crowd who would talk. The man I sought was the one who in the attempt to escape arrest and keep his lifestyle from being made public and out in the open to the penetrating eyes of those friends and or family who knew him. This man would be frightened enough that the thought of charges being laid by police; would do anything rather than suffer the humiliation of seeing his name in the newspaper. Standing in front of a large fellow who reeked of bourbon, I looked into the man's eyes to see if alcohol may have induced the change of attitude I was looking for.

"You, got, no right to barge in here and treat us this way, we ain't done nothin!" The man shouted.

Out of the corner of my eye, I saw Sergeant Davis bolt down the line up of men.

"Keep your bleedin' mouth shut until you're spoken to!"

I almost felt sorry for the man as Davis shouted, issuing spittle in the man's face with every syllable.

Looking at all the faces of the men in the lineup, I saw; one man standing a little out of line, his body language spoke volumes. The man stood back and slightly out of my line of sight. The man's brow was furrowed, his jaw clenched, and in my opinion, looked to be stressed above the others in the queue. Out of the corner of my eye, I continued to watch the overwrought man wring his cloth cap between his hands, gazing at the floor. Taking a second look, I noticed that the young man's attire did not fit in with the other members with their collars and bowlers and fobs.

"Our man is not here, Detective?"

"No," I answered Davis gruffly. "But let's see what we can get out of the man on the end there, Davis," I nodded in the direction of the nervous man standing to my right.

"Alright, Johnston lets round these blokes up, two by two out the side door, into the paddy wagon with the lot of them."

I allowed Davis to shout his orders; meanwhile, I had strategically placed myself between the man I wanted to question and the rest of the men in the lineup.

"Hold up, there boy; the detective wants a word with you," Davis hauled on the man's arm.

"What's your name."

"Tom Brown."

"Come on you, speak up and give us your real name this time," Davis growled.

I watched the man squirm, and his eyes dart up, making eye contact for the first time. I could see by the man's expression that fear and the desire, to tell the truth, were waging a war within. It was likely that the chap was asking himself how Sergeant Davis knew that Brown was not his real name in the first place.

"Thomas Burns!"

"That's better Mr. Burns, now how long have you frequented this club?"

"Club, I didn't even know it was a club for that, these, the men that were here," Burns stammered.

"What kind of club did you think it was?"

"I came here tonight, for the first time, honest," Burns pleaded. "I thought it was just a place where men drank; I didn't know it was that type of club."

"I see, why didn't you leave when you figured it out what kind of club it was," I continued questioning Burns.

"I was going to, but I need a job, this here bloke says there is a job that pays a tidy sum if I was willing to meet with him to discuss it," Burns continued.

"When did you realize it was a rouse to get you here," I asked.

"When I heard the whistles and the bloke took off out of the room, seconds later you jacks came through the door..." Burns' voice trailed off into silence.

"What was the man's name that you were meeting here tonight," I asked, looking over at Davis.

"Clive, that is all I know, honest," Burns said.

335

"Did this Clive, look anything like this," I asked, unfolding a composite sketch. The sketch was made from the description given to me by the woman who owned the house where Dr. Tumblety was lodging.

"No," Burns looked at the sketch and spoke without hesitation.

Looking over at Sergeant Davis, I could not believe my ears.

"Are you positive boy," Davis spoke up. "Take a good look."

"I don't need to look at it again," Burns answered. "The man I came with has red hair and a full beard."

"Well, do you remember seeing him here tonight," I asked, fishing for any information that may collaborate with Spooner's information.

"I am not sure, it is possible, but I just got here five minutes before you blokes kicked in the door. You have to believe me, I know nothing but what I told you," Burns pleaded.

"Let him go, Sergeant," I said to Davis.

"Are you sure, Detective?" Davis whispered.

"Yes, but I better not see your face here again, is that clear," I shouted at Burns.

"No, sir, thank you, sir!" Burns; shouted, elated to be released, almost running out of the room.

"These blokes are all loaded on the wagon Sir," Constable Johnston reported.

Before I could reply, the distinct sound of a gunshot rang out somewhere close by, stopping me in my tracks.

"What was that?" Johnston spouted.

"That was a gunshot you daft . . .."

The sergeant shouted in reply but, whatever else the man said was lost as Davis raced out the door.

Following Davis, I noticed that the Sergeant counted heads, coming to the same conclusion as I.

"You had better come with me, Sergeant," I said, remembering the young constable that I had sent after the fleeing men.

"Yes, sir," Davis shouted. "Johnston, keep this lot quiet, or I will know the reason why."

Warily we started down Fairclough Street, hesitating at the corner where Fairclough and Batty Streets met. We stood looking for any sign of the constable, not knowing which direction the young man might have taken. We looked at each other waiting, looking for some sort of a commotion, or the constable's whistle in alarm, anything that may help point us in the direction of the shot. Both I and Davis were not only seasoned police officers, but we had also served in His Majesty's Armed Forces and were accustomed to gunfire. We also knew that the sound of a gunshot could carry over a considerable distance echoing among the many surrounding buildings. It was approximately seventy-one yards from the corner of Fairclough Street to Berner Street; taking our time, we split up; one on each side of the street. The fog had not dissipated since entering the club and did nothing to help matters as we searched for the missing constable. With every step, I began to fear the worst. Nearing Berner Street, I heard a faint thud at the opening of an alleyway. Holding up my hand, Davis immediately crossed the road to join me.

The night was deadly still, even those who made their living from the streets had stayed under cover from the cold chill and the dense fog. Not wanting my voice to carry, I used hand gestures to direct Sergeant Davis up the alley, while I went around and would meet him on the other side. I stood waiting as the sergeant answered with a nod of his head and started up the alley without hesitation. I listened as Davis disappeared into the fog. I knew that the passage exited at an old refinery yard. I calculated that by the time that I traveled around the buildings, Davis should be approximately halfway up the alley, then the two would try to catch whoever was in the alleyway between them. Rounding the building, I moved off into the darkness, having a queasy feeling in the pit of my stomach. It was not easy ordering a man up an alley where a culprit could be waiting with a firearm. As I walked, I prayed for a gentle breeze. The dense, swirling fog was unnerving, making visibility within the close confines only a few feet. At the end of Fairclough Street, I entered the fenced-in yard of the old refinery its gates long since rotted and collapsed onto the ground. The yard was cluttered with old machinery, crates, and a boxcar.

Skirting the debris, I stopped and listened. I couldn't be sure, but I thought that I had heard footsteps. I stood for a moment but heard nothing more. Looking around my view was hindered by the fog, scattered junk, and stacks of weathered pallets, some of which towered well over my head. I hesitated, unsure if my mind was just playing tricks on me. Standing perfectly still, I listened to the night sounds. I watched the dense fog as it enveloped everything in its wake, but I heard nothing more. With no sign of the constable anywhere, the urgency was upon me to find the young man that I had sent out into the night alone. Continuing through the yard, I came to the back of the building and a narrow lane. Stopping at the opening between the two buildings, I stood perfectly still, listening. Nothing moved, and there was no sound, I waited for a moment longer, not knowing if the sound that I had heard was the gunman or not. Moving forward, I stopped after a few paces, questioning my order to send Davis up the passage alone. I had heard no sound of an alarm, so I could only assume the sergeant had found nothing and was proceeding towards me from the other end of the alley. Starting up the alley, I put my hand out, touching the slick brick wall to my right. There was no light to help guide my steps, but I could make out the dim outline of pallets and crates that cluttered the passageway ahead of me. Darting, this way and that around the debris, I continued through the maze thinking of the missing constable. After a few feet, I chose to stop behind a stack of old wooden crates, peering around its edge, studying the way ahead. I was annoyed with myself for not taking the time to bring a lantern, but then on second thought, if the gunman was up ahead, the light of a lantern would give my position away. Creeping along; the alley broadened. I was grateful that the dense fog had dissipated a little for the buildings here were vacant, and there was no coal smoke from chimneys to add to the menacing fog. Peering out from around another stack of pallets, I had an unobstructed view for several feet beyond my position and then I saw Davis waiting for me.

"Nothing?"

"Nothing Sir."

"This gunshot has me worried."

"The blokes back there aren't likely to pull a gun, are they?"

I let the question go unanswered because I was thinking of Tumblety. If Tumblety was the man that I figured him to be, the doctor had more to lose than the others.

"Alright go back and arrange a four points search and I will finish up here.

I took my time walking up the alley, returning the way that I had come. The doctor was seen going into the club, but the man was not among those arrested. Although, I knew that I was putting a lot of faith in my informant, my gut told me that Spooner was reliable. Trusting informants and tips went with the job and my gut told me that Tumblety went into the club, we were just too late, that is if, Tumblety and Blackburn were one in the same man. The sound of the gunshot worried me though. If it was due to an unrelated incident; it was most inopportune. On the one hand, Davis was right when he said that the chaps back at the club were not likely to pull a gun to avoid capture. It stood to reason that if the man Spooner saw was indeed Tumblety, the man would be desperate to escape, in my mind, it was enough to kill to avoid the noose.

As far as I knew, the buildings along the top of the alley were all vacant; however, that didn't mean they were not being used by somebody for some sort of illegal activity. Retracing my steps, I began to systematically check doors and look through the soot-stained windows of each building. Walking back the way that Sergeant Davis had entered, I started to check the vacant storefronts on either side of the alley but, there was nothing suspicious-looking, nor did anything look out of place.

After two hours of searching, my efforts were futile. Whoever Constable Turner was searching for had disappeared and Turner was nowhere to be found. As far as the gunshot, it could have come from anywhere. Davis had taken his men and searched the streets surrounding the gentlemen's club; the mood of the constables was somber, the disappearance of one of their own and the sound of a gunshot had put images in their head that none wanted to discuss. After four more hours of searching, the sun was on the rise, and the men had all but returned two by two from their search, the last to return was Sergeant Davis.

"Excuse me, Sir, look who I found and I believe, I have one more for you."

Turning, I saw Sergeant Davis standing behind me, with the young recruit Turner each holding an arm of a dark figure between them. I had to look twice at Davis's prisoner, who stood without a sign of emotion on his face, but the bushy mustache caught my attention. Davis's prisoner was coatless; the collar of his shirt was wide open, and his tie was undone, and for all appearances, the man that Davis had in custody was quite disheveled.

"I think Turner chased this one all the way to the Thames," Davis offered. "I also believe this chap may have left the party too quickly Sir?" Davis said sarcastically.

"Yes, Sergeant, I believe you might be right, it is a pleasure to finally meet you, Mr. Tumblety," I said as I walked closer to the man. "Or should I say, Doctor Tumblety?"

There was a moment when our eyes met and though I did not know the man, there was instant recognition.

"And you Constable Turner," I shouted as the young man snapped to and looked frightened. "Good work, we thought …"

The surprised look on both Turner's and Tumblety's faces almost made me smile.

"What is the meaning of this, Detective! I demand you release me at once," Tumblety shouted. "I was simply out for a walk when this constable dragged me here?"

"Out for a walk, in weather like this," I queried. "Did you forget your coat, or perhaps you left it somewhere?" I replied, looking up at Davis with a wink.

"I simply left it at home; I did not know that it was a crime to walk the streets without a coat," Tumblety, responded defiantly.

"You will have plenty of time to explain what you were up to this evening, Doctor."

I watched Sergeant Davis put Tumblety in the back of the wagon none too gently, and then padlock the rear. The rest of the constables slapped Turner on the back.

"Take them away, Sergeant," I ordered.

Walking up behind Sergeant Davis, I spoke softly over my left shoulder. "Did Tumblety, by chance, have a pistol on him, Sergeant?"

"No, Sir!"

"You didn't see a jacket lying about where you found him?"

"No, nothing, Sir. It appears the doctor left in quite a hurry."

"Yes, it would," I said, slapping the sergeant on the shoulder. "I am going back to the club to take a better look around."

"Would you like me to have one of the lads stay here?"

"No, thank you, Sergeant, attend to your prisoners."

"Alright, lads step lively," Davis roared at the constables to fall in line beside the wagon full of prisoners as the driver snapped the reins over the horse's backs.

I watched the wagon and its guardians disappear into the fog. I walked back into the now empty club where the evening had begun. First, on the list was to find a suit jacket and or an overcoat, anything that would prove Tumblety was in fact in attendance when the club was raided.

Chapter Twenty-one

The interrogation room in the cellar of Scotland Yard, where Doctor Francis Tumblety sat, was approximately eight feet, by eight feet, with only one way in and out. There was a table, and two chairs, and an observation window that was covered in steel mesh. I watched Tumblety through that window, sitting at one of the chairs with hands folded on the table. The man was wide-shouldered, with a thick muscular build, approximately forty years of age with dark wavy hair, and a large oversized mustache, on a round face. I watched the prisoner closely, detecting no sign of anxiety on the man's face. I could very well have been watching Tumblety sitting waiting at a bank and likely seen the same bored expression. The only response conveyed since the man's arrival was a demand to see a barrister.

I looked long and hard at Tumblety for several minutes and wondered about the professed doctor. The man seemed very much in control, and yet, if the doctor was all that Alenka had described him to be, then, Tumblety was a man who wore many masks. The man, I saw sitting passively at the small table, was in my estimation, a person who was cold and calculating, and yet, there were no tell-tale signs that Tumblety was the deviant, that I suspected the man to be. Tumblety seemed unaffected by the turn of events and displayed no signs of being perturbed whatsoever. After being arrested, Tumblety gave his name, made Sergeant Davis painfully aware that the constable was detaining an American citizen that was being falsely accused. However, since Tumblety's arrival, nothing else was ascertained.

After Davis notified, Inspector Abberline of the arrest, the inspector informed me of a file that Scotland Yard had spent two years compiling on Francis Tumblety. I had been shocked, to say the least, when Abberline had told me at Batty Street that Tumblety had been under investigation before; and, the police had been interested in his movements and any ties that the man had obtained in London over the years. Now watching the cold exterior of Tumblety, that surprise was gone. I could see none of the usual signs commonly detected from the first-time offender, which I had the opportunity to observe in the cell many times in the past. The detainee's anxiety was marked by the usual hand, wringing the uncontrollable knee-jerking or the nail-biting. Each one knowing full well they had been caught for the crimes they committed. Although there was something to be said about the one-time criminal who ran from the law and had been wondering when he would finally be caught and arrested. Usually, there was a final breakdown, an elation of being released from their prisons of guilt and conscience. I saw none of these reactions, as I watched Francis Tumblety. There was something mechanical about the doctor whose face showed no emotion. I could see the cold qualities possessed by a man, who would try and strangle, a hemorrhaging young pregnant woman, to escape justice.

I began to study the so-called physician with a newfound interest, wondering what set of circumstances could make Tumblety crack. Incarceration and spending the night in a cold cell had done little to penetrate the dispassionate demeanor of the man. The calm, emotionless features showed no sign of strain or anxiety. On the contrary, the expressionless face, if anything, displayed restraint and self-control. After reading, Tumblety's file, I realized the complexity of the individual who sat before me. Tumblety's occupations included, among other things, ties with a *Fenian group who had bombed an outbuilding at Scotland Yard, housing the Special Irish Branch on May the thirtieth, 1884.* For the time being, the man had been arrested for gross indecency. This approach was Inspector Abberline's idea, as my superior was sure the charge of an abortionist and an herbalist who sold useless remedies as cures to the unsuspecting public could not be easily proven. Although, as of yet, I could not convince Inspector Abberline to pursue my theory. Nor could I persuade Abberline to listen to arguments about bringing charges against Tumblety that would name him the prime suspect in perpetrating the most brutal of murders against five women in Whitechapel.

I watched Inspector Abberline walk into the room and sit in front of Tumblety, laying a file folder down in front of him. Tumblety's only reaction was to look up at the arrival of the inspector with what could only be described as disinterest. Abberline started questioning the doctor about the first time that the man had arrived in England, looking into the man's past as far back as 1857. Most of the questions received little or no response, the doctor showing obvious disdain for the proceedings that were being forced on him.

"Mr. Tumblety, in my hand is a statement from the police in Montreal, Canada reporting that you were arrested on September the twenty-third, 1857. The charge was attempting to induce a miscarriage, by way of selling a prostitute medicines that would most certainly produce a failed pregnancy."

I observed Tumblety as the man sat unmoving with Inspector Abberline opposite, standing off in an arena of wit and fortitude. After several minutes the inspector continued.

"Do you have some particular interest in streetwalkers, Sir?"

Abberline sat for a moment looking at the file before him continuing only when no response was made to his question.

"It seems unnatural for a man of your particular, shall we say appetites," Abberline paused, looking at the man in front of him. "To be always in the thick of these women at every turn, when you display an apparent distaste for the fairer sex," Abberline asked?

I watched Inspector Abberline goad Tumblety time and time again, and the doctor merely looked at the inspector with apathy, displaying no reaction at all to any remark.

After another pause, Abberline continued, still studying the police report, before speaking and resuming his interrogation.

"It also states that a writ of habeas corpus was declined and then reissued one month later, at which time you left Canada immediately," Abberline paused. "I wonder how much that little bit of business cost you? Although, I suppose if you sell a number of these useless medicines to the unsuspecting public at £five a bottle, you could well afford it."

For the first time, since the questioning began, I saw a faint flicker of movement in Tumblety's right eye, something so slight that I almost missed the reaction. It told a story that the man cared little about what people thought or said. It also bespoke of something else, something that may have seemed trivial to anyone else, but, to Tumblety, Abberline had crossed a line. I believed that Tumblety was immensely proud of his herbs and medicines, perhaps trusting that they were genuine. Although the response was hardly noticeable, I could tell that the doctor was bothered when anyone tried to discredit these medicines.

Inspector Abberline shifted in his chair in front of a very subdued Francis Tumblety, a man who had made very little response to any of the statements or questions during the interview. Tumblety had said nothing self-incriminating, nor had the man responded in any way that could be construed as damaging or incriminating. The doctor had not even displayed any body language that could be defined as defensive or filled with irritation or anxiety. For the most part, Tumblety sat with his hands folded in front of him, straight-backed, with his ankles crossed below his chair. The man appeared not to perspire, nor was there was any fidgeting, or the usual finger tapping signifying the uncontrollable responses of the nervous and the guilty.

I continued to stare at the man who, according to the file, was described in social circles as debonair, colorful, with a touch of panache. I could not help but wonder what had turned Tumblety into such an uncaring monster. Before me; was a man that showed no feeling or any sign of emotion whatever. Since the interview had begun, I could not be sure if, I had seen indications of an innocent man, or a guilty man, devoid of all conscience. Although my opinion was formed quickly and based on little evidence, circumstantial or otherwise, I considered Tumblety to be a man, completely without empathy towards others. In my estimation, the doctor was likely capable of almost anything, including murder.

Inspector Abberline, after several minutes of nerve-shattering quiet, continued to question Tumblety. The inspector first disclosed that the police suspected Tumblety of involvement in the planned assassination of Superintendent Williamson. The interrogation then turned to the death of the polish girl Alenka, which received little or no reaction from the man at all. Abberline next asked if Tumblety was connected in any way to performing illegal abortions in the Berner Street area and, finally, the inspector asked the man his whereabouts on the nights in question when the Whitechapel crimes were perpetrated. Abberline next pursued the suspect's reasons for being in London, right down to provoking Tumblety by asking about attending the gentleman's club, and ultimately facing charges of gross indecency. After several attempts, Abberline could not crack the cold exterior of the man accused of many things, but charged with none of them. No remark, question, or insinuation could break the stone-faced exterior of the man. Tumblety's face displayed no sign of strain, or panic, during the entire period of questioning. The doctor's responses were, if anything sardonic, including, *'these accusations are unfounded,' 'I wasn't even in the city at that time,' 'and there is no basis for your arres*t.' When Tumblety asked if the charges against him were for merely taking a walk at night, Abberline motioned to the window. Entering the room, I faced the man that Davis had arrested for the first time in twelve hours. In my hand was a vest and jacket that I had found after the shakedown at the gentleman's club.

"Would you mind terribly, if I asked you to try these on," Abberline asked.

I stood with the suit jacket and vest in hand, and everyone in the room could see that they were of the same fabric and color as the pants Tumblety was wearing.

When Tumblety stood, I came face to face with the man. It was in that instant that I saw something other than the calm and relaxed disposition that had been the façade displayed during the interrogation. Tumblety was about two or three inches shorter than my six-feet and had to look up slightly to make eye contact. I watched as Tumblety's flat expressionless, demeanor weakened, and I detected a rage. A festering, uncontrollable fury, lying just below the surface of the calm facade. I did not know the man at all, but, if I was to guess, judging from what I had read in Tumblety's file, the man opposed anyone in a position of authority. I could only surmise that the man who stood before me was a narcissist, who despised anything or anyone who got in his way. It was at that precise moment that I realized, without a doubt, I stared into the eyes of a coldblooded killer. For a split second, all the fake manners and all of the self-control would have disappeared if they had been anywhere other than the interrogation room at Scotland Yard. For the first time since their meeting, I saw Tumblety for what the man really was, a person tortured, by a world, filled with opposition. Forced to live a lifestyle of conformity, and thinking himself above recrimination. The icy gaze quickly turned into condescension as Tumblety took the article of clothing from me and put the jacket on without a wasted movement. It was quite apparent to both I and the inspector who the jacket belonged to. The jacket; was perfectly tailored for Doctor Francis Tumblety. Taking the coat off, Tumblety sat down and glared at the two policemen without acknowledging for an instant; the coat was his. Picking up the jacket, I walked out of the interrogation room without comment. Inspector Abberline stared at his suspect for several minutes, in his typical manner and then gathered the files, and, without another glance at Francis, Tumblety left the room.

I stood studying Tumblety, thinking of a plan that would perhaps get the man to show his true colors. My sixth sense told me that Tumblety was near the breaking point, and the hard exterior was primed to shatter; however, how to obtain that end, was a mystery. I could only assume that the monster inside Tumblety could lay dormant beneath the icy exterior; the doctor displayed to the world, until it was released to lash out at another prostitute. What set of circumstances made this come about was anyone's guess.

As I watched the doctor, I considered how the man displayed a control that was unprecedented to that usually seen of those who found themselves in the interrogation room of Scotland Yard. I could only guess that this was like old hat to the man that had been arrested from Canada to Washington. The true nature of the man; was caged under the conventions of law and order and disguised by social graces. I suspected that Tumblety had control over his alter ego, keeping it under guard and hidden beneath the surface, always calculating and festering, until that time when the real man beneath would be exposed.

"Detective Stone."

"Yes, constable what is it," I asked, a little irritated to be disturbed and having my train of thought disrupted.

"Inspector Abberline wants you in his office sir."

"Alright, stand here on guard, until I get back," I replied gruffly.

"But I am supposed to…, I mean, Inspector Abberline has ordered me to take this man before the magistrate with the others in custody."

Without another word, I left the constable to perform his duty. Inwardly seething, I took the steps two at a time up to the second floor. With a sharp knock on Inspector Abberline's door, I walked in without waiting for an answer. Abberline did not look up from his desk to acknowledge me. Instead, the chief of detectives maintained his composure and said nothing. After five minutes of waiting, my temper cooled somewhat, and I had gained some control. As I stood waiting for Abberline to acknowledge my presence, I came quickly to the realization whose office I had barged into and stood silently for another few minutes before Abberline spoke.

"Detective Stone, what can I, do for you," Abberline said, cordially not looking up from the papers on the top of his desk.

"Sir, I just heard that Tumblety is to go before the magistrate," I stated.

I waited for the inspector to respond, incredulous of the idea that a murderer was only minutes away from being released on his own recognizance.

"Yes, Mr. Tumblety is going before the magistrate on charges of gross indecency," Abberline exhaled, before continuing. "At which time, I am sure the doctor will be granted bail and released."

"But Sir, what about the other charges, I am certain that this Tumblety is our man," I pleaded.

"I am sorry Detective Stone, I wasn't aware of any other charges being brought against Mr. Tumblety at this time," Abberline snarled.

"I am quite certain that this man is guilty. If I had the time, I could break him and get him to confess that he killed the young Polish woman while trying to abort her pregnancy," I began. "Not to mention the bombings, this man is suspected of being involved. In the meantime, I will have Doctor Openshaw brought to the station to identify Tumblety as the man who tried to procure human organs from the London Hospital. The very organ that has been found missing from three murdered women in Whitechapel, surely that is enough evidence to hold him."

I was irritated by Abberline's lack of interest. I would have expected the inspector to be a little more agreeable, based on the sheer volume of information compiled by Scotland Yard about Tumblety. In addition to this, was the circumstantial evidence which cast all kinds of suspicion on how the man made a living, his known associates, and why the man was in London?

"Detective, I am fully aware of the contents of the file on Mr. Tumblety," Abberline began. "I have also read your reports on the dead polish girl, and the attempted procurement of the specimens from the London Hospital Museum of which I might add is not a criminal offense. However, I am not aware of any evidence against the man in whom you have numerous allegations but no proof to substantiate any charges to be brought formally against this man. Might I also remind you that you are on leave, what exactly were you doing out there this evening?"

Abberline's tone began to rise, and the inspector stood, placing both hands on the top of the desk.

"Sergeant Davis asked me to join him because his informant mentioned a man fitting the description of Tumblety, Sir."

"I see," Abberline said after several minutes. "Well, from this time forward keep a low profile."

"Yes, Sir."

"Now, if you have anything further to report that I am not aware, feel free to report it right now, otherwise, I suggest you put any personal feelings or allegations you have about this suspect aside and start doing your job and get the proof we need to put a noose around the neck of the man responsible."

"Yes, sir."

I knew when to leave well enough alone. As much as I did not like to admit it, I knew that Abberline was right. I had allowed my personal feelings to get in the way of my investigation. Instead of basing my theories on the facts, I had allowed the image of a dying Polish girl to influence my thinking. Walking through the station, I left by the front door. The icy wind of November was not noticed as I walked up to the street, feeling despondent. I had turned a criminal investigation into some type of personal vendetta against a man I had only suspicions about. Walking along the busy street, my thoughts turned to the alleged crimes I believed Tumblety responsible for. Scotland Yard had suspected Tumblety of having Fenian ties, among other things. To top it all off, this individual; was suspected of murdering five women in Whitechapel.

The facts were few, but there was one piece of overwhelming evidence that could not be ignored; Tumblety was a self-professed physician. A profession, which allowed for knowledge of anatomy and dissection. This was the critical point that the medical profession and police had been squabbling over, and it was key in the Whitechapel cases. A doctor charged with these crimes would put the argument to rest forever.

Of course, other factors could support the case against Tumblety. Dr. Openshaw could identify the man who came to the hospital and inquired about obtaining human organs for a medical study in America. Unfortunately, Alenka had not survived her abortion to make an identification; however, if I could find a survivor, perhaps, she could offer some information. Unfortunately, any information provided would be second-hand and viewed by the court as here-say. Unfortunately, the abundance of circumstantial evidence was overwhelming; nevertheless, there was no concrete evidence in which to charge Tumblety as '*Jack the Ripper*' or for any crime, other than the charge of gross indecency. Frustrated, I could see Abberline's point as I looked more closely at the evidence. With no eyewitness and the circumstantial evidence that they had, they could not hold the man. Hungry and cold, I hailed a cab to go to my office.

As the hansom rattled along the uneven road to Whitechapel Road, I plucked my watch from my vest pocket; it was ten minutes to three. The Magistrates Court was only in session on Wednesdays until four o'clock. Reconsidering my plans, I pounded on the roof of the cab with my fist to get the driver's attention.

"Driver take me to the Marlborough Street Magistrates Court!"

Ten minutes later, I was pushing on the eight-foot solid oak door. Entering the court, I pulled off my hat and walked silently into the courtroom. The Magistrate James L. Hannay was in the process of dealing with all of the men arrested late Tuesday night, all of whom; were charged with gross indecency. *John Doughty, Arthur Brice, Albert Fisher, and James Crowley*, these four had no priors, and the gross indecency charge was their first offense so, they were released on bail. Looking up to the front of the courtroom, I saw Tumblety already standing before the magistrate. As predicted, the judge granted Tumblety bail, with a promise to return on the next magistrates sitting on November the sixteenth after signing the release form, Tumblety was free to go.

Smugly, Tumblety walked by, glancing at me with casual disinterest. Waiting for a moment, I sat thinking about what I should do next. My first reaction was to jump up and confront the man, but I fought down the urge. Unable to formulate any reasonable plan, I started to rise from the bench but hesitated. Out of the corner of my eye, I recognized another detective, a Special Branch operative, if I remembered correctly, by the name of William Melville. I maintained my seat while Melville stood and then quietly left the courtroom. Easing from the bench, I followed the detective whom I had seen a few times at Home Office but I had little to do with. Coming to the large doors to the court, I stopped, the smacking of the gavel behind brought something to mind that I had not considered until my seething anger had subsided. Inspector Abberline had known that Tumblety would be granted bail and had already planned for another detective to follow the doctor, a man who Tumblety would not recognize. I watched from the top of the stairs as Tumblety walked up Marlborough Street while; Melville walked parallel to his target on the opposite side of the street. Resisting the temptation to follow, I turned and then stopped briefly noticing Tumblety halt at the corner. I watched curiously as the doctor took out a cigar from his pocket, lighting it with a match struck on the sole of his shoe. With what seemed like reckless abandon, Tumblety turned and looked back at the courthouse. For a long ten seconds, I returned Tumblety's stare and, then with a tip of his hat, Tumblety disappeared around the corner. For a moment, I was tempted to follow, and then, I saw Melville tuck a newspaper under his arm and then cross the street in pursuit of Tumblety. By tipping his hat, Tumblety had made one small error. The doctor had fixed all his attention on me, missing Melville altogether. For the first time, Tumblety had shown a quality that I thought the man too clever to possess. When I had met the man, I had mistaken Tumblety's arrogance for brashness. Now, I realized that I had been wrong. Hesitating, for only a minute longer, I began to feel the fatigue of being up all night. I still had to resist the urge to follow the contemptuous blackheart; however, my fatigue won me over, and I headed for my rooms on Whitechapel Road.

Chapter Twenty-two

"There, you are gentleman, drink the tea while it is still hot." Mrs. Wilson sang.

"Thank you, kind lady," Baxter said, bowing slightly as the widow curtsied and closed the door behind her.

Baxter walked to the window with arms wrapped around his back, the fingers of his large hands, laced together with the thumbs twitching.

"By the way, I stopped by your office the evening before last with a dinner invitation, you were not at your usual post, hovering over your police files."

Baxter made the statement concealing motive and question. Though I had known the man long enough, to know that it was the coroner's way of finding out answers without intentionally prying into my affairs.

"That is right, you haven't heard."

"Heard what," Baxter asked, with a tone of consternation in his voice.

"I arrested the man; I suspect was involved in Alenka's death. His name is Doctor Francis Tumblety!"

"You did What?" Baxter screeched. "Where, and when?"

"Early, Wednesday morning," I explained. "I questioned him, I looked right into his blackheart, and then," I paused, regretting my next statement. "I watched him go free."

I watched Baxter's face go red as the man searched for words, but no audible sound came from his mouth. From the coroner's reaction, I could tell that he was having a hard time accepting what I said.

"You, let him go, why in the devil did you do that?"

"I did not personally let him go, Wynne," I explained. "Tumblety was granted police bail, with a promise to return."

"I still don't understand what judge would grant bail to that murderous wretch?"

Baxter was close to foaming, at the mouth with rage, I watched and listened for a few minutes as the coroner explained how things should have been handled. I wanted to do the same, but after I met with Abberline, I realized that I could no longer allow my feelings to influence how, I investigated the case. After waiting for the coroner to calm somewhat, I continued.

"Wynne, Doctor Tumblety was arrested for gross indecency, not for performing, an illegal abortion or murder, unfortunately, that was all we could hold him on. There were no other charges that we could lay and expect them to uphold in court, that is why bail was granted."

"Gross indecency," Baxter exclaimed. "Where on earth did that come from?" Baxter asked, calming down somewhat.

"I arrested him at a purported gentleman's club," I began. "Tumblety; was then taken back to the Yard, where Inspector Abberline interrogated him for most of the night, and the man held up under the inspector's grilling. Tumblety didn't even flinch when Abberline asked him about the Whitechapel murders. As of yet, we have nothing concrete, no evidence to produce, no eyewitness to bring forth, no fingermarks on a murder weapon, nothing. With no one to bring a complaint, I couldn't even charge him for illegally performing an abortion."

"Sorry, John, I didn't mean to make you feel entirely responsible."

"Don't worry about it, Wynne."

There was a long moment of silence when nothing was said, and only the rattle of cup and saucer could be heard. We had both worked over the case for hundreds of hours. Not to mention, the efforts of two police forces, but no evidence could be found that would lead police to believe that Tumblety was anything but a self-proclaimed physician with questionable acquaintances, who has a dubious lifestyle.

"Well, who is to say that this Tumblety chap won't try again and perhaps slip up, next time John."

"Yes, I suppose we could hope for that, Wynne."

"Well, goodnight my friend."

I watched Baxter walk out of my rooms weary and disheartened. I understood Baxter's view, but I could not help but think, that perhaps the coroner could be allowing himself to become too personally involved in the case. Something I had been accused of recently. Turning, the wick in the lamp low, I watched the fire on the hearth and listened to the wind rattling the panes in the window, thinking about Francis Tumblety and wondering where the doctor was this night.

Awakening hours later, the room was dark, and the faint light of a full moon cast its glow through the window. Discouraged, I looked at my watch, then lay back on the bed, my mind wandering over the details of the night before. Closing my eyes, I walked the patrol of Mitre Square, Berner Street, and Flower and Dean and Thrawl Streets in my mind's eye and wondered where '*Jack*' might strike again.

Up at dawn, my sleep had been plagued by the same recurring dream of meeting '*Jack*' in a dark alley. The dream ended the same way each time, with '*Jack's*' knife poised to slice and my inability to stop the killer. Dressing, I left the house quietly and headed to my office. Sitting at my desk, I reviewed the file that the Metropolitan Police had on Francis Tumblety. Unfortunately, after spending an hour reading, I realized that most of the information that the file contained was filled with unconfirmed accounts with no witnesses. The only reliable source as to Tumblety's true character was from the Canadian police. Tumblety's dealings with the prostitute in Montreal was the only tidbit that carried any suggestion, how the so-called doctor made my living, and the consumers that the man targeted.

Sitting back in my chair, I told myself that Doctor Tumblety was the only candidate for the murders. Unfortunately, there were countless candidates doing abortions in the city of London, and any one of them may have supplied Alenka with the herbs and know how to abort her child.

353

However, it was worth mentioning that Francis Tumblety fit the bill for every description they had on file of the killer in Whitechapel.

As I sat in the quiet of my office, reflecting on the dreams that had plagued my unconscious mind, forcing me to relive the unsavory past. I had often heard that dreams were unconscious manifestations, revealing certain aspects of a man's understanding. Though these nocturnal meanderings were vivid and seemingly real, the nightmares had done nothing to awaken or expose any hidden clue that might help me in my efforts to catch a killer.

Though many credible points made Tumblety a feasible suspect. The one element that was lacking in the case against Tumblety was a witness. Any witness that could testify that Tumblety had committed illegal abortions in the city would be a start to bring charges against the man. Regrettably, there was no such witness to come forth, and alas, the dead tell no tales.

Exhausted, I got up from behind my desk and collapsed on the edge of a cushion on the settee. I tried to erase the images that flashed in my mind of the murdered victims. I thought of Tumblety and the man's colorful past that reeked of collusion and criminal activity. However, without being caught in the thick of his crimes, the doctor had escaped the noose, on more than one occasion. As I lay thinking, the images of the murdered women forced their way back into my mind again.

Death in Whitechapel was as common and as predictable as the sunrise and the sunset. If it was true that anything could be obtained in Whitechapel for a price, then homicide was no exception. Many had paid; a price, to satisfy a vendetta and to see their enemies eliminated. Though the longevity of human life was uncertain at the best of times, each person living in the East End could be at any given moment, holding onto the barest of threads of survival.

The burden of proof was a curious thing. For the innocent the lack of proof in a prosecutor's case could set a man free. However, the burden of proof rested on the same principle for a guilty man. There was no evidence to prove that Doctor Francis Tumblety was anything other than an herb salesman, as the man had stated at his arrest. The fact that some of his herbs could procure an abortion in his patients was circumstantial and seemed a trifling compared to the charge of murder. Although, even the selling of potentially harmful herbs could be pursued if they had a witness that could testify that Tumblety had sold these herbs to someone who had died soon after ingesting them. Unfortunately, the conjecture and hearsay seemed to be tantamount to a witch hunt. The Inquisition, in its day, may have been able to bring about a confession; however, in this day and age, the onus of proof was on the prosecution. The only evidence they had to bring before any court was to have Tumblety charged with gross indecency. Tying Tumblety to any other crime was futile at best, and the inspector using his calculating mind had seen the projected results, had Tumblety been brought before a judge on any other charge. A good barrister could have had most, if not all, the alleged charges brought against his client thrown out of court, and the Metropolitan Police, would once again, be made the laughing-stock; in the public's eyes in their efforts to bring '*Jack the Ripper*' to justice. Closing my eyes, my instinct was to follow Tumblety to the ends of the earth, if necessary but, my professional voice told me to let Melville follow the man and see what transpired. Unexpectedly, I opened my eyes and considered why the inspector had Special Branch follow Tumblety in the first place, and why Abberline had not told me about it. With no answer forthcoming, I concluded that there was more going on than what Abberline had let on. What that might be, I could not guess.

Chapter Twenty-three

It was still early when I rose from the settee and took my seat behind my desk again. The familiar rattle of teacup and saucer could be heard coming down the hall and I wondered why the coroner was in at such an early hour.

"Stone, you are up early, my friend."

"Sleepless night, Wynne."

I had known the coroner long enough to know that showing up at the early hour and the tea offering was all a part of Baxter's apology for storming out of my rooms.

"By, the by, John sorry for the quick exit, no offense intended old bean."

"None, taken, Wynne, don't think anything of it."

With the niceties out of the way, I returned to the file on my desk, while Baxter slurped his scalding tea.

"What are we working on today, Stone?"

"This Tumblety has made me think about looking for a witness who may have used his services."

"I admire your spirit Stone, but do you know how many women use these types of quacks in the city of London," Baxter mocked. "Not to mention, the fact that most of this business is done on the hush-hush. The social deprecation of the thing alone makes these women go underground to get this type of procedure done."

"Perhaps we should look to the doctors themselves, and find out if they have any knowledge of these doctors and where they operate from?"

"Stone, I don't want to burst your bubble, but do you have any idea how many doctors practice in a city the size of London?" Baxter asked.

"No, I have no idea, do you?"

"No, I don't," Baxter replied, sheepishly. "If I were to speculate though, I would say that there would have to be at least one thousand if not twice that many, not to mention all of the midwives that practice their brand of medicine in the lanes and byways scattered about the countryside. There are more than a few of these midwives, that I have questioned at inquests that could treat you as good as any educated city doctor. Next, there are the ships doctors and army surgeons to consider that one in need might have access to." Baxter answered.

I understood that Baxter was only trying to get me to see the futility of trying to find a doctor who may or may not have seen a young girl, fitting Alenka's description in a population the size of London's, but it did not help matters much.

"Not to mention, John, there is the fact that abortion is a criminal offense. Do you think that a doctor of good standing would risk his practice to abort some young woman's baby and get sent to jail for it?"

"No, I suppose not, Wynne. What if...?"

"What if what, Stone?"

"What if our candidate had some kind of medical training, they could be the culprit?"

"I would say you are more tired than you ...," Baxter's voice trailed off. "Are you thinking that this Dr. Tumblety is not a real doctor, and that is why the man sells these herbs and such."

"Yes."

"I suppose you could be onto something there, Stone."

"This is all pure speculation Wynne," I said, looking up from my desk at the coroner. "But I can think of no one else that has come into our hands who fits the bill."

"This Tumblety might be a viable suspect for the death of Alenka but it would be a stretch to fit him for the killer in Whitechapel, John. Besides if these two were one in the same man, what would be Tumblety's motivation for killing these prostitutes?"

"I have no clue at this point, and now that we have let the man go, we will likely never know."

"Tumblety has to return to trial Stone," Baxter offered. "If the man is guilty, perhaps in the interim, this doctor, will tip his hand, and he can be arrested again?"

"I doubt we will ever see Tumblety again, Wynne."

"Why do you say that?"

"Because Tumblety has done it before in Montreal," I said, raising my voice!

After a moment of introspection, I thought about the way I had raised my voice.

"Sorry, Wynne."

"Think nothing of it," Baxter replied. "Stone, you look like you need to get back to bed."

"If sleep came so easy, Wynne, I would close my eyes this instant, but it doesn't. I close my eyes, and I dream of a mad killer who goes about London ripping and slashing his victims."

"I know, John, there are nights that I find myself bathed in sweat from dreams of this madman who lurks in the dark. Do you really think that Tumblety will leave the city?"

I looked at the coroner, unable to give an answer that either of them was comfortable with.

"What if it is this Tumblety, Stone. What proof do you have, and what do you intend on doing about it?"

"There is nothing I can do about it. As you say I have no proof at all, this is all speculation, Wynne. All I know is there is a man out there whom I believe is '*Jack the Ripper*,' and all I have is some very real coincidences that correspond with this doctor being in London and no real proof."

November the ninth was cold and wet; the rain had persevered throughout the night on into the morning. Arriving late to the crime scene, I stepped down from the carriage. Closing the hackney door, I looked up at the threatening sky, thankful for the reprieve in the weather, but at the same time wondering when the deluge would start again. I had seen the crowds of people as the hackney rolled down what was often called 'the wicked quarter-mile' that consisted of Flower and Dean, Thrawl, and Dorset Streets. The entire neighborhood seemed to be hovering about at the front of the court at number twenty-six Dorset Street. The public's ghoulish curiosity was never more prevalent than when it was rumored that another woman had been murdered in a room, at number, thirteen Miller's Court. I passed Doctor George Bagster Phillips, as the doctor was preparing to leave the scene.

"Detective Stone," Phillips said, curtly.

With a nod of my head, I walked past the doctor, seeing Inspector Abberline discussing something with Superintendent Arnold so, I stood outside the door and waited for the room to clear. Making eye contact with the inspector, I waited off to one side of the door while Abberline continued speaking to Arnold. Curiously, I watched as a photographer packed equipment onto the rear of a carriage; while constables were busy holding the crowds back that had gathered in front of the building. I stood silently outside number thirteen, the last room on the right before the narrow passage opened into Miller's Court. Stepping aside to allow Superintendent Arnold to leave the small room, I looked up to see Abberline give a quick nod towards me. Stifling a gasp, I stopped halfway through the doorway. There were no words that could describe the horror that I saw before me.

The room was nondescript, aside from two tables and one bed; there was nothing about the tenement that was inviting in any way. The figure on the bed was female, evident only by the stature; and the visible strands of long hair. The corpse lay stripped on a blood-soaked mattress; with a saturated night garment, placed under the victim's torso. The victim's face had been lacerated beyond recognition, leaving no distinguishing facial features to identify the woman by. I could assume that any identification could be made by someone who knew the occupant of the residence and could recognize the victim's hair and eye color. At first glance, the crime scene appeared to be a helter-skelter of blood and gore. However, after careful study, it could be seen that the killer had arranged the victim's anatomy about the room on the tables, and in different positions around the body for reasons unknown. After walking from one side of the room to the other, I supposed that the scene could have been better described by one unfamiliar with '*Jack's*' work as an attack by some kind of large animal, or a pack of wild dogs. Although even an inexperienced eye could see that, there was nothing natural about this attack, or about the killer who perpetrated the crime. As I studied the macabre scene, I could only describe the assault on the victim as being committed by someone whose character was so depraved that any description of such an individual went beyond mere words.

Taking in the whole room, I could see that blood spatter lay everywhere. A significant quantity of blood was soaked around the back of the victim's head, abdomen, and seeped through the mattress and pooled directly below the cot on which she lay and lay in a two-foot area on the floor under the bed. I recalled seeing the photographer when I first arrived and assumed that a photograph had been taken of the scene for one purpose. That being to have a record of the murder without having to rely on a police report. In my estimation, there were no words that could describe the horror that took place at number thirteen Miller's Court. Only the worst imaginable nightmare or some act of war could be comparable to the scene. So, appalling was the ghastly image that it would be engraved in my memory forever.

Looking around the room, I was horrified to find body tissue scattered about the small space. The spectacle and ferocity of the crime left me feeling nauseous. Turning away from the ghastly scene, I looked around the room to try and find the origins of such a horrid attack. Seeing no signs of forced entry or a struggle, I could only assume that the victim was another Whitechapel prostitute, who willingly invited her attacker into her room. Reverting my attention to the victim again, the nasty gash across the woman's throat was likely the cause of death. The same calling card used by the infamous '*Jack the Ripper.*' Although the method was the same as in the other victims, it seemed the killer had changed; his method of attack from the other victims. In this case, it was probable that the victim's throat was sliced while the killer straddled the body. The assumption was that the perpetrator likely began at the face and moved methodically along the body, cutting, slashing, and dissecting the corpse. After noting the positions of the victim's anatomy around the room, I deduced by the amount of blood spatter; and the dissection done to the body that the killer must have taken some time to do the destruction that was done to the corpse.

Moving closer to the bed, I took out my notebook and began taking notes. The body lay, to the left of the center of the bed, her left arm, lay across her chest while the right lay, at her side, the fingers of the left hand were clenched. The legs of the victim were spread apart with the knees bent, and the feet were drawn up, almost touching. Upon closer, examination the abdomen was empty of all the vital organs, both breasts were severed, and the right arm mutilated. Inspecting the face, I observed long lacerations on both sides. These random cuts severed portions of the eyebrows, nose, and ears. The slash to the throat was deep, as was seen in the other Whitechapel victims.

I did not hear Inspector Abberline come up behind me, being so transfixed on the corpse, and how she has spent the final moments of her life.

"According to Mr. McCarthy, McCarthy, the landlord of the building," Abberline explained. "The room was let out to a Mary Jane Kelly."

"Are we to assume that this is Kelly, Sir?"

"She has already been identified by McCarthy and his man Thomas Bowyer, who first found the body," Abberline replied. "Both men, identified the corpse as the occupant. First by way of the victim's hair, and then her eye color. Given the limited means by which we are left, I am inclined to take them at their word that they are certain that the victim is the woman who lodged here."

"When Dr. Phillips arrived," Abberline continued. "The pieces of the victim's anatomy were just as you see them, all around the body. Phillip's identified, the liver, which was found by the feet, the victim's entrails were on her right …"

"As in the case of Catharine Eddowes," I interrupted. "I wonder if Dr. Llewellyn still thinks our killer is left-handed," I said bitterly, without thinking.

Seeing Abberline's perturbed expression, I thought better of making any more critical remarks.

"Sorry, Sir."

"The breasts were cut off, one was found under the head, the other by the right foot," Abberline continued.

"Any reason to think that the arrangement of the body parts might be some clue, Sir?"

"Your guess, Detective, is as good as mine," Abberline shrugged. "I have to say Stone, I have never seen anything like this in all my years as a policeman."

"Nor I, Sir."

"Having said that, Detective, don't rule out some pattern, but I doubt you will find anything in that."

"Are there any pieces of Kelly's anatomy missing, sir?"

"The uterus and the kidneys were found, under the head of the victim," Abberline continued and then paused. "The heart is missing, Stone."

I did not hear the constable draw the inspector away; nor, did I hear the commotion that a room full of investigators made, all gathered for the same purpose, to catch a killer. In my mind, I kept hearing the words *'the heart is missing.'*

I stood back re-enacting, the crime in my mind trying to make some kind of sense for the murder, however, even though most crimes were viewed as senseless, the motive that fueled any offense was ever-present no matter how trivial or menial the reason. The missing heart told me for certain that the latest victim had fallen prey to the same man that had killed the women in Whitechapel. I had long ago grown accustomed to viewing *'Jack'* as someone who had deep-rooted hatred towards women, with enough anger that would fuel a rage that would keep him killing women until the madman was incarcerated. Still, after seeing such an atrocity, I wondered what type of rage could make the killer go on hacking and slashing his victim even after the woman was obviously dead and no longer a threat. The maniacal way the perpetrator continued to mutilate the body was clear, at least, to me that death was obviously not the end the killer wished to achieve. The slice to the throat, was the primary stage to some sadistic ritual, but killing these women was obviously not enough for *'Jack.'* If I was right, the type of rage witnessed in the murders could be seen from the very first victim, Martha Tabram, who had received thirty-nine stab wounds to her upper body. What I saw with this latest victim was the same type of rage but, at the same time, something altogether different from the others. It appeared that the killer was trying to totally obliterate the entire persona of the woman who lay before me. It was staggering to try and explain away or rationalize the set of circumstances that would bring about the transformation of a person into some indescribable monster that could produce the troubling end I looked upon. I wondered what twisted gratification or release, or perverted desire was inwardly satisfied once the killer had finished hacking and slashing the corpse. The only consistent pattern to each of the murders aside from Emma Smith and Martha Tabram had been the slitting of the victim's throats. I had long ago ascertained that '*Jack*' hated the struggle with his victim, or perhaps the man did not like looking into the eyes of his victim after they drew their last breath. That is if one man, killed all seven women. The dissection of the corpses in five of the crimes had been the sole factor that had escalated in all of the subsequent cases. The stab wounds to Martha Tabram could be the tell-all of the pent-up rage that the killer felt, perhaps seeking at first only the death of his first victim. In my opinion, the killer had come a long way from simply stabbing his victim to death. I couldn't help but wonder if all the victims were a likeness of someone that the killer hated. If that was the case, then this latest victim had taken the brunt of that rage. Perhaps Kelly was chosen because of some characteristic, physical, or otherwise, that reminded '*Jack*' of someone else, which drove the killer to such lengths to want to utterly destroy the woman. Either way, there were underlying issues that my gut told me went far beyond the murder of a prostitute in Miller's Court. This could be seen in that all of the prostitutes had the same build and hair color. It was possible that these victims could be the personification of the one person, perhaps a mother, a wife, or some other family member that '*Jack*' hated most. Although admittedly the body that lay on the bed before me seemed to have taken the full brunt of this anger, so much so that the perpetrator had tried to erase the woman's entire existence with the sharp edge of a knife. The truth of the matter was that I had no clue what passion controlled this psychopath. Perhaps the man was possessed by a demon, like Wynne Baxter suggested, a killer that lusted only for the blood of prostitutes. I visualized the killer straddling the body, knife in hand looking down at his victim. The man's clothing bloodsoaked, the spatters of Kelly's blood, covering his arms and face, sitting looking down at his handy work while; the victim's blood seeped into the mattress below her body. As I stood picturing the scene, the man I saw holding the knife was none other than Francis Tumblety.

It occurred to me that if the killer was allegedly this, Dr. Tumblety, perhaps the man was trying to send the police some sort of a message, through the letters and the crime scenes. I could only imagine that said message was to inform the authorities that they could not apprehend '*Jack*' no matter what they tried. Whatever the prompting, or whatever the reasons behind the latest murder, the ability of the killer to thwart law enforcement was shocking. As I looked around the room, I could not help but think the placement of the organs and skin around the body and room may have been done for some reason. The slitting of the women's throat was the '*Ripper's*' signature, but the placing of the organs around the space appeared to look like the crime was staged, or perhaps was just made to look that way. As I studied the manipulation of the crime scene, I had to wonder if the killer was trying to flaunt his ability to both murder and horrify. As I stood in the close confines of the hovel, I did my best to ignore the pungent odor of death. Days earlier, I felt like I was on the verge of a breakthrough of some kind in understanding '*Jack*'. But now this latest twist in the killer's modus operandi made me second-guess all that I thought I knew about the man.

Of course, one thing that had not changed, at least for me, was the identity of the killer. Each time that I put a face to the man known as '*Jack the Ripper,*' I saw Francis Tumblety. If I was right in my assumption that Tumblety was leaving a message to police, it was to display there were no limits in the potentials or lengths the man was prepared to go to shock and terrify Londoners. As horrific and unprecedented as the crime might be, there were still recognizable traits from the other crime scenes. The cutthroat was the most obvious clue that the killer's method to kill instantaneously had not changed. There were the entrails placed on the right side of the body, then there was the missing heart. I wondered if there some specific reasons that '*Jack*' chose the heart?

"Stone what do you make of this?"

Abberline's shout from across the room drew all the occupant's attention. Joining Abberline, I knelt in front of the fireplace, I watched the inspector with poker in hand, pulling articles of clothing from off the grate. Holding my hand close to the grate, I felt the waning heat coming from the cast iron. The grate was still warm to the touch. The fireplace must have been raging to have melted the kettle handle, which was hung on a hook nearby. On the floor, I examined the charred remains of what appeared to be a woman's skirt, several pieces of charred clothing, and the remains of a brim of a hat.

"Was the killer trying to hide, or destroy something," I commented.

"I could see him trying to hide evidence of his blood-soaked clothing, but these appear to be all, women's clothing," Abberline answered.

"With this amount of blood, and if the killer presumably straddled his victim, our killer would most likely be covered in blood. Did the man have a change of clothes, or could it be that this wretch lives somewhere close by?" I reasoned.

Seeing the inspector shake his head in answer, I waited for another opinion.

"Even if the culprit lives close by, there is no way the man could have left this room without someone, a neighbor or a passer-by seeing something, Stone," Abberline rationalized.

"I have to maintain my theory, Sir, that our man changes his clothes at the scene or there is a carriage waiting close by, this could be the evidence needed to corroborate that."

"If this blackheart has a carriage, then someone will report seeing it in the area, Detective."

Abberline stood his ground.

"I am not so, sure Sir," I retorted. "If this killer is as smart, as I think, then the carriage is parked somewhere close by and no one is the wiser."

After spending the better part of an hour in the room, we left, no further ahead than when we entered. They had learned that the perpetrator had entered the room with the apparent consent of Kelly and had slit her throat and mutilated her body. The crime was estimated to have occurred sometime between half-past three and a quarter to four in the morning. Elizabeth Prater of room number twenty, the room directly above Kelly's, told constables that she thought that she heard a woman cry out, [sic] "*Oh... Murder*".

At forty-five minutes to nine in the morning, Caroline Maxwell stated that she saw Kelly outside of the Britannia Public House talking to a man at about half-past eight when she was on her way to Bishopgate Street to get her husband's breakfast. Kelly was still there when she returned fifteen minutes later. The door to Kelly's room was locked, so it was then assumed that the killer used a master key to lock the door upon exiting, or left by the window with the broken pane and fastened the latch by reaching his arm in through the broken window; the latter explanation being the consensus.

Leaving a potential suspect for the moment, there were still several missing pieces of the puzzle that were bothering me. How did the killer leave Kelly's room without drawing attention to himself, was the first on the list? Did the man carry a bag, as a physician would, and have a change of clothes inside? Had he burned those and used some of Kelly's clothes to obliterate what he had done. Or was my theory about a carriage waiting close by the crime scene, the only explanation? With so much blood everywhere in the room, the killer must have been covered from head to toe in the victim's blood. How did the killer leave the room without being seen? Witness accounts proved that there were several people in the area around the time of the murder. If there was a carriage in waiting, then there must have been a driver, and if so, there was a man somewhere in London who knew that a murder had been committed at Millers Court. Why had this man not come forward to give evidence?

Unfortunately, the idea that the perpetrator of the crime had access to a carriage suggested several distasteful scenarios that no one wanted to entertain. If the killer was a gentleman, how could such a man go about killing prostitutes? The very idea for some was, so outrageous to consider, they would not even broach the matter with an open mind. For most, the culprit was depicted as an unkempt, creature of no social standing, who was most likely to be of an unstable mind. For others, the killer was viewed as some drifting vagabond from another country. An individual who had entered the city with no ties. No matter what view of the killer that was brought to mind, it was generally believed that it was no English gentleman, riding about in a carriage in the East End looking for prostitutes to spill their blood on London's walks.

Chapter Twenty-four

It was evening when I returned to my office, it had been a grueling morning of witness hunting and statement taking. At my desk, I poured myself a cup of tea and watched the steam rise from the rim of the cup to evaporate in the air.

"Was it as bad, as the gossip infers John?"

Baxter spoke almost in a whisper, the tone representative of the morose way in which every officer of the law was feeling this day.

A nod of my head was all the response that I could muster as the coroner sat down in the chair opposite and started to pack his pipe. Reaching for the teapot, I poured a scalding cup of tea for Baxter.

"I have never seen anything like it, Wynne," I said, pushing the cup and saucer across the desk towards Baxter. "I have seen my share of horror, but nothing compared to this."

"The streets in the East End will be lit with the torches of the Vigilance Committee this night," Baxter said, still using a whisper.

"Will you be the presiding coroner in this inquest?"

"Not likely," Baxter huffed. "I believe it will be the M.P., Dr. Macdonald, the coroner for the North-Eastern District of Middlesex," Baxter said grimly.

"Is this man, as thorough in his duties, as you are, Wynne?"

"Macdonald is a politician, Stone, what do you think?"

"All afternoon, I have tried to understand the reasoning behind such brutality, but alas, I have given up. I am inclined to believe as everyone else, that this is some fiend wandering the streets crazed, lusting for blood."

"John, you are a detective, what does it matter the whys or what for; you uphold the law and bring the criminal to justice, let others more equipped seek out the reasons why criminals force their own demented will upon the weak or unwary."

"Ours is not the question why, is that it, Wynne?"

"Not entirely, but we need not think there is some logic behind these atrocities, this fiend as you call him is like some mad dog or a diseased cow, an offense to all that is good or natural. One does not question or seek answers from the Creator asking why it was created, the community separates the diseased creature from the rest of the healthy stock, and you put it down."

I watched the muscle along Baxter's jaw, tighten as the man spoke, and then harden as the coroner clenched his teeth.

"Wynne, I agree that the killer must greet the hangman's rope, but that can never happen as long as we treat this criminal like some crazed animal or a lunatic. To catch a killer of a motiveless crime, we must, first, try and understand the mind of the man."

"Why," Baxter said, throwing up his arms. "How, could we possibly get inside the mind of a deranged killer?"

"Wynne, if we can try to understand what motivates him to kill, perhaps we can guess where '*Jack*' will strike next."

"What sort of motive could this animal have," Baxter shouted. "This madman slices up women like a butcher does a carcass, I do not think there is any understanding a deranged mind like this man has, Stone?"

"I think you are wrong, Wynne. It is entirely possible that this man has suffered something horrific, or damaging that has altered his personality."

"Stone, are you saying that, Tumblety has an alternate ego of some kind?"

"In essence yes."

"Let me get this straight," Baxter said. "Are you suggesting Tumblety's alternate ego is this 'Jack the Ripper' and it is this repressed part of Tumblety that is manifest in this killer?"

"If, I am right and Tumblety is our man, then the doctor seemingly has no apparent design, aside from what we guess to be the obtaining of his specimens. If that is the case, then, we must try to figure out what his method of choosing his next victim?"

"That sounds like a tall order Stone," Baxter said, finishing stuffing his pipe. "You might as well suggest that we put ever brunette in London under lock and key."

"It is not as difficult as you might think Wynne," I explained, ignoring the sarcasm. "I believe the man's motive derives from his hatred of women, prostitutes in particular."

"If you look at everyone who hates streetwalkers Stone, you would have a long list indeed."

"I do not believe that these crimes were random, Wynne. I think our man handpicks these individuals, perhaps, because they are a reflection of the woman, whom all his hatred is directed."

"I think you are grasping at straws now, Stone?" Baxter mocked.

"Perhaps, Wynne, but there has to be some reason '*Jack*' picks these women. I believe that our killer is a man who has replaced natural affection with some other form of demented gratification and simply killing no longer satisfies him."

"Are you referring to Tumblety's preoccupation with prostitutes and gentleman's clubs."

"Yes."

"The man is a killer, I think you presume too much, Stone" Baxter argued. "Besides, how much premeditation can you accredit a man who chooses doxies seemingly at random?" Baxter interrupted.

"Do you remember the crude cuts to Nichol's abdomen?"

Baxter nodded his head.

"How about the thirty-nine stab wounds in Tabram's chest, was that a killer gone wild, or perhaps his savagery had not been realized yet. Perchance, Tabram cried out, as '*Jack*' reports in the '*Saucy Jacky Post Card,*' '*the first one squealed a bit.*' We know this man Tumblety has no desire for women judging by the company the man keeps and by the statement '*down on whores.*' Perhaps Tumblety starts planning his strategies after his victim is chosen. '*Jack*' then begins to enjoy enticing them with gifts or plying them with promises, remember the '*Dear Boss Letter*,' which refers to his '*funny little games.*' Then at a particular time and place, specific to his plans '*Jack*' ends their life quickly. With a quick slash of my knife '*Jack*' slices and their lifeblood drains out on the ground in front of them. Only then does our man dissect their bodies when no blood can spill on him, which also explains how this man can leave the scene without drawing any attention to himself."

"If this wretch is the hater of women that you believe him to be Stone, why end their life so quickly? Why not torture them and make them pay, so to speak, for their transgressions before killing them," Baxter asked tapping, the mouthpiece of his pipe against the arm of the chair.

"I believe, Wynne it has to do with the blood. Like I said in previous conversations, I think this individual has come a long way developing into the 'Ripper.' I think there has been a burning hatred festering within '*Jack*' until finally the man has been transformed into someone where simply killing is not enough. I believe that our man has some other sick fascination with the female body, coupled with his anger for prostitutes. That is why we have seen his dissection turn from the procurement of organs into the utter disfigurement of the women's bodies."

"For heaven's sake, Stone, you make it sound as if this '*Jack the Ripper*' is using these women like some lab experiment!"

"Perhaps, in his own twisted way, '*Jack*' sees his killing as ending the miserable existence of each woman."

"Detective, are you telling me that this killer has taken something from this latest victim as well?" Baxter shouted, sitting up on the edge of his seat, horrified.

"This time, the killer took the victim's heart, Wynne."

"Bloody awful!"

"I am certain that there is a tie between the women, some common link each have, but what that is I can't put my finger on it."

"This all sounds neat and tidy Stone, but what bond could the women have," Baxter asked. "We could not find even a close friend between each victim. Although, I should think that one strumpet is the same as the next to most men?"

"Perhaps to those that frequent the back alleys, Wynne. But I think that there is something specific about each victim, some characteristic, or it

370

could be as simple as some mannerism the women have that our man has seen in his victims that reminds him of a particular woman."

"So far, there have only been consistencies in hair color, and the age of the victims, Stone, nothing else."

"There has to be something more specific to put our finger on, Wynne. I am convinced of it. There is something we are missing."

"Maybe, but so far, we cannot find anything specific," Baxter commented. "Perchance, it is just as simplistic as time and place and the fact that they are prostitutes, Stone. What then?"

"I don't think so Wynne. There are over a thousand prostitutes in the East End, why go from one corner of Whitechapel to another to kill Stride, and then kill Eddowes?"

'Yes, I never thought of that, Stone."

"I believe '*Jack*' studies these women and chooses each one carefully after meeting them. It might just be the age and hair color that is the attraction, as you suggest. However, beyond that, it is something the victims might have said in conversation. There has to be something specific about each one, something that draws them to him?"

"Unfortunately, only the killer knows what that is, Detective."

"We have to start thinking differently, Wynne," I responded. "Although clever in many ways, this '*Jack*' may think more literally. Perhaps, the victim's features are based solely on a vague reminder of a woman from his past."

"What the devil are you referring to now, Stone?"

"Perhaps it is just attraction, as you say." I answered.

"Detective this '*Jack the Ripper*' is mad; there is no other explanation," Baxter, growled in response. "Why this man kills, or for whatever the reason, we may never know," Baxter said, reaching for the teapot.

"That might very well be, and maybe as you say there isn't anything specific about these women. Perhaps the only thing they have in common is that they are all prostitutes and...." I retaliated.

I was irritated by Baxter's constant narrowmindedness and was about to change the subject when suddenly something occurred to me. Something that I had never paid any attention to before.

"And, what Stone?"

"What if it is as simple as all of his victims have been drinking in public houses on the night '*Jack*' looks for his next victim?"

"Do you think; he finds his victims only in public houses?" Baxter asked.

Reaching for my files, I opened each and found what I was looking for before moving onto the next file.

"Alright, Wynne," I said, finally. "We know now that our latest victim Mary Jane Kelly was last seen outside of the Britannia house, by the witness Caroline Maxewell. Tabram was seen entering the White Swan public house, by Ann Morris the night she was killed. Nichols was last seen by Mary Ann Monk at seven o'clock entering a public house on New Kent Road. Timothy Donovan, the deputy of the common lodging house at 35 Dorset Street, said I had words with Chapman about *'having money for beer but not for lodgings.'* Chapman was last seen going in the direction of Brushfield Street, where there is a public house. Elizabeth Tanner, last saw Elizabeth Stride, at the Queen's Head public house. Eddowes was arrested for public drunkenness by Sergeant Byfield on the night of her death."

"Stone, there are hundreds of public houses in the East End," Baxter offered. "And, might I add, Detective, if his victims are chosen because they are of dark hair, in their forties and visit public houses the list of potential victims just grew enormously."

I nodded in agreement, realizing immediately that the coroner was right, and perhaps, I was just grasping at straws.

"Wynne, we have to do something, our failing here is in treating this thing too lightly," I explained. "We strut around like this thing just shouldn't be happening on English soil. Well, it is, and the longer we keep looking the other way because the women are prostitutes, or because these crimes are not affecting the better half of the population, this mad man will keep killing."

Looking at the startled look on Baxter's face, I realized I was taking my frustration out on the wrong person.

"Sorry, Wynne."

"Where do we begin?"

"Not we, Wynne, me. I am going to talk to Inspector Abberline and get some men on this. We will need a number of constables placed in every public house in London if we are going to catch this killer!"

Chapter Twenty-five

The following evening, I met with Inspector Abberline, and, before long, the feelings that my work in Whitechapel, was of little or no consequence had returned. After giving the inspector a brief report on my investigation in the Mary Jane Kelly murder, in which I included notes on Francis Tumblety, the only plausible suspect, the Yard had in connection with the murders in Whitechapel. I also gave the inspector my notes on the '*Jack the Ripper*' letters, and anything pertinent I could think of adding in the cases of the seven dead women. All that remained to bring the file up to date was to attend the inquest into the Kelly murder.

In the hackney, my thoughts returned to the details of my meeting with the inspector. I had been rushed through my reports, and the session had ended without a comment on my suggestion to keep Tumblety under surveillance. Any ideas about where I suspected Tumblety selected his victims and how the investigation should turn also seemed to fall on deaf ears. Along with my suggestion to place detectives in all the public houses in the area of Whitechapel. Aside from the inspector commenting on the limited manpower and given the size and area to be covered, '*the task was simply impossible*' and not warranted. When I left the Yard, I had an empty feeling in the pit of my stomach brought about by the quick dismissal of my recommendations and the feeling that whatever evidence I might uncover would most likely be met with the same excuse no matter what it was.

Wynne was nowhere to be found, and the offices in the building had closed. Passing on going to my rooms, I boiled water for a pot of tea on Baxter's stove and sat alone in my office listening to the sound of the rain as it hit against the thin pane of glass in the window, and wondered when '*Jack*' would strike again. With the overwhelming feeling of helplessness came the feeling of dread so, my thoughts quickly reverted to my meeting with Inspector Abberline. My theory that Doctor Francis Tumblety was '*Jack the Ripper*' had been ignored. I could not understand the inspector's stubbornness in the matter. Tumblety had already drawn attention to himself as a person of interest in several crimes against the crown. There was no good reason why, suddenly, that importance had been laid to rest. They had viable proof of Tumblety's past involvement and association with prostitutes. Not to mention, the man performing abortions and the selling of herbs was enough in my opinion to have the doctor seriously looked at as a plausible suspect in Alenka's murder. The fact that the Canadian government had sent information on Tumblety was proof that someone thought investigating into the man's past was pertinent. As far as, I knew there was no other prime candidate that fit the bill for the deaths of the half dozen women to date. I could not believe that the one man that was not above suspicion was allowed to roam the streets a free man.

As I sat in the gloom of the fading light of dusk, worrying about the inspector's response to my conclusions in the investigation, I wondered if Tumblety would be ignored as a suspect if the man showed up at The Yard, covered in blood and confessed to murdering another prostitute. Among other things, I also wondered if it was time for me to tell Abberline to put forth my resignation.

The inquest was held at the Shoreditch Town Hall; on Monday the twelfth day of November. Dr. Macdonald M.P., Coroner for the North-Eastern District of Middlesex, presided over the inquiry. The first minutes of the inquiry was hindered by questions from the jury as to why Dr. Macdonald was presiding over a Whitechapel murder victim when in their eyes, they thought it should be Wynne Baxter.

374

Seated in a corner both, I and Wynne Baxter sat listening intently to the discussion. Baxter nudged me with his elbow, obviously excited by the turn of events and the loyalty of the Whitechapel constituents to his office. After a subsequent amount of discussion, Macdonald informed the jury that Mary Jane Kelly's body was found dead in his jurisdiction. Because the body was taken to a mortuary in Whitechapel was not a concern for the jury to worry about. With the continued unrest of the jury and fearing the loss of control over the proceedings so early on the first day, Dr. Macdonald spoke forcibly over his officer Mr. Hammond, threatening the jurors to do their duty and leave official matters to those qualified, thus quieting the room. Without any further delay, the coroner proceeded with the inquest.

Joseph Barnett was the first to be deposed having, last saw her on Thursday night before her death.

[Sic] Joseph Barnett deposed: "I was a fish-porter, and I work as a laborer and fruit- porter. Until Saturday last, I lived at 24, New-street, Bishopsgate, and have since stayed at my sister's, 21, Portpool-lane, Gray's Inn-road. I have lived with the deceased one year and eight months. Her name was Marie Jeanette Kelly with the French spelling as described to me. Kelly was her maiden name. I have seen the body, and I identify it by the ear and eyes, which are all that I can recognize; but I am positive it is the same woman I knew. I lived with her in No. 13 room, at Miller's-court for eight months. I separated from her on Oct. 30."
Coroner: "Why did you leave her?"

Barnett: "Because she had a woman of bad character there, whom she took in out of compassion, and I objected to it. That was the only reason. I left her on the Tuesday between five and six p.m. I last saw her alive between half-past seven and a quarter to eight on Thursday night last, when I called upon her. I stayed there for a quarter of an hour."
Coroner: "Were you on good terms?"

Barnett: "Yes, on friendly terms; but when we parted I told her I had no work, and had nothing to give her, for which I was very sorry."
Coroner: "Did you drink together?"

Barnett: "No, sir. She was quite sober."
Coroner: "Was she, generally speaking, of sober habits?"

Barnett: "When she was with me, I found her of sober habits, but she has been drunk several times in my presence".

Coroner: "Was there any one else there on the Thursday evening?"

Barnett: "Yes, a woman who lives in the court. She left first, and I followed shortly afterwards."

Coroner: "Have you had conversation with deceased about her parents?"

Barnett: "Yes, frequently. She said she was born in Limerick, and went when very young to Wales. She did not say how long she lived there, but that she came to London about four years ago. Her father's name was John Kelly, a 'gaffer' or foreman in an iron works in Carnarvonshire, or Carmarthen. She said she had one sister, who was respectable, who travelled from market place to market place. This sister was very fond of her. There were six brothers living in London, and one was in the army. One of them was named Henry. I never saw the brothers to my knowledge. She said she was married when very young in Wales to a collier. I think the name was Davis or Davies. She said she had lived with me until I was killed in an explosion, but I cannot say how many years since that was. Her age was, I believe, 16 when she married. After her husband's death deceased went to Cardiff to a cousin."

Coroner: "Did she live there long?"

Barnett: "Yes, she was in an infirmary there for eight or nine months. She was following a bad life with her cousin, who, as I reckon, and as I often told her, was the cause of her downfall."

Coroner: "After she left Cardiff did, she come direct to London?"

Barnett: "Yes. She was in a gay house in the West-end, but in what part she did not say. A gentleman came there to her and asked her if she would like to go to France."

Coroner: "Did she go to France?"

Barnett: "Yes; but she did not remain long. She said she did not like the part, but whether it was the part or purpose I cannot say. She was not there more than a fortnight, and she returned to England, and went to Ratcliffe-highway. She must have lived there for some time. Afterwards she lived with a man opposite the Commercial Gas Works, Stepney. The man's name was Morganstone."

Coroner: "Have you seen that man?"

Barnett: "Never. I don't know how long she lived with him."

Coroner: "Was Morganstone the last man she lived with?"

Barnett: "I cannot answer that question, but she described a man named Joseph Fleming, who came to Pennington-street, a bad house, where she stayed. I don't know when this was. She was very fond of him. He was a mason's plasterer, and lodged in the Bethnal-green-road."

Coroner: "Was that all you knew of her history when you lived with her?"

Barnett: "Yes. After she lived with Morganstone or Fleming - I don't know which one was the last - she lived with him."

Coroner: "Where did you pick up with her first?"

Barnett: "In Commercial-street. We then had a drink together, and I made arrangements to see her on the following day - a Saturday. On that day we both of us agreed that we should remain together. I took lodgings in George-street, Commercial-street, where I was known. I lived with her, until I left her, on very friendly terms."

Coroner: "Have you heard her speak of being afraid of any one?"

Barnett: "Yes; several times. I bought newspapers, and I read to her everything about the murders, which she asked me about."

Coroner: "Did she express fear of any particular individual?"

Barnett: "No, sir. Our own quarrels were very soon over."

The Coroner: "You have given your evidence very well indeed.

(To the Jury): The doctor has sent a note asking whether we shall want his attendance here to-day. I take it that it would be convenient that he should tell us roughly, what the cause of death was, so as to enable the body to be buried. It will not be necessary to go into the details of the doctor's evidence; but I suggested that I might come to state roughly the cause of death."

The jury acquiesced in the proposed course and the coroner was inclined to agree with the proposal.

[Sic] Thomas Bowyer stated, "I live at 37, Dorset-street, and am employed by Mr. McCarthy. I serve in my chandler's shop, 27, Dorset-street. At a quarter to eleven a.m., on Friday morning, I was ordered by McCarthy to go to Mary Jane's room, No. 13. I did not know the deceased by the name of Kelly. I went for rent, which was in arrears. Knocking at the door, I got no answer, and I knocked again and again. Receiving no reply, I passed round the corner by the gutter spout where there is a broken window - it is the smallest window."

377

Charles Ledger, an inspector of police, G. Division, produced a plan of the premises. Bowyer pointed out the window, which was the one nearest to the entrance. Thomas Bowyer then continued his testimony.

[Sic] I [Bowyer] continued: "There was a curtain. I put my hand through the broken pane and lifted the curtain. I saw two pieces of flesh lying on the table."

Coroner: "Where was this table?"

Bowyer: "In front of the bed, close to it. The second time I looked I saw a body on this bed, and blood on the floor. I at once went very quietly to Mr. McCarthy. We then stood in the shop, and I told him what I had seen. We both went to the police-station, but first of all, we went to the window, and McCarthy looked in to satisfy himself. We told the inspector at the police-station of what we had seen. Nobody else knew of the matter. The inspector returned with us."

Coroner: "Did you see the deceased constantly?"

Bowyer: "I have often seen her. I knew the last witness, Barnett. I have seen the deceased drunk once."

By the Jury: "When did you see her last alive?"

Bowyer: "On Wednesday afternoon, in the court, when I spoke to her. McCarthy's shop is at the corner of Miller's-court."

[Sic] John McCarthy, grocer and lodging-house keeper, testified: "I live at 27, Dorset- street. On Friday morning, about a quarter to eleven, I sent my man Bowyer to Room 13 to call for rent. I came back in five minutes, saying, 'Guv'nor, I knocked at the door, and could not make any one answer; I looked through the window and saw a lot of blood.' He accompanied me, and looked through the window himself; saw the blood and the woman. For a moment, I could not say anything, and I then said: "You had better fetch the police." I knew the deceased as Mary Jane Kelly, and had no doubt at all about her identity. I followed Bowyer to Commercial-street Police-station, where I saw Inspector Beck. I inquired at first for Inspector Reid. Inspector Beck returned with me at once."

Coroner: "How long had the deceased lived in the room?"

McCarthy: "Ten months. She lived with Barnett. I did not know whether they were married or not; they lived comfortably together, but they had a row when the window was broken. The bedstead, bed-clothes, table, and every article of furniture belonged to me."

Coroner: *"What rent was paid for this room?"*

McCarthy: *"It was supposed to be 4s 6d a week. Deceased was in arrears 29s. I was to be paid the rent weekly. Arrears are got as best you can. I frequently saw the deceased the worse for drink. When sober she was an exceptionally quiet woman, but when in drink she had more to say. She was able to walk about, and was not helpless."*

[Sic] Mary Ann Cox stated, *"I live at No. 5 Room, Miller's-court. It is the last house on the left-hand side of the court. I am a widow, and get my living on the streets. I have known the deceased for eight or nine months as the occupant of No. 13 Room. She was called Mary Jane. I last saw her alive on Thursday night, at a quarter to twelve, very much intoxicated."*

Coroner: *"Where was this?"*

Cox: *"In Dorset-street. She went up the court, a few steps in front of me."*

Coroner: *"Was anybody with her?"*

Cox: *"A short, stout man, shabbily dressed. He had on a longish coat, very shabby, and carried a pot of ale in my hand."*

Coroner: *"What was the color of the coat?"*

Cox: *"A dark coat".*

Coroner: *"What hat had he?"*

Cox: *"A round hard billycock".*

Coroner: *"Long or short hair?"*

Cox: *"I did not notice. He had a blotchy face, and full carrotty moustache."*

Coroner: *"The chin was shaven?"*

Cox: *"Yes. A lamp faced the door."*

Coroner: *"Did you see them go into her room?"*

Cox: *"Yes; I said 'Good night, Mary,' and she turned round and banged the door."*

Coroner: *"Had he anything in his hands but the can?"*

Cox: *"No."*

Coroner: *"Did she say anything?"*

Cox: *"She said 'Good night, I am going to have a song.' As I went in she sang 'A violet I plucked from my mother's grave when a boy.' I remained a quarter of an hour in my room and went out. Deceased was*

379

still singing at one o'clock when I returned. I remained in the room for a minute to warm my hands as it was raining, and went out again. She was singing still, and I returned to my room at three o'clock. The light was then out and there was no noise."

Coroner: *"Did you go to sleep?"*

Cox: *"No; I was upset. I did not undress at all. I did not sleep at all. I must have heard what went on in the court. I heard no noise or cry of 'Murder,' but men went out to work in the market."*

Coroner: *"How many men live in the court who work in Spitalfields Market?"*

Cox: *"One. At a quarter-past six I heard a man go down the court. That was too late for the market."*

Coroner: *"From what house did I go?"*

Cox: *"I don't know."*

Coroner *"Did you hear the door bang after him?"*

Cox: *"No."*

Coroner: *"Then I must have walked up the court and back again?"*

Cox: *"Yes".*

Coroner: *"It might have been a policeman?"*

Cox: *"It might have been".*

Coroner; *"What would you take the stout man's age to be?"*

Cox: *"Six-and-thirty".*

Coroner: *"Did you notice the color of his trousers?"*

Cox: *"All his clothes were dark."*

Coroner: *"Did his boots sound as if the heels were heavy?"*

Cox: *"There was no sound as I went up the court."*

Coroner: *"Then you think that his boots were down at heels?"*

I saw Wynne Baxter stifle an outburst, out of respect for his colleague, and then turned and whispered across his shoulder.

"How does Macdonald expect the witness to answer that fool question, Stone?"

"I think the Macdonald may have been caught up in the moment, Wynne," I answered. "Perhaps, the coroner wanted to know if she heard the heavy heal of a constable's boot."

380

"Bollocks," Baxter whispered. "I think the man is trying to prove himself a better investigator than I, given the circumstances at the beginning of this inquiry."

I understood Wynne's feelings, I had listened to the questioning, though thorough, the laymen could not give an informative answer to such a question.

"Perhaps, Macdonald was just testing her answers to see if she was telling the truth." I said to quiet my friend.

When the crowded room quieted after seeing the Macdonald's glare at their outburst, Cox answered the question.

[Sic] Cox: "He made no noise."
Coroner: "What clothes had Mary Jane on?"
Cox: "She had no hat; a red pelerine and a shabby skirt."
Coroner: "You say she was drunk?"
Cox: "I did not notice she was drunk until she said good night. The man closed the door. By the Jury: There was a light in the window, but I saw nothing, as the blinds were down. I should know the man again, if I saw him. "
By the Coroner: "I feel certain if there had been the cry of 'Murder' in the place I should have heard it; there was not the least noise. I have often seen the woman the worse for drink."

[Sic] Elizabeth Prater, a married woman, said: "My husband, William Prater, was a boot machinist, and he has deserted me. I live at number 20 Room, in Miller's-court, above the shed. Deceased occupied a room below. I left the room on the Thursday at five p.m., and returned to it at about one a.m. on Friday morning. I stood at the corner until about twenty minutes past one. No one spoke to me. McCarthy's shop was open, and I called in, and then went to my room. I should have seen a glimmer of light in going up the stairs if there had been a light in deceased's room, but I noticed none. The partition was so thin I could have heard Kelly walk about in the room. I went to bed at half-past one and barricaded the door with two tables. I fell asleep directly and slept soundly. A kitten disturbed me about half-past three o'clock or a quarter to four. As I was turning round I heard a suppressed cry of 'Oh - murder!' in a faint voice. It

seemed to proceed from the court."

Coroner: "Do you often hear cries of Murder?"

   Prater: "It is nothing unusual in the street. I did not take particular notice."

Coroner: "Did you hear it a second time?"

   Prater: "No."

Coroner: "Did you hear beds or tables being pulled about?"

   Prater: "None whatever. I went asleep, and was awake again at five a.m. I passed down the stairs, and saw some men harnessing horses. At a quarter to six I was in the Ten Bells."

Coroner: "Could the witness, Mary Ann Cox, have come down the entry between one and half-past one o'clock without your knowledge?"

   Prater: "Yes, she could have done so".

Coroner: "Did you see any strangers at the Ten Bells?"

   Prater: "No. I went back to bed and slept until eleven."

Coroner: "You heard no singing downstairs?"

   Prater: "None whatever. I should have heard the singing distinctly. It was quite quiet at half-past one o'clock."

[Sic] Caroline Maxewell, 14, Dorset-street, said, "My husband is a lodging-house deputy. I knew the deceased for about four months. I believe she was an unfortunate. On two occasions I spoke to her.

The Coroner: You must be very careful about your evidence, because it is different to other people's. You say you saw her standing at the corner of the entry to the court?

   Maxewell: "Yes, on Friday morning, from eight to half-past eight. I fix the time by my husband's finishing work. When I came out of the lodging-house she was opposite. "

Coroner: "Did you speak to her?"

   Maxewell: "Yes; it was an unusual thing to see her up. She was a young woman who never associated with anyone. I spoke across the street, 'What, Mary, brings you up so early?' She said, 'Oh, Carrie, I do feel so bad.'

Coroner: "And yet you say you had only spoken to her twice previously; you knew her name and she knew yours?"

   Maxewell: "Oh, yes; by being about in the lodging-house".

Coroner: "What did she say?"

Maxewell: "She said, 'I've had a glass of beer, and I've brought it up again;' and it was in the road. I imagined she had been in the Britannia beer-shop at the corner of the street. I left her, saying that I could pity her feelings. I went to Bishopsgate-street to get my husband's breakfast. Returning I saw her outside the Britannia public-house, talking to a man."

Coroner: "This would be about what time?"

Maxewell: "Between eight and nine o'clock. I was absent about half-an-hour. It was about a quarter to nine."

Coroner: "What description can you give of this man?"

Maxewell: "I could not give you any, as they were at some distance."

Inspector Abberline: "The distance is about sixteen yards."

Witness: "I am sure it was the deceased. I am willing to swear it."

The Coroner: "You are sworn now. Was he a tall man?"

Maxewell: "No; he was a little taller than me and stout."

Inspector Abberline: "On consideration I should say the distance was twenty-five yards."

"What do you make of that Wynne," I asked, moving closer to Baxter and whispering in the man's ear.

"I haven't the foggiest," Baxter commented. "The inspector's outburst is quite unprecedented; it is almost like the man is trying to establish that there is no possible way that she could have seen the deceased?"

"Is Abberline interfering so that Maxewell's testimony can be refuted," I asked Baxter.

"I don't know what the inspector's motive could be, Stone? I would expect something like this from a constable, not from the inspector." Baxter whispered.

"I agree, Wynne," I spoke sharply, in reply.

Looking across the room at Inspector Abberline, I wondered what reason the man had to disrupt a witness in testimony, especially after the man had already told the jury his own calculated estimate of the distance in question. The crowd had finished whispering back and forth, only then did Macdonald continue his questioning of the witness.

[Sic] The Coroner: "What clothes had the man?"

Witness: "Dark clothes; he seemed to have a plaid coat on. I could not say what sort of hat he had.

Coroner: "What sort of dress had the deceased?"

Maxewell: "A dark skirt, a velvet body, a maroon shawl, and no hat".

Coroner: "Have you ever seen her the worse for drink?"

Maxewell: "I have seen her in drink, but she was not a notorious character."

By the Jury: "I should have noticed if the man had had a tall silk hat, but we are accustomed to see men of all sorts with women. I should not like to pledge myself to the kind of hat."

[Sic] Sarah Lewis deposed: "I live at 24, Great Pearl-street, and am a laundress. I know Mrs. Keyler, in Miller's-court, and went to her house at number 2, Miller's-court, at 2.30a.m. on Friday. It is the first house. I noticed the time by the Spitalfields' Church clock. When I went into the court, opposite the lodging-house I saw a man with a wide awake. There was no one talking to him. He was a stout-looking man, and not very tall. The hat was black. I did not take any notice of his clothes. The man was looking up the court; He seemed to be waiting or looking for someone. Further on there was a man and woman - the latter being in drink. There was nobody in the court. I dozed in a chair at Mrs. Keyler's, and woke at about half-past three. I heard the clock strike."

Coroner: "What woke you up?"

Lewis: "I could not sleep. I sat awake until nearly four, when I heard a female's voice shouting 'Murder' loudly. It seemed like the voice of a young woman. It sounded at our door. There was only one scream."

Coroner: "Were you afraid? Did you wake anybody up?"

Lewis: "No, I took no notice, as I only heard the one scream."

Coroner: "You stayed at Keyler's house until what time?"

Lewis: "Half-past five p.m. on Friday. The police would not let us out of the court."

Coroner: "Have you seen any suspicious persons in the district?"

Lewis: "On Wednesday night I was going along the Bethnal-green-road, with a woman, about eight o'clock, when a gentleman passed us. He followed us and spoke to us, and wanted us to follow him into an entry. He had a shiny leather bag with him."

384

"What do you, think was in the bag, Stone?" Baxter whispered over his shoulder.

Looking over at Baxter, I said nothing for a moment but by, the buzz of the crowd, their suspicions were a match with his, only a physician carried a black bag, and that was what everyone in the room was whispering about. It had long been the subject of every gossip in London for weeks now as well. Everyone, in turn, was wondering if the killer was some doctor that had taken leave of his senses and had ignored his Hippocratic Oath?

"By the sounds of this crowd, I would guess they concur with you Detective, that the bag is some kind of physician's bag," Wynne continued, not waiting for a response.

"Wynne, there was a lot of blood in Kelly's room," I responded. "If I were to guess, which, seems to be, all I do these days anyway, I would say the bag contained another suit of clothes along with whatever else the killer used to hack that poor woman up with. There is no way the killer could have got out of that room at Miller's Court without blood on him," I whispered over my shoulder to the coroner.

[Sic] Coroner: "Did he want both of you?"

Lewis: "No; only one. I refused. I went away and came back again, saying he would treat us. He put down his bag and picked it up again, saying, "What are you frightened about? Do you think I've got anything in the bag?" We then ran away, as we were frightened."

Coroner: "Was he a tall man?"

Lewis: "He was short, pale-faced, with a black moustache, rather small. His age was about forty."

Coroner: "Was it a large bag?"

Lewis: "No, about 6in to 9in long. His hat was a high round hat. He had a brownish overcoat, with a black short coat underneath. His trousers were a dark pepper-and- salt."

Coroner: "After he left you what did you do?"

Lewis: "We ran away."

Coroner: "Have you seen him since?"

Lewis: "On Friday morning, about half-past two a.m., when I was going to Miller's-court, I met the same man with a woman in Commercial-

street, near Mr. Ringer's public-house (the Britannia). He had no overcoat on."

Coroner: "Had he the black bag"

  Lewis: "Yes".

Coroner: "Were the man and woman quarrelling?"

  Lewis: "No; they were talking. As I passed, he looked at me. I don't know whether he recognized me. There was no policeman about."

[Sic] Mr. George Bagster Phillips, divisional surgeon of police, said, "I was called by the police on Friday morning at eleven o'clock, and on proceeding to Miller's-court, which I entered at 11.15, I found a room, the door of which led out of the passage at the side of 26, Dorset-street, photographs of which I produce. It had two windows in the court. Two panes in the lesser window were broken, and as the door was locked, I looked through the lower of the broken panes and satisfied myself that the mutilated corpse lying on the bed was not in need of any immediate attention from me, and I also came to the conclusion that there was nobody else upon the bed, or within view, to whom I could render any professional assistance. Having ascertained that probably it was advisable that no entrance should be made into the room at that time, I remained until about 1.30p.m., when the door was broken open by McCarthy, under the direction of Superintendent Arnold. On the door being opened it knocked against a table which was close to the left-hand side of the bedstead, and the bedstead was close against the wooden partition. The mutilated remains of a woman were lying two- thirds over, towards the edge of the bedstead, nearest the door. Deceased had only an under-linen garment upon her, and by subsequent examination I am sure the body had been removed, after the injury which caused death, from that side of the bedstead which was nearest to the wooden partition previously mentioned. The large quantity of blood under the bedstead, the saturated condition of the paillasse, pillow, and sheet at the top corner of the bedstead nearest to the partition leads me to the conclusion that the severance of the right carotid artery, which was the immediate cause of death, was inflicted while the deceased was lying at the right side of the bedstead and her head and neck in the top right-hand corner."

[Sic] The jury had no questions to ask at this stage, and it was understood that more detailed evidence of the medical examination would be given at a future hearing. An adjournment for a few minutes then took place, and on the return of the jury, the coroner said: "It has come to my ears that somebody has been making a statement to some of the jury as to their right and duty of being here. Has anyone during the interval spoken to the jury, saying that they should not be here to-day"
Some jurymen replied in the negative.

The Coroner: "Then I must have been misinformed. I should have taken good care that I would have had a quiet life for the rest of the week if anybody had interfered with my jury."

"Stone, do you have any idea what is going on. At the onset, there has been a dispute about the jury being dissatisfied with the venue of the inquest, and now this; it seems somebody is tenaciously trying to see this inquest deemed improper," Baxter said, looking more than a little agitated by the way the inquest was being handled.

"I couldn't agree with you more, Wynne. Something is a trifle odd about this jury. I think Macdonald is making a mountain out of a molehill though. This isn't a trial, who could gain by manipulating an inquest jury," I replied.

"I believe, Detective that there is something amiss here," Baxter said, twirling his mustache. "Something that perhaps we have not been made privy to."

Unable to comment, I watched the faces of the jury and wondered if the disgruntled juror from the beginning of the proceedings was the culprit, but, after looking at each individual, there was no telltale sign to show that any one of the jurors had any idea what the coroner was referring to. After studying their faces for several minutes, I could see the only shock from the jury at the insinuation that there was any interference going on.

"Wynne, the jury truly looks as surprised as most of the spectators in the room," I commented. "I don't think they have a clue what the coroner is talking about."

As the crowd quieted, I wondered what exactly Macdonald had been told to make a special point of threatening to stop the inquest at so late in the day. I could only guess that someone had whispered in the coroner's ear at some point during the inquest, informing Macdonald that a witness's testimony had been fraudulent, although; I would have been hard-pressed to recall such an incident taking place.

[Sic] Julia Vanturney [Van Turney], 1, Miller's-court, a charwoman, living with Harry Owen, said: "I knew the deceased for some time as Kelly, and I knew Joe Barnett, who lived with her. He would not allow her to go on the streets. Deceased often got drunk. She said she was fond of another man, also named Joe. I never saw this man. I believe he was a costermonger."
Coroner: "When did you last see the deceased alive?"
Vanturney: "On Thursday morning, at about ten o'clock. I slept in the court on Thursday night, and went to bed about eight. I could not rest at all during the night."
Coroner: "Did you hear any noises in the court?"
Vanturney: "I did not. I heard no screams of 'Murder,' nor any one singing."

"I think, I now know what, Macdonald was referring to, Wynne, when the coroner cautioned the jury about anyone interfering with the jurors."

Baxter leaned closer, interested in hearing the explanation.

"What do you think it was that made him do it, Stone?"

"Vanturney's testimony," I replied. "Macdonald must have asked her some questions during the break and found out that she had slept in the courtyard and heard nothing strange or out of the ordinary the entire night in question, which in turn would conflict with Prater, and Lewis' testimony of hearing 'murder'."

"What makes you say that, Stone?" Baxter asked.

"It appears as if Macdonald might be worried about upcoming testimony. Perhaps the coroner thinks someone is lying."

"Lying, about what, hearing Kelly singing on the night of her death?"

"Not about the singing," I whispered. "Perhaps Macdonald is wondering how one witness could hear the deceased singing, and another who was right outside in the courtyard did not hear a peep. If I was to guess, I don't think Macdonald trusts the witnesses."

"It would also appear as if Doctor Macdonald wants this inquest wrapped up today for some reason," Baxter commented.

Before Baxter could continue Macdonald, suddenly asked Vanturney in a raised voice, about what she heard the night of Kelly's death.

[Sic] Coroner: "You must have heard deceased singing?"
Vanturney: "Yes; I knew her songs. They were generally Irish."

[Sic] Maria Harvey, 3, New-court, Dorset-street, stated: "I knew the deceased as Mary Jane Kelly. I slept at her house on Monday night and on Tuesday night. All the afternoon of Thursday we were together."
Coroner: "Were you in the house when Joe Barnett called?"

Harvey: "Yes. I said, 'Well, Mary Jane, I shall not see you this evening again,' and I left with her two men's dirty shirts, a little boy's shirt, a black overcoat, a black crepe bonnet with black satin strings, a pawn-ticket for a grey shawl, upon which 2s had been lent, and a little girls white petticoat."
Coroner: "Have you seen any of these articles since?"

Harvey: "Yes; I saw the black overcoat in a room in the court on Friday afternoon."
Coroner: "Did the deceased ever speak to you about being afraid of any man?"

Harvey: "She did not."

[Sic] Inspector Beck, H Division, said that, having sent for the doctor, I gave orders to prevent any persons leaving the court, and I directed officers to make a search. I had not been aware that the deceased was known to the police.

[Sic] Inspector Frederick G. Abberline, inspector of police, Criminal Investigation Department, Scotland-yard, stated: "I am in charge of this case. I arrived at Miller's-court about 11.30 on Friday morning."
Coroner: "Was it by your orders that the door was forced?"

Abberline: "No; I had an intimation from Inspector Beck that the bloodhounds had been sent for, and the reply had been received that they were on the way. Dr. Phillips was unwilling to force the door, as it would be very much better to test the dogs, if they were coming. We remained until about 1.30 p.m., when Superintendent Arnold arrived, and I informed him that the order in regard to the dogs had been countermanded, and I gave orders for the door to be forced. I agree with the medical evidence as to the condition of the room. I subsequently took an inventory of the

389

contents of the room. There were traces of a large fire having been kept up in the grate, so much so that it had melted the spout of a kettle off. We have since gone through the ashes in the fireplace; there were remnants of clothing, a portion of a brim of a hat, and a skirt, and it appeared as if a large quantity of women's clothing had been burnt."

Coroner: "Can you give any reason why they were burnt?"

Abberline: "I can only imagine that it was to make a light for the man to see what he was doing. There was only one small candle in the room, on the top of a broken wine-glass. An impression has gone abroad that the murderer took away the key of the room. Barnett informs me that it has been missing some time, and since it has been lost, they have put their hand through the broken window, and moved back the catch. It is quite easy. There was a man's clay pipe in the room, and Barnett informed me that he smoked it."

Coroner: "Is there anything further the jury ought to know?"

Abberline: "No; if there should be, I can communicate with you, sir."

We left before Doctor Roderick Macdonald gave his summation, leaving the crowds behind, in less than an hour, we were seated comfortably in my office sipping hot tea, each consumed with his own thoughts when Baxter finally broke the silence.

"What do you suppose was MacDonald's motivation for warning the jury, Stone. It was late in the day, and as you said, there is no trial, nor should we expect to see one in the conceivable future, and at the rate, we are going, it seems rather doubtful that there ever will be one," Baxter said, revealing the consensus of everyone in Whitechapel.

"I have been thinking about that all afternoon, Wynne. It appears from the very beginning of the proceedings, Doctor Macdonald suspected the jury would be discounted for some reason, placing him on the defensive to see to it that it did not occur."

"Why do you think Macdonald, suspected that the jury's findings or actions would be put into question if you ask me the very idea sounds preposterous?"

It was obvious that Baxter found the idea inconceivable though, I could only guess that a lot was riding on the inquests to make sure they were handled professionally.

"You would know better than I, Wynne."

I sat thinking for a moment before making my feelings known to the coroner.

"Wynne, if a jury's ability to perform their duty is put into question, is the inquest unaccepted in some way?"

"The role of a jury at an inquest is quite simply to be the voice of the community, Stone. They swear by an oath that they will listen to the testimony of witnesses without prejudice and see to it that the inquest into a suspicious death, in all its efforts, are in accordance with the law. Although directed by the coroner in charge, the jurors are given free rights to intervene at their own discretion, to see to it the law is upheld. The jury's duties are limited though in as far as having no special power other than to witness testimony given under the supervision of the coroner."

"What if the jury refutes testimony or finds the proceedings tampered with or something along those lines materializes?"

"Then it is up to the coroner to note their objections and proceed accordingly. However, I might add most jurors are not interested in the intricacies of the law; they are interested in the basics of right and wrong. You saw what happened when the juror tried to question the decision of the inquest of the venue at the beginning of these proceedings," Baxter replied with upturned eyebrows.

Yes, the juror was put in his place, right smartly."

"For the most part, they are average people doing a duty that they really don't want to do. In the end, they are ultimately asked to merely agree with the coroner's findings. Why do you ask?"

"Simply because Macdonald very early on in the proceedings made it known that he was not going to have anyone tampering with the jury, the coroner then makes a spectacle of his feelings to the entire room. Doctor Macdonald did everything in his power to broadcast his apparent lack of faith in either the witnesses or the jury."

"It does seem a bit unorthodox, Stone?"

"It seems that Macdonald was making his feelings a matter of record, should any questions arise in the future to cause doubt as to the inquest's inability to find the truth. Now, it would seem that Macdonald has covered himself from any misconduct."

"If Macdonald did suspect that someone was trying to interfere with the jury, it would make the way clear for him to rush through the proceedings, which would ultimately limit any further tampering." Baxter piped up.

"Not only that Wynne, but the coroner wasn't just warning the jury that no tampering would be allowed, Macdonald was warning the instigator of the suspected tampering."

"Do you think Macdonald had someone in particular in mind, Stone?" Baxter asked excitedly.

"I have no idea, but it would seem some of the evidence given could have been rehearsed especially in the Vanturney testimony."

"I think, I see know what instance you were referring to Stone," Baxter replied, pipe in hand. "From the beginning, Vanturney testified she heard nothing all night, then after a pause, she states to Macdonald that she heard Kelly singing," Baxter replied.

"I am not sure what to make of it, Wynne. Her change in her testimony suggests that she may have been coerced to change her testimony?"

"I don't follow, Stone?"

Baxter leaned closer as though to understand more thoroughly.

"Vanturney replied when questioned if she heard anything unusual, or out of the ordinary from the courtyard. Everyone else, who testified, either heard singing or people coming and going, from behind their closed doors. Then when Macdonald questions Vanturney, someone who was in the courtyard sleeping, who was also in the position to hear, '*If she heard the deceased singing, Vanturney replies yes.*' Then Vanturney adds that Mary Jane Kelly sang Irish songs. Vanturney did not stipulate that she heard Kelly singing Irish songs on the night in question, did she?"

"No, and Macdonald didn't try to elaborate?"

"That's right, Wynne," I responded. "The coroner in keeping with the rest of the witness testimony asked the question in such a way only wondering if Vanturney had ever heard Kelly sing, she answers forthrightly yes, then as if in an afterthought she comments '*they were Irish songs,*' as if she was corroborating other witnesses testimony."

"Perhaps Macdonald was only trying to make his point clear that Kelly was heard singing." Baxter lifted his hands in the air, in bewilderment.

"Macdonald wasn't giving testimony, Wynne."

"No, you are right there, Stone."

"What result was Macdonald searching or hoping for," I asked. "The coroner is not supposed to interpret testimony either."

"No, of course not," Baxter spoke outright. "The coroner at an inquest has a duty to the district to take the testimony of witnesses involved and submit that testimony to the proper authorities. Any manipulation of jurors or testimony given by witnesses would constitute prejudice and impropriety on the coroner's behalf in the keeping of his civic duty," Baxter said defensively. "Besides that, John, what personal or otherwise gain would there be in it?"

"That may very well be, Wynne, albeit this inquiry has the makings of a debacle from the very beginning. The scheduled witness testimony in my opinion was rushed through, and the coroner, threatening the jury of some type of tampering has left the appearance to both jury and spectator that witness testimony has been coerced or manipulated. Not to mention, the other key witness, Doctor Phillips who was allowed to give the most superficial of testimony with a promise to later return at a future date. What date, the inquest has since been summed up."

"Detective, I certainly would agree, and I am of the same mind," Baxter said approvingly. "The facts should be laid out on the table, so the jury and officials can continue as they see fit, although the coroner is allowed to call a future inquest if some pertinent evidence does arise to make that type of demand."

"I still feel that there was some influence coming from somewhere in that room playing juror and coroner against each other, perhaps to see some impropriety."

"I have been thinking about what Doctor Macdonald said," Baxter interrupted, changing the subject.

"About what, Wynne?"

"Macdonald gave comment along the lines of the jury should not be in attendance for some testimony." Baxter offered.

"I was wondering if you were going to bring that point up, Wynne," I mused. "You suspect the witness to be Doctor Phillips."

I looked over at the coroner who refrained from commenting; however, I did detect a quizzical glance in response.

"It was not too difficult to figure it out who you were referring to, Wynne, given your feelings about the doctor and the fact that Phillips is so hesitant giving medical testimony when asked to testify. Especially in a case like this one, where such a gruesome account would turn the stomach of even the most hardened of spectators."

"I didn't say that, Stone, however, it is suspicious that the coroner mentioned this immediately after the doctor's statement."

"If anything, Wynne, it is more likely that Doctor Phillips would have commented to someone previous to his testimony about his professional misgivings in this area of giving exact medical testimony and a juror overheard his comment and then mentioned it to another juror."

"That is a lot of speculation, Detective," Baxter said smugly.

"Given Phillips' high moral command, do you think that the doctor would tamper with a jury?"

"Perhaps Doctor Phillips considers himself above reproach in his area of expertise and should not be subjected to questioning given the nature of the crime."

"Regardless, Wynne, it seems in the very least that the coroner, as you said at the beginning, has for some reason rushed through this entire affair. The question that remains is, why?"

"I can think of no good reason except that Macdonald was preoccupied with trying to keep the Justice of the Peace from declining to pay for the proceedings, and Macdonald rushed through any testimony that might be questioned later on in order to keep the inquest from being subjected to scrutiny."

"Do you think that Macdonald had any real grounds at all to support his recrimination to the jury and witnesses and only speculated that something was amiss, to make a grandiose spectacle simply, so the Justice of the Peace would pay for the inquest in his district?"

"It is hard to say, but I agree with you about Doctor Macdonald rushing through the proceedings, but the rest is all speculation, Stone. Inquests are not a perfect measure; I have had to live with that fact for years. Sometimes we find the appropriate answers, and a culprit is convicted, and other times we realize that we are only human and we have our limitations. We cannot allow those unfortunate circumstances to steer us into thinking that these inquest proceedings are fruitless."

"Maybe you are right, Wynne; but I think some outside influence may have intervened here and prohibited the reading of the medical evidence."

"How can you be so sure, Detective?"

"I am not completely sure; however, I do not think that the entire onus should be placed simply on Dr. Phillips' refusal to testify about distasteful evidence."

"Aside from those who are pursuing some moral high ground and have the power to restrict those in the scientific community, what possible reason would anyone else have to want to interfere in this inquest?"

"My guess would be anyone who wanted to stop any impending violence that is on the verge of erupting on the streets of Whitechapel. I believe that there may have been some political influence that may be involved here that rushed this inquest from the onslaught to stop the spreading fear that is resonating on London's streets."

"It sounds to me, Stone like you're making a case for a full-fledged conspiracy. Do you realize how many politicians would need to be involved to make such a conspiracy a reality?"

"It may sound furtive, Wynne, but perhaps the coroner's concerns are not unwarranted."

"How so, Detective?"

"The popularity of the Metropolitan Police Department is at an all-time low," I explained. "They are looking more and more like bunglers to the community and that same consensus is being passed on to the politicians in office, from their constituents. Perhaps by keeping the most horrific of details from the public eye, they are hoping to keep peace between London's society and the East End."

"That would be where Doctor Phillips would lend his part." Baxter paused. "Something; I know by past experience the doctor is more than willing to cooperate with. However, are these measures sufficient, Stone?"

"It depends on which vantage point you are willing to look from, Wynne."

"Alright, suppose you are right and due to the horrid details of this latest crime, these facts are being kept quiet, it wouldn't be enough to just stop the publishing of specifics or from allowing them to be publicly read at the inquest, sooner or later, Stone, they will come to light, gossip being what it is, the details of this latest murder will eventually be known."

"Yes, of course, Wynne, but I am not referring to those who are immediately affected in Whitechapel."

"Who then, Detective, the crimes are happening here not somewhere else, who could gain if not someone in office, in this district."

"I can imagine that after this latest victim, the Vigilance Committee will have used every single option available to them to get their point across to every politician who will listen about the effects this murderous rampage is having on Londoners. The Vigilance Committee's opinion is that this murderer is not being pursued by police to the limit of their abilities, and they are failing miserably in their responsibilities to the community."

"Are you serious, Stone?"

"I am, and I guarantee that things in Whitechapel are going to get a lot worse before they get any better."

"Stone, I hope you are not suggesting that things will get worse than what we already have now, with some deranged killer running unbridled about our city spilling the blood of doxies from one end of Whitechapel to the other," Baxter sighed.

"Things could get worse, however, not because of '*Jack the Ripper*,' but for other reasons."

"Such as, Detective?"

'Such as those using this murderer's exploits to influence change."

"Stone you sound as though someone has hired this killer to do his bidding and create havoc," Baxter shouted.

"I believe that '*Jack the Ripper*,' is being used, Wynne."

"By Jove old man, it sounds as though you have a name to pin to this political puppeteer. Or are you just surmising again?"

"No, name Wynne, but when the majority voice speaks, action is taken."

"Stone, you look as though you are ready to bust, what news have you heard?"

"The Commissioner of the Police, Sir Charles Warren has posted notices all over the East End police stations stating that they will grant the Queens Pardon to any accomplice other than the person who committed the murders for information leading to an arrest, and I have just heard that Sir Charles has tendered his resignation."

"Resigned!"

"Yes, a resignation that more than likely the man was forced to submit. One does not give up a position like that willingly, Wynne. Changes are being made all around us by those of influence, and the lives of those in Whitechapel are being affected by more than a deranged killer wreaking havoc in the back alleys of the East-End."

Chapter Twenty-six

The message read:

Detective Stone: Your presence, is requested immediately at Home Office.
Inspector Abberline.

With no hint as to why my presence was required, the cab ride to the Home Office allowed me time to think. The thought of yet another murder having been committed was predominant in my mind by the time the cab reached its destination. The door to Inspector Abberline's office was opened; however, I still gave a swift, sharp rap of my knuckle on the door jamb.

"Detective Stone come in," Abberline spoke, looking up from what seemed like an endless surplus of files on his desk that never seemed to diminish. "Stand at ease, Detective."

With a nod of my head, I waited for the inspector to finish whatever was occupying my time. Looking over Abberline's shoulder, I noticed the rain had started up again.

"If you were asked what your thoughts were about the guilt or innocence of Francis Tumblety, how would you respond?"

I watched Abberline sit back in his chair and fold his hands across his belly. The clock on the wall ticked loudly, as I took a few seconds to review every file in the murders in Whitechapel and seemingly every shred of evidence on Francis Tumblety, whether it was circumstantial or not.

"Tumblety is a charlatan, Sir, who profits by selling useless remedies to people who are gullible or those who cannot afford real medicines. The man professes to be a doctor and administers abortifacients and herbs to young girls who are in a family way to help them end their pregnancies. As we have discovered by the Montreal Police, Tumblety has been doing this for upwards of twenty years or more. He has also been charged with the wrongful death of a prostitute there. In my file, there are accounts from the American Union Army C.I.D., who had suspicions of his involvement in President Lincoln's assassination plot, given the nature of his relationship with David Herold. Here in England, our own investigation into the man has discovered Fenian ties and his suspected involvement in the bombings at the Yard. I also believe without the burden of proof that Tumblety is '*Jack the Ripper*' or is somehow involved with the murders of the seven women in Whitechapel, who also happen to be prostitutes. I believe that Tumblety has killed these women due to some uncontrollable desire to kill or by design for the purpose of some fictitious medical study, to collect specimens of the female anatomy. Either way, I would bet that Tumblety is our man."

I stood listening to the clock on the wall, wondering what response was coming from the inspector before speaking again.

"I realize that the evidence stacked against Tumblety is all circumstantial; however, the man's past and his association to prostitutes cannot be overlooked. Another point to be considered is Tumblety's lifestyle."

"How so, Detective?"

"Tumblety has a devil-may-care attitude, going from town to town, making a substantial living selling his herbs but is never around long enough to be made accountable for placing young women's lives in danger. Tumblety is a man of means, which allows him to afford to go from place to place under the guise of a practitioner. Tumblety also travels with a cavalier attitude for the law, and as soon as charges are laid against him for a crime or some kind of misconduct, the man hires a barrister, and within days he picks up and leaves town."

"This circumstantial evidence that we have against Tumblety could amount to nothing more than slander if the man had a good enough barrister."

I had known Abberline long enough to understand that the seemingly offhand statement was the man's way of thinking out loud.

"If the prosecutors are worth their salt, we should be able to find someone from his past to substantiate some charge. With the proof about the death of the prostitute in Montreal and all we know about these medicines and herbs Tumblety sells; I think we have a responsibility to stop him. It is my opinion that we would be saving a lot of young women's lives if we put him in jail. However, ...," I paused, struggling to find the right words to put forth to the inspector without sounding cheeky.

"However, what, Detective?" Abberline snapped.

"Well, Sir, if we wait too long, Tumblety will skip the country and likely head back to America, where we may never get him. We already know that Tumblety has questionable connections from here to Canada, and money is not an object."

"Do you think you can find him, by week's end?"

"Yes, sir."

"Bring him in," Abberline said without hesitation.

"Sir!"

"Detective, Francis Tumblety was scheduled in court today to answer charges of gross indecency; at his last appearance, the man entered a plea of not guilty and paid a substantial bail. Tumblety failed to appear in court today. If our suspicions are correct, then I want the man brought in. Take Sergeant Davis and two others, start with all the clubs and public houses near his last address. In the meantime, I will have men stationed at every station and dock in London that has a boat leaving for the Americas."

"Yes, Sir," I said, starting for the door. "Sir," I said before leaving.

"Yes, Detective?"

"What is Doctor Tumblety charged with, failing to appear, or the gross indecency charge?"

"Let me worry about the charges, for now, we will bring him in for failure to appear before the magistrate," Abberline responded.

"Yes, Sir," I said, walking out of the inspector's office.

From early morning on into the night, constables and detectives alike searched every public house, every lodging house, every alley, and every nook and cranny in London's East End; but Dr. Francis Tumblety was nowhere to be found. Tip after tip received by police informants was followed up, but none of the information led them to Tumblety's whereabouts. Docks were under surveillance, ships manifests were inspected along with their crews, and every possible escape route was covered, and, still, Tumblety somehow managed to slip through their fingers.

For two days, the search went on, at the end of each day discouragement, loomed over the heads of those involved in the manhunt, and the reality that the alleged Whitechapel killer had skipped on his bail and fled the country seemed to be a real possibility. Then on November twenty-third, the police received a tip from Mr. Spooner, the petty thief whose information had aided them in Tumblety's arrest at the gentleman's club. Sergeant Davis had tracked the petty thief down, and Spooner had told him that Tumblety was seen in a public house two nights before talking to a drover who was an acquaintance of his. According to Spooner's information, Tumblety was looking for transportation out of the city but did not want to go by train or by carriage. The drover told Spooner that his passenger paid him well to take him to Dover for passage on a ship, unfortunately, the man did not know to where. The man dropped Tumblety off in Dover and never laid eyes on him again.

With the mystery of Tumblety narrowly escaping through the Yard's fingertips and the man's whereabouts solved. I was painfully aware that the doctor had likely planned the entire scheme from the onset. I thought of Tumblety relishing in the victory, and even appreciated the irony of the doctor using an Irishman to help in his escape. I imagined that Tumblety must have gloated over the prospects of seeing the copper who arrested him defeated at every turn.

I began to think like Wynne Baxter and wonder if Tumblety was a will-o-the-wisp and able to vanish into thin air whenever the man wanted. The more I thought about the occurrence, I began to muse about the whereabouts of Detective Melville. If Tumblety was under surveillance, how could the man disappear and left the country?

During the search, detectives found a man from France who recognized a sketch of Tumblety that was handed about all the docks. The sailor swore that a man fitting Tumblety's description had indeed boarded a Channel Steamer of which he had recently been a passenger. Further questioning revealed that the steamer was headed for La Havre, France. With this knowledge, I immediately went to the Home Office with the information. Abberline, soon after, dispatched several detectives for France. Disappointed by not being one of those sent to France, I left the business of running the Yard's C.I.D division to the inspector and left for my rooms on Whitechapel Rd.

Later that evening, I sat thinking, nursing a cup of tea in my palms. I was disappointed, not so much, for allowing Tumblety to slip through my fingers, but more for feeling so inept. It had been a feeling that had not left me since the man had appeared in court. If it had been up to me, I would have had Tumblety arrested the moment the man did not show for court. Although, at the same time, I had to appreciate the man's cunning. To escape capture, Tumblety had boarded a Channel Ferry for France, using an alias. By reviewing the steamer's passenger logs, detectives discovered that Tumblety had boarded the ferry by using the name Frank Townsend. Presumably, the passage to France was, as it so happened, the same day that detectives had arrived in Dover. Once in France, it was assumed that Tumblety would most likely seek passage onto a ship to America. What made matters worse, was the feeling of responsibility, I had for not apprehending Tumblety before the doctor had a chance to flee to France. Though I had to live with my failure, there was still a light at the end of the tunnel. The Yard was working closely with the French Sûreté to capture Tumblety before the man had an opportunity to flee French soil.

Stubbornly, I refused to alter my position that Francis Tumblety was guilty of the crimes in Whitechapel. Albeit, there was much opposition to my theory, and very little support seemed available to help me try to prove the fact. It appeared at first glance that Inspector Abberline had given me a free hand in the case; though the more I thought of the circumstances leading up to my failure to bring Tumblety in, the more, I considered that I had been merely used by Inspector Abberline from the beginning of my assignment. In fact, it seemed that my primary role was to be a spy in Wynne Baxter's office. It was common knowledge that Baxter was known as the people's friend; and it was believed that someone in the East End knew who 'Jack' was. It was obvious now, that my placement in the coroner's office was to ferret out any knowledge, about the Vigilance

Committee or anything else that I could pass onto The Yard. Now, it seemed that I was the proverbial fly in the ointment, the scapegoat that everyone, including the top brass at Home Office, could blame for allowing Tumblety to escape. To top it all off, what was disappointing to me, was the idea that Inspector Abberline had been in on it from the beginning. Even though I had failed to apprehend Tumblety before the man left London and escaped to France, somewhere in the back of my mind, I felt like that the likelihood of such a thing happening was expected. Perhaps when I was given the assignment to pursue Tumblety, no one really expected me to accomplish the task in the first place. I might have been never expected to be able to get the information that led me to Dover, much less expected me to find out that the man was in France.

Complicating things all the more was the fact that the man was on foreign soil. There was now the involvement of a foreign police force and judicial system to obtain Tumblety's arrest and extradition. Although to me, all of this seemed a necessary evil to bring the villain to justice, but somehow that did not seem to be a priority for my superiors.

After much thought, I was nowhere closer to figuring out a plan to get Tumblety back on English soil, especially with the evidence that I had. It was in my mind to find out what had prompted Inspector Abberline`s sudden change in wanting Tumblety to be brought before a judge in the first place on such a trifling charge, if the goal was not to follow through with arresting the man. Granted, the man had skipped bail, but the charge was so insignificant that it hardly seemed warranted to produce a manhunt unless some new evidence could be provided. It appeared of late, I was spending more and more time trying to convince my colleagues of Tumblety`s guilt than anything else. The more I chewed on the problem, the more I realized that there was more here than what met the eye. Tumblety had proven to be smarter than what I would have first anticipated. The pretended doctor had slipped through the authority's fingers more easily than I would have initially given the man credit. Tumblety had chosen an avenue of escape least expected by going to La Havre France. In fact, it would seem that the man's plan appeared to be the actions of a man knowing pursuit was imminent, not the plan of a petty criminal running scared for his life. The more I reviewed the events of the last week, the more I began to see that the approach of the Irishman was all a part of an elaborate game that Tumblety must have put into motion from the time that the man found out about being pursued by police. It became blatantly clear to me that Tumblety's Fenian ties were more significant than what anyone had initially believed. The Irish had proven their resourcefulness in the past, but this may have proved to be much more than that. Perhaps all of the events leading up to Tumblety leaving the country had been little more than a cat and mouse game that Tumblety had been playing for many years with authorities.

As I sat in the dark nursing my tea, I wondered if there was something else going on, something, in which I had been kept entirely in the dark. Tumblety's ultimate plans of leaving London may have been a topic of conversation behind the closed doors at Home Office, long before the doctor failed to appear before the magistrate. It was quite conceivable that Inspector Abberline, and others in command, were merely using Tumblety to gain knowledge about any Fenian ties and associates that they would not otherwise have known about. It was conceivable that my superiors had discovered by their surveillance that Tumblety was preparing to leave the country well in advance. What if Tumblety had been pursued and watched at every turn since the doctor left Dover. Special Branch may have sought the Fenian connections that the man had gained on his many trips to Europe? It sounded incredibly like fiction, but there had to be a reason why Inspector Abberline had not instigated Tumblety's arrest until the doctor had skipped the city and was subsequently willing to allow Tumblety to waltz out of France to America, where chances of extradition were slim, if not impossible.

It was now evident that Tumblety would need some type of connection, not only to leave London but to also find passage aboard a French steamer. The Fenian connections that the man was suspected of having were just the type of associations that Tumblety could use to provide other means than public transportation. They could provide the necessary documents, a boarding pass, all under an assumed name to escape the country. Being an American, Tumblety would also need someone in La Havre that could set him up with accommodation and the times and dates of ship departures for America. Although Channel steamers were making trips to France regularly, having someone in France that could help with the language barrier would be an asset. These connections could give Tumblety assistance in paying ship captains to keep his boarding a secret. These types of services would be costly, though Tumblety had the funds to pay from the sales of his spurious medicines. The more I reviewed the events over the last several days, the more I realized that Tumblety's escape had been expected, and likely monitored carefully. What bothered me more than Tumblety's escape was the fact that I had been instrumental in the operation all the time.

The next morning, I was up early, dressed, and headed for my office before the rest of the household had awakened. The leaden sky promised only rain, and the cold morning matched my mood as I boarded a hackney for my office. Recapturing the moments from the previous evening did little for my mood, coupled with no sleep and a headache that refused to leave me, made me feel less than cheery.

"Stone, you are up an at 'em early!" Baxter greeted me in his usual exuberance.

Over tea, I described the events that took place since Tumblety had left London. Unusually, Baxter sat quietly while I spoke, offering little and not interrupting me.

"What do you suppose your Home Office will do now?" Baxter asked, finally.

"I haven't the faintest idea, Wynne."

"If your theory is correct, Detective, what is the result of the waiting game that Inspector Abberline is playing? Does the man not realize his hesitation increases the odds that Tumblety will never be caught?"

"If I am right, Wynne, and I believe that I am, in the grander scheme of things, I don't think that Tumblety's arrest is as important as we might believe."

"Are you saying that the murders of seven women, are not significant, Stone, come now, what could be more important than bringing this alleged murderer to justice?"

"Again, Wynne, I wish I knew."

Two hours later, I took the granite steps two at a time to the Home Office front door. Anxiously, I waited outside Inspector Abberline's office. Forty-five minutes ticked by on the large clock that hung at the top of the hall before the door finally opened. Sir Robert Anderson was the first to exit and then another man whom I knew but had never met. This man's name was James Monroe, who had become commissioner of police sometime in December, replacing Sir Charles Warren. Since Sir Charles' resignation, much gossip had been circulating, most of which told a story about a man who had grown weary of the constant criticism of the press and had given in to the pressure and resigned early in November. Neither man acknowledged my presence; however, Inspector Abberline ushered me in with a cold nod of his head.

"Detective, Stone, what can I do for you?"

"I would like to know what we are doing about the Tumblety situation, Sir."

"What situation is that, Detective?"

I looked at the inspector calmly for a moment, unsure how to broach the topic of going to France and searching for Tumblety myself. The inspector's apparent lack of concern left me uneasy and unsure of what to say next.

"The situation, of extraditing Tumblety back to London, to stand trial, Sir. That is before the man leaves for America."

"No, need to worry about that, Stone, besides there is plenty of cases that need our attention here in London."

"What about Tumblety?"

"What about him, Detective?"

"Are we going to allow him to slip through our fingers without doing anything?"

"No one is allowing anything of the kind, Stone!" Abberline retorted sharply.

Backing down, I felt the sharp edge in the inspector's tone as much as heard it.

"So, I guess that is it then, isn't it, Sir."

"Detective," Abberline began. "Unfortunately, there are things afoot that you were not made privy to, and most likely never will be. It is suffice to say that Tumblety was already in France when you were assigned to arrest him," Abberline replied, holding up his hand to stave off any protest. "We have reason to believe that Tumblety was on a Channel Steamer the day you found out the information about the man leaving London. I received the report from our Special Branch operative William Melville in France. As we speak, I am afraid that Tumblety has already gained passage back to America."

I looked at the inspector without saying a word, although; the look on my face must have been enough that Abberline saw an explanation was warranted.

"We have had operatives in France for some time now. They are a part of a newly formed division called Special Irish Branch. Since the planned attack on the Queen on her Jubilee," Abberline paused. "Again, I must add Detective, that there are certain facts that remain undisclosed to you; however, it has been this department's goal to keep an eye on *Fenian movements since Francis Millen's conspiracy and the attempted assassination of Queen Victoria.* We have several operatives in France seeking out the lengths and the widths of the Fenian organization which is vaster than we would have initially believed. Since that time, we have tried to, shall we say, be more abreast of their movements. The '*Dynamite Wars*' have proved to us that the Fenian movements have sympathizers as far as America, and they grow more powerful every day. These sympathizers have demonstrated that they will supply and fund these criminal activities by any means at their disposal. It is these connections that we are intent on seeking out and eliminating. However, the tentacles of the Fenian organization are far more numerous than we would have believed, and we aim to infiltrate these groups and place ourselves one step ahead of them. Unfortunately, we were late in our attempts to notify our operative in France, and Mr. Melville was unable to intercept Mr. Tumblety. We have since learned that the doctor is already on his way to America."

"Sir, if I may be so bold," I said, without thinking. "Were you intent on catching Tumblety for the murders in Whitechapel, or was the man simply allowed to escape unmolested, so our agents could find out information on these connections you speak of?"

"I will put this as bluntly as possible, Detective, and leave it at that. There are those here at Home Office who, mainly because of the lack of evidence, do not share our enthusiasm with putting an American on trial especially a trial that involves the murders of six prostitutes that have been publicized the world over."

"Murder, is murder, Sir, no matter who the victim is," I said raising my voice.

"Detective, I hope you are not going to stand there and presume to lecture me on the merits of law," Abberline shouted! "I will explain in brief, Detective that foreign relationships are delicate, to say the least without deliberately jeopardizing one with unsubstantiated accusations on an American citizen. Not to mention, as you say, there was the added benefit of finding out any other ties Mr. Tumblety may have in France and America. These are the intricacies that far outweighed any unsubstantiated charges that we could bring against the man which may have been thrown out of court anyway. Having said that, you are now apprised of only need to know information and the outcome, although not superlative, the end justifies the means, and we are well rid of Tumblety one way or the other. I trust this is far from satisfactory to you, Detective, but it will have to suffice."

Hearing Abberline's definitive statement about Tumblety's escape, I knew that to continue to belabor the subject was useless.

"Sir if I may, could I have my resignation submitted."

"Yes, I submitted it this morning Stone, and here."

"What is this?" I asked taking the envelope.

"Your letter of reference Stone."

Abberline extended his hand and nodded.

Shouting for a cab, I sorted through all that I had learned in the inspector's office.

Baxter sat in his office scribbling furiously, when I walked by, with my mind buzzing, I left the coroner to his own work and retreated to my office. Beleaguered from the lack of answers from the Home Office and tired from trying to persuade my superiors about Tumblety, I sat with my chin resting on my knuckles. After several minutes, I heard the familiar rattle of teacup and saucer coming up the hallway.

"Stone, I took the liberty of making tea, after seeing your face as you stole by my office door; I assumed you were of the need of a hot cup," Baxter exclaimed.

"Thanks, Wynne, I could use one."

"I take it your reception at the Home Office was none too amicable?" Baxter said, pouring tea into the cups on the desk.

"Not at all, Wynne," I said, picking up the cup and saucer. "It seems the British Government is more interested in diplomacy and maintaining foreign affairs than bringing a criminal to justice."

"How so, Detective, I was always under the impression that the laws of the land were a top priority to the powers that be, if for no other reason than to keep our great country the power we are today," Wynne answered defensively.

"The law," I huffed. "It would seem, is a fickle maiden, Wynne."

"You seem down on jolly old England what?"

"Not down on England, Wynne, just on the powers in control."

"Why is that, Detective?"

"Wynne, the citizen, is only regarded as a means to get into office, by those who would have us believe we are in control of our electoral government, and our decisions are our own, but in reality, we are only pawns and those we have elected are in office for their own purposes."

"Well, that sounds rather depressing, Detective."

"Wynne, we had a real suspect in our grasp for the first time since this ugliness began. One, who not only has charges against him in a suspicious death of a prostitute, but has a history of all types of criminal behavior, and yet, we allowed this man to walk out of jail knowing there was a strong possibility of a nonappearance for his court date."

"Detective, we all have superiors," Baxter offered. "Even those who are in positions of high authority, still, have the public to answer to."

"That may be, Wynne, but do seven dead women mean less in Whitechapel than they do on Milk Street in the city of London. Their blood runs just as red, and they have families who loved them just like you and I. Don't they deserve the same justice, or should they be treated differently because they were prostitutes."

"Of course, they do, Stone, but...!" Baxter's voice trailed off.

"Don't tell me you are defending these bloody politicians?"

"Don't be daft, Stone, of course, I don't agree with everything our government says or does, however, we have to look at this thing more objectively. Some circumstances demand that certain policies be put into action that protect our future, our allies, and routes of trade and commerce."

"So, trade and commerce are more important than bringing this killer to justice?"

"Absolutely not John, but cooler heads must prevail, sometimes."

"Meaning what, Wynne?"

"Meaning, Detective there is the greater good to consider. Do I think that this Tumblety chap deserves to be in jail, unequivocally and without a doubt? However, do I think that the man should be extradited from

America, based on the evidence that we have," Baxter paused? "Probably not, John."

"Regardless, Wynne, allowances could have been made, until enough evidence was secured."

"And in the meantime, if it was an Englishman in an American prison, what would you expect from our government."

I heard my friend loud and clear, and stubbornly refused to answer.

"Stone, the newspapers have had a field day with these murders, the bloody Americans probably know as much about these crimes as we do. Can you imagine if we tried to bring this Yank over here to stand trial? Given the nature of the crimes and having no murder weapon or eyewitness to speak of, the chances of extradition are unlikely. We would need to catch the blackheart standing over a dead body with a blade and blood on his hands before we could get a conviction. Even then with the funds you say Tumblety has at his disposal, the man would have the best barrister money could buy. Tumblety would probably still waltz out of the courtroom just to avoid an international scandal, and would likely be on a ship in a week without as much as a smack on the hand."

Feeling like a scolded child, I let my temper cool knowing full well that Baxter was right. Slumping in my chair at the desk, I bent forward with my face in my hands. Feeling defeated, I looked Baxter, who sat quietly, preoccupied with his own thoughts.

"I guess you're right, Wynne. The onus ultimately lands back on us," I said, struggling with the truth. "If we had of done our jobs, Tumblety would not have walked out of jail with little more than the charge of gross indecency, we had him on. In any event, if the man was brought to trial as you say his barrister would have had a field day, given the evidence we have. It would appear that Doctor Francis Tumblety is far smarter than we gave me credit for."

"What do you mean by that, John?"

"If I didn't know any better, I would think that Tumblety allowed himself to be caught and charged with gross indecency. Something so trivial that extradition would have been laughed at by the American State Department."

"It would have been a gross miscarriage of justice to have held the man any longer, John".

"Yes, Wynne, but we have been running around like a dog chasing its tail from the beginning, without a witness we have nothing. Although, there is something here that strikes me as familiar?"

"Familiar, how so, John."

"Familiar as in this Doctor Tumblety, has been here before, in front of a judge on similar charges, seemingly of little consequence and then the man makes off like a bandit, either paying for some slick barrister to file a habeas corpus or simply pays some fine and is set free," I said thinking. "I am wondering if this is all part of some game the man likes to play with authorities."

"To what end or gain, John? I thought anonymity was what Tumblety favored above all else, to sell his medicines and do his surgeries?"

"I wish I knew," I answered. "Perhaps out of sheer boredom Tumblety travels about with his medicines and moves from town to town and gets himself arrested on seemingly inconsequential charges to draw suspicion away from himself, and his intended plots and schemes."

"Like some kind of magician's use of smoke and mirrors?"

"Perhaps Wynne, but in the end, for all of our policing and all of our courts, we have failed these women by not bringing the culprit to justice."

"That seems a rather dismal picture of our efforts, Detective," Baxter groaned. "I would also like to think over the years that I have done some good, for king and country."

"Of course, Wynne, but there should be allowances for law enforcement in circumstances like Tumblety who are repeat offenders and get away because our court system demands that if we don't catch a killer with a smoking gun standing over a victim, or in this case a bloodied knife, they walk free with no fear of reprisal."

"I am not criticizing, Detective, but if we do that for one, then we have to do it for the masses, don't we?"

"Yes, of course."

"I am on your side, Stone, and feel just as responsible as you do, but there are reasons why we have the laws in place that we do so that we don't put a noose around the wrong man's neck. It is up to us to prove beyond a shadow of a doubt that the man we have in custody is guilty of the crime we have arrested him for. Albeit, our court of law alone has not proven to be a foolproof method of demonstrating the twixt of right and wrong."

"You are right there, Wynne and in the matter of the case against Doctor Francis Tumblety, we can't prove that the man killed Alenka with his medicines any more than we could prove that the man is "*Jack the Ripper*" and most likely, never will."

"They say all good things come to those who wait, Detective," Baxter said, trying to console his friend. "Perhaps Francis Tumblety will meet his Maker in some other untimely way."

"Perhaps, Wynne, but what do you say to Alenka's grandmother, that her killer has most likely gone free without any fear of ever being brought to justice?"

"That my dear boy is a burden that we must bear. Although, I thought you were the one that never allowed yourself to become too emotionally attached to your work?

"It is too late for that, Wynne; I am making this personal."

"How Detective, the man you want, has left the country."

"Yes, but…"

"But what, Detective, what are you planning to do?"

"My job, for one thing, Wynne," I said, getting up from my desk. "This isn't over for me, not by a long shot."

"Are you going to be alright, Stone?" Baxter asked.

"I will be Wynne," I said, handing the coroner the letter of reference. "I have just resigned my position in The Yard."

Chapter Twenty-seven

On the thirty-first of May, in the year of our Lord, 1889 body parts began to appear along the River Thames for the second time in London's history. A segment of a thigh, the hip to the knee found wrapped in a woman's undergarment, and a part of a woman's tweed ulster was gathered together and brought to Inspector John Tunbridge of C.I.D. Scotland Yard. The only clue as to the identity of the deceased was the name L. E. Fisher which was written on the waistband of the undergarment. In the following days, more pieces of human remains were found along the Thames. On June the fourth, at half-past ten in the morning, John Regan, a dock worker, saw some boys throwing stones at a bundle floating near St. George's Stair, at Horselydown. Later that day, under Albert Bridge, which connected Chelsea on the north bank to Battersea on the south bank, Isaac Brett, a woodchopper in Chelsea, found another bundle. The bundle contained another leg, which was wrapped in another piece of ulster, held together with a bootlace. On June the sixth, Joseph Davis, a gardener who worked at Battersea Park, found more human remains wrapped in linen under some shrubbery. Two days later, on June the eighth, Claude Mellor, while walking on the road and walkway along the north bank of the River Thames at the Chelsea Embankment, found a bundle that had been washed up between the fence rails on a property belonging to Percy Shelley.

By the end of June, the last pieces of what doctors knew to be a young woman's body had been found. It was estimated that the body parts had been discarded at several destinations along the Thames coming ashore to end up in bushes, gardens, or up against fences in various regions. The gossip on the streets of London was that the city had been cursed, and the monster that refused to leave the city's prostitutes alone had returned.

Due to the varied regions where the body parts were found, several doctors and police surgeons from various jurisdictions were involved in an attempt to assemble the sections of parts collected. It was found that the remains were from one body and were said to have belonged to a young woman in her early twenties. They were, however, unable to identify the young woman for the one essential piece of the woman's anatomy that could make identification fundamentally possible had not yet washed up on the banks of the Thames River, that being the head.

The London Evening Star June fourth, 1889.

[Sic] *"The denizens of Horselydown, on the southern side of the Thames, were thrown into a fever of excitement this morning, by the discovery in the river of the portions of a woman's body cut into pieces. Shortly afterward a parcel of female clothing was found at Battersea. Both the fragments of the body and the clothes were wrapped in pieces of cloth, which together had comprised a pair of woman's drawers. On the waistband of the drawers was the name 'Fisher' in indelible ink. It is evident that the clothing found belongs to the murdered woman. The portions of the trunk showed the woman to have been large and well developed. They had apparently been in the water for ten days. The discovery has revived the excitement which prevailed during the period of the Whitechapel horrors, and is generally believed that 'Jack the Ripper' has resumed his bloody work."*

I reread the Evening Star article several times before tossing it across my desk. The body parts kept showing up on the banks of the Thames, and there was nothing new found by investigators that could pinpoint who the killer or killers were. To make matters worse, the segments were found at

413

different locales, leaving police guessing as to the origins of the murder and where the pieces of the murdered woman had been placed into the Thames after the killer had dissected his victim's body. With no witnesses to the crime, the fact remained that there was nothing police could do but wait for the killer to be seen dumping parts of his victim's bodies into the river. After enjoying a lull in the bad publicity that police had been getting, with the discovery of the body parts along the Thames, a whole new onslaught criticism erupted from every newsagent in London. The police confronted these new criticisms with several excuses, among which was the size of London's boundaries and the limited manpower at their disposal to police these boundaries. Nothing more could be done until a viable witness came forth and gave evidence as to who was committing the murders.

"I see you are reading the papers, Stone?" Baxter said none too enthusiastically, spreading the rolled-up London Times on my desk, slapping the flat of his hand across it. "This Thames killer has been at it again," Baxter thumped the paper with a meaty finger, pointing to the article.

"Yes, I know Wynne," I said, looking at the article that the coroner had pinpointed. "I have been going over the area that the body parts were found, trying to make heads or tails of it. However, as near as I can figure, the body parts seemed to have been dumped all along the Thames, having not one point, but several points of entry where the severed pieces were deposited."

"How can you be so certain, Detective?" Baxter asked, picking up the copy of the London Times perusing it again.

"There is nothing specific in the article, Wynne, but I have been thinking about the Thames and its bridges, in conjunction with where the body parts were found."

"Are you thinking that this monster may have dropped the pieces off more than one bridge?"

"Do you have a map of the Thames in your office, Wynne."

I knew full well that the coroner's office held a veritable treasure trove of investigative tools that the man had accumulated over the years. The coroner had to be prepared for any set of circumstances while in the performance of his duties.

"I should say I do, Stone," Baxter said, rising out of his chair.

414

As I waited for Baxter to return, I thought of the Thames and the serpentine flow the river took into the North Sea.

"Sorry old boy, it took me some time to find this." Baxter placed a rolled-up map on the desk and turned, "By, the by I have started a spot of tea." Without another word and not waiting for a response, Baxter was gone.

Unrolling the four-foot square map, I placed a paperweight on one corner and held the other side with the palm of my hand. Tracing my finger along with the map that showed sections of the Thames as it snaked its way along the many districts of London.

"Here, we are dear boy," Baxter said, returning after a few minutes with a tray in hand setting it on the edge of the map, holding its rolling edge flat.

With pen in hand, I went to work, scribbling on the map the several bridges and districts that bisected the Thames.

"Now, let's see," Baxter said, pouring tea and sliding a cup across the desk. "There is Wandsworth Bridge, Albert Bridge at Chelsea and Battersea, Westminster Bridge at Westminster and Lambeth, Waterloo Bridge, Blackfriars Bridge, Southwark Bridge at Wapping and Southwark, and then, of course, London Bridge, and Tower Bridge."

Slurping on his tea, the coroner looked over the rim of his cup.

"Did, I miss anything?"

"No, Wynne, but I think, we should concentrate on the bridges from Wandsworth Bridge to Waterloo Bridge."

"Why is that, John?" Baxter stood and poured himself more tea.

"I am thinking of the flow and ebb of the Thames, Wynne," I said, tapping the map with the tip of my finger.

"The Thames flows west to east, and," Baxter said. "I know the spring tides occur every two weeks."

"How do you know so much about the Thames, Wynne?"

"I have, from time to time over the years as coroner, held several inquests into deaths occurring in the Thames, she has taken the life of many a Londoner, Detective."

"Alright, the currents flow from west to east, which could mean that this killer could throw his bundles off of Wandsworth Bridge or Albert Bridge, for that matter and the current could carry the segments of the body as far as London Bridge."

415

"Don't forget tidal flow, Detective," Baxter offered, rising and setting his cup and saucer on the desk refilling it from the pot. "I have seen the Thames rise and drop as much as twenty feet."

Lifting my cup to my lips, I sipped the scalding tea as Baxter sat down opposite.

"Twenty feet!"

"Yes."

"This really isn't helping, Wynne. This bloke could be dropping his collection of body parts anywhere along the Thames. There is no way we could guess any point of origin, even if there was only one."

"I am sorry to be the bearer of bad news, Stone," Wynne apologized.

"There is no need, Wynne, it is just the idea that here we are left sitting and waiting until this creature strikes again. Unless this villain is spotted dropping pieces of his next victim off a bridge into the drink, we are left with no other recourse but to wait for him to kill another innocent, and there is absolutely nothing we can do to stop him."

The Graphic, Saturday June 22, 1889, Issue 1021,

Illustrated Newspapers.

[Sic] The Thames Mystery: The Coroner's inquest on Monday, among other evidence given, was that of Mr. Thomas Bond, surgeon at Westminster Hospital to the A. Division of police, in whose hands had been placed the mutilated remains found from time to time in the Thames. I added to my first report that all the parts examined belonged to the same body, that of a woman, whose age was between twenty-three and twenty-five. The condition of the ring-finger of the left hand showed that a ring had been removed soon before or after death, and from the hands themselves it was clear that the deceased was not accustomed to manual labor. The division of the parts displayed, not the anatomical skill of the surgeon, but the practical knowledge of the butcher or the knacker. There was a great similarity between the condition of the remains and that of those found at Rainham and at the new police buildings on the Thames Embankment. The head had not been found, if it had been thrown into the

river it would probably have sunk. As the police are pursuing their hitherto result less researches, the inquiry was adjourned to Monday July first."

I sat staring at the article for several minutes, contemplating the age of the latest victim, thinking it was a definite stickler for me to convince anyone of my theory behind the motive into all the unsolved murders happening along the Thames. It would appear that the maniacal killer had either relaxed his strict guidelines for choosing victims, or the killer chose each victim whenever and wherever the opportunity presented itself. There was also the possibility that a murder was committed and the body cut up like the others to draw suspicion from the culprit. The one aspect that appeared consistent was the limbs that kept appearing up and down the Thames were from women who had not seen the rough toil of a workhouse. The other factor mentioned in the article that I found most eye-opening was the ring that was missing from the victim's hand; certainly, robbery was not a plausible motive. Taken before or after her death, mattered little I truly believed that the killer still sought some type of reminder of the occasion. To my way of thinking, the killer displayed the need to show his superiority or power over these women. I pondered if the ring was a wedding ring or some promise ring given by a sweetheart? I remembered distinctly the testimony given by Dr. George Bagster Phillips at Annie Chapman's inquest. The doctor said, *'There was an abrasion over the ring finger, with distinct markings of a ring or rings.'* No matter how I looked at the comparisons between the cases, there was something cohesive to all the murders, whether in Whitechapel or up in down the Thames, there was still a small shred of similarity, nothing conclusive, but something that kept tying the crimes together.

Not for a moment did coincidence cross my mind. A coincidence was a word used only when any other explanation failed to present itself. However, no matter how I looked at each case, there were definitely significant differences between the Whitechapel murders and the Thames murders. It went without saying that *'Jack the Ripper'* did not hold his victims against their will, kill them, dissect their bodies, and float the pieces down the Thames. Which brought me back to why there were so many similarities in the murdered victims, and why the killer cut up his

417

victims? The only conceivable reason was to hide the evidence of the crime. So, what underlying desire led this man to kill these women in the first place? No matter what case or which set of circumstances I examined, the same questions went unanswered. Were the women prostitutes, was the killer a medical student or was the man, a butcher by profession who hated women?

There was only one thing that I was utterly sure of though in the Thames murders. The killer chose women of class and distinction. This particular trait was made evident by the lack of callouses and distinctive marks on the hands that would come from hard labor. Other than that, of the women found, there was not a specific hair color, or a particular age, or any trait that would reveal why the victim was chosen in the first place. I believed that this killer chose his quarries based merely on gender and solely to kill them. I was confident that the only way to catch such a killer was to somehow capture the man in the act.

The primary differences in the Thames deaths brought me right back to where I had left off in the Whitechapel murders. I ascertained that in both cases, they were dealing with a man who was most likely a hater of the female gender, and that was the extent of the knowledge of the person or persons behind either crime. *'Jack, the Ripper,'* killed only prostitutes, and they were no closer to catching him then they were after the first victim was found. In both cases, the victims were all female, and that was where the similarities ended. The motive and opportunity for each crime would be forever lost to investigators until they had a suspect in custody.

As I looked at the names of the victims and the nameless victims that had yet to be identified, I was horrified to think that the city of London was filled with any number of potential murderers ready to copy *'Jack, the Ripper'* or this Thames killer, to cover up any number of unrelated murders.

The Times July 4, 1889

[Sic] Yesterday afternoon Mr. Wynne E. Baxter Coroner for South-east Middlesex, resumed his adjourned inquiry at the Vestry hall, Wapping, respecting the finding of a portion of the remains of a human body, supposed to form part of the limbs of a woman named Elizabeth Jackson,

which were found in the river Thames ... Detective Inspector Tonbridge (Scotland Yard) and Detective Inspector Regan watched the case for the Criminal Investigation Department. On the last occasion a witness proved having his attention down to something wrapped in a portion of a pair of woman's drawers, which some boys were throwing stones at while it was floating in the water near the foreshore off Wapping. The witness got it ashore, and, finding the parcel to contain the remains of a human body, I called the attention of the Wapping police to the discovery, and they took charge of the portions and removed them to the mortuary, where they were seen by the divisional surgeon. Dr. Michael M'Coy, of three hundred Commercial Road, assistant divisional surgeon, said on Tuesday the fourth of June last, I was called to the Thames police station, Wapping, where I was shown a portion of a human body. I found it to be two pieces of flesh of the front of a woman's abdomen and the uterus. Witness should say the woman had been pregnant about eight months. Inspector J. Tonbridge stated that the portion of a woman seen by the jury was taken after the inquest to the Battersea Mortuary. Other portions were subsequently found in the Thames – the whole body, with the exception of the head, a hand, and some internal organs. An inquest had been held at Battersea, and Dr. Bond had proved that all the portions, including the part in question, belonged to the same body. The latter had been recognized by the clothing and marks as that of Elizabeth Jackson, aged twenty-four years, a single woman, of no occupation, whose last known address was fourteen Turk's road. The medical evidence proved that the cutting up took place after death, and there was nothing to show what was the cause of death. There was no evidence as to how the parts got into the river. The coroner said that was all the evidence I proposed to receive. Other portions had been found at the West End and an inquest had been held and adjourned at Battersea. I suggested that the jury return a formal verdict. The jury returned a verdict to the effect that the portion of the body found at Wapping was part of the body of Elizabeth Jackson but how she came by her death or how the parts got into the water there was no evidence to show."

The evening was well upon the city, and the lamp on my desk hissed as I turned up the wick. The outcome of the inquest into Elizabeth Jackson's death was predictable. Held strictly as a formality since only two of the

419

pieces of Jackson's bundled up body had been found in Baxter's district. Nothing new was brought to light as far as the circumstances of how a twenty-four-year-old woman had been killed and then cut up by a person or persons unknown and have her body tossed into the Thames.

Whether by accident, or design the piece of the woman's anatomy to wash up in Baxter's district was the portion containing the young woman's abdomen and lower extremities. The other disturbing aspect of the case was the fact that doctors were able to reveal after the autopsy of the anatomy was that the young woman had been eight months pregnant, making the case a double murder. The rap at my office door was simply a courtesy, not waiting for an answer, Baxter shuffled in, paper in hand.

"I see you have already read it, John," Baxter huffed.

I watched Baxter settle into the seat opposite tapping, the rolled-up newspaper against his knee.

"Yes."

Not feeling like talking the thought of the unborn child murdered before his or her eyes were able to see the light of day had sickened me. It was at these times when I relived those moments in the cases; surrounded by so much death that I truly began to hate all the dark and horrid things I was subjected to as a police officer. It physically repulsed me to think that the world could produce something so despicable and vile, that the life of a child mattered so little. For it was undoubtedly the world and all its influences that had created this monster, for God never intended HIs creation to turn out the way that it had.

The London Times, July 5th, 1889. The Thames

Mystery.

[Sic] Yesterday Mr. A. Braxton Hicks the Mid-Surrey Coroner, resumed for the third time at the Star and Garter, Battersea, as to the death of Elizabeth Jackson, whose mutilated remains were found in various parts of the Thames, on the Embankment, and in Battersea Park. The first witness called was a Margaret Minter, three Cheyne-row who said she had received from Mrs. Girard's an ulster, which she gave about two months ago to Elizabeth Jackson. Witness had known her and her sisters about

two years. Two months ago, she had seen Elizabeth in the street looking very shabby, and had given her three pence to buy food. Witness recognized a skirt produced as one worn by the deceased girl. The girl said she had been living with a man who had been unkind to her, and had finally left her. At this interview witness recommended her to go to the union, but she said her parents were there, and she did not want them to know she was with child. She also said she had no home, and had slept on the Embankment the night before. On the twentieth of May witness gave her the ulster and some food. The twenty-first was the last time witness saw her, and she was wearing the ulster. Johanna Keefe sister to last witness, said she had known Elizabeth Jackson and saw her at her sister's where she gave her some black cotton to sew a string on an under-garment which witness identified, as well as the skirt and ulster. Having recapitulated much of the evidence given by her sister, noticed nails of the victim were bitten to the quick. Annie Dwyer, of fourteen, Turk's-row Chelsea, said she kept a lodging house there. She had known the deceased about two years and last saw her about eight weeks ago, said she was very dirty and untidy. Jennie Lee, of fourteen, Turk's-row said she had known the deceased Lizzie Jackson two years. Confirmed former evidence of the destitution of the girl. Witness last saw her on the Monday before Whit Sunday, and she was then with a man who had on light moleskin trousers, dark cloth coat, and a rough cap, and she thought I was a navy. She was wearing the check ulster and skirt produced and went away with the man to Battersea. Elizabeth Pomeroy gave similar evidence. Kate Paine of five, Manilla-street, Millwall proved letting a room to a man and the deceased on the eighteenth of April at four shillings per week. He used her very roughly, and knocked her about and he left her on the twenty-eighth, and the woman went away on the next day. They owed six shillings, and took a quilt off of the bed. The man was called John Fairclough, and deceased, who wore a ring, said he was her husband. She was five months advanced in pregnancy at the time. She remembered the man Fairclough, otherwise known as Smith, and had thus described him to the police: - Age about thirty-seven, height five feet nine inches, complexion, fair, clean shaven, slightly pitted with smallpox, and deaf. His nose was twisted as if it had been broken, and had steel marks on the left hand. When last she saw him, he was dressed in a light green and black striped jacket, light striped trousers, with a piece of light check sewn into the waist. He also

421

had on a blue and white striped Oxford shirt, a white muffler, laced boots, light gray or mouse colored felt hat and also carried a soft cap with a peak of some material. The Coroner added that in the police description he was stated to be a native of Cambridgeshire a miller and millstone dresser, and had been discharged from the third Battalion Grenadier Guards. The Inquiry adjourned for three weeks."

Baxter finished reading the Times and then laid the paper across his knees, resting his arms on the creaking rests of the chair. After several minutes Baxter methodically started to stuff his pipe, speaking only after finishing, and the pipe was firmly placed in his mouth.

"What do you make of that bit of business, Stone?"

"I take it, you are not a fan of Mr. A. Braxton Hicks, Wynne?"

I commented, watching Baxter strike a match and touched the flame to the tobacco in the bowl of his pipe. I waited, watching the match flare and the tobacco ignited by the flame.

"On the contrary, John, I found Hicks to be totally professional in all his capacities," Baxter answered, speaking between the drawing on the pipe and the blowing out of the vibrant blue smoke above his head.

"What is it, that is bothering you than, Wynne?"

I asked, wondering whether it was the inquiry that Hicks had held in Elizabeth Jackson's death or the article that covered the inquiry.

"Here we are with five of the most brutal murders that I have ever witnessed, or the world for that matter, has ever heard of, and we have several witnesses that had seen the victim only moments before she was murdered and they could not give as good a description of an apple as these women have done of this Fairclough chap."

I watched Baxter clench his teeth around the pipe and suck more of the tobacco smoke into his lungs.

"I was thinking about that myself, Wynne. I too, find it incredibly hard to believe that these women could remember so much detail of a man they saw for only a few minutes in passing."

"Age, about thirty-seven ...." Baxter picked up the paper and began to read aloud.

"I know, Wynne, five-feet-nine-inches in height, fair complexion, everything right down to the felt hat. The only thing missing from Fairclough's description that could make him a tangible suspect in the

Whitechapel murders is a mustache. Though that alone would have been no real obstacle to get around, Wynne; however, I dismissed any and all other thoughts after I contacted, Detective Inspector Tonbridge about any leads they may have on John Fairclough's whereabouts on the night in question."

"Well, don't leave me in suspense, Stone; what did Tonbridge have to say?" Baxter asked as he peered over the top of the newspaper.

"The inspector sent me a cable. Fairclough was not even in London at the time of the murder. The man was as far away as High Wycombe when Jackson was murdered, which is approximately thirty miles from London," I said, scribbling on a pad in front of me.

"That is a bit of a stretch isn't it Stone."

"Yes, it is. Not to mention, the fact that Fairclough had been looking for work every step of the way, so there is no question of an alibi for his whereabouts. Several witnesses can testify as to his whereabouts at the time that Jackson was killed."

"It only stands to reason that this Fairclough should have the perfect alibi, we have no witness in Whitechapel, and no real evidence as to who committed any of these Thames murders, why should things change now."

"I will tell you one thing, Wynne," I said, ignoring the coroner's sarcasm. "I think there are a couple of clues that we may have been overlooking."

Reaching into my desk drawer, I retrieved a sheet of paper.

"Such as, Detective?"

"The witness, Margaret Minter, testified that Elizabeth Jackson told her she had resorted to sleeping on the Embankment, as a result of Fairclough leaving her," I commented, studying Baxter as the coroner furiously scanned the article in The Times for the witness's statement.

"By, Jove you are right, I don't know why I shelved that bit of information so quickly, Stone."

"The Embankment gives us a position on the Thames where not only the victim said she had been sleeping, but finding her remains in the vicinity would substantiate that information."

"Yes, but the Embankment covers a lot of ground," Baxter responded.

"The Embankment covers," I paused, taking up another piece of paper from off of my desk. "From Battersea Bridge up to Victoria Tower

Gardens, near Lambeth Road. Taking in Cheyne Walk, Chelsea Embankment, Grosvenor Road, and Millbank, correct?"

"Yes, I suppose it does, Stone."

"Well, Wynne, in your expert opinion, how many miles encompasses the Embankment would you say?"

"Well, I would be guessing of course, but I would think it would be just over five miles from Battersea Bridge to Tower Bridge. Victoria Gardens is, I suppose, just over halfway between, so I would estimate three miles of the Thames to cover."

"That narrows the search a bit, doesn't it, Wynne?"

"Three miles, on both sides of the Thames that is Detective. Making it more like six miles, if my math is correct," Baxter said, cocking an eyebrow.

"Yes, of course, Wynne, but I am willing to bet that Elizabeth Jackson did not travel much further from Cheyne Walk where Mrs. Minter talked to her and Turks Row, where she lived with Fairclough."

"That wouldn't be much of a distance to cover, only about three-quarters of a mile, John," Baxter spouted.

"That is what I estimate as well. The union workhouse on Arthur Street is also in Chelsea, where Jackson said her parents resided. This girl was seemingly alone for the first time and being pregnant, I am guessing that she would not want to travel more than a couple of miles from any familiar surroundings."

"By, Jove, I think you are onto something there, Stone. Being alone and with child for the first time, she would have likely been frightened, not knowing what to expect. She would have wanted to stay close to her family, even though she was embarrassed because she was in a motherly way. That was probably why that Fairclough chap left her in the first place, not having a job, the man did not want the responsibility of raising a child," Baxter huffed his disdain thinking about Fairclough.

"If we are right, another obvious piece of the puzzle has come to light."

"What is that, John?"

"What bridge is just off the Embankment, near the Union Workhouse, and is in the area of several other unsolved murders?"

"Battersea Bridge, John!"

The inquest into Elizabeth Jackson's death was different from all the other dismemberment (or '*torso murders*' as the newspapers had been calling them) in that the head of the victim had not been discovered. Despite the difficulties that this would cause in identifying the victim, police were able to obtain a positive identification. It had been established by police that the reason why the killer chopped up his victims was primarily to prevent the identification of the victim. Having made identification by other means, the police were now able to find out about the victim's background, relatives and retrieve a list of friends, acquaintances, and any place Jackson frequented to establish her whereabouts from the time when she was last seen to the time of her death. The inquest also cleared John Fairclough of any wrongdoing.

Scotland Yard was able to establish an alibi for the man's whereabouts. The undergarments, having the name "L. E. Fisher" written on the waistband, was later discovered that it belonged to the person who had sold the articles for rags and was subsequently purchased by Fairclough at a lodging house in Ipswich. The inquest also revealed police efforts in the investigation, including dragging the Thames for the head of the victim from Albert Bridge to Battersea Park. However, their efforts ended with no favorable results. The final day of inquest was to be held on Friday, July the twenty-fifth.

Leaving the inquiry at the Star and Garter, I felt strangely satisfied for a change concerning the inquest proceedings. Although the case was far from concluded, it was the first time in my experience that a victim had been successfully identified without the victim's head being found. The area in which the woman had lived and frequented had been established, and known relatives and acquaintances had been interviewed, maintaining an area where she was last seen and frequented. Allowing for these parameters, they felt sure in their assumptions that the killer lived and or worked in this area for him to be able to meet Jackson.

Unable to attend the final segment of the inquest, they were content to read about A. Braxton Hicks' summation in the newspaper.

The Birmingham Daily Post: The Thames Mystery

[Sic] Mr. A. Braxton Hicks (coroner for Mid-Surrey) resumed his inquiry, at the Star and Garter Battersea, into the circumstances attending the death of Elizabeth Jackson, aged twenty four, single woman, late of Turk's Row, Chelsea, where mutilated remains were found in various parts of the Thames, in Battersea Park, and in a garden on the Chelsea Embankment last month. Inspector Tunbridge who again appeared to watch the case on behalf of the C.I.D., was called and stated that he had, had charge of the case. When a portion of the body was first discovered, instructions were given to the river police to keep special watch on the Thames to see what other parts of the body were not disposed of. A woodcut of the name found on a pair of drawers in which one of the legs was wrapped was supplied to the press, who very kindly inserted it, and, in fact, it was through the assistance rendered by newspapers that the body was identified. All the important parts of the body had been found except the head. As soon as the body was identified it was necessary to have Fairclough the man with whom the deceased had been living and a full description of him together with a woodcut obtained from a photograph which was taken at Ipswich, was sent to every police station in the United Kingdom. By means of this he was traced by police. Witness discovered that the name on the drawers was that of a person living near Ipswich, whither he proceeded. He found that the drawers had been sold amongst other white linen for rags, and in this way came into the possession of the man Fairclough who bought them for the deceased. In reply to the Coroner, witness said that he and his assistants had been in many parts of the country to obtain information in the case. The Coroner said that was all the evidence. The case was somewhat different from the cases they had, had unfortunately, in Whitechapel. It was a case in which a woman had died under circumstances which in themselves were excessively suspicious, and to the mind of ordinarily reasonable persons it would suggest that whatever the cause of the death it was the result of some unlawful act on the part of someone. Everything found on the body pointed to the conclusion that the body was that of Elizabeth Jackson. He suggested that the jury should return a verdict that Elizabeth Jackson was willfully murdered by some person or persons unknown. Mr. Hicks passed a high compliment on the police for the energy they had displayed in working the case. A verdict in accordance with the coroner's direction was returned. The jury also passed a resolution complimenting the police engaged in the

case on their vigilance and the ability which they had shown bringing the matter to an issue."

"It seems like Inspector Tonbridge has deemed it necessary to leave the case as it stands, Detective," Baxter said, folding the newspaper across his legs.

"What makes you say that Wynne?"

"I find it incredible to think that the police are not scouring Chelsea, night and day now that they know where this poor waif was last seen," Baxter explained. "It is where her parents reside, and where her friends who had last seen her before her death are, right down to where she laid her head at night."

Baxter rustled the newspaper, frantically out of frustration, and tossed it across the desk. I picked it up before answering.

"Wynne, if you were…"

"I beg your pardon, Detective?"

"Excuse me, Wynne," I dismissed the interruption with a smile. "If you were the madman who had been killing up and down the Thames for over fifteen years, successfully, I might add, what would you be inclined to do, after you committed a murder, I mean?"

I looked up from the newspaper and waited for the coroner's reply.

"Well, I suppose, I would be so, inclined to lay low, and wait for the police to cool their heels and put the case on the back burner."

"Precisely!"

Setting the paper on my desk, I gave some thought to what they knew to date.

"The murderer has been very successful, concealing his victim's identities thus far."

"That is, up until the Elizabeth Jackson murder!" Baxter exclaimed.

"That is right, Wynne. This maniac has been killing women seemingly without fear of being caught. It is possible with the fervent newspaper reporting, our man now knows that the police have a positive identification of what could be his last victim, I think for the first time this killer could be scared the police are getting close."

"What do you think this man is up to now, Stone?" Baxter asked.

427

"I would not be in the least bit surprised, Wynne, if this man is watching the police as they investigate this murder, perhaps waiting on the streets of Chelsea, obtaining what information can be had by listening to the gossip."

"I doubt that this chap has that much brass, Stone. I wouldn't be surprised if this animal hasn't crawled under a rock somewhere," Baxter said, lighting his pipe.

"On the contrary, Wynne, we have not given this man enough credit, that is why police haven't a clue as to who is killing these women."

"Well, what do you propose Tonbridge should do," Baxter asked, twisting the chair around.

"Not Tonbridge, but you and I, Wynne," I answered, waiting for Baxter's reaction, of which the coroner did not disappoint.

"Us, are you daft, Stone? What do you think you and I can bloody accomplish that an entire brigade of police could not?" Baxter said, pulling his pipe from his mouth.

"We will never know unless we try, Wynne," I said, grabbing my overcoat from the hook beside the door.

"Stone, where are you off to now?" Baxter shouted, shaking out the burning match that threatened to burn his fingers.

I heard Baxter's question but didn't reply. Glancing over my shoulder, I saw Baxter with overcoat and walking stick in hand following close behind as I started down the stairs heading for the door.

Chelsea was covered in a thick fog that could almost be cut with a knife. The evening was upon them when the carriage stopped in front of the Prospect of Whitby Public House on the bank of the Thames River at Wapping. It had been the topic of conversation during the carriage ride between detective and coroner that the two would be in character, portraying themselves as two strangers passing through and content to be in out of the fog and the damp-chill, to have a mulled cider and warm their bones. They planned to listen to the local conversation and to keep their identities a secret in hopes they might unearth some clue as to how a close-knit community like Chelsea did not know they had a murderer in their midst. It was common knowledge that the maritime attitude was to be closed-mouthed and protect their own, no matter what they had done, not interfering with the law but offering no helping hand either.

Thick tobacco smoke could be seen hanging from the ceiling when I followed Baxter into the Prospect of Whitby. Every eye turned to look up from their drams and pints to sneak a peek at the strangers who entered the pub. The occupants knowing all who frequented their home away from home and knowing full well any late arrivals were strangers to them. Baxter turned and snatched a glance at me, who also detected the decibel of conversation as it fell to a whisper when they entered. The room fell silent as they passed by the first row of tables and proceeded to the bar. The public house was the center of information for most small villages. It was also a place where tales were told and retold, and where young men talked about their adventures and where the old men lied about theirs. Most in the small communities barely ventured more than a mile from their home at any given time, and any outside news was a welcomed distraction that broke up the monotony of small-town life. However, they were painfully aware when they enter the pub that most outsiders were thought of as intruders and not to be trusted.

They nodded a greeting to the bartender who stood behind a large wooden bar top, which was supported between two columns. The tender was middle-aged, balding with a set of whiskers that started on his right sideburn, wrapped along his jaw under his nose and connected to his other sideburn on the left side of my face, leaving his chin cleanly shaven. His thick hands, scarred and, broken matched the hook in the man's nose, which spoke of a past life that was used to the bare-knuckle brawling on ship's decks and docks.

"What can I get you chaps?"

I looked at the bartender who spoke with a thick brogue that offered neither hospitality nor slight.

"Two mulled ciders, my good man," Baxter spoke up quickly, slapping his hands together and rubbing them furiously to warm them. "That is a bitter night, what?"

The bartender poured the cider into each glass, without comment, and then walked to the hearth and jabbed a hot poker into the first one flagon and then the other, and then set the cider on the bar in front of them without a second glance. Without a word between them, I followed Baxter to a chair at an empty table near the back of the room and sat down. The flurry of conversation had all but disappeared as the coroner sat down opposite an old sea dog, judging by the gray hair, and, from the lines on the man's face, the man must have been near the age of seventy, if not older. Content to face the hearth, I watched Baxter from a chair opposite, warming the palms of my hands. The pub was not quite full for the hour was late. The patrons were all aged from their late forties to their mid-sixties. Each face carrying the distinct tan only those who had spent their lives on the sea, each face had been weathered by decades exposed to the elements. The conversation slowly returned to normal, perhaps, a little hushed when Baxter leaned forward and spoke in a hushed tone.

"Nasty bit of business, with these body parts popping up all over the Thames, what, John?"

Baxter spoke in an audible voice and winked and then slid back into his chair.

Seeing the old man tilt his head in Baxter's direction, I decided to play along with the coroner's less than subtle tactics for the moment.

"Yes," I said, peering out of the corner of my eye at the old fisherman. "They say that all the pieces recovered of this last one, all came from the same woman," I responded, making eye contact with the coroner and then glancing back to the old mariner.

"It is ghastly to think that Chelsea's daughters are being cut up into so many pieces, and there seems no stopping this animal."

Baxter commented, taking another sip and then glancing at the old man out of the corner of his eye looking for a response.

"It is a-bleedin' shame that's what I say!"

The old man slammed down his pint with a sinewy arm and an iron fist that still held the strength of a man half his age startling me.

"My name is, Wynne this is, John. Can I buy you a drink, to warm your insides old friend?" Baxter offered the old man whose gaze softened at the offer of another libation.

"Name's, Turk."

The old man spoke through broken and tobacco-stained teeth, the tuft of beard on the sagging chin turned to a dingy yellow.

After Turk took another sip from his glass, Baxter caught the eye of the bartender and held up a finger.

"You chaps are not from around here," said Turk.

With the interruption of the bartender dropping the glass of the amber liquid, none too gently in front of him, the old man's gaze, turned in Baxter's direction, ignoring the sharp glance that the bartender gave him, and stared at the glass. The old mariner took the glass from Baxter, with a nod of the head and cradled it in his two palms, drinking a generous portion, closing his eyes as the burning liquid soothed his throat.

"No," Baxter answered. "Just passing through to the city," Baxter answered, sliding his glass towards the center of the table untouched, in reach of the old man.

"What, I can't understand," I said, looking over at Baxter, then turning my attention to the old man. "Why you chaps haven't started one of them Vigilance Committees like they have up in Whitechapel?"

I turned my gaze back to Baxter and then glanced back at the old mariner, waiting for a response that never came.

With the glass pressed against his bottom lip, the old man gulped down the last of the cider as Baxter held up another finger to the bartender, who responded by bringing another flagon.

"That warms the insides, doesn't it, my good man?"

Baxter winked at Turk who eyed the amber liquid on the table across from him with a yearning that was satisfied as Baxter pushed the flagon towards the old man. A wolfish grin appeared on the man's face as a wrinkled hand snatched it from the table as though there was a time limit on the offer.

"The thing I don't understand in such a small community like Chelsea, how a man could ill-treat one of his own by killing their daughters?" Baxter offered another comment. I grimaced at Baxter, making eye contact, trying to warn my friend not to go too far and perchance insult the old man.

"Hmm," Turk growled.

With his second drink half gone, Turk set the flagon, softly on the table, and then looked over his shoulder, peering around the room.

"It ain't no Chelsea man, nor one from Battersea I'll wager," Turk snarled, taking the last of the cider in one gulp.

"Two more mulled ciders my good man!" Baxter shouted to the bartender.

The glint in the mariner's eye was all the enticing that Baxter needed.

"Who then, would be committing such atrocities down here?"

"Who can tell, it ain't none of these, good men, one and all," Turk gestured around the room to his comrades seated nearby. "But I will tell you it is some blackheart that travels these waters often enough though."

431

I looked up at Baxter as Turk began to mumble an old sea song slapping his hand on his thigh to some unheard beat from a bygone day and realized that there was no more information to be had from the mariner.

"Well Wynne, shall we be getting on our way, the hour is late, and we still have far to travel."

"Right oh," Baxter rose, slapping a hand on the old mariner's shoulder on his way by. "What do we owe, old boy?" Baxter asked the bartender, walking to the bar, to pay the bill.

Waiting for the coroner, I stood watching the old man sing his tune, reminiscing of better times with those around him. Tremendously loyal and ready to stand up for one another at the drop of a hat if nary a word was spoken against any they knew. The song that Turk caroled was picked up by a couple of more old-timers, and, soon, the entire room was filled with the tune and the cheer between those that had worked, fought, and suffered the same hardships together would get them through the next round of misfortunes.

Aboard the carriage, Baxter tapped his walking stick against his heel, as the carriage rumbled over the broken cobbles that had suffered the ravages of time and the elements.

"Well, Stone, what do you make of what the old mariner said?

Rubbing the three-day-old stubble on my chin, I counted the lamps up and down the embankment contemplating what the man Turk said.

"It has a ring of truth in it, Wynne."

"What does, Detective?" Baxter asked, stopping the incessant tapping on his shoe.

"These people are a close-net group," I said, thinking about the men they had just seen in the pub. "Their families go back generations, living closely together, making their living from the sea, and relying on one another when their fathers and sons are at sea?"

"Yes, I suppose so," Baxter said, taking a handkerchief from an inside pocket wiping his nose. "What does that prove though Stone; there are anomalies in every society, why not here?"

"Yes, that is true enough, Wynne but brutal murder in a close community like this one would not be allowed even if they had to handle it themselves. For these murders to have gone on for such a long time, I am inclined to believe what this Turk said, that our man is an outsider."

"Why would these people not hunt the wretch down and give him their own brand of justice then?"

"I think Turk is right," I said, looking over at my friend. "I believe that this killer is someone who travels up and down the Thames, using the river to come and go, not staying very long in any area."

"That could mean that our killer is well-known in the area, and could be living under their very noses, Detective.

"Perhaps you are right, Wynne, and this man is someone familiar or lives in a community close by, but I hardly doubt that we would find this man living among them."

"Where does that leave us then, Stone?" Baxter said, returning to tapping the end of his walking stick against the side of his shoe.

"I don't know where any of this leaves us," I said, feeling frustrated. "I do know the longer this killer is left unchecked, the less likely we are of ever catching this madman."

I turned to look out the cab window, not liking my conclusions.

"Why do you say that, Detective?"

"Well, if we are to assume that there has been one killer all along, starting with this Battersea killing, and if that crime was committed over fifteen years ago," I said looking over at Baxter. "Depending on the killers age, health, and any other crime that the man could get nicked for, we could be running out of time."

433

Chapter Twenty-eight

The days turned to weeks, and the weeks turned to months; my feelings and belief that Doctor Francis Tumblety was their man had not changed. I has learned the news days earlier that P. C. Alfred Long had been sacked from the department for drinking on the job. Wynne Baxter had been sitting in my office when I entered looking forlorn.

"Have you heard the news then, John?"

"Are you talking about Constable Alfred Long, Wynne?"

A nod of the head was all the gumption that Baxter could muster in response to my question. I did not want to say 'I told you so' to Wynne, about being right. The idea of being right did not make me feel any better. Constable Long's whereabouts on the night of Catharine Eddowes murder had been put into question by Detective Halse. Halse had been in the Goulston Street area at the same time when Constable Long was supposed to be, but the detective had not seen Constable Long anywhere in his search until around two in the morning. At which time Halse, found Long-

434

standing over a fragment of blood smeared apron that had belonged to Catharine Eddowes. The fact that Constable Long had been sacked for drinking on the job could explain a point I had made three years ago about the whereabouts of patrolling constables and the discrepancies during the times when the murders occurred. It was unfortunate that Constable Long incident had to take place, but it also explained the inconsistencies in the times the bodies were found by patrolling constables and the times when doctors estimated the time of death of some of the victims occurred. Though that is not the first time that constable patrol times and their whereabouts had been under examination. The first time was on the night when Mary Ann Nichols was murdered, and the location of Constable Neil had been the topic of scrutiny when the murder was committed. Constable Cross had put out the alarm at the time of the discovery; however, Constable Neil could not be found anywhere in the vicinity after Nichols' body was discovered. It now looked quite damning for the police that in some cases where the murders of the women were committed that constables had been quite lax in their duties. Some had even gone so far to speculate that the constables on the nights in question were not anywhere near where they were supposed to be on their patrols when the murders were committed, giving the murderer ample time to kill and make good his escape. There were other ramifications as well. The doctors who had testified at the inquests had established that the dissection of the victims could be done within the parameters that the patrol times had established, making their testimony have the appearance of being rehearsed. It went without saying that coppers were human, and they fell into the same temptations as the rest of the population. Although these types of shortcomings were not an excuse, nor could these examples of dereliction be excused when a tragedy could have been avoided, and a life could have been saved.

"I guess that clears up a lot of the timing problems when P.C. Long and Detective Halse were in the area of Goulston Street and Halse did not see Constable Long anywhere during his search for the murderer."

"Unfortunately, yes, as ugly as the truth is sometimes, Wynne."

"You have been the lone advocate all along maintaining the fact that the 'Jack' had been aware of constable patrolling times and any, shall we say, discrepancies in their route times. I guess it also goes without saying that you were probably right in your theory about how fastidious this madman

435

was in his planning as well. The wretch was most likely aware of these constables ducking in and out on their routes and used it to his advantage to murder these women. It also puts an end to the argument of discrepancies between the time of death and the finding of the body by constables. The constable's dereliction of duty also explains how the murderer could complete the mutilations on the bodies and escape undetected."

"Wynne, this is only one instance, and, regrettably, Constable Long had to be terminated for his patrol times to be scrutinized, it still makes me feel no better."

"I wonder if we, like Bagster Philips, have allowed our stubborn proprieties to overrule our good sense?"

"What, do you mean, Wynne?"

"I wonder if the rest of us have been wrong all this time, and 'Jack' is a doctor, as you have been suggesting all along."

"Oddly, that should make me feel better, but it doesn't, Wynne. To be honest, it makes me feel like my time as a detective is finished."

"Retire, Stone?"

"Yes, Wynne," I sighed. "Perhaps it is time."

"Well, John, whatever you decide your job as investigator in the coroner's office, is here as long as you want it."

I watched Baxter leave my office, thinking long and hard about what my friend said.

Only days later on July the seventeenth 1889, the body of Alice McKenzie was discovered at ten minutes to one in the morning by Constable Walter Andrews.

The case sparked a hue and cry because the victim was discovered with more than one slice to the neck. Although the act of slicing the throat caused some to speculate that the *"Ripper,"* although inactive for some months, was still somewhere lurking in the shadows of the East End. Investigators braced themselves for another string of dead prostitutes, although several inconsistencies made some skeptical.

It was well known to anyone who had heard the gossip or could read a newspaper that *'Jack the Ripper'* sliced the throat from left to right, and presumably from behind his victim. According to Dr. Phillips, the attending physician at the scene, Alice McKenzie was lying on her back when her throat was cut, much like Mary Jane Kelly. It was established that the first cut of the knife probably caused her to be in shock and prevented her from screaming; it was the second slice of the knife that had caused her death. At the inquest, on Wednesday, July the seventeenth, Wynne Baxter had the opportunity to question Doctor Phillips again on the stand.

[Sic] Dr. George Bagster Phillips, divisional surgeon of H Division, was recalled and deposed, - On the occasion of his making the post-mortem examination, the attendants of the mortuary, on taking off the clothing of the deceased woman removed a short clay pipe, which one of them threw upon the ground, by which means it was broken. I had the broken pieces placed upon a ledge at the end of the post-mortem table; but it has disappeared, and although inquiry has been made about it, up to the present time it has not been forthcoming. The pipe had been used. It came from the woman's clothing. The attendants, whom I have often seen there before, are old workhouse men. There were five marks on the abdomen, and, with the exception of one, were on the left side of the abdomen. The largest one was the lowest, and the smallest one was the exceptional one mentioned, and was typical of a finger-nail mark. They were colored, and in my opinion were caused by the finger-nails and thumb nail of a hand. I have on a subsequent examination assured myself of the correctness of this conclusion."
The Coroner: When you first saw the body, how long should you say she had been dead?"
Dr. Phillips: "Not more than half an hour, and very possibly a much shorter time. It was a wet and cold night. The deceased met her death, in my opinion, while lying on the ground on her back. The injuries to the abdomen were caused after death."
Coroner: "In what position do you think the assailant was at the time?"
Dr. Phillips: "The great probability is that he was on the right side of the body at the time he killed her, and that he cut her throat with a sharp instrument. I should think the latter had a shortish blade and was pointed. I cannot tell whether it was the first or second cut that terminated the woman's life. The first cut, whether it was the important one or not, would probably prevent the woman from crying out on account of the shock. The

whole of the air passages were uninjured, so that if she was first forced on to the ground she might have called out. The bruises over the collar-bone may have been caused by finger pressure. There were no marks suggestive of pressure against the windpipe.

Coroner: "Did you detect any skill in the injuries?"

Dr. Phillips: "A knowledge of how effectually to deprive a person of life, and that speedily."

Coroner: "Are the injuries to the abdomen similar to those you have seen in the other cases?"

Dr. Phillips: "No, Sir. I may volunteer the statement that the injuries to the throat are not similar to those in the other cases."

The Foreman: "Do I understand this pipe you speak of was in addition to the one produced on the last occasion?"

Dr. Phillips: "Yes. I cannot tell from where it came, but my impression is that it came from the bosom of the dress. The knife that was used could not have been so large as the ordinary butcher's slaughter knife.

Coroner: "Were the finger-nail marks on the body those of the woman herself?"

Dr. Phillips: "My impression is that they were caused by another hand. These marks were caused after the throat was cut."

Dr. Phillips' autopsy notes revealed what I had maintained all along, that the murderer did have some anatomical experience. That the cause of death was the severance of the left carotid artery, and that the bruising found on the chin was probably done after the first cut of the woman's throat was inflicted, and the; perpetrator lay his victim on the ground and most likely performed the second cut stranding over her. Seven scratches beginning at the navel pointing towards the genitalia and a small cut across the mons veneris. The mutilations were not superficial, nor were they deep enough to penetrate the muscle. Dr. Phillips proposed that the marks on McKenzie's left side were made with the perpetrator's right hand while the left made the cuts. It was also assumed by most in the medical community that the reason for Dr. Phillips's speculation in the killer's experience in the anatomical field was based primarily due to the type of cuts to McKenzie's abdomen. They were not searching deep penetrating wounds, but those of a hand that had experience in piercing the skin without damaging the muscle below.

Wynne Baxter summed up the inquest on Wednesday, August the fourteenth. The crowded room knew Baxter well and respected him for his professionalism and integrity. The clearing of Baxter's throat closed every mouth in the place, and all eyes were at the front of the room.

[Sic] "Then we have practically come to the end of this inquiry. Opportunity has now been given to ascertain whether any further light could be thrown upon this unfortunate case. The first point the jury have to consider is as to the identity of the deceased woman, and, fortunately, in regard to that there is no question. There is an interval of nearly five hours from when M'Cormack saw the deceased until she is seen between half-past 11 and 12 by some women in Flower and Dean-street. This is the last that was seen of her. At a quarter past 12 a constable had his supper under the very lamp under which the deceased was afterwards found, and at that time no one was near. Another constable was there at 25 minutes past 12, and the place was then all right. The officer next entered the alley at 12:50 and it was between those times that the murder must have been done. When the body was discovered, there was no one about, and nothing suspicious had been seen. Had there been any noise, there were plenty of opportunities for it to have been heard. There is great similarity between this and the other class of cases which have happened in this neighborhood, and if this crime has not been committed by the same person, it is clearly an imitation of the other cases. We have another similarity in the absence of motive. None of the evidence shows that the deceased was at enmity with anyone. There is nothing to show why the woman is murdered or by whom. I think you will agree with me that so far as the police are concerned every care was taken after the death to discover and capture the assailant. All the ability and discretion the police have shown in their investigations have been unavailing, as in the other cases. The evidence tends to show that the deceased was attacked, laid on the ground and murdered. It is to be hoped that something will be done to prevent crimes of this sort and to make such crimes impossible. It must now be patent to the whole world that in Spitalfields there is a class of persons who, I think, cannot be found in such numbers, not only in any other part of this metropolis, but in any other metropolis; and the question arises, should this state of affairs continue to exist? I do not say it is for

439

you to decide. The matter is one for a higher power than ourselves to suggest a remedy. But it certainly appears to me there are two ways in which the matter ought to be attacked. In the first place, it ought to be attacked physically. Many of the houses in the neighborhood are unfit for habitation. They want clearing away and fresh ones built. Those are physical alterations which, I maintain, require to be carried out there. Beyond this, there is the moral question. Here we get a population of the same character and not varied, as in a moderately-sized town or village. Here there is a population of 20,000 of the same character, not one of whom is capable of elevating the other. Of course, there is an opinion among the police that it is a proper thing that this seething mass should be kept together rather than be distributed all over the metropolis. Every effort ought to be made to elevate this class. I am constantly struck by the fact that all the efforts of charitable and religious bodies here are comparatively unavailing. It is true a great deal has been done of late years, especially to assist the moral development of the East-end, but it is perfectly inadequate to meet the necessities of the case. If no other advantage comes from these mysterious murders, they will probably wake up the Church and others to the fact that it is the duty of every parish in the West to have a mission and localize work in the East-end; otherwise, it will be impossible to stop these awful cases of crime. Here is a parish of 21,000 persons with only one church in it. There are not only cases of murder here, but many of starvation. I hope at least these cases will open the eyes of those who are charitable to the necessity of doing their duty by trying to elevate the lower classes."

I waited, sitting in my chair, watching the crowd slowly sift out of the room. The remarks that Wynne Baxter had finished with were compassionate; however, though I was moved by the coroner's benevolence, in all honesty, the statements probably fell on deaf ears. Not only had London's east been driven into the bottomless pit of despair, but it also seemed that the rest of London was willing to stand back and watch the people there wallow in that pit. These feelings seemed to run deep in the fabric of society, and the occupants of the ghetto's and slums had become accustomed to their plight. Whilst the rest of London could see that the only answer was to tear down the slums and rebuild, there was, however, a recurring issue that no one had the answer to. What to do with those who congregated in the East End once the slums were torn down?

Subsistence was forever on the minds of those who lived in the ghetto. Anyone can examine the social aspects of those who live in poverty and cast aspersions at their lifestyles or make assumptions on why they chose to stay in the slums. It did not change the fact that a bed in the lodging house was four pence for a single and eight pence for a double; for some without jobs, it was the difference between eating or sleeping on the streets. Most chose to walk the dark roads and eat for two days or more, while others chose a booze-addled existence wandering from public house to public house, earning a few pennies by using their natural talents and lying with sorted strangers to make money for lodgings each night.

The crowded room had emptied; while I remained, wondering what my next step should be. I waited as Wynne Baxter finished gathering the papers on his desk, and then I saw my friend look up and shrug his shoulders. We walked out of the Working Lad's Institute on High Street in Whitechapel together, saying nothing. In the Hackney, the silence, continued for the entire trip until they separated content with a wave when the cab came to a halt. I watched Baxter climb the steps of his home until the cab lurched and started up the road to my flat. On the trip to my rooms, I replayed Baxter's closing remarks in my mind. I understood that the coroner's heart was in the right place, and; the man wanted the record to show the plight of the east and arouse the compassion of London to not just understand the problem, but be moved to do something about it. Unfortunately, knowing about a problem and doing something about it were two entirely different things. The world over, in every age and every culture, there were those of affluence and those who suffered need. The few pennies that the compassionate tossed at the problem were too inadequate to do any real good but ease the conscience of the giver. The social reforms in place without the proper guidance to the needy; seemed to only worsen the problem, and the cycle continued generation after generation. In my mind, I could not see any solution to the human condition, simply because there was not a common consensus to fix the real problem. The truth of why things remained in a state of brokenness was due to the corrupt nature of the flesh, and the selfish desire to satisfy the flesh, above satisfying the need for a proper relationship with their Maker combined with the healthy attitude of everything in moderation.

The Fall of man had its beginnings with satisfying self, and; that nature had not changed; it was why the '*Jack the Rippers*' existed in the world and would continue to exist until the end of time.

It was a year to the day after the death of Annie Chapman that the women of Whitechapel again began to fear the streets where they plied their trade in their desperation to survive. Whitechapel had become accustomed to the false security that came with the disappearance of '*Jack the Ripper*'. It had been almost two months since the death of Alice McKenzie, a.k.a. clay pipe. Then on the tenth of September, 1889, the female torso of a prostitute was found under a railway bridge at Pinchin Street. The body, or what could better be described as a torso, was missing both head and legs and was found in a state of severe decomposition at fifteen minutes past five in the morning, by P.C. William Pennett. Given the condition of the remains, which had been covered with some type of sacking, led the police surgeon to believe that the body had been there for several weeks. I arrived at St. Georges mortuary where the victim had been sent. Examining the gruesome remains, I tried to focus mainly on the cuts made to sever the limbs from the trunk; however, the smell was so overpowering, it was hard to concentrate.

Standing alone in the narrow room for several minutes, it was hard not to recall the other dead women; I had seen in the mortuaries of Whitechapel in the not too distant past. Examining the torso.

My thoughts turned to the Battersea cases. There was no way to know how many women over the last fifteen years or more had been murdered, and their body parts scattered around London. The torsos of both the young and old had started to pile up with no answers as to who the culprit was or why the victims were killed. After spending a year looking for one killer, the Metropolitan Police had not come to any definitive conclusions on any aspect of the case, let alone narrowed the field to a list of plausible suspects. All this time, they might have been looking for a man who used the Thames to come and go like the old mariner Turk had suggested.

It was needless to say that one of the killers chose victims who wouldn't be missed, their disappearance would create no alarm, nor would it arouse any excitement from anyone in the community. This man could be a recluse and one who perhaps lived in and around the Thames. This killer kept a low profile, disposing of the remains of his victims in a place where the body parts may not surface for weeks or months and who had remained unabated for all this time with no person suspecting him of any crime.

The second killer, I imagined was a more ostentatious type. A man who seemingly hated prostitutes and relished in the idea that police found his victims right under their noses. This man enjoyed the newspaper's stories, with their vivid descriptions of my exploits, and the appellation '*Jack the Ripper.*' In my mind's eye, I saw a man who was charismatic and lived a lifestyle outside the mores and custom of the time. I envisioned a man who lived a life that bordered on the fringe of the immoral. Someone who used deceit and charade to make a living, choosing to live in the slums to have access to the less fortunate. Here in the east, amongst the smattering of cultures and moral degradation, this man could maintain the anonymity that his profession demanded. '*Jack the Ripper*' was a faceless man in the crowd, but at the same time, this killer craved recognition and was bent on achieving it.

I had been standing staring at the body for some time, realizing the description that I had formulated in my mind was that of Doctor Francis Tumblety. I had been struggling for several minutes trying to put another face to '*Jack*' before I realized that Wynne Baxter had come into the room and was standing beside me.

"What do you think, John," Baxter asked, awkwardly.

I looked at Baxter, realizing that a mortuary was a place where my friend would never grow accustomed, and; yet the man had chosen a profession that warranted his presence near the dead almost daily. I could only guess what Baxter was thinking, knowing when the coroner used my first name, the kind of mood he was in because, I too had been thinking and feeling the same way. Suppose the two of them had been wrong about Francis Tumblety. If so Tumblety's, jumping bail could not have been more opportune. Perhaps if the man had been intercepted before reaching France, Tumblety might very well have had a noose about his neck and given up the ghost.

"I am in a quandary, Wynne."

"About what?'

"How to prove Tumblety is our man for the courts in America to extradite him back to London."

"Stone, I think you are missing one very important fact," Baxter said somewhat ominously.

"What is that, Wynne?"

"If you still maintain that Tumblety is guilty and his capers include the torso found near the Thames Embankment, and if this torso has the same characteristics as the others, tell me how it possible is that Francis Tumblety is '*Jack the Ripper*' as well as this killer who chooses to operate along the Thames," Baxter asked, bluntly.

"I will not deny, Wynne, that the discovery of this torso does arouse some questions. Before you arrived, I was toying with the idea of two murderers. Something, I think, at this stage, I could get my head around," I answered.

Walking towards the torso, I ignored the smell and examined the segmentation around the limbs.

"The Thames' torso had ligature marks around where the limbs had been. There is none here; there are also different characteristics in the mutilation Wynne, as was observed in the case of Elizabeth Jackson. According to Doctor Phillips' examination, the knife used in the murder was long, probably longer than eight inches, and no organs were missing. I was just toying with the idea that there are two killers in London, one as dastardly as the other. In the one case, we have Doctor Francis Tumblety an alleged killer who has left the country and whose exploits have ceased, and presumably so have the deaths of the prostitutes in Whitechapel.

The other killer is this fiend who is using the Thames River to deposit his victims, allowing for an area so large the man could be anywhere along the rivers two hundred and fifteen miles. This madman not only likes to kill women but enjoys hacking them up beyond recognition, leaving police guessing at the victim's identity. Wynne, you are more acquainted with these cases than I. What are your thoughts?"

"How can you be sure this Battersea killer is still out there, John?"

"We know this wretch is still out there Wynne, for the most obvious of reasons, torsos are still turning up all around this area. "

"Yes, Detective, that seems the obvious conclusion, but this body obviously was not dumped in the Thames!" Baxter offered.

"The Thames is only a couple of miles from here Wynne, and it may be that this whole area is used by a couple of killers, this torso has several dissimilarities, distinguishing it from the Whitehall torso."

"What does that prove, Stone?" Baxter threw up his hands. "It is quite possible, that the Thames killer dropped this corpse here to simply throw police of his scent."

Wynne Baxter was a top-notch investigator who could hold his own with the best, although even the best had their limits. The past year of investigating the horrific murders had apparently begun to take its toll. Baxter had become frustrated by yet another victim that has fallen prey to a faceless murderer.

"The murderer did not take his time and sever the legs and head in the same way, by tying the limbs off to stop the flow of blood. It proves that whoever killed this woman was different from the others. Not to mention, the fact that there was nothing taken from the body, so there was no purpose for the murder; other than to dispose of the body and perhaps to obstruct the police in their efforts at finding the identity of the woman."

"So, what do you propose to do now," Baxter asked, thumping the bowl of his pipe against the palm of his hand.

"I haven't the foggiest idea, Wynne. Doctor Phillips has given the time of death as September, the eighth; marking the anniversary of the death of Annie Chapman. Perhaps that could be significant?"

"What if Tumblety has returned to England?"

"It is possible, but I don't think the man would risk his neck."

Turning on my heel, I had to get out of the small room, the smell had become almost intolerable.

Aboard a cab, the mood was sullen and quiet. Back in my office, we found solace in the warmth of the stove and in a steaming cup of hot tea; however, before long, a pounding at the door shattered the peace. Reaching for the knob, I stopped seeing a large envelope that had been pushed under the door from the hall. Pulling on the knob and swinging open the door, I found the hall empty, with no sign of the deliveryman.

"What is it Stone," Baxter asked, curiously.

"Hmmm."

"Stone, what on earth is going on?"

"Wynne, you are not going to believe this."

The Envelope contained what appeared to be a witness statement and the rough notes of a newspaper column. Reaching across my desk, I handed the envelope to the coroner, who began to read out loud.

445

"Matthew Packer keeps a shop in Berner St. and has a few grapes in the window."

[Sic] *On Saturday night about eleven pm a young man from 25-30 about 5' 7" with long black coat buttoned up – soft felt hat, kind of Yankee hat rather broad shoulders – rather quick in speaking, rough voice. I sold him half pound grapes 3d. A woman came up with him from Back Church end (the lower end of street). She was dressed in black frock & jacket, fur round bottom of jacket with black crape bonnet, she was playing with a flower like a geranium white outside and red inside. I identify the woman at the St. George's mortuary as the one I saw that night-*

They passed by as though they were going up Commercial Road, but-instead of going up they crossed to the other side of the road to the Board School, & were there for about 1/2 an hour till I should say 11.30 talking to one another. I then shut up my shutters. Before they passed over opposite to my shop, they waited near to the club for a few minutes apparently listening to the music.

I saw no more of them after I shut up my shutters. I put the man down as a young clerk.

He had a frock coat on - no gloves. He was about 1 1/2 inch or 2 or 3 inches - a little higher than she was."

Opening the file drawer in my desk, I pulled the file on Elizabeth Stride, and opened it on my desk.

[Sic] *"Elizabeth Stride was wearing a long black cloth jacket which was fur trimmed at the bottom with a red rose and a white maiden hair fern pinned to it. A black skirt, a black crepe bonnet, and a checked neck scarf, knotted on the left side."*

"Who do you suppose sent this," Baxter asked, studying the contents of the envelope.

"I guess it is someone who wants to draw our attention to this shop keeper, Mathew Packer."

Reaching into my desk drawer, I pulled out my witness statement file. I knew from experience that at the scene of a crime, there could be several eyewitnesses; very seldom did more than one witness account match that of another. More often than not, only fragments of a statement could be counted as reliable, thus making the eyewitness very unreliable.

"Follow along with me, Wynne," I said, shuffling through the files. "Elizabeth Long's statement was this: the man she saw with Annie Chapman appeared to be a little taller than Chapman, and approximately forty years of age. Chapman was five feet tall. Joseph Lawende stated the man that was with Catharine Eddowes was shabbily dressed, about thirty, of fair complexion, having a small fair mustache. James Brown noted that the man with Elizabeth Stride was five-foot-seven inches tall, stoutly built, with a long overcoat. J. Best stated the man attacking Stride was about thirty years old, five foot five inches tall, hair dark, complexion fair, a small brown mustache, full-frame, and broad-shouldered. The second was about thirty-five years old, five-foot-eleven inches tall, fresh complexion, old black felt hat with a wide brim. Mary Ann Cox stated the man with Mary Jane Kelly was approximately thirty-six and five-foot-five-inches tall, having a fresh complexion and blotches on his face, small side-whiskers, a thick carroty mustache, and dressed shabby, with a dark overcoat, and a black felt hat. George Hutchinson stated Kelly was with a thirty-four or thirty-five-year-old man, who was five-foot-six inches, having a pale complexion, dark eyes, with a slight mustache curled up at each end, and dark hair.

"So, Wynne, what do we have," I asked, looking at the coroner who had been scribbling wildly on a pad of paper.

"We have a man who is between, thirty and thirty-six years old, and between five-foot-six-inches and five-feet-eleven inches tall, with red to dark hair, a mustache, with the ends curled up, a fresh complexion with blotches on the skin, with dark eyes, wearing a long dark coat and an old felt hat."

"Tumblety, is a man of approximately five-foot-ten inches tall, with broad shoulders, and a black mustache, that could be thinned at the tips by wax. I never saw him with his shirt off but judging by his build, the man is solid."

"Stone, forgive me but, you haven't exactly disqualified Tumblety from the eyewitness accounts, but you have not positively identified the man as the culprit either," Baxter said. "And lest you forget, you told me that in the Scotland Yard file, Tumblety had been a person of interest as far back as 1857. If that is the case and we assume that Tumblety was in his twenties then, and over thirty years have passed that would put Tumblety in his late fifties."

I listened to Baxter and what the man said was absolutely right, however, the man that he had seen in the interrogation room at The Yard looked more like a man half that age.

"You are right Wynne, but the man I arrested did not appear to be a year over thirty-five. He was dark-haired and robust. He did not have any of the graying or wrinkles that a man of that age might have. How do you explain that?"

"I don't know Stone," Baxter confessed. "Hair can be darkened these days, perhaps he is just one of those persons who don't show their true age."

"There are other things to consider here Wynne."

"Such as?"

"Well, first of all, it was after dark when the eyewitnesses made their accounts. In addition to that, we must consider that all the areas in and around where the victims were killed were all poorly lit. The witnesses' accounts agree that the man they saw wore a long overcoat, had a fresh complexion and a mustache, correct."

"Are you supposing that these people, are just surmising due to the poor lighting." Baxter replied.

"What if the eyewitnesses remember seeing someone but were unable to make a positive identification of the man standing with the victim and then drew tidbits from the papers?"

"Do you think that the witnesses were influenced by the inquest reports?"

"Perhaps, Wynne."

"But the witnesses believed that they were giving an accurate statement, how do you, account for that?'

"Wynne, you are aware, as well as I, that most witnesses are unreliable in their accounts. What if they noticed the man, they described because of some distinguishing feature that made the man stand out from the crowd."

"Do you mean to say, John, that this fellow had some physical characteristic that was noteworthy enough to cause the witnesses to focus on that person, and they filled in the gaps from what they read from the papers?" Baxter asked.

"It is possible Wynne," I said, glancing at the witness accounts. "It might also have been as simple as something the man did to draw the attention of the witness."

"What do you mean?"

"It is possible that it was a mannerism that drew their eye to one individual over the other. Or perhaps the man coughed, spoke with an accent, or wore colorful clothing that drew the witnesses' attention. It could also be as trivial as the man they remembered wore a big black felt hat?"

"I get your point now," Baxter said excitedly. "The black felt hat was what they remembered most, and the rest of the details they assumed, or remembered from the inquest accounts."

"It is possible the eyewitnesses mistook the man's height as well. A long black coat can be deceiving, especially in the dark."

"Distance, height, and depth perception can be hampered or miscalculated after dark by someone who is flustered or unused to making those estimations in a snap judgment," Baxter commented.

"I have observed that more than once in my experience dealing with the untrained eye," I agreed. "However, Wynne, I am also interested in the other man that Israel Schwartz said was standing off to the side when Stride was attacked. That man was described as approximately five-foot-eleven, fresh complexion, dark overcoat, felt hat with a wide brim."

"Now you are back to the possibility of two killers again, Stone?"

"No, I don't think there were two killers involved in the murders in Whitechapel. One killer, there is perhaps an accomplice."

"How do you explain witnesses seeing at least two men with more than one of the victims before they were murdered?"

"I will agree with you, Wynne, that two killers are working in and around London's East End, each one working in a different area from the other and each having two totally different modes operandi. Although there might be one other thing, we might be overlooking here, Wynne?"

"What is that," Baxter asked.

"The murdered women are all prostitutes; how many men would stop just to talk to these women?"

"I would think there would be the usual salutation by a regular user, not that I would know, but for the most part, I would think that idle chatter would not be something that most clients would expect." Baxter rationalized.

"How many men would you estimate that would seek a prostitute out and pay for their services in an evening?"

"These women might see two or three customers a night, a few more at week's end, I should think. Some might want to buy them a drink, but I doubt any could afford to just pay for conversation," Baxter answered with a shrug of his shoulders.

"If that is the case, the man, our witnesses; saw with the victims before their death was a man who could afford to romance them and give them money, just to talk."

"Yes, I suppose so, where does that leave us, Detective?" Baxter questioned.

"It is one more piece filled into this puzzle, Wynne."

"Unfortunately, we have more spaces than we have answers, John."

The speedy inquest into the Pinchin Street torso answered very few of the questions that Wynne Baxter needed answers to. I watched as the coroner shouted for the crowded room to come to order. Looking around the room, I examined the faces of the jury and those of the audience that had packed the room just as they had done so many other times before. Each person looked on hungrily searching for news that everyone dreaded to hear, that another murderer had come to Whitechapel.

[Sic] *"I should like to ask Dr. Phillips whether there is any similarity in the cutting off of the legs in this case and the one that was severed from the woman in Dorset-street?"*

Dr. Phillips: "I have not noticed any sufficient similarity to convince me it was the person who committed both mutilations, but the division of the neck and attempt to disarticulate the bones of the spine are very similar to that which was affected in this case. The savagery shown by the mutilated remains in the Dorset-street case far exceeded that shown in this case. The mutilations in the Dorset-street case were most wanton, whereas in this case it strikes me that they were made for the purpose of disposing of the body. I wish to say that these are mere points that strike me without any comparative study of the other case, except those afforded by partial notes that I have with me. I think in this case there has been greater

450

knowledge shown in regard to the construction of the parts composing the spine, and on the whole, there has been a greater knowledge shown of how to separate a joint."

"In summing up, observed that they had not been able to produce any evidence as to the identity of the deceased, but the evidence of both medical gentlemen engaged in the case clearly showed that the unfortunate woman had died a violent death. It was a matter of congratulation that the present case did not appear to have any connexion with the previous murders that had taken place in the district, and the body might have, for ought they knew to the contrary, been brought from the West-end and deposited where it was found."

The jury returned the verdict of willful murder against some person unknown.

Sitting across from each other, absorbed in their own thoughts, in the familiar way that both coroner and his officer had grown accustomed. It was quite disturbing to think that on the one hand, I wanted nothing better than to say that his two killer theory was correct. All medical conclusions aside, there was evidence to show inconsistencies found in the examinations of the torso murders. While one doctor was prone to one theory, another was disposed to have another. For all intents and purposes, it appeared that London had an unknown man cutting up women and dumping the limbs of his victims in the Thames. On the other hand, they had another madman who seemingly held his victims and killed them in a manner as of yet, unknown. To later dissect his victim in a way that would appear as though some medical experience was used. They had, up until the Pinchin Street torso was discovered, grown accustomed to the idea that two killers operated in London. However, after putting to rest their fears that another killer had surfaced, the truth remained that a woman, who was a known prostitute, had been brutally murdered by someone unknown, and the killer was still at large. Proving or disproving one particular theory or aspect of the case over another was of little concern to me, what did concern me was the undeniable fact that police officials had done a miserable job protecting the community from not one killer but as many as three or four. The only consolable point that did little to comfort either coroner or detective was the immutable fact that they were not alone in their failures. Time after time, they had sat through almost a dozen inquiries into the deaths of women, and repeatedly they had been confronted with the phrase '*willful murder by person unknown*' leaving each man cold. The other immutable fact, that remained, was the Whitechapel murderer known as '*Jack the Ripper*' had presumably killed his last victim and had not resurfaced since the death of Mary Jane Kelly.

Consumed by the pursuit of one killer who left not a trace of evidence had proved to be taxing enough, but; the pursuit of three faceless madmen now seemed an impossibility. One man or three, the knowledge that such a brute lurked in the dark did nothing to deter those women who freely chose to walk down the darkest alleys of London at night with strangers.

Chapter Twenty-nine

It was almost two years to the date since I had resigned my position at Scotland Yard to be the chief investigator for the coroner of Middlesex. It was only minutes that passed since I had entered my office when the coroner shoved open the half-opened door carrying several newspapers with the head line's reading '*Has London's 'Jack the Ripper landed in New York*,' at the top of every paper.

The New York Times, 26 April 1891

"Carrie Brown, nicknamed 'Old Shakespeare' was found dead in her room at the East River Hotel on Manhattan Waterfront on April twenty-

fourth. The Hotel is located on the S. E. Corners of Catharine Slip and Water Streets. She checked in on April twenty-third between half past ten and eleven in the evening with a man. She was found the next morning by Eddie Harrington, the night clerk. Upon opening the room, I found the deceased strangled, the murderer using Brown's own clothing with cuts and stab wounds all over her body."

It was several seconds before Wynne Baxter looked up from the paper.

"Well, what do you think of that bit of business?" Baxter asked.

"I think that there is a murderer in New York, Wynne."

"That's it," Baxter screeched. "That is all the response that you have?"

"That is, it, Wynne."

"Sometimes, I don't understand you Stone," Baxter huffed. "You have been going on and on about Tumblety slipping through your fingers and him being trailed to New York by police after leaving Ellis Island. Now, a similar murder has been committed in New York, of all places, and you don't seem, in the least bit, interested."

Slumping in his chair, the rattle of the folded newspaper drowned out the rest of Baxter's comments.

"Wynne, first of all, there are several differences in the cases."

"Oh, and what did you ascertain from the brief story, I have just read to you?"

"Well, first, Carrie Brown was strangled by her own night clothing; she was not stifled by an arm about the neck. Second, she did not have her throat cut. Third, the victim was sliced, not mutilated, and no organs were missing. However, ..."

"However, however, what, Detective?"

"I am going to send a cable to the Chief Police Inspector Thomas Byrnes, of the New York City Police Department."

"What on earth for?"

"To try and get any details that may not have made the papers."

"What are the odds of his responding?"

"I guess we will have to wait and see."

Two months later, Wynne Baxter threw a copy of the New York Times newspaper across my desk.

The headlines read that Inspector Thomas Byrnes of the New York City police had arrested a man in the Carrie Brown murder.

"*Ameer Ben Ali*, nicknamed, '*Frenchy*' was living in the hotel at Catharine Slip and Water Street in room thirty-three, across the hall from Carrie Brown. Blood was found on the door and into the entrance of his room. "Frenchy" was arrested one day after Carrie Brown's murder, in keeping with Byrnes' boast six weeks previous, when the inspector announced that no murderer would be allowed to work in New York City the way that the London Police had allowed '*Jack the Ripper*' to go unmolested."

I let my words fall on the coroner's ears for a moment before I broke the silence.

"That was quick, wasn't it, Detective?" Baxter said, waiting for a response that did not come.

"Yes, wasn't it?"

"Do you think this, Byrnes has the right man, John?"

After several more minutes of silence, Baxter persisted in his questions.

"Stone, where the devil are you?" Baxter shouted.

"I am sorry, Wynne, what were you saying?"

"I said, do you believe that this Inspector Byrnes of the New York City Police has the right man?"

"It does seem likely, blood on the door and in the hall between both rooms, seems rather incriminating, doesn't it?"

"Alright, John, what is bothering you?"

"Nothing; I just received a cable from the New York City Police, Wynne."

"What does it say?" Baxter asked, sucking furiously on his pipe.

"*Detective John Stone, formerly of Scotland Yard,*

In response to your cable, Dr. Tumblety landed at Ellis Island on December the third. New York City's Chief Inspector Byrnes soon discovered Tumblety was lodging at 79 East Tenth, Street at the home of a Mrs. McNamara, and had him under surveillance for some days following. Byrnes could not arrest Tumblety because, in his own words, 'there is no proof of his complicity in the Whitechapel murders, and the crime for which the man was under bond in London, is not extraditable.' We have had him under surveillance until He suddenly disappeared from his lodging house and has not been seen since; it is suspected that Tumblety has left the city.

Yours sincerely, A. Todd NYCPD.

"Tumblety, disappeared," Baxter exclaimed, through blue clouds of smoke that drifted across the room. "Do you think Tumblety was still in New York at the time of the Brown murder?"

"He might have left the city, but who is to say."

"What would Tumblety be afraid of; New York is as far from London as anyone running from the law could go."

"Extradition, I suppose, but it seems the doctor waited for some time before deciding to give the police, the slip?"

"How so?"

"If one is afraid of extradition for crimes committed in another country, and the papers are reporting your whereabouts, why wait so long to skip town? Why wouldn't Tumblety leave soon after discovering the surveillance on the house?"

"Perhaps, Tumblety was aware that the police were keeping an eye on him and was none too worried about them?" Baxter replied.

"That is exactly what I was thinking, Wynne. What better alibi could a person want than to be under police surveillance when a crime is committed?"

"I suppose, Tumblety has the New York City Police to thank for that."

"I think, Tumblety was thanking them. We have already established that Tumblety has the wherewithal to move about whenever and wherever the notion comes on him. If we have learned anything about the man, then we have learned that Tumblety can change his appearance. I think Tumblety stayed at the lodging house to establish his alibi."

"Knowing full well the police were outside his door," Baxter agreed. "Tumblety could have ducked out of the Lodging House, perhaps in some type of a disguise. If that is the case, then it is quite possible that Tumblety could have killed this prostitute nicknamed Shakespeare then returned without police knowing. Tumblety not only clears his name with the New York Police, the man would now be able to move about at his own free will without being followed."

"That is, a possibility, Wynne."

"We are under the assumption that Tumblety was in London when all the murders were committed. We are also under the understanding that the man most likely tried to procure human specimens for some fictitious medical study. We can only comprehend that if Tumblety had nothing to hide then why skip out on his bail," Baxter said while walking around the room. "We know Tumblety fled London under an assumed name, presumably because the doctor was aware of being pursued by police to arrest him. We know by this article that it was the body of a prostitute that was found murdered in an area of New York not much different from one that could be found in London's East End. She was with a client, presumably, and she was strangled and cut up and left dead in her room."

"That is right, so let's figure out the unique differences in the murders," I said, gathering my files as Baxter reached for his lukewarm cup of tea, and settled in his chair.

"Alright, John, we know her throat wasn't cut."

"We also know, Wynne, that this woman was strangled with a piece of her own clothing that the killer used to wrap around her neck. She was cut but not mutilated, and no organs were missing."

"Perhaps the killer was disturbed in some way?" Baxter intervened.

"I don't think so, Wynne, the night clerk never went up to the room until the morning, giving the killer the entire night without being disturbed."

"Oh, yes, you are quite right," Baxter answered, lighting another match and returned to trying to light his pipe again.

"The newspaper also reported that the knife," I paused, rummaging through the newspapers on my desk. "*The knife used to kill Brown was a filed down cooking knife and it was found at the crime scene, lying on the floor next to the bed.*"

"That is not much of a description," Baxter retorted. "A cooking knife could be as small as a paring knife and as long as a butcher's blade."

"We also understand that this man, this *Ameer Ben Ali*, was arrested for the crime of murder."

456

"That is right, Detective, so do you believe that this Inspector Byrnes has his man?"

"Let me read this to you," I said, looking over the clipping I held in my hand. "This is something, I read some weeks ago. *[Sic] 'it would be impossible for crimes such as 'Jack the Ripper' committed in London to occur in New York and the murderer not to be found,'* that was published in the New York Times some six weeks before the Carrie Brown murder was committed."

"I see, so you think this Byrnes chap might be trying to make a name for himself?" Baxter enquired.

"I don't know the man, but it does seem convenient for this *'Frenchy'* character to have blood smeared from one end of the hall to the other and not try to flee."

As in the case of the Whitechapel murders, the American newspapers were full of the murder of Carrie Brown and the trial of Ameer Ben Ali, the hype around the grisly murder and the speed that the New York City Police had apprehended the monster who committed such an atrocity.

Carrie Brown, a sixty-year-old prostitute, found dead in a hotel room, in a bawdy district of the slums of New York, ordinarily would not have caused anyone to utter any fascination on the topic. Murder, like any other crime, was not uncommon in the ghetto, in New York, or any other metropolis in the world, nor was it exclusive or reserved to the area where the prostitute was murdered. However, the details of the way she was killed aroused the morbid curiosity in New Yorkers just as the *'Jack the Ripper'* murders had in Whitechapel.

The accused, an Algerian man named Ameer Ben Ali, alias 'Frenchy' had checked in to the room across from Carrie Brown's under the assumed name of George Frank. Ameer Ben Ali was arrested on April thirtieth and indicted by a grand jury by May eighteenth. Ameer Ben Ali's trial began on June twenty-fourth, 1891, but it seemed, for all intents, and purposes, the newspapers, and the police had already established the man's guilt. The prosecuting attorney's primary evidence against Ameer Ben Ali was the blood trail leading from Carrie Brown's room to Ali's room, and by July third, it was proven that it was all the evidence the prosecutor needed. Ben Ali, was convicted by a jury of his peers, of second-degree murder and sentenced to life in prison.

457

There was, however, one vital piece of information that interested the coroner's officer across the Atlantic Ocean in Whitechapel. It was that one piece of information that I had gleaned from the newspapers that I held onto like a dog worrying over a bone. The article was from the New York Times.

New York Times, dated April twenty-sixth, 1891

[Sic] "New York Chief of Detectives Thomas F. Byrnes issues a general alarm for the arrest of a man about five-feet-nine inches high, about thirty-one years old, light hair and moustache, speaks broken English."

The blurb in the newspaper gave the description of a man seen by the clerk in the East River Hotel on the night Carrie Brown was murdered. I reread the description time and again trying to read between the lines, focusing on those details about the man that were not written in the article. The description was close to the one given of the man last seen with at least two of the murdered victims in London nearly thirty-five hundred miles away. It would be most naïve not to consider the possibility that it was the same man considering the chief suspect in the crimes in Whitechapel had fled and was known to be in New York City around the same time. Although, I knew it was little enough to go on, I also knew it was hard for an investigator not to grasp at straws when there was a killer on the loose. Little things, even the most trivial, begin to seem important while investigating a murder in hopes that even the smallest tidbit of information could be the one thing that could lead the investigation onto the trail of the killer. That one thing, in this case, was the height of the alleged man last seen with Brown. The average height of a man for the period was around five-feet-five inches. Standing in my socks at six-feet tall, I had grown used to being the tallest man in any room. Tumblety, compared to others in a crowd, stood above the average. Size and stature are not something that can be concealed, though a clever man could wear a long coat to deceive any who might take notice. Broken English was another characteristic that could be easily fabricated, as could an accent. Grasping at straws, was okay for a green policeman, though; I had long ago tempered any rash behavior and over-eagerness, so not to go off half-cocked and follow a clue even after the evidence produced no good result. This, however, was one of those times when the clue though valid enough to take notice of, was still a far cry from solving a crime that was committed half a world away.

The details of the newspaper article would haunt me for ten years and it did not become more poignant then when a copy of the New York Times landed across my desk.

"Wynne listen to this," I said, back-folding the newspaper and placing it flat on my desk.

New York Times, April twenty-second 1901

[Sic] "Ben Ali is released from Matteawan State Hospital for Insane Convicts at Dannemora after serving nearly eleven years of a life sentence. Journalist Jacob Riis, of the New York Sun, *who had arrived at the scene of the crime shortly after it was discovered. The Riis affidavit states that there had been no trail of blood leading from Brown's room to Ben Ali's room. The other affidavit is from George Damon, a Crawford, New Jersey, man, stating that shortly after the crime a Danish servant in his employ disappeared, presumably leaving the country, shortly after the crime. In the man's room, Damon says I found blood-stained clothing and a key from the East River Hotel."*

"Well, how do you like that, the press is the good bloke for a change!" Baxter exclaimed.

"They sure came through for this Ali bloke, Wynne. It is too bad that he spent another two years in custody after Governor Benjamin Odell had pardoned him."

"Of course, you know what this means, don't you, Stone?"

"What, what means, Wynne," I asked, looking over at the coroner, wondering where the conversation was headed.

"It means that the killer is still at large, Detective!" Baxter shouted.

"Yes, I suppose it does, Wynne," I answered. "I was just thinking about this George Damon chap, it appears to me the New York City Police Department should be tracking this Danish lad down, but the newspaper article does not disclose any results of the search for him, nor does it give a thorough description of the man."

"Perhaps the police are keeping that information to themselves for now, Stone?" Baxter offered.

"For what reason, Wynne?"

"Perhaps to give this Dane a false sense of security."

"I suppose, it is possible, Wynne. It would seem that this George Damon has some type of intimate knowledge about the fellow that rented a room from him. Whom at some point and time came into possession of a key belonging to the East River Hotel, the very hotel where Carrie Brown was found murdered."

"It does seem rather damning, coupled with the bloody clothing found in the man's room."

"All this information that leads to a probable suspect and, yet, this article reveals no information about the purported suspect, only that the man is possibly of Danish descent, and that police assume this chap has left the country."

"At least, the police seemed to have a legitimate suspect in mind for the crime?"

"If the police have a legitimate suspect, why did they not put a description of him in the newspaper like they did before? This information all sounds too good to be true, Wynne, the murder has been all but solved and wrapped up because this man is suspected of leaving the country."

"John, perhaps the police have it upon good authority that this Dane did in fact leave, and the only thing left for them to do is to watch the ports to see if the man returns?" Wynne said optimistically.

"I just find it hard to believe that the New York Police would have this type of lead about an alleged suspect and they are downplaying it by saying the suspect has likely left the country and they are not pursuing it. I think this is just fantastic reporting."

"Really, Stone, sometimes you are hard to please?" Baxter huffed. "At times, I think you want everything bound in a pretty little bow."

Ignoring Baxter's comments, who continued proclaiming some theory of his own, I shuffled the files on my desk, studying the newspaper article from the New York Times.

As I mumbled the contents of the article to myself, my thoughts turned again to Dr. Francis Tumblety and how the man could still possibly be in New York City somewhere, hiding. After digging deeper into the doctor's past, the man had turned out to be a creature of habit. Tumblety often returned to areas that would be receptive to not only his lifestyle but to those people who would require his services. Tumblety in more ways than one had also proven to be a slippery character, mostly by being able to elude police. Rummaging through the newspapers on my desk, I found another article about Tumblety, who between the years *1860 and 1864 had masqueraded as an Indian Herb Doctor, in Brooklyn New York, living in and around the Fifth Avenue area* which could be a good reason for the man to want to stay in the city. Tumblety in other publications was described as an '*outlandish character speaking with an English accent.* One such account described Tumblety *as a physician in the company of his companion and manservant David Herold,'* who soon after the article was printed, was hung in July of the same year for his involvement in the President Lincoln assassination.'

The Evening Star Washington Dc. May 11, 1865

The Alleged Conspirators
More about Doctor Tumblety – New Facts
[From Rochester Union, 9th.]

As Tumblety resided in Rochester many years, and is well known here to almost all our citizens .... His name is J. H. Tumblety, and Blackburn is an alias he has assumed somewhere. His mother resides here still, and he has other relatives, all respectable citizens. He is of Irish origin, ... and has no Indian blood.... He will be remembered by many, some fifteen years or

461

more, since, as a peddler of books upon the cars…. He once had an office in Smith's Block, where he went by the name of Philip Sternberg, and treated a certain class of diseases. When one R. J. Lyons, an "Indian Herb Doctor," had an office over the Post Office, Tumblety used to be with him, and he probably picked up the information requisite to start him in his profession there. When ready to go abroad as a full-fledged 'yarb' Doctor, he procured a certificate of character, signed by a dozen or twenty of our most respectable citizens, who gave their names not knowing he intended to practice medicine. Tumblety went to Toronto and there put out his shingle as a physician, and published the names he had procured here. When the papers came back those who had signed the certificate of character were much annoyed.

Subsequently Tumblety was arrested at Toronto on the instigation of the regular faculty as a quack, and he was taken before a court. There he produced some kind of a certificate which he had obtained from a Philadelphia College, and escaped with a fine of twenty pounds, which he paid, and resumed practice with considerable éclat. Subsequently he had a difficulty in Montreal, which cost him a considerable sum to get out, but all tended to give him the notoriety he sought, and he probably made a great deal of money by being prosecuted by the "regulars." …

When the war broke out, he appeared at Washington, and was once gazette as a surgeon on the staff of General McClellan, but this was subsequently denied and explained. Tumblety has not been here that we can hear of in three or four years. Reports state that he was arrested in St. Louis. He will probably get notoriety enough out of his last arrest to gratify his ambition in that direction for a lifetime, if he is able to show that he is innocent. Those who knew him best say that he was no politician, and they think he would not be likely to engage in such a diabolical scheme as that which his man servant, Herold, was concerned. This is, we believe, a truthful sketch of "Dr. Tumblety," so far as it goes.

Tapping my fingernail on the handle of my teacup, I had a hard time believing that it wasn't Tumblety that was described by eyewitnesses as the man they saw with more than one of the victims before their deaths. Physical descriptions were tenuous, to begin with when dealing with witnesses who were asked to describe a suspect in the heat of the moment.

It was also worth mentioning that in all the cases, the eyewitnesses questioned were all making physical descriptions of the suspect at night in poorly lit areas. Taking into account that a person could slouch or lean, thus giving the appearance that they were shorter. It was also reasonable to take into account the faulty recollection of a witness who, for all intents and purposes, did not know they would be asked to recall what they saw hours later or, in some cases, days later. Albeit, it did seem unlikely that all witnesses could be wrong having pinpointed five-foot-six inches to five-foot-nine as the height of the unknown suspect. The other aspect that concerned me was the mustache that witnesses described by witnesses.

In some cases, witnesses described the man they saw as having a narrow and thin mustache. Tumblety had a dark mustache, wearing it with both ends turned up in the handlebar fashion of the day. It dawned on me suddenly that the man's mustache could have been dyed using the chemical, silver of nitrate. Of late, I had heard that both the vain men and women of London were using the chemical to darken their hair. Despite all of the variables in the eyewitness descriptions, one constant remained that there was no denying. Since Francis Tumblety had fled the country, no other murder had occurred in Whitechapel with the same modus operandi as the '*Jack the Ripper*' cases.

"What if the doctor was using a disguise?"

"What! Who was wearing a disguise?" Baxter asked.

Looking over at the coroner, I held up my finger for Wynne to be patient one moment.

"Listen to this for a moment, Wynne," I said, running my finger across the newsprint. "*In Brooklyn, Tumblety was traipsing about the streets dressed as an English lord, using a fake accent, covered in jewels, and selling his fake medicines as an Indian herb doctor.*"

"Yes, what of it?" Baxter sat up; sleepily in his chair.

"What if, the man traipses around like some actor of some kind,' I answered. "Perhaps, Tumblety got the idea from this Herold, chap, or his associate, John Wilkes Booth?"

"You are not making any kind of sense, John."

"Listen for a moment Wynne," I said, trying to explain. "Everything about the man is a charade of some kind, his dress, his accent, his role-playing, everything."

"I am not following you, Stone, you make the man out to be some type of theatrical character."

"That is precisely it, Wynne. Listen to Bond's comments in the profile the doctor was working on.

[Sic] *"Assuming the murderer to be such a person as I have just described he would probably be solitary and eccentric in his habits, also he is most likely to be a man without regular occupation, but with some small income or pension. He is possibly living among respectable persons who have some knowledge of his character and habits and who may have grounds for suspicion that he is not quite right in his mind at times. Such persons would probably be unwilling to communicate suspicions to the Police for fear of trouble or notoriety, whereas if there were a prospect of reward it might overcome their scruples."*

"Solitary, in their habits, would that foot the bill of someone who entertains at gentlemen's clubs, Detective?"

"Wynne, what would you call a man who perhaps lives a lifestyle not considered the norm by the rest of society?"

"I guess being seen as an outcast, would cause that man to become solitary, what? Being ostracized by society because of one's feelings or beliefs has been the cause of many, a man's downfall," Wynne answered, sitting back in his chair, listening more carefully.

"Eccentric, I would say yes. Anyone, who walks about with gold chains, and jewelry on a military type jacket could be accused of being eccentric, wouldn't you agree, Wynne?"

"I should say so, especially in the slums, where Tumblety chooses to live. I wonder if the man craves attention or if the man is eccentric to a fault seeking a fight to prove his superiority?" Baxter puffed on his pipe that had long ago extinguished.

"Tumblety would be the only man who could answer that Wynne. Who incidentally could also be a man like that which, Dr. Bond describes as one who does not have a regular occupation?"

"Selling phony remedies and medicines that have no medicinal value, to a gullible public certainly fits that bill, what?" Baxter answered excitedly.

"How about living among respectable persons, Wynne," I asked the coroner, wondering what his friend's sharp mind may deduce from that statement.

"Posing as a doctor might qualify him in certain circles to be thought of as a respectable person, calling himself a physician and a healer and being portrayed as a servant to the masses, so to speak, could also cause the man to be revered by those who don't know his true nature."

"That makes sense, Wynne; however, there is this knowledge of those who may know who and what Tumblety really is underneath that fake persona. This individual that Dr. Bond speaks of, sounds more like a family member to me or at least somebody that is in Tumblety's confidence, what do you think?'

"Could this Herold fellow you referred to as Tumblety's friend, companion, and servant fall into that category. That chap sounds like someone who would be close enough to be in the doctor's confidence, a quality that I am sure there are few available for such a position, Detective."

"Yes, a confidant who may or may not have been emotionally involved with Tumblety, posing as a servant or friend, to those outside their personal circle of, shall we say, friends. I was considering David Herold, and wondering if such a relationship ever existed."

"What would make you think that, John?"

"Tumblety has traveled extensively, and I would think a close personal relationship would be difficult to have for one accustomed to moving around so much. Not to mention, a special relationship such as one referred to by Dr. Bond would have to be a family member, I would think. Any other type of relationship Tumblety might have, would arouse suspicion and make him the topic of any gossip, something the doctor may try to avoid while trying to promote himself as a physician in certain circles wouldn't you agree, Wynne?"

"So, where does that leave us, Detective?"

"Well, if Herold was involved intimately with Francis Tumblety, the man was obviously not too influential in the relationship, at least not enough to have Tumblety involved in his plots and conspiracies. Not to mention any and all of his knowledge of the doctor was lost the day Herold was hung for being a conspirator in the Lincoln assassination."

"I was just thinking, Stone, birds of a feather flock together; perhaps Tumblety was far too intelligent to become involved in a plot that had no good end."

"That does seem likely, Wynne. Maybe," I considered my next words carefully. "Perhaps the doctor was involved in the infancy of the planning of this little scheme, but unlike Herold who saw the rope, Tumblety was far too clever to stick it out to the end. Tumblety left the country before the scheduled night of the assassination."

"It seems that a lot of people who come in contact with this chap end up that way Stone, dead, I mean," Baxter said, thoughtfully.

"Yes, it does, but doesn't that make sense, Wynne?"

"I don't follow, John?"

"This man poses as a physician, takes money for medicines that have no healing effect, and for performing illegal procedures. The man's actions speak for themselves, sooner or later they have to catch up with him, forcing him to move from town to town and country to country unable to stay anywhere long. I have to assume after a while those who buy his herbs find out that Tumblety is a charlatan and no more a physician than you or I."

"That could qualify with Doctor Bond's comments on the perpetrator of these murders as not being of sound mind. Being on the move constantly, having to move from country to country could establish that Tumblety is involved in some type of criminal activity not just selling his counterfeit cures, but perhaps going as far as involvement in the Lincoln assassination. There are likely more sinister activities that the man is involved in than what we are aware. As you say, Scotland Yard's Special Branch has already suspected some connection in the plot to kill the queen. Perhaps these societies and criminal acquaintances are the man's way of seeking notoriety. It would also mean that these types of relationships, make it impossible for the man to have any kind of a normal life. Tumblety has already established himself as having an indifferent attitude towards his patients, established by the fact that the medicines administered to these poor creatures could harm or kill them. That behavior alone could label the man as not being in charge of all his faculties," Baxter trumped up.

"Yes, it does. The man's inability to forge friendships could offer a small insight into Tumblety's character," I agreed.

466

"It does make you wonder how this fraud has been left to carry on his charade for such a long time, John. Perhaps Tumblety's ability to get away with the crimes in the past has allowed him to ripen into the rogue we suspect him of being."

"I think there is more behind the criminal element that Tumblety seems to become entangled, in every city."

"Do you mean the Fenian connection you spoke of?"

"Yes, and no, Wynne. Tumblety seems to wear many hats, none of which fit and the man seems to be able to get himself out of scrapes before permanent damage is done."

"How so, John?"

"I read in the man's file that Tumblety was verbally attacked in America for running around in a soldier uniform displaying an illegitimate rank and medals, on a uniform to a regiment that the man did not belong. Apparently, the man was able to do some fast talking and was able to get himself out of trouble before being placed in jail. Tumblety posing as a Union Officer could indicate that the doctor was more involved in Lincoln's assassination than what could be proven; however, I have been unable to find anything to indicate that Tumblety and Herold were anything more than acquaintances. The fact remains that Tumblety has his fingers in many pies, and seems drawn in by the excitement of the chase that his activities bring or the intrigue that his associates are involved, who can guess. It could very well be that Tumblety is criminally insane."

"This is all beginning to sound rather trumped-up, or too surreal to be believed, what?" Baxter grimaced.

"Perhaps, Wynne, but we have confirmation from Montreal, that Francis Tumblety left that city because of circumstances involving an illegal abortion on a prostitute there. Tumblety then fled St John's in 1860. It seems a man named James Portmore died after taking medicine that Tumblety prescribed, after it was claimed it would cure the man. Unfortunately, this is the only documented information that we have to rely on Tumblety's practices. After the man arrived in Liverpool, I believe his movements and his activities were a closely guarded secret. Scotland Yard Special Branch had cause to keep Tumblety under surveillance for some time because of the man's Fenian ties. Regardless of the man's present activities, I believe the doctor's past speaks for itself. However, like you have suggested Wynne, Tumblety's relationships do not last long, and his patients may or may not survive their ordeal after taking his prescribed elixirs. Even if there was a patient, who did survive one of Tumblety's many procedures, how in the world would we ever find that person?"

"What of these herbs, why hasn't some authority stopped him from selling these medicines that have no medicinal value and put people's lives in danger?"

"Perhaps that is how Tumblety has become so assured of himself, Wynne."

"What do you mean, John?"

"I believe Tumblety, thinks himself untouchable by authorities. This man has been living his particular lifestyle for a lot of years, Wynne. It seems that every time Tumblety comes before a judge, there is a bribe involved or his barrister by some technicality of law can get the doctor released on some type of bail, after which Tumblety leaves before being arrested. It seems that Francis Tumblety has had a long and distinguished career as a swindler and a cheat. Not to mention his involvement in more than one suspicious death."

"It would seem that this quack, as you call him, has become calloused in some way, Stone, so much so, that murder in whatever shape or form it takes; does little to faze him?"

"I believe his indifference would have started somewhere in his past, there must have been someone of influence in Tumblety's youth who has set him on this path, a path, it seems that there will be no turning back from."

"Stone, you do have a knack for painting a dismal picture." Baxter sighed.

Chapter Thirty

Two days later, I looked up from my desk to see Wynne Baxter carrying a tray into my office. My office had become a sanctuary, a place of discussion, a quiet place away from the hustle and bustle, and away from the comings and goings that occurred on a daily basis in the coroner's office. Both men had now become accustomed one to the other each man had used the other as a sounding board on more than one occasion, firing their theories and formulating strategies to catch the allusive killer that had become so much a part of their daily lives.

The business of a coroner never stopped in the metropolis. We had just finished investigating a wrongful death of a man run over by a runaway team of horses the day before. I had just arrived at my office moments before when the familiar rattle of teacup and saucer made me put what I was reading down.

"Wynne, I was going over some of Doctor Thomas Bond's notes again."

"Notes, Detective," Baxter asked.

"Sir, Robert Anderson had asked the doctor to write a paper on his professional medical opinion on the type of personality, we should be trying to identify in our search for a suspect."

"Oh yes, the doctor's professional views and thoughts on what type of personality '*Jack the Ripper*' might possess."

Looking up, I could see a rather disturbing look on the coroner's face.

"Sorry, Detective. I still shudder when I think of what would possibly prompt Doctor Bond to end his life and do it in such a horrific manner?"

"I wish, I knew, Wynne. I too have trouble understanding the reasons why Doctor Bond would take his own life. I have heard reports that he had been suffering from some drastic bout of insomnia."

"Insomnia!" Baxter shrieked. "The newspaper reports said nothing of insomnia; here I still have the article in my office, Stone."

Baxter was only a few minutes in returning with a folded newspaper in my hand.

"Here read away, Detective." Baxter said, handing me the newspaper.

Penny Illustrated Paper and Illustrated Times
Saturday, June 15, 1901

[Sic] *Doctor Thomas Bond, the well-known surgeon and eminent analyst, committed suicide on June 6 by jumping from the third-floor window of his house at Broad Sanctuary Westminster. Dr. Bond, who was a P.R.C.S. and an M.D. and formerly attached to Westminster Hospital, held a high reputation in his profession. He was extremely popular; the Doctor was aged fifty-eight. For a long time, Dr. Bond has not been well, and had not always been able to attend regularly to his practice. On the night of June 5, however, he appeared somewhat better. Shortly before seven the next morning the nurse attending the doctor left the apartment for a moment. No sooner the attendant's back turned then the doctor got out of bed, and wearing only his night clothing, threw himself out of the window. He fell a distance of fifty feet, alighting upon his head in the area. It is thought that when help first arrived the unfortunate gentleman was not dead, but he died on the way to Westminster Hospital, just opposite to the Sanctuary. Dr. Bond leaves a widow and five children."*

"I guess you're right, Wynne, it says nothing of insomnia, but I did hear it upon good authority if that means anything."

"You don't suppose Bond was self-medicating, do you?"

"Your guess is as good as mine, Wynne, it would be a temptation hard to resist for someone, if medication was readily available to them. Perhaps Bond had started to experiment with some of these new medicines that are available now. As to what would prompt a prominent doctor to end his life in that manner, I am at a loss for words?"

I put the article down, unable to get the image of the distraught doctor jumping from a window.

"John there are a dozen ways to end your life; poison, an overdose of pills, which Bond could lay his hands on any variety of medicines that would do the job, a lot neater. Though, I would think if someone was in a position that needed to end everything quickly for some reason, a quick bullet, would sum things up a lot nicer than a fifty-foot plunge."

"Something obviously made the good doctor irrational enough to act in that impromptu manner. I am certain that Bond was not sitting around that morning wondering about jumping out of his bedroom window."

"If a man wanted to kill himself by throwing himself out a window, Stone, I think if anything it would be spontaneous no thought process at all," Wynne retorted.

"That seems reasonable Wynne; however, what was the doctor's frame of mind. Perhaps instead, we should look at the reasons behind why someone would want to commit suicide?"

"Well, the article mentions some illness; I suppose this insomnia you spoke of, could have been a side effect that the man suffered from. There was that chap in Cheapside, who took his life over gambling debts; however, I must say, it was done using gas. Perhaps, this insomnia was a cover for some dementia that Bond was suffering," Baxter offered.

"Well, I can understand a situation like that making a man desperate enough to take what might seem like the only way out. But I was wondering, Wynne, how long can a person go without a fitful night's sleep before losing their ability to cope or think straight?"

"I don't know, Detective; at first glance, it seems a trifling to make a man want to end it all. Having said that, I must say, I do fancy a good night's sleep. I suppose sleep deprivation over a long period could make even the strongest of minds go loopy."

"For whatever reason, something prevented Bond from seeking outside help, or maybe the doctor had a darker secret than anyone could possibly fathom. Something that drove him to the brink of insanity, a thing so horrible, if found out, it would destroy him. Perhaps Bond saw death as the only way. Whatever it was, it caused Bond to jump from that window."

"What are you saying Stone, do you know something that you are not telling me?"

"No, let's drop it Wynne; it hardly seems worth pursuing; besides it would only be conjecture."

"Stone, you are not suggesting Bond committed suicide due to this '*Jack the Ripper*' case, are you?" Baxter said aghast.

"I am not suggesting anything. All I am saying, Wynne, it does seem odd that of the five women who are '*Jack the Ripper*' victims, Doctor Bond was involved, in some way, in all their cases. Aside from the Battersea torso murder. Bond is the only doctor that still maintained that the killer demonstrated no anatomical experience in the dissection and subsequent mutilation of the bodies."

"Are you proposing that the doctor had something to hide, that perhaps the man was proclaiming some falsehood to draw attention away from the cases or in the very least Bond knew something about the case that went with him to his grave?"

"Wynne, I am not suggesting anything, I am simply trying to understand what set of circumstances would prompt a prominent doctor to end his life, and to end it in that way. I have investigated several suicides, and, as you said, it seems odd that Bond would end his life over lack of sleep. Having said that, the few homicides that I have investigated; involving gravity, the victim is almost always found on his head like they were diving into the water or something of that nature."

"Stone," Baxter interrupted. "Did you just hear yourself, you said homicide, not suicide, you don't believe that Bond was murdered do you?"

"Sorry, Wynne, but it is my experience that if a person commits suicide, the victim most often jumps feet first and it is usually from a distance of more than fifty feet."

472

"Very well, Detective it is your plight in life to question what you must. The rest of us will have to remain content to accept those things that are out of our control."

"Wynne, a physician, is a man who by taking the Hippocratic Oath, vows to save human life with all his efforts and by any means available to him; that alone is a responsibility that the average man would find hard to perform all of their life. The human life is something of value hence the oath, and the sustaining of life is why someone would want to become a doctor; it is not something they take lightly. Is the sanctity of life not just as highly regarded if that life is the physician's own?"

"I would think so, but can a tormented mind distinguish between right and wrong?"

"Wynne we are now in a new century where new medicines are being discovered, doctors are finding out more about how the human body works, but there are still a lot of unanswered questions. A physician must at times feel inadequate or in the very least feel as if their hands are tied trying to appease those who are unwilling to give up witchcraft and the bloodletting frame of mind that the medical profession has been hampered with for over a century. Sometimes the chains that society places about those seeking a more scientific route can force men to do things that they may deem for the greater good; however, they may be looked on by those of authority as monsters that should be taken out of society and caged."

"That is all very well and good, John, but you still have not answered my question. You have made some sweeping insinuations that I believe demand an answer when it comes to sullying the good name of a prominent physician."

I knew that the conversation had gone further than what I had initially intended. I had suspicions that like everything else, had not been verified by fact, which in my mind was nothing more than guesswork.

"Well, John," Baxter persisted. "Do you think that Doctor Thomas Bond was guilty of some impropriety or was murdered because of some knowledge that the man might divulge?"

I looked across my desk at my friend and thought of the greater good that both I and the coroner had spent countless hours trying to uphold and maintain in looking for the truth. My speech to Baxter while defending Doctor Thomas Bond could be used at the same time as a defense for Doctor Francis Tumblety. However, I could not think of two men more opposite in their pursuit of preserving human life. I thought of Bond, a trained physician and respected in his field. Then I considered Tumblety, whose credentials were questionable and had little or no respect for the law and found it better to let sleeping dogs lay.

"No, Wynne, I think not, for whatever reason the demon that haunted Doctor Thomas Bond and tormented him many a sleepless night; had ultimately won whatever battle that waged inside the man. God only knows what anguish the Doctor was subjected to that made him end his life in that way, but that will have to be between him and his Maker."

Chapter Thirty-one

Two years later, on May twenty-eighth 1903, Francis Tumblety died in St Louis, the article in the St Louis Republic Newspaper told of Doctor Francis Tumblety`s death and the probate of his will. It was revealed that one portion of Tumblety`s vast estate consisted of one hundred and forty thousand dollars in cash, strangely enough deposited in a New York bank. The New York Tribune reported that Tumblety had relatives in Rochester, New York, and Liverpool. Small tidbits came flooding over my desk over the next few years; of them all none were more fascinating than an article from the McCook Tribune (Neb.) more than two years after the death of Carrie Brown. Printed, May first 1891, I found the article while rummaging through a box of old newspapers at a coffee house, no doubt left by an American traveler anxious for news from home.

McCook Tribune (Neb.) May 1, 1891:
'Jack the Ripper In America,' New York, April 25.

[Sic] *'Jack the Ripper' is believed by the police to have at last come to this city. Yesterday morning in the East River hotel, the body of a wretched woman was found with her abdomen horribly cut and her bowels protruding. Her name is not known. The resort in which the body was found is one of the lowest in the city. It is located on the southeast corner of Catherine and Market streets. The woman was known about the neighborhood as one of the half drunken creatures who hang about the low resorts of Water Street and Riverside. She came to the hotel last night in company with a man who registered as Knickloi and wife. The couple were assigned to a room on the upper floor and went to it at once. Nothing was seen or heard of them during the night. No cry or unusual noise was heard. This morning the attendant rapped at the door of the room occupied by the couple. There was no answer and he rapped again with no better result and finally broke in the door. A horrible sight met his gaze. On the bed lay the woman in a big pool of blood. She had been dead for hours. Her abdomen had been fairly ripped open with a dull, broken table knife that lay in the pool of blood. The viscera had been cut, and from appearances a part was missing. The woman's head was bandaged. A cloth had been tied about her neck and face, but whether for any foul purpose or to hide any other traces of murder the attendant did not wait to see."*

The newspaper article brought new light to the Carrie Brown case, giving further information to the gravity of the mutilation of the prostitute's body. The one identifiable aspect of the murder was the *'protruding bowels'* of the victim; however, I would have given one of my eye teeth if the reporter would have revealed which side of the body the entrails were placed. Although the Carrie Brown murder was distinguished by several other points when compared to the *'Ripper'* murders in Whitechapel. There were still several other features of the case that drew my attention. One fact that did not escape me; was that anyone living in New York could have read about the *'Jack the Ripper'* murders in London in the newspapers that had flooded around the world. That individual, could very well have, tried to imitate the details in this murder in New York City. It would not be the first time that such a thing had happened. If anything, an intelligent man would consider the similarities and logically conclude that there appeared to be several killers similar to the deviant in London rather than consider that there was one lone man perpetrating the crimes. Who for all intents and purposes, had left England and fled to America, arriving in New York and leave it as it lay? However, I was not thinking just logically, I was thinking like a detective, and I was thinking about one man, Francis Tumblety. It seemed to me that I would be remiss in my duties not to consider how extraordinary; it was that a similar crime was committed in the very city that an alleged criminal had fled. The very particulars of the crime, the victim, where the crime was committed, and the details of the crime scene rang too close to the Mary Kelly murder not to take notice. It would seem that the killer in New York also possessed the ability to disappear without a trace in keeping with '*Jack*' in Whitechapel.

Over the next few months, I was able to compile more articles but none that was more absolute than the last and final newspaper clipping that had found its way to the coroner's desk by an acquaintance of his who had been traveling to America on business. The article was from the St. Louis Republic, dated Wednesday, November the eighteenth 1903.

St. Louis Republic, Wednesday, November 18, 1903.

[Sic] *"Local Attorney Gains Victory in, Tumblety Estate.*

Public Administrator Garrard and Strode was notified yesterday that about 140,000 belonging to the estate of Doctor Francis Tumblety had been deposited with the National Bank of Commerce of New York to his credit. It will be paid through the Third National Bank Strode, who Is administrator of Doctor Tumblety's estate. The transaction is the sequel to a victory for Strode in the courts of New York where my administration of the estate was opposed by Dr. Tumblety's heirs. Dr. Tumblety died at St. John's Hospital, in St Louis May twenty-eighth last, at the age of 82 years. He had come here short time before, from Hot Springs. Ark., where he was treated for heart disease, which, caused his death. He was supposed to be a stranger, but it developed that he had lived in St

Louis, and had spent several years traveling, after having made a fortune as an advertising physician. He sent for an attorney and made a will bequeathing about half of his fortune. He had intended to make another will containing the same bequests as in the first will, and providing for the disposition of the first will of his estate."

I read the article stopping at the paragraph that talked about Tumblety's age. The reporter had Tumblety at age eighty-two, having arrested the man, I would have guessed that Tumblety would have been in his thirties or early forties at the latest. I could only imagine that the Francis Tumblety referred to in the article was the father or grandfather to the man I had arrested, almost fourteen years before. However, perhaps Wynne Baxter had been right. If in 1857 Tumblety had been in his late thirties, then the article would have his age right. There were other interesting details about the man's life, such as spending '*several years traveling*' and going about as an '*advertising physician.*' It could very well be an explanation on how Francis Tumblety, the younger, had gotten experience and his career choice.

For me, the door had closed on the murders after Mary Jane Kelly and news that Tumblety had fled to America. Unfortunately, for the families of the victims, that door had remained open long after the victims had been buried and their names and the peculiar circumstances in which their lives had ended were no longer remembered by the rest of the world. Life had gone on, but the knowledge that a killer had slipped passed the arm of the law, had left Scotland Yard and the Met. Police Dept. with a bad taste in their mouths. Now staring at the crinkled newsprint, one chapter was closed, but the fact remained that the murders committed by '*Jack the Ripper*' went unpunished.

The weeks turned to months, and the months to years, the lives of those who had been affected by the horrendous crimes in London between 1888 and 1889 took the time to mourn. Over the years, the victims affected by the crimes had learned to deal with the effects of the pain suffered during the rampage of murders perpetrated by '*Jack the Ripper.*' The killings were looked upon by the world, as fantastic. In their eyes, the citizens of London had been judged for their depravities and its police were ridiculed. The newspapers did little to subdue the curiosity, making the murders in London the talk of the world. Though the passing of season after season usually helps to heal the wounds of the sufferer. In Whitechapel, the passage of time did little to help those who took part investigating the vicious crimes. They sought the solace that can only be offered by a closed case, and a convicted felon punished for his crimes, which had not happened. Over time, the most that Scotland Yard could look forward to was a time when they would finally be out of the critical eye of those who saw them as failing to do their duties.

For Whitechapel, it was some time before the sensationalism brought about by the newspaper reporting slowly subsided. Though, now and then some other murder that even hinted come vague similarity to the 'Jack the Ripper' murders, would give some reporter with a sharp pencil the opportunity to dredge up the past again. Then the newspapers would be filled with some fact or coincidence, and 'Jack' would find his name back in the newspapers, and, London's citizens would be forced to relive the past again, when murder was the only attribute of the city that people found interesting to talk about.

Time does eventually take its toll, and soon a generation of policemen who had lived through those horrific days, who had spent countless hours in pursuit of the killer had finally retired to their country homes. By then even the newspapers relented and stopped trying to keep the stories alive, much to the appreciation of those few who sat night after night in their armchairs reliving the murders over and over in their minds. They would remember those rain-drenched cobbles and the dark alleys where 'Jack the Ripper' would creep in the night seeking out his next victim. Only after that generation of police had gone could the members of the Metropolitan Police hold their heads up and excuse the failures of their grandfathers, due to the poor criminal investigation techniques and the lack of the amenities that were now available to them in the modern twentieth century. They would boast that if the crimes were perpetrated, in their day, they would have caught the killer in a snap of their fingers. There were still those who remembered a similar boast made by the New York City Police, who had a similar crime in their city, which like those in Whitechapel, remains unsolved to date. However, those who remembered the days of their youth, when night after night they hunted the elusive murderer. They understood that no police force in the world, modern or otherwise could have caught the perpetrator of what seemingly was a motiveless crime.

The *Thames Mystery* and the '*Jack the Ripper*' cases were crimes that ostensibly had no beginning and no end. Some said five women were killed by Jack, others said seven. There was no way that police could beyond a shadow of a doubt, deduce if all the crimes were committed by one hand or multiple killers. The doctors argued that there was no degree of anatomical knowledge in any of the dissection done to the victims. However, not one of them could explain how a layperson could dissect a human kidney or any other organ from a corpse in the time that was estimated, in the poorly lit areas where the crimes were committed. They excused the technique used by '*Jack*' as those knife strokes used by a butcher, rather than consider some practiced hand of the medical profession was responsible. Or, in the very least, the dissection was done by someone who chose to disguise the technique of a skilled surgeon to put investigators off his trail.

The victims that the killer's preyed upon were those who had no close ties to family or friends. If robbery was a motive, the police could have searched nearby areas for those items taken, but; the victims in most cases were destitute having pennies on their person and none of the worldly possessions that were worth stealing, much less killing for. It finally became apparent that the victims had only the living tissue in their bodies that was coveted and taken by the hand that sliced their throats and left them to bleed out on the cold cobbles of London's walks.

The crimes perpetrated on the prostitutes of London were regarded as heinous with no rhyme or reason. They were excused away by some who persisted that the murders were committed by some escaped '*lunatic*' from some unknown asylum. However, after exhausting every lead and investigating the patients in every hospital, the police came up with no such establishment nor any escaped patient that could have organized and committed the crimes and have the facilities to escape from the police without a trace. The only logical explanation was that two killers perpetrated the Whitechapel murders and the Thames torso murders. One homicidal maniac who took his hatred out on the prostitutes of Whitechapel, for reasons known only to him. This killer was a man who stifled his victim's screams with his left arm wrapped around their throat, and then with a sharp knife in his righthand sliced through the carotid artery, the blade of his knife cutting around the neck so deep into the tender flesh of the throat that the edge glanced off the victim's vertebrae.

This 'Jack the Ripper' as the newspapers called him; would then lay the body down while their lifeblood sprayed away from him. The killer would next roll his victim over and calmly unbutton their clothing and proceed to slash at the face and torso, ending by performing a crude dissection on the body and, for some unknown reason, take a piece of the victim's anatomy before leaving. The scene of his crime was chosen specifically so that the killer could perform his duties under darkness and so that his victim could be found only a short time later by patrolling police.

The other villain who stalked the women of London was assumed by some to be a man who chose to take those newly released from workhouses or prisons or those who begged on London's streets. Housing them in some secret place for an undetermined amount of time, to later kill them and cut up their remains, tossing the pieces in the Thames. It was believed that this was done to hide the crime and the victim's identity at the same time. The reason for committing the crime, was a mystery, just as the cause of each individual's death. It was speculated that this madman was one who sought out those indigent women in particular who had nothing and no home to go to, and no one to look for them, much less any that cared for them. This killer chose only those who were destined to live a life of begging and living on the streets. However, it was also speculated that there was more than one killer who perpetrated the *torso murders* as they were often referred to because of the missing head and limbs. What set these crimes apart were the ligature marks found on some of the trunks. These were marks found on the body that signified that the limbs were tied before the killer used a sharp knife and saw to dismember his victims. Their parts were later discovered in and around London wherever the rising tide of the Thames deposited them.

As in all ordered societies, there were separations between the classes, and there were those calloused citizens who were fortunate enough not to have to live in the slums of London's East End that commented that the killer was simply doing his victim's a courtesy, thus ending a life of begging, disease, and starvation.

Whatever the demented reason, the killings started, and there were no eyewitnesses that could give evidence that could bring the killer or killers to justice. Each crime was carried out by one or more persons who, in leaving no victim alive to testify, allowed his (their) criminal activity to continue unabated. With no physical evidence and no witness accounts available, the police were left guessing for a possible motive for the crimes and wondering where the killer or killers would strike next. In one of the largest cities in the world where crime was widespread in the slums of the East End, there was no way to close the streets or stop the women from practicing their trade any more than police had the ability to patrol both sides of the entire length of the Thames River night after night seeking out a killer who used the river as a dumping ground for his victims.

Long after the turning of the new century, Stone still maintained Francis Tumblety's guilt for the murders of the prostitutes in Whitechapel. For the balance of his career, he opted to stay Wynne Baxter's investigator.

Soon the '*Jack the Ripper*' case slowly faded into memory, although sometimes at night, the detective would still dream of chasing the allusive figure down the dark alleys of London. It wasn't until fifteen years later when he had moved from the ever-growing metropolis of London that the real story of Francis Tumblety's life came to light.

It was a fine spring day in the year 1918 when I received a rolled-up newspaper from my friend Wynne Baxter in the mail. Sitting in my favorite chair on the front porch, I could feel the sun's penetrating rays through the trellis over my head the rains had stopped briefly allowing the intense rays of sunshine through a scattering of gray clouds. Unrolling the newspaper from its wrinkled brown wrapper, I saw that the paper was an American publication from Rochester New York, inside the wrapper a note slid from the folds of the paper and fell into my lap.

Dear John

I received this paper from a colleague in Kent, who had recently come from America on business. How this man came to be in possession of this newspaper I will leave that story for a later date, but be content to know that I think this article will satisfy any doubt that you may have had in the past about your endeavors to prove Dr. Francis Tumblety's guilt.

Your Friend Always
Wynne E. Baxter

Cradling the newspaper on my lap, my heart started to pound as I anxiously placed my spectacles on my nose and wrapped the arms over my ears. With shaking hands, I opened the newspaper and found the headline and proceeded to read.

[Sic] The Rochester Democrat and Chronicle Monday December 3, 1888.

THE MISSING TUMBLETY

An American Quack Suspected of the Whitechapel

Crimes.

He Probably Seeks America

A Braggart and Charlatan—Circumstance Against Him—

Details of His Adventurous career. A Rochester Boy. His Life in

This City.

Special to the New York World.

LONDON, Dec. 1 —The last seen of Dr. Tumblety was at Havre, and it is taken for granted that he had sailed for New York. It will be remembered that the doctor, who is known in this country for his eccentricities, was arrested some time ago in London on suspicion of being concerned in the perpetration of the Whitechapel murders. The police, being unable to procure the necessary evidence against him in connection there with, decided to hold him for trial for another offense against a statute which was passed shortly after the publication in the Pall Mall Gazette of 'The Maiden Tribute' and as a direct consequence thereof Dr.

Tumblety was commuted for trial and liberated on bail, two gentlemen coming forward to act as bondsmen in the amount of $l, 600. On being hunted up by the police to-day, they asserted that they had only known the doctor for a few days previous to his arrest.

TUMBLETY'S CAREER

A London detective wishing to get information about the man, now under arrest for complicity in some way with the Whitechapel crimes has only to go to any large city the world over, describe the curious garb and manners of Francis Tumblety, M. D., and he can gather fact and surmises to almost any extent. In London, he calls himself Tumblety. In this city there are scores who know him, and not any has a kind word to say for the strange creature, but from those most intimate come rumors, reports and positive assertions of the practices of the man. In this city he had a little experience with the law, and this enabled lawyers to worm out something of his life history. William P. Burr, of No. 820 Broadway, speaking of the man yesterday, said: 'I met him on July, 1880. He brought a suit against a Mrs. Lyons, charging her with the larceny of 17, 000 worth of bonds, and I was retained to defend her. It seems that several years before he met the son of Mrs. Lyons while walking on the Buttery. The lad had just come from college and was a fine-looking young man. He was out of employment. Tumblety greeted him and soon had him under complete control. He made him a sort of secretary in the management of his bonds, of which he had about $100,000 worth, mostly in governments, locked up in a downtown safe-deposit company. He employed the youth as an amanuensis, as he personally was most illiterate. On April 23, 1878, the 'Doctor,' as he was called, started for Europe by the Union line steamer Montana. There is his name on the passenger-list, Dr. Tumblety. He gave a power of attorney to the young man, and under that some South Carolina railroad bonds were disposed of, as it was claimed and shown, under an agreement that they were to be taken as compensation. When Tumblety got back the young man had disappeared and the mother was arrested, charged by the 'Doctor' with having taken the bonds. I remember the examination to which I subjected him at the police station. James D.

McClelland was his lawyer, and he went into history of the doctor's life I remember well how indigent he became when I asked him what institution had the honor of graduating so precious a pupil. He refused to answer, and was told the only reason which he could refuse was that the answer would tend to incriminate him. He still refused to answer, and I thought I would spring at him to strike. There was quite a commotion in court. The case fell through and the old lady was not held. The son returned and brought a suit against the doctor, charging vicious assault, and the evidence collected in this case was of the most disgusting sort. The lawyer who had the matter in hand is now dead, but I remember that there was a page of the Police Gazette as one exhibit, in which the portrait of the doctor appeared, with several columns of biography about him. This suit was not pushed, and though came another suit brought by this Tumblety against William P. O'Connor, a broker, for disposing of the bonds. Boardman and Boardman, defended and gathered up a great mass of evidence against the doctor, Charles Frost and Charles Chambers, detectives of Brooklyn, had evidence against him. At this time, he kept an herb store, or something of that sort, at No. 77 East Tenth Street. The suit did not come to anything, and I do not know of any other law matters in which this notorious man was concerned.

HIS LIFE HISTORY NOT KNOWN.

'I had seen him before that time hovering about the old post office, where there were many clerks. He had a seeming mania for the company of young men and grown-up youths. In the course of our investigations about the man we gathered up many stray bits of history about him, but nothing to make a connected life story. He had a superabundance of cheek and nothing could make him abashed. He was a coward physically, though he looked like a giant, and he struck me as one who would be vindictive to the last degree. He was a tremendous traveler, and while away in Europe his letters to young Lyon showed that he was in every city of Europe. The English authorities, who are now telegraphing for samples of his writing from San Francisco, ought to get them in any city of Europe. I had a big batch of letters sent by him to the young man Lyon, and they were the most amusing farrago of illiterate nonsense. Here is one written from the West. He never failed to warn his correspondence against lewd women, and in doing it used the most shocking language. I do not know how he made his

484

money. He had it before he became acquainted with the Lyon family, and was a very liberal spender. My own idea of the ruse is that it would be just such a thing as Tumblety would be concerned in, but he might get one of his victims to do the work, for once he had a young man under his control, he seemed to be able to do anything with the victim."

HIS CAREER IN WASHINGTON.

Colonel C. A. Dunham. A well-known lawyer who lives near Fairview, N. J., was intimately acquainted with Tumblety for many years, and, in his own mind, had long connected him with the Whitechapel horrors. 'The man's real name,' said the lawyer, 'is Tumblety,' with Francis for a Christian name. I have here a book published by him a number of years ago, describing some of his strange adventures and wonderful cures, all lies, of course, in which the name Francis Tumblety, M. D., appears. When, to my knowledge of the man's history, his idiosyncrasies, his revolting practices, his antipathy to women, and especially to fallen women, his anatomical museum, containing many specimens like those carved from the Whitechapel victims—when, to my knowledge on these subjects, there is added the fact of his arrest on suspicion of being the murderer, there appears to me nothing improbable in the suggestion that Tumblety is the culprit. He is not a doctor. A more arrant charlatan and quack never fastened on the hopes and fears of afflicted humanity. I first made the fellow's acquaintance a few days after the battle of Bull Run. Although a very young man at the time he held a colonel's commission in the army, and was at the capital on official business. The city was full of strangers. 90 per cent, of them military men. All the first-class hotels resembled beehives. Among them were many fine-looking and many peculiar-looking men, but of the thousands there was not one that attracted half as much attention as Tumblety. A Titan in stature, with a very red face and long flowing mustache, he would have been a noticeable personage in any place and in any garb. But, decked in a richly embroidered coat or jacket, with a medal held by a gay ribbon on each breast, a semi-military cap with a high peak, cavalry trousers with the brightest of yellow stripes, riding boots and spurs fit for a show window, a dignified and rather stagy gait and manner, he was as unique a figure as could be found anywhere in real life. When followed, as he generally was, by a valet and two great dogs, he was no doubt the envy of many hearts.

The fellow was everywhere I never saw anything so nearly approaching ubiquity. Go where you would, to any of the hotels, to the war department or the navy yard, you were sure to find the 'doctor.' He had no business in either place, but he went there to impress the officers whom he would meet. He professed to have an extensive experience in European hospitals and armies, and claimed to have diplomas from the foremost medical colleges of the Old World and the New. He had, he declared, after much persuasion accepted the commission of brigade surgeon at a great sacrifice pecuniary; but, with great complacency, he always added that, fortunately for his private patients, his official duties would not, for a considerable time, take him away from the city.

WHY HE HATED WOMEN.

"At length it was whispered about that he was an adventurer. One day my lieutenant colonel and myself accepted the 'doctor's' invitation to a late dinner-symposium, He called it-at his rooms. He had vary costly and tastefully arranged quarters in, I believe, H. Street. There were three rooms on a floor, the rear one being his office, with a bedroom or two a story higher. On reaching the place we found covers laid for eight—that being the 'doctor's' lucky number, he said—several of the guests, all in the military service, were persons with whom we were already acquainted. It was soon apparent that whatever Tumblety's deficiencies as a surgeon, Amphitryon he could not really be excelled. His menu, with colored waiters and the et ceteras, was furnished by one of the best caterers in the city. After dinner there were brought out two tables for play—for poker or whist. In the course of the evening some of the party, warmed by the wine, proposed to play for heavy stakes, but Tumblety frowned down the proposition at once and in such a way as to show he was no gambler. Someone asked why he had not invited some woman to his dinner. His face instantly became as black as a thunder cloud. He had a pack of cards in his hand, but he laid them down and said, almost savagely: "No, Colonel, I don't know any such cattle, and if I did I would, as your friend, sooner give you a dose of quick poison than take you into such danger." He then broke into a homily on the sin and folly of dissipation, fiercely denounced all women and especially fallen women. Then he invited us into his office where he illustrated his lecture, so to speak. One side of the room was entirely occupied with cases, outwardly resembling wardrobes, when the

486

*doors were opened quite a museum was revealed—tiers of shelves with
glass jars and cases, some round and others square, filled with all sorts of
anatomical specimens. The 'doctor' placed on a table a dozen or more
jars containing, as I said, the matrices of every class of women. Nearly a
half of one of these cases was occupied exclusively with these specimens.*

THE STORY OF HIS LIFE.

*"Not long after this the 'doctor' was in his room when my lieutenant-
colonel came in and commenced expatiating on the charms of a certain
woman. In a moment, almost, the doctor was lecturing him and
denouncing women. When he was asked why he hated women, he said that
when quite a young man he fell desperately in love with a pretty girl,
rather his senior, who promised to reciprocate his affection. After a brief
courtship he married her. The honeymoon was not over when he noticed a
disposition on the part of his wife to flirt with other men. He remonstrated,
she kissed him, called him a dear, jealous fool—and he believed her.
Happening one day to pass in a cab through the worst part of the town he
saw his wife and a man enter a gloomy looking house. Then he learned
that before her marriage his wife bad been an inmate of that and many
similar houses. Then he gave up all womankind. Shortly after telling this
story the 'doctor's' real character became known and he slipped away to
St. Louis, where he was arrested for wearing the uniform of an army
surgeon. Colonel Dunham was asked whether there was any truth in the
statement of a city paper that Harrold, who was hanged as one of Booth's
confederates in the assassination of Lincoln, was at one time the 'doctor's'
valet. The reply was that it was not true. The gentleman added that he
could speak positively on the subject, as he knew the valet well. Colonel
Dunham also said that Tumblety had not been arrested on suspicion of
having guilty knowledge of the assassination conspiracy. 'He was arrested
in St. Louis' said the Colonel, on suspicion of being Mr. Luke P.
Blackburn, lately governor of Kentucky, who had been falsely charged
with trying to introduce yellow fever into the northern cities by means of
infected rags. It is perfectly clear that Tumblety purposely brought about
his own arrest by sending anonymous letters to the federal authorities to
the effect that Blackburn and himself were identical. His object, of course,*

was notoriety. He knew he was too well known in Washington, whither he felt certain be would be sent, to be kept long in custody.

UNMASKED ON THE STAGE

"Tumblety would do almost anything under heaven for notoriety, and although his notoriety in Washington was of a kind to turn people from him, it brought some to him. Let me tell you of one of his schemes. At that time there was a free—or it may have been a 10-cent—concert saloon known as the Canterbury Music hall. The performance embraced music, dances, farces, etc. One day Tumblety told me, apparently in great distress, that the management of the Canterbury Hall had been burlesquing him on the stage. An actor, he said, was made up in minute imitation of himself, and strutted-about the stage with two dogs something like his own, while another performer sang a topical song introducing his name in a ridiculous way. That night, or the next, I went with some friends to this concert ball, and, sure enough, about 10 o'clock out came a performer the very image of Tumblety. In a minute a dog, that did not resemble the 'doctor's sprang from the auditorium upon the stage and followed the strutting figure. The longer I examined the figure the greater became my surprise at the perfection of the make- up. Before I reached my hotel, I began, in common with my companions, to suspect that the figure was no other then Tumblety myself. The next day the lieutenant-colonel told the 'doctor' our suspicions. The fellow appeared greatly hurt. He at once instituted an action against the proprietor of the ball for libel. The action was another sham, and three or four nights afterwards the 'doctor' was completely unmasked. When the song was under way a powerful man suddenly sprang from the auditorium to the stage, exclaiming at the figure: "See here, you infernal scoundrel, Dr. Tumblety is my friend, and I won't see him insulted by such an effigy as you are. Come, off with that false mustache and duds", and quick as a flash he seized the doctor's hirsute appendage and pulled it for all it would stand, threw his cap among the audience and otherwise showed the fellow up. The 'doctor' though a powerful man, made no struggle except to get behind the scenes as soon as possible.

"Tumblety's book contains, as subscribers to testimonials to his right social standing and medical-skill. In Canada, the names of some of the

best-known people in the Dominion and elsewhere. Evidently the testimonials are bogus. The book was doubtless intended for distribution among persons who would never suspect or discover the fraud, and there was little or no danger of its reaching any of the parties whose names accompanied the lying commendations. Tumblety, I am sure, would rather have lost $1,000 than that a copy should have fallen into my hands. I obtained it in this way: Meeting me one day in Brooklyn, near my office, I urged him to go in for a chat. As I was standing by his desk, about to leave, I voluntarily picked up the book and, while I was yet talking, mechanically turned over the leaves. The name of a friend having suddenly caught my eye and aroused my curiosity, I asked the 'doctor' to let me take the book. This he good naturedly objected to, making various excuses for refusing. I, however, insisted, and when be found me in dead earnest he reluctantly yielded."

AS A BOY IN ROCHESTER

Captain W. C. Streeter, an old resident of Rochester, N. Y., is quite sure that Tumblety is a native of that city. Captain Streeter is now the owner of a fine canal-boat that plies between this city and Buffalo, but in his youth lived in Rochester. A World reporter boarded his boat at pier 5, East River, yesterday, and found the Captain in his snug cabin surrounded by his wife, daughter and son. 'The first recollection I have of him,' said the Captain, 'is along about 1848. I should judge he was then something like 15 years old and his name was Frank Twomblety. I don't know when he changed it to Tumblety. He was selling books and papers on the packets and was in the habit of boarding my boat a short distance from town. The books he sold were largely of the kind Anthony Comstock suppresses now. His father was an Irishmen and lived on the common south of the city on what was then known as Sophia Street, but is now Plymouth Avenue and is about a mile from the center of the city. There were but few houses there then and the Tumblety's had no near neighbor. I don't remember what the father did. There were two boys older than Frank and one of them worked as a steward for Dr. Fitzhugh, then a prominent physician."

"Frank continued to sell papers until 1850, I think, and then disappeared, and I did not see him again for ten years, when he returned to Rochester as a great physician and soon became the Wonder of the city.

He wore a light fur overcoat that reached to his feet and had a dark collar and cuffs, and he was always followed by a big greyhound. When a boy he had no associates, and when he returned, he was more exclusive and solitary than ever. I don't remember ever having seen him in company with another person in his walks. When I met him on his return, having known him quite well as a boy, I said, 'Hello, Frank, how d'ye do?' and he merely replied, 'Hello Streeter', and passed on. He had become very aristocratic during his absence. The papers had a great deal to say about him, and he created quite a sensation by giving barrels of flour and other provisions to poor people. Afterwards he went to Buffalo and did likewise, and I understand he visited other cities. I think Frank was born in Rochester. He had no foreign accent when I first met him, and I understood at the time that he was a Rochester boy. I remember after he became famous my two brothers quarreled because each imagined the other was thought more of by the 'doctor.' I have not heard anything about him for fifteen years, as he moved away from Rochester. He was about five feet ten inches high, of rather slight build, and fine-looking, but evidently avoided society. I thought then that his mind had been affected by those books he sold, and am not at all surprised to hear his name mentioned in connection with the Whitechapel murder.

TUMBLETY GREW UP LIKE A WEED ON THE CANAL BANK AT ROCHESTER.

WASHINGTON, Dec 1. Mr. Edward Haywood, of the Bureau of Accounts in State Department, has known Tumblety since boyhood, and when it was first mentioned in the newspapers that there were suspicions connecting Tumblety with the Whitechapel murders Mr. Haywood immediately said that the theory was quite tenable. "I am in my fifty-second year" said Mr. Haywood to a World correspondent today, "and I fancy Frank Tumblety must be two or three years older. I remember him very well when he used to run about the canal In -Rochester, N. Y., a dirty, awkward, ignorant, uncared-for, good-for-nothing boy. He was utterly devoid of education. He lived with his brother, who was my uncle's gardener. About 1856 he went west. Tumblety turned up in Detroit as a 'doctor.' The only training he ever had for the medical profession was in a little drug store at the back of the Arcade, which was kept by a Doctor Lispenard, who carried on a medical business of a disreputable kind.

"A few years later I saw him here in Washington and he was putting on great style. He wore a military fatigue costume and told me he was on General McClellan's staff. Lieutenant Larry Sullivan, who belonged to a Rochester regiment, came up to him one day. He tried to palm the same tale off upon Sullivan, but the latter being perfectly familiar with McClellan's staff, told the imposter plainly just how great a liar he was. During the war and for some time after Tumblety remained In Washington and played the 'doctor' as he had done in Detroit. he got op some sort of a patent medicine, and at one time the walls were covered with large posters advertising the virtues of the Tumblety Pimple Destroyer. He must have made money, for he was able to spend plenty and live in the most extravagant elegance. 'Knowing him as I do, I should not be the least surprised if he turned out to be Jack the Ripper."

My nimble fingers shook with the crinkling newsprint that rattled with the warm spring breeze. Taking my spectacles off, I massaged the bridge of my nose where the nose pieces left an imprint and wished I had been in Wynne Baxter's office with my old friend and read the newspaper dated December the third, 1888. It seemed like a lifetime ago since the murders and my arrest of Tumblety. Now, I found the news most bittersweet, and the smile faded from my lined face. Feeling the sun's rays as they penetrated through the dismal sky, I closed my eyes, enjoying the warmth on my tired bones and thought about the article and what it meant some twenty years too late. After receiving the news, I would have thought that I would have felt like basking in the new found knowledge of Tumblety's bizarre collection of the female anatomy, but strangely I was left with the thoughts of being cheated out of bringing the madman to justice. After some minutes of thinking about the contents of the article, I found there was no consolation in the knowledge found out too late. There was not even the satisfaction of seeing the man brought to justice on some other charge, in respect to his possession of the female anatomy, even though the jars filled with the macabre remains could in no way be proven to be the remains of the murdered women in Whitechapel. There was little solace in the fact that the article mentioned the ghastly trophies and the story behind Tumblety's hatred for women due to being spurned by a woman of ill-

491

repute. The exposé did, however, answer a lot of questions that had remained unanswered until now about the probable motive for the murders in Whitechapel and perhaps the reasons, if that is, what they could be called behind the missing organs taken from the Whitechapel victims. In addition to the twisted viewing of the jars, arranged in the social class, spoke of an individual far more deranged then I could have ever imagined. Given the personal knowledge that Tumblety possessed about the social types of the individual specimens in the jars alone was evidence that left no shadow of a doubt that the doctor had personal knowledge about the donors, if not, the perpetrator of the crimes. How else could the man have obtained such intimate information, without the knowledge of where the donors came from? Thinking about the dinner party where the macabre remains were displayed, I found it atrocious that the gentlemen in attendance at the party did not question the origins of the trophy jars. Or in the very least, I would have thought the incident would have prompted some conscientious guest perhaps sickened by the contents of the jars to have given the authorities the knowledge that such a collection existed in Tumblety's possession given the many reports in the newspapers all over the world mentioning Francis Tumblety in connection with the Whitechapel murders. As before, I suspect, that politics would have played an integral role in the man's extradition anyway. Tumblety being an American citizen and a self-proclaimed; doctor, could justify having such a collection in his possession for medical study. However, another hurdle to cross was proving how Tumblety came into possession of such a collection in the first place. Having the knowledge that such a ghastly collection even existed was only a small piece of a vast puzzle, leaving authorities with the impossible job of how to provide proof of their origins, which would have been a substantial feat. I could see many obstacles in their effort to build a case based on suspicion alone, which left me back where I had been some thirty years previous. Any case built on supposition alone without proof would be difficult to convince the state department to agree to extradite an American citizen. Although, to point fingers now having the knowledge that the specimens even existed seemed moot, now that Tumblety could be dead for all I knew, and there probably was not more than a handful of people that would even care.

There was nothing perfect about the judicial system, it had seen countless men and women hung by the neck in London's past on charges as frivolous as heresy. The law demanded that the courts prove a man guilty beyond a doubt and it had been up to the Metropolitan Police to gather the facts and pronounce them before a judge and jury, which was something they neglected to do. Had there been even one single collaborating witness found or even an eyewitness that might have seen the perpetrator, that may have been something, but they had not one piece of physical evidence that could have kept Tumblety in London. If Tumblety's museum of human anatomy had been found that perhaps would have been enough to hold Tumblety for questioning. If some connection could have been made between the specimens and the anatomy taken from the murdered women, that would have been something. As it was the newspaper article had come all too late, and the hands of time wait for no man.

From September 1888 to November of the same year there were five women brutally murdered in Whitechapel by apparently one man, during that time another thirteen women right up until the year 1891 were murdered, and not one shred of evidence was obtained to point the finger at Francis Tumblety or anyone else for that matter. The coroner on several occasions had asked me if I thought Tumblety had returned to London after his escape to France, and my answer then would have been the same today, I had no way of knowing. The Thames murders from 1873 to 1888 had claimed at least three lives that they knew of, and by 1889 another three torsos could be added to that count. In total, over twenty women were murdered mysteriously, and both police and coroner had come up with one conclusion, that these women were murdered by person or persons unknown and more than a few murdered by some means unknown.

The cases I reviewed in my head as I sat in the warm spring sunshine brought a familiar uneasy feeling that there was far more happening behind the scenes in those days then what I was able to prove. My views on the killer had changed little over the years. Just as my idea that '*Jack's letters*' held some clue as to who was behind them and the reasons why they were sent, for I was certain that they were written by someone other than the murderer. However, Francis Tumblety's frequent search for notoriety seemed to make him a perfect candidate for the first two letters.

The question of competence was forever in my thoughts, though, I stubbornly dismissed the idea because of my own personal knowledge of how many hours, I alone spent in pursuit of both killers. This knowledge, however, did little to console my mood.

The newspaper rattled in my hand with a passing breeze as I sat and dozed in my chair on the porch of my Colchester home. I could faintly hear my neighbor next door clipping and scratching in his garden while a cart rumbled up the street some distance away. I was content for the moment, though it would have been nice to tell the relatives of those five women that were viciously murdered that I had caught the man who had taken their loved ones from them. That, at least, would have been something, and it would have been a nice closing chapter to my career. As I dozed, the rolled-up newspaper slipped from my hand and rolled across the porch. My last thoughts were that somewhere along the Thames at least one of the men who killed up and down the river may still be alive and that man, just as the man known as 'Jack the Ripper' had to live with the guilt for the deeds done in this life. The only satisfaction that remained was something I thought about more than once, as I sat on the porch in the afternoon sun. There was the satisfaction that one day the man or men who perpetrated these murders would one day stand in front of his Maker and Judge, only, then would justice finally have its day, and until that time, I was content to leave it in God's hands.

For many years on dark nights in public houses, there were those who had lived through the horror in Whitechapel during the fall of 1888 and they would bring up the allusive figure, wondering if 'Jack the Ripper' still prowled in the dark shadows of London's East End. They told ghost stories of the fiend lurking in the dark like some chained figure, waiting to be released seeking the tender flesh and the warm silky blood of some young woman that chose to walk the streets alone at night to make a few pennies for lodgings. There were still those who chose to ignore the warnings and take heed that a killer once stalked the women in Whitechapel. A fiend; who sliced the tender throat of his victim with a sharp knife seeking their lifeblood, and then viciously taking pieces of their anatomy. A man who had never been caught, one who only waited in the fog for the time to be ripe to continue his killing spree and once again bathe the streets of London in blood.

THE END

Bibliography:

London, Jack, The People of the Abyss, first printed by Macmillan, 1903, The Workhouse Press, 2013.

Bismarck Weekly Tribune, Friday, Dec. 21, 1888.

Evening Star, Washington Dc. May, 11, 1865.

The New Ulm Weekly Review, Dec. 5, 1888.

The St. Louis Republic; Wednesday, November 18, 1903.

The Sun June 26, 1904.

The Evening World, June 5, 1889

The St. Louis Republic, Friday, May 29, 1903.

The Great Falls Leader; Morning Ed. Friday, January, 11, 1889.

Nephrol Dial Transplant (2008) 23: 3343–3349 doi: 10.1093/ndt/gfn198 Advance Access publication 11, April 2008 Special Feature – A kidney from hell? A nephrological view of the Whitechapel murders in 1888, Gunter Wolf.

Inquests Reports as Printed in the London Times and the daily Telegraph.

The Daily Telegraph, Tuesday, October 9th, 1888, Day 1, Monday, October 8th, 1888.

The Daily Telegraph, Tuesday, October 23rd, 1888, Day 2, Monday, October 22nd, 1888

An autumn evening in Whitechapel: From: Littell's Living Age, 3, November 1888, From the Daily News

The Times September 10, 1888, page 6, Another Murder at the East-End.

The London Times - September 1, 1888, Another Whitechapel Murder.

The Times November 10, 1888, page 10, Another Whitechapel Murder.

The Daily Telegraph, 3 September 1888

The Daily Telegraph, 14 September, 1888

The Times, 3 October 1888 5

The Times, 4 October 1888

Coroner's inquest (L), 1888, No. 135, Catherine Eddowes inquest, 1888 (Corporation of London Record Office)

The Daily Telegraph, 13 November

The Times, 18 July 1889

The Times August 15, 1889

The Times, 24 February 1891, 13

The Daily Telegraph, 24 February 1891

The London Evening Star June fourth, 1889.

The Graphic, Saturday June 22, 1889, Issue 1021, Illustrated Newspapers.

The Times July 4, 1889

The Times, July 5th, 1889. The Thames Mystery.

The Birmingham Daily Post: The Thames Mystery.

The New York Recorder, 13 May 1891.

The New York Herald, 25 and 26 April 1891.

The New York Times, 26 April 1891

Pall Mall Gazette of 'The Maiden Tribute

The Rochester Democrat and Chronicle Monday December third, 1888.

It would be remiss not to mention Casebook and their sites corroborative assistance on newspaper clippings that I obtained in my research that were difficult to read. https://www.casebook.org/

Printed in Great Britain
by Amazon

30984575R00283